EVA CHASE

ROYALS OF VILLAIN ACADEMY

BOOKS 1-4

Royals of Villain Academy: Books 1-4

This is a work of fiction. Any resemblance to actual persons, living or dead, or actual events is purely coincidental.

First Digital Edition, 2020

Cover design: Saintjupit3r

Ebook ISBN: 978-1-989096-86-4

Hardcover ISBN: 978-1-998752-03-4

Created with Vellum

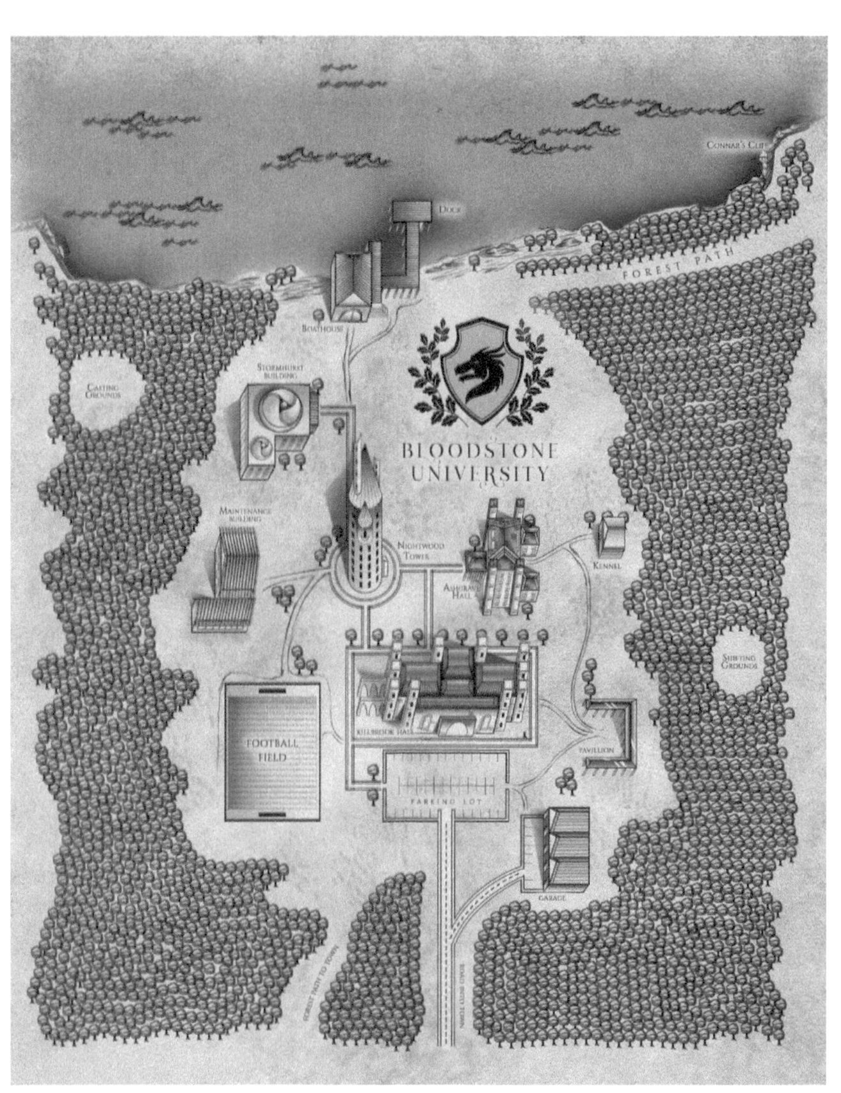
Connar's Cliff
Dock
Forest Path
Boathouse
Stormhurst Building
Casting Grounds
Bloodstone University
Maintenance Building
Nightwood Tower
Kennel
Killbrook Hall
Football Field
Shifting Grounds
Pavillion
Parking Lot
Garage
Forest Path to Town
Road into Town

CRUEL MAGIC

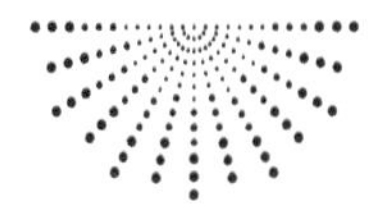

ROYALS OF VILLAIN ACADEMY #1

CHAPTER ONE

Rory

If I'd known my parents would be dead in an hour, I'd have done a few things differently that Sunday morning. Made sure to fit in a hug or two. Offered at least one "I love you." And not dredged up the same old argument we'd been having for the last half a year, which didn't end up mattering anyway.

But I didn't know, so I took what appeared to be my moment. The three of us were sitting around the square white table in the breakfast nook just off the kitchen, warm California sunlight streaming through the broad windows. Dad was finishing up his French toast and eggs equally drenched in syrup, a contented smile curling his lips. Mom poured herself another cup of coffee and inhaled the steam with a pleased sigh.

I dabbed my last corner of toast in the runny yolk left on my plate and washed it down with a gulp of my own bitter coffee. "I was looking at the listings online," I said. "There are a few apartments not too far from here that I can afford."

Mom let out a very different sort of sigh and gave me a look full of fond exasperation. "We've talked about this, Lorelei. You should be saving that money for your future."

She only pulled out my full name when she intended to end the conversation. I barreled onward. "I've really appreciated having the basement. You know that. But I just turned nineteen. Isn't my future supposed to be starting *now*?"

The first time I'd brought up the idea of moving out, they'd offered me the small basement apartment they'd been using for storage as a compromise. But the whole point had been to get a little independence, and it was hard to feel like an adult with my parents literally over my head. After being homeschooled most of my life, now that I was attending a few classes at the local college—and seeing how my classmates lived—it was becoming more and more obvious that I had to make a real break if I was going to figure out my future for myself.

Unfortunately, while I was making more than enough to cover rent and the rest, an artist with no credit history didn't look like the safest bet to potential landlords. To get a lease, I was going to need Mom or Dad to sign on as a guarantor. Which meant, somehow or other, I had to convince them it was a good idea.

Dad leaned his elbows onto the table. "You know the drill," he said with a teasing glint in his eyes. "Pros and cons. Go."

We'd been playing that game whenever I'd proposed something my parents weren't sold on since I was seven years old. I'd like to think I was pretty good at it by now.

"Pros," I said, ticking off fingers as I went. "It'd be an important transitional step to becoming a completely independent adult. I'd be forced to learn how to look after myself. I could get a place that's closer to the college so it'd be easier for me to participate in the extracurricular stuff there and save maybe an hour in transit. I'd be building my credit score and a rental history. I'd have more space and more freedom to… to figure out who I am without you looking over my shoulder."

I hadn't let myself say that part before because I'd known it'd make Dad wince the way it had just now. Mom set down her coffee, knitting her brow. "You should feel like the apartment is completely yours, hon. We don't want to stifle you."

"I know." My hands fell to my lap, and I twisted one of the glass beads on the charm bracelet they'd given me for my tenth birthday and that I'd added to every year since. Each charm was a symbol of a love or a dream I'd shared with them. Why couldn't they understand this longing? "All you have to do is look out the window to see who's coming and going. Sound travels up. Even if you're not *trying* to monitor what I'm doing, I can't forget that you're right here."

"All right," Dad said. "That's fair enough. Maybe we should have taken that more into consideration. And then cons?"

I held back a grimace. He wasn't going to let me fudge this list. "I'll be spending money I could otherwise be saving. If I have a few bad months in selling my figurines, I'll have to dip into the savings I already have. I won't be able to just pop up here and grab something to eat if I'm feeling hungry and lazy, but maybe that's a good thing?"

"It won't be as safe," Mom said. "You'd be living around strangers."

"I'm going to have to sometime, aren't I?"

"It'll be extra stress when you have your studies to focus on," she went on. "And you'll have a lot more pressure to keep going with your current job because you need that money, even if you decide you want to try something new that's more of a risk. In some ways, you'll have less freedom."

"It's not that we're trying to keep you here forever, Rory," Dad said. "We just want to make sure you get the best start we can give you. Why not wait another couple years until you can really launch a career for yourself, and in the meantime we can try to find ways to help you feel more independent here?"

It was hard to argue with that. There were tons of cons. I didn't know how to express how important the one main pro was to me in a way they'd accept without hurting them a whole lot more than I wanted to.

As I bit my lip in thought, Mom smiled, her voice falling into the softer lilting tone it often did when she was about to work her magic. "I know you've been getting a little stir-crazy, wanting to do some traveling too, so I thought we could finally take that trip to New York City this summer—see the Met and MoMA."

Her words did exactly what she'd intended. A spark of delight lit in my chest at the idea of jetting across the country to some of the most respected art galleries in the country. We'd done a bit of traveling as a family before, but only within the state.

With that joy came a knot of guilt as well. I was already planning my own solo trip—a week in Florence, Italy to see all the amazing galleries and architecture there—and I didn't need parental sign-off to do that. I hadn't decided yet whether I was going to wait to tell them until I was heading out the door or not until I was actually on the plane. Telling them now, months in advance, would only mean more arguing.

Mom couldn't feel the guilt, though. As a mage, she drew on joyful feelings to perform her magic, so she was finely attuned to only that aspect of my emotions. With a soft murmur and a flick of her hand, she set my cooled coffee steaming again. A bit of comfort to ease the sting of their disagreement.

"Thanks," I said. "And that trip sounds fantastic."

"I'm looking forward to it too," Dad said with a grin. "I'll see if the Conclave has any special projects I can take on. I expect we'll have plenty of energy to work with."

He was a mage too. The two of them could turn any joy they stirred up in each other or me—or anyone else we ran into—into power. Dad's specialty was healing. Around his ordinary accounting job, he volunteered at a nearby hospital, nudging people's recovery along. *Always be open to happiness*, he'd told me when I was little, half playful and half serious. *Every time I make you smile, it could save someone's life.*

Letting them turn my happiness into magic was as close to any kind of supernatural power as *I* got. From what I'd gathered from the little bits and pieces they'd revealed over the years, being a mage was hereditary. As an adoptee, I hadn't gotten the genetic benefit, and there was no way for them to teach me when I didn't have the power already inside me.

Maybe that was another reason I wanted to take at least a few more steps away from the house I'd grown up in. No matter what I did, I was never going to be as special as they were. Most of the time, I was okay with the fact that I was just a Nary, which was what Mom and Dad called regular people—short for ordinary, or as Mom had said when we'd had The Talk about their talents, *Nary a bit of magic.* Sometimes, though, the yearning prickled so deep it made me queasy.

I *was* ordinary, and eventually I was going to have to build a life with no magic in it at all. Might as well get it over with.

"We'll come back to this conversation when I can convert some of those cons into pros," I told my parents, getting up. Maybe they hadn't been able to teach me magic, but they'd definitely taught me stubbornness.

I brought my coffee downstairs and through the laundry room. On the threshold of the basement apartment, I paused for a moment, taking a sip and contemplating the space.

I really did appreciate having it, and I wished it'd done the trick. Even though the apartment was cramped and dim with storage boxes stacked against one wall, it wasn't *awful.* I just couldn't shake the growing sense that the longer I stayed this tied to my parents, the harder it was going to be to stand on my own when I really needed to. Until I'd started the college classes this fall, Mom and Dad had been the only people I'd regularly spent time with. I had a lot of catching up to do.

My pet mouse, Squeak—not the most original name, but it was her first owner who picked it, not me—was scurrying around her cage, nuzzling at the bars. The sunlight coming in through the little window over her perch made her fur shine: pure white other than a splotch of black on her left flank. I popped open the door and let her scramble up my arm to my shoulder while I considered how I wanted to spend the rest of my morning.

I *could* finish the last bit of the History of Modern Design essay that was due on Thursday… or I could get to work on that phoenix figurine idea that had come to me last night.

I wavered for approximately two seconds before grabbing my bin of polymer clay and my sketchpad off my desk. Squeak's whiskers tickled the back of my neck as she wriggled under the dark waves of my hair. Sometimes she liked to hang out back there like it was a nest or something, which, given how much trouble I often had getting those waves to behave, was kind of fitting. I started up one of my favorite playlists on my phone and sat down at the little kitchen table.

The first stage for any figurine was working out the design with pen and paper. I had to see what I was going to sculpt before I could start working on the actual pieces. My fingers flew over the sketchpad, bringing to life a fiery bird soaring up from a burst of flame. A giddy shiver ran through me as I filled in the details. Perfect.

It was going to be hard to part with this one, but now that I'd spent a few years building a name for myself online, I could make twice as much money selling just one of my little creature sculptures than I did with my three shifts a week at the art supply store downtown. I needed to pay for that Florence trip—and maybe to put down enough advance rent that some landlord would be willing to skip the whole guarantor thing.

When I was satisfied with the sketch, I started warming up the orange clay that would form the base of the phoenix's body. Its tangy waxy smell filled my nose. The feel of the clay softening under my fingers always took me into a sort of trance that felt almost magical. My art was the closest thing I had to a special power.

I was shaping the lump of clay, humming faintly with the song that had just come on, when the ceiling shook.

Bang. Bang. Two sharp thuds echoed from upstairs in quick succession, so violent my skin jumped. The clay slipped from my fingers.

Voices barked loud enough for the hostility to travel through the ceiling, but the words were indistinct. I jabbed the music off, my heart thumping. What the hell was going on?

One of the voices upstairs yelled again. Something made of glass or china smashed. I swallowed hard and grabbed my phone. As I slipped out of my apartment to the stairs at the other end of the laundry room, I dialed 9-1-1.

"What is your emergency?" said a woman on the other end, who managed to sound both pert and deadly serious.

"I don't know," I said, fighting and failing to keep my voice steady.

"It sounds like someone broke into my parents' house. I'm in the basement—I can hear a commotion upstairs. It doesn't sound good."

"What is your address?"

I rattled it off.

"All right," she said. "We'll have the police there as soon as we can. You hang tight. Stay on the phone with me—and stay out of whatever's going on."

That was easy for her to say. It wasn't *her* parents going through God knew what up there. I kept the phone clutched by my ear, but I also slunk halfway up the stairs, placing my feet carefully so the steps wouldn't creak.

The voices got clearer. They must be in the kitchen—Mom and Dad often lingered there for a while reading or chatting after breakfast.

"...is she?" a man was demanding. "Out with it, or this can get much worse."

There was no sound of impact, but Mom let out a pained gasp as if she'd been hit. Was this some kind of home invasion? Couldn't she and Dad use their magic to turn the tables on these assholes?

I guessed there wasn't much joy in the room for them to draw on.

I couldn't help myself. Maybe some other girl would have stood by while thugs smacked around her parents, but not this one. I eased up another step so I could peek through the mudroom into the kitchen.

Mom and Dad were hunched on the floor at opposite ends of the room, Dad farther away with his back against the fridge, Mom closer to me, braced against the oven. Five figures stood over them, three men and two women, all dressed in posh black shirts and slacks like they should have been out at some exclusive dinner party and not here threatening random innocent people.

Except, what were they threatening them *with*? I didn't see weapons in anyone's hands. What the fuck was going on?

Footsteps thumped down the stairs at the other end of the house. "Second floor is clear," a guy hollered.

Clear of what? What had they thought might be up there?

"Check the basement," said the man who'd been warning Mom earlier.

Mom's back stiffened. A strange look came over her face, frantic but fierce.

"You don't have to," she said with a rasp. "I'll tell you where she is."

Two suspicions clicked into place in my head: The assholes were looking for *me*. And Mom was only pretending to give in to get the satisfied smile that crossed the man's face in that moment. A brief jolt of happiness was all she'd need to break out her powers.

Heaving herself to her feet, she thrust her arms out with a swift murmur. The man and the woman next to him stumbled backward. My heart leapt with hope in the instant before the man caught himself. He slashed his hand and spat out a word that wasn't from any language I recognized.

Mom's flesh tore open from the base of her chin all the way down her throat. Blood gushed out, streaming down the front of her pink cotton tunic. Her legs gave way beneath her as the color drained from her face. She sagged over in front of the oven.

My mind went blank with horror. *No, no, no*. I dropped the phone and threw myself toward my mother.

The man had already been swiveling toward Dad. "You deserve far worse for the crimes you've—"

He cut himself off as I hurtled into the room. I managed to catch Mom's head before it hit the tiled floor. Her blood washed hot over my forearms and flowed across the tiles. Her head lolled in my hands, her eyes glazed and lifeless.

My stomach flipped. I pressed my palm against the raw gaping wound on her throat instinctively, as if any part of me really believed I could still save her. "Mom," I choked out.

"Rory, get out of here! Run to—"

The woman closest to Dad said a word and twitched her fingers, and his mouth snapped shut. Several hands grasped my arms to haul me away from Mom's body.

I tried to wrench away, to hit the people around me, to stop them somehow, but my feet tripped under me. One of the figures spun me around to face him. His fingers clamped on my shoulder, his bright hazel eyes catching my gaze from where he'd tipped his head close to mine.

"It's okay," he said in a low, gentle tone that penetrated the roar of anguish inside me. "We've got you now. You won't be trapped here anymore. We're going to take you home."

The words sounded as if they should have been comforting, and he said them like he meant them. With a weird rush of warmth, my body stopped shaking. I blinked, registering that he looked younger than the others, not much older than me. And he was one of the most striking guys I'd ever seen. Even if I hadn't been in the middle of the most horrifying scene in my life, with one glimpse that smooth face with its slicked-back black hair and those brilliant eyes would have burned it into my memory.

The most horrifying— Wait, had he cast magic on me to calm me down? My mind recoiled.

I didn't want these people to "get" me, and this was my home right here. That was my mother—

"I feel we need to send a message," said the man who'd murdered Mom from where he was walking toward Dad.

My heart lurched with a fresh jolt of panic. I yanked myself away from the gentle guy just as the man sliced both hands through the air in an X.

A matching X gouged through Dad's plaid shirt right into his chest. A spasm jerked his body, and a cry seared up my throat. I lunged at his attacker.

More hands caught me. The murderer muttered something under his breath that sounded like a curse.

"Knock her out," he said. "We've got to get going."

A few harsh syllables reached my ear with the swipe of a palm across my forehead, and my mind fell away into blackness.

CHAPTER TWO

Rory

I came to with a sway of the surface beneath me. My body was lying on firm padding, a smooth material against my cheek. My next breath brought the smell of leather into my nose. The thrum of an engine and another swaying sensation told me I was in some kind of vehicle.

My eyelids felt too heavy to lift. My thoughts were muddled. What had they done to me? The people in the kitchen—the man who'd ripped Mom and Dad open like animals in a slaughter house—

Nausea surged through my gut at the memory. I stiffened against the seat. Those monsters had killed my parents and dragged me off… somewhere. I didn't have any idea why or what they wanted, but every particle of my being clanged with fear.

The haze in my head gradually retreated. I eased my eyes open just a crack to take in my surroundings.

Some of my hair had fallen across my face, hiding my gaze from anyone watching. Between the dark brown strands, I made out thin sunlight seeping through the windows onto an empty burgundy leather seat that faced my own. I was in the back of a limo.

My only company was two figures up in the front, the backs of their heads just visible above the tops of the seats. The sunlight glanced off a glass privacy divider between me and them.

As I took that in, the woman in the front passenger seat turned to glance back at me. My breath stopped in my throat as I held myself perfectly still, watching her through my eyelashes. After a second, she looked away again.

The divider must have been a thick one. I didn't hear her speak, but a hint of a laugh carried through as if in response to a comment.

My captors wanted to keep an eye on me, but I guessed they didn't want me to hear whatever they might say about me or where we were going. Okay. A faint ache was spreading through my shoulder from lying prone, but I'd just have to pretend I was still unconscious until I decided what the hell to do next.

None of this made any sense. Mom and Dad had never given me any reason to think they had enemies, let alone the kind of enemies who'd want them *dead*. They'd spent their lives working with joy, for fuck's sake.

This morning—if it was still the same day—I hadn't seen any sign that they were worried about an impending attack. Everything had seemed so normal.

A lump rose in my throat. I shut my eyes against the burn of tears. That breakfast was the last time we'd really talked, and I'd spent most of it badgering them about letting me move out. If I could have erased the last day and stopped any of this from happening, I'd have happily stayed in the damned basement for the rest of my life.

I was pretty sure I was still wearing the same clothes, but no blood clung to my hands or arms. Someone had washed Mom's blood off me. Somehow that felt like a betrayal in itself.

A small shape shifted against the back of my head. I had to tense up to restrain a flinch. Then tiny claws prickled against my scalp in a familiar sensation.

Squeak—had she been holding onto my hair the whole time? I'd been so caught up in the attack that I hadn't thought about where she might have ended up.

A wry wisp of a voice tickled into my head. *Good, you're awake. We need to talk, sweetheart.*

I almost choked in surprise, and my mouse's claws pinched deeper into my scalp. *Quiet. Don't let them know you've come to. If you stay still and whisper to answer me, we should be able to have a decent conversation without them realizing.*

"Squeak?" I murmured, my thoughts spinning. My mouse could talk—or telepathically communicate, at least? Since when? She'd never acted like anything other than a regular rodent back home.

The name's actually Deborah, but when we're around anyone else, you're better off sticking with the mousey one. Sorry to spring this on you so suddenly. I'm just glad I managed to hang on to you while these bastards were hauling you off.

What…? Who…? I didn't know where to start.

Maybe Squeak—Deborah?—picked up on my confusion, because she nestled into her favorite spot at the nape of my neck and went on.

Here's the quick version: I used to be a joymancer like your parents. The Conclave worked some magic so that my mind could take up new residence in this mouse body. It's not such a bad trade, you have to understand, because I was just about dead from cancer when they offered. All I had to do to get a bunch more years was play pet and do my bit as your familiar if anything went wrong. I just wasn't expecting anything to go quite this wrong.

I couldn't wrap my head around most of that. Dad had brought Squeak home from one of his stints at the hospital, saying she'd belonged to a kid there he'd failed to save whose parents hadn't known what to do with the pet. He'd asked if I'd mind looking after her for a bit while he found a permanent home, and I'd ended up enjoying the little animal's company so much I'd told him I'd keep her.

"My parents knew?" I said quietly.

The deal was that I'd watch out for you and signal them if you needed help.

"You called yourself a 'joymancer.'" I hadn't heard that term before.

That's what we all call ourselves—the mages who take our magic from joy. I take it your parents never told you about the other kind. The ones that grabbed you are fearmancers. The same way we draw on happiness to power our spells, they draw on terror. As you've already seen, that leaves them with a pretty warped sense of morality.

Fearmancers. A cold shiver ran down my back. Mom and Dad had never said anything about other kinds of mages. I'd never even met any of their colleagues under the Conclave.

I forced myself to keep my voice low. "Why would these fearmancer people want *me*?"

I'm not sure, Squeak/Deborah said. *But I do know where they're taking you. They were talking about it while you were out on the plane. You've been down for the count for hours. They brought us on a private jet to an airfield in what I've gathered is northern New York. This is just the last step of the journey.*

"A journey to where?"

The fearmancers have a school where they teach all their awful practices. The Conclave has known about it for a long time, but they keep it well-hidden enough that we've never been able to shut it down. They've got some fancy name for the place, but most of the time we just call it Villain Academy. A lot more accurate, in my humble opinion.

Villain Academy. Another chill trickled through me. "I still don't get it. Why are they bringing me anywhere at all? I'm not even a mage. I'm just a Nary."

Deborah made a sound like a sigh. *Oh, Lorelei. Your parents really should have told you that part. The thing is—*

The limo jerked to a stop. Deborah froze and then scurried down under the collar of my T-shirt to hide beneath the fabric on my back.

My pulse raced as my captors stepped out of the vehicle. Someone opened the door by my head with a rush of cool damp air. No, this definitely wasn't a California April anymore.

I narrowed my eyes to slits. A shadow fell over me. "We can't bring her in like this. Ashgrave, wake her up."

There was a pause, and then a low measured voice I recognized said, "She's already awake." Feet shifted against the ground outside as the familiar speaker crouched next to my seat.

"Hey," he said in the same gentle tone he'd used in my parents' kitchen. "I know you're probably really confused, but we're here. You just need to come inside, and we'll get everything sorted out."

Sorted out? Were they going to sort out the way they'd murdered my parents? The fact that they'd kidnapped me and dragged me from one end of the country to the other?

But the young guy with the gentle voice and the striking face hadn't carried out the killings. Okay, he'd tried to dull my panic with his magic, but then and now, he'd talked as if he wanted to help me. Was it possible not everyone here was a total villain?

Whatever the case, he could clearly tell I was faking.

I eased myself upright as if I'd only just woken up. The guy's black hair was a little rumpled from the trip, but his face was still as stunning and his eyes as brightly alert as before. He offered me a little smile with perfect cupid's bow lips. "Let's go. The headmistress is waiting for you—she'll explain everything."

I wouldn't mind a few explanations, but I wasn't in any hurry to go anywhere with a bunch of villainous mages. I didn't feel all that safe in the limo, though.

The guy backed up as I scooted forward. I stepped out onto the smooth asphalt of a parking lot. Immediately, the cool air raised goosebumps on my bare arms. I wasn't dressed for northern weather, especially now that the sun was sinking low.

A couple spots away from the limo, a posh gunmetal gray sedan was parked. The other figures around me must have arrived in that. All six of the creeps—the fearmancers—who'd stormed in on my parents stood around me, watching.

Directly beyond the sedan lay a field framed by a dense forest that wrapped around to my left. The road my captors must have driven up veered away between the trees there. That was my chance at escaping.

To my right, a massive stone building loomed, looking like the illegitimate offspring of a medieval castle and a Victorian manor house. Turrets jutted here and there, their windows shuttered. A gargoyle hunched over the arched front doorway. Um, yeah, I'd rather not set foot in there, if I had a choice in the matter.

The trouble was, I didn't think I had any choice at all.

"Why am I here?" I said. "What do you want with me?"

The fearmancer who'd killed my parents stirred impatiently on his feet. "As he said, Ms. Grimsworth will do the explaining. That's how she wanted it."

I guessed what I wanted didn't figure into his plans. I glanced toward the road again, and his underlings tensed around him.

I'd be kidding myself if I tried to pretend I wasn't generating plenty of fear to fuel their magic with every thud of my heart. I'd seen how easily the one man had slaughtered Mom and Dad. If I made a run for it, what were the chances I'd even make it across the parking lot before they caught me?

I squared my shoulders. They'd brought me here for a reason. I'd be able to come up with a better strategy for getting out of here if I knew what that was. *Know thy enemies.* Dad used to say that, jokingly, when talking about working around the hospital administration.

A punch of grief hit me in the gut. I clenched my jaw, holding myself steady against it.

I didn't have a clue what was going on, but I did know one thing for sure: no way in hell were these assholes getting away with what they'd done to my family.

"Okay," I said, hugging myself against a chilly lick of breeze. "Let's go."

My parents' murderer, who appeared to be in charge of this little squad, made a dismissive gesture with his hand, and three of his followers got back in the sedan. He, the young guy, and one of the women escorted me up the stone steps to the building. As I got closer, I could make out a crest carved into the peak of the stone arch just beneath the gargoyle. The crest was framed by prickly leaves, and at its center was a dragon's head. Not ominous at all.

Our shoes rapped loudly against the polished hardwood floor inside. The huge front hall smelled like mahogany with a whiff of smoke, the former from the broad curving staircases on either side and the latter from the flames dancing in sconces along the stone walls. Their glow gave a wavery quality to the daylight that streamed from the high windows.

The man led us past the staircases and down a narrower, dimmer hall beyond them. It opened to a second entrance room with gold-gilded wallpaper and a single mahogany staircase directly in front of us.

Voices filtered from a side room, but we weren't headed there. The man strode up the stairs. I climbed after him, fidgeting with the glass charms on my bracelet as I went.

"That's right," a smoothly amused voice rang out from above us. "Let's see how you move with a real fire under your feet."

My head jerked around. Down by the right-hand end of the second floor landing, four guys were standing in a cluster. Or rather, as I reached the top of the stairs and could get a better look, three guys were standing in a semi-circle around a fourth.

My legs stalled as I stared. If my hazel-eyed "friend" was striking, the three young men looming over their target were heart-wrenchingly gorgeous. The kind of stunning I'd have assumed had been tinkered to perfection in Photoshop if they hadn't been standing before my eyes just ten feet away.

One appeared to have been built entirely out of muscle, with a chestnut-brown crew cut that emphasized the chiseled planes of his square-jawed face. Another held his lean body with a languid grace, his dark copper hair shadowing boyishly angular features that were made mature by lavishly full lips currently curved into a smirk.

Between them, directly in front of the scrawnier kid they'd caught, was the guy who'd spoken. I could tell it'd been him from the haughty tilt of his handsome face, which managed to look divinely innocent and yet devilishly hot at the same time, a mix of soft and hard lines so perfect that my fingers itched to try to capture them in clay. His golden-brown hair was just long enough to show a hint of curl, and his dark eyes, fixed on the kid, glittered with satisfaction.

The kid, who I'd have placed at sixteen or so, backed up a step, and the divine devil moved his hand. A spurt of fire shot up beneath the boy's shoes. He yelped, scrambled backward, and lurched forward again as the flames seared higher and hotter at his heels. His eyes had gone wide with terror. His tormentors laughed.

Fearmancers. What a fitting demonstration of their talent. Horror twisted tight in my chest. My three escorts had started across the landing in the opposite direction, but the last shaky thread of composure I'd been holding onto snapped.

This morning I'd been totally useless while one asshole had flayed my family. I didn't have to watch another one flambé this kid. I could at least create a distraction that'd give the boy time to flee.

"Leave him alone!" I said, marching toward them. "You're hurting him."

Three startled gazes leapt to me, the flames flickering down. The divine devil grinned.

"I'm teaching him a necessary lesson. Are you aiming to get schooled too?" His eyes skimmed down over my body, and I was abruptly aware of my wrinkled tee and loose jeans in comparison with the pressed dress shirts and slacks everyone around me was sporting. "You look like you could use it."

My eyes narrowed. "You're welcome to try."

Before I'd even finished speaking, his lips moved and his fingers twitched, and a streak of flame darted across the floor toward me.

If he'd thought he was going to shock me, he had no idea what I'd already been through today. I stomped my foot down on the fire, restraining a wince at the flare of magical heat, and glared. "Is that the best you've got?"

The copper-haired guy let out a laugh. The divine devil's mouth curled into a sneer, his expression as cocky as before, but a quivering sensation flitted through the air between us. It wriggled through my ribs and up to the base of my throat, sharp and heady, as if I'd bitten my tongue.

The guy whipped another lick of flame at me and the kid, and one defiant word crackled over my tongue. "*Freeze*."

The quivering jolted out of me—and a sheen of frost raced across the floor, swallowing the flames and fixing the guy's loafers to the floor with a glint of ice. The kid dashed away.

My pulse stuttered. What the fuck? How did that— Had *I* done that?

Where had that power come from?

The jitter of uncertainty that hit me was my undoing. The guy recovered in a flash. He stomped his heel, the ice crinkling away under it, and the entire surface beneath me turned slick and hazy. I moved to take a step, and my feet shot out from under me. I landed on my ass with a sting of pain up my spine. The frigid layer of ice bit into my palms.

"Do you really want to keep going?" the divine devil said, managing to sound both teasing and menacing.

I scrambled up, and the woman from my escort grabbed my arm to steady me.

"This isn't the time," the man said, and motioned to the hazel-eyed guy. "Maybe you'd better fill them in. And you." He jabbed his finger at me. "*This* way, please."

"I look forward to seeing you later," the divine devil called after me as my two remaining escorts ushered me across the landing and around a corner.

As fascinating as he'd been to look at, I couldn't say I returned the sentiment.

I inhaled and exhaled slowly, trying to settle my nerves. I *couldn't* have conjured up that frost, right? I'd never shown the slightest hint of magic before. There had to be some other explanation.

We strode down a gloomy hall with varnished wooden doors lining both sides. The killer stopped at the door at the very end of the hall and rapped his knuckles against it.

"Come in," a woman said in a cool voice, as if she'd been expecting us.

The man opened the door and motioned me in ahead of him. I stepped onto a thick crimson-and-ocher rug in a room as big as my entire basement apartment. Built-in mahogany shelves lined the walls, stuffed with aged books, jars of indeterminate powders and oils, and assorted trinkets.

In the middle of it all, a prim woman of about fifty sat at a matching desk carved with a vine around the edge. Her eyes had a beady quality, her nose pert and her lips thin. Her long graying blond hair was wrapped into a thick coil at the nape of her neck, resting against the collar of a fitted indigo dress-suit.

She stood up as we came in with a bob of her head to my escorts. "Well," she said, fixing her beady gaze on me. "Here you are." She sounded satisfied but somehow not quite pleased, as if she was happy with the situation but not that she had to be a part of it.

"Go on, then," she said in the same cool tone, waving the other two off. They vanished, shutting the door behind them. The woman extended her hand toward one of the two velvet wingchairs that faced her desk. "Please, have a seat. As I'm sure you were told, I'm Headmistress Grimsworth. I'd imagine you have a lot of questions."

I allowed myself to drop into the chair, careful of the mouse clinging to my shirt between my shoulder blades. It seemed like I should probably pretend Deborah hadn't told me anything, or they'd wonder how I knew, but acting clueless didn't feel all that difficult. All the trauma and the confusion of the day washed over me in one huge wave. It took a moment before I could speak.

"Where is this, and why the hell am I here?"

Ms. Grimsworth's mouth curled into a narrow smile. "You're here because this is where you're meant to be. This is the Bloodstone University for Magical Edification, and you are Persephone Bloodstone."

CHAPTER THREE

Malcolm

"Who the fuck was that?" I said, my gaze following the new girl as she slipped out of sight. "And where the hell did she grow up that she comes here dressed like a feeb and jumping into other people's business?"

The junior we'd been playing with had scampered off. If he started spreading the word about how some random chick had saved him from Malcolm Nightwood, he'd find a whole lot more than his feet on fire.

Jude swiped a hand through his dark red hair, his lips curved with his typical smirk. "She looked pretty nice landing on the ground ass-first when you were done with her, I'll give her that."

Connar's grim expression broke with a soft snicker. His brawny arms flexed as he crossed them over his chest. "You know, she did. She should have realized she was outmatched the second she saw you."

I'd admit the new girl had a nice ass in general, even in her baggy jeans. I'd gotten a good look at it while she was leaving. Maybe she'd be fun to have around if she removed the stick she apparently had shoved up there.

We could certainly help her with that.

Declan fixed me with what I'd come to think of as his professor look. He'd always had a bit of a know-it-all vibe that must have come with being the oldest of us and the only one close to full baron. It had intensified since he'd gotten the teacher's aide gig this fall. I gave him a pass on it because he generally put that knowledge to use greasing whatever wheels we needed greased.

"*That*," he said in an authoritative tone, "was the long-lost heir of Bloodstone. So whatever you're imagining doing to her right now, you might want to revise those plans."

I blinked, momentarily losing my grasp on my composure. *Only* momentarily, of course. "The Bloodstone scion? They found her? Holy shit."

Jude cocked his head, his dark green eyes lighting up with curiosity. "Was she living with feebs, hence the clothes?"

"With joymancers," Declan said. "Which as far as I can tell amounts to almost the same thing. Their house could have fit in the front hall three times over. They do like to show off their modesty."

"Wait," I said, prodding him in the chest. "Did you get yourself invited along on the rescue party? Why the hell didn't you tell us anything?"

Declan's chin came up. "They asked me at the last minute. Said it'd be good for her to have one of the other scions there—someone who'd have an idea what she might have gone through. We weren't supposed to tell anyone until we'd pulled it off."

Declan's mother had been killed in the same confrontation-turned-massacre where joymancers had claimed the lives of both the Bloodstones of our parents' generation. Sometimes I forgot that little piece of his past, because I'd only been three when it'd happened, so I didn't really remember it in the first place.

No one talked about the skirmish much anyway. It was kind of a sore spot among the older mages.

"You could have introduced her and saved her a little trouble." I peered toward the hall the girl had disappeared down, a tickle of exhilaration rising through my chest. So, that was the Bloodstone scion. She hadn't had any more idea who we were than we had about her. Totally fitting that she'd have started asserting dominance the second she'd walked into Blood U.

She'd be embarrassed when she found out who she'd actually been messing with. I had to smile, imagining her reaction.

Despite the shabby clothes, she'd been awfully easy on the eyes. And that brash spirit… Oh, yes, spring term had just gotten ten times more exciting.

"No one knows how much *she* knows about who she is or what happened to her," Declan said. "From the way she was acting, I don't think she had any idea. Grimsworth wanted to talk with her first."

"We'll give her a little time to settle in," I said magnanimously, rubbing my hands together. "Find out what dorm they stick her in. We can stop by after dinner and give her a chance at re-doing first impressions."

Having a Bloodstone at the school… I wasn't going to let that tip the balance very much. The four of us who ruled Blood U and would someday rule the whole fearmancer shebang together—we'd had each other's backs for years. She'd have to prove herself ready to respect and return that kind of allegiance before we'd fully welcome her into our circle, the final point on the pentacle.

We'd make it clear who ran things around here and go from there. Once she got the picture, I had the feeling it'd be a productive friendship.

My thoughts slid back to the fierceness in her dark blue eyes when she'd tried to stare me down, the flush of color in her pale cheeks. Maybe more than friendship if I got my way. And, let's be honest, I usually did.

CHAPTER FOUR

Rory

I stared at the headmistress of Bloodstone University for the space of a few heartbeats before I regained control over my vocal chords.

"I think there's been a mistake," I said. "I would definitely remember if my name was something as weird as Persephone Bloodstone. I'm Lorelei Franco. Usually I go by Rory. Nice to meet you." I raised my hand in an awkward little wave.

Maybe I should have said "horrible to meet you," but from Ms. Grimsworth's pinched expression, I had the feeling that wouldn't have gone over well. I still didn't have a lot of options here.

The headmistress looked down at a few papers spread in front of her on her desk. A sharp ashy smell drifted past my nose from a cone of incense set on a burner on a nearby shelf. It made my stomach turn.

"You've been living with Lisa and Rafael Franco, yes?" she said. "For how long?"

"For—for as long as I can remember. They adopted me when I was two years old."

Ms. Grimsworth hummed to herself. "They or their colleagues

kidnapped you, Miss Bloodstone. Did you know that they were mages—that they could wield magic?"

I nodded slowly. "Yes. They didn't keep that a secret from me. But why—"

"There are two types of magic-workers in this world," Ms. Grimsworth said. "The people who raised you were joymancers, working with feelings of elation. You've now met the first fearmancers I'd imagine you've had a chance to associate with in your memory."

"Fearmancers. Mages who use fear?" I said, as if Deborah hadn't already explained that much. Otherwise she might wonder why I wasn't more surprised.

"Exactly. Our communities have often been at odds. Seventeen years ago, a group of joymancers interrupted several fearmancers in the middle of conducting their business. Your birth parents were there, along with you. They were killed in the attack, and the joymancers took you with them when they fled the scene. We've spent significant resources over those years trying to track you down. They hid you well, but not well enough to foil us completely."

Her beady eyes glinted with satisfaction, as if the brutal murders of my *real* parents, the ones who'd raised me, were something to celebrate. My stomach churned.

Even if everything she'd just said was true, why the hell *wouldn't* mages like Mom and Dad have wanted to get a little kid away from a "community" like this? They'd been trying to give me a better life.

"You've been affected by your time with them, naturally," the headmistress said. "But as you realize how much they were denying you, how much they stole from you, I expect you'll adapt quickly. There's a reason this university is named after your family, Miss Bloodstone. The Bloodstones are one of the five ruling families among the fearmancers. You'll have great magical gifts that I doubt your kidnappers ever allowed you to use."

"I don't have any—" I started, and stopped, shutting my mouth so sharply my teeth clicked. On the landing, with those gorgeous asshole guys, I'd conjured ice. Not a lot of it, but… I hadn't known what I was doing.

The sensation of power that had come over me hadn't been joy—

that was for sure. No, for one fleeting instant, the divine devil had been *afraid*.

And I'd drunk in that emotion and transformed it into power, as easily as breathing.

Fuck.

"I'm a fearmancer," I said quietly as the understanding sank in. "But I never—when I was living with my parents—"

"They would have had ways of suppressing your natural talents," Ms. Grimsworth said. "Mages of both kinds normally see their magical ability emerge sometime between their fifteenth and sixteenth birthday. For most of your childhood, they wouldn't have needed to even worry about it."

Between my fifteenth and sixteenth birthday. Icy fingers wrapped around my gut. The mouse currently nestled against my back, clinging to my shirt—Dad had brought her home just a couple of weeks after my fifteenth birthday.

Deborah had said her job had been to protect me, to let them know if I needed help. Had that really been just a nice way of saying she'd been my guard, watching to make sure my fearmancer magic didn't emerge despite whatever they were doing to hold it in?

Oh, God. No wonder they hadn't wanted me to move out or to travel anywhere without them. They must have needed me to stay close so they could work their spells on me.

I closed my eyes against the horror welling up inside me. No. My parents *had* been protecting me—protecting me from these people who they must have known were searching for me. From the dark magic they practiced. Any horror I felt shouldn't be because of them but the blood the fearmancers had spilled in my house this morning.

Somehow I didn't think I could simply say, *Well, that's all lovely, but I'd like to head back to spend the rest of my life with the non-psychopathic mages now*, and the fearmancers would fly me back on their private jet in a jiffy.

I looked down at my hands clasped together on my lap. The light from the ornate fixture on the ceiling glinted off the charms along my wrist that Mom and Dad had bought for me over the last nine years. Another wallop of grief hit me without warning.

How long would it take for someone to find them where the fearmancers had left them ravaged? Or had the mages who'd taken me magicked my parents' bodies away so the murders would never be discovered, and they'd simply vanish from existence?

All the pieces of my life with them, from my childhood through to this morning, were hundreds of miles away. All I had of *myself*, of my history as their daughter, was that bracelet and the old T-shirt and jeans I'd thrown on for a lazy Sunday morning.

And a telepathic mouse that was part guardian, part guard. Deborah's furry back shifted against my skin as she adjusted her position. I couldn't forget her.

Ms. Grimsworth had been waiting in silence as I'd wrestled with her revelations. I sucked in a breath and raised my head. "All right. What happens now? What do you expect me to do?"

She gave me a tight smile that might have been slightly sympathetic. It was hard to tell, her face was so rigid. "It seemed best for you to come here and remain until your education is complete. As the heir to the Bloodstone legacy, you'll have certain responsibilities. You're greatly behind in the training you'll need to complete to fulfill those responsibilities. The Bloodstone properties will be yours when you're ready to take your full place in society. They're currently inhabited only by maintenance staff paid for by your fortune."

I had properties. I had a *fortune*. This morning I'd been worried about making a couple hundred bucks on a figurine. A hysterical giggle bubbled in my throat.

"Aren't there any other Bloodstones around who can handle this stuff?" I had to ask.

The headmistress pursed her lips. "Your grandfather served as temporary baron, despite being aged out, until his death seven years ago. He had a brother who took up residence in Portugal decades ago and who hasn't been heard from in almost as long. Your mother's younger sister passed away before you were born—a boating accident. By that series of unfortunate circumstances, you are the only definite living Bloodstone in existence."

Wonderful. Exactly how pissed off would she be if I chose this moment to vomit all over her expensive rug?

I dragged in a breath. Maybe the best option was also the easiest. I could play along for now, right? It wouldn't be such a bad thing to learn the basics of the magical talent I'd only just discovered. I'd wait for my moment, and then I'd run for the hills—or rather, for California. My parents had friends in the Enclave. Someone had to know what the hell to do.

"I guess it's up to me, then, huh?" I said with a weak laugh, and stood up. "How do I get started?"

Ms. Grimsworth said something under her breath and made a small gesture with her hand. "I've summoned the professor who'll serve as your mentor to show you to your dorm room. He'll explain more of the workings of the school along the way. Tomorrow morning, we'll conduct your assessment to determine your areas of greatest strength, and then he and I will draw up a course plan for you to follow. You'll find we aren't rigorously focused on classroom work here at the university. We find students learn best with a mix of assignments and more self-directed practice."

Like setting younger students on fire? I bit my tongue rather than mention that.

The headmistress got up and motioned at me from head to toe. "It also seems worth mentioning that the team that liberated you cast a locating spell on you to ensure we don't lose you again. You'll be able to roam the entire campus grounds and visit the town down the hill, but if you should find yourself whisked farther away, we'll be alerted and arrive as quickly as possible."

As she spoke, a shiver ran over my skin that might have been an echo of that magic. I thought I read a subtle threat in her gaze. If I tried to make a break for it of my own accord, I wouldn't get very far, no matter how stealthy I was. Shit.

There had to be a way to undo a locating spell. I'd just have to learn it.

A knock sounded on the door. Ms. Grimsworth swung it open.

In the hall stood a man I'd have put in his mid-forties. Tufts of light red hair—really it was orange—stuck up in various directions over his round head and along his equally rounded jaw. Like every other fearmancer I'd encountered so far, he was dressed to impress: a blue linen shirt that downplayed his barrel chest and gray dress pants.

"Miss Bloodstone," the headmistress said, "I'm pleased to introduce you to Professor Banefield, one of our specialists in Insight. He'll be acting as your mentor for your first year at the university, and perhaps longer if you get along well."

I didn't want to think about being stuck here for a whole year, let alone more than that.

Professor Banefield gave me a smile that had more warmth than I'd gotten from all of the other fearmancers I'd met combined and stuck out his hand. The warmth startled me so much it took me a second to realize he was waiting for me to complete a handshake.

"It's a pleasure to meet you, Miss Bloodstone," he said with a brisk pump. "Or if I might call you Persephone—"

"Rory," I said quickly. "My name is Rory." Maybe I couldn't argue the Bloodstone part, but I'd be damned if they were going to take away the first name my parents had given me too.

Banefield's gaze twitched to the headmistress and back to me. "All right then. Rory. I'm so glad to have you returned to us. You must be overwhelmed. Why don't you let me show you to your room here on campus, and then you can take some time to absorb everything you've learned?"

"That sounds good," I said, because it really did. If there was a place here I could be alone with my thoughts, let me at it.

"I hope you'll consider this school a home for as long as you're with us," Ms. Grimsworth said as I stepped out of her office. "If you should have any concerns, you can always come to me."

Professor Banefield set off down the hall with a rhythmic stride. After walking alongside him for a minute, I realized he was a bit bowlegged.

"This building houses the staff offices and residences as well as the junior dorms—for students aged fifteen to seventeen," he said, and pointed at a door with a gleaming bronze name plaque. "If you need me, you'll be able to find me here. You'll be living in the adjacent Ashgrave Hall, which contains the senior dorms—for our students aged eighteen to twenty-one—and our extensive library."

That name rang a bell. When I'd gotten here with my parents' attackers, the head guy had called one of them "Ashgrave," hadn't he?

"Why Ashgrave?" I asked.

Banefield gave me a quizzical look but answered easily enough. "Each of the ruling families had a hand in creating this university. Yours had the distinction of giving their name to the entire school, but the others each adopted a building."

Someone who'd been part of the attack was a member of another ruling family. I wasn't sure what to do with that information.

"Bloodstone, Ashgrave... What are the other ruling families?" That seemed important to know.

"Nightwood, Killbrook, and Stormhurst. This is Killbrook Hall we're in right now. The classrooms are in Nightwood Tower, which forms a triangle with the two halls. And closer to the lake you'll find the Stormhurst Building for Physical Fitness."

Banefield rambled on as he led me down the stairs. "The university seeks to provide all students with both privacy and a communal experience. The senior dorms are set up with ten individual bedrooms around a common living and kitchen area, with a bathroom shared just by the ten or fewer in that dorm. Because of your status, you'll naturally receive one of the few corner rooms with a little more space and a view of the lake."

"Naturally," I muttered, and snapped my mouth shut when he shot me another of those puzzled glances. "So, what happens in this 'assessment' thing tomorrow?"

"Nothing for you to worry about. All you need to do is be present, and the assessors will take care of the rest. From what I recall, it feels like a brief, mild tingling."

If he was telling the truth, I could probably handle that much.

We stepped out through a side door into the cool spring air. The sun had dropped below the trees, and the shadows sprawled long across the ground. A paved pathway swerved through the neatly trimmed grass to another medieval-ish stone building that rose five stories to a gable roof.

Another path rambled across the way to a narrower cylindrical structure nearly twice as tall that easily earned the label Tower.

Banefield pointed between Ashgrave Hall and Nightwood Tower toward a squat building topped by a dome farther across the green.

"Assessments take place in the main gymnasium," he said. "I'll come by your dorm to escort you there at nine o'clock tomorrow. We all understand it'll take you some time to get your bearings."

And yet they seemed perfectly happy to throw me into this life with hardly an acknowledgement of the one they'd ripped me out of. Did fearmancers have so little conscience that it didn't occur to them that I might still be bothered by my parents' deaths even now that I knew Mom and Dad had supposedly kidnapped me? Was that fact supposed to erase an entire childhood of love?

The first two floors of Ashgrave Hall held the library. A few students were ambling between the shelves, glancing our way and then going back to their business. We hiked up three more flights to the top floor. No elevators to speak of, apparently. I was going to have killer legs if I stayed here very long.

"It's important to note," Banefield said as we climbed, "that we welcome a number of Nary students to the university to assist with certain aspects of our programming. They wear a gold pin shaped like a leaf that they believe simply marks their scholarship status. You must be careful to avoid discussing any magical subjects while they're within hearing and to ensure they don't pick up on any spells you cast on or around them. Discipline is rather strict in that regard."

I blinked at him. "You let Naries into your university of magical studies?"

He shrugged. "We prepare you for every aspect of the world you'll be venturing into. None of us can exist without some dealings with the Nary population."

The fifth floor landing offered four doors. Banefield swiped a keycard over a panel for the one marked C1, and the lock clicked over. He handed the card to me and pushed the door open.

The square room on the other side was four times the size of my living room back home, with a similar aesthetic to the headmistress's office, just fewer books and more seating. A thick rug covered most of the floor under the clusters of sofas, armchairs, and coffee tables. A ten-seater mahogany dining table stood between the living area and a kitchen with two stainless steel fridges along the far wall. Five wooden doors stood along the walls on either side of me, and another door next to the kitchen must have led to the bathroom.

A couple of girls around my age were sitting at one end of the table finishing off their steak dinners. The rich smell of sirloin laced the air. A few others were sprawled on the sofas. All of them had been looking toward the open bedroom door in the far left corner when we came in. Their gazes jerked to me and then back to the bedroom.

Another girl was poised just outside that door with her hands planted on her curvaceous hips. Perfectly neat waves of auburn hair spilled down to the middle of her back.

"I didn't agree to this," she was saying in an acidic voice.

"You can take it up with the headmistress then," a woman said from inside the room. She came out carrying a box, a stiletto heel protruding from inside. "Or them, I suppose," she added, lifting her chin toward Banefield and me. She walked along the line of doors to deposit the box in the bedroom closest to us.

The girl spun around. The beauty of her angelic face, pale and smooth as porcelain, was ruined by the narrowing of her eyes and the disgusted curl of her lip.

"That was *my* room, Professor Banefield," she said, crossing her arms over her chest as she strode over. "It's been mine since I moved to senior last year. I don't see why I should have to give it to her." The disgusted curl deepened as she looked me over. I bristled automatically.

"Victory," Banefield said in an even voice, "this is Per— Ah, this is Rory Bloodstone. As a scion, she's owed the best room we can provide for her. If she'd been with us from the start, you wouldn't have gotten to enjoy the room for as long as you did." He turned to me. "This is Victory Blighthaven, one of our most talented students."

His compliment bounced right off Victory. From the glare she was shooting me, she wished the fearmancers hadn't found me at all.

That makes two of us, I wanted to tell her, but I couldn't figure out how to express my profound desire to be anywhere but here in a way that didn't offend her and every other mage around me even more.

The fact was, though, that I didn't really care about the room. If I had my way, I wouldn't be staying in it very long anyway. If having it would keep this witch out of my way, let her have it.

"I don't need a special room," I said to Banefield. "It's fine. I'll take whichever one was empty."

Victory brightened for the instant before Banefield shook his head. "We have standards for a reason. You've been denied your heritage too long, Rory. We aren't going to hold you back from it even here. I believe Victory's things have already been moved over?"

The woman who'd carted the box out reemerged. "Yep, we're good to go. I set up the wardrobe like Ms. Grimsworth wanted, too. Come on, Miss Bloodstone. Let me show you."

Victory's eyes burned a hole in my back as I followed the woman over.

With the two of us and Banefield in the bedroom, there wasn't much standing room left. A queen-sized bed filled about half of the space. Across from it, a small mahogany desk and chair sat beneath a huge picture window that showed the field between the hall and the athletic building as well as the sparkling water of a huge lake farther beyond that. A wardrobe that stretched almost to the ceiling stood against the wall next to the door.

The woman tugged open the wardrobe's doors. Silky blouses and dresses and several pairs of slacks hung in a row. Every piece was sleek and posh. A fearmancer's clothes.

"I bought undergarments and the like for you—new, of course," the woman said, motioning to the drawers at the bottom of the wardrobe. "They said you wouldn't be coming with much. If the sizing's off, just pass on the word to someone from maintenance. We had to go by the initial observations. There are a few pairs of shoes in there too—you can see if they fit. Harder to tell feet sizes. From the looks of you, they were right that her clothes should work."

"*Her* clothes?" I repeated.

"Your mother's. We picked out a selection from the estate that seemed appropriate for university life." The woman flashed me a grin. Then her expression turned more serious. "We wanted you to have something from your family as you get started here."

My mother. Something from my family. The Bloodstones, they

meant. The birth mother I couldn't even remember. Not the one whose literal blood had drenched my hands less than a day ago.

A prickling rushed up behind my eyes before I could catch it. "Thank you," I said, as quickly as I could manage without being a total ass. "I, um, this is great. I think I just need to lie down for a few minutes."

"Yes, of course. I'll see you in the morning." Banefield ushered the woman out of the room and closed the door. The second it thudded shut, I sank onto the edge of the bed.

Deborah scurried down the back of my shirt and poked her little white head out from under the hem. *Lorelei, if you—*

"Not right now," I whispered hoarsely, and just like that, the tears I'd been holding in from the moment I'd woken up spilled out in a torrent. I bowed my head into my hands and let grief take over.

CHAPTER FIVE

Rory

The first sound that penetrated my cloud of grief was Victory's caustic voice carrying through my bedroom door, pitched in a low but pointed way to give her plausible deniability while she fully intended to be overheard.

"I heard the Bloodstones have always been bitches. 'Oh, really, I'll take whatever room's available,' as if she didn't know they'd already kicked me out of the one she wanted. Looks like the line runs true."

At least a couple of someones twittered with laughter in response.

I rubbed my stinging eyes and pushed myself upright where I'd curled up on the bed. My head was muggy, and my stomach pinched with hunger. It had to be well past my usual dinner time now.

Mom had been planning a roast. I'd seen it thawing in the fridge this morning, less than a day and what felt like hundreds of years ago.

I inhaled shakily and resisted the pull of another wave of tears. Crying wasn't going to help me. If I was going to get through this, I needed to pull myself together.

Tiny claws tickled the back of my hand. Deborah the mouse peered up at me from the bedspread. *I'm sorry I wasn't able to prepare you better. I didn't know about you being a scion. I was going to tell you the fearmancer part in the car, but there wasn't time. If I communicate with you like this around them, they might pick up on it.*

"It's okay," I said under my breath, with sharp awareness of how easily voices could travel through the door. "If you can talk to me like that, can you cast other kinds of spells too?"

Unfortunately, no. It's part of the familiar bond. A mage can tie their spirit to an animal, and there's a certain mental connection… Regular animals wouldn't be able to communicate in words like this, of course. I only can because my mind is human.

"My parents created the bond," I said. They must have, in some way I hadn't noticed at the time.

So I could watch out for you in ways you didn't realize you needed, Deborah said.

"Yeah." I wished they'd thought they could trust me with those revelations. "I guess we should find a home for you somewhere in here. I don't want to know what the assholes here would do if they found out I've brought a disguised joymancer along with me."

Yes, good thinking. I'd rather not discover the consequences either. Her furry body shivered.

I poked around the room with Deborah perched on one of my palms, and we decided my sock drawer would make an ideal hiding spot. The notch in the front for pulling the drawer open was just big enough for her to squeeze in and out, and if a few mouse hairs got on my socks, I didn't think anyone would be looking closely enough to notice.

My stomach grumbled more insistently. Was there anywhere to get food on campus? Professor Banefield hadn't mentioned a cafeteria.

I went to venture into the common room, and my pulse jumped at how easily the doorknob turned. Banefield had given me a keycard for the dorm, but my bedroom door didn't appear to have any lock at all. No keyhole on the knob, no bolt I could slide over from the inside.

I'd assume respect for personal belongings operated on an honor system, except from what I'd seen honor wasn't a quality fearmancers valued highly.

When I came out, two different girls were at the dining table, perched at opposite ends. One fidgeted with her mousey-brown ponytail as she hunched over the bowl she was eating from. The other was cutting into a filet mignon, her tawny waves pulled back from her face with a silver clip in the shape of a raven. The girls who'd been eating steaks earlier had moved to a sofa at the other end of the room where they were paging through a fashion magazine together.

And Victory was lounging on the sofa closest to my room, her bare calves sprawled over the lap of a girl with a shiny black bob. She'd thrown her head back in a laugh at some comment made by her other friend, whose ice-blond french braid was streaked through with purple and pink. At the click of my door, her gaze shot to me. I ignored her, but I could feel her narrowed eyes studying me as I tested my doorknob from the outside.

"No locks in here, your highness," she cooed. "But I'm sure someone as special as you can figure out other ways of keeping your door secure."

Oh. They must all use magic to prevent intruders. And if someone was better at magic than you, they'd be able to break in no matter what you did, if they wanted. Of course that was how security would work at Villain Academy.

At least I didn't have much in there I wanted to protect. The only things that actually belonged to me, I was wearing. Deborah could hide herself just fine.

I turned away from my room, fighting the urge to hug myself defensively, and considered which of my dormmates would be the safest to ask where I could find my own grub. I hadn't gotten any farther than eliminating Victory and her sidekicks when the dorm door whipped open, and four guys who definitely didn't belong to this room strolled in. Apparently even that lock opened to the right spell.

The guys moved through the common area with total confidence, as if they walked into girls' dorm rooms every day. Which for all I knew, they did.

At the head of the pack was the divine devil from earlier, his wickedly flawless face split with an easy grin and a small cloth bag dangling from one hand. He was flanked by the redhead and the musclehead from before, which was no surprise, but ambling along behind them was the striking guy with the swept-back black hair and hazel eyes who'd tried to reassure me during my parents' murders.

"Mal!" Victory cried. She and her friends sprang up, and she sashayed over to give the divine devil a kiss on the cheek while the other two batted their eyes at the whole pack. Her hand lingered on his forearm.

"Hey, Vic," he said, his expression pleased if not exactly warm. The fact that he enjoyed this girl's attention only solidified my initial opinion of him.

The guy with the dark copper hair tugged on the end of Victory's friend's braid with a teasing smirk. "Does your hair just grow this way, Cressida? I never see you with it down."

The other girl arched her eyebrows, but an eager flush colored her cheeks at his touch. "Maybe someday you'll get to, if you prove yourself up to the challenge."

"What, you haven't been sufficiently impressed so far?"

The divine devil—Mal?—shot his friend a *knock it off* look, and the copper-haired guy let go of her braid with a breezy flick of his fingers. Victory gazed up at the ringleader coyly. "To what do we owe this visit? Got big plans you need company for?"

His gaze found me where I'd stiffened just outside my bedroom door. He aimed his smile my way with no hint of his earlier animosity. "I figured a little housewarming was in order for our newfound scion." He lifted the cloth bag higher. "We come bearing dinner, made by Jude's family chef. Best roast duckling you've ever tasted."

That wouldn't be hard, considering I'd never tasted roast duckling before, period. Why was this guy being so friendly now? Victory's smile had tightened, and she was as close to shooting daggers from her eyes as she could get without actually fileting me.

I'll admit that being homeschooled most of my life had its downsides, the main one being the isolation. The only people I'd socialized with on a regular basis were my parents. I liked to think that these days I didn't put my foot in my mouth anywhere near as much as I had in the first few months of college, but my capacity for complex social navigation was still pretty limited. And if the tricky situations I'd encountered at my old school had been algebra, this right here felt like advanced calculus.

"Um," I said brilliantly.

The divine devil's gaze darted across the room and settled for a moment on the mousy girl hunched at one end of the dining table. He murmured a few words with a clench of his hand. She slumped back in her chair, her eyes glazing.

My shoulders came up. I didn't need any practice to know how to respond to *that*. "What the hell did you do to her?"

He cocked his head as his gaze came back to me. "We can't talk freely when there's a feeb around. When I snap her out of it, she'll just think her thoughts wandered off for a minute."

For the first time, I noticed the gleaming leaf pin by the neckline of the girl's shirt. She was one of the Nary students Professor Banefield had mentioned.

And this jerk had talked about putting her into a stupor the same way you might mention leashing a dog.

He was already sauntering closer to me, leaving Victory to trail behind him. He tossed the cloth bag onto the dining table, and I caught a whiff of a meaty, citrusy smell that made my mouth water. My stomach probably would have gurgled again if it hadn't balled into a knot of repulsion.

"I think we got off on the wrong foot earlier. I'm Malcolm Nightwood, the Nightwood scion." He made a grand gesture toward himself and pointed to the copper-haired guy who'd come up beside him, who offered a cheeky wave. "This jackass is Jude Killbrook." Then to the beefy guy, who was watching me with a small smile that didn't really fit his otherwise stern expression. "Our resident blockhead, Connar Stormhurst." Then my former captor/rescuer. "And the stuffed shirt over there is Declan Ashgrave."

My eyes leapt to the guy with the bright hazel eyes, whose voice had been so gentle in the midst of the carnage this morning. "We met earlier," he said, in an even tone I couldn't read. "Welcome to the pentacle of scions."

So *he* was the Ashgrave I'd heard the head of the group talking to. He stood a little more rigidly than the others, but he didn't look any more bothered by Malcolm's casually insulting description of him than the other two did. Did he actually like this guy?

They were waiting—for me to return the introduction, obviously. "Rory Fra—I mean, Bloodstone," I said, stumbling. "Rory Bloodstone." For now. I motioned to the dinner he'd brought. "You really didn't have to."

Victory let out a sound like a muffled snort. The guys ignored her.

"You're one of us," Malcolm said. "We look after our own. You've made it to the right place, with the right friends—good-bye to the prissy joymancers."

That last remark took me from bristling to furious in an instant.

"What if I'm not interested in being friends?" I said.

Malcolm chuckled. "Who are you going to hang out with, then—the feebs and the wimps like you had before? We know where you belong."

My voice came out taut. "No. *I* know where I belong. And it's nowhere near jerks like you. So why don't you get the hell out of my dorm room and bestow your 'friendship' on someone who wants it?"

The room fell into total silence, all of my dormmates watching us. Connar's folded arms tensed. Jude let out a low whistle, but his smirk had hardened.

"You just got here, darling," he said. "It's a little early to start drawing battle lines."

A flush colored Malcolm's neck. His coffee-brown eyes flared with anger. "I think you need to remember who you're talking to."

"I know exactly who I'm talking to," I said. "A superficial, insecure asshole who cares more about family names than who someone is and has to resort to insulting and tormenting everyone he thinks is less than him just to feel good about himself. Why the fuck anyone would want that in their life, I haven't got a clue."

One of the girls gasped. If Malcolm could have incinerated me just with his gaze, I think he would have.

Despite his expression, his voice came out cuttingly cold. "If that's how you want to play this, be my guest. We'll see how quickly your feeb-dressed untrained ass comes begging us for a hand up when you see what the world is really like. And when you do, you'd better be on your knees and ready to open wide."

He spun on his heel and stalked out. The other three guys followed him, not even Declan glancing back. My chest twisted as he disappeared out the door.

It looked like he was just as much of an asshole as the rest of the scions. Why the hell had he tried to be kind to me this morning if he was going to stand by while his friend talked trash about everyone and everything that had mattered to me?

"You do know how to make an impression, don't you?" Victory said with a sharp little smile that looked a bit smug.

The adrenaline rush of my anger ebbed, leaving me empty. I gestured to the bag Malcolm had left behind. My stomach panged, but I knew if I ate one tidbit of the meal he'd brought, Victory would be running to him to crow about how I'd already accepted his charity.

"If anyone wants extra dinner, you're welcome to it," I said, and ducked back into my room where I could be alone with all the painful sensations inside me.

CHAPTER SIX

Jude

Saying Malcolm was pissed off was like suggesting the Atlantic Ocean was a tad damp. He kept his head high and his gait steady as we crossed the landing to his dorm room, but I'd known him my whole life, and I could read his anger in every tensed muscle and flick of his gaze. He strode into the common room, where a few of his dormmates were chatting around a coffee table, and swept his arm through the air.

"Everyone out. We need this space."

His smooth baritone penetrated the doors. It was nearly nine o'clock at night, but every guy in here knew better than to argue with Malcolm Nightwood.

The three in the living area scrambled up and hustled past us without a word or even eye contact. A couple of guys who'd been in their bedrooms slipped out and fled too.

Malcolm rolled a few syllables off his tongue that had meaning only to him, his fingers rippling like a piano player's as he scanned the room. He was confirming no one else was still in residence. When the spell had satisfied him, he spun around to face the rest of us.

"That brainless bitch," he snapped.

Everyone at Blood U knew better than to argue with Malcolm Nightwood… except our newfound Bloodstone scion.

I might have laughed at the memory of her trying to take Malcolm on, like a lamb bleating at a fucking lion, if Malcolm hadn't been so furious about it. If the conversation had happened in private, he might have brought her down a few pegs right there and left it at that. But she'd torn into him in front of the daughters of some of the most powerful families below the pentacle five, thrown his graciousness in his face, and he hadn't been prepared for a fight.

It was better that we'd left with one quick jab than stay and risk a larger fumble.

"She's brainless, all right," I said, flopping onto the arm of one of the sofas. "She's never worked a bit of magic before today, and she thinks it's a good idea to go up against the four strongest mages in the school? She'll regret that in no time flat."

"I should have flipped her on her ass right there," Connar muttered, cracking his knuckles.

Declan held up his hands, always the voice of reason. "But you didn't, because no matter what she said, she's still a scion." He turned to Malcolm. "She didn't really understand what she was getting into. She's only been here a few hours."

Malcolm scowled. "Somehow I don't get the impression she's going to turn all sunshine and roses as she settles in."

"So we teach her what her proper place is," I said. "And teach her quick, before she gets even farther into bad habits." I didn't care where she'd grown up or how ignorant she was, she couldn't walk in here and do whatever she wanted expecting everyone to accept her like that. We all had our parts to play, scions more than anyone.

If I'd pulled a stunt like she just had in front of that many witnesses… An uncomfortable prickle wrapped around my gut. The less I thought about that, the better.

Years of searching to finally pluck her from our enemies' grasp, the crown of scionhood dropped just like that onto her head where it should have been all along… You'd think she could show a little more gratitude.

"We'll teach her, all right." The eagerly brutal light that was my favorite look on him came over Malcolm's face. The corners of his lips curled upward. "Of course we will. We won't even have to work that hard. She's got a lot of catching up to do and an entire senior class looking for ways to earn for their leagues. A few well-placed blows, and she *will* come running to us begging us to have her back and help her learn the ropes. She might be a scion, but this place is ours. *We* decide what goes."

"Any blows you strike are going to need to be a lot more subtle than lighting a kid's feet on fire if you don't want Ms. Grimsworth cracking down," Declan said. "Having the Bloodstone scion back under her watch is a big deal to her. You can… *educate* her, but we don't want to come close to crossing any lines."

Malcolm scoffed. "Give me a little credit. She won't even know what hit her."

Connar looked from one to the other like a pit bull ready to spring. "What's the plan, then?"

I leaned back against the sofa. I knew what *my* role here was. If any of these guys would still give me the time of day if they had the full story—which was doubtful—it'd be for my ability to provide the entertainment. So I'd keep delivering.

"I don't think she should get to do much other learning until she's proven she can learn to give respect where it's due. She'll have a class schedule after her assessment. I can already think of a few fun ways we can make her wish she had us on her side."

"Do you have some new illusions up your sleeve, Jude?" Malcolm said.

I spread my hands. "Hey, might as well earn for my league at the same time."

He chuckled. "Whatever. As long as it's good, I'm down. What have you got?"

CHAPTER SEVEN

Rory

Professor Banefield had said he'd come get me for my assessment at nine in the morning. It hadn't occurred to me in the moment that I'd dropped my phone back in my parents' house and my dorm room didn't appear to have any clock. Maybe the other fearmancers had a magical way of telling time?

In any case, at least it gave me one reason to be thankful that I slept so restlessly that I was up with the rising sun.

When I ventured into the common room again, it was empty except for the Nary girl—the one Malcolm had called a "feeb"—who was eating a bowl of cereal in the same hunched defensive position I'd seen her in yesterday.

Now that I'd seen how the mages around her were inclined to treat her, I could understand why she might take that stance. She didn't appear to have suffered any ill effects from Malcolm's daze, which one of the girls must have finally snapped her out of after he'd left, but what the hell did I know about the effects of that kind of magic?

"Hey," I said tentatively, stopping by the edge of the table. She wasn't magical—she didn't even know magic existed—and weirdly that made her the only person I'd met so far that I could really trust. "I didn't expect anyone else to be up this early."

The girl gave me a wary look as she chewed the spoonful she'd just popped into her mouth. "I like to get out of here before anyone else wakes up," she said, in a tone that hinted at a whole lot of hassling she'd gotten when she didn't.

I glanced toward Victory's bedroom door with a grimace. "I can understand that. I'm Rory, by the way."

She bobbed her head, her ponytail swinging with the movement. "I heard. Ah, my name's Shelby. Sorry you ended up stuck with this bunch."

My mouth twitched into a smile, and her shoulders relaxed a little. Her gaze followed me as I puttered through the kitchen. The sink was stacked with dirty dishes, a sour smell rising off them.

"Doesn't anyone clean up around here?" I asked.

"The housekeeping staff come through in the middle of the day and take care of everything," Shelby said. "That's one thing I like about this place."

Because the posh fearmancers couldn't bear to pick up after themselves? Lovely.

I opened one of the fridges and noted the names sharpied onto every container. "I guess there isn't any common food."

"No. There's, um, a cafeteria for the juniors in Killbrook Hall, and seniors are allowed to eat there too, but… no one does. It's basically social suicide."

I was pretty sure I'd already committed that at least twice since setting foot on campus. "Oh, well. Will you at least still talk to me when I'm shunned?" My smile shifted into a wry grin.

Shelby looked as if she was surprised to find herself grinning back. She rubbed her hand across her mouth and then blurted out, "If you want, you can have some of my cereal—and milk too, of course. It's nothing fancy."

A tiny spot of warmth formed amid the ache that was still squeezing my heart. "Thank you," I said. "That would be really nice. Fancy's not really my thing anyway."

By the time I'd poured myself a bowl, Shelby had already

disappeared into her bedroom. How did the staff of Villain Academy convince Naries to come here? Or, maybe more pertinent, how did they convince them to stay here after the hell the regular student body must put them through?

Questions I guessed I'd have to save for another time.

I scooped an extra handful of cereal to carry in to Deborah and headed back to my room. She wriggled out when I opened the sock drawer. Her *Thank you* as I set down the cereal brought a pinch of guilt into my gut.

"What do you actually like to eat?" I asked, feeling a little ridiculous. She'd chowed down on the pet food and bits of cheese and fruit I'd brought her happily enough the four years I'd thought she was just a mouse, but maybe there was something she'd prefer now that she could tell me about it.

A hint of amusement crept into her dry voice in my head. *Oh, any kind of human food is wonderful, really. Although I have to admit I was particularly fond of cheese even before I became a mouse.*

"I'll see what I can do about getting you some then."

The woman who'd brought my birth mother's clothes had also thoughtfully left for me a basket of basic toiletries. In the bathroom, I stayed in the shower under water scalding enough to dull the inner burn of grief until I heard someone else come in. I wasn't sure I wanted to find out who. I waited until whoever it was had ducked into their own stall and then made a dash back to my bedroom.

The thought of wearing any of the clothes that had belonged to my fearmancer mother made my skin crawl, but my tee and jeans from yesterday kind of smelled, and maybe I'd get what I needed here faster if I looked more the part.

I pawed through the wardrobe until I came up with a silky blouse with a subtle print and navy slacks that matched. Neither showed a ton of skin or clung to my body too tightly, but my eyebrows went up when I looked at myself in the mirror mounted inside the wardrobe's door.

Holy shit. I was all sleek and professional-looking—I'd totally pass for a fearmancer now.

The sight made me want to tear the clothes right back off. I reminded myself of my plan, confirmed that my birth mother's old shoes were too small, and slipped on my sneakers from home. The black suede didn't look *too* weird with the dressy outfit.

Good luck, Deborah said when I brushed my fingers over her soft fur, giving the black splotch on her flank an extra rub the way she'd always liked.

"Do you want me to get you, like, a book or something?" I whispered. Now that I knew my mouse had a human consciousness residing in her, leaving her to trundle around aimlessly for hours on end felt ridiculously cruel.

Don't worry about me, sweetheart. I just relax while the mouse instincts take over, and I don't really get bored.

I still hesitated before closing the wardrobe, but I did have to get going.

Rather than wait around while the other girls bustled around the common room, I headed downstairs so I could meet Professor Banefield by the entrance to the hall. I flipped through a design book in the library for about half an hour before I spotted his barrel-chested form pushing past the doorway. I hurried over to meet him.

"Rory," he said, no stumbling over my preferred name this time. "You're looking well."

I don't feel it, I thought, but I just gave him a smile.

"Are you settling in all right?" he asked as we set off along the path to the Stormhurst Building.

"I think so." Other than the fact that I'd managed to piss off the school royalty in less than twenty-four hours. A minor detail.

The athletic building smelled like floor wax and a lingering whiff of sweat that apparently not even magical cleaning practices could quite remove. We found Ms. Grimsworth and four other people who I took to be professors, two men and two women, waiting in a huge gymnasium. It looked bizarrely normal with the starkly colored lines crisscrossing the pale wooden floor and the basketball hoops perched partway up the walls. I'd gone to watch a couple of the volleyball games one of my classmates was competing in at my old college, and the gym there had been pretty similar.

"Good morning, Miss Bloodstone," the headmistress said, her voice echoing off the high ceiling. "Are you ready for your assessment?"

"I guess," I said. "What do I have to do?"

Her lips quirked into a wry smile. "Not a great deal. The process tests your innate proficiencies. The types of magic we do are divided into four major domains: Physicality, Illusion, Persuasion, and Insight. Knowing where your strengths lie will help us guide your studies. Most students here have one or two strengths. Your fellow scions each revealed three. I wouldn't be surprised if you show the same."

So Malcolm and his friends really were the most powerful mages around here. And I'd made enemies out of them in two seconds flat. Nice work, Rory!

"Okay," I said. "That sounds simple enough."

"Stand in the circle there," Ms. Grimsworth said, pointing to a blue shape marked halfway across the room. As I walked over to it, I realized the four professors formed a square around it, each an equal distance from me. I was right in the middle.

I came to a stop in the circle and let my arms hang at my sides, trying to stay relaxed.

"Just take it in and let your body react the way it will," the headmistress said.

I nodded, and the professors raised their hands.

Each of them spoke simultaneously, their voices blending together as they reached my ears. An erratic quivering of energy raced over my skin from all sides and delved into my flesh.

My body tensed instinctively. Something shuddered inside me, down in the place behind my ribs where I'd reacted to Malcolm's brief flash of fear yesterday. It whipped up like a whirlwind. For several seconds I couldn't breathe, the energy burst so forcefully against my lungs. Then it fell away as quickly as it had risen.

I'd closed my eyes without realizing it. When I opened them, the professors I could see were frowning. They walked over to consult with Ms. Grimsworth.

A faint draft raised goosebumps on my arms, and I rubbed them as I waited. Had they seen something about my magical capacity that bothered them? Maybe after having my abilities suppressed for years, I wasn't on the same level as the other scions. Oh, well. I'd work with what I had. I only needed enough to get the hell out of here.

The headmistress beckoned me over. "Miss Bloodstone," she said, "it appears we have a rather unusual result. The assessment revealed no effect at all."

I hadn't expected *that.* "No effect?" I repeated, wondering if the words meant something different than they should. I'd definitely felt plenty affected.

"It's the sort of response we'd expect to see from someone who has no magical ability at all," she said.

I blinked at her. "But—I could feel something reacting inside me."

"That might have been simply the magic of the test."

I didn't think it was, and besides— "I've already used my magic. Yesterday. I… had a disagreement with one of the other students about how he was treating a younger mage. I conjured ice on the floor, enough to freeze his feet to the ground for a few seconds."

Ms. Grimsworth raised her eyebrows. "Well, then. Do you happen to know which student this was? Perhaps we can get a testimonial."

Did I *want* a testimonial? It occurred to me, too late, that maybe I should want her to think I didn't have any magic. The fearmancers wouldn't have any use for me then, so I wouldn't have to stay here, right? But I'd already barreled on ahead. Too late to backtrack now.

"Ah, it was Malcolm Nightwood," I said, restraining a wince in anticipation of her reaction. "His friends—Jude and Connar—they were there too." I didn't know if Declan or my other escorts had been close enough to see what I'd done.

The headmistress only looked vaguely amused. "Ambitious, aren't we?" she murmured with a little shake of her head. "Well, you are a Bloodstone." She gestured to Professor Banefield. "Get Mr. Nightwood, Mr. Killbrook, and Mr. Stormhurst down here, will you? I don't imagine they should be too difficult to track down at this hour."

I sat on a bench by the wall while we waited for the guys to arrive, and Ms. Grimsworth fell back into conversation with the other professors.

How could I have shown *no* magic? It didn't make sense—not to me, and not to them either, obviously. Deborah was proof that even my parents had expected me to develop a power.

Finally, the divine devil and his cohorts swaggered into the gym. Even knowing what a callous, sadistic asshole Malcolm was, I couldn't stop the flutter that passed through my chest at the sight of his shockingly gorgeous face. Overnight I must have downgraded his looks in my memory to match his personality. With two more epitomes of hotness on either side of him, it was hard to look away.

Malcolm gave the headmistress a cherubic smile. "What can I help you with, Ms. Grimsworth?"

The headmistress motioned for me to rejoin the group. I walked over, watching the three guys uneasily. Their gazes skimmed over me as if they'd never seen me before. Somehow that unnerved me more than if they'd been glaring at me.

"Miss Bloodstone has informed us that she conjured ice in your presence yesterday," Ms. Grimsworth said. "I was hoping you could verify the incident."

"Ice?" Malcolm said, knitting his brow.

I gritted my teeth. "On the floor. Under your feet."

He shook his head. "I remember sending a little ice under you to interrupt your tirade, but I don't recall you throwing any magic at me."

"I think Miss Bloodstone must have gotten confused, Headmistress," Jude said helpfully, flicking back his floppy copper hair. "Maybe she was trying to summon some ice at the same time Malcolm did. But I heard him cast the spell."

"Mr. Stormhurst?" Ms. Grimsworth said.

The brawny guy's chiseled face stayed blank. "As far as I saw, only Malcolm used any magic."

Oh, for fuck's sake. Malcolm shot me a triumphant flicker of a smile, and I forced myself to bite my tongue. What could I say? It was the three of their words against mine, and I was the newcomer here.

"All right, boys," the headmistress said. "I'm sorry to have interrupted your day."

"It was no trouble at all, Ms. Grimsworth," Malcolm said sweetly.

The three of them sauntered out. I turned to the headmistress. "I swear to you, I used magic yesterday."

She sighed. "Even if you did, if it isn't enough to register on the assessment, it might as well be none. This test has never failed us before."

"Could it be… My parents—the joymancers—were suppressing my magic before."

"Your rescuers examined you for lingering spells on your journey here," Ms. Grimsworth said. "By the time of your arrival, any magic used on you had already faded away. Spells of that sort are difficult to maintain without regular reinforcement."

No wonder my parents had kept me so close. Had they been casting magic on me every single night—or even more often than that—without me knowing?

"Then what do we do?" I asked. Despite the tightening of my throat at the thought of all those secret spells, my hopes stirred. Maybe I could get out of this hell right now after all.

"Well…" The headmistress rubbed her chin. "It's a highly unusual situation. In light of your heritage, I don't believe we should make any decisions hastily. We'll continue with a general spectrum of courses for the next month and see if we can't wake up your talent from whatever depths it descended to thanks to your captors' suppression."

A month. Okay. "And if I still don't show what you're looking for in this assessment after that?"

"I suppose we'll deal with that when we come to it. Most likely we'd have you take up residence in your family's properties with some private instruction on our society, and when you're ready to marry, we'll hope that your children fare better."

My *children*? Were they going to turn me into some kind of broodmare?

Ms. Grimsworth was studying me. "Were you hoping for something else?"

I opened my mouth and closed it again, thinking over my answer. These people hated the joymancers. I couldn't tell her I wanted to go back to my parents' people.

"I spent my whole life that I remember in California," I said. "If I'm not any use here, I'd kind of like to go back there." The fearmancers couldn't stop me from reaching out to the Conclave for help if I was in the same city.

The headmistress pursed her lips. "I don't think that would be at all advisable, Miss Bloodstone. The southwest is the epicenter of joymancer activity in this country. They've already ripped you away from your community and kept you prisoner once."

"But if I don't have any magic—"

"Do you think they'd believe that? You had no magic when you were two years old, but they knew you were a bargaining chip all the same. They're afraid of us, and people acting out of fear find it very easy to ignore rationality. You'll be safe as long as you're among your kind."

You're not my kind, I wanted to snap. But with her words, a sense of dread was sinking in. Not about Mom and Dad—I knew they'd cared about me. They might not have wanted me roaming too far out of their reach, but they hadn't treated me like a prisoner the way she was saying.

The other joymancers, though… If I was so important, why hadn't any of my parents' mage colleagues ever come by to talk to me? It was almost as if the rest of the joymancers had avoided meeting me. So I couldn't identify them if I defected back to my real "kind"? So they didn't have to worry about revealing any secrets?

Or so there was no chance I'd use my villainous fearmancer powers on them?

If they hadn't trusted me even while I had my parents there monitoring everything I did, what were the chances they'd trust me now? They might even think I'd *helped* those murderers kill Mom and Dad.

I swallowed hard. "Okay," I said. "I see your point."

Her expression softened just slightly, which maybe was as soft as that pinched face ever got. "We'll do our best to bring out whatever talent you have in you, I can assure you. It'll take us a few hours to work out your preliminary schedule. Why don't you take the rest of the morning to acquaint yourself with the campus at your leisure?"

"That sounds good."

I didn't set off exploring the campus, though. I headed straight back to my dorm, finding the common room thankfully empty for the moment, and shut the door to my bedroom as firmly as I could.

"Deborah?" I murmured.

Her little white head nudged the wardrobe open a few seconds later. I knelt down to scoop her up when she scampered to me and cradled her as I flopped on my back on the bed.

Trouble? she asked. *Other than the crapload of trouble we were already in, I mean.*

"I..." I inhaled slowly. "The joymancers were afraid of what I might do if I came into my powers even a little, weren't they? That was why my parents suppressed my magic—that was why they had you watching me."

She was silent for a moment. *They didn't want your magic to lead the fearmancers to you.*

"It couldn't have been just that, though. They never even told me. I'd have been so much more prepared if they had, but it mattered more to them that there wasn't a chance I'd turn against them. They didn't even tell *you* the whole story."

I'm sure they did what they thought was best for everyone involved, Deborah said, which wasn't exactly reassuring. She obviously didn't have anything to say that would prove the joymancer community would give me the benefit of the doubt now that I'd discovered who I was.

No way in hell was I staying here with these psychos any longer than I had to. But I was probably screwed if I ran back to California empty-handed too.

How could I show that no matter what my heritage was, I was on their side? That I was the girl—the woman—my parents had raised me to be?

How could I make sure the bastards who'd slaughtered my parents got what was coming to them?

The idea hit me so hard I tensed against the feather duvet.

"Deborah," I said slowly, "when you were telling me about this place, you said the joymancers had been trying to shut it down for ages, right?"

They just never got close enough to manage it, yes. Why?

"Well… you can't get much closer than this. What if *I* took down Villain Academy for them?"

Saying the words aloud sent a cool shiver through me. Dad's voice rose up in the back of my head. *Pros and cons, Rory.*

Pros: I'd destroy the institution that trained mages to become heartless killers. The information I could bring to the Conclave might help them interrupt all sorts of other fearmancer villainy. I'd avenge my real family. Oh, and as a side benefit, I'd get to see the cocky smile wiped right off Malcolm Nightwood's way-too-handsome face.

Cons: I might fail and face a fate that I couldn't imagine getting any worse than what I already had to deal with living with these creeps.

Yeah, when I laid it out like that, my decision couldn't have been clearer.

Are you sure about this, Lorelei? Deborah said, nuzzling my fingers. *If they catch you, fearmancers aren't exactly known for mercy.*

"That's a chance I'll just have to take," I said. "I'm the best shot my parents have at getting justice. The best shot the joymancers have at tackling this place." Just because I'd been born a fearmancer didn't mean I had to subscribe to their philosophies.

I sat up, resolve coiling inside me. I was going to topple this place, but that meant I had to stick around long enough to pull off what might be the most epic betrayal in mage history.

In one month's time, no matter what, I had to pass my second assessment.

CHAPTER EIGHT

Rory

You'd think a building like Nightwood Tower would be easy to navigate, considering it was pretty much straight up and down. Unfortunately, the perverse architect who'd designed it had decided to include two staircases, one on the north side and one on the south, each of which only gave access to two of the four classrooms on each floor.

I'd hiked up seven flights on the north side before I realized there was no way to reach my Seminar in Persuasion, room 704, from there. I had to hustle back down and up the other side.

Thankfully I'd set off for my first real class at Villain Academy with plenty of time to spare. My nerves had been twitching too much for me to sit still. I'd spent the last two days in one-on-one sessions with Professor Banefield between his regular classes while he tried to get me up to speed on the basics of fearmancy, but I still didn't feel particularly ready.

The trouble was it turned out I wasn't very good at being scary. Just as mages like my parents had to spark joy in someone around them to work their magic, I had to provoke fear. I'd done it with Malcolm the other day completely unintentionally. Approaching someone or something with the primary purpose of scaring them made my gut clench up. Especially when Banefield kept sticking things like adorable floppy-eared bunnies in front of me and expecting me to terrify them.

I managed to get a little reaction by stomping my foot or giving a shout, but the jab of guilt that shot through me afterward made it hard to concentrate on doing any casting or conjuring. After a while, Banefield had put a pause on applied magic and switched to theory and history to give me a break.

"You'll adjust to the process," he'd said with the confidence of a man who'd been taught his whole life that freaking out every conscious being around him was a totally admirable goal. "Another option would be to take on a familiar. Most of us end up taking one. The magical bond allows any fear your animal provokes to fuel your magic as well."

"Oh," I'd said. "Maybe later, if I can't get the hang of this on my own." I couldn't admit I already had a familiar who wasn't likely to terrify anyone. I got the impression the girls in my dorm weren't the type to scream at the sight of a mouse. They were the type to skewer it. I'd rather not risk her life to test that theory.

By the time I reached the seventh floor for the second time, my breath was coming short. I leaned against the cool plaster wall beside the classroom door to recover, and who should come strolling up the stairs but Malcolm Nightwood, looking as devilishly hot as ever and not the least bit winded. How was that fair?

He grinned when he saw me, but the curl of his lips had a hard edge. "If it isn't Glinda the good witch," he said wryly. "Finally came out of hiding?"

"I wasn't hiding," I said. "Strangely enough, I *do* have a little catching up to do."

"Hmm." He set his hand against the wall about a foot from my shoulder and looked me up and down. That close, I could practically feel his gaze traveling over my body with a flicker of heat I couldn't say I enjoyed. He might be the most gorgeous man I'd ever set eyes on, but he was also clearly dangerous.

"You cleaned up well," he said. I was wearing another of my birth mother's outfits: tapered pants and a V-neck blouse. It'd looked professional enough to me when I'd put it on this morning, but under Malcolm's gaze my chest felt abruptly exposed. He trailed a finger down my forearm to my charm bracelet, drawing a sharper line of heat to the surface. "Everything except for this. Did you buy it in some feeb dollar store?"

I jerked my arm away from him. "Just because something didn't cost thousands of dollars doesn't make it cheap. It was a gift from my parents."

He guffawed. "From your parents? As if the Bloodstones would ever—" His voice cut off, and his grin turned into a grimace. "You mean the joymancers. The ones that incarcerated you. Why the hell would you want to hold on to a memory of that? They weren't your parents; they were your jailors."

"You've got no idea what it was like," I retorted, and changed the subject before he could insult my parents any more than he already had. "Why did you lie to Ms. Grimsworth at my assessment? You *know* I conjured that ice."

Malcolm shrugged, his mouth shifting back into his previous cocky grin. There was more of an edge in his voice now. "Just living up to your expectations, Glinda, since you've already decided I'm an asshole. We play by our own rules at Villain Academy."

My body went rigid. How did he know—had he heard me talking with Deborah, or had someone else heard and told him?

Malcolm chuckled at my reaction. "Did you think we don't know what those sanctimonious pricks call us while they're looking down from their high horses? Let them think that."

Oh, okay, so the nickname was just common knowledge. "It doesn't bother you?" I couldn't help asking.

"Why should it?" He shrugged. "You know, if we were being really accurate, it wouldn't be about fear and joy. It'd be truthmancers and liemancers. We lean into what the world really is, how it really works. At least we're not pretending it's something it's not. If that makes us villains to them, who cares?"

"Says the guy who just lied about me in front of the headmistress."

Malcolm leaned a little closer with a glint in his dark brown eyes. He'd left the top two buttons on his perfectly fitted dress shirt undone, and the fabric gaped to reveal a triangle of toned chest. His voice came out smooth and silky.

"I was speaking a higher truth: thanks to the jailers you're still honoring, you don't have enough magic for us to bother acknowledging. If you want to change that, the other scions and I are ready to accept your pleas whenever you're ready to get down on your knees."

"I'd rather jump out that window," I said, jabbing my thumb toward the opening behind him.

"We'll see."

He pushed away from me and sauntered into the classroom with a completely carefree air. Fuck, he had the Persuasion seminar now too? I'd been hoping he'd just been passing by on his way to a different class.

The room I stepped into after him held three rows of three desks each—individual-sized, but the same posh mahogany as most of the furniture around Villain Academy. Three of them were already taken, the one in the middle by Victory's friend with the purple-and-pink-streaked french braid. Cressida, Jude had called her.

Malcolm dropped into the seat at the far back corner, so I took the one at the front closest to the door. Maximum distance seemed like a wise idea.

Professor Banefield had told me that most of the classes included students with a mix of experience levels so that those farther in their studies could develop a more thorough understanding of the subject by teaching the newer students. How many of these seminars was I going to end up sharing with Malcolm Nightwood—or the other scions, for that matter?

The teacher, whom my schedule told me was Professor Crowford, ambled in and stopped behind the larger desk at the front. He was obviously getting on in the years, only a few black streaks standing out against his silver hair and fine wrinkles creasing the corners of his eyes, but still attractive enough with his Roman nose and heavy-lidded eyes that you could tell he must have been a heartbreaker in his younger years.

His gaze came to rest on me, and he dipped his head in

acknowledgment. "Miss Bloodstone, it's a pleasure to have you joining us. I'll do my best to make up for the delay in your studies."

"Thank you," I said, trying to shake the impression that an enormous spotlight had just been trained on me. Maybe I should have sat at the back after all.

A few more students filed in, only one of whom I recognized: the tawny-haired girl from my dorm. She had her shoulder-length waves pulled back with another silver clip today, this one a leaping fish.

Everyone gave me a curious look as they took their seats around me. I curled my fingers into my palms so I wouldn't fidget.

Word must have spread around campus by now. They'd be able to guess who the new girl was. Did they also know I'd flunked my first assessment?

Persuasion, I thought to steady myself, remembering what Professor Banefield had told me about this specialty. *Any magic that directly influences what another being thinks, says, or does.* Wonderful. I didn't think I wanted to do any of that unless it was to convince someone here to stick me on a jet back to California.

"For this morning's seminar, I'd like us to go back to basics," Professor Crowford said, and I felt several gazes turn my way again. "It's always useful to remind ourselves of the foundations of our magical practice. The core of persuasion is will—imposing our own will on another. Which is why..."

As he went on with his explanation, the surface beneath my butt started to prickle. A thin heat seeped through the fabric of my pants. What, was this place so fancy the chairs came with seat-warmers? I hadn't been particularly cold before. An off switch would be nice.

I shifted my weight, and the heat intensified. It crept up my back, sharp enough that a trickle of sweat rolled down my neck.

Crowford was gesturing to his temple. "...when choosing the angle of this sort of spell, it's important to consider the perspective of the target. How does the world look through their eyes? What's likely to be going on inside their mind? Naturally, insight can be a useful co-component, but even if you're weak in that area, you can still..."

My ass started to sting. I braced my feet against the floor as more sweat beaded on my forehead. This had to be a trick, a spell to unsettle me. Whoever was doing it—Malcolm? Cressida? Some other enemy I didn't even know I'd made?—they wouldn't actually injure me in front of one of the professors, right? They were just trying to shake me up.

It was working. Professor Crowford was still talking, but I was only catching bits and pieces of his lecture. Too much of my attention was focused on tuning out the growing pain spreading along the bottoms of my thighs.

It couldn't get much worse than this. They'd have to stop soon. They couldn't—

The heat flared with a knife-like searing that cut me to the bone. I flinched and stumbled out of my chair with a choked yelp. Crowford's mouth snapped shut. Just like that, he and every student in the room was staring at me.

"The newbie seems like she doesn't really want to be here, Professor," Malcolm remarked. "She's very distractible."

Well, that answered the question of who. I swiped at the sweat on my forehead, restraining myself from glaring at him.

Crowford ignored Malcolm's comment. "Is something the matter, Miss Bloodstone?" he said.

No, I just liked to fling myself out of my seat at random moments for fun.

"My chair," I said, the ache still running through my backside. "It burned me."

The professor's mouth twisted in a way that could have been bemused or irritated—it was hard to tell. He stepped around his desk and walked up to mine, bending to touch the seat I'd vacated.

"It doesn't feel unusually warm at the moment," he said. "Are you sure?"

Of course I was sure that my ass had just about been scorched off my body. I opened my mouth to say so and hesitated.

The pain had faded away. When I adjusted my weight, letting my thighs brush together, the movement didn't provoke the slightest sting.

Oh, fuck, had that all been in my *head*?

I sat back down gingerly. No raw skin. No prickling blisters. No injury, like I'd assumed from the start.

A different sort of heat flooded my face. "I guess it wasn't real," I said. I wasn't going to pretend it hadn't happened.

Professor Crowford scanned the room. He definitely looked bemused now. "I suppose one of your classmates decided to fully initiate you into Bloodstone University, by an interesting choice of methods given the class. Credit to Illusion."

It took a second for his last words to sink in. "Credit?" I repeated.

His gaze slid back to me. "Did your mentor neglect to explain that aspect of school life? Every student is assigned to a league based on their primary magical strength after their assessment—or gets to choose one if they have multiple strong talents. Well-cast spells in that vein earn credits toward your league. At the end of each semester, the league with the most credits gets a feast prepared and served by the losers." The crinkles around his eyes deepened with a smile. "As you develop your abilities, you'll find such incidents are valuable opportunities to practice your defensive skills."

I sank lower in my seat as he returned to the front of the room. Of course this place didn't just look the other way but outright rewarded students for tormenting each other. Why would I have expected anything else?

Did they get *extra* credit for managing to mess with a scion? Until I could figure out how to get those defense skills into gear, I had the feeling I was going to be prime target number one.

CHAPTER NINE

Connar

One thing I could admit: from the moment I'd arrived at Blood U, it'd been easy for me to strike fear when I needed it. Also when I didn't need it. Pretty much all I had to do was walk into a room to set off a whole bunch of jitters of nervous energy.

No one talked about the reasons. No one dared to. But as I hurtled across the football field, I felt that energy expand inside my chest with the whites of the other guys' eyes and the tensed expressions as I wove between them.

Would Connar Stormhurst decide to blast right through them or fling them off their feet? Was there going to be blood spilled on the field today? Who knew?

I didn't think I'd used magic against anyone in the middle of a game in the entire time I'd been at the university, but that didn't matter. The possibility was there, lurking in everyone's minds.

The uncertainty could clear a path for me even without my really doing anything. I veered toward one of the juniors who'd joined in, baring my teeth, and he scrambled out of my way so quickly you'd have thought a hellhound had just snapped at his heels.

The goalpost loomed up ahead. I spun around, adrenaline from the run thumping through my veins, and raised my hands. "Open!"

Chandler Viceport hurled the ball toward me. No doubt he whispered a word or two to steady his aim. If he'd been off anyway, I'd have tossed out a little magic to swing the ball toward me, but it was flying straight into my arms. I yanked it to my chest and sprinted the last short distance to the goal.

"Touchdown!" one of my other teammates hollered for me.

As the teams gathered to regroup, I raised the undershirt I'd stripped down to and wiped the sweat from my face. The cool spring breeze was a relief after a workout.

I ambled over to join the other guys, and a few of them glanced up. I couldn't miss the way they braced themselves a little at the sight of me, even though we'd been playing on the same team for almost an hour. It twisted my gut and made me want to fake a lunge at them just to freak them out. Might as well meet their expectations and get that extra heaping of fear.

"Conn!" a voice hollered from across the field. The late afternoon sunlight glanced off Malcolm's bright brown hair. He waved to me, standing in his usual relaxed pose.

"I'll be right back," I said to my teammates, and jogged over to see what the heir of Nightwood wanted.

"Don't you ever get tired of dashing across the same field over and over?" Malcolm said, but his smile showed the teasing was good-natured.

"I never have to worry about losing my way," I tossed back.

He knuckled me on the shoulder. "You know I respect the hell out of you, but let's be honest, you probably would if they took the game someplace else. Will they survive a few plays without you?"

I shrugged. "If they don't, that's their problem. What's up?"

"I had another idea for our good witch. You're out here pretty often. If you see the Bloodstone scion heading into the woods on her own—even on the road into town—give me a shout right away?"

"Sure. What are you planning?"

"I'll share the story if it comes to be." His grin turned devious. "If I decide I need back-up, I'll let you know."

"And you know I'll be there," I said automatically.

I kind of wanted to ask what he planned on doing if none of his machinations brought her begging for forgiveness. Rory Bloodstone might have been new here, but she was a scion. I wasn't sure she was any more likely to back down than Malcolm was. She had been a bitch to him, and I'd be happy to see her brought down a peg for that, but the thought of their squabble turning into some kind of war within the pentacle didn't sit well with me.

What the hell did I know, though? Malcolm's teasing was based on truth. Between the four of us, I was the last one anyone would call the brains. Even expressing a doubt felt like it'd be a breach of loyalty.

Sometimes I wasn't sure how much even Jude or Declan liked having me around. Jude's jokes strayed into caustic territory from time to time, and I'd seen that familiar wary look on Declan's face more than once.

Malcolm was the only person I knew who'd always treated me like he did, as he'd put it, respect the hell out of me, without concern or questions about what I or my family might have done. As if he simply assumed, because he knew me, that no matter how horrible the stories might be, there must have been good reason.

I wasn't a horrible person. And I knew that mostly because I'd have this guy's back or die at his side, no matter what came at us.

Despite his joking, Malcolm also gave me more credit for brains than even I generally did. He tipped his head to me. "If you notice a window of opportunity and think of a good ploy, feel free to jump right in there too. Gotta keep her on her toes until she gets the picture."

"I'll be watching," I said. It seemed unlikely, given that so far I hadn't crossed paths with Rory except briefly, but I'd do what I could for the cause.

"Excellent. A bunch of us are heading into town for drinks later. You in?"

"Absolutely."

He sauntered away, and I loped to rejoin the players on the field. The first rule everyone learned at Blood U was you didn't mess with

Malcolm Nightwood. One way or another, Rory Bloodstone was going to figure that out too.

CHAPTER TEN

Rory

I knew something was wrong before I opened my bedroom door. A hint of scent burned my nose. I braced myself and shoved.

The door swung open into the dark room, and a wave of the smell, thick and choking now, gushed over me. It was the putrid sour stench of rotting food, like a restaurant garbage bin left out in the sun for a week.

Bile surged up my throat. I clamped my hand over my nose and mouth.

Deborah's voice reached my mind thinly across the distance between us. *Believe me, I have never wished more that I could still work my magic. Not that I can see there's much joy to be had here.*

Even with my stomach still roiling, the corners of my lips twitched upward at her disgruntled tone. Okay, it smelled awful. How did it look? I'd better find out what the full damage was.

I edged into the room, breathing through the sleeve of my blouse, which only filtered out a tiny bit of the stench. My pulse lurched when I flicked on the light, half expecting to see my bed drenched in butchered meat, but it looked… exactly the same as it had when I'd left it: the comforter rumpled, the curtain pulled back from a window that was now shadowy with dusk, and the wardrobe shut tight. I'd have sworn even the glass of water I'd left out for Deborah's use hadn't moved an inch.

I tugged open the wardrobe just in case, but my clothes hung untouched in their neat row. The only problem was the stench, then. Conjured, or maybe an illusion that only affected me. Would my familiar tap into any illusions that targeted my mind?

I heard them talking about the spell before they cast it, Deborah said, still hiding in the sock drawer—I couldn't really blame her. *The girl who was upset about you taking her room and a couple of her friends. If I could have stopped them...* A sound like a little growl carried into my head.

"It's not your fault," I said. So, it'd been Victory, presumably along with Cressida and the girl with the black bob whose name I'd determined was Sinclair. I couldn't say I was shocked.

The stink congealed deeper into my lungs, and nausea clutched my stomach. It didn't really matter that the room didn't contain any real source of the smell. I wasn't sure I could sleep in that space. I wasn't sure I could stand here five more minutes without vomiting. The hasty dinner I'd eaten before holing up in the library was churning around way too fast for my liking.

I closed my eyes for a second, fighting to get my bearings. My knees stung from falling on the paved path after someone's raccoon familiar had darted between my feet—on purpose or just a coincidence? The owner had smiled as they'd called the animal back.

At least a few times every day now, an eerie whispering would flit around my ears, murmuring words like "Pathetic" and "Keep on failing!" I couldn't count how many times I'd felt a finger prod my back or my ribs in class or walking across campus, but when I'd spin around I'd find there was no one close enough to have touched me—with their hands, anyway.

I couldn't defend myself. Six days after arriving here, I still hadn't managed to work any magic since my first encounter with Malcolm.

Had he sicced the entire student body on me, or had the others just observed him and followed his lead after the hot seat in our

Persuasion seminar? Victory had her own separate beef with me, obviously. I wasn't sure it mattered with everyone else. This was what he'd wanted: for me to be badgered and berated into regretting that I'd snubbed his offer of "friendship."

I'd have asked Deborah if she had any idea how I could fix this, except I knew I didn't have the magic to combat this spell either. Should I risk sleeping in the common room on one of the couches? Should I go to Professor Banefield?

God, I didn't want to run off to the teachers like some kind of kindergarten tattle-tale. That'd make me look even more pathetic. Anyway, from what I'd seen of things here so far, he was more likely to tell me to suck it up and give credit to the appropriate league than to come to my aid.

I had to fight my own battles. I just… didn't have any idea how.

Footsteps rasped across the floor outside my room. I tensed up.

As I turned around, the girl with the tawny hair and ever-changing silver clips—today's was a stag—peered into my bedroom from about a foot outside. She waved away the air in front of her nose. "Wow. They really outdid themselves, didn't they?"

Definitely not just an illusion then. Credit to Physicality for the conjuring.

"Yeah," I said. "I think I need to get out of here."

She backed up to make room for me to leave. Her mouth twisted with what looked like sympathy as she considered the putrid space. "I guess you still haven't got the hang of magically locking the door?"

"I haven't gotten the hang of magically anything at all," I admitted.

She twisted a lock of her hair around her finger. "I'd offer to lock it for you, but then *you* wouldn't be able to open the door. The smell feels like a pretty powerful spell, so I don't think I can just… turn it off, but I can encourage a breeze to wash it out the window if you want?"

That was the first help any other student had offered me since Shelby the Nary had shared her cereal with me my first morning. Relief punched me in the sternum, but at the same time, after the barrage of subtle tests I'd faced across the last few days, I found myself eyeing the other girl warily. "Are you sure you don't mind?"

She smiled, simply and genuinely. Her clothes were nice, but she didn't put on the same airs as the girls like Victory. Maybe she was okay.

"As long as you open the window for me," she said. "I don't want to set one foot in there."

"Fair enough."

Holding my breath, I dashed across the room to the window, yanked it up, and raced back out again. The other girl laughed at my haste and rolled a few syllables off her tongue.

I'd gathered from Professor Banefield that once a fearmancer had a handle on their abilities, they started coming up with their own private words for the spells they wanted to cast. *Eventually you'll be able to come up with the sounds and connect them to your meaning on the spot,* he'd said. *If no one can understand what you're saying, no one can predict how you're working the magic before it hits them.*

The air stirred. A light wind drifted past us into the room. The girl stepped back. "I don't know how long it'll take to clear that all out, but the smell will get better, anyway."

"Thank you so much," I said.

She ducked her head, a faint flush coloring her freckled cheeks, looking suddenly shy. "I'm Imogen, by the way. I, ah—I really hated how they messed around with you in Persuasion the other day. I'm sorry about that."

"It's not your fault." What could she have done even if she'd tried to step in? The professor had been fully aware that someone was harassing me, and he'd given them credit for it, for fuck's sake. "The whole week has been… Well, it's been. Let's leave it at that." I let out a short laugh. "Getting a little help makes for a definite improvement."

I expected her to slip away into her own bedroom, but she stayed with me as I walked to one of the sofas. "You really didn't know anything about this place before you got here, did you?" she said, sitting down at the opposite end. "I can't even imagine."

"I didn't know fearmancy even existed," I said. "I thought all mages worked with joy, like my—" My throat closed in hesitation after the response I'd gotten to calling Mom and Dad my parents before, but they *were*, and I wasn't going to let jerks like Malcolm browbeat me into denying it. "Like my parents."

"I guess it makes sense they wouldn't have wanted you to know where you were really supposed to be."

Here? I was never going to belong here. But saying that would have felt like throwing her kindness back in her face.

I wasn't going to be like so many of the mages here. They automatically sneered at the mention of joymancers, dismissing people because of the powers they were born with no matter what else they were like. I wouldn't do the same to fearmancers. Not every one of them was necessarily a villain. And I could use whatever friends I could get around here.

Not to mention, Imogen probably knew things that could be useful for my whole taking down Villain Academy plan. I tugged at the hem of my blouse, deciding on the best way to ask some of the things I'd been wondering about.

Deborah had said the main reason the joymancers hadn't already shut down this place was that they hadn't been able to find it. The fearmancers must be using magic to hide it. If I could break those protections somehow or other once I had my own magic under control…

"From what people have said about my birth parents, it sounds like there's a lot of animosity between the two groups," I said. "Isn't anyone worried that joymancers will attack the school?"

Imogen snorted. "They couldn't even if they wanted to. My dad works here, you know—he's the head of the maintenance team. He says Blood U is the safest place any fearmancer can be in the whole country, there are so many wards around it."

That didn't sound like an easy job. "Does he help keep the wards up as part of maintenance?" I couldn't help asking.

"No, Ms. Grimsworth handles that in coordination with the blacksuits." Imogen paused. "They're basically the bodyguards and defenders for the whole fearmancer community, not just the university. The team that came to rescue you—they'd have been blacksuits."

Blacksuits. My mind flashed back to my supposed "rescue," to my parents' murderer in his posh shirt and slacks that had, yep, been black. My throat tightened. Add them to the list of people to take down.

"So, what is—" Imogen started to ask, and the dorm-room door clicked open. Shelby came in, her head ducked so the fall of her mousy-brown bangs hid her face. The rest of her hair was pulled back in her habitual ponytail. She saw me with Imogen and veered straight toward her bedroom.

Had Imogen hassled her before just because she was a Nary? Or did she simply assume I wouldn't want to talk to her if I already had company? There was one quick way to check whether Imogen was a fearmancer I'd actually want on my side.

"Hey, Shelby," I said, raising my hand to wave her over. "How's it going?"

She stopped but didn't move toward us, sucking her lower lip under her teeth for a fleeting nibble. "Um, okay. I saw you got your food situation figured out?"

I smiled. "Yeah. Thanks for saving me from starvation the other day." After my first mentoring session with Banefield that morning, he'd arranged for one of the chauffeurs the school had on staff to take me into the nearby town so I could do some grocery shopping. It'd felt a little weird getting driven around like some rich snob and even weirder when I looked at the balance on the Bloodstone bank account I'd gotten access to and realized I *was* rich.

Imogen looked from me to Shelby and back again, a faint furrow creasing her forehead as if she was puzzled by the fact that I'd even acknowledged Shelby's presence. She didn't say anything snarky, though.

"You should get the double-chocolate brownies at the bakery counter the next time you're in the grocery store," Shelby said, her stance relaxing. "They're freaking amazing."

"With a recommendation like that, I think I'll have to."

"I've had those a couple times," Imogen said, slowly but warmly enough. "They are really good." She perked up, her focus narrowing in on me again. "Hey, why don't we go grab a drink in town? It's not like you'll be able to use your room for a while. You've got to get off campus now and then."

She obviously had only been including herself and me in that "we." Shelby started to turn away again. She didn't even look hurt, just resigned.

"Sure," I said. "Shelby, you want to come too?"

Imogen opened her mouth, surprise flickering through her expression, and seemed to catch her reaction. "Yeah," she said. "Why not? The more the merrier, right?"

Having Shelby along with us would mean we couldn't talk openly about anything magical, but the trade-off was worth it for the way the Nary girl lit up at the invitation. My heart wrenched at the thought of how many times she must have been shunned by our other dormmates in however many months she'd been living here.

"Yeah," she said. "For sure."

"Do we need to call for one of the school cars?" I asked.

Imogen waved that suggestion away. "No one bothers with those unless they're so wasted they're falling over. It's like a twenty minute walk. Come on."

Outside, night had fully settled in. Thin streaks of cloud blotted out most of the stars, but here and there a few tiny sparks twinkled down at us. The breeze that ruffled our hair had a cool edge to it that made me glad for the trim jacket I'd put on today, courtesy of my Bloodstone mom.

We skirted Killbrook Hall and meandered across the parking lot where I'd first arrived at the university to the narrow road that led through the woods into town.

"There's a walking path through the forest a little ways over too," Imogen said, gesturing. "But it's a little spooky for my tastes at night."

"I'm fine with the road," Shelby piped up.

We fell into awkward silence as we set off along the gravel-strewn shoulder toward town. Imogen seemed unsure how to talk with Shelby there.

From what I'd seen, the mage students avoided the Naries if they could rather than integrating them into their socializing. Even with my homeschooled background, I might have more conversational experience with non-magical types than any of my peers, just from days at the park and the past year of university classes.

"How long have you two been at the university?" I asked.

"I started right when I turned sixteen," Imogen said. A bit of a late-bloomer with her magic then, I guessed. "So, almost four years now."

"Wow," Shelby said. "I just started in the fall. It's pretty amazing, the set-up they have, even if people are kind of… intense."

Imogen glanced at her. "What's your concentration?"

"Music," Shelby said. "You guys have the best instruments I've ever played on here. I'm mostly cello. And theory, of course. The library has books I never could have gotten on loan back home."

Right. Professor Banefield had mentioned something about the Nary students coming under the pretense of individualized study around a few select areas. They shared a couple classes with the fearmancer students—in general areas like business and literature—and the rest of the time they kept to their own little pockets of focus. While we practiced our magic.

"Maybe we'll get to hear you play sometime," I said.

Shelby ducked her head, but with a smile. "Yeah. The five of us seniors in the music program, I think we're putting on a short concert at the end of term. What about you guys? What are you studying?"

Oh. Er.

"Biology," Imogen rolled off her tongue, answer at the ready. "Mostly human."

"Like, medical stuff?"

"I haven't been able to specialize that much yet, but yeah, heading that way."

A fearmancer healer? That was interesting. Shelby turned to me, and I grasped onto the one subject I knew I could talk about with university-level depth. "Environmental design. Which is basically like architecture, except you're focusing on how places are going to look on the inside. Or the design of outdoor areas like gardens or whatever."

That's what area I'd thought I was going to get into before all of this craziness had happened, anyway. The breeze picked up, and I hugged myself against the chill.

"That's cool," Shelby said.

We lapsed into silence again. A twig snapped under my foot, and a shiver of energy pierced my chest. I stopped with a jerk.

"What?" Imogen asked.

"I just…" I didn't know what I'd felt. I peered into the darkness between the trees. Some small creature rustled in the brush. Then everything was quiet again. "I guess I'm just jumping at shadows," I said sheepishly.

It wasn't that I'd been scared, though. The sensation had felt almost like… like that moment on the landing when Malcolm had realized I wasn't going to back down easily. The brief tremor of fear that had turned into power at the base of my throat.

Was it coming from the other girls, anxious about wandering along here in the night? But everything I'd learned said any power I gained had to be fear that *I'd* provoked directly.

I paid close attention to my internal reactions as we walked on. After a minute, a softer tremble reached me, one I might have missed if I hadn't been waiting for it. My toe hit a particularly large chunk of gravel, and as it rattled across the shoulder, a volley of tiny quivers pricked at my sternum. Something scurried away deeper into the forest.

The realization clicked into place with such a rush of relief I almost laughed out loud. I *was* provoking fear—in whatever forest animals were close enough to hear us passing by. It was a subtle effect. They weren't terrified of us, but we definitely made them nervous. Imogen must be feeling it too, or maybe she was so used to larger whiffs of fear that these little tidbits barely registered.

"Actually, hold on a second," I said. As the other girls paused, I left the road.

I only ventured a few steps between the trees, but that was enough to set off another round of fearful glints. I drank them in, my heart thumping a little faster with the faint buzz of energy collecting behind my collarbone.

I had power. Maybe not a lot, and maybe not enough to defend against everything this school wanted to throw at me, but more than I'd had before.

"Rory?" Imogen said.

"Just checking something," I said quickly, and hurried back. Before either of them could think too much of my weird behavior, I jumped into a new line of conversation. "So, what's the best place to get a drink in town anyway?"

"There are a few places that are pretty decent," Imogen started, and we spent the rest of the walk discussing the features of the various town eateries and our personal favorite drinks. I was abruptly grateful for the handful of parties I'd gone to with my former classmates to have some idea what my options were.

The trees thinned, and the town came into view up ahead, the streetlamps beaming brightly. We wandered past a couple of residential streets and then onto the main strip. Imogen glanced into a bar with a glossy black sign and made a face.

"Well, we're skipping that one tonight. The scions always stake it out when they head down here. It's run by a Blood U alumnus."

In the amber light on the other side of the window, I made out a whole lot of familiar faces lounging in a few of the booths. That explained why our dorm's common room had been so empty tonight.

Malcolm had Victory perched next to him, stroking his forearm as he said something to Jude, who laughed and slung his arm around the shoulders of a girl who'd been in at least one of my classes. Cressida and a couple other girls from our dorm were squeezed in with Connar and another guy, throwing back shots.

My gaze caught on a sweep of black hair. Declan was tucked into the back of Malcolm's booth. He raised his lowball glass to his friends with a small smile.

A pang echoed through me as I jerked my eyes away. It might be stupid to have counted on anything from a guy who'd been part of the attack on my parents' house, but part of me felt abandoned by him.

"Where to, then?" I said, picking up my pace to leave Declan and the others behind.

Imogen pointed out a more modest-looking pub a few blocks down the street. We'd just reached the door when a jolt of panic hit me.

"I've never actually gone out to a bar before," I admitted. "Are they going to check my ID?"

"You don't have a fake one?" Shelby said, patting her wallet pocket.

"No problem." Imogen gave my arm a gentle squeeze. "I'll take care of it if they ask. I'm *very* good at distracting bartenders." She winked at me.

She'd slip me by with magic, she meant—probably the same way she got herself by.

I laughed. "Then what are we waiting for?"

As the three of us pushed past the pub door, the good humor stayed with me, side-by-side with the hum of my newfound power. This was a different kind of power right here: people who'd lend me a hand when I needed it, people I could turn to.

If Malcolm wanted to break me, he was going to have to try a whole lot harder.

CHAPTER ELEVEN

Rory

My heart sank the second I stepped into my tenth floor Seminar on Insight and spotted Jude's dark coppery hair at the far end of the room. I'd been starting to think maybe I'd managed to avoid any classes with him.

Of all of the scions, I found him the hardest to figure out. Was he pissed off at me like Malcolm was? Did he find the whole situation entertaining in a sadistic sort of way?

Between the two of them, right now I trusted Jude even less.

Unfortunately, thanks to my door becoming mysteriously stuck this morning until Imogen had heard my banging on it and magicked it open, I'd gotten here at the last minute. The only remaining seat was right next to him, smack in the middle.

My heart sank all the way through the floor when I noticed Victory at the desk behind it. She shot me a sharp little smile with a tilt of her angelic face. "For a girl with so much catching up to do, you cut it awfully close," she said with just a hint of venom in her coy voice.

Three guesses who had sealed my door, and the first two didn't count.

"I'll aim to be more punctual next time," I said, and dropped into the chair. My legs were a little wobbly from my sprint up the stairs. Holy crap, why didn't these magical assholes invest in elevators?

"If it isn't our ice queen," Jude said in an affected drawl, his lanky body sprawled out as if it didn't quite fit the desk. "No, wait, you didn't exactly rule over that ice. Maybe I'll just call you Slip'n'Slide."

"If that makes you happy," I said, not even bothering to look at him. If I looked at him, I'd have to notice how irritatingly stunning that angular face of his was. Under my desk, I twisted the charms on my bracelet, one tiny way to relieve my nerves.

A petite woman with coiffed blue-white hair and owlish eyes stepped into the room—Professor Sinleigh, I assumed. Like the teachers in a couple of my previous classes, she was joined by an older student who was acting as a teacher's assistant. Unlike the previous classes, today's assistant was Declan Ashgrave.

I tensed in my seat as he leaned his slim frame against the wall to the side of her desk, his bright hazel eyes sweeping over the room. I hadn't had any classes before this with two of the scions in attendance. But then, all Declan had done so far was *not* do anything while Malcolm ripped into me. Maybe he'd feel a little more responsible for students' well-being while he was in this professional role.

A girl could hope, right?

"Miss Bloodstone," Professor Sinleigh said, peering at me as if through glasses even though she wasn't wearing any. "I understand you've had several private tutorials at this point to establish the essentials. Do you have any complaints if we jump right in?"

Would she really teach things differently if I said no? The faint buzz of magic I'd collected walking by the forest quivered at the base of my throat.

I hadn't known how to even start unraveling whatever spell Victory had cast on my door—Banefield had warned me that messing with other people's spells was a lot harder than casting your own—but Insight sounded like the simplest of the fearmancer skills. You figured out what people were thinking, what they wanted, and what they cared about, like normal people tried to all the time. We just had the benefit of magic to sharpen our perceptions.

And I was tired of looking like a clueless newbie around the people who were so eager to see me that way.

"No," I said. "That's fine."

"Good. If you find yourself confused, you can let me know—or Mr. Ashgrave, my aide, is available for extra assistance after class."

She clapped her hands. "As the rest of you know, we normally get started with a practice exercise. Middle row, turn to the student at your right. Left row, you two at the back work together. Pierce, Mr. Ashgrave will offer himself up for your use. Take turns reaching out to your partner's mind and mentioning one internal observation you're able to make."

It was clearly my lucky day. I glanced to my right and found Jude smirking. He swiveled in his seat to face me. "Looks like it's you and me, Bloodstone."

I turned like he had. I'd done a few exercises in "reaching out" with Professor Banefield, so I had the basic idea, but I'd never had enough magic in me to do more than get the briefest of glimpses. I couldn't say I was looking forward to what I might discover inside this guy's head if I managed to open it up.

Jude's dark green eyes fixed on mine for a second before traveling up to my forehead as if he was going to look right inside my head. He murmured his private casting word. I didn't know how to connect meaning to my made-up words yet, so I'd been using regular words that captured the right impression for me so far.

"Did you eat a Twinkie for breakfast?" he asked, his lips curling with disgust. "You might as well chow down on dog food. You're putting scions to shame here."

A couple of the other students glanced over at us, obviously having overheard him. A flush crept up my neck.

I *had* eaten a Twinkie, because they'd been one of Mom's guilty pleasures and a reminder of home, and the only food I'd had around that I could grab quickly to gulp down on my way to class. The sticky sweetness had gone a bit sour in my mouth, but the crinkle of plastic as I'd hustled up the stairs was still fresh in my memory. Was that how he'd picked up on that memory?

"I was in a hurry," I said flatly. "I suppose this is your specialty—your 'league'?"

He laughed. "Not at all. I'm an Illusion man myself."

Illusion. My mind leapt to the burning sensation that had seared my nether regions days ago. Jude hadn't been in that class, but maybe he'd helped Malcolm with the spell.

"Like Malcolm?" I suggested to see his reaction.

"Nah, Malcolm's strong there too, but he leans most to Persuasion. Of course, there's nowhere any of us are *really* weak."

Right. Ms. Grimsworth had said the other scions were strong enough across the board that each of them would have been picking between three of the four leagues.

Jude dragged in a breath as if to go again.

"Hey," I said. "It's my turn now, isn't it?"

He gave me a languidly amused look. "Go ahead and give it your best shot, then, Cold Feet."

I'd take that nickname over Slip'n'Slide. I gazed back at him, trying to see him as a collection of features—a straight nose, a jutting cheekbone, the sharp edge of a jaw—and not the dazzling picture those pieces created. A gold earring glinted in one of his earlobes, shaped like a tiny dagger.

I drew my eyes to his forehead, the skin pale where it peeked through the fall of his hair, like he had with me. "Look inside," I whispered, compelling a wisp of the energy inside me toward his mind.

For a second, I was worried nothing would happen, despite the fizzing of power behind my collarbone. Then, with a little thrill, the sensation rushed over me of falling forward into a vast space—before my awareness slammed into a solid, blank surface.

My mind reeled backward, and I found myself staring at Jude. "You've got a wall up," I accused him.

His smirk came back. "Those who can, do. It's part of the exercise. But you're an all-powerful Bloodstone, right? You should be able to find a crack."

I glowered at him, and his smirk only grew. At the same time, I noticed the shadows beneath his eyes, the skin there just a little darker than looked totally normal. And the tilt of his head wasn't entirely relaxed, but kind of stiff, as if he were having to concentrate on keeping up.

Those weren't magical observations, just the kinds of things Mom or Dad would have pointed out to each other if they were coming up for a strategy for their joymancy together. To figure out how to stir up the deepest joy, you had to determine what a person was missing first.

"You're tired," I said, taking a gamble. "You didn't sleep very well last night."

Jude's mouth tightened. He looked annoyed, but I caught a fresh jolt of energy to join the dwindling supply in my chest. The fact that I'd hit the mark unnerved him.

Good.

I felt satisfied for the approximately second and a half it took before he started talking again.

"*You* cried yourself to sleep," he said, his wry voice taking on a razor's edge. "Finding the pressure of meeting expectations is getting to be a little too much, are you?"

I couldn't restrain a flinch. I'd been feeling more confident since my night out with Imogen and Shelby a couple days ago, but the grief and the general sense of being under attack still gnawed at me. He'd read right.

Before I could respond, someone snickered. Victory leaned her elbows onto her desk. "She hid her feeb clothes in the back of her wardrobe because she's scared someone will want to steal the hideous things."

"Wow," Jude said, launching right back in. "You nearly pissed yourself when that cat came at you yesterday. You're scared of an awful lot, huh?"

Victory picked up the thread with a note of triumph. "She thinks you're completely gorgeous even though she's *terrified* of you."

"Doesn't everyone?" Jude shifted back in his seat with a sly grin. "Poor girl, practically a virgin. Only one tumble between the sheets."

The idea of attractive guys must have jostled free memories I'd rather have kept buried. Jude's words brought them flying to the forefront, chased by a surge of panic that would only feed their magic more.

Victory shook her head. "And the guy ditched her right after. A Bloodstone gave it up for a feeb, and he wouldn't even look her in the eyes after in their stupid feeb school."

Every student in the room was watching the duo's little game now. I jerked my head around to seek out the professor, but she was watching us with an analytical eye, no sign she had the slightest intention of intervening. And Declan, across from her, was watching too, his expression so impassive it felt like a slap to the face.

Did you "rescue" me just so you could feed me to a bunch of fucking wolves?

My assailants weren't done. "And after all that, you've really thought about trying to run away from campus back to that awful place?" Jude tsked his tongue mockingly.

"She's all about the feebs, though. The one in our dorm is the only person here who makes her feel *safe*." Victory made the last word sound utterly pathetic.

My pulse skittered wildly. If they kept going, they might see something damning—they might find out about Deborah, or my plan to see the school shut down, or—

No. I couldn't let that happen.

Gritting my teeth, I shoved all the magic that had collected in my chest into a shield around my mind. I pictured it spreading out, solid and seamless, impenetrable as steel, to encase my entire brain. Every bit of strength and energy I had went into that wall.

Jude opened his mouth and hesitated. Victory fell silent too. For a minute, the three of us held there in a motionless, wordless battle of will. A prickling ran down my spine at the sense of fingers prying at my barrier.

It held firm. Victory backed off with a sniff and returned her attention to her partner. Jude gave me a slanted smile that had no warmth at all in it.

"So you can learn, Bloodstone. We'll just have to see if you can learn the right things."

He sank back in his chair. My shoulders slowly came down, my heart still thudding. The space behind my collarbone felt unbearably empty.

I'd defended myself this once before the class had turned into a total catastrophe, but now every bit of the magic I'd been holding onto was gone.

CHAPTER TWELVE

Declan

I nodded to Jude when he got up at the end of the seminar. As I turned to ask Professor Sinleigh a question about our junior class tomorrow, I kept my gaze carefully away from any of the other students.

I'd hoped that once she'd answered it and headed out, everyone else would already have left. No such luck. One student had stuck around for my extra assistance.

Rory Bloodstone stood in front of the rows of desks, her slim arms folded over her cinched silk tunic. The indigo fabric brought out the blue of her eyes, so vibrantly dark they were almost the same hue. The loveliest part of her generally stunning face.

I tried not to let my mind stray to the pain I'd watched cross that face less than an hour ago, to the way she'd looked to me as if I could shield her from it. It had reminded me too much of the distraught girl I'd done my best to reassure in her captors' home.

I *had* wanted to shield her from the shock and brutality of that moment. Seventeen years ago, she'd lost so much more than even I had. But this, now—our situations were infinitely more complicated. Or at least, mine was.

"Did you have some questions about the material we went over today?" I asked in my most neutral voice, staying on the other side of the teacher's desk. That distance helped me maintain my own internal shields.

"Maybe just one." Her tone was direct and unassuming, but the slight huskiness to her voice touched me like a caress. Her gaze flicked to the door as if to confirm no one had lingered outside and then returned to me. "But not about the material. Why did you come with the mages who took me from my parents' house? You're not one of those blacksuits or whatever they're called."

Where was she going with this train of thought? "No, I'm not," I said. "The blacksuits thought, given the circumstances, it might help your transition to have someone along who had at least a little idea what you'd been through. The confrontation where your real parents were killed—the joymancers took down my mother too."

I'd only been four, just barely old enough to have kept a few blurry memories of her face, sometimes stern and sometimes grinning, and the rumple of her hand in my hair as she laughed at some childish thing I'd said. Rory mustn't remember her Bloodstone parents at all.

She let out a faint sound that might have been a restrained guffaw. "So, they made you come."

"No. They tossed around the suggestion. I said it sounded like a good idea and volunteered."

"Because you wanted to help me?"

Suddenly I felt as if I'd walked into a trap I hadn't seen until the barred walls closed around me. Rory's eyes held mine as she waited for my answer. It was probably too late to backtrack anyway. I'd rather not lie to her any more than I had to.

"Yes," I said. "Maybe I don't really have a clue what it's been like for you the last seventeen years, but I knew finding out the truth about your history was going to be hard for you, and if I could make it even a little easier, that seemed worth doing."

She leaned against the edge of the desk behind her. "I have another question, then. Why did you only care about helping me until I stepped through the front doors of the school? At what point did I stop being 'worthy'? When I wasn't going to put up with your friend's bullshit?"

An edge had come into her voice, but it sounded more hurt than angry. I swallowed hard.

"It isn't about Malcolm," I said. "Although you should probably figure out some way to make peace with him, because he's just going to make your life hell until you do. Insult a scion, and all bets are off. That's just how it works here. That's how it works out there." I gestured toward the window to indicate the wider world. "You have to learn how to defend yourself where there are more rules and boundaries, or you'll be eaten alive the second you leave campus."

I should know that better than just about anyone at Blood U.

"I see," Rory said. "You're staying out of it for my own good. Is that how you look at it?"

"Essentially, yes." We could leave all the other factors out of this conversation. "You're learning, aren't you? You managed to shut them out today."

"I guess it's too much to expect that I get a bit of buffer while I'm catching up."

"There *are* rules," I said. "And one of them is that as part of the teaching staff, I can't favor one student over another."

She raised her eyebrows at me. "Even a scion?"

"Believe me, if you ever manage to turn the tables on Jude and drag out a bunch of his uncomfortable memories for everyone to hear, I won't jump in on his behalf either." I couldn't stop the corner of my mouth from quirking upward at the thought. I'd defend him from any *real* threat—hell, I'd been protecting him and the other two from the moment I'd entered the realm of barons—but that didn't mean I always appreciated the guy's incisive approach to humor.

"All right then." Rory straightened up and headed for the door.

I should have stayed where I was and let her leave, but an impulse grabbed me. Before I could catch myself, I was striding over to open the door for her.

There wasn't a great deal of space by the door. Her sleeve brushed my arm as she slipped past me. She glanced up to meet my eyes one more time, so close now I lost my breath for a second.

She wasn't just beautiful. I'd never seen the kind of determined ferocity with which she'd pushed back at Malcolm before. She had principles, and she was willing to fight for them, hard.

It made me want to fight for her. To hold her like I had so briefly in her parents' house. To find out what those lips tasted like when she wasn't using them in battle.

But I couldn't have that without destroying everything I'd spent my whole life working toward, so it was better I kept as much distance as I could.

She'd need to be a fighter to make it through her time at Blood U unscathed. At least there was that.

A question of my own tumbled out with the memory of Jude's comment about running away. "You aren't really thinking of leaving the school, are you?"

Rory stopped just outside the door and looked back at me. "Not until I've learned everything I need to," she said. "I'm not scared off that easily. Why? Would you miss me?"

She said the last question wryly, but the answer jabbed me in the chest. Maybe she'd only been here a week, but I'd seen enough of her to know that, yes, I would. She'd brought something different to this place.

"You belong here," I said instead.

Her mouth tightened, and she turned away without responding. I let the door swing closed as her footsteps tapped down the stone steps. I had a few minutes to gather myself, and then I needed to be off to my next class, as a student rather than teacher's aide.

I'd gotten about half a minute when my phone rang. I dug it out of my pocket and grimaced at the name on the display.

"Hello, Aunt Ambrosia," I said. "To what do I owe the pleasure?" *What the hell do you want now?*

"Declan," my aunt said with forced sweetness. "I just wanted to make sure you're fully prepared for the ritual next weekend. You did read up on all the proper procedures, didn't you? They're very particular."

Sure, they were. And she'd made *particularly* sure to include a few contradictory documents in the write-ups she'd sent my way in the hopes of tripping me up. As if she shouldn't know by now that I always did my own research straight from the source.

It was the sort of thing you learned to do when the aunt who'd been regent-baron in your place since you were four decided she was going to do whatever she could to hold on to that title. There were rules, yes, and I couldn't afford to break a single one.

"You don't have to worry at all," I said. "I'll be ready."

CHAPTER THIRTEEN

Rory

As I set my dinner plate in the dorm room sink, still a little uncomfortable with the thought of just leaving it there for someone else to wash up, Imogen sidled over and snagged my elbow.

"Hey," she murmured. "There's a senior party down at the lake tonight. First outdoor one of the year now that it won't be painfully cold after dark. Let's go."

I couldn't help tensing. "The scions will be there, won't they? And Victory with her crew?"

Imogen shrugged. Today's silver clip, a rearing horse, glinted against her tawny hair. "You're a scion too. Anyway, *every*one will be there. It's hardly exclusive. Well, other than…"

She glanced across the room, and I followed her gaze to where Shelby was just ducking into her bedroom. No Naries at this party, then. When I glanced back at Imogen, she made an apologetic face.

"We need to cut loose every now and then without having to worry about what they'll see. It's fun. We make sure they don't even realize they're missing anything."

Part of me balked, but another part of me wondered how much

talk there'd be if every mage in the senior class *other* than me showed up. Would Malcolm and Victory and the rest assume they'd cowed me into hiding?

Pros: I'd prove I wasn't scared off. I might learn more about how things worked around here while the students were more relaxed. I could even have some fun, maybe.

Cons: Various people might harass me some more. I was getting pretty used to that. Otherwise, none that I could think of.

Imogen would be there with me. If anyone got too obnoxious, I could always head back to the dorm.

"Okay," I said. "I'm in."

Imogen gave me a nudge toward my bedroom. "Go put on a dress —nothing too fancy—and I'll meet you downstairs."

As far as I was concerned, everything I'd inherited from my mother's wardrobe was fancy. I settled on a soft knee-length halter dress in pale lavender and grabbed a trim black jacket to pull over it, since I was pretty sure it was still going to be chilly down by the water.

The charms on my bracelet rustled as I pulled the sleeve over them. I hadn't taken it off except to shower since I'd gotten to the school, and I planned to keep wearing it all the way through, like a physical manifestation of the promise I'd made to my parents: I would get them the justice they deserved.

Deborah poked her head out of the sock drawer. *You look nice*, she said, her voice more distant in my head because she wasn't touching me. *Special fearmancer occasion?*

"Just a student party," I replied. "I've got to keep up certain appearances."

Maybe it'd scare them a little that I was still confident enough to show up at all, and I could collect some more magic just like that.

When I reached the front entrance to Ashgrave Hall, Imogen was waiting, her athletic figure hugged by a mint-green dress that flared out halfway down her thighs. Maybe I was underdressed. But she gave me a thumbs up and a grin, and motioned for me to follow her out the door.

As we left behind the main triangle and came up on the Stormhurst Building, the tang of wood smoke reached my nose. A bonfire flickered in the distance, its light stuttering with the silhouettes of dozens of bodies moving around it.

"How are the Naries not going to know they're missing out?" I said. The dressier flats I'd picked up at a little shop in town whispered over the grass when we veered off the main path onto a trampled dirt one. Strains of music carried across the field along with the smoke and the light.

"Oh, they can't see any of this," Imogen said in an offhand way. "You know that parts of the school are magically disguised so the Naries don't even know they're there, right?"

Professor Banefield had filled me in on that. "So they don't stumble in on us in the middle of turning each other into toads or something. But the whole *lake* isn't hidden."

Imogen laughed. "Of course not. Just for the party nights—we usually have one or two a month while the weather's warm enough—the teachers give us the go-ahead to put up a temporary illusion and repelling wards. Any Nary who looks this way will see the regular quiet lake, and they'll feel a distinct lack of desire to get any closer."

I appreciated the kindness Imogen had extended to me over the last few days, especially when she clearly didn't need to, but the flippant way she talked about the Naries still itched at me. At least she didn't call them "feebs" like most of the students here seemed to. When I'd finally asked Banefield about *that*, he'd admitted it was short for "feeble."

We don't encourage that sort of derogatory slang, but we don't believe in censoring the students' self-expression either, he'd said in a very responsibility-dodging sort of way.

It really did look like every senior on campus had come down to the lake for the party. Most of students drifted around the blazing bonfire, chattering and drinking. Several had wandered down the dock to the wide platform at the end, a few of them daring to dip their feet into the cool water. Others hung out on the rocky shoreline.

Someone had pulled a table out of the boathouse and laid it out with bottles of wine and platters of hors d'oeuvres that would have seemed more fitting at a dinner party than a college bash. A couple of ice-filled coolers with the necks of beer bottles poking from them gave a more down-to-earth touch.

I wasn't sure I wanted to risk getting tipsy, but I let Imogen grab me a beer. One shouldn't affect me too much. As she opened hers and then mine with a clink of the lid, a lightly sardonic voice piped up.

"Oh, look, even Frosty has come out. Watch you don't get too close to the fire! We wouldn't want you to melt."

My head jerked around to find Jude smirking at me from near the fire pit. The other scions stood around him, and Victory, Sinclair, and a few other girls from their crowd lingered nearby, all of them watching me. Jude took a swig from the bottle of wine he appeared to have confiscated for private consumption and handed it to Malcolm.

"It's the wicked witches who melt," Malcolm said, the firelight turning his hair an even brighter gold. "I'm not sure what'd happen to Glinda. Maybe she'd burn." He sounded as if he was considering finding out.

My gaze darted to Declan just a little behind him, even though I knew better than to expect anything from him now. His hazel eyes glinted with reflected flames under the sweep of his black hair, and then he looked away.

For a moment when we'd been alone in the classroom the other day, I could have sworn something had sparked between us. A hunger in his expression that had set off an answering flare in me, no matter how annoyed I'd been with him. But it had vanished as quickly as it'd come. Whether he cared more than he was willing to show or not, he was as walled off to me as Jude had been during the Insight exercise.

I returned my attention to Malcolm. "*You're* not melting," I pointed out.

He laughed and sauntered up to me. "If you expect me to deny that I'm wicked, I'll have to disappoint you." His smile sharpened as I stood my ground, my heart thumping. "It's good to see you without the feeb in tow. Now if only you'd left behind everything you should have." His hand leapt too fast for me to react, tugging at my charm bracelet.

I jerked my arm away and took a step back. "Thankfully I don't dress to earn your approval."

The girls started twittering. "Easy to make excuses for not going after what you're never going to get anyway," Victory remarked to the others with a sneer.

"You still haven't figured out where your allegiances ought to be," Malcolm said. "I guess we'll just have to keep working on you."

I'd actually be totally okay with you giving up, I wanted to say, but I could picture how much they'd laugh at that idea.

Malcolm turned on his heel and ambled back to his friends without waiting for my response. Imogen sipped nervously from her beer. I was searching for the right words to toss out before I found some other, very distant area of the party to visit, when a couple of guys having a tussle careened between me and the scions.

The one guy let out a drunkenly triumphant holler and pushed the other, but his sparring partner caught hold of his wrist at the last second. They spun around, and the first guy tripped on a beer bottle. Malcolm and Jude sprang to opposite sides, only just barely avoiding getting slammed into the bonfire.

"What the fuck are you doing?" a voice bellowed. I'd barely noticed Connar hanging back alongside the other scions, but all at once the guy was right there at the forefront, knocking the two interlopers back with a heave of his brawny arms. The line of his square jaw flexed as he clenched it. "Do you have eyes, or do you need me to remind you where they are?"

The guys cowered, backing away from the scions as quickly as their feet would take them. "Sorry. Really sorry. Total accident."

"Go have your fucking accidents somewhere else." Connar glowered at them like he was imagining exactly what shape he'd crush them into if they so much as brushed against his friends again. A shiver ran down my back. I hadn't had any direct run-ins with him, and I was abruptly very glad for that.

"You see," Malcolm's smooth voice said, so close behind me that I flinched. He'd circled around while I was staring at Connar. He set his hand on my waist, a spot of warmth my skin cringed away from. "We know how to look out for each other."

I whipped around, out of his hold, and crossed my arms over my chest. I didn't think it'd be wise to broadcast what I was about to say to the entire student body, so I pitched my voice low enough that only he would hear. "I'd take the joymancers over all of you any day."

Fury flashed across Malcolm's face. I dashed away to where Imogen had started backing toward the refreshment table, and to my relief, the divine devil didn't follow me.

"All in a night's fun?" Imogen said with a weak smile when I reached her.

"It's fine," I said. "They got to say their piece. Let's see the rest of this party."

We grabbed some food, and I drank a little of my beer as we wandered along the shore. I was starting to see what Imogen had meant about cutting loose without the Naries. Along with the college party antics I'd experienced back home, like that drunken playfight and the girls who were now egging a few of the guys into jumping off the dock into the lake, fearmancers found plenty of ways to up the ante.

Over here, a small crowd was whooping in encouragement while a guy gulped wine from a bottle that was floating magically several feet above his open mouth. Over there, someone had conjured a glowing illusion of a dragon that was doing battle with a lion made out of flames. Every time the creatures swerved to snap at some student's face, the casters would be drinking in jolts of fear along with their beverages of choice.

I realized after we'd made a rambling circuit of the party that everyone was giving the two of us a wide berth. The clusters of students shifted a little farther away from us as we passed by, though lots of them were happy to stare at me.

I raised my beer to my lips, and a taste so gaggingly bitter hit my tongue that I almost choked. I managed to spit it back into the bottle discretely. Someone had worked a malicious little transformation on my drink.

What was I even doing here? I hadn't decided to stay at Bloodstone University to party with the villains. I was screwing up any real fun Imogen might have been having while she stuck loyally by my side and accomplishing zip for myself and my plans.

"Hey," I said, touching Imogen's arm before we came back around to the bonfire. "I think I'm going to take a step back, maybe go for a little walk by the lake to clear my head."

"Do you want me to come with you?" she asked.

"No, I'll be fine. You enjoy yourself. And thanks for making me get out of the dorm."

She smiled with a hint of relief I had the feeling she was trying to conceal. "Text me if you need me."

Forestland stretched out along the edge of the lake on either side of the open area that held the fire pit, the dock, and the boathouse. A narrow dirt path led off through the trees on the east side. I set off along it, my shoulders coming down as soon as the sounds of the party faded behind me. The fresh night air washed my lungs clean. I felt safer here, alone in the dark, than I had in the middle of all those students back there in the firelight. Especially because with each muted thump of my feet, those tiny flickers of animal fear found their way to me.

I'd gone my whole life without magic, but now that I'd had it, I couldn't imagine ever being at ease without at least a little at my beck and call.

The path had veered far enough from the lake that I couldn't make out the water anymore. I stopped and tipped back my head to peer at the intermittent stars between the leaves overhead. A twinkle here, a twinkle there. Too bad I didn't think wishing on one was going to get me anywhere.

Maybe some of the wards Imogen had talked about were out here around the boundaries of campus. Would I even recognize one if I passed it?

As I lowered my head to study the forest around me, footsteps crunched into the brush. I stiffened, but after a moment I could tell they weren't coming my way. A figure mostly hidden by the shadows and the tree trunks was pushing away from the path through the vegetation, heading toward the lake.

I paused for a few seconds and then slipped between the trees after them. My nerves jittered, but if someone was up to stealthy activities out here, it might be useful to know what. Then at least this night wouldn't have been a total waste.

The ground slanted upward. As I picked my way carefully through the underbrush, trying to make as little sound as possible, the figure ahead of me completely disappeared from view. I kept following the slope up, scanning the trees, until they fell away around a narrow clearing.

I stopped in the shelter of the forest. Less than ten feet away, the grassy rock-scattered ground fell away in a cliff over the lake. The music and voices from the party carried faintly over the water, but before me there was nothing but open water framed by arcs of trees and the sprawl of the night sky.

Near me, a log stretched across the clearing to the cliff edge. I looked past it and spotted the figure I'd been following sitting on the ground with his back against the trunk of a broad maple. In the dim moonlight, I could make out enough of his form to recognize him from the breadth of his muscular shoulders and the chiseled planes of his face.

I'd followed Connar Stormhurst.

My body tensed automatically. Why the hell had he left the party and his friends to come up here?

In the back of my mind, I saw the flash of his bared teeth as he'd run off the guys who'd nearly crashed into Malcolm and Jude. But the Connar in front of me didn't look rabid. He'd tipped his head back against the tree trunk, closing his eyes, and his hard features had somehow turned peaceful.

I had a little magic in me now, and he didn't have any of his friends to make for a completely unfair fight, if it came to that. Curiosity nipped at my heels and nudged me out into the open.

"What are you doing up here?"

Connar startled, his eyes popping open and his brawny body shoving off the tree in an instant. He caught himself at the sight of me, holding in a crouch. His brow knit.

"What are *you* doing up here?" he shot back.

"Strangely enough, I didn't feel incredibly welcome down at the party, so I figured I'd take a little hike. Somehow I don't think you had the same problem."

He hesitated and lowered himself back to the ground, not relaxing against the tree trunk like he'd been before, but not poised to attack either.

"I like this spot. It's completely away from… from everything else."

I wouldn't have thought Connar Stormhurst had an "everything else" he'd need to get away from, but he didn't look as if he wanted to delve any deeper into that answer. I shifted my weight and then asked, "Do you mind if I stay for a bit?"

He eyed me. I'd never been close enough to him to make out the color of his eyes, and now I found myself wishing I knew.

"You're not worried?" he said.

My pulse was thumping away, so he could probably taste how nervous I was, but I made myself smile. "Should I be? Are you in the habit of tossing people off cliffs for simply existing?"

The upward twitch of his lips felt like a victory. "No. Only if they really piss me off."

"Then I'll make sure to step well back if I'm going to do that."

To keep a safe distance from him, I hopped over the log and sat down there. The lake lapped at the jumbled rocks along the edge of the cliff about thirty feet below us. I couldn't make out the bonfire in the distance, only a hint of its reflected glow on the water and the dark line of the dock. The breeze licked over the bottom of my dress and my bare calves.

It was an incredibly peaceful spot with no one around and the murmur of the lake rising up from below. What made a guy like Connar seek it out still puzzled me. I glanced over at him and found him watching me. His expression was more curious than anything else, but my skin prickled anyway.

"What's your league?" I blurted out, just for something to say.

His eyebrows rose. "You can't guess?"

Oh. Er. "Physicality?" I ventured.

He grinned at me, and damn did his face transform when he really smiled. I hadn't seen it before. In his usual stoic mode, he looked gorgeously distant, look-but-don't-touch. That grin gave him a warmth that brought him to life. My heart skipped a beat despite myself.

There really should be laws against *anyone* being that good-looking, especially four of them in the same damn place.

"Did you each pick a different one, then?" If Connar was Physicality, Jude was Illusion, and Malcolm was Persuasion, then that meant Declan was Insight. Which made sense, given that he was TA-ing for that subject.

"A little friendly competition," Connar said. "And even though we're strong in other areas, you usually end up strongest in whatever type of magic you give the most focus. It seemed like a good idea to spread the talent around for when we're the ones in charge."

In charge. My skin prickled again with a different kind of nerves. I was heir to one of the five ruling families. What that fact meant for life beyond this school hadn't really sunk in until just now.

Someday the four guys and I were supposed to reign over all fearmancer society.

I definitely didn't want to stick around for that. I wet my lips, wavering between finding some new line of conversation or calling it a night, and Connar shifted forward.

"What would you be doing if you weren't here?"

"I— You mean, like, here on this hill?"

"Like Blood U. If the blacksuits hadn't found you. What would you have been doing?"

He sounded as if he was genuinely interested in knowing. I hesitated, but I couldn't see any trap in answering. It was a straight-forward what-if.

"Working on assignments for the college classes I had back home," I said slowly. "I was studying design. Or making—I did these little sculptures of different fantasy creatures—people on the internet would buy them." My hands moved as if to form the shape of the half-started phoenix I'd left on my table, and nausea pooled in my stomach.

"Kind of like conjuring," Connar said. "Maybe you'll end up on the Physicality side too."

"Maybe." I hadn't thought about it that way. Physicality wasn't just about what you could do with your own body but creating solid things too. What kind of figurines could I create with magic as my clay? "I guess it must be easier to decide quickly if you've grown up knowing that you'll need to. And having an assessment that's not a flop probably helps too."

I shut my mouth before I babbled on any more, but Connar just kept watching me in that mildly curious way.

"It's hard for you, isn't it?" he said. "Dealing with everything here."

Possibly I shouldn't have been honest, but no one else had acknowledged that quite so frankly, and the words spilled out with a surge of relief. "Of course it's hard. I wasn't ready for any of this."

I looked away from him toward the lake, swiping my hand over my mouth. Connar leaned against his tree again.

"While you're here, you can leave all that behind too," he said after a moment.

We sat in silence for a few minutes after that, but it had a weirdly companionable quality to it, as if we were leaving each other to our own thoughts rather than simply unsure of what to say. Connar closed his eyes, his posture relaxing even more. I didn't know who he was down there with the other scions, but up here, away from everything, he didn't seem like a bad guy.

He was the only one of the four of them who'd acted as if my life before I'd gotten here might have been of the slightest bit of importance, for starters.

Imogen would probably be worried if I didn't turn up soon, though, and I did have a session with Banefield tomorrow morning. With unexpected reluctance, I stood up.

"I'd better get going. But—thank you for sharing this spot with me."

Connar blinked at me in apparent surprise. "Thank you for trusting me not to toss you off a cliff," he said after a couple beats.

It sounded like a joke, but as I headed back through the forest, I couldn't help thinking that his expression had been awfully solemn in that moment.

CHAPTER FOURTEEN

Rory

Professor Banefield answered his office door beaming with excitement.

"I think I've found just the thing for you," he said, ushering me into the book-lined space with its cluster of four armchairs at one end and desk at the other. He'd pushed the chairs and the coffee table that usually stood between them off to the walls. The click of clawed feet from the other side of the desk told me we were back to playing with animals.

My heart sank. "I don't know… I'm not sure terrifying furry creatures is ever going to be my forte." It was one thing to give them the unavoidable anxiety that came with any human presence in their natural habitat and another to purposefully scare an innocent being right in front of me.

Banefield didn't sound fazed. "But that's the trick of it." He ran his hand over his uneven orange hair. "You don't want to hurt them—you don't want them to be hurt. What if you were scaring one animal to protect another?"

He ducked behind his desk and dragged a large cage into view.

This one held a plump house cat that was pacing restlessly behind the bars. Then he pulled out another cage from the other side of his desk: quite possibly the same adorable bunny I'd been unable to torment much before.

His meaning clicked in my head, and a smile crept across my face. "The cat tries to eat the rabbit, and I scare it away. Okay." I paused with a fresh twinge of guilt. "But it still doesn't seem fair to the bunny to put it in that position in the—"

"Which is why we're just going to dive right in," Banefield said, and snapped the cages open.

The cat sprang out in an instant, its gaze already fixed on the rabbit. The rabbit's nose trembled. It let out a squeaky sort of yelp and backpedaled to the corner of its cage as fast as it could go.

Banefield had known what he was doing—I'd give him that. My stomach flipped at the sight of the terrified animal, but this time I wasn't the one provoking the terror. I could be the one to save it.

"Shoo!" I hollered, stepping between the cat and the rabbit's cage. I flung my arms at it to motion it away. "Get away! Leave the bunny alone."

The cat hopped backward with a startled arch of its back. As it hissed at me, a waft of fear, sharper and more potent than any I'd felt yet, rushed through my ribs to collect at the base of my throat.

The cat moved as if to try to dodge past me, and I stomped my foot. "Forget it! It's not your breakfast."

Another jolt of anxiety flowed into me with the smack of my shoe against the floor. The cat stalked away behind the desk. I straightened up, my pulse thumping giddily. Magic hummed from my throat all the way down my sternum. I didn't know how much it was compared to what fearmancers normally used, but it was a hell of a lot more than I'd had to work with before.

"Excellent!" Banefield said with a pleased clap. "There you go. The first hurdle crossed." He murmured something to the cat, and it allowed him to scoop it up and place it back in its own cage. "It may be more of a complicated process, but it'll serve our ends for now. We can arrange scenarios as you need to accumulate energy for your magic, and you should keep an eye out for parallel opportunities in your day-to-day life."

Like when I'd stood up to Malcolm to defend the kid he'd been harassing. Hmm. There were probably dozens of opportunities to scare off bullies from their targets every day here at Villain Academy, but I had the feeling taking up that banner was going to make me even more a target myself than I'd already become.

Not that I had any interest in becoming Miss Popularity—Victory was welcome to that title—but I really wasn't going to learn anything if my classmates turned every class I was in into a "let's beat up on Rory" session.

"Now what?" I asked.

"Now we can move past theory and get into the hands-on practice." Banefield sat down behind his desk. "Where would you like to start? What areas do you feel you could use the most additional work in before your next seminar?"

My mind leapt to that Insight seminar where Jude and Victory had picked apart some of my most vulnerable memories, but I'd managed to put up a wall they couldn't penetrate. All I needed was enough magic to sustain that. And my mentor's use of the term "hands-on" had brought up another memory—of talking with Connar last night.

"I have my first seminar in Physicality this afternoon," I said. "Can I try to, like, build something? How does that even work? Can I turn this energy into *anything*?" I tapped my collarbone.

Banefield chuckled. "I wish that conjuring were so easy. No, Physicality work mainly involves drawing on what you already have and, in essence, re-shaping it. You can make things appear out of thin air only if the materials are already on hand. So, for example, if you did conjure ice the other day, you'd have been pulling water molecules out of the air to create it."

Oh. "I didn't feel like I was doing anything that complicated." I hadn't really thought about it at all; it'd just happened.

"That's the beauty of being a mage," Banefield said. "To some extent, our powers naturally convert our will into the action we're seeking. We're simply honing them, learning how to use them more efficiently and effectively."

I nodded. "Got it. So… if I wanted to make a little sculpture of something with magic, I'd need to have the material I was going to use around. Or I guess I could make it out of ice and just pull that out of the air again?"

"Absolutely," Banefield said. "And don't get too tied to your literal ideas of what any given material can do. That's something you'll branch out into as you get into advanced Physicality, if you pursue that line. There have been great mages who can transform their own bodies into animals that appear twice their previous size or conjure a massive sword from the soil beneath a field. At their base level, many things contain the same essence as many other things, and what exists can always be stretched around our will."

I wasn't sure I could wrap my head around that idea just yet. "Let me just try…" I dragged in a breath. "Freeze," I murmured, letting some of the magic I'd absorbed vibrate up my throat.

Ice shimmered across the surface of Banefield's desk, which thankfully was mostly bare. But I didn't want some thin sheet just lying there.

I groped for the right word to capture my intention. "Together," I said, cupping my hands to model the motion.

The ice quivered and rolled up into a lump right in front of me. A laugh slipped out of me. I'd done that.

Let's see how far I could push this before my magic ran out. I focused on the phoenix I'd imagined all those days ago and made a stroking gesture on either side of the icy lump. "Shape," I said.

The lump erupted into a head and wings and tail. The outlines of feathers rippled over its surface. A beak protruded from the figurine's head and sculpted flames licked up at its base. Every detail I trained my attention on in my mind's eye burst into being, with another "Shape" whenever my momentum started to falter.

The energy inside me seeped away until my chest felt hollow. I stared at the ice sculpture I'd conjured. The phoenix was flinging itself up out of the fire just as I'd pictured it, even more perfect than if I'd tried to form it out of clay.

Banefield offered a round of applause. "Not bad at all for your first conscious attempt. I can see your artistic background coming into play."

"Is it going to start melting?" I asked, cocking my head at the icy figurine. Exhilaration shivered through me. I'd made something beautiful. Something beautiful out of fear.

"The magic you put into it will hold the chill for at least a little while," Banefield said. "Don't worry yourself—I'll disperse it before I end up with a puddle on my desk."

The thought of my creation being "dispersed" brought a little ache into my chest—but hey, if I could do that while conjuring ice out of thin air, imagine what I could do if I found myself a nice chunk of clay. Or maybe even some granite… So many possibilities.

A white shape loped past my chair. The bunny had decided to brave the world outside its cage now that the cat was shut away. I watched it, the wheels in my head spinning. If I let the cat out now, I'd *really* have to scare it to stop it from getting its paws on the rabbit. The amount of energy—

My excitement dampened in an instant with the image of the bunny squealing in terror as the cat pinned it down. What was I thinking? I might not be fast enough. Even if I was, the rabbit would be scared out of its wits.

I'd been enjoying this magic so much that for an instant I'd been willing to risk that poor animal's life to get more of it.

My gut constricted around a lump of guilt. Banefield was studying me. "Is everything all right, Rory?"

"I just— Can we put the rabbit back in its cage before I face off against the cat again? Just to make sure I can protect it?"

"Of course." He didn't get up, though, just leaned over his desk with his hands steepled. "Maybe there's something else we should talk about first, in light of this experiment, and—I understand you've struck up something of a friendship with the Nary student in your dorm."

"Shelby," I said automatically. "Yeah. What about it?"

"I simply want you to be aware of how you're training your mind. With the kind of magic we work, the kind of mages we work around, identifying with those weaker than us is a weakness in itself."

I frowned at him. "Are you saying I shouldn't care about people?" Or fuzzy bunnies?

"No, of course not." Banefield sighed. "Living in secret as we do, our lives are already rather limited. As you've seen acted out here, fearmancers often prey on each other to develop their powers. The strong rise to the top, and the weak…" He made a falling motion. "When you care about someone or something that can't defend itself, you open yourself up to being hurt through that thing. Care about this rabbit, and any mage could draw fear from you by threatening it."

"So, what? We just let the weak get eaten?" Every piece of me balked at that idea.

"That's the way of the entire natural world, isn't it?" Banefield said, calmly enough. "We can work around your sensitivities for now. Just consider that you are the scion—and technically the baron, as soon as you've completed your schooling—of a ruling family. It's your *duty* to stand firm against any attempts to shake you. What might seem like kindness is an indulgence that fails both your community and yourself, and puts the object of your 'kindness' in more danger than if you hadn't intervened."

Because I'd make them a target too. Had the other girls been harassing Shelby more since I'd gotten friendly with her? I hadn't seen enough of how they'd treated her before to compare. Shit.

Some of what he was saying made sense, no matter how much I hated it.

Banefield stood up. "Shall we continue? You've got another half an hour with me."

I got up as well, squaring my shoulders. None of that political awfulness would matter if I saw my quest through and destroyed this place. The joymancers didn't work like that. I could prove to them I didn't either.

But for now, I had to work with what was in front of me.

I shooed the bunny back into its cage. "All right. Release the tabby."

CHAPTER FIFTEEN

Rory

Dad gurgled. Blood spilled over our kitchen floor in a flood that seemed to spread and spread, across every tile and past Mom's already limp body.

No. Please, no.

I lunged to reach him but couldn't seem to move, a scream bubbling in my throat—

And woke up, sweaty and shaking under my fluffy duvet in my Villain Academy dorm room.

Thin morning light seeped around the edges of the curtain to haze the ceiling. I stared up at it and sagged into the mattress as my pulse slowly settled down to normal speed and the images that were half memory, half nightmare faded from my mind.

Was that the fourth time or the fifth I'd revisited my parents' murders in my sleep? Enough times that I was losing track, anyway. The repetition hadn't dulled any of the pain or the panic, but at least I knew those would fade too, at least to the point that I could keep going.

When I sat up, the first thing my gaze landed on was a square of white paper fixed to the inside of my door. A paper that hadn't been there when I'd gone to bed last night. I leaned over to yank open the curtain and let the full sunlight in, and then peered at the note.

It's time, it said in bold black handwriting.

Well, wasn't that a charming sentiment and not at all foreboding.

"Deborah," I whispered, eyeing the floor in case whoever had left me that present had messed around with other things in my room. I'd made my best attempt at magically locking the door last night, but apparently it hadn't been good enough to keep vaguely threatening notes out. I wasn't sure whether the paper had been teleported through the door or placed there by hand by someone who'd opened it, or which of those possibilities was more disturbing.

Deborah poked her pale mouse face out of the wardrobe. She darted across the floor to scramble up a dangling fold of duvet and came to rest her front paws on my wrist. It was only a faint pressure, but her touch brought a little comfort all the same.

She was the only person here who had any idea what I was really going through, and she was hardly even a person.

What's the matter? she asked.

"Someone left a note inside my door overnight," I said. "Did you hear anyone come in or feel any magic being worked?"

I was asleep a lot of that time myself. I expect I'd have woken up if someone had actually opened the door. But if they conjured it there by magic, I could have missed it. I'm sorry, sweetheart.

"It's okay. I just figured I should check." I exhaled, only a bit of the tension inside me dispelling with my breath.

What does it say?

"Just 'It's time,' whatever that means. I guess I'll find out." I swiped my hair back from my face, the dark brown waves so rumpled they were nearly curls. "Can you feel any other magic around the room?" I couldn't, but I didn't trust my own ability to sense it.

Deborah scurried away to traverse the foot of the bed, her whiskers quivering. She came back to my hand. *I think this room is safe enough. I could do some investigating, as well as I can, while you're going to your classes today. Perhaps I'll overhear something useful for you—who left the note, or what else the other students might be scheming about.*

The thought of her leaving the already precarious security of my bedroom to roam around the rest of the school made my chest tighten. "I don't think that's a good idea. Even if you could manage to stop any of the students from seeing you, a lot of them have familiars roaming around that would see you as a meal."

I'm pretty fast on my feet. Don't worry about me. My mission was supposed to be to look out for you, and I'd like to do a better job of that.

A lump rose in my throat. She'd had no idea she'd end up in this treacherous situation when she took on that mission, but she was willing to risk her life to keep protecting me however she could in her diminished form anyway. I couldn't help thinking back to the comments Professor Banefield had made yesterday about how caring about people could hurt both you and them.

Caring about me was putting Deborah in danger. I should be able to protect myself.

"You've done a great job," I said firmly. "I don't know if I'd have been able to hold it together without you here with me. You just focus on keeping out of sight around any of the assholes we can't trust. I'll look after me."

I tugged the note off the door, crumpled it, and tossed it into the garbage can under the desk. My charm bracelet clinked as I jerked open the wardrobe. Time to pick what to wear to face this day, whatever it was going to bring.

I set off for that morning's seminar in a collared ivory shirt and sleek slacks that made me feel like I was some kind of kickass lady CEO, ready to tackle the day with fierce professionalism. I'd put on the other pair of dressier shoes I'd bought: black Mary Janes with low clunky heels that hit the floor with a satisfyingly solid smack. The few remaining tremors of magic I'd held onto after my attempts at a locking spell swirled behind my breastbone.

The sun beamed brilliantly through the first-floor windows around the library. I stepped out into the warming air to cross the green to Nightwood Tower, and my strides slowed.

It was normal to see several students and maybe a few teachers passing between the triangle of the campus's three main buildings at any given time. This morning, a whole crowd had gathered around the fringes of the green. There were dozens of students, most of them faces I recognized from my classes, and many of the teachers too. I even spotted Ms. Grimsworth lingering near a cluster by the back doors of Killbrook Hall.

I set off for the Tower anyway, trying not to let their presence unnerve me, but as I walked along the paved path, more and more gazes turned to follow me. My skin prickled.

I'd just reached the middle of the green when Malcolm came sauntering out of the crowd to meet me.

He had his hands slung in his pockets, the sleeves of his button-down rolled to his elbows, his entire stance radiating casual confidence: every bit the divine devil I'd pegged him as the first moment I'd seen him. His sly smile fit his aura perfectly.

My heartbeat thumped faster. I moved to dodge him on the path, and he sidestepped to block me, his smile widening.

"Hold on there just a minute, Bloodstone."

I halted, holding myself rigid so my nerves wouldn't show. He'd obviously called all these people here. I had to guess he was the one who'd left the note in my room. If I tried to make a dash for the Tower or even back to my dorm, how many steps would I make before he stopped me like we both knew he could?

Just enough to make me look as ridiculous as possible, no doubt.

So I stayed where I was and raised my chin. "'It's time'?" I said, quoting the note. "Time for what, Nightwood?"

"Time you finally recognize what you are and who you should owe your loyalty to," Malcolm said, his voice ringing clear across the green. "Time you stop carrying around an emblem of the self-righteous bastards who killed your family and would like to wipe us all out if they could. Time you got off that imaginary high horse." He raised his hand, and his voice shifted into a silky lilt. "Take off the bracelet the joymancers gave you."

Every bone in my body resisted, but his words wound through my body, loosening my muscles and jolting my nerves into motion. A startled gasp slipped from my lips as my hand moved of its own accord to undo the clasp on my charm bracelet.

Jude had said Malcolm's primary focus was Persuasion. Here was my first-hand demonstration. Professor Crowford had mentioned that the more your instructions went against the person's own will, the more power you had to bring to your magic for it to work. He must be expending an awful lot on me right now.

"Stop," I said. My protest held no power at all. I had to save the little bit of magic I had for when it could matter the most. My fingers curled around the dangling strand of charms. He couldn't take it. I couldn't *let* him.

But that wasn't what Malcolm wanted after all.

"Drop it," he said, as if I hadn't spoken.

My fingers twitched and released. The bracelet fell to the strip of smooth concrete with a rattle of the glass beads. I strained to snatch after it, but my body wouldn't respond.

"Smash them," Malcolm said in the same silky tone, but with a triumphant note now. "Smash every last one, like those fucking joymancers should be smashed."

Oh, God, no. I tensed every limb, calling on the threads of magic I'd been saving up, but my foot lifted against my will. I gritted my teeth and strained to pull it back.

The magic wisped through me to no effect. My heel slammed down on the bracelet. Glass crunched against the pavement. I flinched, tears springing to my eyes despite my best efforts. The words tumbled out. "Please, don't—"

"Keep going."

My foot rammed down again. Another crunch, another jab of pain right through my gut. Memories swam up of the trips to the jewelry shops, picking out each year's addition, Mom listening avidly as I explained what this or that one meant to me. Hope. Adventure. Creativity. Love.

Crunch, crunch, crunch, crunch.

I thought I heard Jude's mocking laugh somewhere to my left. The breeze cooled the damp streaks down my cheeks. My foot twisted, grinding the glass beneath my heel. Malcolm chuckled, low and satisfied, and all our spectators just stood and watched the show. Watched him reduce me to the pathetic weakling mage he saw me as.

My hands clenched at my sides. I wasn't weak. My parents had taught me that from the first days they'd revealed their magic to me, when I'd been just a little kid. *You don't need magic to be powerful, Rory. If your will is strong enough, you can do just about anything.*

I had my will, and now I had magic too, if I just reached out and took it.

As I blinked the glaze of tears away, my gaze darted over the crowd. It caught on Declan standing back amid the spectators, his shoulders tensed, his mouth set in a grim line. He didn't look happy, but he wouldn't step in now any more than he had before. *You have to learn how to defend yourself.*

I could end this now. I could roll over like Malcolm wanted and prove him right, but every particle of my being screamed against that idea. He wanted this to be a fight. I'd give him a real one, by whatever means I could.

Fuck him and the assholes turning this torture into a spectacle. Fuck them all.

"Now let's give that one last—" Malcolm started, and I swiveled toward the nearest cluster in our audience.

"*You* want to try me?" I snapped at them, taking a menacing step forward. The breeze had dried the few tears that had trickled down my cheeks, and all my fury and frustration rippled through my voice. A few of the younger kids jerked back with a flash of fright that shot into my chest.

That was all I needed.

I spun back to face Malcolm, who was sucking in a breath to give another command, not looking at all fazed yet. Why should he be? Even with that whiff of power, I couldn't take him on head to head.

So I'd have to hit him hard and fast where it'd hurt the most, just like he had with me.

"Inside," I murmured, focusing on his forehead the way I had with Jude in the Insight seminar. What was he thinking about right now? What about this really mattered to him?

I caught an impression of an older man with the same golden-brown hair mixed with gray, a low measured voice saying, *Now that's a win befitting a Nightwood*, and a flicker of pride. His father?

Malcolm's expression shuttered. A wall hurtled up, jarring me out of his thoughts, but I had something to hold onto now.

"Hear his disappointment," I whispered, the first words that came to mind to fit my intention. I wasn't even sure if I was conjuring a real sound or the illusion of it for only him, or what it would say—I just threw all the magic I had into tearing through that sense of approval.

That low measured voice warbled across the space between us. "What the fuck were you thinking, Malcolm? How do you think you'll ever stand up among the—"

I wasn't sure if anyone could hear it other than him and me, but for an instant Malcolm's face stiffened in a mask of horror. A tremor ran through him before he could catch his composure. He snapped his stance into place again and spat out a syllable with a swipe of his hand. The voice fell away.

He jerked his hand again with another brief mutter, and a wallop of air shoved me backward. I fell on my ass on the pavement.

"I think I've made my point," the Nightwood scion said, all cool disdain again, but I didn't think I was the only one who'd have noticed his momentary lapse. He must have realized that too. His eyes blazed for the second they met mine, promising there'd be hell to pay. Then he stalked off across the green with a wave of his arm. "The show's over, folks! I hope you enjoyed it."

The show was over, but he hadn't totally won.

"Credit to Persuasion," Ms. Grimsworth said in a voice that carried. She sounded weary.

I eased myself back onto my feet as the crowd dispersed. The glinting shards of my charms scattered the pavement in front of me. Even the chain had snapped apart under my stomping foot.

A fresh wave of heat burned behind my eyes. I swallowed hard, fighting back the tears. As the last figures slipped away at the corners of my vision, I stayed crouched, staring.

Most of the charms were nothing but little shards. There was no fixing them by regular means. Maybe magic could have done it, but I had none left. Anyway, I wasn't sure I'd want to wear whatever my wavering talent could produce even if I summoned some more power. It'd remind me too much of this moment now.

But one shape wasn't quite as mangled as the others. I'd interrupted Malcolm soon enough to mostly save one. The little dragon bead I'd asked for on my fifteenth birthday lay amid the broken chunks, the coil of its tail snapped off but its head and body still intact.

My lips twisted as I looked at it. That was the only one Mom had balked over.

A dragon? she'd said. *That doesn't seem to fit you.*

It's courage, I'd said. *And strength. I want… I want to feel strong.*

She'd grasped my arms and squeezed them gently. *Of course you're strong, honey.*

Then I should have a dragon.

How could she have argued with that?

I fished it out of the broken bits. Had she been thinking that a dragon was too close to the predatory mage I'd been born to become? Was it a good sign or a bad one that this was my only surviving memento of their love?

I hadn't exactly fought fair just now. I'd threatened people who hadn't really been hurting me to scare them, and I'd hit Malcolm with the lowest blow I could. That wasn't who I wanted to be.

It was who I'd had to be to survive. To get the justice Mom and Dad needed, to make my way back home, the ends justified the means.

I stood up, and a movement caught the corner of my eye. My head jerked around. One member of our audience hadn't left after all.

Connar had lingered outside Ashgrave Hall, his hard face set in its usual impenetrable expression. My fingers tightened around the dragon charm. I didn't have any magic left, but I'd fight him with everything else in me if he tried to take this one last token from me.

For a moment, neither of us moved. Then his lips curled just slightly upward in a hint of a smile, as if we were up on the cliff again in that secret spot away from the rest of the world. My heart skipped a beat.

Without a word, he headed into the hall.

I turned back to Nightwood Tower. I still had a class to get to. Clutching the dragon charm, I set off.

To get through the rest of my time here, I couldn't think of anything I was going to need more than a whole lot of strength and courage.

CHAPTER SIXTEEN

Malcolm

The first thing I heard when I answered my mother's call was my little sister crying in the background.

That sound was nothing new. Agnes was coming up on thirteen, and she still broke down way too easily. You'd have thought across all the years of our parents testing our limits and throwing our fears in our faces, she'd have developed more armor, like I had. That was why they did it in the first place: to harden us up before anyone else had a chance to take a jab at us.

Taking on the Nightwood name didn't come easy. She *needed* to toughen up, or someone outside the family might destroy her. If I'd been able to think of a way to prepare her that would have been more effective than my parents' tactics, I would have. Even at a distance, those sobs made my throat tighten.

She was old enough to be better at this, but she *was* also only thirteen.

"Hello, Malcolm," my mother said in her tersely blasé voice, without any hint that she was aware of and most likely responsible for the muffled weeping.

I leaned against the hard mahogany back of my desk chair, my legs stretched out in front of me, one of my dormmates' thrash metal songs filtering through our shared wall. He'd have turned it down the second I thumped on the wall, but I hadn't bothered because it fit my current mood.

"Hello, Mother."

I had the urge to ask her what had gotten to Agnes now, but showing concern wouldn't help me or my sister. It would simply be an opening for some new attack. My mother knew I could hear Agnes; she'd called me in the right proximity as a reminder that no matter what Agnes had been through in the last half hour, I could find myself in even deeper shit twice as fast.

The first thing I remembered learning from my parents was, *Never let your guard down*. Taught with the sting of a conjured electric zap up my four-year-old arm at random moments when my attention strayed too far from the adults in the room.

Another early lesson had been, *Hold your own counsel.* I wasn't going to ask her why she was calling either. She'd tell me when she was good and ready. Impatience looked like weakness.

"I trust your studies are going well," my mother said, a cursory formality.

"I haven't heard any complaints."

"I understand you've had some chance to acquaint yourself with the recovered Bloodstone scion."

There was the motivation behind this call. My gaze lingered on the view from my window across campus toward the lake. The rippling water reflected the pink haze of the sunset. On the other side of this floor in her own corner bedroom, Rory Bloodstone might be looking at nearly the exact same view right now.

Rory fucking Bloodstone, who kept throwing her preference for the pompous joymancers in the rest of our faces. Even this morning, she'd fought me. For what? For the pricks who'd slaughtered her real parents and Declan's mom, who'd left my grandfather with a twisted scar instead of an eye before I was born, who'd fucked up Dad's last big business venture, all of that no doubt with self-satisfied smiles plastered on their faces?

Cracking down on us every way they could, just as vicious as they accused us of being. At least we could own what we were. If Rory could have brought all her grit and fire to *our* side… But no, we obviously weren't quite there yet.

"I have," I agreed, slinging one foot over the other.

My mother had probably heard at least a few details of my clashes with Glinda the good witch. My family made sure to have at least a few staff members in their pocket at any important fearmancer institution, and if some of the witnesses had dished the dirt with their parents, as girls like Victory always did, word would have passed along through those channels too.

She cleared her throat meaningfully. "Are you sure this feud you've encouraged is the wisest approach? We need her ear—we need her to follow our lead once she's among the barons, or we'll never get anything done."

As if I hadn't heard her and Dad complaining about that enough times to know that. "You've managed for seventeen years without a proper Bloodstone baron on hand," I had to point out.

"We've been forced to delay policies we'd have liked to move forward with thanks to the uncertainty about her fate. We're tired of waiting. You'll have to deal with her even longer than we will."

I was the one already dealing with Rory's irritatingly stubborn ass and the power she managed to pull out of it at the most frustrating moments.

"I *started* with an offer of friendship," I said. "She threw it in my face. All that time with the joymancers screwed up her priorities. She'll come around. I've been breaking her down. It shouldn't be much longer now before she comes begging for mercy and forgiveness."

I wasn't going to talk about the defiance that had been etched on Rory's face when we'd stared each other down this morning or the tiny chink in my armor she'd managed to strike me through. She just hadn't learned yet that hitting back at me meant I was going to come down on her twice as hard next time.

"A cowed ally is certainly easier to mold than one on equal footing," my mother said. "See if you can't hurry the process up, though, won't you?"

"If you or Dad think you can do a better job of it, you're welcome to drop by and take a shot at her yourselves," I said dryly.

My mother's tone turned acidic. "Surely we can rely on you to accomplish this one small task without assistance?"

"I said I'm on it, didn't I?" My fingers tightened around the phone.

I should have been able to answer this call with triumph after this morning's exhibition. I should have been able to report that I'd reduced the Bloodstone heir to a sobbing mess and then hooked her with a promise of redemption on my terms. But no. Even after I'd had Rory dancing to my orders, she still thought she was better than us. She still thought she could win.

"I hope to hear a more productive report soon, then," my mother said. "Your father would love to see you assert your leadership where it counts."

My stomach balled at the words. Didn't he see how much I was living out the principles he'd taught me? Maybe he'd be more satisfied with me if "where it counts" hadn't proven to be a constantly moving target that the two of them kept shifting out of reach.

There would be a day, before it was time for me to take over as baron, when he'd look at me and I'd be able to see in his eyes that he was finally totally convinced his heir could fill his footsteps.

When I'd hung up the phone, I tossed it on my desk. The sky outside had deepened to purple, the lake echoing it. The color of a bruise.

The joymancers must have broken something in Rory for her to resist the natural instincts we all had so persistently. She thought she could prove the sanctimonious jackasses right if she beat us. We'd just have to break her all over again so we could put her back together right.

So she could be the marvel I'd caught glimpses of behind the front she put on, infuriating but so fucking tantalizing.

Everyone had points of weakness. It shouldn't be hard to figure out more of hers. She could talk back to me all she wanted, strike her blows where she could, but she didn't have the grounding of growing up with fearmancers, of knowing how to build her own armor.

I'd find the right vulnerable spot, and then I'd bring all her defenses crashing down.

CHAPTER SEVENTEEN

Rory

When I returned to the dorm after another morning seminar, it was a relief to find no one but Imogen in the common room. She looked up from the book she'd been reading and immediately waved me over. "How are you doing?"

I sat down when she insistently patted the sofa cushion next to her. "Oh, you know, getting by."

"Malcolm was horrible yesterday." She glanced around as if to double-check that no one else was in hearing distance. "I mean, he's always been kind of an asshole, but since you got here…"

"I bring out the worst in him?" I filled in. Lucky me.

"No one's ever stood up to him like you do." Imogen paused. "You know, if you ever feel like you just want it over with, and you did back down and at least pretend to grovel a bit, he'd lay off of you. The scions push people around plenty, but they don't keep kicking once they've knocked someone down."

Honor among fearmancers. I guessed the problem was I kept getting back up for more. I looked down at my hands. "I think I'd find groveling harder to stomach than anything he can throw at me."

Her lips curled with a slanted smile. "I was kind of hoping you'd say that."

I glanced over at her, studying her pretty freckled face. "Why are you so nice to me?" I asked abruptly.

Imogen blinked. She looked away for a second and then shrugged. "Maybe it'll sound kind of pathetic but—I've never been 'in' with the favored families. My dad might be head of the school maintenance team, but that isn't exactly the kind of position that draws a lot of respect. And then on top of that, my magical ability didn't kick in until later than most… I learned to keep my head down and my shields up, but I was hassled a lot when I was a junior."

I made a face. "I can only imagine."

"Anyway, I'm sick of watching people like Malcolm and Victory walk all over the rest of us, even though I'm too much of a coward to do anything about it. I really admire the way you push back." She scooted a little closer to bump her shoulder playfully against mine. "And I figure it can't hurt to have one scion on my side, right?"

I laughed and rubbed my hand over my face. "We'll see if that ever works out in your favor."

Shelby slipped into the room then, a book of sheet music tucked under her arm. She took in the two of us together, and her forehead furrowed with concern. "Is something wrong?"

By whatever means, Malcolm had arranged that no Naries would witness his spectacle yesterday. I sucked in a breath, trying to decide what to tell her, and Imogen jumped in.

"One of those assholes broke Rory's charm bracelet," she said. "Just shattered all the charms. It was awful."

Shelby's eyes widened with so much horror that I felt the need to reassure her. "I managed to rescue one," I said, pulling the dragon charm out of my pocket. I'd kept it on me since yesterday morning, afraid that if I let it out of my sight, someone would destroy it too. "I'll have to start a new bracelet or something when I have the chance."

"You know… Just a second." Shelby disappeared into her bedroom with a swish of her ponytail. When she re-emerged she was clutching a thin silver chain.

"It isn't anything fancy," she said, bringing it over to me, "but I don't like wearing necklaces when I'm playing so I haven't really been wearing it. You can borrow it as long as you want."

My heart squeezed. "Thank you," I said. "You don't have to."

"It's no big deal. Really."

The chain slid light and cool across my fingers as I took it from her. I strung the glass bead on it like a pendant and clasped the chain around my neck. The dragon settled against my sternum, as if guarding the magic inside me.

"I really appreciate it," I said firmly, holding Shelby's gaze. Everyone else here was a jerk to the Naries, which only made it feel more important that she understood how honestly grateful I was.

She flushed as if embarrassed and bobbed her head. Imogen checked her phone. "Shit, I'd better get going, or I'll be late for class. Hang in there." She squeezed my shoulder with a quick smile and took off.

Shelby meandered over to the kitchen area to make lunch. She'd just reached the dining table when a shiver ran through her and her hand shot out to grip the top of the nearest chair.

I stood up. "Are you all right?"

"Yeah, yeah, I'm okay." She pushed herself straight again and swiped her hand across her forehead. Her earlier flush hadn't faded away, I realized. "Just a little under the weather. I think I've got a fever. Nothing huge."

Huge enough that I could see a bit of a wobble in her walk. "Isn't there a medical center on campus? Why don't you get them to check you out?"

Shelby shook her head vehemently. She ducked to grab a premade sandwich out of one of the fridges. "They'll either say I'm fine or tell me I need to stay in for treatment, and I can't risk missing any classes. It only takes a couple and they kick you right out of the program."

"Even if you're sick?"

"I don't know. They're pretty strict about dedication and all that. I don't want to take the chance."

She was running herself ragged to stay in a place where nearly everyone treated her like dirt. The pressure around my heart clenched tighter. "Is it really that important, if they're going to be assholes about it?"

"Yeah," Shelby said simply. "It is. There's no other school that offers the kind of specialized individual training they do here. Lots of people end up dropping out because it's tough, but the ones who make it through—I could get a spot in any orchestra I want, pretty much. I'm not losing that opportunity. I promise, it's nothing serious anyway." She sighed as she headed back to her room. "I just wish they'd fix that tree."

"Tree?" I repeated.

She waved toward the far wall. "There's a big oak by the west field. When the wind picks up, it's making this weird sound. That happened back home once, and it turned out the tree had gotten hollowed out by a parasite—it crashed all of a sudden when I was walking home and practically gave me a heart attack." Her eyes glazed in memory or maybe with the fever. "I told one of the maintenance staff, but I don't know if they cared. My skin keeps jumping every time I hear it."

She drifted into her bedroom with her sandwich and her music book. I debated marching her down to the medical center myself, but maybe it was just a cold, nothing serious. She'd know better than I would.

Of course Villain Academy would have to offer a huge reward to offset the torture the university put its Nary students through. I couldn't blame Shelby for wanting to hang on. But would she still think the torment was worth it if she knew just how much she was being used?

I wavered for a minute, torn between the impulse to help her somehow and the worry that I'd ruin her dream if I intervened. In the end, I headed out of the dorm.

My own pickings in the kitchen were getting awfully slim. A walk into town to get away from this place and stock up on groceries—including plenty of cheese for Deborah—sounded appealing. I could take the path through the forest where I'd send plenty of wild creatures scurrying and stockpile some more magic.

Some seniors were playing a casual game of football on the field by the front of the school. It was warm enough that a bunch of the guys had pulled off their shirts. Most of them were pretty fit, but Connar's brawny form still stood out among them, the planes of his muscular shoulders and chest as much chiseled perfection as his face was. I watched him for a moment, wondering if I'd catch a hint of the connection that had seemed to be there yesterday, but his gaze slid right over me.

It'd be silly to expect more than that. I let all thought of him and the other scions go as I started along the winding woodland path.

It had rained overnight, but I only had to dodge a few puddles. As the rustling quiet of the forest closed in around me, something in my chest released. I drank in the fresh spring air and the tiny quivers of nervous wildlife.

I could keep doing this. I'd held firm this long. I was learning, getting stronger. Soon I'd be fully enrolled in the school, and as I expanded my powers, I'd be able to figure out how the teachers kept the campus protected. How to bring those protections down. How to remove whatever tracing spell the blacksuits had placed on me.

One step at a time, all the way home.

Browsing the grocery store alongside all the ordinary shoppers grounded me even more. By the time I set back off toward campus, two bulging bags slung over my shoulders, a little spring had come into my step.

The past was the past. I just had to let the garbage they threw at me roll off me and move forward.

Then a dark shape hurtled out of the woods with a growl and a flash of gleaming fangs.

A shriek escaped me with a lurch of my pulse. I stumbled backward, not fast enough to dodge.

The creature sprang at me, its massive paws shoving me back under its weight. I fell in a patch of mud by the side of the path with a smack of pain through my back and hot breath by my throat.

I lay there frozen as the creature glowered down at me, still growling. It was a wolf. A large one, with mottled gray-and-black fur and gleaming amber eyes. It snapped its teeth at me, and I flinched.

A whistle cut through the forest. The wolf's head shot up and around. A cool, smooth voice tinged with amusement reached my ears.

"I see you've met my familiar." Malcolm gave a shorter whistle and snapped his fingers by his side, and the wolf wheeled. It leapt off me and trotted over to join the Nightwood scion where he'd come to a stop on the path.

"Good boy," he said, scratching the fur behind its left ear. The smile he gave it was the softest expression I'd ever seen on his face. I couldn't expect him to aim anything like affection at me.

I shoved myself upright, abruptly aware of the damp stickiness coating the back of my shirt—and, ugh, my hair was full of mud too—now that I wasn't in imminent danger of having my throat torn out.

"Maybe you should keep it on a shorter leash," I snapped. I wanted to keep my composure, but my nerves were frayed. Fuck, he'd probably gotten ten times more power from my terror in the last minute than I had during the entire walk through the forest.

"That would defeat the purpose of bonding with an animal with such well-honed natural instincts," Malcolm said nonchalantly. "Wolves will be wolves."

And boys would be boys? I eyed him warily as I grabbed my bags from where they'd fallen. Cold droplets of moisture ran down the back of my neck, but the chill inside me ran much deeper.

We were completely alone. No witnesses, no one to comment if a rule or two were broken.

I didn't think Malcolm wanted me *dead*, but at this point that was about all I'd count on when it came to my well-being.

His gaze slid down my body, and a spark of panic lit inside me at the thought that he'd notice the dragon charm and force me to smash it too. But in my fall and recovery, it'd slipped under the collar of my shirt, out of sight—one small bit of good luck in an otherwise godawful situation.

"I'd rather have the wolf for company than you," I said.

Malcolm gave me a grin that was plenty wolfish itself. "Eventually you're going to have to face the facts, Glinda. Some of us are predators and some are prey, and it's obvious which camp you fall into, no matter how big a front you try to put on. If you want to learn how to run with the wolves rather than getting chewed up, you've got to submit to the leader of the pack."

"Well, you can just keep waiting on that day," I said, hefting my bags over my shoulders. "Don't get your hopes up."

I walked past him, a prickle running down my spine as I left him behind. He could catch a whiff of how nervous I was, but I wasn't going to let it show any other way. My ears stayed perked for any sound of attack.

Malcolm didn't move to follow. "Careful when you're out in the woods again," he called after me. "Next time I might not be close enough to call him back. One of these days you could lose something you can't live without."

I didn't give him the satisfaction of a response.

The football game had dispersed by the time I reached the campus. A cluster of junior students had staked out the edge of the field with their lunches, and their stares followed my muddy back as I passed them. Cressida and a couple other girls from Victory's crowd noticed me crossing the green. She covered her mouth with a snicker.

"Love the new fashion statement," she said. "I didn't realize you could hit a bar even lower than feeb."

I ignored them and trudged into Ashgrave Hall. Halfway up the stairs, I ran into none other than the Ashgrave scion himself, on his way down.

Declan stopped at the sight of me, his eyebrows rising. "Are you okay?" he asked, with just a touch of that gentle concern I'd heard in his voice that morning in my parents' house.

The last of my patience disintegrated. I looked at him, letting all the frustration running through me burn in my gaze. "If I'm not, are you actually going to do anything about it?"

He opened his mouth and hesitated, his hand twitching at his side. That was all the answer I had to see.

"All right then," I said, and marched on past him without a backward glance. An uncomfortable sensation sank deep into my gut —maybe not the lesson Malcolm had wanted me to learn, but one that was nearly as wrenching.

No matter what little kindnesses Imogen and Shelby extended to me, neither of them could offer any real protection. I was on my own.

CHAPTER EIGHTEEN

Rory

For the first time, my schedule directed me to the basement level of Nightwood Tower. I hadn't even realized there *was* a basement, but it turned out a little door stood around the side of the north stairs that opened to a second flight heading down. The air cooled as I descended, my footsteps sounding eerily loud in the tight space between the stone walls.

At the bottom of the stairs, I found a small room with wooden benches on either side and a large oak door at the opposite end. A girl I recognized from my Physicality class was sitting on one bench, so I guessed we weren't supposed to stroll right in. I sat down across from her. She didn't acknowledge me, but she didn't take any jabs at me either, so I'd take that as a win.

It didn't look as if this space, which had been marked on my schedule simply as Desensitization, was going to hold the usual eight or nine students that made up most of my seminars. More than four was going to be a tight fit.

Just as I thought that, our third classmate reached the bottom of the stairs with a flick of his dark copper hair away from his eyes. Jude looked at me, and his lips curled upward with his usual smirk. "Hey, Snow Cone. This should be interesting." He propped himself against the wall rather than sit on either of the benches.

I fought the urge to squirm on my seat. I had no idea what "Desensitization" entailed or why it might be interesting. Unfortunately, I hadn't had a chance to ask anyone who'd know since my updated schedule had arrived at the dorm this morning. Deborah hadn't had a clue. Somehow I didn't think I was going to get a helpful answer from the scion who'd enjoyed stringing up my embarrassing memories for everyone else's amusement.

One more student joined us: a gangly young man who eyed both Jude and me with apparent anxiety. He'd just sat down on the bench next to the other girl when the door swung open.

Four junior students filed out. One girl was hugging herself, her face wan. Another hurried for the stairs with a clenched jaw and red-rimmed eyes. One of the boys let out a laugh that sounded forced as the other flinched at the squeak of the hinges.

That didn't say "interesting" to me. That said, "Get me the fuck out of here."

A tall gaunt figure with a sheen of silver on his long jaw appeared in the doorway. He beckoned us in, his gaze lingering on me.

"Miss Bloodstone," he said. "This is your first session."

"Yeah," I said. "I'm… not totally sure what this is."

He chuckled under his breath, a weirdly warm sound in the chilly space, and motioned me after the others into a round domed room that I suspected filled the entire circumference of the tower. From the glossy tiled floor to the curving brick walls, every surface gleamed starkly black, making the space feel even larger in the pale light cast from the fixture at the peak of the dome.

"I'm Professor Razeden," the man said. "And the work you'll do here is a vital part to your education as a fearmancer. The rest of you have much more experience with this subject than Miss Bloodstone does. Who can explain for her why we go through desensitization sessions?"

The other girl raised her hand. "Learning how to prevent other mages from using our fears is just as important as learning how to provoke fear for our own use," she said confidently. "A mage who doesn't know how to control their emotions will find themselves controlled by others."

"Precisely," Professor Razeden said. "And why do we conduct these sessions in a small group rather than individually?"

"Because you need as much time off as you can get," Jude said sardonically, and the younger guy let out a nervous laugh.

Razeden cocked his head, but he didn't look bothered by the joke. "The real answer, please, Mr. Killbrook."

Jude took on a singsong voice as if reciting a quote. "Because one of the greatest fears to master is the fear of having our vulnerabilities exposed."

"But nothing we see about each other in here gets talked about outside the chamber," the other guy jumped in, shifting on his feet. "What happens here stays private."

Razeden nodded, but I suspected if Jude caught a glimpse of anything juicy to do with me, he'd be passing it on to Malcolm within five minutes of us leaving the Tower. Not much I could do about that. And mastering my fears, making sure people like him and Malcolm *couldn't* turn me into a power source while they tormented me, sounded like a great idea.

I glanced around the otherwise empty room. "So, how exactly does that work?"

"You go one by one while the rest of us observe," Razeden said. "The magic in this room is a honed combination of insight and illusion spells. When I activate it, it will latch onto a point of fear in your mind and bring that impression to life, literally or more symbolically depending on the specificity of your emotions. Your fear will continue feeding the illusion until you can manage to control it. Then it will disappear, and your turn will be over. I will, of course, offer guidance as it appears you need it."

He gestured for us to step back to the wall and considered the four of us. "Since Miss Bloodstone is newly with us, I think we should let her do a little observing before throwing her into the lion's den. Mr. Killbrook, you seem quite energetic today. Why don't you start us off?"

Jude gave the professor a mock salute and strode into the middle of the room without hesitation.

What would he be afraid of? I had even less of a sense with him than I did with Malcolm.

"Begin," Professor Razeden said.

The light overhead blinked off, throwing us into total darkness. A hazy image swam into focus: Jude perched on the top of a crystalline spire.

He was swaying, bits of the glittering rock crumbling away beneath his feet. A chunk gave way beneath his heel. He stumbled and toppled off with a warble of wind I could hear even if it didn't touch me. He plummeted, falling and yet suspended before us at the same time.

Jude's hands flailed out with a flash of panic, and then his expression firmed. He stretched his arms out deliberately and spun his body around. His feet hit the ground with a loud but steady thump. He didn't even stumble.

The light came back on. Jude swept down in an exaggerated bow, his eyes glinting with triumph when he straightened up. He was afraid of heights? Of sudden falls? Whatever that imagery had represented, he obviously didn't need any help tackling it.

"Very nice, Mr. Killbrook," Professor Razeden said. "You continue to hone your reactions. Miss Scarlow, let's have you up next."

The fear the girl tackled must have been symbolic as well—I sure as hell hoped so, anyway. A bristling monster twice her height loomed over her and slashed at her with a razor-clawed hand.

As she dodged it, sweat broke out on her brow. She bobbed and ducked and dashed from side to side, but the beast kept after her. Her breath turned ragged. My legs tensed with the urge to run in there and defend her somehow.

"Remember, you must defeat it to overcome it," Razeden called out from the darkness. "How would you slay this creature?"

The girl fell on her side escaping the monster's grasp. She winced as its claws passed through her shoulder, even though the contact didn't appear to tear her clothes or flesh. It was an illusion, but I knew pain that was in your head could still hurt plenty.

She drew in a shaky breath and slid her palm across the floor. A narrow shining sword leapt into her hand from the same place the monster had emerged from. She sprang up and battered its claws away, weaving around the room for several more seconds. Her mouth pressed flat. She lunged forward and stabbed the thing straight through the chest.

Monster and sword disappeared. The light came on, and the girl walked back to the wall without any fanfare, wiping her damp forehead.

"Have you been practicing those exercises I gave you between sessions?" Razeden asked her.

She nodded. "It's just—it's harder when I'm right in the moment."

"More practice, and you'll get there. It's all a matter of training the mind." He turned to me. "Well, Miss Bloodstone, let's see how you fare your first time out."

Oh, God. I forced myself to move into the middle of the room, wondering what embarrassing scenario the room would conjure out of my head. What if it threw an illusion of Malcolm at me? Or even the scion currently in the room? Jude would have a field day with that.

"Begin," Razeden said.

The light went out, and suddenly I was surrounded by white. White tiles, white cabinets. And my mother, flung back against one of those cabinets as a dark shape just beyond my view slashed open her throat.

"No!" Not again.

I threw myself at her, pressing my hand against her neck. I had to be able to do something. I had magic—I was a fucking scion. I couldn't just watch her die all over again.

But where my fingers touched her skin, it flayed open even wider. The blood gushed faster. Mom's dulling eyes stared at me, horror twisting her expression.

I yanked my hand down with a gasp. It brushed her sternum, and her chest cracked open, ribs jutting up into the open air, more blood splattering my arms. I tasted a fleck of it in my mouth.

"No. No, no, no, no, no," I mumbled. My heart was thudding so hard and fast I couldn't make out anything else.

Professor Razeden's voice reached me as if from miles away. "Take deep breaths. Steady yourself. You can handle this. It isn't really happening. It isn't real."

"Yes, it fucking was," I shouted back in a voice gone raw.

The surge of anger that came with that retort gave me something other than terror to hang on to. Fury at the assholes who'd slaughtered my parents, who'd dragged me to their university to fend for myself among these villains, who put their students through horrors like this.

I would not let them beat me. I would *not.*

A thump sounded at the other end of the room. Dad slumped over, innards spilling from the gouge in his chest. My rush of anger fell away beneath a cold surge of fear like a tidal wave.

I shoved myself away from Mom and ran to him. My feet skidded on the blood-slick tiles. I tumbled down next to him, my fingers grazing the side of his head and just like that smashing open his skull.

His face crumpled. Bits of bone and gray matter mashed together beneath my hand. My stomach heaved. A sob caught in my throat.

I wasn't helping them—I was ravaging them even worse than the blacksuits had.

I crouched down, tucking my arms around my head to block out the sight. The sickly metallic scent of the blood filled my nose and mouth as I gulped for breath. Far away, someone was shouting at me, but the words all blurred together in the haze of my misery. A sound like a strangled whimper escaped my lips.

You killed them, a louder voice said, right inside my head. My voice. You *killed them.*

A hand touched my back, and I flinched. The next breath I drew in smelled only like damp basement air. The tiles beneath my feet were black again, and black walls loomed all around me. Not a speck of blood clung to my trembling arms.

Professor Razeden had bent down beside me. "The first few times, when you're not used to it, can be very intense," he said in a quiet, detached voice that offered neither sympathy nor judgment. "Now that I've seen what sort of scenario you may face, we can discuss strategies that should better prepare you to cope and rise above in the moment."

He must have ended the illusion. I certainly hadn't conquered my fear. I held there for a second longer, afraid to test my legs, and then straightened up shakily.

My throat stung when I swallowed. Had I been shouting—or screaming—more than I remembered?

When I blinked, I saw my parents' distorted faces, and the blood —so much blood…

I avoided meeting my classmates' eyes as I hurried back to the wall. Professor Razeden went to talk with the other guy before beginning his session. Jude sidled closer to me.

I tensed up, but the Killbrook scion's comment came out oddly tentative. "You really did love them."

He sounded… puzzled. My gaze jerked to him, but he wasn't even looking at me, his attention focused on the middle of the room where he'd have watched me go through that horror.

The fearmancers really didn't get it, did they? They had no concept of how the same people who in their minds had kidnapped and imprisoned me had also been the people I'd cared about most in the world. Had *earned* that love with all the love they'd shown me.

At least, it'd seemed like love at the time. All my memories were jumbled in the aftermath of that almost-memory.

"If you only just figured that out, maybe you're not as smart as you like to think," I said, but without much rancor.

His eyes flicked to me then. He studied me for a moment, so intently my skin started to itch. I couldn't tell if he found what he was looking for. It was only that moment, and then another smirk slipped across his angular face.

"Had to get the teacher to bail you out of your own head," he said, with a tsk of his tongue. "Doesn't bode well for your academic success, now does it?"

"Shut up," I muttered, which was the cleverest retort I could come up with while my nerves were still scraped raw. Then, to my relief, the light switched off for the final session.

When I got back after Desensitization, I shut my bedroom door and braced the desk chair against it for good measure. Then I opened the wardrobe and sat down in front of it. As I tugged open the sock drawer, Deborah squirmed out from between the rolled pairs. She scrambled across them onto my waiting hand.

What did they do to you now, sweetheart? she asked without preamble, her dark mouse eyes peering up at me.

The tenderness in her tone made my throat constrict. It took me a second to speak.

"I just realized that I killed Mom and Dad."

Deborah made a sound like a snort in my head. *What are you talking about? I was there. You did everything you could to help them, putting your own self in more peril than I can really approve of, as admirable as it might have been.*

"I know. But I also— If they hadn't taken me in, the fearmancers never would have attacked them. If they'd never adopted me, they'd still be alive."

The last words came out ragged. I swallowed hard.

Deborah's tiny whiskers quivered against my palm. She nuzzled the heel of my hand. *That's hardly the same thing.*

"It's the same end result."

Do you think they didn't know the risks? It was their choice to make.

"Because they thought they had to protect the rest of the world from what I might do if they didn't suppress my powers."

No. I'd never heard Deborah sound so firm. *Listen, Lorelei… I can tell you something that'll show you what really mattered to your parents. I told you that I was brought on right after you turned fifteen, remember?*

"Yeah," I said. That was just further proof that they'd seen me as some kind of threat.

Well, after they did the whole consciousness transfer, I woke up in this body a little earlier than I think anyone had expected. I heard them arguing with a couple mages from the Conclave who were overseeing the process. The Conclave wanted you to be moved to a more secure location, where several mages could keep an eye on you and your potential fearmancer powers.

A chill rippled down my back. If the other joymancers had felt that way about me back then, how much would it take for them to welcome me back now that my powers had awoken?

"They wanted to treat me like a literal prisoner," I said.

Deborah tickled my palm with her claws. *They were worried. They knew you'd be powerful. At the time, I didn't realize the heritage you came with. I didn't tell you about this before because I didn't want you thinking* they're *the enemy.*

"It's not exactly a stretch," I muttered.

My point is that Rafael and Lisa refused. They fought *to keep you with them, to keep raising you as their daughter, because that's how they saw you. Lisa said it just like that: "She's our daughter now." They couldn't imagine sending you off like some kind of delinquent for something you hadn't even done. For what your background was. Keeping you in their family for as long as they could mattered more to them than any danger that could come with that decision.*

"Oh." I ran my thumb over her back instinctively, as if she were still my pet mouse and not a person in mouse form. Deborah arched into the touch, so maybe she was mouse enough not to mind. I rubbed the black splotch on her flank. "They really said all of that?"

And a whole lot more. It was a long argument. But obviously they argued it well, because I went back with them to your house where you stayed for the next four years.

The ache inside me wasn't gone, but the story had eased it a little. I hadn't imagined the family I'd thought I had. They'd wanted me, risks and all.

I closed my eyes. "Thank you," I said, curling my fingers around Deborah and tucking her against me in the closest to a hug I could manage.

My fear had been a lie. But then, an awful lot of fears were, weren't they, no matter what Malcolm had said?

I couldn't let myself get so wrapped up in this place that I forgot who the real villains were.

CHAPTER NINETEEN

Rory

As Imogen and I came into the dorm room after a dinner in town, Victory and a few of the other girls brushed past us on their way out. Victory's lips curled into a sharp little smirk. Cressida let her purse smack my arm on her way past, and the girl at the back of the pack tossed over her shoulder, "Sleep well!"

The door shut between us with a mix of giggling and a hissed admonishment. I looked toward my bedroom door with a sinking sensation in my gut.

"Might as well see what the damage is," Imogen said.

"I thought I had a pretty good lock on the door this time," I said as we headed over. My abilities obviously weren't developed enough to stand up to Victory's yet. It'd probably take a while before they were. Professor Banefield *had* said she was one of the university's top students.

The door swung open easily. I braced myself for another stink, but the air smelled clean enough, a hint of freshly mown grass traveling through the window I'd left an inch open. The dim light of the falling evening didn't catch on anything overtly concerning. I reached over and switched on the overhead light.

The fixture blinked on, and my entire bedspread started glittering. What the hell? I walked over.

Every inch of the duvet was scattered with tiny shards of glass, many of them burrowed right into the fabric. I'd slice open my fingers trying to dig them out. Somehow I had the feeling there were more underneath too.

A shudder ran through me. Victory had styled her conjuring to provoke emotional pain as well as physical. The mess on the bed echoed the smashed bits of my charm bracelet.

"For fuck's sake," Imogen muttered, coming up beside me. "I can give my dad a call. The maintenance staff can clean this up for you."

Resolve tightened around the hum of magic in my chest. "No," I said. "I don't want to have to go running for help. I think I can handle it."

I focused on the glinting slivers of glass, remembering how I'd pulled ice right out of the air the other day. This should be easier, right? I wasn't conjuring so much as simply moving.

"Come together," I murmured, drawing my hands toward one another at the same time. The shards quivered. Some of them rose off the bed, collecting in a clump near the foot. Others seemed to stick in the fabric.

I dragged in a breath and focused harder. "Come together." Willing every bit of glass from within the duvet and beneath it, pulling them toward each other with the energy vibrating at the base of my throat. Prickles raced across my skin as I worked them all free.

"Come together," I whispered one last time, but I couldn't sense any more glass in the bed. I turned my attention to the floating ball I'd made of them.

What to do with them now? The hum in my chest stuttered. I didn't have much accumulated power left.

I could leave Victory a different sort of present. A smile tugged at my mouth, and I pressed my hands even closer together. "Mold and stick."

The shards melded together into a solid lump, all the sharp edges melting away. I released the shape, and it dropped onto my bed with a muffled thump.

Imogen picked up the thing and laughed. "It looks like a very posh version of a poop emoji."

I grinned back at her. "That's what I was going for. Might as well let Victory know exactly what I think of her attempt."

Imogen tossed it to me, and I brought the lumpy mass over to Victory's room. I didn't have a chance against her locking abilities, so I left it sitting just outside her door. She'd figure out what it meant.

"Let's see if we can really keep her out from here on," Imogen said when I rejoined her. "How did you seal the door last time?"

"I tried reshaping the latch so it wouldn't slide out when the doorknob turned." I twisted the knob to examine it. "I guess she smoothed it back out."

Imogen nodded. "You'd think a physical mechanism would be the best defense, but mental ones are actually harder for people to break. Next time, see if you can mix a combination of persuasion that they really don't want to come in and the illusion of feeling sick or scared or something like that. Scared is the best, of course, because then you get magic out of it too."

"Of course," I said, with a pinch of real queasiness. I wasn't sure I was ever going to get used to the casual way in which the students of Villain Academy fed off each other's distress.

My gaze slid to the wardrobe. So far I'd been lucky and none of my tormentors had messed with that. I couldn't count on staying that lucky. I owed it to Deborah to make sure I defended her as well as I could.

"I could use a little help figuring out another spell," I said, motioning Imogen into the room and closing the door. "If I wanted to make sure anyone who looked in my wardrobe didn't see one specific thing in there… That'd take an illusion, right? Are there any special tricks to doing that effectively?"

Imogen cocked her head. "What are you trying to cover up? It makes a difference."

I hesitated. But if I couldn't reveal this to Imogen after all the ways she'd been here for me so far, why was I even hanging out with her? I didn't have to tell her the whole story about technically having smuggled a joymancer into the school, only the part that would seem relatively normal for a mage.

"I have a familiar," I said. "But she's—well, she's a mouse, and it seems like the vast majority of the other animals around here would happily have her for dinner, so I've been keeping her out of sight. I don't really want to know what Victory or the rest of them would do if they found her."

Deborah's voice reached my head distantly. *Are you sure about this? This girl is a fearmancer, isn't she?*

I couldn't answer her without raising questions I didn't want to answer. Imogen raised her eyebrows. "A mouse? Interesting choice."

"It's a long story." I knelt down by the sock drawer and eased it open. "I don't want anyone seeing anything other than socks in this drawer, even if they start digging around in there. How hard would that be?"

Deborah stayed hidden amid the rolls of fabric. She didn't risk saying anything else to me. Maybe Imogen thought I'd gone completely around the bend and was hallucinating this mouse, but she crouched down beside me, humoring me.

"If you want the illusion to hold even when things are moved around, the easiest way to make that stick is to take everything out of the drawer and start from there. Cast an illusion that people will see the bare base while you're looking right at it. Then add a few socks and layer another illusion on top. And so on in a bunch of stages until it's full again. Unless a person is paying really close attention, they aren't likely to notice they're being misled."

"Okay." That sounded like it was going to take a lot of energy. Maybe it was time for another walk in the woods.

Imogen straightened up. "Let me know if you run into any problems, and I'll try to troubleshoot. I've got to get writing this essay for Modern Politics." She grimaced and headed off to her room, leaving me glad that I'd at least gotten a break in that area. Ms.

Grimsworth had decided I was exempt from the general education courses until I got my magical abilities reasonably up to speed.

"I'll be back when I'm all charged up," I whispered to Deborah.

Outside, the clear sky had gone almost completely black, a half-moon gleaming amid the stars. I left behind the glow of the sconces around the university building doors and wandered toward the lake. Alone at night, I'd rather not meet Malcolm and his wolf in the wider woods on the other side of campus.

A few kids—juniors, from the sound of their voices—had gotten a rowboat out of the boathouse and were laughing and rocking it as they drifted across the water. Watching them, the realization crept over me that I could give them a good scare in a matter of seconds simply by flipping the boat over and dunking them. Just like that, I'd bet I'd have enough energy to fuel all the protections I wanted to put down in my room with more left over.

That was the strategy most of the other fearmancers would have taken. My stomach twisted, and I turned toward the strip of forest instead.

As unnerving as it could be walking around in the woods at night, there were also a lot more animals roaming around than there were by daylight. Wafts of fear fluttered into my chest with each step I made through the brush where I'd veered off the path so I'd make more noise to disturb them. Still, after everything I'd been through in the last week, Malcolm's voice echoed up from the back of my mind.

Some of us are predators and some are prey, and it's obvious which camp you fall into.

How was I ever really going to stand up for myself against him and the others if I only gathered power in dribs and drabs, meandering around like this or startling Banefield's cat now and then?

How was I ever going to gather as much power as they did without becoming just as much an asshole as the people I wanted to take down?

I passed the spot where the ground sloped up toward the cliff and paused. The memory rose up of the weird sense of peace that had come over me looking over the lake. Maybe if I left everything else behind, the right answers would come to me.

The underbrush was so thick that it took a little while to find the best route up the slope. No wonder Connar had found he could count on a certain amount of privacy up there. I guessed I hadn't made the quietest approach, because when I reached the edge of the little rocky clearing, I found him standing on the other side of the log, watching the forest for my arrival.

I halted, feeling abruptly awkward. "Oh. Hi. I didn't realize you were here. I just—it was nice up here last time, and I thought—"

He waved his hand to dismiss my fumbling explanation. "It's fine. There's room for two."

He moved farther along the log to leave plenty of room where I'd sat before and hunkered back down himself. I hesitated. When he glanced back toward the lake, my lips moved instinctively, forming the word for one bit of magic I was coming to trust in the faintest whisper. "*Inside*."

My attention focused in on Connar's head. The stretch of my awareness bumped up against a barrier—but it didn't feel as daunting as the one Jude had blocked me with. I narrowed my eyes with a tremor of the energy I'd just collected in my walk through the forest.

I didn't exactly push through, but I had the sense of the wall thinning to something more like a membrane. Impressions seeped into my head of calm and curiosity and something that tasted like… gratitude?

Was he *glad* I was here? I found that hard to believe, but I definitely didn't feel any hostile intentions in him. That reassured me enough to clamber over the log and sit down a few feet away from him.

A crisp but not unpleasantly cool breeze drifted off the lake. The rustling of the leaves behind us nearly covered the distant laughter of the juniors in their boat.

Connar glanced over at me, and his gaze settled on my new necklace for a second before lifting to meet my eyes. "You like dragons, huh?"

I touched the glass charm instinctively, my thumb catching on the rough edge where the tail had fractured. Strength and courage. "What's not to like?"

That slow, breathtaking grin he'd offered me the night of the party crossed his face. "I completely agree. Take a look."

With zero self-consciousness, he started unbuttoning his collared shirt. Heat rushed over my face. "Er," I began, but he stopped halfway and tugged one side down to reveal only his left shoulder.

I hadn't seen his whole back the other day when he'd been playing football. The moonlight caught on a dark shape etched on his skin. I leaned closer, and the shape came into focus as a dragon, wings unfurled across Connar's shoulder blade, not one but four narrow horned heads peering at me from their sinewy necks.

At least, I assumed it had to be a tattoo. The tiny green and bronze scales rippling across the dragon's body looked so vividly solid I couldn't stop myself from extending my hand to brush my fingers across them. For all they appeared to be real, all I touched was warm smooth skin.

The warmth quivered up my arm. I yanked my hand back. "That's amazing. Why the four heads?"

Connar tugged his shirt back up but left it unbuttoned. I couldn't say I minded the partial view I got of his sculpted chest. "It's to symbolize the barony," he said. "The four of us scions who'll rule together when it's time. My real family."

"Except there's five of us," I had to point out, even though I had less than zero interest in ruling over anybody.

He shrugged. "Sorry. When I got it, we had no idea when they'd ever find you or how that whole situation would play out. The guys—I grew up with them. Even before we started here, we'd see each other all the time."

"I suppose I'll forgive you," I said, and he smiled again. I wanted to prod him about how his chosen family had responded to me—what did he think of Malcolm's and Jude's harassment?—but that was what he came up here to get away from, wasn't it? All of the conflict and the jockeying for power back on campus.

He'd grown up with that too. He probably saw it as normal. But even so, here he was being friendly with me rather than taking up Malcolm's mantle.

"So, Blood U must be pretty different from the schools you went to before," Connar said into my silence.

Understatement of the year. "I haven't gone to schools much, period," I admitted. "My parents mostly homeschooled me. I guess so they could keep a close eye on me." I hugged myself against that uneasy thought. "It was just recently that I started doing a few classes at the local community college. That place was… a lot more straightforward." I could be diplomatic.

Connar chuckled as if he could guess how much I wasn't saying. "Maybe it's complicated," he said, "but it's got to feel right, too, finally getting in touch with your magical power. Realizing all the things you can do that you couldn't have known before. Doesn't it?"

"Yeah." I looked toward the lake, debating how much I wanted to tell him. Nothing that would hurt me if he happened to pass it on to Malcolm, but at this point, my skin was pretty thick. Why shouldn't I be honest, if he wanted to know? "My parents were open about their magic. With me, I mean. I thought I was Nary my whole life, and I wanted so badly to have the same kind of power they did. I just wish I could have found out differently."

Connar was quiet for a moment. "It's a pretty big deal even for us. We know we should come into our powers because they run in our families, but until you taste that first wisp of fear and direct it into a spell, you can't be completely sure you won't turn out to be some kind of dud. Fifteen years or more is a long time to wait to find out."

Maybe he could understand the awe of the discovery to some extent then, if not the pain of what I'd lost in the process.

"How old were you?" I asked.

"Just a month past my fifteenth birthday. For the families with the strongest bloodlines, it usually kicks in pretty quick. I've been here a little more than five years now. Can't say I'll be sorry to leave and get on with the rest of my life."

He set his hands on the log, leaning back a bit. It occurred to me that while he was being this open with me, I really ought to dig for the information that would help *me* get out of here.

"One of the girls told me there's wards all over campus to stop joymancers from finding the school," I said, which was technically true, because Imogen had told me that. Connar didn't need to know I'd prompted the information. "Why would we be worried about that? What would they even do if they found the place?"

What could *I* do that the fearmancers wouldn't want to happen?

Connar tipped his head to one side, his forehead furrowing. "It's never felt like a pressing threat while I've been here. But I suppose—joymancers can be brutal when they figure they're in the right. And they'd definitely disagree with a lot of the things we're taught here. They've killed fearmancers before—they've destroyed property… Basically the entire younger generation of fearmancers from across America is here most of the time, along with the best teachers in the magical arts. If they attacked the university, it could be devastating."

I didn't want to think about killing anyone. I doubted the Conclave would approve that kind of brutality anyway. The fearmancers assumed everyone operated the same way they did, just like they couldn't even conceive of the fact that I might object to anything they did. The joymancers might have ways of imprisoning the teachers and other major figures, though.

"But if the place was compromised and everyone got out, we could just set up school someplace else?"

"I don't think it'd be that easy. Not on the same level. My great-grandfather told me it took them fifty years for the staff to get the illusions and other barriers perfect so they could bring in Nary students without worrying about revealing ourselves. He was one of the first mages to attend with them. The desensitization chamber took a while to construct too. We couldn't just recreate everything like that." He snapped his fingers. "Better not to let them get at the place at all."

Well, that was certainly useful to know. A twinge of guilt ran through me for using him when he so clearly had no idea I had a hostile agenda, but I hadn't lied to him. I'd just asked, and he'd answered.

"Good thing for all the wards, then," I said.

"You're safe here," he said agreeably, which was such a ridiculous statement that it took all my self-control not to burst out in hysterical laughter. Maybe he caught a whiff of it anyway, because he added, "You don't seem to scare very easy anyway."

He could only say that because he'd never been the one scaring me. "Maybe I'm just good at hiding when I'm freaked out."

"It amounts to pretty much the same thing in the end. You've been getting the hang of things, from what I've seen."

"More or less."

"Hey," he said. "You're a Bloodstone, even if you didn't know it most of your life. You were born for this. And it shows."

The smile he gave me then was softer around the edges in a way that sent an odd flutter through my stomach. "You were born for it too," I said, just to break the moment.

A shadow flickered through his expression. He turned back to the lake. "Yeah. You could say that."

I had the impression I'd made a misstep, but I had no idea what it was. I shifted on the log. "If you'd rather have this spot to yourself again, I can—"

He held up his hand. "Wait. Watch. This is the best part."

The breeze had died down completely. The lake's ripples expanded. Then, with one last tremor, the surface of the water went still. The stars glinted down toward the glossy depths, and the lake reflected them back. Tiny glimmers speckled the dark water as if a whole galaxy lay down there as well as above us.

My breath caught in my throat. Right then, Villain Academy and all its horrors fell back even farther in the distance.

"You can see how amazing that is too, right?" Connar said quietly.

It took me a second to find the wherewithal to speak. "Of course. It's beautiful."

His gaze slid from the lake to me. He paused for a beat and then said, "So are you."

His low voice passed over me like a caress. My eyes jerked to him as the breeze rose again, shattering the underwater galaxy. "What?" I blurted out. "Why would you say that?"

He laughed and eased closer on the log, bringing his hand to my cheek. An eager shiver passed through me at his touch. "Because you are," he said. "Especially when you're refusing to take anyone's shit."

I was groping for an acceptable response to that when he leaned in and kissed me.

I'd only ever kissed two guys before: the boyfriend of two months who'd ditched me after the first time I'd slept with him, as Victory had gleaned from my memories, and some guy at a party a couple weeks later when I was trying to convince myself I didn't care. Connar blew them both away in an instant. His mouth pressed hot against mine, with a hunger that drew out an answering need in me.

My hand clutched the half-open front of his shirt in the instinctive urge to pull him closer. He looped his arm around my waist as he kissed me again. His other hand lingered against my cheek, his thumb grazing over my cheekbone in a gesture that was almost as giddying as his kiss.

The taste of his mouth and the heat of his body dizzied me. What the hell was I doing? Why wasn't I doing more? After days on end of staying constantly on guard, the sensation of my body melting into his was nothing short of addictive.

It was just kissing. It couldn't hurt anything, could it? *He* hadn't hurt me, not really, not once. And his mouth on mine felt so fucking good.

He tipped his head, his tongue parting my lips at the new angle. I welcomed it to twine with mine. His fingers stroked a burning line over my jaw and down my neck. I adjusted my grip on his shirt, and my knuckles brushed his bare chest. He made an encouraging growl.

I dared to slip my hand right under the fabric to run right over those chiseled muscles, so hard under skin that was unexpectedly soft.

Connar kissed me harder, and his hand dipped lower. He teased his fingers along the curve of my breast through my shirt.

A pang of desire spread low through my belly. I pressed into his touch. His thumb swept over the peak, my breath stuttered, and a sense of alarm finally pealed out loud enough to wake me up.

This wasn't just kissing anymore. If I didn't get my head together fast, it was going to be a *hell* of a lot more than kissing. With a fearmancer. With a guy who called two of my most avid tormentors his family.

I pushed away from Connar with a sting at the loss of contact and scrambled to my feet. My whole body felt feverish, my lips raw, the air shockingly cool against them.

Connar stared up at me, his eyes dark with the same desire still echoing through me. His voice came out rough.

"Rory—"

"I think—I think I should go now," I said, and hurried down the slope before he could say anything that might make me forget myself all over again.

CHAPTER TWENTY

Jude

No one could ever mistake me for a cuddler. I rolled off Sinclair, she let out a satisfied sigh, and I motioned her toward her clothes where they'd fallen beside the bed.

She gave me a narrow look. "Can't a girl relax for a second?"

"If you wanted to relax, you should have picked a different time to come calling. My parents are due for the annual meeting in half an hour."

She sat up with a fluff of her black bob and reached for her panties. "You could have told me before."

"But then we might not have had this excellent quickie. It's not as if I didn't make sure you got yours." I grinned at her.

She made a face in response, but she couldn't stop her gaze from sliding down to take another admiring look at my naked body.

Sinclair knew what she was getting into. We ended up in my bed together once every month or two, and other than that we barely spoke. She hooked up with other guys. I enjoyed various other girls as the mood struck me. We weren't even friends, just two people who found each other attractive enough to make our initial banging after one of last year's parties an occasional repeated occurrence.

No drama, no responsibilities. The perfect sort of intimacy.

She squeaked on her way to the door, and I caught a little spark of fear. "Your stupid familiar nipped my heel," Sinclair grumbled.

I laughed. "She's just helping you get going. Good work, Mischief."

My ferret chortled from where she'd darted under my desk. Sinclair glowered at me as she slipped out of my bedroom, and I got up to shower and pick out my clothes for the appointment. Better look snappy for the old man, or he'd have one more excuse not to look at me at all.

I swiped a bit of gel through my hair to keep it out of my eyes, tugged the sleeves of my gray button-down halfway up my forearms, and set off for the hall that bore my family's name.

It seemed a little ridiculous that we continued to have parent conferences once we were seniors. I was just a few months shy of twenty—men had waged actual wars at my age without having to check in with Ma and Pa first.

But that was the way things were done at Blood U, since we weren't considered fully qualified mages until they sent us off into the wider world sometime during our twenty-first year. Every year before that, on the anniversary of our arrival at the university, every student's parents dropped in for a chat with Ms. Grimsworth about our progress.

I found mine waiting in the front foyer right on time. My mother's face lit up when she saw me, and she held out her arms for a hug. My father's gaze followed me as I ambled over to her with the sort of expression a person might direct at a cockroach they'd have stepped on if only they hadn't been in bare feet. Then it flicked away. I gave Mom a quick squeeze and Dad an even quicker smile as if I hadn't noticed.

Every time he saw me these days, he looked as though he were finding it increasingly hard to swallow. Not that he'd ever been a cuddler either. The closest thing to a hug I remembered getting from *him* was a fleeting moment when he'd patted my head after I'd pulled off some reckless childhood stunt to impress him—absently, his hand snapping away when he'd realized what he was doing.

Most of the time I got nothing from him at all. I might as well not even exist. It was fitting, in a way he didn't know I could understand.

"Shall we head up?" I said brightly. "Wouldn't want to keep the old bird waiting."

I caught a slight wince at the flippant way I'd referenced the headmistress, but otherwise Dad didn't react, let alone speak.

As we climbed the stairs to the teachers' residences and offices, Mom peppered me with questions about my latest pursuits, and Dad remained stolidly silent. Over the years I'd come to the conclusion that she filled the space around me with twice as much chatter and energy to try to make up for his void.

Ms. Grimsworth's secretary was waiting by the door to see us in. The headmistress stood up behind her desk with a respectful bob of her head, presumably a little lower than she'd have offered a parent who wasn't a baron. My father smiled thinly at her.

"Well, Baron and Mrs. Killbrook," she said as we all sat down, "I'm sure you realize this is mainly a formality at this point. Jude continues to perform at expected levels in all his classes, in line with his excellent initial assessment. He has earned many credits throughout the year for his chosen league, and he commands deference among the student body with ease. The only small matter that was brought to my attention…"

She shuffled through the reports on her desk, and apprehension pinched my gut. I had a feeling I knew what she was going to say.

So what? Let it come out. Let's see what Dad made of it. How good a poker face could he keep? Would he dare to berate me for *this* supposed failing?

"Ah, here we are." Ms. Grimsworth peered at the paper. "Professor Viceport has noted that Jude is not progressing at the pace she'd expect in some of the more advanced areas of Physicality. Durability appears to be a particular concern." She looked up at me. "Do you have any thoughts on what might be holding you back in that area, Mr. Killbrook?"

I spread my hands with a shrug. "The knowledge that it would be unfair if I topped everyone at everything?"

Or, more accurately, the fact that durability was the one aspect of shifting and conjuring it was particularly hard to fake with an illusion. I could make something look and feel real in the moment, but anything meant to last after I left the room… If I stretched myself too far and the spell fell apart in a revealing way, Professor Viceport would realize I'd been faking all over the place.

Dad could probably guess that. I glanced over at him, debating how pointed to make my look. I wasn't really sure what I'd want him to do or say, but I couldn't get sicker of the way things were.

He was nodding at Ms. Grimsworth, his expression bland. "It builds character when not everything comes easy to you. I'm sure he'll find his way over that hurdle in time."

"Well, if you should decide you want to arrange for extra assistance, I'm sure you're aware of the summer training session in Maine…"

The headmistress went on for a little longer about my options for magical development, and Mom thanked her profusely on our way out. Dad barely waited until we'd crossed the hall before muttering, "Quite the drive out here just to hear a lot of nothing for fifteen minutes."

I'd thought about how useless these conferences were myself, but his vacantly dismissive tone lit a flare of rage in me on the pile of kindling he'd been building since he arrived. I bit my tongue, but in my mind's eye I imagined his head smashing in like Rory Bloodstone's joymancer father in her desensitization session, all with one swipe of her hand. Skull cracking, blood spurting…

My mouth stretched into a grim smile. What a lovely picture that would make.

The satisfaction I got from it dimmed at the memory of Rory's pretty face crumpled in anguish. What was it like to have a parent you cherished that much even after finding out they'd told you the most horrible lie?

I didn't have a clue, but the question lingered with me as I saw my parents to their car and waved them off. Dad didn't take his eyes off the road for a second. Mom waved back until she had to twist around in the passenger seat. I turned away from the parking lot and meandered around the side of Killbrook Hall, the memory of Rory trailing after me. Rory after the session, her voice taut as she said, *Maybe you're not as smart as you like to think.*

Her breakdown in the chamber should have been perfect fodder to spread around the school. I hadn't told anyone, though. Every time I remembered it, my stomach clenched with the impression that what I'd seen wasn't real weakness at all.

She was a strange one, the Bloodstone scion. Unconventional and unpredictable, and that made her interesting. I could set her off with a few well-placed words, but underneath that defiant temper she had an iron core. And no one could have denied she was particularly stunning to look at when she was pissed off.

I found myself smiling again and shook myself. Why the hell was I giving her this much thought? As long as she refused to make amends with Malcolm, she was a thorn in all our sides, undermining our authority with every day that went by.

The way she'd slipped past my shield somehow that first day in the Insight seminar… I had no idea how she'd managed it, but if she'd dug very far, lord. The thought nauseated me.

She hadn't gotten any farther, though. I'd stabbed back hard—enough to both stop her and to make her terrified of trying again, I'd imagine. Until she was ready to surrender, we'd just keep tipping her off balance.

I snatched at the first idea that crossed through my mind and said a few words under my breath over my closed hand. When I opened it, an illusion of a wasp flitted off into the air to find its target. Only Rory and I would be able to see it, hear it—feel it. She was going to have some trouble concentrating for the next few hours.

Oh, yes, she'd be begging for a change in tune soon enough.

CHAPTER TWENTY-ONE

Rory

"You've been coming along well with the casting skills," Professor Banefield said as we strolled across one of the campus fields together. The spring day was so clear and bright that he'd suggested we take my mentoring session outside for a change of pace. "I suspect at this point it's just your blocks around generating the fuel you need that are holding you back."

My reluctance to terrify random people and creatures out of their wits, he meant. *I think that's called a conscience. Most of you here should look into that.*

I kept that snarky remark inside and searched for one that was more diplomatic. "Everyone here grew up practicing this stuff. It's a pretty big mental shift when you didn't."

"I realize that, and I've been thinking about the progress we have made. Clearly, you find it much easier when the fear serves a constructive purpose. Perhaps we can do more with that framing."

"What did you have in mind?"

He stopped and pointed to a boy who was sitting in the grass with a book about ten feet away from us. The kid looked like he might not be any older than fifteen, still a bit childishly chubby.

I might not have been raised by fearmancers, but I'd absorbed enough of their perspective in the last few weeks to be able to look at the boy and immediately recognize him as prey. In a cat-and-rabbit scenario, he was definitely the bunny.

Who was the cat, though? I glanced around, but there was no one else in view who appeared to have any interest in tormenting the kid.

"You know why your peers have been practicing provoking fear their entire lives," Banefield said. "It's what our community runs on. Those who are the most in control of others' fears—and their own—are the greatest masters of their own destiny. Don't go over and terrify that junior because you'll enjoy it. Terrify him because he needs to learn, in every possible way, how to deal with being terrified so that he can handle himself in the world beyond this campus."

Every muscle in my body balked. "I don't know."

Banefield cocked his head at me. "Look at it this way: Who would you rather see as that boy's teacher—you or Malcolm Nightwood? You don't have to be vicious about it. Just shake him up a little for his own good."

Okay, so my mentor knew me pretty well. Of course, at some point Malcolm probably would terrify this kid in his callous way no matter what I did right now. But… was it possible that the kid would cope with *that* better if he'd already seen he could survive a more restrained offensive from me? That did make a certain kind of sense.

I didn't want anyone to be terrorized, period, but if they had to be, maybe it wasn't such a horrible thing for me to insert myself into the process. I just had to find the right way.

"I'll see what I can do," I said with a nervous jitter in my stomach.

I walked over to the boy. His head jerked up as my shadow fell over him, and just like that, a jolt of sharp fearful energy raced past my ribs.

Wow, human fear was so much more potent than animal. That one instinctive emotional reaction topped a half hour walking through the woods.

This didn't have to be hard. The kid was already scared without my saying anything. I didn't have to threaten him or hurt him. Just remind him that people could.

And ignore the fact that he'd be assuming I was talking about myself as well.

"Do you really think this is a good place to take a break?" I asked in the coolest tone I could summon, folding my arms over my chest. "Look at how easily I came right up on you. You've got nothing at your back. A lot of people around here would take that as an invitation."

The boy scrambled up. More of his fear flooded me with every shaky movement of his body. "Sorry. I'll get out of your way," he said, and hustled toward the nearest building.

I watched him go with shame tainting the exhilarating rush of power flowing through me. I'd hardly done anything. I'd made perfectly good points.

It wouldn't always be that easy, though. And I could taste how that sense of power could start to override even a solid conscience.

Professor Banefield came up beside me. "There you go. That was satisfying, wasn't it? Deal out a little tough love once or twice a day, and we can really get going with your magical work."

"Yeah," I said. It seemed wrong to feel this excited and this uncomfortable at the same time.

Banefield nodded to a couple of girls walking along one of the paths not far away. Gold pins glinted by the collars of their shirts. "You can always use a similar strategy with the Nary students. They may not need to be prepared for quite our level of competition once they leave here, but being toughened up a little can only benefit them in the long run."

Assuming they didn't leave here outright traumatized. Or dying. I remembered Shelby in the common room, swaying with her fever.

"Don't you think the university is a little hard on the Naries?" I said. "At least the regular students know what they're getting into. They shouldn't be killing themselves just to stay here so we can torture them."

Banefield's eyebrows jumped up. "What makes you put it that way?"

I gestured toward Ashgrave Hall with a jerk of my hand. "The Nary student who's in my dorm—she's pushing herself to go to classes even though she's sick. She won't even go to the medical office to get checked out because apparently the teachers are so hard on the Naries they threaten to kick them out if they miss a class or two to look after themselves."

"I'm sure under extreme circumstances, exceptions would be made," Banefield said. "We keep high standards because of the benefits an education here offers them in the end."

That was how Shelby had justified it too. It still didn't sit right with me. "We've got to cut them a little slack. They're not mages—they don't have the same talents to help them cope. They *can't* perform at the same level. It's cruel to expect them to and then punish them for not managing."

"I'm sure Ms. Grimsworth would be happy to entertain your thoughts on the matter if you want to take it up with her." Banefield's dry tone suggested that she'd entertain my thoughts for about five seconds before filing them away as nonsense.

I exhaled in a rush as we headed back toward Killbrook Hall. "She—the Nary student—said there's a problem with one of the trees on campus too. It's making some strange sound like it's going to fall over soon."

Banefield hummed to himself. "I can mention it to the maintenance staff, but I wouldn't be surprised if it's only some students playing pranks. If nothing else, we do teach every student here to be very cautious about taking anything they've believed for granted."

He stopped by the door to the hall and turned to me. "I think this has been a productive session. No need for you to come back to my office. Everything appears to be coming along well for your second assessment."

I paused with a skip of my pulse. "What?" I said. After the work I'd been doing in class, I'd started to put the idea of another assessment out of my mind. "All of my professors have seen me work magic by now. *You've* seen me work it. No one thinks I'm some kind of dud anymore, do they?"

The corners of Banefield's pale eyes crinkled with amusement. "I'm sure they don't. But the assessment process is a formality we can't simply skip. While you have demonstrated emerging magical talents, the faculty still needs to confirm you possess at least one area of ability strong enough to warrant using our resources to continue teaching you. From what I've seen, you have nothing to worry about. I expect you'll show at least two or even three like your fellow scions."

His confidence didn't settle my nerves. "And if I get the same weird result as last time?" I'd been able to cast magic before the last assessment too, and that hadn't helped me any.

"I highly doubt that," Banefield said. "But if you did, then it's nothing to be ashamed of. It wouldn't be your fault if your talents were stunted by your upbringing. You would return to your family home and could engage the services of a private tutor to continue encouraging what skills you have along."

Banished from the university named after my own family. Yeah, I was sure none of the fearmancers would see that as shameful at all. And how the hell could I work at exposing the place if I wasn't allowed to stay here?

Banefield patted my shoulder. "Focus on your studies, and don't worry about the rest," he said as if it were that simple, and headed inside.

I dragged in a breath and might have steadied myself if a well-built figure with a head of gleaming golden-brown hair hadn't sauntered around the edge of the building just then with a vicious grin.

"Well, well, well," Malcolm said in his smooth voice. "For all your 'goodness,' your position here at Blood U is awfully precarious, isn't it, Glinda?"

Of all the people who could have overheard that conversation, why had it been him? My shoulders tensed. "I plan on sticking around."

"I guess we'll have to see if you can handle the heat when push comes to shove." His dark eyes glittered with cold amusement. "You know what happens if you screw up and they send you off? The only way you can get back in here and take a spot with the real mages is with permission from the barons. That's my family, and Jude's, and Connar's, and Declan himself. So, you bow down now, or you do it later. Either works for me."

"Keep dreaming," I said, swiveling on my heel.

"I'll see you in our seminar," he called after me.

Oh, fuck, I had Persuasion with him in just a couple hours.

At the very least, my legs were getting stronger. I reached the seventh floor of Nightwood Tower without more than the slightest burn in my calves and only a little out of breath.

I'd shown up just before the start of class, preferring not to extend my time around Malcolm. All the seats were taken except one at the back, across the room from Imogen, but that was just fine. Malcolm had chosen one in the front row by the big window that overlooked the south field. It had been pushed fully open, letting a warm spring breeze saturate the room and ruffle the papers on Professor Crowford's desk where he was reading over a chart of some sort.

I started for the empty seat, and Malcolm's voice rang out. "Where do you think you're going?"

"Maybe if you give it a little thought, you'll—" I started to retort, and he flicked his hand.

"You're going to stop right there," he said with the lilt of a persuasion spell, and to my frustration my feet jarred to a halt under me, so abruptly I had to catch the desk next to me to keep my balance. The girl sitting there glared up at me.

Professor Crowford glanced up, his heavy-lidded eyes shifting from me to Malcolm. He didn't say anything, though. I guessed as far as he was concerned, this was just Malcolm putting his lessons to use.

"Is this really necessary?" I said, keeping my voice as steady as I could despite the hitch of my heart. "Haven't you got anything better to do?"

"Oh, I think this is pretty important," Malcolm said. "We all need to be aware of our limitations. You seem to figure you've gotten pretty strong, but the truth is, I'm more in control of what you do than you are. I could make you jump right out that window if I wanted to. *Walk.*"

The thrum of magical energy in his voice conveyed his full

meaning. My feet turned under me. One lifted and then the other, carrying me toward his desk and the window beyond it. The window with a seven-story drop on the other side.

The breeze didn't feel so warm anymore. I groped for control over my limbs, but my legs kept walking, one firm step at a time. The fear I'd absorbed this morning buzzed behind my sternum, but I didn't know how to use it to stop him. Was I supposed to be able to understand that instinctively? How the hell was I going to pass any assessment if I couldn't even summon enough power to keep myself *alive*?

No doubt that was exactly the point Malcolm intended to make.

I concentrated on the churning energy inside me and willed it into a steel shield around my mind like I had with Jude in the Insight seminar. My feet kept moving. Malcolm kept grinning. His spell had already wormed its way inside my mind. How could you dig something like that out?

I'd almost reached his desk. The window stood just a couple steps past that. My gaze darted to Imogen, rigid in her seat—she might not have had the power to stand up to Malcolm even if she'd dared too—and to Professor Crowford, who was watching the situation unfold with detached curiosity.

He wouldn't let me climb right out the window and jump. Right? Would Malcolm even try to push things that far? I had to think he only wanted to make the point. He'd bring me to the brink and benevolently let me off the hook while I teetered on the edge of the deathly fall. The fearmancers hadn't gone to all this work to rescue their stolen heir of Bloodstone just to see me break my neck less than three weeks later.

That was one tiny scrap of security in the middle of a heap of shit. I didn't want his fucking benevolence sparing me. I wanted to *stop* him.

"Good girl," Malcolm said as I reached his desk, in the same tone he'd used with his wolf. "Just keep on going."

"Out," I murmured as quietly as I could. Find the persuading spell inside my head and then tear it out of me.

My own magic prickled through my mind, but Malcolm's must

have been woven in too deep, too tightly. I took another step. My blouse quivered with a waft of the breeze. I could see across the field all the way to the forest and the spire of the town church in the distance beyond it.

Sweat trickled down the back of my neck. If I couldn't break his spell, what else could I do to control myself?

It was hard to unravel someone else's magic-work. Easier to cast your own to oppose it. That was one of the first principles Professor Banefield had told me.

"Wall," I whispered with a rasp of magic over my tongue. The breeze snapped away, the air stilled, and my knee smacked into an invisible barrier not around me but in front of me, blocking my body from continuing across the last short span to the window.

Even so, my legs kept trying to walk. My foot and then my other knee banged against the wall I'd conjured.

I must have looked ridiculous, but I didn't care. All I cared about was the narrowing of Malcolm's eyes.

He muttered something, and the wall shuddered. I spat out the word again, focusing all my attention on holding the barrier in place.

Magic coursed up my throat. An ache spread through my chest at the speed with which I was throwing it forward, but I could feel the pieces of my security net crumbling as quickly as I was rebuilding them.

This was the best I could do. I could catch myself on the verge of catastrophe for however long I could sustain my magic. I couldn't snap out of Malcolm's hold. I couldn't walk away. And as soon as my limited reserves wore out, he'd have complete control again.

I might have helped him make his point even more thoroughly than if I'd just gone along with his stunt.

A sense of hopelessness quivered into my voice. Malcolm leaned forward, clenching his hand with a tight utterance, and my wall smashed. My foot swung forward. I gasped the word, heaving the barrier back into place, but the effort wrenched the remaining hum of energy up from my chest. This was my last defense. When he shattered that too—

"That's enough," Professor Crowford said evenly. He waved his hand, and just like that, both my wall and the compulsion to walk through it disintegrated. "A very fine demonstration of persuasive ability warping natural instincts, and a decent effort at creative countering. Credit to Persuasion and Physicality. Let's give the other students a chance to do some work now, shall we?"

I stumbled backward and then whipped around to find my seat. My legs were trembling.

Did Crowford know how close I'd been to losing the battle? If I'd somehow moved one of the professors of Villain Academy to pity, I was worse off than I'd been afraid of.

Malcolm shot a smirk my way as I sank into my chair, not looking all that disturbed by the interruption. He knew he'd landed his blow. And I knew it too.

Nausea crept through my stomach as I sat back to take in my next lesson, however much I'd get to use it.

CHAPTER TWENTY-TWO

Rory

You'd think a library twice the size of the public one near my house back home would have *something* useful in it. I scowled at the pungent leather-bound volume I'd just flipped through and slid it back onto the shelf carefully so the cover didn't crumble any more than it already had.

This whole section of the library on the second floor was devoted to magical texts, bespelled to ward off the Nary students. Apparently most writings on magic had been compiled centuries ago, from the look—and smell—of the books around me. Some of them were written in languages I couldn't read or lettering I didn't even recognize. Maybe there was a spell to conjure a translation? Simply pointing at the table of contents and saying, "English!" hadn't gotten me anywhere so far.

The ones I could read prattled on about energy transfers and conduction of intent with a complexity of terminology that left me feeling like a sixth grader trying to decipher a graduate-level engineering textbook. Fearmancers sure did like to talk a lot in very flowery language about how amazing their abilities were.

What I could really use was an introductory treatise or two—magic for kindergarteners. I'd sat through a lot of seminars in the last few weeks, but for the majority of my life I'd done most of my learning on my own with books or on the internet. Homeschooling might not have given me the greatest social skills, but the various assignments Dad had set up for me had left me an expert at independent study.

I just had to find a book that started with the basics.

I wandered farther, my gaze skimming the titles, and swift footsteps scraped against the hardwood floor. Declan ducked into my aisle, his black hair falling forward by his temples, his hazel eyes oddly frantic. He grabbed me by the elbow.

"Come on," he said under his breath. "We've got to get you out of sight."

"What?" I protested, but his urgency made me lower my voice too. I hurried with him down the aisle.

"I'll explain after—here, this'll have to do. They were right behind me."

He muttered something at a door in between two of the bookcases and shoved it open. At his tug, I darted after him into the tight space on the other side. He yanked the door closed, and the room went dark except for a thin line of light that seeped in along the doorframe.

The smell of old books was even stronger now. A shelving unit pressed into my back and the shape of another loomed behind Declan. Beside us, a table and chair took up the rest of the space. When I squinted, I made out a book sitting there with a gaping split down its spine. Maybe this was a repair room?

The space was so narrow that Declan and I had ended up just a few inches apart. When I shifted on my feet to get a better sense of balance, my chest almost brushed his. A warm cedary scent rose off his body, cutting through the dry leather tang. I had the unfortunate urge to lean into it.

"What the hell is going on?" I whispered instead.

His gaze stayed fixed on the door as if he could see through it. "I overheard Victory and a couple of her friends going by downstairs. They knew you were in here—they'd figured out some way to get you in trouble with the teaching staff. Something to do with the rare books, I think. I only heard a little."

"So you came racing over to find me first?" I couldn't keep skepticism from creeping into my voice. Declan didn't have the best track record when it came to rescuing me from trouble.

"Just because I'm not going to fight all your battles for you doesn't mean I want to see you expelled. You don't deserve that."

He really should have a chat with his good friend Malcolm about the subject, then. I'd be willing to bet the large sums of money I now possessed that none other than the Nightwood scion had suggested expulsion to my other harassers as an ideal cause to take up.

"Why didn't you drag *them* off into some dark room where they couldn't be assholes, then?" I said, and the answer came to me before the words even finished leaving my mouth. "Because we wouldn't want anyone to think you're showing me any 'favoritism.' Right."

Declan sucked a breath through his teeth as if he were going to argue with my conclusion—or maybe just with the tone I'd taken—but then he jerked a finger to my lips to silence anything else I might say. My mouth tingled at his touch.

Cressida's voice filtered through the door. "She's got to be around here somewhere. We'd have seen her if she headed out."

"Maybe Sinclair wasn't paying enough attention," Victory muttered. "I should have left you to keep an eye on the stairs instead."

"Well, if she's gone, it's not as if she'll never set foot in the library again. We'll just..."

Their voices faded away as they left our nook behind. I sighed in relief where I'd tensed against the shelves. Declan's hand dropped from my mouth. I resisted the impulse to lick my lips to sustain the impression of his touch.

"They might not have totally given up," he said. "We should give them a little while to leave, and then I'll go out first to make sure the coast is clear."

"And then I just never set foot in the library again? Wonderful solution."

"Once you've passed your assessment and been officially enrolled, it'll take a lot more for anyone to call your place here into question."

"That would be great," I said, with an edge I didn't bother restraining, "if I wasn't in here specifically because I'm trying to make sure I pass that assessment."

He turned his head. It was too dark for me to make out more than the vaguest impression of his expression, but I could tell he was looking at me.

"Where do you feel you need extra help?"

The frustration of the last several days bubbled over in a flood. "Oh, I don't know, how about not having to spend every class fending off whatever new harassment technique your friends and their sycophants have thought up next instead of actually learning? That would be pretty nice, but it's not going to happen, is it? Because torture trumps everything else at Blood U. What do you even care?"

"I'm trying to help you the best way I can," Declan said, his own voice going terse.

"Yeah, right," I shot back. "You're trying to help me the *easiest* way you can. Out of sight, where no one might actually find out you disagree with what they're doing. But hey, you get to feel good about 'doing your best'."

Declan adjusted his weight, resting his hand on the shelf beside my shoulder. "I haven't had a single thing easy my entire life. Everything I have, I had to fight for, and I have to keep fighting, or I'm going to lose it all over again. You have no idea what the hell you're talking about."

"Of course I don't. How would I? You've barely said anything to me since I got here. Go ahead, why don't you tell me about it?"

He was standing so close I felt his hesitation in the tensing of his body. I grimaced. "Of course not. Talking to me like an equal would be treading just a little too far outside the party line, wouldn't it? God forbid you act on your own conscience even when we're totally alone in the fucking dark without a single person watching."

I waved my hand at him, and my fingers swept across his chest. A surprisingly solid chest considering how slim he was. I was abruptly twice as aware of just how little space remained between our bodies.

Declan caught my wrist. His thumb swept over my palm with a flash of heat.

"You—" he said in a rasp, and then his voice cut off as his mouth collided with mine.

I was still angry with him, but I'd also wanted to kiss Declan Ashgrave from the first moment that striking face had appeared in front of me in the midst of the worst horror of my life, and both of those facts in combination were… confusing.

My lips parted in surprise, and he tipped his head to kiss me harder. My free hand shot up to push him away, but somehow instead my fingers just closed around the folds of his shirt, clutching onto him.

His mouth tasted like sugared coffee, perfectly bittersweet. He kissed as if he were searching for something in the claiming of my mouth. I wanted to give it to him, and I also wanted him never to find it if it meant he'd keep kissing me like this.

He pressed forward, his body aligned with mine from head to foot and scorching hot as he held me against the shelves. A little noise that was somewhere between a protest and a plea for more worked from my throat.

Maybe it was the sound that shook him out of whatever had come over him. All at once, he was shoving back from me as far as he could go, which wasn't far. His back smacked into the opposite shelves. A book fell to the floor with a thump.

"*Fuck*," he said, sounding so pissed off my body went rigid. "Stay right there. Don't move. Don't touch me."

My own anger flared back to the surface. "What the fuck are you talking about? *You* kissed *me*. It wasn't my idea."

"Do you think I don't know that?" he snapped.

"No, from the way you're talking, it isn't immediately obvious."

"Just—just stop." He inhaled raggedly. "It isn't going to happen again. It shouldn't have happened at all."

He paused, and a sensation rolled over me that snuffed out my anger in an instant. A waft of fear, thick and prickling, surging up through my chest from where he stood.

"Could you please not tell anyone about this?" he said quietly.

"It'd be your word against mine anyway," I muttered, but I couldn't put much force behind the remark.

Declan Ashgrave was *scared* of me. Scared of what I could do if I revealed this moment of indiscretion.

That was what a fearmancer would do, wasn't it? Make use of every weakness they could.

"And it won't be my word at all," I added before he had to say anything else. "I'm not interested in hurting you. I don't want to hurt *anyone*. That's not who I am."

A ragged laugh escaped him. "It's too bad you ended up here, then, isn't it?" He leaned close to the door. "I think it's been long enough. I'll go out. If I haven't come back in five minutes, assume you can get out of here without Victory coming at you." He turned back to me just for a second. "And after this, stay away from me."

He ducked out without another word, leaving me alone in the dark.

CHAPTER TWENTY-THREE

Rory

It was a good thing I had to stop for a second to fish in my purse for my dorm keycard, because that gave me the chance to hear Victory gloating on the other side of the door.

"And *then* when he was done begging, I told him I'd consider going out with him again only if he can get us into Fuchsia next time."

Her minions laughed approvingly. I backed up a step, dropping my keycard back into my purse.

I'd had a few hours to simmer down from the close call in the library—in all the assorted ways I needed to—but I wasn't sure I could take another round of the Victory treatment tonight without probably screaming and possibly doing something that would get me in trouble without any scheming necessary, like setting her hair on fire or choking her with the lovely glass sculpture I'd made for her.

Better that I found something else to occupy myself with until she either headed out for a night on the town or went to bed.

I meandered back down the stairs uncertainly. The library was a no-go zone in case an ally of hers spotted me going in and alerted her. It was getting dark out, the sun having just dropped below the western treetops. I guessed I could discover how much the social suicide of having dinner in the junior cafeteria could lower my already rock-bottom status. I didn't feel all that hungry yet, though. My stomach was still twisted up from this afternoon.

Just beyond the main doors to Ashgrave Hall, a lean figure with dark red hair was standing at the edge of the green. As I halted, debating between retreating or making a show of not being fazed, Jude crouched down and clucked his tongue. A sleek brown ferret with a dark mask across its paler face came darting through the grass to meet him. It had a little gray-furred body clamped in its jaws, a dribble of blood coloring the tiny chest.

"That was a quick hunt," Jude said to the ferret. "You must have been hungry. Eat up."

He straightened up again as the animal tore into its meal. I jerked my gaze away from the raw flesh to his face. "Your familiar?"

He didn't startle before he looked at me, so he must have noticed me coming out even if he hadn't acknowledged me. "A handy companion," he said breezily. "What do you figure we should get for you, Ice Pop? I can think of all sorts of creatures that would make excellent meals for the existing university menagerie."

The question echoed my worries about Deborah too closely for comfort. "I think I'm fine without one for now," I said stiffly. "Don't let me interrupt your dinner."

I had even less interest in eating anything myself now. I set off toward the fitness building, thinking maybe I could work out a little of the tension coiled inside me on the machines.

"FYI, I'd steer clear of the lake if I were you," Jude remarked to my back. "Connar headed that way a few minutes ago looking pretty fierce, and I'm sure you've seen what he's like." He phrased it like a warning, but his eager tone suggested he hoped I'd take it as a dare and find myself in a tough spot with his fellow scion.

He didn't know that I *had* seen what Connar was like—and that the guy had a hell of a lot more to him than the "blockhead" Malcolm used as a bodyguard.

That meant Connar hadn't told the other scions anything about what we'd talked about or what had happened between us in that spot over the lake. Whether he'd guarded that secret for himself or for me, I didn't know, but suddenly I was sure that the lake was exactly where I wanted to go.

I didn't even bother walking down to the open area of shore. I veered straight into the forest, cutting across the path and making my way up the slope. My heart beat faster as I neared the peak with a potent combination of anticipation and apprehension. Was this really the best idea? I didn't know. I just—

I stepped out from between the trees, and my feet stalled.

I was alone on the clifftop. The clearing was vacant.

Wherever Jude had seen Connar heading, it hadn't been up here.

My spirits crashed as if they'd been pummeled by a wave way bigger than anything the lake could produce. I swallowed hard.

It shouldn't matter. It wasn't as if I could even really call Connar a friend. But I'd wanted an escape, and as peaceful as this spot was, it wasn't the place that had made me feel momentarily at home.

It'd been him.

I started back down the slope, disappointment condensing into a heavy lump in my chest. I'd made it about halfway down when a snapped twig farther below brought my head up.

Connar stopped several feet below me, catching sight of me at the same moment as I noticed him. For a second, I just stared at him, a little dazed.

His chestnut brown crew cut gleamed even darker than usual, the short strands lying damp along his forehead. His pale green dress shirt clung to his muscular chest in a few places as if it were damp too.

He must have gone swimming. The thought made me shiver. I'd dipped my feet in the lake from the dock a couple days ago and winced at the chill of the water.

"Hey," he said.

"Hey. I—I just thought you might be up there. Jude said something about you coming to the lake…"

"I'm heading up there now. I felt like I needed a quick swim first." His forehead furrowed. "Are you all right?"

After weeks of putting on my best brave face for everyone, even

Imogen and Shelby, even Deborah, something in me cracked open with the honest answer.

"No."

He crossed the ground between us with a few quick strides, but he stopped with a couple feet of distance still between us. "Do you want to go up there now?"

"Yes." Apparently I only had the capacity for single-word answers at the moment.

Connar didn't seem to mind. He touched my wrist to nudge me to follow him, and rather than pulling back, he let his hand slide down to clasp mine. My pulse sped up again, but this time it was only eager.

With each step, the cracking sensation inside me expanded. By the time we reached the clearing, I could hardly breathe. I turned to Connar, and his jaw tightened at my expression. His arm came up around my back tentatively.

I let myself tip my head against his chest and then lean into his embrace. The smell of him filled my lungs, slightly watery from the lake but with a smoky edge that reminded me of one of the essential oils in my parents' collection. Vetiver, maybe.

The pressure in my chest didn't exactly release, but it did ease. Everything about Connar's reaction told me that I hadn't been crazy to come here. Maybe it was *only* here that we could be this close, but that was enough. He hadn't jerked me around. He cared not just about how I was now but who I'd been before. I could be real with him in ways I wasn't sure I could be real with anyone else in my life right now.

God, did I need that.

"Do you want to talk about it?" he asked after a bit.

I shook my head. "Leave everything behind, right?"

I heard his smile in his intake of breath. "That's the beauty of this place."

The word "beauty" tugged my mind back to the last time I'd spent here with him—the way he'd talked to me, the way we'd kissed. A giddy quiver ran down through my belly, but there was something I needed to know before I ended up repeating that moment.

I pulled back and looked up at him. For once, it was still light enough, with the sun only just about to set, that I could make out the color of his eyes. They were pale blue like the sky on a slightly hazy day. I wanted to drift in his gaze like a cloud.

"Last time," I made myself say, "why did you kiss me?"

Connar's eyebrows drew together. "Because… I wanted to?" he said, as if he had the feeling he'd stumbled into a test and that the only answer he had might not be satisfactory. But that was exactly what I needed to hear. No sign of ulterior motives or regrets. He'd wanted to, and I'd wanted to kiss him back, so that was that. Honest attraction.

"Excellent," I said. "A perfectly good reason."

He relaxed with a chuckle. "Is that an invitation to give it another shot?"

My innards were still too tangled up for me to jump right in. "Can we just sit for a bit and see how it goes?"

"Sitting is pretty much all I usually do here, so I don't see why not."

At the far end of the clearing stood a tree that looked as if it'd once been two that had grown too close together and merged into one trunk. We sank down with our backs to it, Connar keeping his arm looped around my waist. I carefully let my shoulder rest against his.

Despite his swim, his body was plenty warm. The heat of it flowed into me everywhere we touched.

"So, you're okay with what happened last time?" he said. "You left in a pretty big hurry."

"Yeah, I—" I struggled to decide on the right words. "I guess I'm a little… jumpy, with everything being the way it's been."

Connar could obviously translate that vagueness just fine. His mouth twisted. He hesitated for a moment. "You know, I think there might be a way to end this before it gets any worse. A way that'll leave both you and Malcolm happy. If you knew him better—and he knew you better— There's definitely some common ground. I'm still figuring things out, but—"

An ache squeezed around my heart. I touched his chest to stop him. Was he really offering to negotiate with Malcolm on my behalf?

"I don't care about making Malcolm happy," I said. "I'd be happiest if he just left me alone. Maybe you shouldn't worry about him so much either—he seems to look after himself pretty well."

"That's not— The way it is with the scions—"

"I know," I said, softer than I'd have thought I'd be able to talk when the subject involved Malcolm in any way. "Four heads of the same dragon."

An idea struck me with so much certainty that I sat up straighter. Connar watched me curiously as I leaned forward and spread my hands over the ground.

"Hold on," I said. "I want to give you something."

Energy whirled behind my collarbone. Closing my eyes, I reached it out into the earth beneath me, the acres of rocky terrain all around, and murmured, "Metal. Together."

Shivers raced up my arms as the shreds of material wriggled up through soil and stone. I gathered it in the air between my hands like I had the shards of glass on my bed, like the ice I'd conjured in Professor Banefield's office. The lump of metal grew until it felt the right size.

"Shape." A fresh wave of energy surged through me as I molded the lump with my mind and instinctive motions of my fingers into the form I was picturing.

When I opened my eyes, I held a little dragon figurine of mottled gray metal, half the length of my palm. Its wings curved around it and its single head peered forward on its arched neck, its stance defiant but its expression gentle.

I held it out to Connar. He accepted it from me, his eyes wide with awe, and turned it over in his hand gingerly as if he were afraid he might break it.

"I hope you don't forget that you're *you* too," I said quietly. "At least some of the time, that's got to come first."

He inhaled sharply. "If you knew *me* better, you might not say that."

"I know that you're more than your 'friends' give you credit for. I know you're the only one who's bothered to really listen to me—to acknowledge who I am and what I've been through—since I got here. Why do you think I came to you?"

He looked at me with so much emotion shining in his eyes that my breath caught. "If I can be that guy for you everywhere you need it —I'll try. I'll do what I can."

"You're here," I said. "That's a start. That matters."

Connar glanced down at his dragon again. He tucked it into the pocket of his slacks. Then, in one smooth motion, he stroked his fingers over my hair and drew me into a kiss.

The press of his mouth against mine brought just as much of a thrill as it had the other night. I gripped his neck, wanting closer, wanting more.

With a careful nudge, he eased me around and onto his lap without breaking the kiss. My ass settled onto his thighs, and the heat between our bodies turned searing. A tremor both nervous and needy tingled between my legs.

He kissed me harder, and I slid my hands up under his shirt to explore the muscular planes I'd only briefly gotten to know last time. He groaned against my mouth. My lips parted with his, and he took the opportunity to capture my mouth more fully, his tongue sweeping hot over mine, his teeth grazing my lower lip. A shaky groan of my own slipped from my throat.

He tugged my blouse free from my slacks and trailed his fingers up over my ribs to the band of my bra. As I ran my thumb over one of his taut nipples, he traced the line of the band to the clasp at my back. His mouth left mine to nip my jaw and devour my neck. His fingers pulled, and my bra released.

My skin caught fire all along the path he charted with his lips. As he nibbled the crook of my shoulder, his hands slipped under my loosened bra to cup my bare breasts. My nipples pebbled against the shifting fabric as he stroked the undersides of those curves. The faint friction, the longing for more, and the flick of his tongue over my neck left me gasping.

A sharper heat was kindling low in my belly. Maybe I didn't have a whole lot of experience in this area, but I knew that sensation. I wanted him, simple as that, insane as it might seem.

Pros and cons, I thought automatically, and whimpered as his thumbs swiveled over the peaks of my breasts with a heady spark of sensation. *Pros...*

Fuck it. It *was* simple, simple and straight-forward. I wanted him, he wanted me, and I could already tell how good it would feel. No promises, no expectations like I'd had last time. Just whatever it was in the moment, without any strings attached.

Could I have asked for a scenario more perfect, really? Tomorrow if I crossed paths with this man he'd pretend nothing had happened between us, but I'd pretend it too. It'd be a secret we shared together. Completely the opposite of the jerk who'd discarded me without warning like a piece of trash.

I yanked at Connar's shirt, and he leaned back so I could peel it off him. The sight of his naked torso up close made my mouth water. I took it in, resting my hands against his ridged abdomen and drawing them up his body to his pecs. Then I flexed my hips to sink deeper into his lap. His chest hitched at the same time mine did when the bulge in his pants met my core. The pang of need that shot through me then was nothing short of ecstatic.

"Rory," Connar said roughly, and tugged my mouth back to his. We kissed, wild and hungry, and then he stripped off my shirt and bra in a couple of brisk motions. The cooling evening air teased over my breasts. He gazed down at them, flicking one of my nipples with a jolt of pleasure and smiling when it perked up even more.

"So fucking beautiful," he said. He cupped that breast and lowered his mouth to it.

I tried to suppress a moan as his attentions sent a surge of bliss through my chest. I didn't know if anyone else was down by the lake, but a loud enough sound could travel all the way to the dock.

Connar sucked my nipple harder into his mouth, and I decided I didn't care who heard. I dug my fingers into the short but soft strands of his hair and arched my back to meet him.

He lay me on the ground with a murmur that spread a cushiony feeling beneath me. The wonders of magic. It occurred to me to question where he'd learned that trick and who else he might have used it with, but I shoved those thoughts away.

He was with me right now. He was looking at me as if he'd never wanted anyone more.

Connar hooked his fingers into the waist of my pants. His voice came out thick with desire. "I want to worship you, Princess Bloodstone."

I nodded, only half understanding what he meant but happy to take anything he'd offer when he said it like that. He slid my pants and panties down together and bent over me, kissing my belly, the dip just below my navel, and finally the sensitive center of my core.

My hips jerked up with a gasp at the brilliant pulse of pleasure. Connar stroked my thigh and brought his mouth to me again.

The heat of his breath and the movements of his tongue sent flash after flash of ecstasy through me, building into a heady flame that simply burned on and on. It flickered hotter and sharper as his tongue dipped right inside me. He grazed his teeth over my clit and then sucked hard, and I burst with a cry I couldn't restrain, bucking against his mouth.

Bliss washed over me, but the release didn't delve quite deep enough. I grasped Connar's shoulder to urge him up my body. "Please."

The mumbled request lit a fire in his eyes. He kicked off his slacks and boxers in two seconds flat. But he took his time easing down over me, one arm braced next to me, the other hand caressing my cheek.

All the concerns that had been drilled into my head woke up. "Do we have to worry about—"

He shook his head with a grin and wiggled his fingers. "Magic. I'll look after you."

After the way he already had, I believed him. He kissed me hard on the mouth and on the corner of my jaw. His cock slid against my core, and I raised my hips to meet him. With a breathless murmur that sent a faint tingling through me, he gripped my thigh and dove into me.

"Fuck," I said at the blaze of pleasure that came with him. He filled me with a delicious burn.

He laughed raggedly and kissed me. "Fuck, yes, absolutely." Then he was pulling back and plunging into me again, and both of us lost even that limited vocabulary.

I rocked up to meet him, clutching his arm, stroking his dampening chest, lost in the feel of him inside me and over me. Connar groaned and thrust faster. My second climax swelled with a quivering like magic all through my nerves.

His lips crashed against mine, and his cock pushed deeper than ever before. I clenched around him. Ecstasy swept through me, curling my toes, sizzling through my mind.

For one instant, as he made a choked sound and followed me over, not even the cliff or the lake or the ground beneath me existed. Only Connar and me.

CHAPTER TWENTY-FOUR

Connar

Nestled against me, her head tucked under my chin, Rory's body felt so delicate it sent a weirdly thrilling pang through my chest. She *wasn't* fragile—I'd seen plenty of evidence of her incredible strength—and I wouldn't have wanted her to lose that toughness. But she'd let down her guard with me, out of everyone she could have turned to. She'd let me in both emotionally and in ways that made my groin stir at the memory.

It was a brand-new sensation, one that left me a little short of breath. Alongside the exhilaration, I couldn't help wondering how long this could possibly last.

There were so many things she didn't know. *I* could leave them behind when I came up here, but I doubted anyone else would do me the same favor.

For now, I might as well enjoy every bit of the grace I'd been granted. I kissed her forehead, inhaling the caramel-sweet scent that laced her skin and her silky hair. Rory scooted even closer to me and raised her head to catch my lips with hers. The kiss was soft and tender, but my cock did a whole lot more than just stir at that.

Dear God, I did hope we got to do this again after tonight.

"I should probably go," she said, with enough regret in her voice that I couldn't have taken it as any kind of rejection. "I've got an early class tomorrow, and I haven't even eaten dinner yet."

That should have been my cue to offer to go grab a bite with her. My stomach knotted.

She grabbed her clothes and carefully reassembled her outfit, her beautiful body disappearing piece by piece beneath layers of fabric. I sat up. The night air had cooled, and it raised goosebumps on my skin now that I'd lost her warmth.

"Sometime," I said, "after I've had a chance to smooth things over, I'll take you out to dinner in town."

Her gaze snapped to me, startled. Then a smile that could have wrenched my heart in two and stitched the pieces back together spread across her face.

"I'd like that."

I watched her go, slipping into the forest both wary and confident, comfortable in the dark. The image lingered in my mind after she'd disappeared from sight.

When she'd first stumbled on me up here, I hadn't expected us to end up like this. My first instinct had been to scare her off from the spot I'd come to think of as mine. But she'd stood there so uncertain and yet defiant, not half as nervous as most of the people back at the party were of me while she asked my permission to stay a while, and it'd hit me that I could play a different part for once.

Whenever the scions had a problem, I was the automatic bad cop: the intimidator, the implicit and sometimes explicit threat. With Rory Bloodstone, Malcolm and Jude already seemed to have that role covered between them. Which left an opening for me to be the good cop. Put her at ease. Get her talking about her thoughts and feelings. Figure out how to lead her into the fold where she belonged. End the war without any more bloodshed.

That'd been the plan, anyway. Maybe it was a stretch for me, but I'd figured it was worth a shot.

The problem was, the more we'd talked, the more I just wanted to keep talking with her for the sake of getting to know her. She wasn't like anyone I'd ever known.

And she didn't see me like anyone I'd known ever had.

I reached for my shirt and pulled it on, considering my best move with Malcolm. There had to be a way I could make him see he'd taken his campaign far enough. Wouldn't it be better to have a fierce woman like Rory Bloodstone on our side, unbroken, than to keep battering away at her strength?

He was pissed off because he thought she'd attacked him first in an attempt to challenge our authority here. To him, this was a battle for dominance. But everything I'd seen and heard from Rory told me it wasn't like that for her at all. She didn't give a shit who ruled Blood U. She was fighting tooth and nail just to survive.

I knew what that kind of desperation tasted like.

The others didn't. The three of them had been scion from the day they were born. I just had to figure out how to put it to Malcolm so he'd understand. I was still working on that part.

After I tugged on my pants, I touched the left pocket to make sure Rory's dragon hadn't fallen out. The feel of it under my fingers brought a smile to my face.

I texted Malcolm on my way down from the cliff, and he replied that he was in "the basement." I headed to Ashgrave Hall.

Before we'd even been moved over to seniors, Malcolm had found out about the half-empty storage rooms under the library and demandingly cajoled Ms. Grimsworth into letting him turn one of them into a private lounge area just for the scions. When I came in, he and Jude were standing around the pool table, Jude bent over to take a shot. The leather couches at the other end of the room around the widescreen TV and video game systems were unoccupied.

Sometimes we brought down other students we were feeling friendly toward, but it was nice to have a space that was only ours.

Jude's shot sunk two balls. He laughed at Malcolm's disgruntled curse and turned to face me. "Conn! Cooled off sufficiently? Our Ice Queen headed your way not too long ago—I hope you didn't take her head off."

"As far as I know, it's still attached to her neck," I said in as mild a tone as I could manage, and went to the bar cabinet that the maintenance staff kept stocked for us.

I had to find the right way to explain myself soon or this mess would just keep getting bigger. I poured myself a scotch and tossed back a gulp that burned all the way down to my stomach.

Malcolm sank a ball with a clatter. He leaned against the pool table as Jude considered his options.

"Darksend was making noises about shipping you off to that tourney again," Malcolm said. "The man doesn't know when to quit. I reminded the administration how *very* important it is to the rest of the scions that we continue our education together."

My stomach had dropped at the mention of the professor's name. Since I'd been in his class two years ago, Professor Darksend had been campaigning to have me join an international tourney in Physicality that basically amounted to a magical MMA competition. "It's only a couple of months away from your studies!" he'd go on. "An excellent opportunity to show off your skills and make a name for yourself."

It didn't seem to matter to him that I'd prefer not to build my name beyond where it already was by bashing around people I didn't even know and had nothing against. And unfortunately, my parents loved the idea. If it hadn't been for Malcolm's periodic interventions whenever the registration re-opened, I'd have already found myself in a deathmatch either in the ring or at home.

"Thanks," I said, that one word not enough to cover the rush of relief and gratitude that swept through me.

"Hey," Malcolm said with a grin. "I need you here, not off on a rampage for some stupid title."

He'd never made me explain why I wasn't interested. I'd just told him I wanted nothing to do with it, and that was all he'd needed to know.

Jude took his next shot with an extravagant flourish that bit him in the ass—he only nicked the ball he'd wanted to hit. He spun the pool cue in his hand as if he didn't particularly care, which knowing Jude he might not.

"What's the next step in our rampage against the Bloodstone?" he asked. "We've only got a week before she's up for re-assessment."

"I've got Victory gathering intel so we can make the next big hit really count," Malcolm said. "She was incredibly happy to pitch in to the effort. I'll hassle her if she doesn't report back soon. In the meantime, just keep on keeping the good witch on her toes."

"Not a problem." Jude smirked. "I've been enjoying the view along the way."

Malcolm smacked him in the leg with the end of his cue. "Don't get any ideas," he said in a tone that made my insides clench up.

"Who, me?"

"I know what you're like, Mr. Hit and Split."

"Oh, and you figure this girl's too good for that?"

Malcolm gave him a narrow smile. "She *is* a scion. There's a lot more to her than a pretty face and a nice ass. I'm looking forward to finding out what she can do with all that spirit once we smash the spite and show her what it's like to be a real part of the pentacle. On the off-chance that my charms have no effect, you're welcome to step in and see if she likes yours better. Until then, she's off limits."

Jude rolled his eyes, but with only casual annoyance. "I didn't realize you had a crush."

"Oh, please. As if you hadn't noticed she's the most interesting thing to walk through those doors since we started here." Malcolm's smile softened slightly around the edges, and my gut constricted into one huge lump.

I hadn't realized he was thinking about Rory as anything other than an opponent. He'd been so intent on his campaign to knock her down that it'd never occurred to me he might want her by his side after he'd brought her to her knees.

While my best friend had been looking out for me tonight, I'd been betraying him without even knowing it.

There must have been signs; I just hadn't picked up on them. I'd been too caught up in getting to play good cop—and thinking with my dick rather than my head. Fuck.

What the hell did I do now?

CHAPTER TWENTY-FIVE

Rory

If I had to pick a favorite class at Villain Academy—because while I was stuck here, I might as well—it should have been my Seminar in Physicality. My instincts seemed to be strongest in that area, probably because I'd spent so much time bringing my imagination into reality in my former life, and it was my only class that didn't force me to deal with any of the scions or Victory and her main gang.

Basically, everything was perfect except for the fact that I was starting to think that Professor Viceport hated me.

I couldn't have pointed to one obvious piece of proof. It was just a whole bunch of little things. Whenever she called on me or answered a question I asked, her tone sounded several degrees chillier than with the other students. Her nose appeared to wrinkle in mild distaste when she examined anything I'd conjured or transformed. And even though I'd managed to work more magic in this class than any other, she hadn't offered a single encouraging word.

I'd have thought she simply wasn't the encouraging type, except right now she was gushing over a spoon the girl next to me had transformed out of a stick. It didn't look like an especially amazing spoon to me. Maybe there was some special hurdle in spoon creation that I wasn't aware of.

In any case, after three classes of that treatment, I figured it couldn't hurt to bring up the subject. If I was screwing up in some way I hadn't realized, I'd like to know before my impending assessment.

When Professor Viceport dismissed the class, I waited until the other students had filed out of the smaller gymnasium in the Stormhurst Building where we'd gathered today. The professor crouched down to gather the supplies she'd brought along. As I approached her, she peered at me over the top of her rectangular glasses. She was skinny in a way she managed to make look elegant rather than awkward, her ash-blond pixie cut wisping along her forehead. It didn't soften the ice in her eyes.

She straightened up. "Can I help you, Miss Bloodstone?" she asked in a tone that said she really didn't want to.

I clamped down on my nerves. I was a freaking scion. It was her job to teach me. I shouldn't be anxious.

"Yes. I just—I've gotten the impression that you're not totally happy with the work I've been doing," I said. "I'm trying my best, but obviously it'll take some time for me to get the hang of things after being out of the loop for so long. If there are any factors you think I should focus on more, or any other corrections I should make…" I trailed off at the pursing of her lips.

"If you're 'trying your best,' I'm sure that's all I can expect," she said crisply. "You are a Bloodstone, after all."

What was that supposed to mean? It wasn't as if I'd gained any benefit from a family I'd never known.

"I only meant, if I'm missing something—" I started.

"Don't worry yourself about it. You've got all the advantages you need." She spun on her heel and strode out of the room, cutting off any further conversation.

Okay, then. That hadn't been the most productive conversation of my university days. She *definitely* had a problem with me, but she also definitely didn't want to talk about it, so I guessed I was shit out of luck if I wanted any advice from that corner.

I shouldered my purse and slipped out after her. April showers had rolled in again late last night, and the sky was still clotted with clouds. I tugged my jacket closer against the damp wind.

Two clusters of guys had gathered on the field near Ashgrave Hall. The farther bunch I didn't recognize at a distance, but the one closer to me was made up of the four scions. Wonderful.

As I eyed them, a dark shape swooped down out of the sky. A hawk. And then another, diving from a different angle toward the same spot. Both groups of guys let out a cheer, urging them on.

The first hawk jerked up at the last second, its feet skimming the ground. It rose again with a chipmunk clutched in its talons. The scions let out another whoop. The other group muttered with frowns all around. The first hawk soared over to Declan, dropping the limp chipmunk at his feet and coming to land on his shoulder. The other bird perched on the wrist of the boy at the head of the opposing group.

"Best two out of three!" that guy hollered.

"If you want to get beaten that badly, how can we turn down the invitation?" Jude called back.

Just another one of their cruel little games.

My gaze lingered for a moment on Connar at the back of the pack, but he didn't glance my way. All of them were so focused on the competition that they hadn't noticed me heading toward them.

I wasn't sure I'd have wanted them to. Remembering the way Declan had told me to stay away from him yesterday after he'd kissed me made me queasy. Veering to the left, I gave them and their playing field a wide berth.

I kept my eyes fixed on the stone side of Ashgrave Hall looming ahead of me, as if I hadn't noticed them either. The guys were having a hushed discussion about the "bait." Ugh. I picked up my pace even faster.

Then a harsh voice carried across the space between us. "Yeah, just keep running, Princess."

My head snapped around with a lurch of my heart. That had sounded almost like—

Not almost like. Exactly like. Because it was. Connar had turned, his arms crossed tight over the expanse of his chest, his gaze burning into me so fiercely my pulse stuttered a second time. He was the one who'd made that snarky remark, calling me "Princess" like he had last night.

My mind refused to compute. If it'd been any of the other scions, I'd have given him the middle finger and walked on. But—Connar— This had to be a mistake. He'd never torn into me before, no matter where we'd been. He'd said—

The other guys had turned to watch. Malcolm clapped his hand to Connar's shoulder. "You tell her, Conn," he said with an amused grin.

"What are you staring at?" Connar said, so sharp the words stung my skin. "Do you need another reminder of who you're messing with?"

A lump rose in my throat. "Connar—"

He cut me off before I could get out more than his name. "How about it, Princess? We're still going to need to see you on your knees. You don't mind getting down in the dirt, do you? You can start begging any time now."

I backpedaled and swung around on abruptly shaky legs. The other guys' laughter pealed after me. "Nice," Jude said to Connar.

That wasn't the guy I'd talked to last night. But it was. It was exactly who I should have known he was.

My earlier nausea surged up from my gut. I clenched my teeth and all but ran the last several feet to the building. Heat prickled behind my eyes.

No. I was not going to cry over that bastard. That fucking bastard who'd been so tender with me before and then—

Why had I let myself trust him? I *did* know what everyone in this place was like, the scions especially. How had I been so stupid to think the affection he'd shown me was genuine?

Just like the guy before him, he'd gotten what he wanted and kicked me to the curb. Only the fearmancer version of the kicking was a lot closer to literal—and much more painful.

A few of my dormmates were hanging out in the common room when I burst in. Imogen was carrying a cup of tea from the kitchen to her bedroom. Her steps faltered when she saw me, and a flicker of emotion I couldn't decipher crossed her face.

"Hey," she said. "I was about to head down to the library to grab a few books. You want to come with?"

She hadn't looked like she was heading to the library, and her voice was weirdly bright. Or maybe I was doing a better job of hiding my inner turmoil than it felt like.

"No," I said. "That, um, that's okay."

"Come find me if you change your mind," she said, raising her cup of tea, and breezed past me out the door.

The girls who were sitting in a cluster in the lounge area leaned closer to each other with emphatic murmurs that might or might not have been about me. I glanced toward Shelby's door, but a hoarse coughing filtered through it at the same moment. My stomach twisted even harder at the thought of turning to her. She'd looked pretty out of it when I'd seen her this morning. She needed *my* help more than I should need hers.

I couldn't tell her even a tenth of the things that were bothering me anyway.

I hustled into my own bedroom. My magical security system was still in place, at least. I ducked inside, recast the spell with a few muttered words, and collapsed onto the bed.

The tears I'd been fighting started to leak out despite my best efforts. I squeezed my eyes shut as if that would keep them in.

A faint rustling sounded from the wardrobe. A moment later, Deborah burrowed between my arms and my chest. Her whiskers tickled my palm.

What happened, sweetheart?

"Nothing important," I whispered. Was it stupid even to feel this hurt when I hadn't expected last night to mean all that much anyway? How had I gotten my head turned around so badly?

I stroked my thumb over Deborah's fur. "I hate it here. I hate all these people. I don't—"

I didn't know what I was doing. I didn't know if I could keep doing it, keep going, until I figured out some kind of plan to turn the tables on everyone here. But where could I go that would be any better?

They're awful, Deborah agreed without hesitation. *You've learned some tricks. We could make a run for it now. If we plan it right, we could probably get to California before they catch up.*

And then what? The joymancers would throw me in whatever jail they had, and the fearmancers would slaughter them like they had my parents to drag me back out.

Until I brought down this center of fearmancer society and as much of the rest as I could, there was nowhere I could run that would do me or anyone else any good.

"No," I said softly, petting Deborah again. "It's okay. I'll be okay." But for the first time since I'd decided to destroy Villain Academy, I couldn't shake the cold wash of fear that had come over me.

CHAPTER TWENTY-SIX

Rory

There was something deeply unnerving about meeting a figure in the flesh whom you'd only before seen in a sort-of dream. As I headed out of Ashgrave Hall, a man fell into step beside me. I glanced up at him, and my pulse hiccupped. I stopped in my tracks.

I'd seen that golden-brown hair flecked with gray and those familiar features grown tighter with age in my brief venture into Malcolm's mind. His father, because that had to be who this man was, looked even more like the Nightwood scion now that he stood before me in reality.

The apple didn't fall far from the tree. My stance tensed.

The man gave me a smile that was about as warm as his son's usually was—so, not particularly. "Miss Bloodstone. I take it you know who I am."

"Mr. Nightwood," I said automatically.

"*Baron* Nightwood," he corrected in a firm tone that suggested I'd better remember that title next time. "I was hoping we might speak for a bit."

A chat with one of the four current rulers of the fearmancer world.

With the most powerful current ruler, if the dynamics between the scions were anything to go by. I swallowed against the sudden dryness of my mouth. Why was Malcolm's dad coming to me here and now?

What were the chances he was any less of an asshole than his son? I'd have to assume pretty much nil. He'd had at least a couple more decades to perfect his cruelty.

I'd never thought I'd wish to have Malcolm Nightwood in front of me, but I'd have been overjoyed if he'd swept in to replace Baron Nightwood in this moment.

"What did you want to talk about?" I said, relieved just to hear my voice stay steady. Was he going to remove me from the university before I even had the chance to complete my assessment? Malcolm had said the barons were the only ones who could reverse a dismissal, so no doubt they could also impose one.

Baron Nightwood ushered me away from the entrance to stand near a windowless portion of the building. I'd have taken more comfort from the fact that we were in view of the green if I hadn't seen how enthusiastically a Nightwood could make use of an audience for amplified torture.

"I apologize for not introducing myself and welcoming you home sooner," he said. "I thought it best to give you time to settle in before making more impositions on your attention than you must already be facing."

I blinked at him. Baron Nightwood was… apologizing… to me? Was this part of some weird reverse psychology voodoo?

"Um," I said, "that's totally okay. I've kind of had my hands full."

The corners of his mouth twitched so slightly I couldn't tell whether he'd mastered a smile or a frown. Maybe he was amused thinking of all the ways his son had contributed to my preoccupation.

"Well, now that you've had the chance to adjust, we of the barony wanted to invite you to begin stepping into your ultimate role as baron yourself."

For the second time in as many minutes, I found myself lost for words. "I thought—I was told that I couldn't become baron until I graduated."

This time Baron Nightwood definitely smiled, as coolly as before.

"Not officially. But we've been without a true fifth in our pentacle for nearly two decades now. It has made effective governing somewhat difficult. We'd like to see you transition in as quickly as you're able to. The rights and the authority are unquestionably yours. Why should you be denied them even longer?"

This didn't make any sense. I'd been defying his son at every turn. Why would he want to give me *more* authority? I had to be missing something here.

"I'm not sure I'm ready for that," I said cautiously.

Baron Nightwood waved off my hesitation. "We wouldn't expect a lot from you to begin with. And this situation isn't without precedent, you know. Declan Ashgrave has been acting in nearly all respects as baron for a few years now even though his position isn't entirely official yet."

Something Declan had said before clicked into place in my head. His mother had died in the same altercation that my birth parents had. She must have been the previous Ashgrave baron. He'd been thrust into this role way earlier than I had.

Not that the fact gave him an excuse for being a jerk.

"What exactly are you looking for me to do at this point?" I asked. This guy did know that I wasn't even officially enrolled as a student here yet, didn't he?

"We have a meeting of the pentacle in two days," Baron Nightwood said. "We'd like you to attend so that you can… get up to speed on our current concerns. I can arrange your transport from and back to the university. Ms. Grimsworth has already approved your absence from the one class you'd miss."

He'd thought of everything, hadn't he? Why was it so very important to him—and maybe the other barons—that I get involved now?

Uneasiness prickled down my back. I didn't want to go anywhere in a vehicle owned by the Nightwoods, and definitely not into a meeting with the four most powerful fearmancers in the country. And it was conveniently right before my assessment. Could they do something to make sure I failed, something I wouldn't even be able to identify?

Malcolm had grinned when he'd talked about the pentacle families having me in their power.

On the other hand, it was possible the barons just wanted to get on with their politics, and I might find out something useful there.

As I wavered, Shelby came out the doors of the hall, her ponytail swishing and her stride light with more energy than I'd seen from her in about a week. Whatever she'd been sick from, it must have passed. I caught her eye and raised my hand in a wave with a relieved smile. She bobbed her head with a shy smile in return.

Baron Nightwood followed the exchange with narrowed eyes. His lip curled with distaste when his gaze came back to me. "What was that about?"

"She's a friend," I said. Had he never seen someone wave hello before?

"A friend," he repeated in the same tone. "I realize your upbringing was rather unusual, but one of the first things you need to learn is that a mage of your standing does *not* associate with the feebs any more than you have to. You certainly shouldn't be considering them friends. It appears our guidance would be of a lot of use to you."

My hackles came up in an instant. There was the familiar Nightwood attitude. The words came out before I had a chance to think them through.

"I'm about as interested in the kind of guidance you're talking about as I am in your son's, which is not at all. The only person who'll decide who I'm friends with is me."

Baron Nightwood sighed. "Miss Bloodstone, I meant no offense, only counsel. Once you get to know the wider forces of our society—"

"And I will," I said. "Get to know them. This just isn't a good time. I've got too many other things to concentrate on." *Like making it through the next few days without getting crushed by your son and* his *asshole friends.* "Get back to me after I've passed my assessment and know what I have to offer, and then I'll see about attending one of those meetings."

A flicker of anger passed through the baron's eyes, but I wasn't inclined to stick around to find out how much I might regret the decision I'd just made.

"Now hold on a moment," he said, his voice going from cool to chilling, and I took a few steps back.

"Sorry, I've got to run. My mentor's expecting me for our morning session."

And then I took off toward Killbrook Hall as quickly as I could walk without literally running.

The barons wanted something, and whatever it was, I had trouble believing it meant anything good for me. Maybe I'd be better equipped to tangle with them later, but right now I was having a hard enough time just defending myself against their heirs.

I hadn't quite escaped yet. Baron Nightwood rolled a sharp syllable off his tongue, and my feet jolted to a halt beneath me. The soles wouldn't lift from the ground. I twisted around to see him striding over to me. The haughty expression on his face and the brutal gleam in his eyes brought out the same divine devil I'd seen in his son.

He stopped in front of me and peered down at me for just long enough that I wanted to squirm.

"I'll give you a reprieve in light of your current circumstances and your history," he said, low and cutting. "But the next time I call on your attendance, it'll be an order, not a request. You're not baron yet, and you don't defy the barons you have. Are we clear, Miss Bloodstone?"

Provoking him further didn't seem like the wisest idea, at least not if I ever wanted to use my feet again.

"I understand," I said. And I did. I understood that he was the biggest asshole of them all.

"Good." He snapped his fingers, and the magic holding me released. "Run along then."

The breeze chilled the sweat that had formed on the back of my neck as I hurried the rest of the way to Killbrook Hall. Professor Banefield was waiting for me on the landing outside the staff residences.

"Sorry I'm late," I said quickly, my heart still thumping double-time. "I—I got a little delayed."

"It's all right," he said, motioning me back down the stairs. "It just means I'll explain what I have planned for today on the way over. I've arranged a private session for you with Professor Razeden."

My feet nearly tripped over each other. "For Desensitization?"

Banefield nodded. "I understand your first session was rather traumatic, and I know you've been under a lot of stress with your approaching assessment. It hardly seemed out of line to allow you a chance to navigate your fears without an audience. Professor Razeden will be able to give his full attention to guiding you through."

I should have been grateful. It would be a real help to get a handle on the whole desensitization process without Jude and whoever else looking over my shoulder. But the thought of facing that murder scene all over again, especially right after my clash with Baron Nightwood, made me want to vomit.

I just had to get through it. That was the whole point—learning how to make it through. With every fear I found the tools to withstand, there'd be one fewer way for the scions to hurt me.

Baron Nightwood had already departed from the green. I breathed slow and steady as we came up to the tower that bore the same name, working to calm my nerves.

No one was going to see this except my mentor and the professor who must have seen all kinds of fears over the years. There was nothing to be self-conscious about. And at least this time I knew what to expect. It wouldn't be real. Nothing could hurt my parents ever again.

Not even me.

Professor Razeden met us in the room with the benches outside the main chamber. He dipped his head to me in greeting. "Miss Bloodstone. I'm glad we'll have the opportunity to develop your baseline coping skills in a more intensive fashion."

He didn't look all that glad, but I wasn't sure that gaunt face was capable of looking really happy. "Okay," I said. "I'd like to cope better next time too."

"I want you to listen to my voice now," he said as he led us into the chamber. His dry, even tone echoed through the room. "Focus on it, and keep listening for it after the session begins. I'll walk you through the steps to shutting down your fear. If you start to get overwhelmed, go still and avoid interacting with your surroundings until you have a plan of action. Shall we begin?"

I nodded, swallowing the lump in my throat. If we were doing this, better to get it over with ASAP.

My shoes rapped against the glossy tiles as I walked into the center of the chamber. Razeden took his spot near the door, Banefield standing a little awkwardly on the other side of it. Maybe it'd help him understand where I was coming from better when he got a glimpse of how horrible my "rescue" had really been.

"Begin," Professor Razeden said, and the light went out.

A glow spread out around me. I braced myself, but… it wasn't the shiny white of my parents' kitchen. The room seemed to have expanded into a vast space lit by yellowish panels overhead. Four figures stepped into the light in a ring around me, and my stomach flipped over.

I was in the large gym in the Stormhurst Building where I'd had my first assessment. But it wasn't the professors who'd conducted the test before who surrounded me. It was the scions.

"*Dance*," Malcolm said with a vicious smile, and snapped his fingers the way his father had. My legs leapt up beneath me, springing this way and that in a ridiculous cavorting. They spun me toward Jude.

The other guy's smirk looked even sharper than usual under his dark copper hair. He raised his hands, and a searing heat shot up over me, an illusion that set my nerves screaming as if they'd actually been set on fire. A cry broke from my mouth.

Declan's voice rang out behind me. "You know you're not good enough. Stop kidding yourself, Rory. I can see every thought in your head. You're hanging on by a thread. Any second it's going to snap, and we'll see exactly how weak you really are."

My dance was more like a flailing now. Tears welled in my eyes at the burn still racing under my skin. I stumbled around toward Connar, whose face was as hard as stone. He stomped on the ground, and a metal disc as high as his waist rose up, gouging the floor with its razor edges as it screeched toward me.

Through the blur of pain and panic, I managed to make out Professor Razeden's voice. "You can do this, Miss Bloodstone. It's their power that frightens you, but you have power too. Summon your own magic to push theirs back."

Right. They weren't real. I just had to prove to myself that I was strong enough to withstand them. I pressed my hand to my chest, trying to feel the hum of magic there amid the burning.

My legs ached as they jittered on beneath me. "Don't make me laugh," Declan went on with a sneer. "Everything you've done since you got here has been a mistake. You keep shooting your mouth off without a clue how to back it up."

I dodged the razor disc, and Connar swung his arm. The air shoved me into the spinning edge as if he'd pushed me from across all that space. The blades sliced through my side all the way down to my ribs. I cried out again at the spear of pain that shot through my chest.

"Fight back!" Razeden hollered from beyond my view. "Shield yourself and hit them hard."

"Stop," I mumbled, but the word didn't catch any magic inside me. I tried to concentrate on the steel wall I'd snapped into place around my mind the other day, but at the same moment Jude switched up his illusion. The heat fell away just in time for a cloud of shrieking wasps to descend on me. Fresh pain pinched all over my body where their stingers jabbed me.

Where was my magic? I did have it. I should be able to do *something.*

"Away," I murmured, with a surge of energy from behind my sternum. The wasps shuddered, several of them disintegrating into the air like the nothing they were.

Then Malcolm's voice rang out again. "*Hand to your throat.*"

My arm jerked up before I could stop it. My fingers clamped around my throat. I tensed my muscles to wrench them away, but they didn't budge.

"*Squeeze,*" Malcolm said.

My hand clenched. My breath cut off with a ragged gasp. A deeper ache shot through my throat and the sides of my neck as I fought for air. I had to stop him. I had to shut them all out.

"You think you're so perfect, but you know we have the real power here," Declan said. "You're on your own. Why would anyone want to help you when you can't even hold yourself together?"

I strained, but I couldn't reach my magic past the choking pressure on my throat and the panicking through my chest. I couldn't grasp hold of one more shred of the energy inside me.

My head started to spin. I dropped to my knees.

The Desensitization session faded away around me, leaving only the bare floor, the black walls, and the two professors watching my hand fall limply from my throat.

I'd failed an imaginary assessment. If I didn't perform better at the real one, I'd end up in an even worse position than the torment I'd just survived.

CHAPTER TWENTY-SEVEN

Declan

Every time I stepped into the room where the meetings of the pentacle were held, a little vise closed around my gut and didn't let go until I was in my car driving away again. The other barons dipped their heads with due respect and smiled their thin smiles, but I could hardly call any of them friendly colleagues.

And then there was Aunt Ambrosia, both my closest living blood relative and the person who'd most like to see my blood spilling all over this fine hardwood floor, always hovering at my side watching for the slightest slip.

She still had the right to sit next to me at the large rowan-wood table with its pentacle etching, the two of us on either side of the Ashgrave point. Until I finished my last year at Blood U, her word would hold some weight here.

"You look a little tired, Declan," she said in her syrupy voice as we took our seats. "I hope the additional workload isn't wearing you out too much."

Today, her black hair coiled in loops over her ears before cascading down her back. It was a style my mother—her sister—had often worn when she'd been baron. I'd seen it in many of the old pictures. Aunt Ambrosia's dress, heavy velvet that didn't fit the season, recalled my mother's fashion sense too. It made me feel ill watching her trying to transform herself into the long-gone woman whom I'd barely known, as if the imitation would make it easier to take my mother's place.

I'd taken on the teacher's aide position specifically to show how much work I could handle, and I didn't imagine I looked any more tired than usual. If I did, it had nothing to do with schoolwork. More likely the memory of a hot mouth against mine in the dark.

"Everything is going well, but thank you for your concern, Aunt Ambrosia," I said.

"Have you heard from your brother lately? It is such a shame having him so far away when we have an excellent school right here."

I resisted the urge to clench my hands. Needling me about how I'd influenced my younger brother's life since I'd taken over guardianship of him from her three years ago had been one of her favorite bones of contention.

Marguerite Stormhurst, Connar's mother, jerked open the curtains to let what light and warmth the windows allowed to enter the gloomy space. She moved with the same athletic power he had, but her body was wiry rather than bulky with muscle.

"Do you still have Noah in that school in France?" she asked me in her blunt way. "Do you really think they'll teach him anything over there he won't learn just as well here?"

"I figure it broadens his horizons to spend some time studying with fearmancers he'd never have met otherwise," I said. "And now that I'm an aide at the university, it wouldn't be right to risk inadvertent favoritism. When I graduate, I'll have him transfer over here the following semester."

All of that was true, but the larger reason that I'd never have said to anyone in this room was I'd wanted to keep Noah away from the politics at home and the potential threats that circulated alongside them. The kid was only seventeen. He'd been just an infant when our mother had died, but he was nearly as much a target for Aunt Ambrosia as I was. The longer I could ensure he stayed far from this vicious circle, the better.

Baron Stormhurst wouldn't have understood my concern at all. She was only baron because she and her husband had destroyed her older brother's family thirteen years ago. No one had any proof that the series of accidents and illnesses had been their fault, of course, because that would have been sloppy, but everyone *knew*.

Just like everyone knew what had happened between Connar and his brother right before they turned fifteen.

Edmund Killbrook, Jude's father, rested his elbows on the tabletop where he'd already taken his seat. He was even more sharp angles than his son, his hair a sandy blond. Jude's deep red came from his mother.

"I hope he doesn't come back with the airs the European mages like to put on," he said flatly.

Julian Nightwood, Malcolm's father, strode to his seat with a click of his dress shoes against the floor. Looking at him was like looking thirty-two years into the future to the middle-aged man Malcolm would become.

Baron Killbrook's gaze slid to the empty point of the pentacle where a chair sat waiting for the next Bloodstone baron. He turned to Nightwood as the other man sat down. "I thought you were going to bring the Bloodstone girl."

Nightwood frowned. "The Bloodstone girl is in need of several good slaps before she sets foot in this room. The joymancers clearly addled her head. The sooner we can wring that influence out of her, the better." He glanced at me. "You've had plenty of chances to observe her and intervene, Ashgrave. It appears she's proved beyond the abilities of both you and our sons."

"She lived with the joymancers for seventeen years," I said, as impassively as I could. "She's only been at the university for four weeks. Retraining instincts and inclinations takes time."

Stormhurst let out a huff as she dropped into her chair. "We've given it enough time. We've been *waiting* seventeen years. To be on the verge, and then—" She sucked a breath through her teeth. "There has to be a way to speed the process along."

"From what Malcolm's said, he's come up with an idea he expects to throw her off before her assessment," Nightwood said. "If her magic fails to activate fully, it's likely she'll be dismissed, and then we'll be in a much better position to direct her."

"Are we going to leave it to the scions again, then?" Killbrook said.

Nightwood leaned back in his chair, his gaze going distant for a moment. "Malcolm has made some progress. He's intimidated her enough that she was frightened just seeing me. I think we should be above meddling with the university procedures." He raised his eyes. "But if his next gambit fails, we'll want to turn to other tactics. I agree that we've waited long enough already."

Other tactics. I didn't know exactly what the rest of the pentacle had been waiting for or how Rory would fit in, but it must have been big. It was only the core laws of our society that couldn't be overturned without the agreement of five rightful barons—which meant when you only had three or four, there wasn't even any point in talking about it. The best I'd gathered was that the pentacle had been preparing to make some major move before the confrontation that had left them missing one and with only a regent for another.

Whatever their intention was, I didn't think my mother had agreed with it. I had vague memories of her venting to my father about "the four of them" and how they meant to "destroy everything" in the weeks before she'd vanished from my life.

Sometimes I wondered if her death had really been entirely at the hands of the joymancers, or if someone else in the vicinity might have shoved her into the line of fire with the thought that a child would be easier to mold to the attitudes they wanted.

Stormhurst grimaced. "All right. I trust you're prepared to carry out the necessary measures as needed, Ashgrave?" Her cold eyes met mine.

Whatever the other barons were after, they wanted it badly. I could taste the current of impatience that ran through the room. The vise around my gut tightened.

Challenges between students was one thing. All of us mages on campus stood on at least somewhat equal footing. If the *barons* started sabotaging Rory's progress, that wasn't just natural squabbling or familial in-fighting. That was plotting treason against the sole remaining member of one of the pentacle families. We were supposed to each govern our own.

My frustrations with Rory were far more my fault than hers. That moment in the library—so close to her with so many emotions stirred up, her scent everywhere and her hand brushing over me like a caress—I'd lost control for one reckless, blissful, stupid moment. *So* fucking stupid.

It wasn't just my brother I was shielding as I staked a claim at this table but the other scions too. They deserved to be able to complete their time at Blood U unencumbered by the weight I'd had to shoulder so much earlier than most barons did. Rory deserved better than a double-edged welcome home. She'd barely had a chance to find her feet. Given a little more time, I had the feeling she'd become something magnificent, just perhaps not in the way these people wanted.

But if I said anything against the suggestion that we undercut her position, I'd be putting my neck—and my brother's—on the line. No one here liked Aunt Ambrosia. I'd seen that quickly enough, and it'd worked in my favor more than once. But if I actively protested the other barons' plans, I expected I'd find those treasonous intentions turned against me in two seconds flat. They'd hand her the knife and point out exactly where to stab it.

So when Nightwood's gaze came to rest on me too, I smiled the same thin smile back at them and said, "I'll do whatever I can in support of our interests on campus."

CHAPTER TWENTY-EIGHT

Rory

The morning of my second assessment, I stood under the shower for several minutes with the hot water cranked. Steam hazed the air and filled my lungs, but the heat didn't melt the nervous tension in my chest.

It had to be okay. I'd felt tons of magic since that last assessment. I'd cast all kinds of spells. Maybe I was still getting the hang of it, but there was no denying I was a mage.

But what if I wasn't enough of one? What if whatever had gone wrong last time went wrong again?

I dashed across the common room to my bedroom and slipped into the outfit I'd already laid out on my bed. My dragon charm settled against my collarbone. Then I turned to study myself in the wardrobe's mirror.

Still damp despite my efforts with the towel, my hair looked almost black as I combed my fingers through the tight waves. My dark blue eyes stood out starkly against my pale face. The black pantsuit I'd picked out had struck me as powerful on the hanger, but seeing it on my body only emphasized my overall impression.

That was a fearmancer staring back at me. Powerful or pathetic, every inch of me fit the role now.

No matter how hard I fought, Villain Academy was absorbing me.

The uncomfortable thought made the tension in my chest twist sharply. I shook it away and knelt down to get a little last-minute encouragement from my familiar.

"Deborah?" I murmured, waiting for her to poke her little white head from between the socks.

She didn't emerge. Maybe she'd gone for a walk around the room to stretch her legs? "Deborah?" I said again, as loud as I dared while a few of my dormmates lingered in the common room.

No streak of white fur darting toward me. No patter of mousey feet. No reassuring voice popping into my head. The twisting sensation turned into a knot of fear.

She'd never left the bedroom before. She'd have told me if she'd decided to, wouldn't she, so that I wouldn't freak out?

I inhaled deeply and tried to exhale my nerves along with my breath. Jumping to conclusions wouldn't do me any good. She'd probably just fallen asleep somewhere and hadn't woken at my voice.

I pawed through the socks gently, my spirits ready to leap at the sight of her curled body. It never appeared. I checked the other drawers and then all around the bed and the baseboard, my heart thumping harder with each spot I found vacant.

Either she'd suddenly gone off exploring without giving me any warning, even though she knew this morning was the key to my future, or… someone had taken her.

I'd replaced the security spell on the door before I'd gone to the shower, hadn't I? It'd become so automatic, I couldn't remember whether I'd needed to take it down when I'd come back in afterward.

Of course, even if I had, there were at least a few mages around here strong enough to break through my work.

My stomach listed as I came out into the common room. One of the girls sitting at the kitchen table looked up. She took me in, and her mouth flattened.

"Victory and Malcolm Nightwood were doing something by your

room while you were washing up," she said quickly, as if she'd been waiting to spit out that line.

My stomach, my heart, and the knot in my chest—they all plummeted to my feet. "Do you know where they went?" I asked, my voice sounding weirdly distant to my own ears.

"They mentioned hanging out in the basement," the girl said with that same reciting sort of tone. Had she volunteered to tell me, or had Malcolm persuaded her into it?

It didn't really matter. I ran for the door.

The basement. What basement? The question chased after me as I raced down the stairs, wishing I had a few fewer flights to descend instead of my lovely bedroom view. Was there even a basement in this building? Had she been talking about the Desensitization chamber in Nightwood Tower? I couldn't imagine anyone hanging out there, and the girl hadn't said it that way.

At the bottom of the stairs, I circumnavigated the library, following the curve of the lower hall. I'd never gone that way before, assuming it was for maintenance. At the far end, I found a narrow door. The sign hanging on it held a pentacle symbol and the words, *By Invitation Only*.

Fuck if I was going to wait for an invitation to crash the scions' party.

The door swung open easily. Maybe they expected the sign to be deterrent enough, or maybe they wanted me down there. Even if it was the latter, I didn't have a whole lot of choice.

I barreled down the steps and swung around the corner to find a tableau of my least favorite people in the world poised for my arrival.

The space was set up as a games room, a pool table at one end, a cluster of sofas and loveseats around a widescreen TV at the other, a substantial mahogany bar cabinet standing against the opposite wall. A vent over my head gushed warmth and a faint piney scent. The ceiling was high enough and the artificial lights strong enough to make the space feel much airier than your standard basement. But looking back at the assembled figures, I had trouble drawing in any air at all.

Victory and her two most devoted friends were sitting on one of the loveseats facing me, the lackeys on the seat cushions and Victory perched on the arm with her shapely legs crossed and her mouth already curved into an amused smile.

Declan and Connar had propped themselves at opposite ends of the sofa kitty-corner to the girls. Declan's posture was stiff, and his gaze didn't quite meet mine. Connar looked tensed to spring, his jaw tight.

Malcolm stood behind the sofa, leaning his arms casually against its back. A spark of triumph lit in his eyes at the sight of me, and his grin stretched wider. He nodded to Jude, who'd been lounging against the wall next to the TV with his hands slung in his pockets.

As the Killbrook scion pushed himself upright, my attention snagged on the one other person in the room—the last person I'd have expected to see in this company. Imogen shifted on her feet where she stood near the bar cabinet, her lips slanted at a pained angle. Understanding clicked in my head.

"You told them," I said with a flare of anger and betrayal.

"Rory," Imogen started, her voice wavering.

Victory sliced her hand through the air. "Shut it."

I couldn't tell whether she'd cast a spell or whether Imogen was just scared that she would, but my supposed friend's mouth snapped shut.

"Told us about what?" Jude said languidly. "Oh, you mean this little treasure?" He drew his hand out of his pocket with his fingers curled around a trembling white mouse, his little finger resting against the black splotch on her left flank.

My heart just about leapt up my throat. "Give her back to me," I said, marching over.

"*Stop*," Malcolm said in his casting voice, straightening up behind the sofa. My feet halted. The same fucking trick his dad had used on me. I turned toward him as well as I could, seething and trying not to shake, and he just grinned back at me. "Hid a whole familiar from us. Very sneaky. Well, maybe not so very sneaky when it is so very small."

My gaze jerked back to Jude. "If you hurt her—"

"Then what?" he asked, cocking his head. "What do you think you can do to any of us, Snowflake? You don't really deserve a familiar when you haven't even got the power to take care of it. Better to put the poor thing out of its misery in a constructive way."

He clucked his tongue, and the hairs on the back of my neck stood on end. His ferret familiar wriggled out from under the sofa and bounded across the thick rug to Jude's feet. It peered up at the mouse with an eager guttural sound.

"You'd like this tasty treat, wouldn't you, Mischief?" Jude crooned. As he adjusted his grip to dangle Deborah by her tail, the ferret's head bobbed.

"Leave her alone!" I said, the words catching in my throat before I could force them out. "You don't know—" I couldn't tell them how much more she was than just a mouse. They'd definitely kill her then. I turned to Declan frantically. "Isn't this against the rules you like to uphold so much? You can't let them do this."

I was sure when Professor Banefield had gone over the school policies with me, he'd mentioned that students were forbidden from purposefully harming another student's familiar. Officially, at least. Apparently that didn't mean much. Declan looked down at his hands, saying nothing.

Malcolm chuckled. "He's just as sick of you thumbing your nose at us as the rest of us are. The only *real* rule at Blood U is not to get caught if you break the other ones. No one here is going to go running to the administration on your behalf. You can't even prove you had a familiar, can you?"

I couldn't. A shiver ran through me. Jude swung Deborah gently through the air, and the ferret stood up on its hind legs, its upper body swaying to follow the movement.

"You'd better listen to him," Connar said, his voice low and rough.

The question dropped ragged from my mouth. "What do you want?" Because there had to be something. This wasn't purely torture. This was a negotiation—one where they held all the cards.

"That's more like it." Malcolm crossed his arms over his chest. "If you want your squeak toy back, first you're going to grovel on your knees right here, telling us all about how you now recognize that we're the real powers in the school and begging us to help you find your way. Then we'll take it out to the green, and you can do another demonstration while everyone's on their way to class. And *then* we'll head over to your assessment, and you can prostrate yourself while the professors and the headmistress watch. Do that, and we'll make sure you pass too. We're generous when people deserve it."

I hugged myself to hold in a shudder. Throw myself at their feet not just in private but in front of the entire campus… I'd never recover the higher ground after that. I'd have proven to students and teachers alike that Malcolm and the other scions owned me.

"What's more important to you?" Jude said, waggling his eyebrows. "Your pride or your familiar's life?"

"Just—just give me a second," I said, as if I was going to see some way out of this if I just stood here a little longer.

"Nah, I think you've had long enough. You obviously need a bit more motivation."

He flicked his wrist, and the mouse sailed through the air to land at the edge of the rug. I cried out, lunging after it, but Malcolm's magic held me firm. The ferret pounced. "Slowly, Mischief," Jude said softly. "Take your time."

It sank its teeth into Deborah's delicate shoulder, and she squeaked in pain.

"You can feel it, can't you?" Malcolm said, his voice rolling over me as an echo of pain did bite into my muscles. "Through the familiar connection. Everything it feels, you feel too."

"Stop it," I said. "Stop it!"

"On. Your. Knees. And let's hear that groveling loud and clear."

Victory and her friends snickered. "Watch the mighty fall," she said.

Deborah squealed again. My legs wobbled, my knees starting to give. My gaze darted across the room in one last-ditch attempt to find something, anything, that could fix this. It settled on Imogen's face.

Her lips were still pressed tight, but her eyes were wild. The weird thing, though, was that I didn't see the same hopelessness I felt reflected there. Her expression was more frustrated, as if she already knew the answer and it was killing her not to be able to say it.

My lips moved instinctively, forming a word under my breath as I focused on her forehead. "Inside."

If I'd tried an insight spell on anyone else in the room with my mind in its current turmoil, I'd probably have smacked into a shield I had no hope of breaking. But Imogen wasn't guarded against me. I tumbled right into the whirl of her memories and emotions, flashes of hand gestures and laughter, and one thought so clear I heard it like her voice ringing in my ears.

...all a fucking trick.

I jerked my awareness out of her mind and caught my balance before I reeled backward. A trick. A trick?

"You feel how much Jude's familiar is hurting that little thing," Malcolm went on, and this time I recognized the faint casting lilt beneath the words. "Are you going to just stand there and ride out its last breaths?"

A fresh knife of pain ran through my chest, but it wasn't coming from the mouse on the floor, was it? He was persuading me to feel the pain I'd have expected to.

He'd only need to do that if... if the mouse on the floor wasn't really my familiar.

It might not even be a mouse at all. Jude specialized in illusion.

Something Professor Banefield had told me during our preliminary lessons came back to me. *The four magical foci exist on a sort of axis of opposing pairs: the inward Insight against the outward Persuasion, the concrete Physicality against the ephemeral Illusion.*

I'd seen through Malcolm's persuasion by leaning on insight. Now I needed something concrete to challenge Jude's illusion.

I *should* have a connection to Deborah, wherever she was. We were tied together with a magical bond. That was why she could talk to me inside my head. If I just reached out to her the way I'd drawn ice from the air and metal from the ground...

My hand came up in front of me. "Where," I murmured, and closed my fingers to my palm.

A tremor of sensation tingled over my skin from somewhere beyond the walls. She was down here. Down here, but not in this room.

I dropped my hand back to my side and aimed a glare at Jude. "That's not my familiar. You can stop now."

Malcolm muttered a curse. Victory let out a disgruntled sigh.

Jude gave me a sickly smile and flicked his fingers. The mouse his familiar had been toying with blinked out of existence, leaving the ferret jerking its head back and forth trying to figure out what the hell had just happened.

"It doesn't really matter whether we feed it to the ferret or not," Malcolm said. "You're not getting it back until you get your act together."

"Then I'll just find her myself," I said. I shifted my attention to the floor, wondering if I could apply the same principles to freeing myself —how could insight unlock my legs? To my surprise, Malcolm released the spell with a wave.

I didn't get a chance to feel relieved. "You won't be finding anything right now," he said, his smile returning harder than before. "If you don't hurry, you're going to be late for your assessment, and *that* definitely won't be good for your chances of sticking around here, now will it?"

Fuck. I wavered on my feet. For whatever reason, Malcolm had decided he couldn't get away with actually hurting Deborah. That meant he wasn't going to feed her to the ferret now, right?

But who knew what else he might do with her once I was gone?

What would happen to both of us if I got myself kicked out of the university?

Malcolm glanced at the time on his phone. "Tick tick tick."

With a wrench of my heart, I made my decision. I spun and dashed for the stairs. Guilt squeezed around my chest as I bolted up them and ran for the main doors.

I needed to stay if I was going to get justice for Mom and Dad. I needed to stay if I was going to end all the horrors that happened here. Deborah would understand the risk I'd taken with her safety.

I had to believe that.

Passing students stared as I sprinted across the green. I slowed to a jog as I crossed the field and came up on the Stormhurst Building, my breath raw in my throat. Showing up hyperventilating wasn't going to be a mark in my favor either.

I strode into the gym just as the clock mounted on the wall clicked over to nine o'clock. Ms. Grimsworth looked up from where she'd been talking with Professor Banefield near the door. The four professors from before were already standing in their positions around the central circle.

"There you are, Miss Bloodstone," the headmistress said. "Ready?"

My legs felt like jelly and my breakfast was threatening to erupt from my stomach, but there wasn't much I could say other than, "Yes."

I walked to the testing circle, trying to shut out the clamor in my head. Fear for Deborah. Embarrassment that the scions had managed to trick me again so thoroughly. And doubt. So much doubt, worming through every other thought in my head.

The professors raised their hands. My body tensed automatically. "Just relax and accept," Banefield called to me.

Ha ha. Right.

I exhaled shakily and willed my body to loosen up as much as it could. The effort seemed to satisfy the assessors. They murmured together, and those simultaneous waves of energy blazed into me.

Their magic whipped through me like it had the first time, but this time I felt the responding thrum behind my ribs more clearly. It pushed and pulled in the same moment, a straining of power against itself. *An axis of opposing pairs.*

A giddy rush of possibility shot through my mind with my sort-of victory against the scions fresh in my memory. What if *that* was what had gone wrong last time? Physicality vs. illusion, insight vs. persuasion—my abilities so closely matched at either end that they'd cancelled out each other's effects?

I didn't have time to interrogate that theory. I needed to let the professors' spells register every bit of my strengths. If my magic still wasn't enough, well, at least I knew I'd been assessed fairly.

I closed my eyes and trained my attention on the whirlwind inside me. The threads of energy that brought the solid sensation of conjuring a physical thing or the opening up of another person's mind—I tamped down on those as hard as I could, holding them back.

Two bolts of magical energy sang through me at a higher pitch and flung themselves back toward their casters. I released the impressions I'd suppressed and instead reached toward the quivers that spoke of shifting of a person's senses or the warping of their will. I yanked those down in turn.

The rest of the assessment energy crackled out of me rather than bursting inside me like it had a month ago.

When I opened my eyes, the woman across from me looked a bit startled. My stomach sank. Had my attempt to show my abilities failed after all, and she couldn't figure out how I'd given the same result again? I swallowed hard as the four professors moved across the room to consult with Ms. Grimsworth.

The follow-up conversation went on for longer than before, with a protesting "But—" here and an emphatic "Hold on!" there. My earlier nausea curdled in my stomach. Finally, the professors stepped back, and Ms. Grimsworth beckoned me over.

Professor Banefield was beaming. Seeing that lightened my spirits a little as I approached the headmistress.

"Did I do okay this time?" I said.

She laughed, but with an edge to it that set my nerves off all over again.

"Miss Bloodstone, your performance was far more than 'okay'," she said. "Even with much debate, no one can deny the results. You show great and equal strength in all four domains. This is the first time any of us has encountered a power that balanced or that potent in our time."

For a second, I could only stare at her. A smile crept across my face, and then a laugh of my own spilled out of me. "So, I'm staying?"

"I think you'd better," she said, with just a hint of a smile of her own. "Come along. I think there may be quite a few people interested to hear your results."

She was right. When we emerged from the Stormhurst Building, a few dozen students had gathered on the field. They all perked up at the sight of me, their expressions avid. The scions, who maybe had encouraged the audience in the hopes it'd be for my downfall, stood at the edge of the crowd, watching just as intently.

It really hit me then. I'd won. They weren't getting rid of me. And I now had official confirmation that I was not just a powerful mage, but that once I got a grip on my abilities, I'd have more strengths than any of them.

Ms. Grimsworth set her hand on my shoulder and pitched her

voice to carry. "I'm pleased to announce that Miss Bloodstone will officially be joining us here at Bloodstone University as the only student currently or recently in residence with a strong talent in all four domains of magic."

A shocked but excited murmur spread through the gathered students. I caught a flash of fury in Malcolm's face, and then the headmistress was calling my attention back to her.

"You have your pick of the lot, Miss Bloodstone," she said. "At this point a student would generally pick a specialty and league to associate themselves with. What is your choice?"

I hadn't even considered that in depth before, I'd been so focused on just making it through the assessment. My thoughts immediately leapt to Physicality.

I'd always found so much joy in the act of creation. But the feelings around that type of magic were tainted now, too tangled up in everything I'd shared with Connar that he'd thrown in my face.

It was Insight that I'd learned from my parents before I'd known it was a skill I'd ever use through magic. It was Insight that had allowed me to stop Malcolm before I'd smashed the dragon bead on my necklace and saved me from giving in to the scions' demands this morning. Insight would have protected me from Connar's betrayal too if I'd pushed harder. I could take it so much farther with the training I'd get here.

I brought the word to my tongue, and everything in me hummed with the rightness of it.

"I'm going with Insight," I said.

Several voices in the crowd whooped in approval. "I'll have a new schedule for you tomorrow," Ms. Grimsworth said. "I think you've earned a day off."

I stepped forward, still a little uncertain that this could all be real, and the other students moved to meet me. At first they all just peered at me as if trying to glean how I'd done it. Then one girl said, "That's amazing!" and the floodgates burst. I was passed from one person congratulating me to another in a dizzying whirl of grins and awed voices.

Some of these people had probably helped trip me up over the last few weeks. I couldn't assume they were my friends now. I'd just been named the most powerful mage to attend the school in decades, and they were seeing how much that shine might rub off on them.

I'd be damned if the approval didn't feel good after all the tripping, though.

Somewhere in the middle of the impromptu celebration, a soft warmth pressed into my hand from behind. My fingers closed instinctively around a small furry body that sent a pang of recognition straight to my heart. Deborah.

I tucked her close to my chest and spun around, but whoever had passed her to me had vanished amid the other students. Had one of the scions decided they'd tortured me enough using her? Or had it been—well, I couldn't imagine it'd been Victory, but one of her minions?

I couldn't tell. Maybe it didn't matter. I held onto my familiar tightly with a sob of relief, and her tiny nose nuzzled my thumb as if to say what she didn't dare speak into my head with so many mages around us. She was back. She was home.

In that moment, I could almost believe that I was too.

CHAPTER TWENTY-NINE

Rory

My new cachet stuck with me throughout the day. Everywhere I went on campus, even in my dorm's common room, people watched me as if fascinated to see what I might do next.

It was a little exhausting. I holed up in my room for a while, and when I got bored with that, I looked out the window and saw that the field to the east of the main triangle was vacant. Next to a low, broad wooden building that I assumed was some kind of maintenance shed, I thought I saw the beginning of a path I'd never tried before at the edge of the woods.

I slipped out of Ashgrave Hall as surreptitiously as I could and hurried across the field. I'd just passed the maintenance building when its door clicked open and a voice I recognized reached my ears.

"Here you go," Malcolm was saying, his tone unusually warm. "About time for a run, don't you think?"

I eased back a step to peer around the side of the building. The Nightwood scion stood with his back to me, giving his wolf familiar a pat on the side as he motioned it off toward the forest. As the dark creature loped off, Malcolm reached to scratch the side of his neck.

The sun shone off his golden-brown hair. The collar of his shirt shifted to the side, revealing an angry mottled pink line across his shoulder that looked like a recent burn mark, large enough that I could see it even from several feet away. His fingernail brushed the edge, and he winced.

I never did have the best control over my tongue. "Are you all right?" I blurted out.

Malcolm snapped around to face me, his hand jerking to his side. "Why wouldn't I be, Glinda?" he asked with a haughty lift of his chin.

"You just looked like you had a burn or something on your shoulder." I sighed. "Never mind. I was about to leave anyway." I wasn't risking a walk in the forest with his wolf on the prowl.

Malcolm chuckled, but it was a dark sound. "So you're picking up the fearmancer mindset after all. Discover every weakness you can possibly exploit. Sorry, but you're never going to find me an easy target."

I stopped in the middle of turning away and met his eyes again. Anger flickered in my chest, but it was restrained by a quaver of a totally different emotion.

It was awfully sad that he couldn't even accept an honest question of concern without searching for an ulterior motive, wasn't it? How did anyone live their whole life like that?

For a second, I thought I saw something vulnerable behind the divine devil demeanor.

"I'm not planning to make you a target," I said quietly. "You know, even though I didn't want to be your friend and I'd rather you stayed as far away from me as possible, I'd care if I saw you get hurt. I'd try to help. Because that's what people with properly functioning hearts do for other people. That's who my parents—my *real* parents—raised me to be. And no matter how much of an asshole you are to me, you're never going to break that part of me."

We stared each other down for the space of several heartbeats. Malcolm folded his arms over his chest. His dark brown eyes bored into mine. "You should remember that no matter how many strengths you have, the guys and I have a much better idea how to use ours. We were holding back before because you couldn't do much to defend yourself. But believe me, we're just getting started."

That might be true. And I still might not know exactly how I was going to make it through the days ahead, but I had a much better idea than I'd had before. I was a fearmancer raised among joymancers, and I was going to hold onto all the joy I could gather until I was ready to burn all the fear away and make things right.

I held Malcolm's gaze and let a smile cross my lips. "So am I."

CRUEL MAGIC - BONUS SCENE

Rory saw the blacksuits' invasion of her family's home as a murder and a kidnapping. To Declan, it was a rescue operation. This bonus scene shows his version of the events in Chapter 1.

Declan

When the blacksuit opened the back door of the van where I'd been waiting, he didn't mince words.

"We've taken down the last of the wards—we're going in. Are you sure you're up for this?"

Was I sure I wouldn't get in the way, the guy really meant. Being very nearly a full baron granted me enough respect that he wouldn't phrase it that way to my face, but *not* quite being a full baron yet meant he couldn't help having the thought.

I didn't blame him for that. I *had* been asked the question directly by a couple of his higher-ups before we'd reached this point, even though those higher-ups were the same ones who'd tossed around the idea of bringing me along in the first place. If I'd thought there'd be a problem, I wouldn't have accepted the proposal.

No, I was more focused on the problems I could hopefully solve. The blacksuits were trained for aggressive assaults and defensive maneuvers, not for diplomacy or emotional support. Persephone Bloodstone had already been violently ripped from her family and forced to endure seventeen years under the sway of our enemies. She deserved to have someone on her rescue team who'd care about more than slaughtering any mage who tried to stand in our way and then hauling her back to New York state as hastily as possible.

Who would have been better qualified for that role than me? I was her fellow scion, a representative of the role she was meant to inhabit, and a fellow victim of the attack that had taken her parents' lives. The other barons might see my skills in insight as the least impressive of the magical specialties, but my talent should help me understand what she needed from us to make it through this operation without suffering even more trauma that she must already have sustained.

"I'm ready," I said.

The blacksuit nodded and murmured a concealment spell over me. I let him, trusting that his specialized training in that area would exceed my illusionary skills. Then he motioned me out, and we headed down the street to join the others where the team had staked themselves out in a second van just one yard over from their target.

The house the blacksuits had finally managed to identify as the one where the Bloodstone heir was held was a modest two-story with a small lawn. A crack ran through the pavement of the front walk, and paint was flaking in a few spots on the clapboard siding. It was such a far cry from the homes Persephone should have grown up in that I grimaced at the sight.

How had the joymancers treated her across all these years? Would we find her broken and bruised, trembling in distress? I'd seen photographs of her parents, of Persephone herself as a toddler, but I had trouble picturing her—how Baron Bloodstone's and her husband's features would have blended together on the now nineteen-year-old woman's face, how those features might have been altered by her experiences since their murders.

Her kidnappers would pay for their crimes. The blacksuits would make sure of that. I was glad no one expected me to carry out the slaughter, but I wasn't going to lament it either.

Losing my mother had been bad enough. The joymancers had stolen *everything* from Persephone.

And now she'd have to find her footing among her own people faster than she could possibly be prepared for. So many expectations, hopes, and resentments rested on a nineteen-year-old girl none of us had seen since she was two. Would those expectations shape her into a woman ready to rule as she was meant to, or had she lost her future as well? There was no room for weakness where she was going.

"We're moving in quickly," the blacksuit who'd brought me over reminded me in a low voice. "Don't want to give them a chance to raise the alarm. You hang back until we have all the joymancers in the building secured and we've located the girl."

"Got it."

The words had barely left my mouth when the rest of the squad spilled out of the van. The concealment spells made them blur against the sidewalk like shadows slipping through the early morning sunlight. Once we were inside, we'd let that magic fade to focus our energy on other things, but out here, we didn't want to draw the attention of the Nary neighbors.

The blacksuit in the lead, a man named Feverwell who was the squad leader and the only one who'd bothered to introduce himself to me, murmured a quick casting by the front door. Then he shoved it open, and the squad barreled inside.

I hurried along behind them, the hairs on the back of my neck rising with apprehension, a defensive spell ready on my tongue. From up ahead, there was a grunt and the thuds of two bodies hitting the floor. The blacksuits spat out casting words like bullets.

They'd spread out beyond a doorway at the end of the front hall. I found myself peering into a bright and homey kitchen. Two figures in ordinary clothes slumped on the floor: a middle-aged man against the fridge and a woman who looked to be around the same age pinned by magic to the oven door. Two blacksuits stood over each of them, others fanning out into the rest of the first-floor rooms.

Feverwell stalked across the length of the kitchen. "Are there any other joymancers in the building?"

The woman shook her head. Her face had paled with fear, but I could read the defiance in her eyes without using magic.

"If you're lying, you'll regret it," the squad leader snapped, and hollered to the other blacksuits. "Anything?"

"First floor is clear. Other than this joymancer junk." The woman responding must have knocked something over, because a smashing sound carried from the room next to the kitchen.

"Heading upstairs!" another yelled.

Feverwell rounded on the joymancer woman again. "Where's the girl you took? Where is Persephone Bloodstone?"

The woman gave her head another shake. One of the blacksuits by the captured man prodded his leg with a booted foot, but the man's mouth only pressed flat.

"We know you've been keeping her here," Feverwell said. "Pretending otherwise only means I'm going to make things more painful until we get our answers."

Both of the captives simply stared at him. He loomed over the woman, not a giant by any means but plenty intimidating. With a muttered spell word and a flick of his hand, she flinched as if stabbed in the gut.

"Where is she? Out with it, or this can get much worse."

He repeated the casting with enough force that the woman gasped and hunched over. Feverwell clapped his hands as if to say, *Let's get on with it.* But not another sound left the woman's mouth.

I shifted on my feet, restless but knowing it wasn't my place to step in. The blacksuit who'd headed upstairs came barging back down. "Second floor is clear!"

Feverwell motioned toward the far end of the kitchen. "Check the basement."

The joymancer woman reacted immediately, her shoulders tensing and her back going rigid. "You don't have to," she said in a ragged voice. "I'll tell you where she is."

The offer was in such opposition to her previous defiance that I didn't trust it for a second. I opened my mouth to shout a warning, too late.

She snapped the magical bonds and shoved herself to her feet, her arms whipping out with a casting of her own. No doubt it was fueled by Feverwell's happiness at the thought of finding Persephone at last.

The squad leader might not have been able to control his emotional response, but he was trained for exactly this kind of combat. The force of the woman's spell propelled him backward only a couple of steps. He whipped his hand through the air with a casting word that sounded as vicious as its effect.

The woman's throat burst open, blood spurting out. Her body went slack. As she crumpled by the oven, Feverwell turned to focus on her partner—

—and a slim, dark-haired figure lunged into the room from seemingly out of nowhere.

The younger woman thrust her hands under the fallen joymancer's head an instant before it smacked into the tiles. Blood splashed across her arms and soaked into the knees of her jeans. "Mom," she said in a strangled voice, pressing her hand helplessly to the wound on the woman's throat.

Mom? Was she this couple's child? Where the hell was—

The joymancer man's voice burst from his mouth. "Rory, get out of here! Run to—"

One of the blacksuits standing over him barked a casting, and his mouth jammed shut. The others had converged on the young woman. As they yanked her to her feet, her head came up. The dark strands of her hair fell away from her face, and my heart stopped.

She wasn't the joymancers' child, and I had no idea why they were calling her "Rory." No one who'd seen a single picture of Baron Bloodstone could have doubted that this girl was her daughter. Those dark eyes, a startling, almost indigo blue, were unmistakable even widened in panic.

She looked healthy and uninjured—and completely bewildered. She struck out at the blacksuits with a cry. As sure as I was that she was Persephone Bloodstone, I could also tell she had no idea whatsoever what was happening here.

Before I had any conscious thought to move, I was striding across the kitchen. The young woman stumbled, and I grasped her shoulder, shooting a sharp look at the blacksuit who'd had the most grip on her. "This is *her*," I said under my breath. "Don't hurt her."

I held enough authority that he gave way, letting me turn Persphone toward me again. Her head came up as I lowered mine, and our gazes locked.

Those eyes were even more breathtaking up close, stark with horror at the scene unfolding around her. It took me a second to regain my voice. I threw the full force of my persuasive power into it. That area of magic wasn't my primary strength, but I had enough skill that I trusted it as my best bet of calming her down.

"It's okay," I told her, sending out soothing energy travel through the words. "We've got you now. You won't be trapped here anymore. We're going to take you home."

Persephone's body started to relax beneath my hand. She blinked at me, the panicked haze clearing from her vision. She'd been pretty even in her frantic state—now, with her face tipped close to mine, she was so gorgeous my pulse stuttered.

My God. So this was what it was like meeting a Bloodstone in the flesh.

I had a moment to take the experience in and for a rush of relief to follow that my spell appeared to have worked. Then her expression tensed all over again. As I opened my mouth to reinforce my casting, Feverwell's voice carried from across the room.

"I feel we need to send a message."

Persephone tore away from me, heaving herself toward the man by the fridge. Feverwell was already moving. With a hissed word and a slash of his hands, a bloody X raked through the joymancer man's chest down to the ribs.

A cry wrenched from Persephone's lips. She grabbed at Feverwell, looking as if she'd have liked to rip *him* open, but the other blacksuits caught her first.

She'd thrown off every trace of my attempt at soothing her nerves. That strength of will would have reassured me more if it hadn't been spurred by her apparent concern for her captors.

"Knock her out," Feverwell ordered. "We've got to get going."

"Wait," I started, but one of the men holding Persephone jerked his hand across her forehead with a hasty casting. She sagged, unconscious, between him and the woman who'd grasped her other arm.

"What the hell are you doing?" I demanded. "That's Persephone Bloodstone—we shouldn't be treating her like a prisoner."

Feverwell glowered at me, looking as though he was regretting having me along. "I know who she is, and I also know that the joymancers could have an assault squad breathing down our necks any second now. The girl is clearly confused—they probably had her under some kind of spell. It'll be a lot easier to check her over for hostile magic and ensure her safety if she's not fighting us at every turn." He raised his voice to reach the rest of the squad. "Move out, people, now!"

I hurried alongside the blacksuits, a series of knots forming in my stomach. When we piled into the van, I squeezed to a spot next to where the squad had propped Persephone's prone body on a couple of folded blankets.

Her head lolled against the thick fabric, her lips slightly parted. The blood that had sprayed her clothes from the woman's throat—the woman she'd called *Mom*—was darkening as it dried. There was something so fragile about her right then that I had to bite back another attempt at persuading her calm, as if she even would have heard me in her current state.

She couldn't afford to stay fragile for long, not in the world we were bringing her into. As soon as news got out that the Bloodstone heir had returned, everyone would be looking to her for a show of strength—and watching for ways to sway her to their ends if they saw an opening.

It was the world she belonged in, but that didn't mean anyone was going to coddle her. That wasn't the fearmancer way.

I'd come here to help her, to make the transition easier for her. Gazing down at her with the knots in my stomach pulling tighter, I couldn't shake the suspicion that I'd already failed in ways I hadn't even realized.

VILE SORCERY

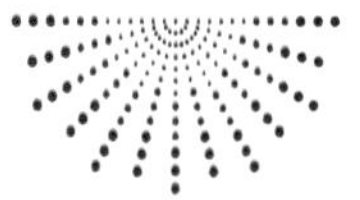

ROYALS OF VILLAIN ACADEMY #2

CHAPTER ONE

Rory

The morning after I was declared the most powerful mage to attend Villain Academy in decades, I dreamed about my parents' murders again.

The moment didn't play out exactly as it had in real life. This time, my legs refused to move as one of the blacksuits slashed his hand through the air with a snapped spell. Mom's throat tore open with a gush of blood, and I stayed locked in place, straining to run to her.

A scream ripped up through my chest but caught in the back of my mouth. I couldn't even force out that sound. Couldn't throw any spell of my own at the attackers. Couldn't take a single step to defend Dad when the man spun on him and gouged an X in his chest.

The smell of blood, thick and metallic, flooded my nose and washed over my tongue. My stomach lurched.

I woke up shaking and watery-eyed with the wrenching sense that I had no power at all—none that mattered, anyway.

Early morning sunlight streamed through my dorm bedroom window, thinner here in upstate New York's early May than it'd be back in California, where I should have been. Where I would have been if I could have saved my parents.

I pulled the duvet up over my head to hide from the day. No part of me felt ready to face it. I'd just spent the last month fighting to make sure I could stay here at the school more properly known as Bloodstone University. The school named after a birth family I'd never known and didn't particularly want a part in. The school that was full of the cruelest people I'd ever met.

I'd won. I'd proven myself more capable than I could have hoped. After yesterday's assessment, I should have been full of confidence. But the truth was, I was exhausted.

The fight was far from over. I'd worked my ass off to stay here so that I could figure out a way to take down the university and the vicious mages who'd destroyed my *real* family, the parents who'd raised me. No one here was going to make that easy for me, least of all my four fellow scions, the sons of the other ruling families. Malcolm, Jude, Connar, and Declan—all of them as brutal as they were gorgeous.

Maybe Headmistress Grimsworth wouldn't mind if I took a whole week off to recover instead of just one day? Ha.

The sheet twitched, and a small furry body nestled against my arm. *How are you doing, sweetheart?*

The voice of a sixty-something woman that traveled into my head came from the pet mouse tucked in the crook of my elbow. Before I'd even known I was a mage myself, my parents' people had arranged for Deborah's soul to be relocated into the animal, and for the mouse to be bound to me as my familiar so that she could protect me… and keep an eye on me. Just in case some of the magic my parents were suppressing in me leaked out.

They and the mages they worked with were joymancers, getting the energy for their spells from the happiness they stirred in others. Like everyone else here at Villain Academy, I was a fearmancer, with powers that came from provoking terror. Having now met a whole bunch of fearmancers, I couldn't exactly blame Mom and Dad for worrying about how I might turn out.

"I'd like to go back to sleep for about a year," I murmured to Deborah. The walls in the dorm room weren't super thick, and while the secret that I *had* a familiar was out now, no one except me knew my mouse had a joymancer's soul along for the ride. Deborah's life depended on my keeping that secret.

"Are *you* okay?" I added. Yesterday she'd been kidnapped by the other scions in an attempt to force me into bowing down to them. I'd managed to outsmart them and get her back, but being in their hands even for a little while couldn't have been fun.

Don't you worry about me, Lorelei, Deborah said with a tickle of her whiskers against my skin. *I'm already on my second life—I'm grateful to have it at all. What matters to me is making sure* you *make it through these trials all right.*

My chest tightened up. I ran my thumb over the soft fur on her back. At least one person here had my best interests at heart… even if she wasn't exactly a person anymore.

"I'll be fine," I said. "I'm just feeling a little overwhelmed. No one knew what to expect from me before. After that assessment, they're going to be watching for incredible things. I still can't cast much if I'm not stirring up fear in people, and I still don't like doing that." I let out a little groan. "And now I'm going to have a full schedule. Even more classes with these assholes."

Don't you think the other scions will back off now that they know how strong you are? Your classmates seemed to respond quite positively to the news yesterday.

"Those ones were just hedging their bets, I guess. Figuring they should fawn over me a bit while I'm in the spotlight. If I can't keep up, they'll go right back to taking jabs at me. And the scions… I don't think I can count on any mercy or respect from them. Malcolm Nightwood made it *very* clear that he's not finished with his campaign against me."

His exact words had been, *We're just getting started.* Definitely not extending a hand in friendship. Not that I'd have accepted his hand any more than I had the first time he'd come sauntering in here, figuring he could simply introduce himself and I'd be honored to enjoy his company.

I couldn't let him or the others get to me. I'd focus on learning everything I could until I was ready to destroy this school and the cold-blooded psychopaths it taught all its students to be, and then I could prove to the joymancers back home that I wasn't like the other fearmancers. That they didn't need to be afraid of my powers. I'd go back to them and back into the life I really wanted.

If it took me a while to get there, so be it.

I pushed back the covers and sat up, careful of Deborah. "We'd better find you a new hiding spot in case they decide to use you to mess with me again," I said under my breath. The sock drawer wasn't going to cut it anymore. "Any ideas?"

I've found some comfortable nooks right in the walls. It'd be difficult for them to catch me in there. And I can keep more of an ear out for anyone coming into your room who doesn't belong.

"Okay, that sounds good."

I should have been able to keep intruders out with all the magical strengths I supposedly had. Unfortunately practice counted for a lot too, and my most enthusiastic enemies had plenty of talent of their own along with their years of experience.

A couple of my dormmates were sitting on the sofas in the common room when I walked through, but not any of the girls I'd really interacted with. They watched me pass by with a curious if wary look and went back to their conversation. When I'd finished my shower and headed into the kitchen to grab breakfast for me and my mouse, those two had disappeared, and Shelby was pouring herself a bowl of cereal.

A smile leapt to my face at the sight of the dorm's one Nary student. Bloodstone University brought in a limited number of Naries —short for *ordinary*, or *Nary a bit of magic*, as Mom used to say—on scholarships more for our benefit than theirs. As mages living in secret among human society, we needed to learn how to act and cast around them without raising suspicions. That was *all* they were supposed to be: a tool. Fearmancers didn't make friends with Naries.

But I wasn't your typical fearmancer, and I'd rather have Shelby's company over that of the mages here any day, even if there were a whole lot of things I could never talk to her about.

"Hey," I said as I opened the fridge to retrieve my eggs and Deborah's cheese. "You're looking better. Totally recovered?"

Shelby glanced over at me with a swish of her mousy brown ponytail and smiled back. A faint but healthy-looking flush colored her cheeks. She'd been suffering from a flu for most of the last week, pushing on with her schoolwork despite a serious fever, because she was scared the teachers would send her home if she didn't seem committed enough to her classes. Despite the chilly treatment she got from most of the student body, the music program here apparently offered her opportunities she'd endure just about anything to hold onto.

"Back in ship-shop shape," she said, and paused. "Other than hearing that stupid tree. The maintenance staff obviously didn't listen to me about it."

"Tree?" I repeated as I cracked my eggs over a frying pan, and then remembered. "The one you think might be rotten?"

"Yeah. It's still making that weird sound when the breeze is moving in the right direction. It's pretty faint—maybe they think I'm making it up. But I swear it sounds just like the one that collapsed on my street way back when, and I'm not feverish anymore, so…" She grimaced.

The fearmancer staff just assumed they knew better than any Nary. I doubted they'd even checked it out. When I'd told my assigned mentor, Professor Banefield, about Shelby's complaint, he'd brushed the sound off as a prank one of the magical students must have been playing on her.

I'd just have to raise the issue again. I couldn't imagine anyone getting enough fear out of some faint weird tree sound for it to be worth keeping up the illusion for days on end.

"I have to talk to the staff about something today anyway," I said, which was only sort of a lie. Banefield was staff, if not maintenance staff. "Maybe if they hear about it from more than one person, they'll take the problem more seriously."

"Thanks. I'd really just like them to take a look. People could get hurt. Anyway… I was wondering… Do you want to go grab drinks in town again sometime? I'm busy with rehearsals for the end-of-year concert the next couple evenings, but maybe after that?"

She eyed me hesitantly. I was the first dormmate she'd had who'd been anything close to friendly. I gave her my warmest smile in reassurance. "That'd be great. I'm still getting to know what the best places are."

We chatted about the town's somewhat meager offerings for food and entertainment as I finished frying my eggs. Just as my toast popped up, a door at the far end of the room opened, and Victory Blighthaven stepped out.

Victory's auburn hair curved in perfect waves around her angelic face, and her blouse and skirt clung to her hourglass figure so smoothly it was obvious they'd been tailored for her. She'd have been lovely to look at if it hadn't been for the pointed glower she aimed my way.

She was one of Malcolm Nightwood's biggest fans, which meant she wasn't a fan of me at all. It didn't help that I'd inadvertently stolen the best bedroom in the dorm from her when I'd arrived. Obviously the announcement about my exemplary assessment hadn't warmed her up to me.

I decided not to find out what Victory might contribute to the conversation and hustled my breakfast into my bedroom. Deborah gave a happy sigh when I set down her plate of cheese, crackers, and blueberries. I sat at the little desk crammed between the bed and the window and dug into my eggs and toast.

As I gulped down the last few buttery bites, my gaze meandered over the green outside toward the domed shape of the Stormhurst Building and then on to the glittering waters of the lake. If it hadn't been for the people, this place really would have been beautiful. I could just imagine…

A haze crept over my mind. I couldn't have said I was thinking about anything, really, only that all at once I blinked and the scattering of clouds had scudded farther across the sky—and my hand was jerking a pen across a paper I didn't remember getting out.

I yanked my arm back with a hitch of my pulse. The scrawled words stared back at me. The same sentence was dug into the paper over and over all the way down its white surface.

I killed them. I killed them. I killed them.

A chill shot through me from gut to throat, just about propelling my breakfast with it. The pen slipped from my fingers, and my hand came up to grip the glass dragon charm hanging from a silver chain around my neck. The last piece of my old life I'd been able to hang onto.

How—What had even just happened there? I'd never blanked out like that before. Even when I'd acted without meaning to in the grip of one of Malcolm's persuasion spells, I'd been conscious the whole time. And there was no one in here with me to have cast any spell on me anyway.

Why had I written *that*? I'd thought it more than once remembering my parents' deaths. The blacksuits who'd come to "rescue" me from the joymancers would never have killed them if they hadn't taken me in and raised me in the first place. But I didn't think I'd ever admitted that guilt to anyone. It'd been in my head during my first desensitization session, but I could have sworn I hadn't said anything out loud. I'd been sobbing too hard to say much of anything.

Had that daze been caused by magic or simply the emotions I'd tried to bury?

Lorelei? Deborah's voice reached me from a greater distance than it normally sounded. She scurried across the floor to touch my socked foot. *Thank goodness! You came out of it.*

"What happened?" I whispered.

You tensed up all of a sudden, grabbed that paper, and started writing. I tried to talk to you, but you didn't seem to hear me. It looked like some kind of spell. I peeked out into the common room, but I couldn't see anyone who looked as if they were casting on you. Of course, who knows what awful magic these fearmancers might be able to work?

That wasn't terribly reassuring. I crumpled the paper into a ball and tossed it into the little garbage bin under the desk.

What were you writing?

"Just..." My throat constricted. "Nothing important. Just gibberish." I glanced at my phone and winced. "I should get going. I'm supposed to meet my mentor in ten minutes."

The chill in my nerves lingered as I hurried out of the dorm. None of my usual tormenters were around. If I'd been in the grip of a spell, *someone* had to have cast it.

I loped down the five flights of stairs to the ground floor with my thoughts in a jumble. I'd just reached the hall by the library when four striking and all-too-familiar figures came ambling my way.

Malcolm Nightwood's voice rang out with its usual smooth cockiness. "Well, if it isn't Glinda the good witch. You look a little frazzled. Is the pressure of all that talent we're expecting to see getting to you already?"

I swiveled on my heel to face the four scions. They must have been coming up from the basement room where they had their private lounge area—which meant, I was pretty sure, that they'd all been much too far away to cast any targeted spell at me.

Malcolm smiled at me with a cool glint in his dark brown eyes. The restrained hostility in his expression eliminated any heat his breathtaking looks might have sparked in me otherwise. His golden hair and his face with its perfect mix of hard and soft lines had made me think of him as a divine devil when I'd first met him. These days I had no doubt that he leaned much more toward the devil side in personality.

At his left, Jude flicked back his floppy dark copper hair and offered me a smirk. The Killbrook scion was just as good-looking as Malcolm in his lean, angular way—and could be just as vicious when he decided to be. But it was the muscular guy at Malcolm's other side who made my stomach clench up. Connar Stormhurst met my eyes, his chiseled face set in a stern expression that didn't waver for a second. I couldn't see any hint that he remembered, let alone cared, about the conversations we'd had away from the others… or the intimacy we'd shared.

I should have known better. Just like I should have known not to have any hopes for Declan Ashgrave the second I'd found out where he and the blackshirts had brought me. The oldest scion, bringing up the rear of the bunch, had shown more than once that he'd protect me only when it didn't interfere with his obligations to the other guys or his job as teacher's aide. Now, he ducked his head, his black hair falling forward to shadow his bright hazel eyes.

"I'm just fine," I said as evenly as I could manage. "Thank you so much for your concern, though."

I spun back around and strode toward the main doors. Malcolm's chuckle rolled after me. "We'll see you around, Glinda!"

He turned that friendly comment into a threat so easily. A shiver ran through me as I headed along the path toward the teachers' offices in Killbrook Hall. Whether someone had magically induced my little episode this morning or not, clearly my first priority needed to be working on my mental shields. If I could be sure of protecting myself from outside influence, I'd be safe from any more unnerving episodes —or I'd know that whatever was wrong was coming from inside me.

CHAPTER TWO

Rory

"Congratulations again on yesterday's exemplary assessment," Professor Banefield said with a grin as he ushered me into his office. "I knew your talent would shine through once you had a little more time."

His warm confidence put me a little more at ease. "You've got my new schedule for me?"

"I do. Lots more learning to be done, but you're clearly up to the challenge. Why don't you look it over before I say my piece."

He handed me a paper showing two weeks' worth of class times, mostly the same across both weeks. A lot more of them than had been on my initial "easing the Bloodstone scion into her magical education" schedule for the last month.

When I'd had a few minutes to read it over, Banefield leaned forward, rubbing the side of his round head. His light red hair stuck up in tufts as if he'd slept on it funny, but I'd seen him often enough to know that was just how it always looked.

"You'll see that you only have one official session with me each week now that you're getting settled in," he said. "You can drop in during my office hours any time you feel you need additional guidance, of course. I'll always be available to you, but my primary role now will be to help you continue to adjust to school life in general rather than magical lessons. From here on, you can see you'll have two seminars a week in each specialty to help catch you up."

"And now a Desensitization session every week… but at a different time?" I glanced at him quizzically.

Banefield's upbeat expression faltered for a second. "Professor Razeden and I felt—and Ms. Grimsworth agreed—that in light of your circumstances, it would be ideal for you to get frequent one-on-one instruction in that area until your control has improved."

A flush rushed to my cheeks. Yeah, my control had been pretty crappy the first two sessions I'd done. The whole point of Desensitization was to master your reactions when faced with your greatest fears—the weaknesses other fearmancers could get the most mileage out of targeting. Both times, I'd needed Professor Razeden to end the illusion for me because I hadn't been able to stand up to it even with his advice.

At least private sessions meant I wouldn't have any scions watching my weaknesses laid out on display.

"We're avoiding placing you in any of the general interest courses with the Naries for similar reasons," Banefield went on, avoiding lingering on my failure. "Not that your use of magic has lacked control, but you haven't been practicing it enough for us to be certain there won't be problems. Better not to risk exposure. I expect you'll move into those in the fall term with the new school year."

"That makes sense," I said. I wasn't in any hurry to add even more to my workload. But the mention of the Nary students reminded me of my conversation with Shelby.

"If you have any other questions…"

I folded the schedule. "I do, but not about this. I was talking with the Nary student in my dorm this morning—she's still worried about that tree I told you about before. Do you know if anyone in maintenance has checked it out—and if they haven't, can we get them to?"

In general, I found Professor Banefield to be one of the most pleasant people at the university. Something shifted in his demeanor whenever the nonmagical people living alongside us came up, though. His jaw tensed beneath his scruffy beard, and his mild eyes took on a harder sheen.

"As we discussed earlier, Rory, I think it's best not to get caught up in the concerns of the Naries. This is an… unusual environment for them, but they accept it because of the benefits we offer in return. We don't want to encourage them to question the unusual occurrences that may come up around them."

They accepted this environment partly because they had no idea we were using them to generate fear and test our magical stealth.

I made a face. "That doesn't mean she's wrong about this. How long would it take for someone to check it out? A falling tree is going to hurt a mage just as much as any Nary who ends up in its path."

"I'm sure the maintenance staff is already monitoring the grounds as per their job."

His voice had gone firm. This was around the point I'd given up last time. Today, resistance prickled through me. Maybe the day I could take down the university felt way too far in the future, but I could make sure at least *one* person was treated properly.

"If one of the magical students had reported it, someone would make sure to look into it, wouldn't they?"

"That's different," Banefield said. "We trust that you would be able to tell the difference between a real problem and a prank."

"Yeah," I said, "and this sounds like a real problem to me. Shelby is a musician—she obviously has a good ear. And she's experienced this before. It makes sense that she might pick up on a sign that most of us would miss, magic or not. I get that fearmancers generally don't want to lower themselves to listening to Naries or whatever, but don't you think there's a certain point where that crosses the line from sticking to your own to being stubbornly stupid?"

A little more irritation than I'd meant to reveal leaked into my tone. Banefield stiffened in his chair. For the first time in the month I'd known him, he looked *angry*. I braced myself with a hiccup of my pulse, but whatever way I'd provoked him, he mastered his reaction.

The first thing he let out was a sigh, and his shoulders came back down.

"*I* have plenty of experience dealing with Naries," he said. "The one thread that has carried through all those interactions is carelessness. They only care about their own individual discomforts and desires without a thought to any larger purpose. We cannot have our staff distracted from their regular jobs to track down a 'weird-sounding' tree on one likely misguided report."

There were a whole lot of things I could have said about fearmancers and their selfishness, but I didn't think most of those paths would take us anywhere productive. I did have to point out, "It's not as if *we're* all that careful with the Naries. At least when they screw up, in my experience, it's usually a mistake rather than purposeful malice."

"And yet mistakes can have such wider reaching consequences compared to malice thoughtfully planned." Banefield gave me a tight smile. "I know you're still adjusting to the expectations and practices of our community, Rory, but I can assure you one thing—we expect every student here to choose their actions with full consideration of the impact."

Was that supposed to be reassuring? I shifted in my seat and opened my mouth again, but Banefield cut me off before I could say anything else.

"Your first new seminar will be starting shortly. I think this discussion has run its course."

We'd see about that the next time I got his ear. I stood up, clutching the schedule. "There was one other thing. I'd like to get in some concentrated practice on shielding my mind. To, ah, reduce the 'impact' of any spells that get thrown at me."

Banefield relaxed a little more with the change in subject. "The timing works out well then," he said. "I believe it's Insight you're off to now. Professor Sinleigh should be able to give you even better advice for advanced tactics—she has a couple of decades' experience on me. And it's best if you're working on your magical techniques with your seminar professors rather than me so they can accurately judge your progress."

I tugged open my schedule again. Yep, I was off to Insight. This seminar was a new addition to my schedule, so I could hope Jude and Victory wouldn't be there, eager to pry open my head.

I set off through the building toward the green at a brisk pace. The sooner I got to Nightwood Tower and my classroom there, the more choice I'd have in seating. Professor Sinleigh liked to pair us up with our nearest neighbors.

Killbrook Hall held the junior residences as well as the staff quarters. I passed several younger students on my way out, and a mix of juniors and seniors heading to their own classes outside. Many of them glanced at me with a glimmer of recognition, their eyes widening a bit or their heads turning to watch after I passed. A cool shudder of sensation rippled up through my chest.

It was fear, I realized as another waft of it hit me. Not one of the kinds I'd felt before: the sharp quivers of animal nerves when I ventured into the forest, the jolts of panic the few times I'd been able to land a jab against one of my tormenters. This flowed through me with a sensation more subtle and yet more sweeping.

Apprehension. Beneath all the awed fawning I'd gotten yesterday, just seeing me made quite a lot of the student body awfully wary. And why not, after the way the established scions with their multiple strengths lorded it over this school?

That thought settled uncomfortably in my gut as I reached the tower and trudged up the stairs. I couldn't say I minded getting this top-up of magical energy, now tingling behind my collarbone, but I didn't exactly like the idea of becoming some frightening figure either.

It was a good thing I'd made it to class a bit early, because I was able to choose a spot between a few students who'd never been overtly nasty to me, just a couple minutes before Cressida walked in. Victory's partner-in-crime lifted her chin haughtily at the sight of me and flicked her white-blond braid back over her shoulder as she took a seat at the opposite corner of the room—a reasonably safe distance.

Of course, sitting at the front didn't give me much distance at all from the other person in the classroom I'd have wanted to avoid. When the professor came in, peering at us with her owlish eyes, Declan Ashgrave arrived right behind her. Insight was his main specialty—the league he'd chosen from his strengths—and in those seminars he was working as Professor Sinleigh's aide.

His gaze settled on me for a second, and I tensed in my seat. He stopped by the far side of her desk.

Declan hadn't been as much of an asshole as the other scions, but he hadn't done anything to stop their torment either, even when I'd challenged him to his face. And then there was the whole library incident when he'd dragged me out of sight of Victory and her crew for my apparent safety, but ended up kissing me and then yelling at me about it.

The kiss had been pretty enjoyable, I had to admit. The yelling, not so much. Better to avoid any possibility of either happening again.

"All right, class," Professor Sinleigh said, clapping her delicate hands. "Today we'll be focusing on narrowing the scope of an insight spell through the use of questions. As some of you will be aware, asking a specific question with your spell can help you home in on more useful impressions, but they are also more hindered by mental defenses. Those of you who are relatively new to the concept, begin with more basic and unthreatening inquiries. Those of you who are more practiced may attempt to dig deeper if you're confident enough. But first let's run through a warm-up exercise..."

By the end of class, I knew that the girl sitting next to me had a fox for a familiar, favored mint tea, and loved the color green. I wasn't sure whether I'd broken through barriers she had up or she just hadn't tried that hard to stop me, but at this point, I'd take the success as a win.

As the other students filed out of the room, I approached Professor Sinleigh. She was so petite I found I was looking down at her from about half a foot—and I was hardly an Amazon.

"Miss Bloodstone," she said in her soft, precise voice. "It's an honor to have you joining us in the League of Insight. What can I help you with?"

"I'd like to work on my mental shielding skills," I said. "Professor Banefield, my mentor, said I should talk with you about that."

Sinleigh nodded. "That's a very valuable skill to develop. We will cover several techniques in class."

"I was hoping to get caught up a little faster, since I've missed so much time here."

"Yes, of course." She tapped her lips. "I think what would work best is for you to begin with some additional tutoring from Mr. Ashgrave. It wouldn't be a bad thing for the two of you to become better acquainted as scions at the same time. Once he's sure you have all the core skills solid, I can arrange some time to coach you on the more advanced strategies." She looked to Declan. "You should be able to fit that into your schedule, shouldn't you?"

Er, that hadn't been the scenario I'd been going for at all. I crossed my arms over my chest instinctively.

Declan trained his bright hazel eyes on me for a moment before turning to the professor. I couldn't read his expression. "I can definitely find the time if that arrangement works for Miss Bloodstone."

Okay, so we were sticking to professional courtesy now, were we? My body balked, but if I refused to work with him, Professor Sinleigh would think *I* was the problem.

I couldn't start my time here as an official student running away scared from the guys I'd spent the last month standing up to.

"All right," I said. "That sounds fine."

Sinleigh considered me as if she'd picked up on my lack of enthusiasm, but she didn't remark on it. "I'll leave you two to work out the best timing. Let me know when you're ready for your advanced coaching."

She slung her bag over her shoulder and slipped out of the room.

I stayed where I was by the corner of the desk, and thankfully Declan didn't come any closer. He looked at the floor and then at me, swiping back his smooth dark hair.

"This wasn't my idea."

"Obviously. I was here for the entire conversation."

One corner of his lips quirked up slightly at my tone. "If you're sure—"

I shrugged. "If you can manage not to be an asshole and just do your job, it'll be fine. Unless you're worried that someone will see the extra tutoring as favoritism."

The hint of a smile disappeared at that little jab. "Sinleigh assigned me to do it. I don't see how anyone can criticize me for that. I only have about ten minutes before I need to head out now, but we can arrange times during my office hours. There's a joint aide office in the staff wing of Killbrook Hall."

"Okay." Despite my claim that all this was fine, my thoughts had scattered too much for me to think through the least awkward way of handling this. "I just got my new schedule. Let me—let me see when I seem to have the best openings, and then I'll let you know."

"Of course." He paused and then backed up a step as if to give me more room to pass him without coming near him. The gesture set off a twinge in my chest. He just couldn't help sort of protecting me in between all the times he didn't, could he?

As I headed for the door, he sucked in a breath. "Is your familiar okay?"

I stopped on the threshold, my head snapping around. "What?"

"Your familiar. It seemed all right, after—they only had it in a cage in another room—but you can't always tell when you don't really know the animal."

Something clicked in my head with his gaze on me and the guilt slanting his mouth. "You're the one who brought her back to me." In the commotion after my assessment announcement yesterday, someone had slipped Deborah into my hand so swiftly I hadn't seen who it was. Declan *had* looked awfully uncomfortable during the charade Malcolm and Jude had orchestrated yesterday, when they'd made me think they were feeding my mouse to Jude's ferret familiar.

"They didn't have the right to hold on to her," he said.

"But they had the right to take her in the first place? What if they'd decided to *really* let the ferret at her?"

"They wouldn't have," Declan said firmly. "You don't have to worry about that. No one here would risk it. To purposefully kill someone's familiar—even a scion wouldn't get away with breaking that rule. Jude might think a lot of himself, but he knows he doesn't have perfect control over his animal."

"But no one knew I even had her." If the four of them and the four girls who'd been spectators hadn't told anyone, then hardly anyone knew even now.

"It wouldn't have mattered. When someone's familiar dies, especially if it's traumatic—it affects you. If you reported it, the staff would be able to confirm, whether they knew you had a familiar beforehand or not." Declan ducked his head. "I know it's not a lot of comfort, after everything, but there are lines we don't cross."

We meaning fearmancers in general or my fellow scions in particular? I wasn't sure it mattered. The twinge in my chest had expanded, filling the space inside my ribs with a faint ache.

"Maybe you should look into finding a few more of those," I said, and left before the growing mix of gratitude and disappointment could wrench at me any harder.

CHAPTER THREE

Jude

My mother tried. I knew she did, and I could summon some gratitude for that. The thing was, most of the time I couldn't help thinking she was trying a hell of a lot more for Dad than for me when by any available metric it should have been the other way around.

Her voice carried tinnily through the phone into my ear. "He's mentioned the comments Baron Nightwood made a few times since the last meeting of the pentacle, and he always looks so grim. I can tell it's bothering him."

I shifted my weight against the worn stone wall I was leaning against and rolled my eyes in the general direction of the green. Of course she could. Dad wore displeasure like a parka, heavy and hooded on his skinny frame. You could practically hear it rustling when he moved around a room.

"Maybe he should take it up with Baron Nightwood then," I said, even though I could tell where this line of conversation was going.

Sure enough: "I just thought, since you see Malcolm so often at school, you could feel things out through him. I'm sure your father would appreciate any insight you're able to offer."

"I don't think the baron would appreciate me poking around in his son's head."

"That's not what I meant. You're friends. You must talk about things."

Yeah, and I knew better than to bring up Baron Nightwood around Malcolm. His dad was a prick on a completely different level compared to mine. When Malcolm got back from visits home, it was a good policy not to talk to him at all until he'd had at least a few hours to let off steam on whoever happened to be in his vicinity.

I tipped my face back to the sun, inhaling the sharp grassy scent from the recent mowing. "If Dad wanted me to look into this for him, *he* should be the one asking me. He's got my number too." Not that I could remember the last time he'd used it.

Mom probably couldn't either. "He doesn't like asking for help," she said in a placating tone.

That was an all-out lie. He'd known perfectly well he was "asking for help" by fussing about the subject in Mom's hearing. He just didn't have the balls to do it directly.

"I'll see what I can do," I said, by which I meant, no way in hell was I hassling Malcolm over this. It was the fastest way to end the conversation.

When I shoved the phone back in my pocket, students were just starting to trickle out of the tower across the way. A smile crept across my lips. I straightened up, scanning the various figures for a good target. A cluster would make for maximum impact. I had to time it right to make sure they were still reacting when the teachers departed after them so someone would be around to award the credit to my league.

There. A clump of five young Naries came straggling along behind most of the others, their gold leaf pins glinting in the sun. They veered across the grass to head toward the football field, and I rolled a few slithery syllables off my tongue, aiming the picture in my mind with a serpentine flick of my hand.

The trick was making the illusion potent enough to be frightening but not so over-the-top I'd be docked for potential magical exposure. I spoke my casting word again, feeling the scales and seeing the pattern along the sinewy body with the slide of the sounds off my tongue.

Bigger than the garter snakes you'd expect to find naturally around here, but not quite as big as Connar's ball python familiar. Just large enough to freak the feebs out without them thinking it was impossible for a creature like that to be weaving through the grass. All I needed was a little more concentration and another quick gesture to draw it fully solid, etching in every impression it needed to offer their senses with a prickling at the back of my skull…

One of the boys yelped and scrambled to the side, nearly tripping over his feet. A girl shrieked as she yanked the guy next to her backward. I couldn't see my creation perfectly from this distance, but their reactions and the rippling of motion through the grass between them gave me a good enough view.

Fear flowed sharp and potent through my lungs with my next breath. Fainter flutters carried from all around me as the other students turned to see what the commotion was.

I closed my eyes for a second, savoring the most delicious sensation in the world. I was never going to get tired of drinking that cocktail of alarm and panic.

All I needed was for one of the teachers to pass by on their way to the offices, and the gambit would have scored in every possible way.

I looked back toward my targets in time to see a familiar slim figure marching up to them. Shit. The breeze tossed the Bloodstone scion's dark brown waves back from her pale face, which was set with a frown. She held out a hand as if to reassure the Naries and bent down.

What the fuck was she— Seriously?

I'd cast the illusion with enough strength for it to stay solid to touch as well as sight for several minutes, and I couldn't dispel it now while the Naries were staring, even though Rory Bloodstone was lifting the snake up from the grass with her fingers clamped just behind its jaws. To avoid getting bitten, I supposed. If she'd taken it for real, at least I'd won that much even if I'd lost my chance at earning a league credit.

The snake's body twisted and squirmed beneath Rory's hand as she scanned the crowd. Several of the spectators hurried on to escape her notice, more afraid of her than of the damned creature I'd drawn for them. Cowards.

Annoying as her intervention was, I had to admit she also looked pretty spectacular standing there, fierce as an avenging angel. Too bad Blood U wasn't any place for angels.

Her gaze settled on me and stopped there. If she thought I was going to run off as if *I* were scared of her, she could forget that. I relaxed against the wall of Ashgrave Hall as she strode across the green to confront me. It was a nice enough view with her hair still swaying across her shoulders and her dress pants swishing against her slender legs below where the fabric clung to her perfectly curved hips.

"I assume this is yours," she said, shoving the snake at me.

There was no one standing close enough to see it except the two of us now. I gave a careless wave, and the snake disappeared from her hold so quickly her fingers clenched into a fist grasping after it. She blinked at her empty hand and then wiped it on her pants as if my magic might have left behind an unpleasant residue.

I offered her a grin. "If you like playing with snakes, you only had to ask. There are plenty to go around."

It was so fucking easy to get that fire to flare even brighter in her deep blue eyes. "I'd just prefer they weren't terrorizing anyone," she said. "Mission accomplished."

She swiveled as if to go. Hardly satisfying. I could get more of a rise out of her than that.

"Hold on a minute," I said. "I was going to get at least one credit out of that. You owe me something in return, Ice Pop."

Rory's gaze jerked back toward me. In that instant, I saw the same searing cold anger that she'd glared at me with in the moment when she'd realized the mouse I was letting Mischief toy with was only an illusion, not her familiar. Apparently it was going to take more than a couple days for her to get over that little transgression.

She took a quick glance around. "I'll give you ice," she said, and muttered a word under her breath with a jab of her hand. Before I had a chance to react, a glittering substance sprang up from the earth beneath my feet to encase them in a chilly coating. Like she'd done to

Malcolm the first time we'd met her—the whole reason I'd gone with those icy nicknames to tease her.

I laughed and moved to stomp myself free, except where Malcolm had been able to crack through the sheen of frost she'd conjured with one jerk, she'd tossed a whole lot more ice at me. Neither of my feet would budge beneath the thick layer.

Rory was already stalking away. She vanished into the hall before I could shout after her. Although maybe I wouldn't have wanted to shout anyway. I didn't need the newbie's help, did I?

A few of the other students were looking my way, having noticed the exchange. With a quick murmur, I drew an illusion over my feet to make it look as if the ice had melted away. Then I leaned against the wall again. With a few more surreptitious murmurs and shifts of my fingers, I tested the magic in the ice.

She sure as hell hadn't held back on me. Damn, that conjuring was tight. Physicality was *supposed* to be one of my areas of strength, but the truth was, I mostly got by using particularly careful illusions. And no illusion could actually dislodge a well-cast conjuring.

A strong talent in all four domains of magic, Ms. Grimsworth had announced yesterday after Rory's assessment. She hadn't been kidding, had she?

Rory's spell hadn't been the most artful ever, and it lacked endurance too. The edges of the ice were already melting in the spring warmth. I'd just have to wait here a few more minutes until it softened enough, and then I'd be able to crack it. Still, if she kept picking up her skills at this speed, as full of righteous spirit as ever and with more capacity for power than even Malcolm had, we might have real trouble on our hands.

The declaration of her strengths clearly hadn't left her complacent. She was going to keep following her own joymancer-tainted moral directive no matter who she pissed off along the way. We hadn't broken one bit of her.

I should have been peeved, standing there waiting for that fucking ice to melt. Instead, remembering Rory as she'd marched across the green toward me clutching the illusion of the snake, an unexpected sense of possibility unfurled in my chest.

She had more power than any of us and all that determination to prove she was better. Different. Not like all the other fearmancers. Why the hell had I ever *wanted* that broken?

I'd let myself get caught up in Malcolm's crusade without thinking through everything her presence here could mean for me.

From the moment I'd arrived on this campus, my life had felt more and more like a trap slowly closing in on me. That girl—that girl could be my doorway out.

I just had to make her want to be.

CHAPTER FOUR

Rory

I was paging through a book on Theories of Deception that my Illusion professor had recommended, propped against the pillows I'd set against my headboard, when someone tapped on my bedroom door.

"Rory, can we talk?"

It was Imogen's voice, low and hesitant. Imogen, who'd been my only friend among the fearmancers during my first month here.

Imogen, who'd sold me out to the scions and Victory's crew. She'd also been the only person who'd known about Deborah and her hiding place. She'd led them right to my familiar so they could enact their game of emotional torture. I hadn't talked to her since then, hadn't wanted to even look at her. My gut twisted into a knot right now at the thought of answering.

But we were sharing a dorm for who knew how long. Maybe it'd be better if we cleared the air.

I left the book on the bed and eased the door open a crack—just far enough to see half of Imogen's lightly freckled face framed by her tawny blond hair. As always, a silver clip held back some of the shoulder-length strands. Today she'd picked one shaped like a crescent moon.

"What do you want to talk about?" I asked.

She clasped her hands together in front of her, her mouth tight with discomfort. "I know I really screwed up, and maybe you're never going to accept an apology, but—but I'd like to at least try to make one. And to explain what happened, even if I can't justify it. If you're willing to hear me out?"

I would actually really like to know what had made her turn on me like that, but at the same time I suspected hearing it wasn't going to be much fun.

Imogen eased back a step. "There's no one else around right now if you don't want me in your space. We could talk out here."

That suggestion loosened a little of the tension inside me. I stepped out, glancing around to make sure Victory and her cronies weren't lurking after all, and followed Imogen over to one of the couches. The lingering scent of someone's rosey perfume rose off the fabric as I sat down. I curled my fingers around the edge of the firm cushion.

Imogen looked down at her hands and dragged in a breath before raising her head. Her light brown eyes met mine pleadingly.

"I never wanted to tell them anything," she said. "I hope you can at least believe that it wasn't my idea at all. I'm *so* sorry about everything that happened—what they made you think they were doing to your familiar—it was awful."

I didn't need her to tell me that. She couldn't imagine how awful it'd been for me, not least because she had no idea I'd have lost not just my animal familiar but the human guardian residing inside the mouse.

"Why did you tell them, then?" I said.

Her gaze dropped again. "Victory had seen us hanging out together. It wasn't really a secret that we were friends. She guessed that I might know something about you that they could use. She must have cast an insight spell on me and seen enough to realize there was something secret in your room. And then she threatened that she'd make up a false complaint against my dad, something bad enough to get him immediately fired, if I didn't tell her the rest."

"So you did."

"I tried not to," Imogen said, her voice strained. "I pretended I had no idea what they were talking about, but they didn't believe me. Victory called up Ms. Grimsworth and was about to say something—I knew whatever she'd tell them about my dad, they'd believe her over him and me. Her family is friends with the barons. We're not really anybody. If Dad lost his job over some scandal, I don't even know if he could find another one in the community."

I leaned back on the couch, rubbing my forehead. She'd thrown me under the bus to protect her dad. I wasn't sure I wouldn't have done the same if our positions had been reversed. I would've given in to Malcolm's demands, gotten down on my knees and offered my unwilling allegiance to him and the other scions, if I hadn't realized that Deborah wasn't really under threat.

Imogen had only known me for a few weeks. How could I expect her to have felt more loyal to me than to her family?

The betrayal still stung, though. Victory knew how to manipulate her now. What was to stop her from doing it again? Regardless of whether I understood why Imogen had done what she had, I could never completely trust her again, could I?

"I really am sorry," Imogen said with a miserable expression. "I was so relieved when you figured out the trick."

I'd seen that too—it was a bit of insight into her frantic mind that had tipped me off about the trick in the first place. She'd been in agony, not gloating like Victory and the others.

"I get it," I said. "I mean, I'm never going to be happy that it happened, but I'm not going to stay mad at you when it was Victory pulling the strings. I believe you that you didn't want to tell her."

Imogen studied me. "But you don't really want anything to do with me now either."

"It's not that. I—" I pulled my hands into my lap where they clenched. "Apology accepted, okay? The rest, we'll see how it goes."

"Okay. That's fair." She sighed and stood up. "Thank you for listening. Most people here would have sooner set my hair on fire than find out what really happened."

"Well, I think we've thoroughly established that I'm not like most people here," I muttered, and her mouth twitched with the start of a smile.

"I need to go into town to grab some groceries," she said. "Do you —do you want me to pick up anything for you?"

A peace offering? A few days ago, she'd have asked if I wanted to go with her, but she could obviously tell I wasn't in the mood to jump right back into our previous friendship. I might have taken her up on the current offer if I *had* needed anything.

"No, I'm good," I said. "But thanks."

She bobbed her head and headed out. I flopped back on the couch. My thoughts were still churning in my head, but it was kind of nice getting to stretch my legs out here in the common room rather than hiding away in my little bedroom all the time like I normally did to avoid dealing with the rest of my dormmates.

How long would it take Victory to come around? She couldn't hate me *forever*, right? As far as she knew, eventually I was going to be one of those barons her parents liked chumming up to.

Well, I was getting the hang of this magic thing, and my mere presence supplied me with a decent supply of fear now. Let her try a few more tricks on me and see how she liked being embarrassed when I turned the tables. I wasn't going to stoop to her level, but she'd better believe I'd be defending myself with every strength I had.

The relative peace lasted about five minutes. Then a knock sounded on the outer door to the dorm.

A measured voice filtered through, clear enough for me to recognize it instantly. "Rory?"

I sat up with a hitch of my pulse. Why the hell had Declan Ashgrave come calling at my dorm?

I walked cautiously over to the door. I'd seen the scions walk right past it when I'd first arrived, but I guessed it'd been Malcolm or maybe Jude who'd magically unlocked it. Declan respected the deadbolt. A minor kindness.

"What do you want?" I asked, hugging myself like I had in class a few days ago, as if the folding of my arms could protect me.

"Can I come in? It'll just take a moment."

What was the worst he could do? I didn't actually think he was out to hurt me, even if he wasn't willing to stop his friends from doing that.

I gritted my teeth and opened the door. He walked a few steps inside and stopped there, his handsome face as striking as ever, his hair neatly swept back above his bright eyes.

Apprehension prickled through me. The last time he'd been in a rush to talk to me, he'd dragged me into that closet in the library where things had taken an unpleasant turn.

"How did you know I was here?" I said abruptly. If I'd been in my bedroom, I might not even have heard the knock. "Aren't you worried about my dormmates hearing you coming calling and wondering what's up with that?"

Declan gave me a crooked smile. "Insight specialist, remember? I guess that might not have come up in any of the seminars you've been to yet. Once you've got enough practice, you can get a sense of how many people are nearby and who they are, if you know them. My dorm is right under yours."

The prickling shot deeper. "You've been *spying* on me from down there?" He was a scion, which meant they'd have given him the corner room—his bedroom would be right under mine. It wasn't as if he could watch me through the floor, but suddenly it felt as if he might as well have.

"No, nothing like that." Declan held up his hands. "I only checked because I wanted to talk. And I can't tell anything other than that you're in the room. I don't know any mage who can look inside someone's head without actually seeing that head to focus on it."

My hackles came down a smidge. I did remember Professor Sinleigh mentioning something about that. And I was glad Declan had waited until my conversation with Imogen was over before coming up. All the same…

"All right, you're here and I'm here. Again, what do you want?"

He gave me a slightly exasperated look that I didn't think was completely fair. "You asked for those extra shielding lessons, but you haven't gotten back to me to set up some times. I thought, considering… everything that's gone on, it'd be a good idea to get started sooner rather than later. I've got time right now, if you want to come back to my office, or you can tell me—"

He broke off at a sharp laugh on the other side of the door. Victory's laugh.

My heartbeat stuttered. Maybe I'd give as good as I got from Victory, but I didn't exactly want to hand her ammunition. That's exactly what she'd make of the idea that I was getting extra help. No doubt she'd use it as an excuse to test my mental shields in every possible way at every possible opportunity.

I already knew Declan wasn't going to be on board with pretending he'd come to visit for non-professional reasons. I grabbed his arm. "Come on." I hustled him across the common room and yanked him into my bedroom just as the lock clicked over.

Declan moved away from me as soon as the bedroom door had closed. I released his arm automatically, and he backed up to stand near the window, leaving plenty of space between him and me. Not really enough, though. The room felt abruptly twice as small, especially with my bed right there less than a foot from both of us. I very studiously did not look at it.

Victory's voice carried in from the common room. "If she tries to make us go over the project *again*, we'll just have to… convince her otherwise."

"You'd think they'd know better by now," Cressida replied, alongside a giggle I thought was Sinclair's.

They kept chatting away, sounding as if they'd gone into the kitchen. I caught Declan's eye where he was standing tensed with one hand gripping the back of my desk chair. Now that he was in here, there was definitely no way he could leave while they were there without raising a whole lot of questions he wouldn't be happy about.

"Sorry," I whispered. "I heard them coming and sort of panicked. They probably won't stay out there too long."

He nodded and inhaled slowly. With his exhale, he raised his hand and spoke a few words made of the nonsense syllables all the more experienced mages used to cast their spells. Once you could create a strong enough association between whatever sounds you picked and the magic you wanted to evoke, fearmancers preferred to ensure no one around could guess what they were casting and prepare.

My back went rigid, but all that happened was the voices from the common room snapped out. The room fell into silence.

"I conjured a sound barrier," Declan said. "Physicality isn't one of my strengths, but as long as they don't go prodding it, it should hold just fine. It's easier if we don't have to worry about them hearing us."

It was. I swallowed hard. "We won't know when they leave."

"I can pay attention to my impression of them out there. Don't worry, as soon as the coast is clear, I'll get out of your room."

Right. "Just like you knew when Imogen left."

He grimaced. "I promise you, I haven't generally been monitoring your comings and goings. It's just a skill that comes in handy from time to time."

He did have a point there. "Maybe you'll need to teach me that too," I said, leaning against the wall to increase the distance between us.

"Shielding seems like the more important skill to begin with." He paused. "Do you have time to come with me now—after they leave—or do you want to decide on another time to meet? We might as well get that sorted out while we're stuck here."

I had a pretty good sense of my schedule now. I probably should have sought him out to make arrangements earlier, but part of me had still been balking at the thought of spending more time in his presence. He clearly intended to hold up his side of the deal, though, and having someone I didn't trust as my tutor would at least give me extra motivation to develop my mental defenses fast.

"I have a seminar in about half an hour," I said. "But if you'll have time later this afternoon…?"

He nodded. "I've got my own classes too, but I'll be free from five onward. Meet me at the aide office then? It's right at the start of the hall by the professors' quarters."

"Okay." There, we had a plan. For everything except how to get him out of my dorm room unnoticed. I tipped my head toward the door. "They're still out there?"

"Yeah. If they don't get going soon, there are a few tricks I can try.

We just have to be careful with Victory, since she's pretty sharp… as I guess you've noticed."

"Kind of hard not to."

He motioned toward the book on the bed. "If you want to get back to your reading or whatever, don't let me stop you. You didn't ask to play host. Feel free to pretend I'm not here."

I definitely didn't want to be *on* my bed with Declan Ashgrave just a few feet away. "I'm fine right here," I said. "We don't exactly have the best track record with tight spaces."

A shadow crossed his face, and his gaze twitched away from me for a second. His jaw worked. "I'm sorry," he said. "For what happened in the library—I handled it badly."

Understatement of the century. But the fact that he'd apologized—and looked legitimately pained about it—softened me a little.

"Is that a big problem of yours?" I said, more wryly than I might have otherwise. "Preventing yourself from kissing your students?"

Declan gave me a narrow look, but a faint flush crept over his cheeks at the same time. He hesitated for long enough that I started to think the glower was the only answer I was going to get.

"No," he said quietly. "Only with the ones I'm strongly attracted to. Or rather, the one."

Heat flared beneath my skin at that remark. I fumbled for my tongue. "Well, um, I'm sorry for existing in your general vicinity, then?"

"No apologies necessary." He exhaled in a rush. "Just to be clear, I'm not saying that as a come-on. It's not going to happen again. I just don't want you to think I go around leching on every girl I see."

"Just me."

"Rory. I can control myself. I'm generally very good at it. That was… a particularly unfortunate combination of circumstances. I promise you, it was the first and last time."

Remembering the kiss, the demanding passion he'd somehow hidden behind that strict and often cold exterior, part of me couldn't help thinking that was kind of a shame. Which was maybe why my mouth kept talking without bothering to consult my brain.

"So… if you weren't a teacher's aide, then this wouldn't be a problem at all? You'd—I don't know—ask me out or something?"

He laughed, but there wasn't any humor in the sound. "No, the circumstances are never going to be *good*, with the positions we're in." He paused at my quizzical look. "Has no one explained about the pentacle inheritances yet?"

"I know there's a pentacle of barons and of scions," I said. "The five ruling families—I think that's how Ms. Grimsworth put it. And the authority is passed on from parents to kids. I don't think anyone's mentioned more than that. Why? Are the families not supposed to mix?" Connar hadn't seemed worried about that, but then, as far as I could tell, he'd simply been stringing me along until he got what he wanted.

"There aren't any rules along those lines. But you can't be part of two families at once, and you're the only living Bloodstone. Whoever you end up marrying, they'll have to be a Bloodstone too. If you partner with another scion, they'd be giving up their barony."

"Oh." That possibility definitely hadn't occurred to me. "Then what happens to that barony?"

"It'd go to the next blood relative, assuming there is one," Declan said. "But I don't have any plans to throw away my position. I've spent my whole life working to make sure I can take it in the first place."

Well, that made sense. I wasn't sure what to say to that, though.

Before I could decide on an appropriate response, Declan's head twitched toward the door. "They're heading out," he said. "I'll give them a minute to go down the stairs, and then I'll get out of your hair."

Now that he'd actually been talking to me like a human being, I didn't completely want him to go, regardless of the circumstances. I'd see him in a few hours for our tutoring session, of course. But the thought of Connar had stirred up too many little knives of emotion for me to ignore.

"I get that the favoritism, and rules, and circumstances, and all that are important to you," I said with a vague gesture. "But—can you pick how you're going to act with me and just stick with that, no matter who's around? Because I would really prefer not to deal with being jerked around between friendly and asshole any more than I already have been, if that's all right with you."

My voice might have gotten a little raw. Declan considered me. "You're not just talking about me."

"I—"

His expression tightened. "Did Malcolm—"

"No," I said quickly. "No, Malcolm has been an asshole the whole way through."

Declan hadn't stopped studying me. With a jolt of panic, I concentrated on the steel shell around my mind I'd pictured before, however useful that amateur shield would be against a guy who'd specialized in Insight for years. "I'd also appreciate it if you didn't go magically poking around inside my head."

He blinked. "I'm not. I was just thinking back. When Connar tore into you the other day… you looked shocked."

Fuck. "I'd really rather not talk about it."

"Okay," Declan said, even though his expression was still puzzled. Given the alternately stern and ferocious demeanor his friend had shown any time I'd seen them together, it probably would surprise him to think Connar and I had somehow found common ground, even if it hadn't lasted. "I'll do my best to be predictable. We're still on for five?"

"I'll be there."

He dipped his head to me and waved his hand, I assumed to bring down the sound barrier he'd conjured. "I'll see you then."

It was only after he'd ducked out that the other implications of his confusion sank in.

He hadn't known that anything had happened between Connar and me. Which meant Connar hadn't told the other scions. Why not, if he'd only buttered me up so he could get his rocks off and then taunt me afterward? Shouldn't he have been celebrating how he'd landed that blow?

And if his betrayal hadn't been part of their whole scheme to knock me down, why the hell *had* he done it?

CHAPTER FIVE

Rory

We were all getting up to head out of my second Illusion seminar of the week when the door shifted. In the space of a second, the wooden surface twisted into a gigantic demonic face, gnashing its teeth at the nearest students, who stumbled backward.

The demon let out a harsh cackle that set my nerves jangling and then was absorbed back into the door. A guy at the back of the class—Alex? Alan? I had a lot of names to pick up—chuckled and gave a bow.

"Very nice detail and combination of visual and auditory components, Mr. Rutland," Professor Burnbuck said in a dry voice. "Credit to Illusion."

And a nice jolt of fear for the caster too.

I hurried on out with the rest of the class, but somehow Alex-or-Alan Rutland caught up with me, sauntering down the tower stairs with a smile that could only be described as self-satisfied.

"I think that was my best work yet," he said.

I glanced around. As far as I could tell, he was talking to me, even though we'd never spoken before. "Ah," I said, with as clear a lack of enthusiasm as I could pack into one syllable. What did *he* want from me?

"I'm strong in Physicality too—it makes for a pretty potent combination. While you're getting the hang of things around here, I'd be happy to give you a few pointers."

If this had been my regular college back in California, populated by regular people who didn't make a living out of terrorizing everyone around them, I wouldn't have blinked at the offer. But I was at Bloodstone University, accurately nicknamed Villain Academy by the mages who didn't attend it, and this was the first time in a month anyone had volunteered a helping hand, unless you counted Malcolm's initial posturing offer of friendship.

There was not looking a gift horse in the mouth, and then there was not being a total idiot.

"Thanks," I said mildly. "I think I'm picking things up okay, though."

"Maybe I could treat you to a night on the town then," the guy said as we stepped out into the cool morning air. The day had started out damp and dreary and was continuing in the same direction. "And not that dinky town down the road. Much better nightlife if we take an hour's drive in my Jag." He slung his hands in his pockets, putting on a casual stance even as he purposefully flexed his arms.

Oh. *Oh*. Was he *flirting* with me?

I had to catch myself before a laugh sputtered out of me. This guy clearly hadn't paid much attention to me if he thought the promise of nightlife and a fancy car was the way to my heart. Why the hell was he even—

Declan's explanation about the fearmancer laws of inheritance came back to me. *Whoever you end up marrying, they'll have to be a Bloodstone too*. Although the way these people jockeyed for power, to anyone not already a scion, that "have to" was probably more like "gleefully get to."

My affections were a ticket straight to the ranks of the barons.

"I don't think that's a good idea," I said.

"You won't know until you give it a shot, will you? I promise I'll show you a good time."

I stopped and spun on the guy. "What do you know about me other than my name and the fact that I was assessed with all four strengths?"

He just stared at me for a second with his mouth half-open. Yeah, obviously nothing, because those two facts were all that mattered to him.

"You don't get along well with Malcolm Nightwood," he ventured after way too long a pause.

I restrained a snort. That fact was almost as obvious as the other two. "I don't think I'm going to get along very well with you either, all right?" I said. An instinct took over to step a little closer, to draw myself up straighter, as I let steel lace my voice. "I'm not here to be your stepping stone, and I don't think you want to find out what'll happen if you try."

A wave of fear raced from him into my chest. He backed up, his eyes narrowing. "Message received," he snapped, but he hightailed it out of there so fast you'd have thought I'd sent a demon charging after *him*.

The rush of power I'd felt in that moment faded with a queasy twist in my stomach. I hadn't needed to be that harsh with him.

Making him scared shouldn't have felt that good.

I was built to enjoy it. Built to seek out every opportunity to absorb people's fear. That didn't mean I had to give in to those impulses, though. I'd just keep a closer rein on myself the next time I got frustrated.

And maybe I'd be less inclined toward those impulses if I made sure I had plenty of magical energy already stockpiled.

Instead of heading to the library like I'd planned, I set off across the field toward the forest that surrounded most of the campus. Making the local wildlife nervous with my comings and goings was an easy way to top up my supply of fear without being a jerk to anyone.

The air in the woods clung even more damply to my skin, but as soon as the trees closed around me, I reveled in the relative silence and solitude. No one watching me, evaluating me, deciding how they could use me or hurt me. Even in my bedroom, it was hard to feel completely alone with just that thin door between me and the common area.

A little melancholy crept in with the peace. The northern atmosphere might not match the one I'd grown up with, but it was hard not to remember the walks I'd taken with my parents on our periodic trips to this or that state park: Mom snapping photos, Dad chatting it up with other hikers we passed, me pulling out my sketch pad whenever we paused to make a quick pencil study of this flower or that interesting tree.

Never again.

That knowledge squeezed around my throat. I walked faster to outpace my grief as well as I could. It wasn't going to help me in this place.

I rambled through the brush until the uneven ground started to make my calves ache and a multitude of tiny quivers had filled the space behind my collarbone. As I turned back toward campus, a heavier crunch of a fallen branch froze me in my tracks.

A figure was picking his way through the trees toward me. It only took a moment for his coppery hair to stand out amid the vivid spring greenery.

Jude cocked his head as he reached me. "I thought I saw someone from the path. There *is* a path, you know."

"Sometimes I like to make my own," I said, my posture rigid.

He laughed, but it didn't sound as mocking as usual. "Fair."

"Well, now you know it's me. I'll be on my way."

"Hold on, Ice Queen," he said as I moved to walk away. His tiny golden dagger earring winked with the sunlight filtering through the leaves overhead.

I raised my eyebrows at him, unable to hold back the question. "I get to be queen after all?"

His mouth had settled into a lazy smile that only emphasized everything that was attractive in his boyishly wicked face. "After that little display the other day, I think you've earned the title."

That was unexpected. After my initial, rather pathetic attempt at freezing Malcolm in place to stop him from harassing some junior student, Jude had made a game out of calling me as many ridiculous ice-themed nicknames as he could. I couldn't tell what he was playing at now.

"Where are you headed?" he asked.

"Back to school," I said, because he'd figure that out soon enough just by watching me.

"So was I. I'll walk with you."

That would be a no. I raised my chin. "I wasn't looking for company. Anyway, I thought you preferred the path."

"Depends on who I'm walking with." He spread his hands in a gesture of appeal. "Can't we get along as fellow scions? You've proven yourself, beat the hell out of the assessment. I respect that. No need for us to be at each other's throats. We *are* going to have to work together someday."

I'd always had a hard time figuring Jude out, but he was outdoing himself today. Did he expect me to believe this white flag was genuine?

I shifted my weight. "Malcolm doesn't seem to think the war is over."

Jude made a show of peering around himself every which way, giving me an excellent view of his leanly muscled body in his dress shirt and slacks. "Just as I thought. The heir of Nightwood doesn't have me on a leash. Malcolm's a stubborn prick, I'll give you that. I see more value in flexibility."

And that would be great, except I don't believe you.

My skepticism must have shown on my face as I debated what to say. Jude waggled a finger at me. "Maybe I shouldn't be telling you about stubbornness. Was I really that awful to you?"

Oh, did he want a list of transgressions? I counted them off on one hand. "You ripped into me in Insight class and made sure everyone heard all the embarrassing memories you dug up. You made fun of me after I had to relive my parents' *murders* in Desensitization. You helped kidnap my familiar and did everything you could to convince me yours was going to eat it piece by piece. And that's only the things I know for sure." Who knew how much he might have helped Malcolm with one scheme or another along the way?

Jude hummed to himself. "It seems to me that my first crime came after you'd already taken a jab at me—"

"I was just completing the exercise!" I said. "And if you're going to get technical about it, *you* still took the first jab."

"—*and* insulted me and the other scions in front of most of your dorm, without any provocation I can think of."

"How about the provocation of you'd been acting like jerks the entire time I'd been around you?" I grumbled.

Jude ignored me, sailing smoothly onward. "I don't recall making any snarky remarks to you after your desensitization session until you'd already insulted my intelligence. And your familiar wasn't the slightest bit hurt."

"It was still a horrible situation to put me in."

"We were testing you. Making sure you'd live up to your title. That's how things work here and out there." He motioned in the general direction of town, but I knew he meant the wider fearmancer community. "You rose to the challenge; I recognize that. It's done."

Was it really that easy for him and everyone else here to shrug off the way they treated each other?

"I didn't grow up like all of you did," I said. "Those aren't the kinds of rules I follow."

"But you're here now, and *we* didn't grow up the way *you* did. You don't join a symphony and get mad that no one will jam along with your ukulele."

I didn't want to "join" at all, I shouted inside my head, but it wouldn't be smart to say that out loud. I still needed to give some appearance of wanting to be here, or I'd never get enough access to figure out how to undermine the place.

"Fine," I said. "You were doing what seemed to you like normal things to do. That doesn't mean I have to like it—or want to see what the hell you might decide to do to me next. Do *you* honestly like living this way, always at each other's throats?"

Jude paused. For the first time, a more serious cast came over his expression. When he smiled again, the edges were sharper.

"Maybe I don't," he said archly. "Maybe that's why I'm here talking to you right now."

I *really* didn't know what to make of that. In my silence, he shrugged.

"Forget all of that, then. Let's make it simple. Your life would be easier having me as a friend rather than an enemy, if you get to choose, wouldn't it?"

"Is that a threat?"

He rolled his eyes. "No, it's just a question. Friend versus person-you-have-nothing-to-do-with, if you're going to get nitpicky."

"I guess it would," I said. If I could have trusted him to be an actual friend.

"There you go. Maybe you haven't developed the fearmancer taste for blood yet, but you're already as practical as one."

I bristled, wishing I could take back my answer, but to my relief Jude stepped back.

"You need some time to stew on it," he said. "I can take a hint. Think hard and well, Ice Queen."

With a jaunty salute, he strolled off toward the path.

I waited until he was out of sight, all my senses gradually easing off of high alert, before I continued toward campus. Had that been the opening to some new scheme from the scions? Or had he actually *meant* what he'd said?

It didn't really matter. I couldn't picture ever calling Jude Killbrook a "friend." But there was some truth to that old saying about keeping friends close but enemies closer.

The wind picked up as I reached the edge of the campus, thick and damp. When I tugged my hair back behind my ears, the currents of the air yanked at the dark waves a second later.

A small group of mages—juniors from the look of them—stood farther down the line of the forest tossing birds I assumed were their familiars up into the air and laughing. To train them for bad weather? To drink in the animals' fear at trying to fly in the growing gale? Lord only knew in this place.

I'd taken three steps across the field when a wrenching groan filled my ears. I spun around in time to see a huge oak topple over right into the group of mages.

I looked up at the sound of footsteps where I was sitting on a stiffly cushioned chair in the reception area of the health center. Professor Banefield stepped inside, his gaze moving straight to me. He sat his barrel-chested form down on the chair across from me.

"I heard you were here," he said. "Did you know one of the injured students?"

I shook my head. "I just—I saw it happen. I wanted to make sure — No one will tell me if they're okay. Do you know if they're okay?" I'd been sitting here for two hours, waiting for news. One of the kids had walked out with a brace on her wrist and a couple bruises, but two others were still off in the inner rooms.

"I believe one has finished treatment and is simply resting as he fully recovers. The other— From what I heard, there was damage to her skull. A brain injury is no easy thing even with magic."

Especially not magic designed for tormenting people. My jaw clenched, but some of the anger in me snuffed out when I looked at Banefield. His shoulders were slumped, his expression as weary as if he hadn't slept in days.

He might have known at least one of the kids. He taught the junior Insight classes. Hell, he probably knew all three of them.

Maybe I did have a taste for blood after all, because I couldn't help saying, all the same, "That was the tree Shelby was talking about. The one she was worried had rotted."

"Yes," Banefield said. "Clearly."

He looked at me like a man before a firing squad, waiting for me to take the next shot. The killing blow. *If you'd just listened to me…*

No, I didn't really want blood after all. There was enough of it already on the ground under that fallen tree.

"They're still people," I said instead. "*We're* still people, not gods or something. Sometimes they're going to be right. Sometimes we'll make mistakes. That's all I was trying to say before."

Which the current disaster had proven amply true. A swell of guilt overwhelmed any remaining anger. I dropped my face into my hands. "I should have pushed harder. I should have gone to talk to the maintenance staff myself."

"Rory…" Banefield cleared his throat and shifted forward on his chair to rest a hand on my head in an almost fatherly gesture. "This isn't on you."

I couldn't stop a little bitterness from leaking into my voice as I swiped at my eyes. "I guess this is just more of that weakness you talked about, caring about other people."

Banefield was silent for a moment. "No," he said. "I don't think it is."

He withdrew his hand. We sat there without speaking for a while as I gathered my composure. Then he got up. "There isn't anything useful either of us can do here. Why don't you go back to your dorm and take some time for yourself? We can talk more later. If you need to reach out to someone in the next day, you can speak to Ms. Grimsworth or any of your professors. I have to take a trip off campus."

A trip? Now—to go where? But he was already heading out the door. All I got was a glimpse of determination tensing his exhausted face before he was gone.

CHAPTER SIX

Malcolm

Taking a run with Connar was always a good challenge. He might be as big as a linebacker, but he could keep up a good pace for an hour without breaking much of a sweat. My own tee was sticking damp to my back by the time we started to slow as we passed the lake for the sixth time. My familiar, loping alongside us, pulled ahead and then glanced back at me with one of those wolf expressions that seemed to say, *Is that all you've got?*

The early morning breeze cooled the sweat on my skin in an instant. I swiped the workout towel over the back of my neck. The burn of the exercise had spread through my calves up into my chest, exactly the way I liked it. You couldn't keep up magical endurance unless you had the physical endurance to support it.

Shadow circled us with a huff. "You need more of a challenge?" I said with a smile, and fished the rubber ball he was oddly fond of out of my pocket. He twitched with anticipation at the sight of it. I whipped it across the field as hard as I could, and he dashed after it in a blur with a joyful panting. My smile stretched into a grin as I watched. He'd have run the whole day if he could.

Connar and I had fallen into the casual jog of our cooldown, which made it easier to talk. "Sometime we'll have to drag Jude and Declan along on one of these runs," I said, mainly for the snort I knew I'd get from him in response.

"They'd fall over before we were halfway through," he replied, but his amused smile only lasted an instant. Insight might be the one area I couldn't claim a strength in, but I thought I could say the guy had been even grimmer and more taciturn than usual in the past week.

I could take a few guesses at the reason. The main one was named Rory Bloodstone.

"All the more reason they should start working up to it." I nodded to the triangle of buildings we were coming up on. "At least Declan's making himself useful in other ways. Sinleigh set him up as our Bloodstone scion's tutor. That should get us some good material to work with."

Connar's jaw tightened. "She's picked herself up pretty well since the assessment. And she was awfully hard to shake before that too."

He didn't need to remind me. A prickle of tension ran down my spine thinking of her dazed but triumphant expression when Ms. Grimsworth had announced her results, my brief encounter with her afterward when she'd answered my threat with one of her own. The way she'd asked about the burn mark I hadn't been hiding well enough, my defenses momentarily lowered because I thought I was alone… I wasn't going to let her see another hint of vulnerability, that was for sure.

I waved my hand dismissively. "Maybe we came on too strong to begin with and that backfired a bit. There are plenty of subtle tactics that can do the trick. Don't worry, we've got this. No way in hell are we letting her spend the rest of her time here reciting joymancer philosophies and mouthing off at us."

I hadn't worked my ass off and endured everything I had to cement my position only to have this girl barge into our lives like a bolt of lightning and bring it all crashing down. She might be riding high now, but I'd seen how quickly currents could shift, especially when there was blood in the water.

Connar hadn't seemed all that concerned at first by the feud that had developed between the four of us and Rory, happy to lend support as needed and otherwise to let Jude and me lay our plans. Apparently her defiance had been gnawing at him underneath. I'd never seen him go off on someone out of the blue like when he'd ripped into her that one day while we'd been matching Declan's hawk against another senior's falcon. His temper could be explosive, sure, but you could generally see it coming with the lighting of the fuse.

Rory hadn't said a word to us, hadn't even been looking at us, as far as I'd been able to tell. He'd simply snapped at the sight of her.

Connar's expression didn't shift. "What plans have you got in the works now?"

"It starts with a slow build, and then we'll ramp it up fast once she starts to wobble. She's still a fish out of water here. She's not going to find much support. We make her feel completely unstable in all those righteous attitudes of hers, and she'll have to turn to the authorities for help. Who better to set her straight than her fellow scions? With Declan there, we've already got one foot in the door."

"She might just crash and burn on her own."

I grimaced. "It already looks bad that she's gotten away with so much crap in the first place. We need her in line before *she* undermines our authority in any permanent way. And the barons want her ready to join in the pentacle as soon as possible—with the appropriate respect in place."

Dad had given me a nice long lecture about that this weekend, along with the cut now scabbed over but stinging on the inside of my arm. As always I'd cast an illusion to hide the injury. More training. A Nightwood should never let anyone see he was wounded. A year after I'd started at Blood U, my parents had started dealing out those sorts of lessons with less care in the expectation that I had the skills to pick up the slack.

"Well, you know if you need anything from me…"

"Of course." I cuffed him lightly on the side. "We just want her to struggle… in quiet sorts of ways. Has she ended up in any of your classes?"

"One of my Physicality seminars," he said.

"Perfect. Even you should be able to do subtle in your own

league." I shot him a teasing grin. "Funny how her conjurings will just keep falling apart for no reason she can see."

"Yeah. I can manage that."

He didn't sound all that happy about the prospect. I eyed him as we slowed to a walk, Shadow running wolfish circles around us. "Is something else eating at you?" If Professor Darksend had been hassling Connar about the stupid tourney again, I'd shove his head up his ass.

"What?" Connar looked momentarily unsettled, or maybe I misread that, because a second later he was smiling his usual quiet smile. "No. I'm good to go, whatever you need."

"There's nothing left to do for this bit. I set up this morning's move last night. We should be just in time…"

With a glance at the time, I motioned for him to follow me toward Ashgrave Hall. It was still so early that only a couple of students had ventured out onto the green. Most of the dorm room windows stood at least a little open to let in the fresh spring air. I expected we'd have heard Rory even without that factor, though.

We were about ten feet distant when the first shout carried from her room at the top right corner of the building, opposite mine. Rory's voice broke through the air hollering a wordless sound of frustration and then sputtered into a flurry of swearing. Connar gave me a quizzical look.

I chuckled. "She's still asleep. She doesn't even know what she's doing."

When I listened carefully, I made out the rasp of tearing fabric. Exactly as designed. Everyone in her dorm would be hearing that commotion. She wasn't the only person who'd think she was getting unstable.

Connar's stance had tensed, but he nodded to me. "Sounds like you got her good. I'd better shower before I have to get to class."

"If you don't mind missing the end of the show."

"I can tell there's lots more to come."

He disappeared into the building. Rory's voice had petered out. She'd have woken up by now. Given the state she should find herself in, I'd imagine it wouldn't take long before she made an appearance.

I whistled to Shadow and crouched down as he loped over. He

dropped the ball at my feet and ducked his head for a scratch between the ears. I gave him a good one, his dark fur coarse but soft beneath my fingers.

Ms. Grimsworth had decreed that because of my familiar's size, he had to keep to the kennel during class hours. I'd campaigned against the idea, but I hadn't won that fight.

It wasn't right. Wolves weren't meant to be kept caged. Leaving him behind in that building on the edge of campus always jabbed a thorn of guilt into my side. When we left Blood U, I'd make sure he had free run all day wherever we ended up going.

"You've got another hour or so, boy," I said, extending the scratching to the crook of his jaw for good measure. "You want to give the woods another roam?"

His ears perked up, probably detecting my meaning as much through our familiar bond as the words themselves. "I can't come with you," I added. "We'll go for a proper hunt tonight."

He trotted off, I straightened up, and the Bloodstone scion came striding out through the main door of Ashgrave Hall, just a few feet away.

Rory's hair was in disarray, clearly not combed with anything other than a swipe of her fingers since she'd woken up. Her blouse hung unevenly over her sleek jeans. And yet she still managed to look so stunning that fuck me if my pulse didn't skip a beat in that moment.

Of course, part of that was anticipation. "Hey, Glinda!" I called out before she'd taken two steps toward Killbrook Hall—off to see her mentor or maybe the headmistress, no doubt. "You don't look so hot. Wake up on the wrong side of the bed?"

Rory spun around. She might have looked flustered, but her dark blue eyes still flashed with that gleam of challenge when they met mine. Somehow that iron will rose up whenever the two of us faced off. Now that I knew to expect it, the sight sent a thrill through me alongside my resolve.

"It was you, wasn't it?" she snapped. "One of your stupid persuasion spells, probably."

I let my eyes widen and held up my hands. "I haven't got a clue what you're talking about. I just got back from an hour's run with my familiar around campus."

Her gaze flicked over me, taking in my sweaty shirt and the exercise towel tucked over my shoulder. Glancing farther, she'd have caught sight of Shadow just before he vanished into the forest.

She let out her breath in a huff. Her voice came out so fierce yet husky that it provoked a deeper thrill straight down to my groin.

"If you are doing something, I am going to find out, and then you're going to regret it."

"I look forward to it," I said with a cheery wave.

She made a face at me and hurried off. Her stride wasn't quite as steady as it usually was. I should have felt victorious as I watched her march into the other hall, but mixed in with the triumph was the same sort of jab as when I ordered Shadow into that godawful kennel.

Rory Bloodstone wasn't meant to wobble. It wasn't a good look on her at all. Why the hell did she have to cling to her pretentious joymancer ideas about heroes and villains so stubbornly?

If she would just fucking admit she needed us, then we could get on with the good parts of having the full pentacle of scions together at long last. And she *did* need us, whether she wanted to accept it or not.

None of us made it alone, not in the field of barons and heirs.

CHAPTER SEVEN

Rory

I stopped just inside Killbrook Hall to take a deep breath and take a stab at tidying my rumpled hair. It was possible I was going crazy, but I'd really prefer not to convince Professor Banefield of that before I even opened my mouth.

He had to be back, didn't he? It'd been two days ago he'd said he was leaving for his "trip." We were supposed to have a mentoring session in an hour and a half anyway. Surely he'd have sent a message along if he'd had to cancel it?

If he wasn't there, I didn't know who I'd talk to. Ms. Grimsworth didn't exactly put me at ease, even if she had warmed up a bit since discovering my many strengths.

Just remembering how I'd woken up turned my innards into one huge knot. The tips of my fingers still throbbed from where I must have dug them into the folds of my sheet, hard enough to wrench the fabric apart. Because that's how I'd found myself when I'd hurtled out of sleep with my throat raw and my ears ringing—tangled up in torn strips, bits of thread clinging to my skin and my pajamas.

I hadn't even been dreaming, as far as I could remember. I'd torn into the sheet for no reason I could imagine, and Deborah had told me I'd been yelling too. Nothing pleasant, from her hesitance in mentioning that part.

I couldn't wake you up, just like I couldn't last week when you got caught up in writing on that paper, she'd said with an anxious paw on my hand. *I couldn't get close as it was, the way you were… moving around. I peeked out into the dorm, but the other girls around all looked startled.*

I'd asked her if she could scurry through the walls to check Declan's room below mine, just in case. Even if I didn't want to believe he would mess with me like that after the tentative understanding we'd come to, one of the other scions might have been able to use his room to get close enough to effectively cast. But she'd returned to report that it'd been empty, no one around.

My dormmates who'd been up had still looked startled when I'd emerged a few minutes later after a hasty change. Even Victory, who'd been standing by the table, had stiffened as if she were wary of what *I* might do even as she'd arched her eyebrows. The other girls had averted their gazes and given me a wide berth, one of them flinching at the tap of my footsteps.

A whole lot of nervous fear had flooded me, but I hadn't gotten any satisfaction from it at all.

And then Malcolm had been waiting outside with his goading comments. Maybe it'd just been an awful coincidence… but if he didn't have anything to do with my weird episodes, and my dormmates didn't either, then the problem was probably me, wasn't it? Something in my own head, nothing magical at all—or a response to the magic I wasn't used to that was now flowing through me more and more potently.

I swallowed thickly at that thought. None of the staff had mentioned any concerns that my time with my joymancer parents, the four or so years while my natural magic had been completely suppressed, might have any negative effects. Had they ever known any fearmancers who'd been stifled like that before, though?

A senior guy I vaguely recognized walked out of the hall that led to the staff wing. Someone with an official early morning appointment with one of the professors, I guessed. His gait slowed when he saw me, and my back automatically went rigid. He clearly recognized *me.*

I caught a flicker of anxiety, and then he was striding up to me, his jaw set. He bobbed his head in a weird almost-bow when he stopped in front of me. "Rory Bloodstone. I was hoping I'd get a chance to talk to you. I—I'm taking part in a challenge on the casting grounds this afternoon. It would be an honor if you'd watch my performance. I do intend to win."

I blinked at him. He didn't sound as if he were happy to be talking to me or he really wanted me spending any more time around him than was happening right now. At least the guy who'd tried to flirt with me the other day had seemed like he thought it was a good idea until I'd told him off. Or maybe this wasn't a come-on but some bizarre fearmancer custom that no one had bothered to tell me about.

"Why?" I said. I didn't have the energy to beat around the bush right now.

A sharper flare of fear shot into my chest. It felt a lot more like panic than nervous jitters. Why the hell was he talking to me at all if I made him this uncomfortable?

His hands fumbled in front of him as if he thought he could grasp onto an answer with them. "I—I think you'd be impressed with what you see. My family has a strong heritage in both Illusion and Persuasion."

Okay, I was pretty sure this was another attempt at dating me. Fearmancers just had really weird approaches to courting.

"Look," I said, as gently as I could manage around my already frayed nerves, "I don't give a crap about your family heritage. I mean, not just yours, but anyone's. All right? And I'm not really interested in having people impress me either. You'll probably do better with your challenge if you're not inviting people you're terrified of."

That last bit might have been a little too much honesty. His expression flickered, and his posture tensed more than it already was. "I didn't mean to offend you," he sputtered, and dashed off before I could tell him he hadn't really.

One of the juniors who lived in the dorms above had come into the front hall while we'd been talking. She glanced after the guy and then gave me a haughty look that reminded me of Victory, although this girl couldn't have been more than fifteen.

"Don't be mad at him," she said in a slightly sneering tone. "His parents probably put him up to it. Landing a scion would be a *big* step up for them."

"Thanks for the… tip," I said, feeling abruptly defensive of the guy. God, if he'd put himself through that conversation despite his fear of me, how much *more* terrified was he of his parents? "Maybe everyone here should practice staying out of other people's business."

At the sharpness in my voice, a flicker of anxiety rippled out of her. She took a step back. I restrained a groan and hurried off toward the staff wing before I could inadvertently terrorize anyone else.

The hall with the professors' offices—each of which led into their personal apartments, from what I'd gathered—was totally quiet. My steps sounded too loud despite the thick carpeting on the floor. I stopped at the door with *Prof. Archer Banefield* engraved on the bronze plaque and knocked, first softly and then, when I didn't get an answer, as hard as I dared.

I didn't hear anything from the other side. I was debating between trying one more time and just stewing in my worries until our actual meeting time when the lock clicked over.

Banefield opened the door looking rather rumpled himself, which was saying something when he never came across as all that neat to begin with. If possible, his light red hair was sticking out in even more directions than usual, his shirt buttons were off by one, and he was still in his socked feet.

"Rory," he said, managing his usual warm tone despite his disarray. "I wasn't expecting you this early. I was still in the process of, ah, getting myself together for the day."

Embarrassment flared in my chest. "I'm sorry. I can come back later. I just—this morning—I needed to talk to someone, but it can wait."

His eyebrows drew together as he took me in, concern shadowing his eyes. I guessed my attempt at composing myself hadn't been a total success. He motioned me in. "No, it's all right. You're here now. Why don't you sit down and tell me what happened?"

Once I was in his office, sitting on the rich brocade of the armchair where I'd spent so many mentoring sessions, I felt even more awkward. "I'm not even sure exactly what's going on," I said. "Whether it's me or someone using magic on me or… or what." Were there other possibilities beyond those two? I hoped not. "If it's someone else messing with me, I know I should deal with that myself. It's just—if it's *me*—I'm not really sure what to do. I thought someone should know, anyway."

Banefield leaned back in his chair with a puzzled frown. "What exactly *has* happened?"

I explained about the time last week when I'd gone into the daze and then how I'd woken up this morning, leaving out the parts about Deborah's attempts to intervene and her observations of the nearby students. When I'd finished, Banefield's frown had deepened. He looked almost… *angry*.

He'd never seemed all that perturbed by the treatment I was getting from the rest of the student body before, and honestly a lot of that had been worse than this, just easier to identify. I hadn't screwed up with how I'd handled the episodes, had I?

"You're right that an immediate casting generally requires close proximity," he said, setting his elbows on his desk with a thump. "Have you checked your room for any objects that might be holding a sustained spell?"

I nodded. Deborah and I both had the first time, and we'd done another quick sweep this morning while I'd thrown on my clothes. "I haven't found anything that I can tell has magic in it."

"You should be able to sense anything that could have that strong an effect on your mind. If there's anything you could have failed to check—clothing, or personal articles that often leave the room with you…"

"I checked *everything*," I said. "The last thing I want is for this to keep happening."

He rubbed his mouth. "Professor Sinleigh told me she arranged for you to begin additional tutoring in mental shielding with her aide. Has that started yet?"

"We've met up twice," I said. "It's definitely helped. I'm getting in the habit of maintaining a low-level shield without needing to constantly think about it—while I'm awake. I guess it'll take more practice before I can keep up that kind of security while I'm asleep. But if there isn't anyone or anything around working the magic, then maybe it's not coming from outside my head, right? I don't know—I never had any teaching or practice with this stuff, and then all of a sudden…"

I faltered before I forced myself to say my deepest fear, but Banefield picked up on the direction I was heading in. He met my eyes with a firm expression.

"There's nothing wrong with you, Rory," he said. "I'm sure of that much. Even if we haven't determined how, what you're experiencing… It will be the work of outside forces."

"How can you know that?" I said. "How often do long-lost scions turn up needing to figure out their magic years later than every other student?"

He paused with a twitch of his jaw. His gaze slipped away from me. His fingers laced together, his knuckles whitening as if he were grappling with something between them. When he finally looked at me again, his words came out low and rushed.

"I don't know how much I'll be able to say. They may have— But we need you, I can see that, and I can't let them— You *have* to stay on guard. There are plans being put into motion, and the—"

His voice cut off with a hitch. The color drained from his face as he pressed his hand to his gut. His mouth tightened into a thin line.

"Professor?" I said with a jolt of panic that was no one's but my own.

He opened his mouth and then doubled over with a violent retching sound. I scrambled to my feet. Before I'd even made it to his side, his body sagged over the arm of his chair as if all the life had gone out of him.

CHAPTER EIGHT

Rory

Will he be all right? Deborah asked from where she was cuddled next to my leg at the edge of my bed.

I ran my thumb over her soft fur, summoning the bits of hope I'd found beneath the heavy weight inside me. The sun was beaming outside the window, but it didn't brighten my mood.

"I'm not sure," I said—quietly, aware of the clinking of silverware as my roommates ate lunch in the common room. "The mages who work in the health center didn't want to tell me anything more this morning than they did yesterday. They did say he was improving, at least, and I think they expected he'd be going back to his quarters pretty soon. But they're talking as if it's just a bad stomach bug and he fainted because it came on so fast."

Hmph. Very convenient timing for a severe flu to kick in suddenly when he was about to tell you something important for your safety.

"Yeah." I'd spent an awful lot of time thinking about that since Professor Banefield's collapse. I just wasn't sure how it could have been a purposeful attack. We'd been alone in the room and talking normally—I didn't think anyone outside could have heard what he was saying.

After the way Banefield had asked about searching my room for spelled objects, I didn't think he slacked off in that area himself. But there was still so much about magic I didn't know.

He was the one I'd have gone to with a question like this, which obviously was out of question. Deborah had shuddered in horror at the idea of someone causing an illness like that—joymancers usually went around curing them, like my dad had during his volunteer hours at the hospital—so she wasn't any help. Who else could I talk to about it without potentially putting Banefield or myself in even more danger if it had been purposeful?

I was an official student now, with a place on campus no one could take away from me and powers everyone was starting to respect, but in some ways I was still as alone and adrift as I'd been when I'd first set foot on campus. Maybe even more so, now that I knew what horrors the people here were capable of.

"Keep listening at the walls," I said, "as far as you can safely go around the building without being seen." It seemed unlikely that any of the students would be involved in a magical assault on a professor, but it couldn't hurt to monitor things. "If someone is hurting him, I have to help him. He was obviously trying to help *me*—it seemed almost like he knew something about the weird stuff I've been experiencing, or at least who might have caused it. 'They' and 'them'..."

Could it be the other scions?

I frowned. "I don't think so. Banefield didn't step in even when Malcolm was being awful to me in front of everyone last month. Why would he suddenly care so much about ripped sheets and random writing? He said he was taking a trip somewhere—he was gone for at least a day—right before this... Maybe that had something to do with it. Or with whatever he found out that he wanted to tell me. I wonder if I should take a trip too."

Deborah nuzzled my knee. *What do you mean?*

"I don't know where he went, but my family—my birth family—has properties I've never seen yet. The Bloodstones could have enemies I don't know about. There might be information out there I can use. I just have to figure out how to get out to them."

Shelby had mentioned that there were buses that stopped by town, but who knew if they'd get me to the right places. Most of the students seemed to have their own cars, or else they had their parents or a chauffeur pick them up when they wanted to go somewhere. The school had a chauffeur or two of its own, but I didn't really want to call on one of those to take me on what could be a day-long road trip. Especially when I didn't know if I could trust *them* either.

"I'll have to talk to Ms. Grimsworth," I said. "I'd need her to loosen up the tracking spell on me if I'm going that far anyway."

Are you sure venturing out there is a good idea? If your family has enemies, which they very well might given the way these people operate, they'll find it much easier to hurt you if you're out there on your own.

"I know. But I can't just sit around here hoping answers will drop into my lap." I gave her fur another stroke of my thumb. "Don't be a Debbie Downer. I've made it this far. I think I'll survive a little longer. It'd be good to have more room to maneuver." At the very least, I didn't think anyone wanted to outright kill the Bloodstone scion. What would happen to their rulership then?

I had to wait for Ms. Grimsworth to finish a meeting before I could see her. She pursed her thin lips in a way that managed to look slightly sympathetic as she let me in.

"If you were hoping for news about Professor Banefield, I can tell you that he's doing well enough to have returned to his apartment. The health center staff have advised him not to engage in any work for the next day or two while he completely recovers, but after that, we have every expectation that he'll be available to you as usual."

"That's good to hear," I said with a rush of relief. "I don't suppose… He mentioned he was taking a trip a few days ago. Do you know where he went?"

The headmistress's beady gaze sharpened. In her fitted dress suit—a deep forest green today—and with her graying blond hair pinned in its usual thick coil by her neck, she always gave off a strictly formal vibe.

"The recreational activities of my staff are beyond my purview," she said. "If the trip related to your studies in some way, I'm sure you can discuss it with your mentor when he's back in full health."

I hadn't really expected her to tell me even if she knew. Hell, maybe Banefield's illness *had* been non-supernatural, the timing simply a coincidence, Shelby had spent a week fighting off a flu not that long ago.

"If that's the only matter you wanted to see me about…" Ms. Grimsworth added, reaching for a notebook on her desk.

"No, actually, it's not," I said quickly. "I was thinking—I'd like to take a trip of my own to see my family's properties. Any of them that are close enough that I could go out there without missing any of my classes, at least. I could use some directions, and I'm not sure of my best way of getting out to them… and I'd need the tracing spell you have on me relaxed so the blacksuits don't go on the alert when I get that far off campus."

Or removed completely, if she was in a trusting mood. If I could have run off from the university without the fearmancers being able to trace my movements, I could make it back to California and the Enclave of joymancers before they managed to catch me, I was pretty sure. Of course, I'd have to be *absolutely* sure before I made an attempt like that. As soon as I revealed just how deep my loyalties to the joymancers ran, these people would never let me walk around freely again.

I wasn't sure I knew enough yet to prove those loyalties to my parents' people either. I should be able to direct them to the location of the university, but I hadn't figured out anything about taking down the wards or otherwise tackling the place. Still, not setting off alarms the second I walked farther than the neighboring town would be helpful no matter how much longer it took for me to work out the rest of my plans.

The headmistress was nodding, so the request must have sounded reasonable. "I can relax the spell's range. We still want to be sure you're protected after everything you've been through."

"Thank you," I said, hoping I didn't sound overly grateful.

"The main Bloodstone home is in Maine, too far to make a day trip of it unless you hire a private plane, but they do have a couple of properties closer by. I'd imagine your grandfather packed up most of your parents' personal items for storage before he passed on, but everything else has been maintained as it was. As for getting to them, we had someone bring by one of your family's cars a few weeks ago in case you wanted to make use of it. Let me get you the key."

I hadn't expected to discover I owned a car, although maybe I should have given the size of the bank account I'd inherited and the fact that there were multiple properties across the Northeast in my name.

Ms. Grimsworth tugged open a drawer on her desk and riffled through it before handing over a car key on a worn leather fob. My fingers closed around it with a flash of uncertainty, but I wasn't sure I wanted to share my doubts with her.

"Thanks," I said.

"The vehicle has been kept in good working order, as with all your family's property, in anticipation of your return." She paused. "I hadn't mentioned it because it was so important that you focus on your studies leading up to your second assessment, but your other grandparents have been asking about seeing you."

I froze. "I thought all my grandparents were dead."

"On your mother's side—on the Bloodstone side. Your paternal grandparents are still much with the living." The hint of derision in her tone made me suspect she'd put these people off for more than just the sake of my studies. She didn't like them. "They have no particular authority among the barons, but they are relatives. It's up to you whether I accept their request and allow them to visit you here."

I had living family among the fearmancers. Maybe I was supposed to be leaping with joy at the idea, but instead I felt sick. Dealing with the expectations of my classmates and teachers had been bad enough. I wasn't sure I was ready to pretend I wanted to take on another family.

Since Ms. Grimsworth didn't appear to like the idea either, at least I wouldn't face any pressure from her. "I think I'd like a little more time to get my bearings first," I said. "It's going to be a little… awkward, meeting people who are supposedly family but are basically strangers."

"Yes. I agree. Better to wait until you're feeling secure in your role."

Ms. Grimsworth nodded to the key I was clutching. "Your Lexus is in spot 39 in the garage. Let me see what I can do with your tracing spell while you're here."

I paid close attention as she came around the desk and walked around me, but the sounds she murmured were her own spell-casting words, indecipherable to anyone else. Most of the time she was behind me where I couldn't even see how she moved her hands, if that made any difference. Other than a faint quiver that ran over my skin at one moment, I wouldn't have known she was adjusting the magic attached to me at all.

I left the headmistress's office with several locations marked on my phone's map and a twist in my stomach. I didn't have any classes until late in the afternoon, so I went to take a look at my new acquisition.

This was the first time I'd had any reason to venture into the garage just east of the parking lot at the front of the school. The trim wooden building didn't look all that big from the outside, but then, that was in comparison to Killbrook Hall, which loomed over the south end of the grounds like a craggy Victorian mansion-slash-castle.

Clearly a lot of the students did have their own cars on hand, because it turned out the garage housed three long rows of parked cars with a lane looping around the middle, leading to a ramp up to a second floor that presumably held even more vehicles.

I found my Lexus just around the curve in the lane: a sleek sedan that shone pale gold in the sunlight streaming through the building's high windows. As I eased toward the driver's seat in the space between it and the neighboring Porsche, a flame-red Ferrari pulled out of a spot farther down and zoomed past me with a girlish whoop. I peered through the driver-side window of my car.

Well, I knew enough about cars to tell that it was an automatic, thank God. I tried to picture Mom in there—she'd done most of the driving back home. What she'd have grasped or pushed first. How she'd have set her hands on the wheel.

A lump rose in my throat. What I wouldn't give to have her or Dad here right now.

I squeezed my eyes shut against the flood of grief. Hold it together,

Rory. Anyway, this was ridiculous. Of course I wasn't going to get anywhere like this. Maybe I could—

Footsteps tapped down the concrete ramp from the second floor. I glanced up, and my gaze locked with Jude's. His eyebrows rose slightly. I braced myself as he sauntered over.

He came to a stop by the rear of the car and let out a low whistle. "Is this yours, then? Bloodstones know how to make a statement, don't they?"

I didn't hear any mockery in his tone, only apparently genuine admiration, but it didn't set me any more at ease than his comments the other day in the forest had. "I can't take any credit for it. It'd have belonged to my—to my birth parents." I wasn't going to start calling the Bloodstones my *parents*, full stop.

"What are you waiting for? You should take her for a spin, make her yours."

"I can't," I said, figuring he'd connect the dots soon enough even if I tried to avoid the subject. "I don't have my license."

He laughed. "Half of us here never bothered. You can always magic up an illusion of one if you need to."

I shoved the key into my purse. "No, I mean I never learned how to drive." One more way Mom and Dad had ensured I'd stay close. There'd never been many places to drive to, with me being homeschooled and pretty deficient in social life. I'd asked about it a couple of times, and they'd made one excuse or another… I hadn't cared enough to push it.

Jude's eyebrows jumped a little higher. He propped himself against the Porsche's trunk. "Good thing I happened to be passing by. That's simple enough to fix. I'll teach you."

I gave him a skeptical look. "Yeah, that sounds like a brilliant idea."

"I'm not joking. Jump in, and we can get started right now. I enjoy living dangerously." He grinned at me when I continued to hesitate. "If that's not a good enough reason for you, consider it my way of starting to pay you back for the shit I put you through."

That framing did make the idea more palatable, but that didn't mean I trusted him to mean it. "I feel like I can find a driving instructor who didn't put me through shit in the first place."

I hoped I could, anyway. The list of people who fit that criteria was depressingly short. It wasn't as if Deborah could teach me.

Jude's smirk suggested he realized how limited my options in that department were. He cocked his head. "What exactly do you think my evil plan is here?"

"I don't know," I retorted. "I just know there's a fairly good chance you have one."

"And there's no way I can convince you otherwise?"

"I can't think of any, and I doubt that's going to change. So why don't you just call it a loss and save us both a bunch more arguing?"

My frustration seeped into my voice despite my best efforts. Jude considered me for a moment, his smirk fading into a more thoughtful expression. Then he wet his lips.

"What if I gave you a free pass? One question, asked with insight, and I'll let you in. 'Do you have any evil plans?' or 'Are you trying to screw me over?' or however you'd want to put it."

For a second I could only stare at him. Jude who kept a wall up that felt solid as a mountainside, Jude who I'd never actually managed to get a read on through magic—the only "insight" I'd been able to glean had been through observations I'd made with my eyes… *He* was offering to let me inside his head? Did giving me driving lessons really matter that much to him?

How could I pass up the opportunity to take a peek at whatever was really going on behind those dark green eyes?

I turned to face him. "All right. Let me know when you're ready."

I'd need to pick my question carefully. Leave the wording open enough that he shouldn't be able to hide any ill intentions.

Jude's expression tightened for a second as if he was regretting the offer, but he exhaled slowly and tipped back his head. "Go for it."

I focused on his temple, the pale skin beside the fall of his dark copper hair, and coaxed some of the energy swirling behind my clavicle up my throat and into the words I spoke. "Why are you offering to help me?"

I caught a glimpse of Jude's mouth twitching, and then I was tumbling straight into a mass of sensations that overwhelmed the rest of my awareness, not even a sliver of a wall to slow my fall.

Images and emotions whirled past me. A glimpse of me standing beside Ms. Grimsworth as she announced to the curious onlookers that I was the only current or recent student with strengths in all four magical domains. A mix of irritation and admiration as Jude shook ice off his shoes. A chuckle at the thought of a pale-haired man sputtering with indignation.

And deeper, underneath all that but so vast and sweeping it rushed over me alongside everything else, a panicked impression of scrambling, of something crumbling away in his hands as he tried to grasp it. *Fear*—but not of me, or I'd have caught it before. The gaping size of it, the frantic fumbling to recover, jolted me back to the Desensitization room, to the metaphorical spire I'd watched disintegrate under Jude's feet.

All those sensations crashed through me in the space of a couple seconds, and then a familiar wall slammed in front of me, hurtling my consciousness back into my own head.

Jude was staring at me, his face taut and his shoulders rigid, looking shaken for the first time I could remember. He shoved himself off the Porsche. His voice came out taut too. "Never mind then. Sorry I bothered you."

He was… walking away. What the hell? Apprehension gripped my chest. I'd obviously gone deeper into his mind than he'd expected, given the way he'd cut me off so abruptly, but maybe I hadn't gotten quite as deep as he thought.

"Wait!" I said.

Jude had already made it past the neighboring car. He stopped and swiveled only halfway toward me. "What?" he said flatly.

I crossed my arms, studying him. "Why are you giving up? What do you think I saw?"

His lips curled into a smile so tight it looked more like a grimace. "I'm aware that desperation is hardly an appealing quality. You don't have to rub it in. I'm going."

There wasn't anything else, then. Fearmancers did make a big deal out of anyone seeing them the slightest bit vulnerable. And maybe it shouldn't be a surprise that Jude would be worse than most, considering how hard he must work to maintain his usual blasé attitude when he had all that turmoil roiling around underneath.

I didn't know how to interpret every part of the insight I'd gotten, but I'd seen enough to tell he wasn't here to hurt me.

"I'm not trying to rub it in," I said. "I just want to understand. What are you so worried about?"

As he eyed me, his shoulders came down. His expression didn't exactly relax, but some of the defensiveness in it softened. "Is the price for giving you driving lessons the full baring of my soul?" he said lightly, his gaze still wary. "You've already gotten a better look than anyone else ever has. You dive in there fast, Ice Queen."

"You offered," I had to point out. "And I think I'd be good with just an explanation of why driving lessons are so incredibly important all of a sudden."

The corner of his mouth curled up, more of the tension seeping out of his stance. He took a few steps toward me again and stopped, still a safe distance away. I couldn't tell what was going on in that striking head of his *now*, but his attention brought a tingle of warmth to the surface of my skin.

"Would you believe it's simply that I'm starting to see I might have ruined my chances with the only person who's ever made me care if I did?"

No, not really. What I'd felt in him had felt way more fraught than I could imagine had to do with just me. "You hardly know me," I said.

He shrugged. "I'm not sure about that. You don't make much effort to hide who you are."

I supposed that was a fair point. I sucked my lower lip under my teeth, trying to sort through the jumble of emotions now residing inside me. My decision no longer felt so clear cut.

Lay out the pros and cons, my dad would have told me.

Pros: It would be really, really useful to learn how to drive so I could make whatever investigations I needed to without anyone looking over my shoulder. I wasn't sure who else I could ask. Jude might have been an asshole to me in the past, but at least I knew what I was dealing with. Everything I'd seen in his mind a moment ago and his reaction afterward told me he did care about getting this chance to make amends, even if the fact that he cared exasperated him. I hadn't caught any hint of a conspiracy with the other scions or anyone else.

And he could be a very useful person to have on my side here at Blood U if I happened to need a rule or two to be broken in pursuit of the justice I wanted to bring down.

Cons: I remembered the humiliation and horror he'd put me through with wrenching clarity. No matter what I'd seen, I wasn't sure I'd ever trust him.

But that might be a pro in its own way. If I never trusted him, I'd never make a mistake out of misplaced trust.

"I don't know about 'chance*s*'," I said, "but I'll give you one. Where do we begin, Mr. Instructor?"

Jude blinked at me as if he didn't quite believe his ears. Then he smiled again, so brilliantly my heart fluttered even with all those memories front and center. He held up his hand. "Key? Garage navigation is an advanced skill. I think I'd better be the one to get us out to the parking lot if you want your car to stay in one piece."

I tossed him the key and moved out of the way so he could take the driver's seat. As I got in on the passenger side, he ran his hands over the wheel with a pleased sigh. "You did luck out with this inheritance."

I couldn't help snorting at his reverent tone. "Are you in this for me or my car?"

"Oh, don't worry, a hunk of steel is no competition. Although you should see the beauty I've got upstairs sometime." He revved the engine without waiting for my response and backed out of the parking spot fast but so smoothly my heart only leapt halfway to my throat.

We cruised out of the garage into the smaller lot just outside. Jude parked so we could swap seats, and I settled in on the driver's side with a flicker of nerves. It took me a few seconds to find the lever to adjust the seat so I could reach the pedals Jude's long legs had found so easily.

"Brake," I said, tapping one with my foot. "Gas."

"There you go," Jude said. "I barely need to teach you anything. One tip: Take the car out of park before you try to go anywhere."

"Um. Right. Obviously." I pulled the gear shift into drive and then, rethinking that move, into reverse. Then I slowly eased on the gas. The car edged backward inch by inch.

"Turning the wheel also helps for steering clear of nearby buildings," Jude said, watching my progress with amusement. "Left to go left, right to go right, even when you're heading backward."

I would have glowered at him if I hadn't been keeping all my attention on the movement of the car. I tugged the wheel to the side, and the Lexus glided around, leaving me with a clear path down the lot. All right, first challenge met. I stopped, switched to drive, and pressed the gas a little harder than before.

My pulse hitched with the lurch of the car, but the engine settled into a not totally terrifying pace.

"Nice," Jude said. "Take us down to the end and then turn around and go back. We'll go in a few circles before we aim for a longer straight line."

Was he thinking we'd leave the parking lot on my first time out? My gut twinged with nerves, and at the same moment someone's cat familiar came darting across the lot in front of the car.

I was going slow enough that it shouldn't have mattered. The problem was that in my jolt of panic, I jammed my foot down—on the pedal I'd already been pressing.

The Lexus surged forward. The cat's sudden terror flooded me. I let out a yelp and yanked at the wheel instinctively. The car roared around toward the edge of the lot.

Jude jerked forward, his hand skimming over my knee. A hasty word tumbled from his mouth, and the car screeched to a halt right at the edge of the pavement. He'd hit the brake with a smack of magic.

He pulled back as quickly as he'd leaned in, curling his fingers into his palm rather than letting them graze my leg the way he could have if he'd wanted to cop a feel, and casually shifted the car back into park. I exhaled my jitters, but my heart kept thumping double-speed. Shit.

Jude glanced over at me and tsked his tongue teasingly. "So ambitious. I know you like to carve your own path, but I think the staff would appreciate it if we avoid literally cutting one across campus."

An unexpected laugh tickled through my lungs and spilled from my mouth. Slightly hysterical, maybe, but it felt good. God, when was the last time I'd really laughed, not in a bittersweet or self-deprecating way but just because of the absurd humor of the moment?

Who would have thought when I did, it'd be because of this guy? Who'd have thought he'd be sitting there looking so happy about it?

I took a shaky breath and leaned back in my seat, adjusting my grip on the wheel. "Okay, let's give that circle another shot."

CHAPTER NINE

Declan

A show-off from the front row topped off the afternoon's Insight seminar with a sudden sprouting of thorns from the tops of all the desks. Professor Sinleigh took in the sight and the startled yelps, looking rather unimpressed by the display.

"I'll give credit to Physicality if you can remove those protrusions as quickly as you conjured them up," she said, and the guy wiped the desks flat again with a few mumbled words and a jerk of his hand.

Rory came up beside me as the other students headed out. "People are really starting to ramp up all the credit-seeking spells."

She wasn't standing particularly close, but my skin still warmed with the awareness of her presence. I directed my focus to slinging my bag over my shoulder. "This always happens as we come up on the end of term. We're halfway through now."

"You mean it's going to get worse?" Rory made a face.

"All part of school life." I couldn't resist glancing at her to raise an eyebrow. "You're an official student now. Better get used to it."

The wry smile she gave me in return reminded me why I should have resisted. It set off a flare of a sharper heat that brought our kiss in the library racing to the front of my mind. I averted my gaze and steeled my defenses to protect my own mind from my idiotic impulses. "Ready for your next lesson?"

"Absolutely."

She followed me down the tower staircase, keeping a couple of steps behind rather than staying beside me through some sort of unspoken agreement. I wasn't sure how aware she was of the delicate balance I was maintaining after the one piece of my struggle I'd confessed to her last week. I was aide and tutor and fellow scion, strictly professional, helpful but not friendly, available but not open.

I couldn't let her find out just how many pressures were attempting to yank me even farther in the opposite direction of my personal feelings. That could be disastrous for both of us.

"The pranks don't just become more frequent—they get bigger too," I said to fill the silence in which my thoughts seemed to blare. "Everyone's always trying to top the ones they've heard about from previous terms… There was a stunt for Physicality my first year here that I don't think anyone feels has really been beat yet—a girl who was adept enough to perform a full shapeshift took on her bear form and charged into the middle of this awards ceremony for the Nary students."

"You mean some people can literally turn into animals?" Rory said, sounding startled.

"No one's mentioned that to you yet?"

"I guess… My mentor did say something along that line, but I didn't really think it through. It hasn't come up in my seminars."

"It wouldn't," I said. "Pulling off a full shift is hard—unless you devote yourself to physicality, you're not likely to get there. Holding it for long enough to rampage around a gathering for several minutes is even harder. The students who practice shifting spells have special sessions devoted to that aspect."

Whatever had gone on between her and Connar, the transformative side of his studies mustn't have come up. *I'd* only seen him shift a couple of times. It was impressive, but also unsettling.

"More surprises to look forward to," Rory muttered.

"At least the better you get with the shielding, the more you can prevent the persuasive gambits from affecting you." I slowed as we came out of the tower, and she fell into step beside me as we crossed the green to the building that held the aides' office. "It'd be exhausting fully guarding against every possible spell all the time, but if you suspect someone might be going to cast, you can always prepare."

"And once you get particularly good, you can cut off an intrusive spell even after it's gotten into your head, right? I think I did that kind of accidentally in my first Insight class."

I winced inwardly at the memory of the way Jude and Victory had torn into her that day. But she'd held strong, gathered the will to shove them back rather than crumpling under the attack.

That moment, watching her stare defiantly back at them while they realized they couldn't break her wall, might have been the point when I'd really started falling for her. She was a fighter, just like I'd had to be—more than anyone else here at the university had.

I yanked my mind away from those thoughts. "Once someone's in, it's harder to kick them back out. It's easier with Insight than with Persuasion spells, where they're not just looking through your mind but actively affecting your thoughts. But anyone who's a master at Insight can block everything if they're in good mental shape—not overly tired or similar. You just might have a while to go before you get there."

"Are you a master yet?" Rory asked in a lightly teasing tone. I didn't let myself look at her, but I heard the smile in her voice.

"Maybe journeyman at this point."

We'd slipped into this dynamic so easily: tutor and pupil, advisor and advisee. The two sessions we'd had so far, Rory had followed my lead, listened to my guidance, and avoided bringing up anything I'd shared during that uncomfortable moment in her room. I doubted she trusted me completely, but the fact that she was trusting me even this much left my gut in a tangle.

If I could see her through this without her taking any permanent wounds, I would. I just wasn't sure *whether* I was capable of it yet. The one thing I absolutely couldn't do was warn her. Someone would find out. My life would be over. A baron who betrayed the other barons didn't keep his title—or generally anything else.

They meant to betray her too, to break her down and mold her to their will. I didn't have the power to challenge three ruling families directly on my own, but maybe behind the scenes I'd manage to give her the chance she deserved to really fight for herself. I'd had my whole lifetime to prepare—she'd only had a month.

Imagine how she could shift the pentacle if she had just a little more time to find her feet.

During our previous sessions, one of the other aides had been working in the large office space that was about the size of one of the dorm common rooms: desks set up along the walls, a couple of tables and a cluster of armchairs in the middle. The chairs were more comfortable, but I preferred the built-in boundaries the tables provided. Especially when we walked into the still, faintly pine-scented air of the office and found the room otherwise empty.

That was fine. I had my own mental defenses built up, made up of the looming mass of responsibilities and goals and people I intended to protect. However much I was coming to admire and care about Rory, it was better even for her if I maintained this distance.

"Have you been practicing the exercises I gave you?" I asked as I sat down at our usual table.

Rory pulled out the chair across from me. "Of course. Pretty much whenever I have a few spare minutes and I don't think I'll be interrupted. They seem to be helping. When I was in class today and we paired off for that one assignment, my partner tried to get a sneaky read on me before we'd officially started, but I had enough of a barrier in place that I noticed it and built it up stronger before she got in."

"Excellent. I figured you'd pick it up fast." She was nothing if not a quick study. I rested my arms on the tabletop. "So far we've been focusing on defensive tactics. Today I want to do some work around active casting."

Rory knit her brow. "What does that have to do with shielding?"

"A lot. The moments when your own mind is most vulnerable are when you're attempting to tackle someone else's. Any time you're casting a spell that involves reaching out your consciousness—to peer inside someone's thoughts, or to influence their behavior with your will—you have to let down your guard. A solid shield wards off magic both ways. Once you get good enough that people know you're generally protected, anyone who wants to get at you will watch for when *you* cast a spell and use that as an opportunity to strike."

Rory's jaw set. She was always pretty, but I didn't think she ever got quite as beautiful as when that spark of determination came into her dark blue eyes.

"All right. How do I make sure that doesn't happen?"

I let myself smile. "You get good at casting as surreptitiously and quickly as possible, so you can have your wall back up before anyone even realizes it was down."

I gave Rory a few simple spells to practice to hone her subtlety and speed. As she launched into them, my pulse kicked up a notch.

This was the part I hated. I watched her concentrating on the exercise—and murmured a casting word of my own with the intake of my breath, so soft she wouldn't hear it.

All I took was a little dip inside her mind during the brief vulnerability in the midst of her casting. No aim, no depth, just skimming the surface for the first few random impressions I could catch. Her resolve to develop this skill as quickly as she had the others. A nip of hunger and a longing for the chocolate brownie waiting back in her dorm room. The image of a round, pale face—Professor Banefield, her mentor—with a ripple of worry.

Nothing all that private. Nothing that could be turned against her as a weapon. Just enough so that when the older barons questioned me, I could honestly say I'd continued working around her defenses, in case any of them happened to slip past mine to gauge the truth of that statement.

Still, if she ever noticed what I was doing, that would be the end of, well, everything. I couldn't imagine there'd be any coming back from it. So I'd better make sure I damn well kept it fast and subtle until I'd built up her defenses every way I could and no one—me, the barons, the other scions—could shatter them.

Just as I was pulling back, she glanced at me, and I caught one last impression. A flicker of a memory—a close dark space, her hand pressed against someone's chest, a mouth hot against hers. A matching heat shot through me. She was remembering our kiss, and with a waft of desire.

I jerked my awareness all the way back into my head and willed my blood to cool. It didn't do me any good remembering that myself —or thinking about what it might mean that she was. She was devoted and determined, unshaken in her convictions even after the battering she'd taken last month, and no matter how much desire that woke up in *me*, there was no fucking universe in which I could really have her.

Those glimpses into Rory's head weren't the only gambit I had to play here, simply the one I disliked the most. After I'd given her a few more pointers and she'd practiced some more, I pulled a sheaf of paper out of my bag.

"I thought you should have this," I said, which was mostly true. Technically presenting Rory with this kind of information had been Malcolm's idea, but I'd chosen the specifics. Whatever campaign he was attempting to wage against her now, I had to stay impartial. That feud, at least, was a clash between equals. I'd teach Rory every defense she asked me to help her with, but coddling her in that conflict wouldn't do her any favors.

Besides, I did agree with him on one point. Rory needed to understand her past before she'd be able to completely accept who she was and what she was meant to do. Not all her convictions were based on reality.

Rory cocked her head as she studied the papers. "What is this?"

"The official report from the blacksuits on the altercation in which your parents were killed," I said. "I had to call in a favor to get it, but I figured you deserved the full story." She'd been horrified by the way the blacksuits had dispatched the joymancers who'd raised her. Would she understand their actions better if she saw just how the joymancers had ravaged our people before they'd taken her? There were photographs in that print-out that made my stomach turn.

Rory's gaze ran over the first paragraph. Then she met my eyes. "This will be the blacksuits version. They'll want to make themselves sound as justified as possible, won't they?"

I looked back at her steadily. "Our people may be brutal when they need to be, but most of us value accuracy. Our side took lives that day too, and the report doesn't shy away from that fact. We know what we are. It's important that you know what we—and the joymancers—are too."

"The joymancers wouldn't have—"

Rory cut herself off. From what Malcolm had said, she'd made her preference for joymancer attitudes quite clear to him, but she might not realize how much he'd told the rest of us. She was being careful, which did her credit, even if she hadn't been able to stop a familiar angry flush from coming into her cheeks.

She'd loved the people she'd called her parents. I wasn't going to blame her for that. The two of them might not even have been bad people as individuals. They'd still had a part in tearing her from her home and her rightful heritage.

"How many joymancers did you know?" I said quietly.

She bit her lip. "Only my parents," she admitted.

"You have to realize there are reasons they kept you away from the others. What you'll read in there will fill in some of those blanks."

Her hand still hesitated over the report, as if she were torn between taking it and shoving it back at me. My gut twisted tighter, but I played the one card I was sure would work with her.

"*You* care about knowing the whole truth, don't you? You've never seemed like the type to shy away from the facts even if they're painful."

"Of course I want to know the facts," she said, grabbing the papers and stuffing them into her purse. "I just wonder what the joymancer account says, that's all. In the interest of covering all the bases."

"Well, if I can manage to scrounge up that too, I'll pass it along."

She guffawed and got up. "Well, thank you again. Are you still good for the same time on Sunday?"

"I'll meet you here."

I lingered by the doorway as she headed down the hall, a hard, heavy sensation sinking through my chest. I'd done everything just as I'd planned it. As far as I could tell, I'd handled the balance just right. But watching her go with the image of her gorgeously resolute expression imprinted in my mind, I was filled with the sickening certainty that one way or another, I was failing.

CHAPTER TEN

Rory

A low, graceful melody carried from my dorm room. I stopped in the hall outside, taking it in as I reached for my keycard. The lilting strains had a mournful quality that seeped right into my chest with the ache of uncertainty that had been lingering there all morning.

The music cut off abruptly when I opened the door. Shelby's head came up with a swish of her ponytail where she was sitting in one of the common room armchairs with her cello propped in front her. She relaxed a little when she saw it was me, but not completely.

"Sorry," she said, getting up. "I can go back to the music rooms in the tower."

I waved her back down. "What are you talking about? I don't mind. You're really good. We should be glad to get the free concert."

She laughed stiffly. "Yeah, most of the other girls don't feel that way. There's usually no one here for an hour or so this time on Fridays, so I stick to that. I like getting to hear how the songs sound in different spaces—you notice different elements."

I could almost see in the hunch of her shoulders the way Victory or her lackeys must have taken their jabs at Shelby over this like so many other things. The only thing they seemed to enjoy more than hassling me was intimidating the Nary students in every way they could.

"Well, don't stop practicing on my account," I said. "I'd love to hear more."

I must have said it emphatically enough, because a smile crossed Shelby's face. "Wait until you hear us all together," she said. "Just a few more weeks until the annual concert."

I grinned back at her and patted the phone pocket on my purse. "I've already got it written in my calendar."

She lifted her bow again. The delicate glide of it across the strings sent an appreciative shiver down my back. She must have worked her ass off to make it into the music program here, one of the special streams Bloodstone University offered just to their nonmagical scholarship students. According to Shelby, the opportunities anyone who graduated got were incomparable, which they'd have to be for anyone to put up with the crap the rest of the student body put them through.

I went to the kitchen to grab a snack. Surprise, surprise, one chunk of cheese and a couple of yogurts I'd left in my section of the fridge had gone sour and spotted with mold. After the second time I'd seen that happen, it'd been obvious someone was messing with my food as yet another power play. Now, with the fifth time, I couldn't even be bothered to get angry about it.

I chucked those items in the garbage and reached for the apples farther back that I'd cast a concealing illusion on. Victory and the others couldn't spoil what they didn't know was there. I had enough of a budget to afford to buy a few decoys. Not letting them get to me felt like the best possible revenge.

When I came into my bedroom, the smell of the cut apple brought Deborah out of the nest she'd built for herself in the wall. I set her half on the bed beside me and took a bite of mine while she started to nibble. The juice that flooded my mouth was perfectly tart, but the ache inside me expanded again with the cello song seeping through the door. My other hand crept up to curl around my dragon bead on its chain.

Courage and strength—that's what I'd told Mom it meant to me. I needed both right now.

"Deborah," I said quietly, "what do you know about the confrontation with the fearmancers where the joymancers took me?"

She paused, and I thought her little muscles tensed just slightly between her sleek white fur. *I didn't have any part in it. I didn't know the Conclave had taken in a fearmancer child at all until they extended the offer of getting out of my cancer-addled body. Those kinds of missions weren't general knowledge if you didn't work closely with the Conclave.*

"But it didn't surprise you that it could have happened. That they could have killed fearmancers and taken one of their kids."

One of our duties as joymancers is to stand up against those who'd destroy the happiness people can find in the world. If we have an opportunity to interfere with a malicious plan, whether it's orchestrated by fearmancers or Naries, we take it.

That was exactly the kind of thing I figured she'd say. I let out a slow breath, my hand dropping to rest on my purse. My purse that contained the printed-out report Declan had given me yesterday. I'd read it at least ten times since then. It hadn't sat any better with me this morning than it had last night.

"According to the fearmancers' report on the fight… my birth parents and the other fearmancers in the building were just there to consider buying the place. That was why the joymancers were able to get the better of them—they weren't expecting any conflict. They hadn't brought along anyone to defend them. They brought *me* along. Obviously they wouldn't have done that if they'd thought they might be walking into a battle."

No doubt they would have used that building for some nefarious purpose, Deborah said. *These people don't know how to do anything* other *than nefarious.*

"I know," I said, even though I couldn't have said that was completely true. I didn't think Imogen was a bad person, even if she'd hurt me. The more time I spent with Declan, the more sure I was that he was doing his best given his circumstances. Like Jude had said the other day, everyone here had simply grown up with different priorities and a different way of looking at the world than I had. That didn't make every single thing they did evil.

Any more than every single thing any joymancer did was necessarily good.

"It just seems pretty… vicious to attack a bunch of people going about their business—with their kid right there too—when those people aren't hurting anyone right then, you know?" I went on after a moment's hesitation. "Shouldn't we be better than that?"

I don't know all the ins and outs of the situation. I'm sure there was more to it. Why don't you put that away, sweetheart? You've had enough to worry about without adding to it with events from years and years ago.

I knew what she meant. This morning I'd woken up again with a sore throat, a mug I'd left on my desk smashed, and nervous glances when I'd come out of my bedroom. Deborah had darted off as soon as I'd started yelling, but she hadn't been able to identify the cause. I wouldn't be surprised if she thought the episodes were my toxic fearmancer magic messing with me from the inside out and not an attack. I didn't really want to think too closely about that possibility.

"I'm not saying they didn't have any good reasons," I said. "I'm not even necessarily saying the joymancers are wrong to stop the fearmancers any way they can. I just—maybe it's not totally bizarre that everyone here hates joymancers as much as they do. If you look at things from their perspective."

And a warped perspective that is, Deborah muttered, digging into her apple again. *Don't let them get in your head, Lorelei. You were raised to be better than that.*

She didn't say that I *was* better. Only that I'd been raised better. I looked down at her for a moment, my stomach rejecting the thought of eating any more of my own piece of apple.

Did she really trust me even now, or was she just as wary of me turning into some kind of monster as the joymancers who'd taken me must have been? She hadn't even liked the idea of me leaving campus to visit the places I'd inherited.

I didn't know how to bring up the other part that had stuck in my head: the pictures of my birth mother and father after the slaughter. And it had looked like a slaughter. They'd been burned to the bone, their skin and clothes crackled black in swaths across their bodies, my father's neck gaping open like a dark second mouth. The building's polished tile floor had been smeared with ash.

In one of the pictures, I'd been able to make out a tiny toddler footprint in that ash where two-year-old me must have stood next to my mother's charred body. The seared remains of her arm had been stretched toward that spot.

My real parents hadn't deserved to be murdered by the blacksuits, blood splashed all over our kitchen. But maybe that violence hadn't been automatic brutality so much as the fearmancers' idea of payback.

Declan's mother had been in those pictures too, her body just as ruined. He must be old enough to remember at least a little about her, even though my memory of the attack was a blank.

The cello music halted. I lifted my head to catch the voices that filtered in from the common room. That sounded like Imogen. I shook away the tension inside me. Now was my chance to dig a little deeper into the possible magical payback that might be happening right here.

When I stepped out of my bedroom, Shelby was just ducking out of the dorm with her cello. Imogen caught my eye and shrugged. "I didn't ask her to stop. I guess she's self-conscious."

And maybe Imogen hadn't always been the friendliest in the past. She'd been tentatively warm when I'd included Shelby in some of our conversations and outings, but she hadn't seemed all that enthusiastic about socializing with a Nary.

That fact served as a useful reminder to be careful how I treaded with her.

"Hey," I said. "I actually wanted to ask you about something... You said you're studying the medical side of physicality magic, right?"

Imogen nodded, curiosity mixing with the wariness in her expression. "Is this about— I know you haven't been sleeping all that well."

Was she going to be weird about my morning episodes, steering clear of me the way the other girls had even more than usual? Shelby hadn't withdrawn from me, but then, she spent as little time as possible in the common room, so she might not have even realized which bedroom the disturbance had been coming from.

"No," I said tentatively. "Well, maybe it'd be useful for that too, but I'm mostly thinking of someone else. Can a mage make a person sick using magic? And if they can, how would that work? Like, are there ways to tell whether it's magical?"

Imogen's eyes widened. She sat down on one of the sofas, and I followed suit. "Why are you asking?"

"The professor who's my mentor came down with something that seemed serious the other day, and I'm probably just being paranoid, but I can't help wondering about that possibility, after everything that's already happened. So it *is* possible, then?"

Thankfully, I didn't need to explain to Imogen why I'd be paranoid about people targeting someone who'd supported me. She'd been on the receiving end herself not that long ago. She brought her hand to her mouth as she considered.

"It's definitely possible. It's actually one of the most common methods of quietly… interfering with people someone wants out of the way but can't challenge openly." She paused. "You've heard about Connar Stormhurst's family, haven't you?"

An icy prickle shot through my stomach. "No, nothing to do with challenges or whatever. Why? What did he do?"

"Oh, it wouldn't have been him. It happened when I was, like, six or seven, so he wouldn't have been much older—no magic yet." Her gaze darted through the room and came back to rest on me. "I'm not saying this to criticize the baron, just to be clear. Everyone knows about it. There's no reason you shouldn't too."

"*What?*"

She swept her tawny hair back behind her ears, making her silver dragonfly clip bob. "His mother wasn't always the Stormhurst baron. Her brother was the one who inherited the position. But there was an… accident that killed him and injured his wife badly, and then their one kid, the scion, got sick… No one could prove it was magic, but she didn't respond to any regular treatments either."

"Their daughter died too?" I said, the chill congealing into a pool of nausea. "Connar's mom wiped out the competition so she could have the baron spot?"

Imogen clasped her hands in her lap. "Like I said, no one could prove anything. If they could, there'd have been sanctions. But everyone *knows.* It's happened before. And then there's the whole thing with Connar and his brother."

I braced myself. "What about them?"

"It's only rumors what exactly happened. But he definitely has a twin brother. I guess if things had gone by official policy, their performance here at the university would have decided who was named the scion. But before their magic kicked in, they had some kind of fight… No one's really seen his brother since then. He was messed up so badly he couldn't come to Blood U. Apparently he's still *alive,* but…" She worried at her lip with her teeth.

Connar had hurt his own brother so badly the guy was a permanent invalid? I restrained a shudder. I wouldn't have thought the guy I'd gotten to know was capable of that… but I wouldn't have thought he was capable of making the caustic remarks he had the day after we'd had sex. He had a brutal side, that was for sure. I'd let myself forget it when we were away from everyone else, but maybe he was the worst of my fellow scions.

"That's awful," I said.

Imogen shrugged stiffly, her expression still tight. "It's how things go. Prove your strength, hold onto your power—or grab it from someone else. Sometimes I wish my family was respected enough that people would care what I think… but a lot of the time I'm glad to pretty much fly under the radar."

Not an option I could take. Maybe my assessment had gotten the casual bullies to back off, but it'd clearly also pointed an even bigger spotlight on me than I'd already had as simply the long-lost Bloodstone scion.

Malcolm had told me once that the only real rule here was to avoid getting caught if you broke one of the other rules. It sounded like that applied to all fearmancer society.

"If no one could prove what happened with his cousin, then I guess that kind of spell isn't easy to identify?" I said.

Imogen shook her head. "Not from what I've read and seen. The magic usually kicks off the problem, but a… 'good' spell of that type will set in motion a bunch of effects that will feed off each other naturally once they're going. Unless you're there to catch the original spell when it activates the process, there's nothing to trace."

I sighed and leaned back on the couch. "Do you think even the victim would be able to tell the difference between a real illness and a magical attack?"

"Probably not. But it doesn't happen *so* often—or leave people living and able to talk about it enough—that we've got a lot of examples. Sometimes you can guess based on the symptoms or the after effects, if they don't totally align with a regular illness."

That was something. I considered her. "Would you know what to look for?"

"I have a basic idea. Why?"

I motioned toward the door. "I was going to go pay Professor Banefield a visit—see how he's doing, bring him one of those double-chocolate brownies Shelby got me addicted to. It's the first day since he got sick I'm allowed to drop in. *I* don't have any idea what signs to look for, but if you're up for coming along… If only just to get my paranoia in check? I'd really appreciate it."

Imogen stared at me for a second as if she expected me to take back the invite. Then she got up with a flash of a smile, looking as pleased as if I'd offered to get her into the hottest party of the month and not to visit a still slightly under-the-weather professor. "Of course," she said. "If you think I might be able to help. I owe you about a thousand times over."

My violent morning episodes obviously hadn't stopped her from wanting to patch up our friendship. She was happy I trusted her enough to bring her along. I hadn't actually trusted her enough to admit the full extent of my fears about what had happened to Professor Banefield, but she didn't need to know that.

I smiled back at her. "Let me just grab that brownie, and we can get going, then."

I'd given Banefield plenty of time to get back to his office after his morning seminar. He answered the door immediately at my knock, looking pretty much his usual stout, messy-haired self if maybe a little paler than usual. His forehead furrowed when he took in Imogen beside me.

"It's good to see you, Rory, and… Miss Wakeburn, is it?"

"Good memory," Imogen said brightly. She'd told me on the way over that she hadn't had class with Banefield in over a year.

"We won't stay long if you've got catching up to do." I held out the brownie in its clear plastic bag. "I brought you a get-well treat. Or, I guess it's an 'I'm glad you got well' treat at this point."

Banefield chuckled as he accepted the brownie. "Really not necessary. I have to apologize for our last meeting. I'm sure I gave you quite a scare."

"It's not *your* fault," I said. "You're really feeling better?"

"Almost one hundred percent." He shifted his weight as if he were going to step back and invite us into the office, but then he stopped. "Has anything come up that you need my assistance with right now?"

I wanted to know what the hell he'd been about to tell me when he'd gotten sick, but I definitely didn't trust Imogen enough to bring that up with her around. Damn it.

"I didn't get to ask you before how your trip was," I said. "I was thinking of traveling off campus when I have the chance. Maybe you can give me some tips on spots to visit."

It was the best way I could think of to prod him to tell me where he'd gone without outright asking a question that was none of my business.

Banefield chuckled again. Was the sound terser this time? I itched to try an Insight spell on him, but the chances of my pulling that off without getting into trouble for working magic on a professor seemed pretty slim, given that Insight was his specialty too.

"It was more of an errand I had to run than anything like a vacation," he said in a tone that didn't invite further conversation. "I'd imagine your peers could advise you best on the most trendy leisure spots in the area. Thank you for coming by, Rory, and for the treat."

I'd been hoping for a bit more of a chat than that, but I wasn't going to hassle a guy I'd watched collapse just last week. Had he forgotten what he'd started saying? Maybe he'd only said it at all because of the sickness coming on—maybe it hadn't even been true, only some wild fever dream.

"I'll see you for our usual session," I said.

As we meandered back down the hall, I glanced at Imogen. She knew what I was wondering before I had to say the question out loud.

"I'm really not an expert on this or anything," she said, "so I can't make any promises. But I didn't notice anything that gave me a bad feeling. At least nothing to do with him being sick."

I stopped in the second floor landing. "What do you mean? Did it seem like something else was wrong?"

Imogen frowned. "I don't know for sure. Maybe he's just unsteady after that illness. I never got into any trouble when I was in his class, so I've got no idea what else it could be. A couple times when he looked at me, I felt..." She touched the base of her throat. "He was *afraid* of me."

CHAPTER ELEVEN

Rory

For mages who often objected to being characterized as villains, the fearmancers sure had a lot of material in their library on the various strategies for dispatching people you didn't happen to like. Whatever they might say about questionable things joymancers had done, I doubted the Conclave library had dozens of manuals of destruction.

I was paging through my fifth volume of the afternoon, several more stacked beside me, when a lean figure swooped in and plucked the top book off the pile.

"Hmm," Jude said, propping himself against the shelves opposite me as he flipped to the table of contents. "This looks very ominous. Suddenly I'm not so sure I want to be spending any more time in moving vehicles with you, Ice Queen."

I rolled my eyes as I looked up at him. "Don't worry. So far I've decided you're useful enough that I'll keep you around."

"Ah, but what terrible fate will befall me when you no longer need my oh-so-generous instruction? So many terrifying options. An enchanted blade? Suicide by Persuasion? A portal into an endless void?" He considered me with mock seriousness. "You don't really seem the void type, I'll admit."

I held out my hand for the book. "Is that even really a thing, or did you just make that up?"

"Maybe a little of both. It depends on how you interpret the material." He tossed the book to me and eyed the rest of the stack. "No, really, dear heir of Bloodstone, what the hell are you plotting tucked away back here?"

I was tucked away in the back of the aisle because I liked it better here than sitting at the tables out in clearer view. Just yesterday, I'd had yet another of the senior guys attempt to impress me into dating him, this one by toppling a group of juniors with a miniature earthquake. I wasn't sure which was worse—that, or the increasingly nervous reactions I was getting from quite a few of the other students whenever they saw me.

I'd had another bad episode this morning, shouting and tearing up the sketchpad I'd bought last time I was in town. Word about the Bloodstone scion's volatility was clearly starting to spread.

"Maybe I didn't want to get asked a whole bunch of questions about my reading material," I said, giving Jude a pointed look. "Also, as you of all people should be able to figure out, who says I'm reading this stuff for offensive use and not for defense?"

Jude hunkered down on the carpeted floor across from me, stretching out his legs to rest just a few inches shy of mine. We'd come into fairly close contact here and there during the three driving lessons he'd given me so far, but only when absolutely necessary. The rest of the time he'd kept a carefully considered distance.

I still wasn't sure what exactly he was after from me, but at the very least, I really had been getting the hang of driving with his help, and he hadn't done anything horrible during that time. I'd actually found myself almost *looking forward* to seeing him when I'd gone out to the garage yesterday, which maybe was a little terrifying in itself. There was something about his don't-give-a-shit attitude—ever present other than that one lapse when I'd peeked inside his head—that made all the other problems I needed to tackle seem smaller.

"I'll admit this school isn't free of idiots," he said. "I may have informed many of those people of their deficiencies in the past. But I doubt there's anyone here quite idiotic enough to try anything in those books on you."

"Why not?" I said abruptly. A question had been creeping up in the back of my mind as I'd skimmed through the books, and Jude was as good a person to ask it as any. He was here, and, well, if I trusted him at all, it was to give me an answer without sugar-coating the way Imogen or Banefield or, heck, even Declan might have. "I'm the last living Bloodstone. What happens if someone does decide to murder me?"

Jude's casual grin faded. "Deep dark thoughts in the deep dark depths of the library?"

"It seems like an important thing to know, as someone who'd rather take precautions against getting murdered if I need to."

"No one will try," he said, so matter-of-factly and firmly I believed *he* believed it. "It wouldn't be to anyone's advantage unless you really, *really* piss them off and they also happen to be extremely good at magic to cover their tracks. We tend to be a practical lot. Violence for gain. All anyone's going to gain from offing you is a death sentence for themselves for killing a baron."

I rested my current book against my raised knees. "From what I've heard, that hasn't stopped other barons from being murdered before."

Jude hummed. "Lines of inheritance. If you can get away with it and you're next in line, some will take that risk. But you don't have any next in line. It's just you. If you're gone…" He snapped his fingers. "The heart of Bloodstone power will leap into whatever fearmancer it deems most worthy."

Interesting. I'd rather have found out I was immortal until I had my own heir or something, but I'd take that explanation as well. "And what's to stop it from jumping into my theoretical murderer?"

"Nothing. It's just an awfully big gamble to make. The few times people talk about a final heir having been killed in the past, the person the heart picked wasn't at all who anyone would have expected. Even if you do really piss someone off, they'd have no guarantee that getting rid of you wouldn't land them with someone who pissed them off even more."

Yeah, I could see how that factor could work in my favor. So, my life should be fairly secure. All the things I cared about in that life… not so much.

"Hey, enough with the morbid thoughts. Bring on the sunshine and sparkles." Jude clapped his hands with a smirk. He must have cast a spell in his last comment, because an illusion rose up, so solid I might have thought it was a physical conjuring if I hadn't known his preferred area of expertise.

The pages of the book I was holding glowed, and a flurry of butterflies burst forth, their wings tickling my hair as they whirled around me. My gaze latched onto one for long enough to see Jude had gifted it with humanoid eyes and a mouth that stuck its tongue out at me. Another wiggled its body in a wobbly jig, its ass waving this way and that, before winking at me.

A snort escaped me. I covered my mouth to muffle a laugh that might have brought the librarian over to shush me. Mission accomplished, anyway. It was hard to think dire thoughts about my mortality when faced with cheeky dancing butterflies.

Jude wiped his hands together with a satisfied smile that beamed brighter when I met his eyes. The illusion vanished with the motion of his hand.

"Much better. I'll tell you what, Ice Queen. From what I've seen, anyone who *really* tries to mess with you will probably regret it." He paused and tapped his chin. "Unless saving yourself requires driving more than half a mile. Then you might be in trouble."

I gave him a light kick in the shin. "If that happens, it'll be your failing as a teacher."

"Oh, and now the natural fearmancer aggression comes out." He winked at me much like his butterfly had and pushed himself back to his feet. "Let's see if we can make it a mile next time."

He sauntered off, leaving me sitting there with a strange fizzing sensation in my chest, not exactly eager but not exactly uncomfortable either. He couldn't have known what I'd planned for my next class, but his interruption had given me a boost in confidence.

Damn right, no one had better mess with me. Malcolm had gotten away with too much already. Now I was going to mess with him right back.

My resolve continued humming through me as I walked to Nightwood Tower for my Persuasion seminar. If I'd had easy access, it was Connar's head I'd most want to open up. Physiological ailments were the domain of Physicality, and he had a family history of removing unwanted people using that sort of magic. But I'd also never seen Connar use the kind of spells that would give me a chance to slip past any shields he had up.

I didn't really know him, as much as I'd started to feel I did. I had no idea how to provoke him in the right direction… and the thought of finding out what he might do if I provoked him in the *wrong* direction made my stomach knot.

Malcolm's favorite trick was exerting his will on my mind. It shouldn't be too hard to encourage that impulse. And he'd been the ringleader from the start. I didn't think Connar would have gone after a professor without at least talking to the Nightwood scion about it.

If one of them was responsible for Banefield's illness, Malcolm should be able to tell me, whether he wanted to or not.

The classroom was half full when I reached it. Malcolm hadn't shown up yet, as I'd expected. He preferred to mosey in with just a minute or two to spare.

Ever since the day a few weeks ago when he'd nearly persuaded my feet to walk me right out of the tower, he'd always taken the same seat next to the window. Maybe to subtly remind me of that moment and the battle I'd have lost if Professor Crowford hadn't called an end to it. No one else touched it, leaving it to him.

Until today. I strode right over and sat myself down.

Cressida, sitting at the back of the class, let out a disbelieving chuckle. A few of my other classmates glanced my way but said nothing. The guy behind me drew back in his seat as if already retreating from a skirmish that hadn't started yet. Professor Crowford didn't give any of us more than a brief glance while he read over his lesson plan, his silver hair slicked down so the black streaks stood out even more starkly.

My heart thumped fast but steady as I waited. A couple more

students trickled in. Then Malcolm's voice carried through the doorway, hollering a wry insult after whoever he'd been talking to on the way up.

He walked into the room, and his gaze shot straight to me. There were two empty desks left, both on the other side near the door. He strolled right past them to the desk I was sitting at, his eyes never leaving me for a second. I stared right back at him.

"I think you've gotten lost, Glinda," he said. "All that fresh air isn't so good for you."

The warm spring breeze wafted over me. I smiled mildly at him. "I'll take my chances with the window. Unless you really think you can move me again."

At the same time, I brought my mental shield into sharper focus: breathing into the image of it around my mind, feeling every inch of it solid and impenetrable, the way Declan had taught me.

Persuasion was Malcolm's league, and as he'd reminded me not long ago, he had way more practice at using his magical skills than I did. But I had a couple of advantages. One: I was a hell of a lot stronger than I'd been the last time he'd exerted his will on me, and he wouldn't be expecting too much of a challenge. Two: I was fast. Fast enough to dig deep into Jude's head before he'd realized how far I'd gotten and tossed me out.

Hopefully fast enough to leap into Malcolm's mind in the brief opening I'd get and set him off-balance before he could take another stab at me.

Malcolm let out a dark chuckle, a glint lighting in his dark brown eyes. "This should be fun. *Stand up.*"

He didn't slack off much. A jolt ran through me as his spell jabbed into my shield—but my defenses held. The instant I felt the impact, I spoke my first personal casting word under my breath.

"Franco."

I hadn't told even Declan what I'd picked. Maybe the word wasn't total nonsense, but using my former last name felt *right* for this purpose. It'd been my parents' name, and Mom and Dad had been the ones who'd taught me how important every kind of insight was—to understand what people wanted and needed and to bring them joy.

Malcolm had let down his own shield to cast his persuasive spell. My awareness soared straight into the jumbled impressions of his consciousness. I hadn't had enough time to risk going for a targeted question with my spell, but he was focused on me right now, so any larger intentions he had for hurting me shouldn't be buried too deep.

Banefield—was there anything at all to do with my mentor in his thoughts? I dove deep as quickly as I could, getting just a glimpse of emotions and images.

I caught a flicker of triumph, not just for the victory he assumed he was going to win right now, but something else—my chaotic appearance when I'd dashed out of Ashgrave Hall the other morning—a small object with a cool smooth surface he'd held in his hands—a tang of something almost like longing—Connar's stern face—Malcolm's wolf familiar loping off into the woods—me sitting right here at this desk, a rush of exhilaration at the challenge—an impression of Crowford's voice saying, *Credit to Persuasion* as Malcolm strode out of the room while the rest of us bowed down so low our foreheads touched our desks—a prickling hint of frustration—

Wham. The force of Malcolm's mental wall flung me out of his head so violently I jerked in my seat, my spine jarring against the hard back of the chair. My own thoughts spun.

Malcolm glared at me, looking all devil and very little divine in that moment. He opened his mouth to aim another persuasive spell at me, and I knew I probably wouldn't be able to hold up my own defenses now that he was pissed off.

I groped through the bits and pieces I'd seen in his mind for something to throw him off balance. That scene with the classroom—that hadn't happened. It had to be something he was planning.

"Everyone had better keep their mental walls up at the end of class," I blurted out, pitching my voice to carry through the room. "Malcolm thinks he's going to have us all bowing to him on his way out."

The anger in Malcolm's eyes flared even hotter. His voice came out even but taut, splitting straight through the barrier I'd yanked back up as solid as I could. "*Get your ass out of—*"

Professor Crowford cleared his throat loudly, cutting the

Nightwood scion off. My muscles released where they'd seized to follow the command.

Malcolm spun toward the professor, barely holding back another glare. Crowford was watching us. Was there a hint of amusement in his heavy-lidded eyes? The rest of his expression was so inscrutable I wasn't sure.

"I think Miss Bloodstone has proven she can handle her chosen seat," he said. "Credit to Insight. There are other fine chairs you may sit yourself down in, Mr. Nightwood."

Malcolm's jaw worked, but he lifted it rather than arguing. He shot me one last look before retreating to the other side of the room, full of smoldering promise. My body stayed tensed.

The sense of triumph I'd seen in him and the images connected to it—I was pretty sure I'd just confirmed that he'd had something to do with the weird episodes I'd been experiencing. I hadn't dug up enough to figure out how, though. And there hadn't been any sign that he knew or cared about any scheme involving Banefield.

I'd better be able to figure out what he *was* up to fast, because that glare had promised payback.

CHAPTER TWELVE

Connar

The Physicality classroom took up nearly the entire half of the third floor of the tower. It held broader desks for conjuring work and room for twenty students, although it was rarely full. We'd generally had eighteen until Rory had started turning up a couple weeks ago.

She had her back to me today, like she usually did. I'd started sitting toward the far end of the room where I could more easily keep an eye on her without her noticing, and she'd always picked a spot that gave her plenty of distance from me. But while I watched the fall of her dark hair and the delicate movements of her hands as she shaped her magic, the memory of her walking in on the first day hovered in the back of my mind.

Her expression when she'd seen me—the tensing of unexpected pain, almost as bad as when I'd laid into her the other day on the green. It'd only been there for a second before her face had hardened and she'd turned away, but I hadn't been able to forget it.

I couldn't dwell on that. I couldn't think about before, about the smile I'd been able to bring to her lips or the tenderness in her eyes when she'd looked at me or the way her body had felt against mine. None of that had really been mine anyway. I'd pretended to be someone else with her, someone who hadn't done the worst of the things I'd done.

I was someone who hurt people. Better she found that out now, before we'd gotten any closer.

My hand dropped to my pocket, to the lump of the metal dragon she'd conjured from the earth for me. For the man I'd managed to briefly convince her I was. But even my friends couldn't really trust me, could they? I'd hidden the fact that I was seeing her from them. I'd told myself I was doing it to help Malcolm, but how much had I really been thinking that plan through and how much had I just been making excuses so I could have her?

He thought we needed to break her before she'd finally accept what she was and let go of all the joymancer ideas in her head. And when she'd come around to our side, he wanted her, if she'd have him. I'd stepped right in the way of both of those goals for my own selfish reasons…

I could make up for that part, at least. I'd screwed up, but I was fixing my mistakes, like Malcolm had fixed so much for me over the years. If I couldn't even do that, then I deserved every wary look the rest of the students directed my way.

So, as Rory conjured a rising patch of fire in the clay bowl on her desk, I kept half my attention on my own elemental assignment and half on picking away at hers. For each murmur I put toward building my flames up, I aimed another at making hers falter. A little chill to dull the heat. A snuffing out of this spark and that one.

The fire wavered and vanished. Rory brushed her hair back behind her ear, and I made out the edge of her frown, the movement of her lips as she tried to work the spell again. Professor Viceport came to a stop in front of her desk. I was watching closely enough to notice the fraction Rory's shoulders came up at the professor's attention.

My stomach balled. I curled my fingers under my desk and sent another murmured spell her way. Subtle and slow but steady. Draining the energy from her conjuring. The new flames in her bowl died.

"I'd expect better from you after that assessment," Viceport said in a cool tone, and walked on.

Rory didn't reply, but her jaw tightened, and the knot of my stomach tightened even more at the sight.

It didn't matter in the long run. I wasn't outright hurting *her*. Just adding a little uncertainty until she gave up on standing apart from us. When she was ready to add her strength to ours, we'd shore up hers in return.

If she'd met Malcolm in some secluded clearing away from the jostling of school politics, she probably would have liked him too. She'd never gotten to see the guy who, at seven, had waved my brother and me over to climb trees with him and the others while our mother joined her first meeting of the pentacle as baron. Who'd smiled at us even as Jude and Declan watched uncertainly. He'd come ready to accept us even if we'd only just been named scions, no matter what whispers were going around about what our parents had done to make that happen.

Rory hadn't been here for my first couple months at the university when I'd been shell-shocked with grief and guilt—for all the times when senior students who'd known the former Stormhurst scion or juniors just looking to stir shit up had tried to provoke me into a fight, and Malcolm had diffused the situation with a few cutting words and his unshakeable confidence. For all the times since then when I *had* lost my temper, and he'd come 'round to find me right afterward and ramble on as if nothing odd had happened until I felt grounded again.

He'd always believed I was worthy of his friendship even when I wasn't so sure of it myself. The least I could do in return was believe that he knew what the hell he was doing. He pretty much always did.

I focused on those memories as I snuffed out yet another of Rory's conjured flames. I couldn't let anything distract me from the loyalty I owed.

By the time class wrapped up, my stomach might as well have transformed into a rock. I ducked out of the room before Rory had even left her desk and strode across campus. I wasn't really thinking about where I was going, but my feet knew where to take me when I was in a twisted-up mood like this. The cool breeze washing over the lake brought the scents of moss and spring flowers.

I was just passing the building that carried my family's name when a voice hollered out. "Connar!"

Declan was just coming out of the building, his hair damp from the pool. I stopped as he walked over to me. He swept a few stray strands away from his forehead and peered at me with his intent eyes. Even if I hadn't known insight was his specialty, he'd have given me the impression he could see right inside my skull. Not that he was in the habit of testing our mental walls. He knew what loyalty meant too.

"We haven't had much chance to talk in a while," he said, which sounded strange to me.

"We were all hanging out in the lounge a couple days ago," I pointed out.

"I mean just you and me." He took a breath, and the wariness *he'd* never totally lost around me flitted through his expression. I'd seen it way too many times on too many faces to need any of my insight skill to recognize it. "What happened with you and Rory?"

Shit. My pulse stuttered with instinctive panic, but I knew how to keep my expression impassive. Just pretend you don't know about it, pretend it didn't happen. That approach had gotten me through plenty of clashes in the past.

I hadn't had to use it with one of the other scions before, though.

"What do you mean?" I said. "What did she say?"

Declan kept studying me. "Not much. Just enough for me to know the two of you got friendly without the rest of us noticing—and that the way you tore into her the other day really shook her up."

I ignored the first part of his statement. "Isn't that what we're supposed to be doing—shaking her up?"

"Sure," he said. "Her attitudes. Her faith in the joymancers. Whatever's getting in the way of her being able to do what she needs to do as a leader here. But she's still a scion. She *is* one of us. She deserves better than cruelty for cruelty's sake. And she's never going to warm up to us if we've been encouraging her to see us as allies and then yanking the chair out from under her when she's willing to."

"I didn't set out to yank any chairs out," I said, which was true enough. The whole situation was an epic fuck-up, one I hadn't intended or anticipated, and that was on me. Declan didn't need to know all the details.

Maybe my expression turned even sterner or some flint came into my gaze, because the Ashgrave scion eased off. "Fine. Just keep in mind that if you break her more than we can build her back up, we lose as much as she does. We need her on our side."

He stalked off, leaving me twice as tense as before.

I tried to put all of it—the conversation, the sabotage in class, the expectations I'd failed and the ones I wasn't sure I could meet—behind me as I pushed into the forest. Finding my way to the clifftop was as easy as breathing. I'd found the little rocky clearing overlooking the lake years ago when I'd stomped off into the woods, purposely veering into the thicker underbrush to give me a distraction from whatever I'd been steaming about. The moment I'd stepped out into that quiet space, nothing but trees and water around me on all sides, the emotions inside me had stilled.

It always worked. Somehow, looking out over the lake made me feel as far away from the rest of my life as if I'd taken a jet across the ocean. Maybe the rest of my life was still there when I returned to the rest of campus, but it didn't weigh on me quite as heavily right after.

At least, that was how it'd always been before. Now, when I emerged from the trees to the glittering expanse of the lake and the frame of trees all around it, a fresh wave of emotion rolled over me.

I could remember exactly how Rory had sat on the log that stretched across one end of the clearing, the way she'd held herself with all the confidence she could exude, determined not to be scared of me. The awe on her face when we'd looked out over the reflected stars. The heat of her mouth. The smell of her hair—

I closed my eyes and shook my head. No. I wasn't going there. I didn't want to go back to any of that. Anything I'd shared with Rory was in the past, far away, like the rest of the weight I carried.

No matter how much I told myself that, though, the impressions of her still lingered. I sat down with my back to a pine and couldn't help thinking that I'd been sitting exactly two trees over when she'd first ventured into this space. When my hand came to rest on the earth, it was with the sensation of how I'd laid her body down on the ground just over there, under mine.

The natural magic of this place had to come back, didn't it? If I just gave it enough time?

Today, I waited it out for half an hour before I was sure I couldn't shake the memories completely. My heart sank as I stood up.

The clifftop wasn't just mine anymore. Rory had come and made it hers too. How could I leave every uncomfortable thing behind when she was tied up in so much of that uneasiness, and she lingered up here in ways I couldn't erase?

I didn't want to erase her. I wanted to sit with her, talk with her, kiss her all over again. What the fuck was wrong with me?

Gritting my teeth, I marched back in the forest without any real sense of destination. If I walked far enough, maybe the crunch of my footsteps would drown out everything inside my head for at least a sliver of time.

CHAPTER THIRTEEN

Rory

Jude showed up in the garage carrying a cloth bag filled out in a vaguely rectangular shape. He tossed it in the back seat when he got in—on the passenger side, because last lesson I'd graduated to maneuvering, very very slowly, out of the parking spot myself.

"What's that?" I asked, settling myself behind the wheel. Faint mingled smells reached my nose: bready and sugar sweet and a tart scent that made me think of fresh strawberries.

Jude stretched his legs out as far as the space allowed and flashed me a grin. "Since we *are* going more than half a mile today, I brought a reward for if you make it to the intended destination. I picked out a picnic spot a little ways outside town."

We'd only driven into town and then back last time. My pulse sped up at the thought of taking the car farther, but I'd managed not to run into anything so far, with no further magical interventions from Jude needed.

"We're going to have a picnic?" I said with skepticism I couldn't disguise.

Jude raised an eyebrow. "They're not really a fearmancer sort of thing, I admit. I was under the impression they were a Nary thing, so maybe you'd appreciate it considering you spent most of your life mingling with them. If I'm wrong and picnics aren't anybody's thing, I can always find something else to do with a tasty lunch."

"No, no, picnics are good." And from the smell continuing to seep through the car, that one was *very* good. "Just unexpected."

He made an extravagant flourish with his hand. "I aim to be inexplicable."

"Well, you definitely do a good job of that," I muttered as I started the engine, and he laughed.

I managed to make it out of the garage and down the road into town with only a few momentary panic attacks. After I pulled off the left-hand turn at the main intersection that would lead us out into the country, my hands started to loosen where they'd been clenching the wheel. Driving really was a pretty simple process once you got used to the basics, at least out here where there wasn't much in the way of traffic or any such thing as rush hour. I didn't think I'd want to brave city streets quite yet.

As we left the last of the houses behind and cruised on along the country highway Jude directed me to, he rolled down his window. The wind ruffled through his floppy copper hair and tossed my brown waves back from my face.

A sly smile curled his lips. He motioned to the farmland around us. "It's awfully flat out here. No blind turns, no pedestrians. I think you can push that engine a little faster."

I glanced at the speedometer. "I'm at the speed limit."

He made a dismissive sound. "*Everyone* drives at least ten over. On a stretch like this, more like twenty. Common rules of the road." His smile curled a little higher. "Show me you've really got control over this hunk of steel, Ice Queen. I wouldn't want to think you're scared of a little asphalt."

My heart thumped even faster, but I knew what he'd said was true. My parents used to complain about how fast they had to go to stay with the rest of traffic rather than getting in the way, which could be even more dangerous than speeding. And that *was* in the city. Better to get used to it out here.

No problem. Just ease a little more weight onto my foot on the gas pedal. There we go.

The engine growled louder. A few pebbles rattled against the undercarriage, and I restrained a wince. The wind warbled past us.

"Not so bad," Jude said. "I think you can handle at least a bit more than this. Don't you?"

I adjusted my grip on the wheel. It felt the same as it always did. The tires sped across the pavement, and the road ahead was clear. But still I hesitated.

Jude's voice came out in a coaxing tone. "Come on, Rory. You've got this."

I did. What exactly was I scared of? I could see for myself there were no obstacles ahead.

I pushed on the gas harder, and the car raced down the road. A jolt of exhilaration ran through me. I'd been so tense and careful while I was driving up until now, I couldn't say I'd really enjoyed it. Right now, like this, it felt like flying.

I *was* in control. This vehicle and the power of its engine responded to my command without needing any magic at all.

Jude didn't prod me for more. He tipped his head back with the wind coursing in from the window and closed his eyes as if losing himself in the sensation.

Only for a few seconds. Then he straightened up again and pointed to a crossroad up ahead. "Just past that road, we're going to want to make a right. Do with that information what you will."

I slowed as we passed the intersection, the thrill of flying along the road deflating. But the reduced speed did mean I was able to spot and pull onto the dirt track a hundred feet farther without any screeching of tires.

The track led through a sparse stand of trees and petered out at the edge of a sunny field dotted with wildflowers. It was about as perfect a picnic spot as I could have dreamed up. I glanced at Jude as I put the car into park. "Are you sure you're new at this whole picnicking thing?"

Jude beamed at me and snatched the bag out of the back. "I'll take your amazement as a compliment."

It turned out the bag wasn't actually a bag but a sheet of cloth folded and tied around a wicker basket. Jude unfurled the sheet over the grass as our picnic blanket and started laying out the basket's contents. He peered up at me when he realized I was still standing there in the grass, staring.

"I can't take credit for the trappings," he admitted. "I just told the family chef I wanted the fixings and food for a picnic, and she sent all this along with the week's meals."

Somehow, that made me feel a little better. "Good," I said, sitting down on one corner of the cloth. "Otherwise I'd have to worry that you'd been possessed or something."

"By a picnic-loving spirit? You should be so lucky."

"You'll have to give my compliments to your chef." The food looked as amazing as it had smelled. There were turkey sandwiches on rolls I could tell were home baked, deviled eggs sprinkled with paprika, a fruit salad of assorted berries, lemon tarts, and bottles of fizzy lemonade. When I lifted one to my mouth, the liquid prickled over my tongue with the perfect blend of sour and sweet.

I didn't know what to say after that, so it was a good thing I had plenty to stuff my mouth with to avoid talking altogether.

When we'd polished off most of the main dishes, Jude sprawled out on his back with his elbows propping him up, squinting against the sun and looking so pleased with himself I couldn't hold my tongue.

"How did you find this spot, anyway? Or did you send your chef to do that too?"

"I am capable of doing some work for myself. I spent a few hours driving around checking the likely sites. The ones not too far away from campus, obviously. I did want to be reasonably sure you'd make it." He smirked at me.

It was hard for me to imagine Jude Killbrook going to that much trouble to set up a picnic—for my benefit, no less. "So where's the catch?" I said. "There's got to be more to this, right?"

"Because I can't enjoy a pleasant afternoon with good company unless I have ulterior motives? I'm wounded." He sighed dramatically and plucked a few berries out of the salad bowl. With a flick of his wrist, he tossed a raspberry in a perfect arc up into the air and down into his mouth. A blueberry careened after it.

"You're going to end up choking like that," I had to point out.

"Concern for my well-being! I'm making a little progress."

I resisted the urge to stick out my tongue at him. "I didn't say I'd *care* if you choked. I just thought you might like to know."

"So chilly, Ice Queen." He mock-shivered and tossed up another raspberry.

I leaned forward and snatched it out of the air in mid-arc, then popped it into my mouth instead. Jude pushed himself upright with a sound of protest. "Just saving you from yourself," I said at his glower, but I couldn't help smirking right back at him.

"In that case," he said archly, "I find I'm suddenly deeply worried that you might choke on that tart." He scooted over to snatch at the last of the lemon tarts that I'd been saving for when my stomach felt a little less full.

"Hey!" I grabbed it first and yanked it out of his reach. "You already had two. Where's your hospitality?"

"Says the woman who just literally stole the food from my mouth." He feinted left and shot out his hand to the right, and I jerked the tart away just in time.

His fingers closed around my wrist. Heat spread over my skin from that point of contact, and my body snapped into awareness of how close we'd gotten to each other, his arm across my abdomen, his knee against my thigh.

His head bowed just a foot away from mine, the sunlight catching in his dark green eyes. His stunning face filled my entire field of view. A momentary dizziness washed over me despite myself.

This was Jude Killbrook. No matter how charming he'd been the last few weeks, I'd seen how cruel he could be. He'd been that cruel to *me*.

In my distraction, he slipped the tart from my grasp and set it back on its plate. "I'm not sure this is what I want after all," he said, low and soft. He let go of my wrist, but he didn't pull back, his gaze searching mine. "I'd like to kiss you, but I'm a little concerned you might punch me."

My pulse hiccupped. I willed my voice to stay steady. "Is there any particular reason why I *shouldn't* punch you?"

"You could give kissing me a try first. I've gotten excellent reviews from multiple sources."

I made a face and gave him a shove to propel him backward, careful not to let my hand linger on his lean chest. "How romantic. Consider working on your sales pitch."

He shifted at my push, but his gaze stayed on my face. "Is the idea really so horrifying?"

"I don't know about *horrifying*, but..." I let out an exasperated sound. "I appreciate your help with the driving, okay? And the picnic. And I'll admit I've actually had fun. But you can't expect me to just forget the whole first month I was here. You've never even apologized for the crap you put me through. You can't just pretend it never happened and expect me to play along."

Jude blinked at me as if startled. As if he *had* thought he could pretend the taunting and the pain away.

"What if I don't know how to be sorry about that?" he said after a moment. "When I think about the way we came down on you, I remember how you rose to the challenge. Every tactic we tried, you pushed back harder. You were fucking brilliant. Do you think I'd be here otherwise?"

A lump rose in my throat. He sounded so sincere, but at the same time I didn't know how to wrap my head around the perspective he was offering.

"It still hurt," I said. "*You* still hurt me. I didn't ask you to put me through hell so I'd learn how to be 'fucking brilliant.' You can't pat yourself on the back for that and not take responsibility for every other part. And don't tell me that's just how fearmancers do things or whatever other excuse."

"I wasn't—" Jude's lips twisted. He lowered his head for a moment and swiped his hand through his hair as he raised his eyes again. "You're right. I hadn't thought about it that way, and I should have. I'm sorry for the pain you went through because of anything I did."

The resistance inside me softened. I hadn't really thought he'd apologize at all. But then, how much did he even mean it?

"Malcolm is still trying to come down on me," I said. "Do you know anything about that?"

When push comes to shove, will you be throwing me under the bus to make him happy?

Jude shrugged. "Malcolm's going to Malcolm. He's said some stuff about going for an indirect approach and finding more subtle ways to shake you up, but nothing specific I could tell you to watch out for. I think he's waiting to make sure whatever he's planning works before he starts bragging about it. I'm pretty sure you already know to watch out for him in general."

"If he did say something specific, would you tell me?"

"Would you want me to, even if I knew you could handle it on your own?"

"I might be able to handle it more easily with a heads up, so yeah."

Jude made a sweeping gesture with his arm. "Then consider it done."

I wasn't quite satisfied yet. Another question spilled out. "What does he think about you taking me on picnics and all this?"

"I haven't seen any point in giving him a play-by-play of our time together," Jude said. "He probably assumes I'm working voodoo on you for the cause. Easier for both of us if he keeps thinking that."

That might be true. If Jude was being sincere in wanting to make amends and separating himself from Malcolm's campaign against me, I couldn't imagine how furious the Nightwood scion would be when he found out, and he'd definitely take it out on me at least as much as his supposed friend. But only if Jude didn't have any sway at all there. Only if he assumed nothing he said would make any difference to what Malcolm did anyway.

Or if he couldn't be bothered to find out whether he could stop Malcolm, with all the trouble that the attempt would stir up.

Exhaustion washed over me just thinking about it. Maybe what he'd just said was all the answer I needed.

I started clearing the blanket, sticking the dishes back in the basket. Jude joined in with glances my way as he grabbed the last few things. He lifted his chin toward the plate by the edge of the sheet. "You still have your tart."

My stomach tightened in resistance. "You know," I said, "I'm not really hungry anymore. You can have it."

Jude didn't look particularly happy to have won that battle. Instead of eating it himself, he tucked the tart into the basket with the rest of the picnic remains. He set the basket on the grass and moved to shake off the sheet as I stepped to the side. His gaze stayed on me as he folded it up.

"I think I should be clear about something," he said abruptly. "The other girls—there aren't any other girls now. That I'm kissing. Or whatever else. There never was anyone else I really wanted anyway. I didn't know what I wanted until you. So I'm in this just for you as long as there's any chance at all. I can make up for what happened before. I *will.* However long it takes."

I stared at him. "Why? What's so special about me?" What could possibly have prompted the desperation he'd acknowledged that first day in the garage?

He dropped the folded sheet onto the basket and gave me a crooked smile. "Weren't you just lecturing me not that long ago about how you're not like us?" He waved in the general direction of the university. "Everyone in that place is so busy fighting over who's got the biggest dick—or whatever it is the girls fight over—that they haven't got room in their heads to think about anything else. You don't give a shit about any of it. You rise up above it all like an angel over the battlefield."

"I wouldn't have thought you wanted an angel."

"One who can go head to head with me, mouth off right back at me, sure." He took a step closer to me. "You know what you want. You say what you mean. You don't let anyone shake you. You're going to have assholes lining up around the block trying to get with you just because of your last name, and none of them will have a clue what really matters about you, and that's a fucking disgrace. You should at least know it."

He said every word so emphatically, his eyes holding mine, that the dizziness I'd felt earlier tingled through me again. He took another step, close enough to touch my cheek now. A jolt of fear ran alongside the heat it provoked, but he didn't go in for a kiss like I'd expected. At least, not that kind of kiss. He eased up on his feet just slightly and brushed his lips to my forehead.

My breath caught, my whole body flushing as if it'd been a much more intimate gesture. Jude dropped his hand. "However long it takes," he repeated. "I'll wait. You're more than worth it, Rory."

Part of me wanted to follow him, to grab him by the collar and find out what those lips would feel like pressed against mine. I held myself in check.

I'd rushed in with Connar. I'd let myself get swept up too quickly, and I'd obviously missed the warnings I should have noticed before. I was *not* going to let another of these guys rip my heart out like that.

"Okay," I said. "I—I guess we should get back to campus."

Jude didn't argue, just carried the picnic stuff back to the car. He sank into the passenger seat with every appearance of serene patience. I inhaled and exhaled slowly before starting the engine, willing the chaotic mess of emotions inside me to chill out.

My heartbeat had evened out by the time I'd gotten the car back onto the highway. Gazing down the empty road ahead of me, I eased my foot down on the gas pedal, inching us faster and then a little faster still. Jude made no comment, but a smile crossed his lips.

His words echoed in my head, though maybe not the ones he'd have expected to stick the most. I knew what I wanted. I didn't let anyone shake me.

I couldn't let myself be scared.

I made it into my spot in the garage without any scraped paint. Jude bobbed his head to me after he got out. "Until next time?"

"Until next time." I could agree to that much.

Outside, he set off toward our dorms, and I turned toward Killbrook Hall. There were answers I wanted, answers I *needed*, and I hadn't pushed for them because I'd been conscious of my mentor's recovery—and the fact that he might have been targeted because of me. Imogen's comment about feeling his fear had lingered with me.

He was perfectly fine now, though. He'd been going to tell me something, whether it'd been feverish nonsense or not. I had to find out what.

I'd have been willing to wait if it'd turned out Banefield was in a seminar, but he answered my first knock on his office door. "Rory," he said with a bemused expression. "You look like a girl with a mission. What can I help you with?"

I waited until he'd shut the door behind me, and then turned to him with my arms crossed. "That's what I need to ask you. What can you help me with? You were about to say something important right before you got sick. Something you were worried would happen—someone you think I should watch out for…?"

His mouth pressed flat before he answered. "That's not— I don't know how much I can tell you. I *want* to help in every way I can. But maybe that's not it."

So there was something real. I caught a flicker of fear from him now too, sharp and quavering. It made my throat close up.

"I don't want to put you in danger over this," I said. "I just want to keep myself out of danger too. Did someone *make* you sick?"

Banefield waved his hand dismissively, but he didn't look startled by the suggestion. "You don't need to concern yourself with that."

"Of course I do, if it's because of me—because you tried to help me." My heart sank. "But you aren't, not really, are you? In case it happens again."

Could I blame him for not taking the risk? Maybe not. But as the realization washed over me, I felt completely alone even with him standing right there in front of me.

Watching me, a resolute expression came over Banefield's face. "I'm so sorry, Rory. This is ridiculous. I'll try—I should at least be able to warn you that the—"

He choked on the next word. "Professor!" I yelped.

His body was already doubling over like it had before with the same sputtering retching sound. I tried to grasp his shoulder, but he fell to his hands and knees before I got a grip. With a shudder, he vomited onto the carpet. His arms gave.

I managed to catch my mentor before his face smacked right into the puddle of puke, my arms straining at his slack weight. I eased him down onto his side, my gut twisting at the smell and the sight of the sweat already dappling his lolling head. Then I scrambled to the door to call for help.

The certainty chased me there, digging deep into my chest. The health center could try to call this a regular relapse if they wanted, but they'd be wrong—or lying. It wasn't some virus or bacteria making him sick. It was me. Somehow my presence and his attempt to talk to me about that particular subject was setting off a magical bomb inside him.

What the hell did he know? And who had gone to these lengths to stop him from sharing it with me?

CHAPTER FOURTEEN

Rory

There were a lot of places I'd rather have been than in one of the Stormhurst Building's gyms while the rest of the members of the Insight league mingled and muttered around me. Unfortunately, league meetings were compulsory even if you didn't give a damn who won the term competition. I just hoped it wouldn't take too long for them to hash out whatever they wanted to hash out.

Declan had turned up a few minutes ago, giving me a slight nod but going to stand at the other end of the room. Keeping everything professional. That was fine. I preferred his distance to the glare Victory's friend Sinclair was shooting at me every time my gaze happened to pass over her. You'd have thought she was offended I'd shown up at all, as if I had any choice in the matter.

It was hard to pay much attention to either of them when my mind kept returning to yesterday's meeting with Banefield. Every time I remembered his collapse, my gut twisted with a queasy mix of guilt and apprehension.

He'd known he'd get sick again if he tried to tell me… whatever he'd been trying to tell me. That was why he'd balked. But he'd tried anyway, done his best to spit out his warning before the spell grabbed him.

Maybe I shouldn't have pushed for answers. But considering how viciously someone was punishing him for talking, I had to think whatever he knew could make the difference between my surviving here and becoming a victim myself.

I had to figure out the spell that was targeting him and how to stop it, for both our sakes. It was my fault he was sick. The staff at the health center hadn't been able to give me even vague reassurances about his recovery when I'd stopped by this afternoon. Would whoever was targeting him go even farther this time?

What if they killed him?

A bellowing voice cut through my worries. A big guy with bristly brown hair had gotten up on a chair at one end of the room so he could see over the entire crowd that had gathered—some fifty or so of us. "Insight League!" he said. "Let's get down to strategy. We've only got one month left in the term, and we're behind all the other leagues."

"As usual," a girl near me said under her breath.

"We've got *two* scions on our team now," someone near the front of the group said, pitching his voice to carry. "That's got to give us some advantage."

"Sure, let's hear what they have to say about it." The guy who seemed to have appointed himself leader of the league scanned the crowd.

"You know I can't make recommendations while I'm a teacher's aide," Declan said from his spot near the wall.

"Where's our Bloodstone?" The guy on the chair spotted me and beckoned me over. "If you've got a fresh perspective, we'd love to hear it."

As I hesitated, the gathering parted to make way for me. Sinclair let out a not-quite-surreptitious snort. Everyone was watching me now. Shit. I'd come because I had to, not because I had any interest in leading the discussion.

Now that the guy had put me on the spot, I couldn't get out of contributing without looking like a total ass. I forced myself to walk over to join him. He went as far as to hop off the chair to offer it to me. Wonderful.

I climbed up and looked uncertainly over the crowd of figures who, other than Sinclair with her sour expression, were looking at me as if I'd shown up at Villain Academy to lead them to victory. It wasn't as if my assessment results had come with a league competition strategy guide.

"Ah, as I guess everyone knows, I haven't been here at the university very long," I said. "I'm not sure what our not-so-fresh perspectives on the league competition are. When was the last time Insight won?"

A murmur that sounded half disgruntled, half amused rippled through the gathering. The leader guy beside me let out a dry chuckle. "Can anyone here remember us ever winning?"

Heads shook all around the room. Declan spoke up with a pained smile. "It's happened a few times, but very rarely—the last time was almost a decade ago. Insight can give us an advantage over the other skill areas in all sorts of ways, but it's not particularly flashy. It's difficult to use it in ways that are both effective and grab the professors' notice. I don't think we should fault ourselves for that."

"We've got to at least try to win," a girl in the middle of the crowd said.

"Okay." I resisted the urge to bite my lip. "I guess no one here knows how we managed to win those times before, then…"

"Why are we listening to her?" Sinclair's crisp voice cut through the continuing murmurs. "She can hardly figure out how to use her magic for herself."

My hackles rose. I hadn't asked to be looked to as some kind of advisor. And I *had* used my magic pretty effectively in the last few weeks, thank you very much. As the murmurs rose, my mind leapt to the other day when I'd managed to get one over on Malcolm Nightwood himself. A spark of inspiration lit in my mind.

"I might still be getting the hang of things, but I'm a fast learner." I didn't give Sinclair my direct attention, focusing on the less familiar faces around me instead. "Maybe we can't do flashy tricks, but we *can* catch on to the tricks the other leagues are planning before they can go ahead with them. Call them out so people around will be on guard and they won't be able to pull it off. I've already gotten credit for using Insight like that."

"Go around acting like a bunch of narcs?" a guy said. "I don't know."

No, it was perfect. For the first time since I'd watched Professor Banefield crumple yesterday, the sense of control I'd had racing my car along that country highway came back to me. I'd earn a little more faith from my league while stopping some of the chaos the other leagues were spreading around campus. I just had to frame it in a fearmancer-appealing way.

"We won't be narcing on them." I let a slow smile cross my face, thinking of Jude's smirk for inspiration. "We'll be getting the jump on them. Showing we know them too well for them to get away with any crap. Reminding them that even what's in their head isn't safe while we're around."

Putting it that way made me feel a little sick, but matching smiles sprang up throughout my audience.

"We could give it a shot," the leader guy said. "Scan everyone around you, looking for schemes. If we're all keeping watch, they won't be able to get much by us."

"Yeah!" a girl said. "Take away the element of surprise, and anything they're plotting falls flat. How're they going to fight back when we can see all their plans?"

I'd done enough here, right? I stepped down off the chair, and after some more enthusiastic conversation, another guy got up to make suggestions about watching for gaps in the professors' mental walls so we could find the best ways to butter them up. No one seemed to mind when I drifted toward the back of the group without commenting on any other strategies.

"We've got a month to turn this around," the leader guy reminded us before we left. "Not a word about any of the ideas we've discussed once we leave this room! You know the other leagues are always hanging around hoping to get a jump on *us*."

I slipped out of the gym ahead of most of the crowd. Outside the Stormhurst Building, the lights mounted over the door cut through the thickening dusk. Several figures were hanging around just outside the building, making an effort to look casual. Spies for the other leagues? They weren't hearing anything from me, anyway.

In California, it would have stayed warm all through the night by this time in May, but here in northern New York, a chill had already crept into the air. I hurried toward the glowing windows of Ashgrave Hall.

I hadn't made my escape quite fast enough. I'd just reached the main green between the halls and the tower when Sinclair caught up with me. "You really think you're so smart, huh, Bloodstone?"

I paused and turned to look at her. She crossed her arms over her chest, the ends of her black bob swinging along her jaw as she raised it at a haughty angle.

What the hell was her particular problem with me today? I hadn't seen her offering any useful comments during the meeting.

Most of the other students had been heading in the same direction as us. A bunch of them came to a halt rather than continuing on, watching the confrontation. My skin prickled. I just wanted to go up to my room and get away from all these people for a while, but I didn't think it'd be wise to turn my back on Sinclair while she was fuming like this.

"People asked me for ideas," I said evenly. "I gave them one."

"That's not what I'm talking about." Her lip curled with a sneer. "Miss Super Special with her four strengths, expert at Insight, and you can't even tell when you're being taken for a ride."

Had someone been messing with *her* head? I knit my brow. "I don't have any idea what you're talking about."

She guffawed. "Of course you don't. Jude wrapped you around his finger so easily, didn't he? Do you really think you're anything more than a challenge for him? He'll play you and then he'll ditch you when he's proven that he can."

My stomach tightened. Jude and I hadn't spent much time together on campus, but he hadn't made any effort to hide our little ventures in my car either. Of course other people had noticed.

Maybe she was telling the truth, or maybe she was just trying to get under my skin. Either way, she obviously wasn't looking out for my best interests, only to jab a knife in. I kept my voice steady.

"Thanks for the warning. I'll keep it in mind."

"You don't believe me. Just you wait. Please tell me you haven't fallen for the whole charade that easily. You can't think he actually *wants* you."

As she spat out the last sentence, a door behind me squeaked. Sinclair's gaze darted to the space beyond my shoulder, and her mouth snapped shut.

"And how exactly would *you* know what I actually want, Sinclair?" Jude asked in a darkly languid voice as he came up beside me.

Her stance tensed. "I was just… I—"

"You were just trying to screw me over and harass Rory at the same time. Although I'm not sure why you'd care so much who I associate with when you clearly have such a low opinion of me."

Sinclair flung a hand toward me. "You can't really like *her*. I know you. That's not who you are."

Jude folded his arms over his chest. "Maybe I'm trying out being someone else for a change. You should give it a shot. It's very refreshing."

Sinclair glowered at him for a second before shifting her gaze back to me. "It isn't going to stick. He'll be back to—"

"Fuck off, Sinclair," Jude interrupted, his voice gone flat and cold, so unlike his usual tone that Sinclair faltered completely. Her hands clenched at her sides, and then she stalked away with a toss of her hair.

Jude swiveled on his heel, taking in the other students who'd assembled to watch. The glow of the overhead lights streaking through the darkness turned his copper hair even darker and his angular face even paler. His eyes had narrowed.

"If anyone else is thinking about taking on the Bloodstone scion, I'd suggest you think again—because you'll get your ass kicked not by me but by her. And if any of you have any problem with *me* or where I choose to bestow my affections, feel free to tell me all about it now." He spread his arms as if offering himself up.

No one spoke. Several figures slunk away into the dusk. Jude clapped his hands together.

"Good. If you have any problems you *don't* want me taking you to task for, consider making sure that I'm definitely not within hearing when you start spouting off about them, and we'll all be happier." He turned to me and gave me a slanted smile. "Sorry to barge in. I'm sure you could have defended yourself, but it sounded as if my honor was at stake too."

"It's all right," I said, a little dazed. Not so dazed that an automatic retort didn't tumble off my tongue right after, though. "I guess you don't have a lot to go around, after all."

Jude barked a laugh. "And now it's under attack from both sides." He set a careful hand on my shoulder and leaned in to press the softest kiss to my cheek. There, in the middle of the green, with at least a couple dozen students still watching. Shock fluttered up through my chest.

"You are all right, aren't you?" he murmured by my ear, and I realized the kiss hadn't even been the point. He was giving me the chance to let him know if I was more affected than I was letting on without having to admit it in front of our peers. Because I was a scion, and scions weren't supposed to show weakness. Because any vulnerability these witnesses observed might be turned into a weapon against me.

With everything he'd said from the moment he'd come out, he'd been careful not to imply I'd needed saving.

"I'm fine," I said quickly under my breath, and he straightened up. His hand lingered on my shoulder for a moment longer before he withdrew it. As the warmth left my skin, it occurred to me that other than Malcolm's pompous welcome my first evening on campus, this was the first time any of the other scions had shown any public kindness to me at all, let alone a declaration of "affection," however Jude expected people to interpret the word.

How long would it take before Malcolm heard about this and figured out Jude hadn't really spent the last few weeks harassing me?

CHAPTER FIFTEEN

Rory

The woman who'd come to the front desk at the health center frowned at me with a pinched expression. "I'm sorry, Miss Bloodstone, but as you've been told before, we don't allow anyone other than family to visit patients undergoing treatment."

I'd come fresh from a morning holed up in the library, hoping I could try out a few strategies to understand how the spell was working on Professor Banefield. Considering all the fuss everyone had made about me being a long-lost scion, you'd think it would at least get me visiting rights.

"He's my mentor," I said. "He's the closest thing to family I have here."

It was true, and saying it sent a pang through my chest. If my real family *had* been here, Dad would have been doing everything he could to save Banefield, like he'd done for so many critical patients at the hospital where he'd volunteered. I didn't think the fact that my mentor was a fearmancer would have stopped him.

The woman in front of me wasn't so flexible. I could tell that gambit hadn't worked before she even opened her mouth. "I'm afraid that's still against policy. I assure you we're giving him the best treatment available."

I grimaced as I turned to leave. Their treatment wasn't good enough for them to have figured out he was under some kind of spell. Maybe if I told them more about how it'd happened—but if I revealed what he'd managed to say to me, that might put him in even more danger.

If I could find something more definite in those goddamn library books, the staff might listen to a suggestion or two even if I couldn't see him. I just had to be as sure as I could get. Before I spent any more time in the library, though, I had to get through my next Desensitization session.

My shoulders came up as I left the Stormhurst Building and started toward Nightwood Tower. My private sessions with Professor Razeden hadn't been *horrible*, and with his guidance I'd actually managed to crack through the illusions inspired by my fears the last couple times, but I doubted I'd ever look forward to those ordeals. They were designed to prepare us to stand strong against any attack an enemy might throw at us—not much fun in that.

I was about halfway to the tower when the ground suddenly tipped beneath my feet. I stumbled, and the path shifted again, rolling as if propelled by waves.

Every time I tried to catch my balance, the ground swayed in a different direction. My stomach roiled. I stared at the path ahead of me, which rippled and dipped.

What the hell was going on? I'd experienced earthquakes and smaller tremors plenty of times in California, but they hadn't felt like this. A few other students had been crossing the green, and their steps looked steady enough. As I stumbled again, the two closest to me glanced my way and started to stare.

Great. Now word would go around campus that on top of her regular screaming fits, the heir of Bloodstone had been tottering around on a Saturday morning like a drunken sailor.

The problem wasn't affecting them too—so it wasn't the whole ground. Maybe it wasn't the ground at all, only my impression of it. An illusion messing with my equilibrium.

I dragged in a breath and closed my eyes, focusing on the bits of my surroundings I knew were real. The hard surface of the paved path under my shoes. The crisp bite lingering in the spring air. The hint of roast chicken carrying in the air from the junior cafeteria where the staff would be preparing lunch for the younger students.

The lurching beneath me faded and then stopped completely, so suddenly I knew I hadn't cut off the illusion's effects myself. I adjusted my feet against the ground as I opened my eyes. A smooth voice cut through the air from behind me.

"Not so sure of your feet today, Glinda?" Malcolm sauntered around me, cocking his head as he considered my face, and my mental shield snapped into place twice as strong automatically. "You look a little seasick."

He was switching up tactics, playing with illusion as well as his main speciality. I didn't intend to give him the satisfaction of showing I was any more unsettled than he'd already seen.

"Mostly just sick of your stupid games," I said.

"Oh, don't blame it all on me. You know you're still in over your head. You're just too stubborn to admit it. Those bad dreams aren't lying, though, are they?"

I raised my chin even though my pulse had lurched. "How do you know what my dreams are like if you're not messing with them?"

"Come on, Bloodstone. Hasn't anyone told you?" He shook his head, his eyes intent on mine beneath the gleam of his golden hair. "You yell so loud I'd bet the whole hall can hear you all the way down to the library."

I swallowed, remembering the now-familiar rawness in my throat this morning. "Fuck off," I said.

The dismissal had sounded a lot more powerful when Jude had shot it at Sinclair last night. From my mouth, it fell flat. I pretended not to notice and moved to stride on past the Nightwood scion along the pathway.

"It doesn't matter how many friends you rope in or how fast you run, not when the problem's in here." Malcolm shifted forward to tap my head, so quickly I couldn't jerk out of the way in time. When I whirled around, he'd already backed up, that cocky smile still curving his lips. "I'm ready to help whenever you're ready to beg for it. Let's see how long it takes you to *wake up*."

His last words had a hint of a casting lilt, like when he was using a persuasion spell. But I hadn't felt any tap at my mental defenses—and he couldn't persuade me to wake up when I was already awake, right? I hesitated, waiting to see if any of my limbs would move without my consent, but as far as I could tell, I still had full control over my body.

I was letting him get to me, reading more into his taunts than was there. "When you beg for forgiveness for being such an asshat, then maybe I'll consider it," I retorted, and marched on.

My legs moved perfectly normally under me, but as I hurried on, a brief wave of dizziness washed over me. A blurry movement at the edge of my vision brought my head jerking around. No one was there, just the empty field leading out to the forest.

Malcolm was watching me act jumpy. I pushed myself onward to the tower.

I stopped again at the top of the stairs leading down to the basement room. The shadows that filled the crevices around the steps and the stone walls unfurled and reached toward me with filmy fingers. My heart hiccupped, I blinked hard, and they snapped back into place.

Okay, Rory, Malcolm's nowhere near you now. Get a grip on yourself.

Professor Razeden was waiting for me outside the desensitization chamber, his tall gaunt figure a little like something out of a nightmare itself. He gave me a subdued smile when he saw me, even though I was giving him extra work on his weekend.

His dry, even voice had guided me enough by now that it centered me pretty much instantly. "Miss Bloodstone, right on time. Are you ready for another go?"

"Absolutely," I said, ignoring the niggling uneasiness that had followed me down. "Let's see if I can make it through with a little less coaching this time."

"There's no shame in needing the instruction," Razeden said as he ushered me into the black walled room with its arching ceiling. "Your peers have had years to build up their defensive strategies. Believe me,

I had to talk every one of them through plenty of sessions. Get into position to begin."

I stepped into the middle of the room beneath the artificial glow of the overhead lights. What lovely horror was my mind going to conjure up this time? The spells on the chamber, when triggered by the professor, worked with a combination of Insight and Illusion, delving into our minds and projecting our greatest fears around us in terrifyingly vivid clarity. People who'd gotten more practice tended to end up with more metaphorical situations, apparently. So far mine had all been disturbingly literal.

"Slow, steady breaths," Razeden reminded me from his post near the door. "Start out calm and it'll be easier to stay there. Whatever comes, remember that you're stronger than it. You're real, and it's only an illusion."

Right. Easier said than done when you were staring your worst nightmares in the face in full living color, but at least I hadn't crumpled into a ball sobbing recently.

"Go ahead," I said.

The room went pitch black. Then a different space wavered into view around me, the lines solidifying with a blink.

My pulse thumped faster as I recognized the scene. There hadn't been many details of the building in the photos from the report on my birth parents' deaths, but a couple sessions ago my mind had constructed its own version of a vault-ceilinged grand hall where a force of joymancers had burned them to a crisp.

Like before, I found myself standing between the two groups of mages, staring up at them from a great height, as if I were a helpless toddler again. The joymancers shouted at the fearmancers, who shouted back. Even though I didn't think they'd been a part of the actual attack, my real parents stood with the intruders, Dad's face flushed an angry red, Mom's hair flying wild. My birth mother jabbed her hand at them accusingly.

I opened my mouth, but I couldn't force out more than a babble of sound. When I waved my arms, they didn't seem to see me. I took a wobbly step and fell to my knees.

No, no, no. I didn't want to go through this whole thing again.

Last time I'd had to watch them slice and sear each other until bodies had littered the floor. My only victory had been willing the images to disappear after the fact rather than needing Professor Razeden to end the illusion for me.

His voice reached me as if from far away. "Don't try to interfere with what they're doing. Accept that you can't stop the confrontation. Focus on walking away."

Walk away. Don't let myself care what they did to each other. It was already done anyway.

I pushed myself back up. One careful step, sliding my foot across the polished hardwood with my shaky toddler balance, tuning out the words whipping back and forth even more viciously around me.

"You fucking bitch!" Mom yelled, sounding like herself and yet like a stranger at the same time, and one of the fearmancers cried out. My arm shot up despite my best intentions as if I could ward off the spells they were starting to hurl at each other.

My hand had been empty a moment before. As it snapped out, the air twitched around my fingers, and a glimmering shape darted from them as if *I'd* flung something.

It whipped across the room and hit one of the joymancers right in the throat with a spurt of blood. A razorblade, metal gleaming amid the scarlet flow.

My stomach flipped. What the hell? *That* hadn't happened last time. I hadn't been able to affect either side at all.

"Don't pay attention to them," Razeden said. "Keep your eyes on that door."

Apparently he didn't have any tips related to my sudden affinity for weaponry. I guessed the same strategy still made sense. Clenching my jaw, I tore my gaze away from the illusionary man whose throat I'd just slit.

One step. Two steps. Someone screamed. My balance swayed, and my arm jerked as I tried to catch myself.

Another razor flashed from my fingers, into the fearmancer side this time. It sank into my birth mother's belly. She flinched and bowed over the wound, blood spreading across the fabric of her dress.

"No," I whispered, curling my fingers into my palms. "No—"

My protest cut off with a gasp of pain. I stared down at my hands, at more razors digging through my palms as if I'd shoved them there. The throbbing echoed up my arms. My head spun.

Razeden's voice sounded even more distant now. "One foot after the other. You can do this."

No special tips for stabbing myself? My next step sent a fresh jolt of pain through my body. Sweat trickled down into my eyes.

A fiery spell whipped past me with a flare of stinging heat. I ducked, my hand bobbed down, and a blade plummeted from it right through my foot. It pinned me to the floor with another spear of agony.

"Keep walking," Razeden said, and a laugh sputtered out of me that turned into a groan. Every part of me ached, and the smell of burnt flesh coated my mouth. My stomach heaved as if to propel what remained of my breakfast up my throat.

I hunched over to pull the razor from my foot, but I couldn't use my mangled hands. The pain radiated deeper, thumping inside my head.

"I can't," I gasped out. "I can't! Make it stop!"

The sounds and smells of the carnage vanished. The pain leached from my body, leaving me simply trembling there crouching on the floor. Fuck, fuck, fuck.

At least I wasn't sobbing. I swiped at my eyes and looked up. Professor Razeden had walked partway over to me, but he stopped at my movement.

"What happened?" he said in his usual even tone. "You looked as if you had a good grip on yourself at first. What threw you off?"

Hadn't it been obvious? I motioned to my hands. "The razors. They just came out of nowhere, and I couldn't stop them, and the illusion of the pain got so intense…"

Razeden's normally impassive expression had turned befuddled. "Razors?"

They hadn't exactly been subtle. "Yeah," I said, frowning. "They hit a couple of the other people, and then they stabbed my own hands… You must have seen them."

The look Razeden was giving me made my stomach churn all over again. "I didn't see any weapons at all—definitely not any on or around you. Are you… are you *sure*?"

"Of course I'm sure. I couldn't exactly imagine—" I stopped. That was what I'd done, wasn't it? They hadn't been part of the room's illusionary effect, the one that projected out for everyone in the space to see. They'd only appeared to my senses. Like the undulating of the ground outside right before Malcolm had taunted me.

How the hell could he have done *this*, though? Even if he could have cast from all the way outside the tower, which from what everyone I'd ever talked to had said was doubtful, there was no way he could know what the desensitization chamber was showing me to make his illusion fit. If it'd been one of the times when he and the other scions had appeared to harangue and assault me, I'd have happily shredded his fake self with a handy pair of knives.

Razeden was still eyeing me as if I'd started talking in tongues. "It was a separate illusion," I said quickly. "It must have been. I swear I saw them—I *felt* them—but if you couldn't, then it wasn't part of the exercise."

"There's no one here who could have cast an additional illusion."

"No one could from outside the room?"

He shook his head. "It's warded. No one wants outside magic influencing the process we go through in here, even accidentally."

But then—

The memory rose up in my head of Malcolm's last ominous remark, the lilt I thought I'd heard in his voice. The ghostly flickers that had crept into my vision when I'd left him behind to head down here. My throat constricted.

He couldn't have known exactly what I'd see, how the shadows would lie on the floor, on my way here either. It was as if my mind had generated those illusions just like it fed into the spells on this room.

"Is it possible to cast a spell on someone's mind that'll kick in when you're not around?" I asked abruptly. "Or, I don't know, that you can quickly trigger after the fact even if they're shielded right then?" Malcolm definitely hadn't broken through my defenses. I knew what that felt like.

Razeden frowned. "I wouldn't say that's unheard of, but it's uncommon. To embed a spell that securely and effectively takes sustained casting over a long period of time while the subject is vulnerable. Even from within the dorm rooms, it'd be difficult for anyone at a student's skill level to direct a powerful enough spell through one of the walls. I assume you've kept your bedroom secure so no one else would have access."

"As far as I know, I have." Deborah would have noticed if anyone was sneaking in and casting spells on me for 'sustained' periods while I slept, anyway.

"There's also a certain level of magic that can be transmitted via a person's familiar," Razeden said, "if the caster has access to the animal and not their intended target."

Yeah, no. Even when the scions had kidnapped my mouse, they'd only had her for an hour at most. Since then, she'd stayed more out of the way than I did.

"I don't know," I said. "Maybe I'm making excuses." Maybe Malcolm had managed to slip past my shield without my noticing? My head was starting to ache just trying to figure it out. "I guess it doesn't really matter in the end. Today was a bust."

"You've made progress. Every attempt teaches you something." Razeden paused when we reached the door. "If you believe someone is interfering with your training, Miss Bloodstone, you must do whatever you can to push back, just as you push back against the illusions in here."

Not, "Come tell me about it and I'll help." Not, "Take it up with the headmistress." Push back. Because that was all part of the Villain Academy training too, wasn't it?

I restrained myself from making a face, but the comment stirred something in me, connecting to the thing Razeden had said about familiars.

I'd been so focused on learning to defend myself and figuring out what was happening with Professor Banefield that I'd set my most important mission aside. No matter what else happened, I still needed to figure out a way to push back against this entire university and the people who ran it like a battle royale.

Almost every mage here had a familiar. All of the scions did, as far as I knew. I might not be able to get into the mindset of a fearmancer all that easily, but animals were animals. How much could I influence what went on here if I made the sort of "friends" no one would expect?

How much could I unsettle the guy who was making a career out of unnerving me?

I walked back to Ashgrave Hall tentatively, watching for new illusions, but if Malcolm had sparked some effect in my head before, it appeared to have faded away. The uneasiness still coursed through me despite my best efforts to tamp down on it. Setting my jaw, I stopped by my dorm room for just long enough to grab some leftover chicken out of the fridge. Then I headed out to the small wooden building at the far edge of the eastern field.

The door wasn't locked. The inside of the building looked bigger than the outside, with a hall and just three doors leading into the inner rooms. Right now, only the one closest to the door had a name tag on it. *Shadow*.

There was a little barred window at waist height. I knelt down and peered into the space on the other side. A dry but distinctly doggy smell tickled my nose.

Nails clicked against the concrete floor on the other side. Bright eyes gleamed with the light filtering through the window on the wall inside the wolf's stall. Malcolm's familiar peered back at me with a huff of hot breath.

"Hey, boy," I said softly, remembering how Malcolm had talked to the wolf after he'd sicced it on me weeks ago. "You must get pretty lonely cooped up in here all day. Thought I'd come keep you company for a little bit. I brought a snack."

The wolf started to growl low in its throat, but the sound cut off the second I poked a piece of chicken through the bars. It snatched the chunk up in a flash and gulped it down. Its muzzle sniffled against the window for more.

"Are you going to be nice?" I asked it. "No more of that growling?"

The wolf let out a thin whine instead. I smiled. "All right, all right. I've got plenty."

After I'd fed it the rest of the chicken, the wolf licked its chops, looking immensely satisfied. My heart thumped as I held my hand up to the bars, braced to jerk it back if need be.

Shadow sniffed my fingers. He bared his teeth for a second before he seemed to think better of that move. Instead, he nuzzled the bars.

"Good boy," I murmured, and dared to give the wolf's snout a quick rub. Shadow held still and even nudged a little closer to accept the contact.

A sense of satisfaction filled my own chest. I wasn't ready to interact with the animal—and all his teeth and claws—without bars between us for protection, but I'd taken a step in the right direction. I'd have to keep wolfish tastes in mind on my next grocery shopping trip.

As I watched Shadow prowl around his stall, another implication of the familiar connection clicked into place in my head.

Did *Banefield* have a familiar? What if his enemies had conjured his illness through it so they couldn't be tracked directly?

I just hoped I could keep my mind steady enough to find out.

CHAPTER SIXTEEN

Jude

I'd known the reckoning would come. It was only a matter of when. Word didn't take long to travel around campus. Less than twenty-four hours after I'd put Sinclair in her place, one of my dormmates knocked on my bedroom door.

"Malcolm's asking for you," he said hesitantly.

I sighed and got up from my desk. Fucking Sinclair letting her fucking claws out. As if she had any right to think I owed her something more than our occasional casual interludes between the sheets when she'd been hanging all over Chandler Viceport last week and who knew how many other guys before that.

Things could have been just fine going as they were until Rory was more sure of me, but no, now we were going to have explosions.

There were a lot of insulting things people could have said about me, and a decent number of them were true, but I wasn't going to be a coward. After all the faith I'd asked Rory to have in me, I owed *her* better than that. So I headed out to meet the self-appointed king of the scions.

Malcolm was waiting in the hall outside, his expression impenetrable, but it was fair to say it wasn't happy. "Come down to the lounge?" he said, his voice as emotionless as his face. He didn't want an audience for this hashing out. Any sign of division between the four of us would only reflect badly on all of us.

"Sure," I said with forced cheer. "I could use a drink."

Malcolm didn't say anything on the way down. When we came into the basement lounge, Connar was at the pool table, taking what looked like an aimless shot at the scattered balls. He straightened up at the sight of us, his jaw tightening. He might not be the sharpest tack in the box, but he knew this conversation wasn't going to be a pleasant one.

Declan hadn't graced us with his presence, but he was no doubt busy with aide business or baron business or whatever other responsibilities he'd added to his plate now. Sometimes I wondered if the guy had started to thrive on stress the way the rest of us were fueled by fear.

I walked straight to the bar cabinet and went about mixing myself a Jack and Coke. Malcolm stopped by one of the couches, folding his arms over his chest.

"What do you think you're doing, Killbrook?"

The temperature of his tone had dropped by about fifty degrees. Between that and the switching to last names, he might as well have aimed the tip of a sword at my throat.

"Making myself a drink," I said breezily. "I'd have thought that was obvious." I lifted my glass as I turned to face him, giving the dark liquid a little swirl.

Malcolm glowered at me. "You know what I mean. What the hell is going on between you and the heir of Bloodstone? We're supposed to be shaking her up, not cozying up to her. And I told you to keep your hands off."

My smile hardened. "You told me not to 'hit and split', if I recall correctly. I'm not planning on splitting. And shaking her up was *your* plan, not mine. It's gotten rather boring, don't you think? I'd rather appreciate who she is than rearrange her into something else."

"*Who she is* is a joymancer-sympathizing, feeb-loving party-crasher who thinks we're all assholes and is doing whatever she can to stick it to us."

"Has it ever occurred to you that maybe we *are* assholes?"

Malcolm tossed his hands in the air. "Fine. We're assholes, which we need to be because we've got a whole bunch of other assholes to keep in line when the time comes. She's chipping away at all the authority we've had here, all the authority we're going to need when we're barons."

I grimaced. "Is that your father talking or you?"

Maybe that hadn't been the wisest jab to make. Malcolm's eyes flashed, and his voice came out even tighter. "We should want the same things. She doesn't give a shit about the pentacle or everything they've built. She'd probably be happy to see it all come crashing down, the way she talks."

He might be right, but then, I didn't think we'd given Rory much reason to be happy to stand beside us either. I took a sip of my drink, the mix of sweet and sour tingling over my tongue. "Well, so far she hasn't seemed very impressed by the authority we've managed to exert over her. I'm comfortable with changing my own approach. You feel free to do you."

"It's starting to work," Malcolm said. "It might have already worked if you'd been holding up your end. We're in this together. We're supposed to have each other's backs."

A sudden surge of anger welled up inside me, hot and prickling. "Are we? And when exactly have *you* ever done anything for *me*?"

For a second, the Nightwood scion just stared at me. "What the hell are you talking about? I'm looking out for the rest of you all the time. I got us this room we're standing in right now, didn't I?"

"Which you enjoy just as much whether we're here or not."

"That's not— Fine. How many times did I get the seniors you kept mouthing off at to back down when you first got here? Or smooth things over with one teacher or another because you'd had one too many of those and couldn't keep your snark to yourself." He motioned to my glass.

My shoulders tensed. I might have hit the alcohol a little heavier than had been smart my first year here, but I'd had plenty of shit I needed to drown. Shit I never could have told the guy in front of me about, because he'd have tossed me out of here faster than I could blink. He was loyal to a fucking concept, not *me*.

"You like playing the big man who has everything under control," I said. "Back then, I let you. I could have handled all that myself like I do now."

"If you believe that, you don't have a very good memory."

Connar stepped closer to us with an appeasing gesture. "Guys, I don't think—"

"How about this?" Malcolm barreled on. "I probably saved your fucking life that one night, making sure you didn't choke on your puke when you downed that whole bottle of scotch. I was the one who found you. The three of us sat there for *hours* working out how to conjure some of the alcohol out of your system to make sure your heart didn't stop beating. Or do you think you could have handled that on your own too?"

I'd shoved that night into the deepest depths of my memory. It came back at his words with a sickening rush of cold. My tongue flew before I'd had time to think about my response. "I'd bet I could have. I wouldn't be the first freshman to ever get blackout drunk. And were you even thinking about me or only the fact that if you'd had to go to Ms. Grimsworth about it, she'd have kicked us out of here and you'd have lost your precious lounge?"

Malcolm's voice came out in a snarl. "You—"

"*Guys.*" Connar stepped between us, shoving us back from each other, his own expression tensed. I'd heard him snap at plenty of other people, but never at any of us. He looked from Malcolm to me and back again. "Just stop. We shouldn't be arguing like this."

"*He* should remind himself what loyalty is," Malcolm muttered, but he turned away with a rough exhalation. Because of course he could get himself back under control just like that. How much could a guy who held himself in that rigid a fist ever care about anyone but himself?

I downed the rest of my Jack and Coke and resisted the urge to toss the glass at Malcolm's head to see how he'd respond to that. "I suppose I'll take my leave, then. Have a wonderful night."

"Jude," Connar said as I stalked to the door, but I ignored him. His first loyalty was to Malcolm, always. I didn't need to hear him explain to me how wrong I was too.

All the buried emotions the fight had stirred up churned in my gut as I climbed the stairs to the main floor. The thought of shutting myself away in my bedroom made me sick. I hesitated in the hall outside the library and then strode out across the green to Nightwood Tower.

The main music rooms for orchestra practice were on the lower floors of the tower, but there were a few smaller ones for private practice tucked away near the top. I'd often thought the layout had been planned that way on purpose to give the scholarship students' lungs an extra work out on the way up. You couldn't really play until you could breathe the music.

No one was in the tower at this time in the evening. I didn't pass a soul on the way up to the piano room, which was exactly the way I preferred it. I'd come to Mr. Hackov, the main music professor, for further instruction beyond what I'd taught myself, but he was the only one in the school who'd ever heard me play. He was the only one anywhere who'd heard me play. I could only imagine what Dad would make of *this* little hobby I'd picked up.

I closed the door, sat down on the bench, and rested my fingers on the keys. My hands moved automatically, falling into the patterns of the Beethoven sonata that was one of my more recent acquisitions.

The muscles in my fingers stretched, and as I leaned into the melody, the world narrowed down to just me and the instrument and the rising song. The notes spilled out around me and through me, washing over everything else and covering it back over much faster and more thoroughly than anything in a bottle had ever been able to manage.

I wasn't quite so lost in the song that I missed the squeak of the door. My body froze, my head jerking up.

Rory was standing there by the door that was just a few inches ajar, her fingers curled around its edge. She froze too, with a guilty expression. “Hey,” she said warily.

If she’d walked in on me getting out of the shower, I’d have felt less naked. And not the kind of naked I’d imagined getting with this girl. Fuck.

I dropped my hands to my lap and cast about for my composure, pulling my mouth into a smile I hoped looked casual. “Hey, yourself. What are you doing up here?”

She eased inside and closed the door gently behind her, but she didn’t come any farther into the room. Her dark eyes searched mine with an intentness that made my mouth dry up. She’d seen more than I’d have wanted her to, that was for sure. A reoccurring theme with the heir of Bloodstone.

“I was in the library—I saw you and Malcolm going downstairs. I figured when you came back up, we might be able to talk.”

I raised an eyebrow. “And instead of talking to me right away, you followed me over to the tower and up to the fourteenth floor without saying a word.”

She bit her lip. “You seemed to be in a hurry. I wondered where you were going.”

“So you snuck along to find out.” I laughed without needing to force it, finding a little comfort in teasing her. “Hell, you must have used magic to stop me from hearing you. You’re getting the fearmancer tactics down pat, aren’t you?”

A blush colored her cheeks. “I’m sorry. I didn’t mean to intrude.”

“Sure you did. That’s okay. I like seeing the sly side of you.” Maybe if we focused on that, we could forget whatever side of me she’d seen before I’d noticed her.

No such luck. She hesitated and then said, “Are you all right? You looked— I know Malcolm can’t be happy.”

“Which is why it’s a good thing I don’t much care what he thinks of me. I’ve got to get my practice in sometime.” I tapped the keys gently.

“I didn’t know you played.”

“It’s not something I widely advertise. People would be lining up demanding I put on concerts and so on, you know. It'd really be too much hassle."

The corners of her mouth twitched upward. Score. Making light of a situation always allowed it to go down so much easier.

"You're good," she said with a teasing note in her own voice. "Maybe you *should* put on concerts."

I made a dismissive sound and shifted over on the bench. "It's not all that hard once you get the basics down. Come here. If I can teach you how to drive, I can teach you piano."

She lowered herself onto the bench leaving a careful few inches between us, but there weren't the built-in barriers the car provided. My arm brushed hers as I leaned over to grasp her hand, positioning it over the keys. Her soft skin warmed my fingers. I focused on that and not how close the rest of her body was to mine.

"You can play the chords. That's C major. This is G major. A minor. F major. Again?"

She repeated them with a couple of adjustments from me. After the third run-through, I gave her an approving nod. "Perfect. Play them in that order, and I'll handle the rest."

"That's a song?"

"It will be."

She started playing the chords at a steady rhythm, and I let my fingers trip over the keys, improvising a melody to match the simple pattern. I could hardly call myself a composer, but my spur-of-the-moment invention wasn't half bad, really.

I sped up, making the song more intricate and adding a flourish here and there, and Rory laughed. In the middle of that, she lost track of her progression and fumbled with the keys.

"Ack," she said. "I ruined it."

"Can't ruin what's just noodling around. You kept up just fine."

She looked down at her lap and then, with a determined air, reached out and took my hand in hers, twining our fingers together as they came to rest on the bench between us. My heart skipped a beat. I was abruptly afraid to say anything in case whatever fell out of my mouth destroyed the moment.

I'd never worried like this with any other girl. I'd just gone for it, and most of the girls I'd gone for had been happy to have my attention for however long I felt like giving it, which I'd admit was generally not very long. But Rory wasn't like any other girl I'd known.

I'd thought, when I set this friendship or whatever it might become in motion, that I was mostly being strategic. How had I become this marshmallow of a guy who simply wanted to see her smile at me, who got giddy over her holding my hand, for fuck's sake?

I didn't know, but I wasn't sure I minded either. I just wished I could be sure I wouldn't fuck things up. This was all unfamiliar ground.

"Malcolm was angry with you," she said. It wasn't a question.

I shrugged, running my thumb over the back of her hand. "He told me to fall in line. I told him to go fuck himself. It was a very productive conversation."

"I don't suppose he mentioned anything about what magic he's been working—or trying to work—on me?"

"No, unfortunately he didn't reveal any of his evil plans. I'm sorry—I should have pushed harder on that." I should have prodded him about exactly what he had going to "shake up" Rory before I'd laid into him. There was no way he'd cough up anything he wouldn't want her to know to me now. Damn it. Thinking before I spoke wasn't a particular talent of mine.

"That's all right. I guess it's a little much to hope that he'd hand you everything I'd want to know just like that." She paused. "I didn't get a chance to thank you for last night."

I looked at her with half a smile. "For what? I told you, I was simply defending my own honor."

She gazed back at me with so much compassion in those deep blue eyes I wanted to drown myself in them. "There were a lot of ways you could have done that. You made a statement. I realize that—and I appreciate it."

Had she leaned a little closer to me? I thought she had. I took a gamble.

"I did get a kiss out of it." I ducked my head to brush my lips against her cheek. Her breath came out with a slight hitch. She didn't pull away. No, she was definitely easing toward me with a tightening of her fingers around mine.

I dipped lower and pressed another kiss to the corner of her jaw, the caramel sweet smell of her skin flooding my lungs. I wanted to taste her everywhere, but this would do for now. I trailed my mouth down to the side of her neck. Her pulse thumped against the gentle flick of my tongue.

"Jude," she said, her voice rough. I pulled back, with only a minor pang of disappointment since I hadn't been sure she'd welcome my affection even that much. I was about to make some flippant comment to carry us through any awkwardness of the moment when she traced her fingers over my cheek and drew my mouth to hers.

Yes, thank God. I could have kept waiting, but Lord knew I hadn't wanted to. I ran my fingers into her silky hair as I kissed her back, reining in the urge to claim her mouth with everything I had in me. Her lips were even softer than the rest of her and just as sweet, and when they parted, the breath that met mine was searing hot.

My Bloodstone scion. My Ice Queen. My avenging angel. Mine, mine, mine. The thought rolled through me with the pounding of my heart, but I wasn't really aiming to make her mine. I was aiming to be hers. Her ally, her friend, her lover, her whatever-the-hell-she-needed-me-to-be, as long as it meant she'd have me, one way or another.

I'd assumed I'd have to fall one way or another, sooner or later, but maybe not. Not if she'd hold me up here with her.

I released her hand to slide my arm around her back, tucking her closer against me. Rory let out a hungry sound and kissed me harder. I could almost feel the power of her magic thrumming through her as if her body were a live wire. It turned me on like a shock of electricity straight to my groin.

My fingers teased through her hair, over her shoulder, and down the side of her chest, just barely skimming the curve of her breast. Rory's breath stuttered—and not entirely with desire. A flicker of anxiety passed from her to me.

I rested my hand on her waist and forced myself to relinquish her mouth. "We don't *have* to do anything." I murmured, our faces still so close together my nose bumped hers. “If it’s too much—if you want to stop—”

“I’ll let you know,” she said before I had to keep going. She gave me a shyly sly smile. “For now… The kissing is good. Please continue.”

I chuckled and caught her mouth again.

Yes, the kissing *was* good. This girl was good—good enough to stake my entire future on.

CHAPTER SEVENTEEN

Rory

"Do you think it's possible?" I asked Imogen, leaning my elbows on the dorm room table on either side of my now-empty lunch plate. "Could a sickness spell be passed on through someone's familiar?"

She tapped her spoon against the bottom of her bowl. The sweet tomato-y smell of the soup she'd eaten still laced the air. "Like I told you before, I'm not an expert at this stuff yet. And offensive magic isn't what I'm specializing in anyway. But from what I do know, I don't see why it *couldn't* be possible. It can't be what's going on with Professor Banefield, though."

I frowned. "Why not?"

"He doesn't have a familiar anymore," Imogen said. "Someone asked him about it in one of my classes with him. He got a little sad-looking and said the one he'd had for a long time had passed on, and he didn't plan on taking another one." We'd already been speaking quietly even though we were alone in the common room, but she lowered her voice even more. "I heard from one of my dad's coworkers that it's because of his wife."

"How so?"

"It's really tragic. She was in a car accident down by New York City years back. A drunk driver came out of nowhere. She was hurt so bad she couldn't call for anyone to help, and the Naries who showed up couldn't do enough to save her. The worst part is, she was pregnant, but not far enough along that they could rescue the kid either." She grimaced. "Anyway, he and his wife got their familiars together—cats that were sisters. I guess for him it was one last connection to her. When his cat died, he didn't want to get another one."

"That's awful," I said. "The whole thing about his wife, I mean." A pang of sympathy ran through me. Banefield had always seemed so warm and easy-going with me—other than when I'd gotten on his case about Shelby and her tree, anyway. The poor guy.

My mind slid back to my own parents with a flash of memory: Mom's defiant face, blood on the kitchen tiles. I closed my eyes for a second as my own grief welled up the way it did here and there without warning. Breathe into it and breathe it out.

I was going to get justice for them. That was the only reason I'd stayed here at the university. Maybe Banefield would help me, whether he realized he was doing it or not—if I could help him first. I owed him either way.

"What about—" I started, and cut myself off at the squeak of the door. Shelby slipped into the dorm room, her face brightening at the sight of us. My jab of resentment at the sight of *her* was chased by a pinching of guilt. It wasn't her fault I couldn't talk about anything magical in front of her.

"One more week until the concert," she said, coming over to the kitchen with springier steps than usual. "We're going to knock your socks off."

I had to laugh. "I can believe it, with all that practicing."

She peered into the fridge and sighed. "I should have gotten more food yesterday."

"I've got some sandwich fixings left if you want," I said. "Although then I should probably get some groceries too." I checked the time on my phone. "I've got class in ten minutes, but when I'm out at two, you want to make a trip of it?"

"Sure." Shelby beamed at me, and even the little bit of resentment I'd felt faded away. Maybe I couldn't talk to—or around—her about one important part of my life, but she was a good friend, and she obviously appreciated my friendship a lot too.

I glanced at Imogen, who would have been an even closer friend if betrayal hadn't soured the pot. She gave me a wry smile as if she suspected my internal dilemma.

She had answered a lot of my questions about the whole magical illness thing, even been willing to look Banefield over herself. And she hadn't acted too weird about whatever commotion I'd been making during my repeated sleep episodes. Maybe we weren't going to be best buddies now, but I could still enjoy her company without giving away anything too personal.

"Do you need anything in town?" I asked. "We could make it a group trip."

She hesitated, and my gut clenched. Her gaze darted away from me. Oh. Apparently she was starting to rethink associating with me, at least outside this dorm room, after all.

"I stocked up not that long ago," she said, getting up. "But thanks."

I tried not to let her retreat faze me. Maybe she really just didn't want to make the walk. Shelby hummed an energetic tune at perfect pitch while I cleared my dishes and retrieved my sandwich materials from behind the illusion that concealed them, careful not to let the Nary student see. I focused on that upbeat sound as I headed out for my afternoon seminar in Illusion.

So, the sickening spell couldn't be coming through a familiar. I'd have to find another angle. If I could have at least seen Professor Banefield… I'd heard he'd been moved to his quarters for comfort but was still too sick to even think about returning to regular work.

An idea tickled up in the back of my head. Maybe it didn't need to be *me* who saw him.

I wasn't so distracted by working out logistics that I forgot my duty to my league when I stepped into the classroom. My gaze darted across the faces of the five students already in the room as I murmured "Franco" with the intake of my breath. I got a burst of imagery from an argument with the parents here and hit a wall there, but the girl in the middle of the room gave me a flash of a scheme to shift into mountain lion form and leap through the room the moment we were all focused on the lesson.

I caught her eye and stepped up to her desk, bringing the best authoritative tone I could to my voice. If I was going to cut down on the chaos at Blood U, I needed to do it in a way these people would respect.

"I'm usually a cat person, but I think you'd better stay in human form," I said, loud enough for the whole room to hear. "No credits for Physicality today."

The girl shrank back in her chair with a stutter of fear to my chest and a glitter of frustration in her eyes. Professor Burnbuck looked up from his desk and tipped his head to me as I sat down in the corner. "Credit to Insight."

A guy who'd been at our league meeting caught my eye from across the room and let out a short but appreciative whoop. I was proving my strategy worked. At least I'd made progress in one area, no matter how minor, today.

Declan's smile when he greeted me at the aide's office door looked weirdly stiff, and everything he said as we got started on our tutoring session was a little more abrupt than usual, as if he were getting it out quickly before he accidentally said the wrong thing. At first I thought maybe it was because one of the other teacher's aides was consulting with a student at the other end of the room. But even after they left, he didn't relax.

"Is something wrong?" I asked.

His gaze jerked to mine, with a tensing of his jaw that told me something definitely was. "No, everything's fine," he said.

I eyed him for a second and then pretended to let it go. But a few minutes later, I said casually, "Can you test my wall right now? Give it a good shove? I think it's strong enough, but it's so hard to tell."

"Of course." Declan fixed his gaze on my head and murmured his casting word that I still hadn't been able to make out. At the same time, I whispered my own.

He had to let down his defenses to try to attack mine. Maybe he'd get a glimpse inside my head while I did this, but that was a fair trade for a quick peek at whatever was pinging around at the front of his.

I fell into his mind with the rush of sensation that was becoming familiar. Only a few scattered images flitted by before he launched me back out again with a slam of his wall—Declan wasn't any slouch—but I'd seen enough: a sliver of a memory of Jude leaning in to kiss my cheek in the hazy light outside Ashgrave Hall.

I hadn't known Declan had been in our audience the other night, but he must have been with the bunch of Insight league-ers who'd been heading back to the dorms. Apparently the moment had stuck with him.

"What was that about?" he said, not just abrupt but sharply now.

"You're acting strange, and you wouldn't tell me why. I'm just practicing my skills. Isn't that what a good fearmancer would say?" I gave him a tight little grin. "Do you have a problem with me and Jude being… friendly?"

Declan ran his fingers through his hair, but he looked as if he'd relaxed a little having the subject out in the open. "It's not really any of my business, is it?" he said, and looked up at me again.

The brilliance of those hazel eyes sent an uncomfortable shiver through my chest. It wasn't any of Declan's business, and I shouldn't have cared whether it affected how he thought about me, because he'd made it abundantly clear that nothing anywhere near that friendly was ever going to happen between him and me. I couldn't deny that I was still attracted to him, though.

How greedy was I? The memory of kissing Jude the night before, alone in the piano room, came back with a rush of heat—I didn't regret that for a second. But I wasn't sure I'd have turned Declan down if he'd gone for a kiss himself. Imagine having both of them. Two mouths on me, two sets of hands traveling over me…

Okay, Rory, back to reality. Clearly that interlude with Jude had woken up all kinds of desires that weren't happy about being kept bottled up. I wasn't going to throw myself into an orgy. Not that Declan was offering in the first place.

Another, much more unnerving thought struck me. "Do you think he's being real with me? He hasn't— You guys have your meetings in the basement all the time. If he's said something—"

Declan cut me off with an emphatic shake of his head. "I don't know what he's thinking or why he decided to change his, er, approach, but he hasn't said anything when I've been there that makes me think he's got ulterior motives. It's not part of any bigger plan, anyway. Malcolm is definitely very pissed off about the whole thing."

That matched up with what Jude had told me. He'd *sounded* like he was telling the truth. And the way he'd looked when I'd first peeked into the room, when he'd had no idea I was even there, his expression so lonely and lost… That hadn't been the face of a guy celebrating the culmination of a plan. That'd been the face of a guy who'd crossed a line with his friends he wasn't sure he could ever cross back over.

And he'd done it for me.

"You know," Declan said tentatively, "no matter how much he means whatever he's said to you right now… He doesn't have any siblings. There's no immediate family for the barony to pass on to. It'd cause a whole lot of chaos if he threw his position away—and I've never seen any indication that he'd want to do that."

Oh. I hadn't thought about that angle—I'd barely accepted the idea that I wanted to kiss Jude, so I sure as hell hadn't been considering future marriage plans. It'd actually been kind of a relief to know that he wasn't making some kind of play because of my status, since he had the exact same clout.

He had sounded awfully serious when he'd talked about what he admired about me, about being willing to wait for me, for a guy who only expected this to be something temporary, though.

"I didn't realize that," I said. "I guess that's something I should talk to him about."

"Yes. Talk to him." Declan let out a dry laugh. "It *isn't* my business, and I've no claim here, but… I don't want to see you get hurt. Not like that." He paused. "How do you feel about him?"

"I—" I brought my hand to my mouth, inadvertently stirring

up kissing memories again. We hadn't gone much farther than that, but just the kissing had been thrilling enough to burn into my mind.

With Jude. Jude Killbrook. Another part of me still balked at the idea.

"Confused," I settled on. "Very, very confused."

Declan's mouth shifted into a pained smile. "None of us has made it very easy for you, have we?"

"Well, at least I know for sure Malcolm hates my guts. That's pretty straightforward."

"I'm not so sure about that," Declan muttered. I guessed Malcolm's maliciousness could be plenty complicated.

Being the guy in charge obviously mattered a lot to the Nightwood scion, and I wasn't surprised that Jude might enjoy that kind of authority, but…

The question tumbled out. "Why is it so important to you? Being baron—ruling over people? Or are you just worried about causing chaos too?"

Declan stiffened. "It's not that. It's—" He paused, his gaze sliding across the room. "I have a little brother. He's seventeen now—he was practically a newborn when our mother died."

I didn't need to ask to know how much his brother meant to him. It was written all over his face. "He could take the barony, then, couldn't he?"

"Maybe. I haven't put him in a position where he had to consider it." Declan looked at me again. "My aunt—my mother's sister—took over as regent baron when I was younger. She wants the position for herself and her family."

I cringed, remembering Imogen's story about Connar's parents. "Has she tried to attack you?"

"So far she's stuck to undermining me in ways my father and I have been able to overcome, and she hasn't risked making too big a move out of fear of being caught, but the older we get… As long as my brother and I are alive, we're the primary heirs. We're a threat to her goals. As long as I'm holding onto the barony, I'll be her main target. She'll leave Noah alone. I've put everything I have into making sure I hold onto my position so she never has any reason to set her sights on him."

Something he'd said in our tense moment in the library came back to me. *Everything I have, I had to fight for.* I'd accused him of taking the easy route, of not caring enough to put in a real effort. No wonder he'd been angry.

He'd made himself a shield to protect his brother. Anything I asked from him beyond the requirements of a job might as well be an attempt to crack that shield.

A deeper emotion stirred beneath the constant flickering of attraction. The fearmancer world must feel as much like a war zone to him as it did to me. All the strictness and the attention to rules that had frustrated me weren't just for his own gain but a set of defenses he no doubt needed to survive.

And he'd done it. He'd kept his position and shielded his brother for how long, without an elder baron to really guide him?

Because the joymancers had killed the baron who should have been there for him, to shield *him* from his aunt's machinations.

"When did you take over the barony?" I had to ask.

"Six years ago," he said, which in my quick mental calculation put him at fifteen. At that age, all I'd had to worry about was finishing my latest homeschool assignments. "I started insisting on sitting in on meetings a few years before that. I'm still not full baron, though. My aunt has the right to stay on as my 'advisor' until I finish my education here."

"So this has basically been your whole life." Had he ever gotten to really be a *kid*?

"It's what I was born for. I'm doing my best with it." His smile came back, small but genuine. "You don't need to worry about me, Rory. I'm happy with my choices."

He just hadn't had very many. I dropped my gaze and rubbed my mouth, abruptly lost for words. "Are we okay to keep going with the tutoring?"

Declan blinked, startled. "Of course. I'm sorry I let my concerns about Jude interfere with our work. I'm not allowed to be jealous—can't get much more straightforward than that."

It didn't sound easy to me, but I wasn't going to try to argue him out of helping me. Especially not when there was a specific way I'd been hoping he could help me deal with whatever crap Malcolm had brewing.

"Good," I said. "There's something else I'd like to focus on for the rest of our time today. We went over some techniques before for basic defenses during sleep, but I'm… not sure they're totally doing the job. Any more intensive strategies you know, let me at them."

CHAPTER EIGHTEEN

Rory

I glanced up and down the hall of wooden doors and murmured as quietly as I could, "Are you *sure* you're up for this?"

Deborah adjusted her position in the loose sleeve of my blouse. Her fur tickled against my wrist. *It feels good to be getting out of that dorm building for once. If I can help you more than I've been able to so far—this is what I'm here for.*

"Okay." I pushed down the twinge of guilt. I wasn't putting her in that much danger. The health center mage who was coming by a few times a day to check on Professor Banefield had left ten minutes ago. I'd watched him exit the building. No one else should be in Banefield's quarters except the professor himself, who I didn't think was alert enough right now to notice one little mouse.

I curled my fingers so my familiar could drop down into them and peek around the hall herself. "Do you see any gaps you could squeeze through? That's his door, the next one on the right."

There's a gap at the bottom of the frame I should be able to manage. I'm discovering the best thing about old buildings is they've had lots of time to warp. Her dry chuckle tingled through my head. *Let's do this, Lorelei.*

I stopped just outside Banefield's office door and knelt as if to adjust the strap on my shoe. Deborah darted from my hand and squirmed through the gap under the door in two seconds flat. My pulse hiccupped as I straightened up again, but I couldn't linger there. I had to give her time to make her investigations and then pass by again when she'd be waiting.

Thankfully, I had a perfectly good excuse to go calling on the headmistress. I hadn't talked to Ms. Grimsworth since Banefield's second collapse, other than briefly right after I'd called for help. She couldn't blame me for having questions now that he'd been sick for more than a week.

I'd made an appointment, so the headmistress was expecting me. To my surprise, she answered the door and immediately ushered me out into the hall instead of welcoming me into her office.

"You're coming by with excellent timing, Miss Bloodstone," she said. "I would have requested your presence later today if you hadn't gotten in touch. Given the uncertain state of your mentor's health and how new you still are to the school, I've decided it's best if I assign you a temporary substitute mentor while Professor Banefield continues to recover."

He was that bad, then, that she didn't think he'd be able to offer me guidance again any time soon? I swallowed hard. "*Is* he recovering? That was actually why I wanted to see you—I know the health center let him return to his apartment here..."

"He has shown progress," Ms. Grimsworth said with a grim expression that suggested it hadn't been much. "They don't feel he's in critical condition at the moment, and he's more comfortable in his own space." She motioned me down the hall.

"Do they know what exactly he's sick from?" I ventured. I wasn't sure it was safe to outright ask about the possibility of malicious magic being involved, but it made sense for me to worry in general. "I saw him in between the two episodes—is it something contagious?"

"From what they've told me, there's no apparent threat to the rest of us. If there was, we'd have him taken to his home off campus." She stopped in front of one of the doors down the hall and rapped her knuckles against it.

I hadn't had a chance to ask her who she was assigning as my new mentor, but the plaque on the door told me in an instant. *Prof. Isla Viceport.*

Oh, shit. The Physicality professor had been chilly with me from my first seminar with her, for no reason I could figure out. When I'd asked her if there was anything wrong with my performance in class, she'd brushed me off with a cutting remark. And since I'd started my new schedule with two Physicality seminars a week, I'd been struggling to keep up. My conjurings and transformations kept falling apart even as I tried to build them up.

Professor Viceport had not been impressed. Her cold disapproval hadn't exactly helped my concentration or confidence.

"I—" I started, fumbling for a protest that wouldn't sound pathetic, but it was too late. Viceport opened the door and peered at us through her rectangular glasses. Stick-thin, her tall frame looked as if it'd been made out of sinew and wire, but she managed to hold it with a certain elegance that made me feel small under her gaze.

"You're already familiar with each other," Ms. Grimsworth said briskly. "I'll let you two discuss how you'll proceed with Miss Bloodstone's mentorship until such time as Professor Banefield can return to his post."

She nodded to Viceport and headed back down the hall, leaving me stranded there with the teacher whose gaze had only gotten icier as she'd studied me.

"Well, come in," Viceport said in a clipped voice, and spun so quickly her ash-blond pixie cut fluttered around her head.

Her office looked a lot like her: sleek, pale, and elegant. She had the same built-in mahogany bookshelves as the other staff offices I'd been in, but her chairs were modern white leather, her desk glass-topped. A light peach rug covered most of the hardwood floor.

I sank into one of the chairs opposite the desk automatically, my hands coming to rest on the cool leather arms, but Professor Viceport stayed standing, her lips pressed into a pinched frown.

"I will assist with any issues you have beyond your classwork as need be. I trust you are mostly up to speed and settled in at this point." She lifted her phone from the desk. "Let's determine the best time for our weekly meetings, and that should cover it for today. Will Tuesdays at four work for you?"

"Um, I have a seminar then. I was seeing Professor Banefield in the morning on—"

"I can't keep to your original session time. Five on Tuesdays or three on Thursday?"

"Three on Thursday should be okay." I reached into my purse to make a note for myself, and Viceport stepped back to the door. She really didn't want to spend any more time with me than she absolutely had to, did she.

I got up as she rested her hand on the doorknob, but my nerves jittered. I'd expected to be able to maintain a decent conversation with Ms. Grimsworth to give Deborah the time she needed. I didn't think she'd have finished her investigations yet. I couldn't just stand around in the staff hallway for minutes on end waiting for her to emerge.

There had to be ways I could stall. I fumbled for another topic—the one I'd brought up with the headmistress should work. Viceport specialized in Physicality, after all, which was the domain any health-related magic fell under among the fearmancers.

"Have you seen Professor Banefield since he got sick?" I asked. "I don't know if you've done much work on the medical side of Physicality…"

Viceport gave me a flat look. "I haven't seen your former mentor. What exactly do you think I could tell you if I had?"

"I just wondered if you had any idea what's wrong. He does seem to be pretty sick—it's hard not to worry."

The professor sighed. Her voice came out not just chilly but frigid now. "Miss Bloodstone, I realize you've gotten much fanfare for your return and your assessment, but regardless of your family, the world does not revolve around your desires. The health center staff are looking after Professor Banefield. He will recover on his own time regardless of how much you'd prefer to continue consulting with him rather than me. His needs come before your own at this particular moment."

My face flushed. "That's not—that wasn't what I meant." Why did she have to take a totally normal expression of concern and turn it into something horribly selfish?

"If you insist." She turned the knob to open the door.

She might have been a professor, but there was only so much of that cool, cutting tone I could take before my temper flared.

"What exactly is your problem with me?" I said. "We're going to have to see each other even more than usual now. Whatever it is, you might as well tell me so I can at least try to do something about it."

Viceport stared down at me, just a hair shy of a glare. "I know Bloodstones well," she said. "The apple rarely falls far from the tree, and I haven't seen any reason to believe it did this time. I will teach you. I will not be your friend."

She tugged the door wide. I wavered for a second and then walked out with no idea how I could answer that. She'd known Bloodstones? Great. I hadn't known any of them. I couldn't even be totally sure whether being like my mother and whatever other relatives I had on that side was a good thing or a bad one by my definition.

I ambled down the hall as slowly as I could without my hesitation being obvious. To my relief, as Professor Viceport's door clicked shut behind me, I caught a glimpse of a tiny nose peeking from beneath Banefield's door.

The hall was empty, but I bent down like before to collect Deborah, making a show of adjusting my other shoe. She scrambled up my sleeve to nestle at the crook of my elbow. The billowing of the blouse hid her small shape completely.

I didn't dare say anything knowing Viceport might come back out at any moment, but my familiar didn't need prompting.

He was in his bed. His breathing sounded hoarse. He tossed and turned a few times, but he seemed to be asleep. I went through the whole apartment and didn't sense any harmful magic. No sign of a new familiar either. She paused. *Every time he turned over, he scratched at his knee. I'm not sure if that's a sign of anything.*

I didn't remember anything in my reading specifically about knees. Maybe Imogen would have some idea, if she was willing to entertain more of my increasingly odd questions about magical illnesses.

At least Declan's latest tips had seemed to work to keep my mind shielded last night. I'd had a nightmare, but only the regular one about the morning my parents died. I'd woken up sweating but with my possessions intact and my throat feeling normal. I didn't think I'd done any shouting this time.

We'd see how long it took my dormmates to forget how ill *I'd* started to appear to be.

As I came up on the dorm building, I spotted my least favorite of those dormmates. Victory Blighthaven's auburn hair gleamed a little even in the shadow around the side of the building, where she was saying something to a guy I'd seen around. From the wave of her hand and her fierce expression, I got the impression they were arguing. As I slowed to watch, she gave him a little shove and disappeared around the back. The guy headed my way.

I wouldn't have given the moment much thought except when the guy saw me, he sped up. He caught up with me before I'd reached the doors and held out a hand for me to wait. I stopped, all my senses going on high alert.

"Rory," the guy said with a smile that was probably supposed to be smooth. "I hear you're a hard one to impress."

"Are you planning on trying? Because really, I haven't asked anyone to, and you should probably save yourself the trouble."

His mouth tightened, and then he barreled onward. "If you saw what I'm thinking about, you might not say that. I also hear you're quite the pro at Insight."

Was he daring me to try to delve into his mind? A wary prickle ran up my back. I didn't like this at all.

"All right, I'll take a peek then," I said, but I kept my mental shields tightly in place.

Either the guy didn't have enough insight skill to tell whether I was prodding his mind, or he was too focused on his scheme to pay attention. "*You want to go on a date with me*," he said, in a raspier version of the sort of tone Malcolm took on when he was working a persuasion spell. "*You're going to walk with me over to my car right now.*"

His effort pinged right off my defenses, but that didn't make me any happier about the attempt. I drew my posture straighter, ready to tell him off, when a brawny form jumped in, grabbing the guy by the arm.

"What the fuck do you think you're doing to her?" Connar demanded, his fingers squeezing the guy's bicep so hard the guy winced.

My stomach lurched. I'd been pissed off at the guy, but I was even more pissed off at the scion who'd intervened.

"I'm fine," I said. "He didn't manage to do anything. Let him go."

Connar frowned, but he released the other guy's arm. I glared at my supposed suitor. Had Victory put him up to using that spell on me? "Get the hell out of here. You try something like that again, and I *will* dive into your head, and I'm sure I can find all kinds of things in there you wouldn't want anyone finding out."

Being caught between two scions had obviously rattled the guy pretty badly. He hustled away without a backward glance—or an apology. I guessed that would have been too much to ask.

I turned to Connar. My gut knotted all over again. "You can get the hell out of here too. I don't know why you bothered stepping in, but I didn't need it. I'm *never* going to need any help from you."

He didn't budge, so I veered around him and strode into the hall. After a moment, footsteps thumped after me. I ducked into the stairwell, but Connar could cover a lot of ground fast. He caught up with me halfway up the first flight. I stopped before he could come up beside me, bracing my hands on the railings on either side, taking a little extra strength from standing a couple steps higher than him. For once, I was looking down at him.

"What?" I snapped. I might have the advantage of height, but being alone in a relatively enclosed space with the Stormhurst scion made my skin want to leap off my body and run away. Deborah was still crouched against my inner elbow, but she couldn't do anything to help.

Every part of me ached with the memory of the tenderness Connar and I had shared and how brutally he'd torn all that to shreds. The words he'd hurled at me echoed in my head.

You don't mind getting down in the dirt, do you? You can start begging any time now.

Connar hesitated, uncertainty sitting strangely on the planes of his chiseled face. The dim light of the stairwell turned his pale eyes from blue to a misty gray. A hint of his familiar scent, musky and smoky like vetiver, touched my nose, and I gripped the railings harder. I was not going to feel sympathy for any supposed vulnerability he showed.

"I don't *like* how this all happened," he said finally in his low voice. "But it's better this way. Okay?"

I bit back a harsh laugh. "No, that's not okay. What would have been okay is if you'd figured that out before you strung me along. Do you expect me to forgive and forget just because you've decided it's 'better'?"

He shifted his weight, his mouth twisting. "It's complicated. Everything here is complicated. You should know that by now."

"There was nothing complicated about us. You convinced me to trust you and then you stabbed me in the back, plain and simple."

A shadow flickered across his face. "You never would have trusted me anyway if you'd known everything about me."

"Is *that* your excuse?" I did laugh then, short and choked. "I know now. I heard all about your parents and how you supposedly destroyed your brother. But you know what? If I'd heard it back then, I would have asked you about it first. I would have listened to what you told me about it. And if I'd still seen the good in you that I thought I did, I'd have trusted you anyway. So don't blame me for judgments I never even made. This is all on you. And I guess your good friend Malcolm too."

Connar's expression hardened at that last comment. "You have no idea who *Malcolm* really is either. I've stood with him because he's earned it."

"And I didn't earn any of that loyalty?"

"It's not— You don't know. He's been there for me for *years*."

"Fine." I eased up a step. "Then go tell him how wonderful he is, and leave me alone."

"Rory..." He reached into his pocket and held up a small glinting shape that sent a bolt of nausea through my center. "I kept it. I remember what you said. Everything I've done, it's just trying to be—"

Fuck that. As I looked at the little dragon figurine I'd conjured for him out by the cliff, that I'd given to him telling him he could be his own person apart from the other scions, tears pricked at my eyes. That right there was the faith I'd had in him—the faith he'd burned to the ground.

"*No.*" That one syllable carried all the power I needed it to. I flicked my hand with a clench of my fingers before he could get any further with his justifications, and the little figure crumpled into the specks of metal dust that had formed it.

Connar let out a rough sound. His fingers snatched after the dust as if he could hold it together.

"If you want credit for being the person I thought you could be, then you need to make it happen for yourself," I said, not caring that my voice was shaking, and spun to hurry up the stairs.

This time, the Stormhurst scion didn't follow.

CHAPTER NINETEEN

Rory

"Credit to Insight," Professor Crowford said with a slightly bemused expression. My fellow student from the Insight league gave a little bow and smirked at the guy whose spell she'd just preemptively diffused by revealing his intentions. Then she glanced at me with an expression I wasn't so used to around here—looking for approval.

I gave her a thumbs up, because why not? I was glad not to have to watch the dude cast his nauseating illusion—no doubt the maintenance staff would really have appreciated the clean-up afterward—and she'd gotten the drop on him at the last minute. The other leagues were becoming more guarded at the beginning of class now that they knew we'd be scanning them. I hadn't read anything from him in my quick skim coming in.

Malcolm hadn't said anything during the whole exchange. It wasn't his league the girl had interrupted anyway. He lounged casually in his seat with a bored expression. But when Crowford motioned for us to get up and go, I felt the Nightwood scion's attention on me.

Fortunately, I'd picked a seat closer to the door. I hustled out and down the stone steps, looking forward to the warm spring air outside. The music department's concert was starting in ten minutes. If Malcolm wanted to hassle me, he could wait until after I'd seen the performance Shelby was so excited about.

Unfortunately, I didn't make my getaway quite fast enough. Maybe the other scion had lent a little magic to his feet. Somehow or other, I'd only come up to Killbrook Hall when his voice rang out just behind me.

"Where are you off to in such a hurry, Glinda?"

I guessed I'd have to get this over with now. I spun around, throwing as much focus as I could summon into my mental shields. "What do you want, Malcolm?"

He prowled around me with a predatory vibe that made me tense up even more. I had to turn to keep facing him. His handsome face stayed calm enough, but a spark of what I thought was anger already glittered in his dark brown eyes.

"I'd like you to answer my question," he said, cool with just a bit of edge.

I set my hands on my hips. "Where does it look like I'm going? The end-of-year concert is happening now. I'm going to listen to some music. So sorry if that offends you."

Malcolm's lips curled, but it was hard to tell whether that tight shape was more a smile or a grimace. "It *is* offensive how quick you are to run off to see what the feebs are going to do."

"I was under the impression most of the school goes to listen. They're here because they're freaking good musicians, aren't they?" I sighed and moved to walk past him.

He caught my wrist, jerking me to a halt. "You really still think you can just ignore me."

I glared right into his eyes. "It's been working all right so far."

"Then you haven't been paying attention. I can still play you like a puppet. You were born for this, but so was I, and I've been *living* it while you were off playing house with the joymancers who slaughtered your real parents."

The words brought back the images from the battle I'd

unintentionally summoned up in the desensitization chamber. The screams, the violence on both sides. My stomach lurched.

I gritted my teeth. "I know who my real parents were, and I'm not afraid of you. As you should be able to tell. Not feeding your magic one little bit right now, am I? So let go of my fucking arm before I have to make you."

Malcolm released me, but he laughed as he did. "I've gotten plenty from you, Bloodstone. You just never know where and when. You're never going to make it, here or anywhere else until you throw in your lot with the right side." He lifted his chin in the direction of the pavilion where the concert was being held. "You might not want to go over there. Things could get dangerous."

My body stiffened. "What are you talking about? What are you going to do?"

"What have I *done*, you mean. It's already in motion. You'll be just fine back here, though. It's not as if there's anything you can do to help."

For fuck's sake. There would be if I knew what the hell he'd planned. I eyed him while he gave me that cocky smile of his. I'd gotten past his own mental defenses before, but I didn't think he'd fall for the same trick twice. Maybe, if I dove in there sharp and fast…

I turned as if I were going to head toward the pavilion anyway. Malcolm chuckled. As the sound reached my ears, I whipped back around and aimed my gaze at his forehead with a hastily whispered word. "Franco."

My magic surged up my throat. My awareness shot forward as fast and narrow as I could focus it—and sliced into the barrier I'd been expecting.

Not quite far enough. I jarred against Malcolm's internal wall before a single impression reached me from his mind. Just as my effort fell away, he spoke the command he must have been holding at the ready.

"*You will do as I say. Stay out of my head.*"

The persuasion spell flitted straight into my mind past my own lowered barrier the instant before I yanked my defenses back up. The commands jangled through my thoughts. Shit. I opened my mouth to try to catch him now that his mind was vulnerable, and my tongue faltered.

He'd ordered me to stay out. The persuasive power of that order was wriggling through my brain behind my mental shields now. I couldn't force the casting word to launch my Insight spell out.

"Give me a little curtsy, Glinda. Let's see how well you can bow if you have to."

My legs swayed despite myself. He hadn't even needed to add the lilt of magic to those words. The impulse to obey him was embedded in my mind as well. I dipped my head to him with a scream of frustration locked in my throat.

Malcolm was outright grinning now. "Not bad. We can work on that. How about a spin?"

My body swiveled in an awkward twirl. I wasn't going to add any more grace to it than I was compelled to. I closed my eyes, shutting him out, trying to train my attention on the energy of his casting moving through my head. All I could sense was a faint quivering through my nerves.

It was almost impossible to diffuse a persuasive spell once it'd hit its target. You either waited for its power to fade on its own—or you put up obstacles to fulfilling it.

I'd done that before, when he'd tried to walk me out one of the tower windows. I could do a more elegant job of it now. "Wall," I murmured, picturing the air hardening into an invisible barrier fit right against my body.

"Come back here," Malcolm said. My muscles shifted and strained as my conjured wall held them perfectly in place. The Nightwood scion sighed. "What have you done to yourself? There's no professor around to intercede just because you tried hard. You know I can break whatever you conjured up."

"Go ahead and try it," I shot back.

The faint strains of orchestral music carried across the field and past the building behind me. Damn it, the concert was starting. I didn't know if Shelby would even notice I hadn't turned up, but if she did, I might lose the one person who'd been there for me since I first got here. The way the other fearmancers treated her, she'd probably assume I'd been faking my appreciation for her musical talent.

My expression must have shown my worry. Malcolm stepped closer, cocking his head. "Getting a little scared now, Bloodstone? I don't even *have* to break whatever armor you've put on. You still can't get to your precious feebs like you wanted to. And you can't stop up your throat. Why don't we have a chat? I'll tell you what I want to know—and you'll answer any question I ask."

Oh, fuck, fuck, fuck. If he started prodding me, he could stumble on information that'd put me in deep shit not just with him but the entire administration in a matter of seconds. Unless…

"What would—" he started, and I jumped in.

"Not if I shut you up," I said, urging my magic into a physical punch of energy to jam Malcolm's mouth closed. I trained all my will on muzzling him. If he couldn't talk, he couldn't activate the persuasive spell any more.

Malcolm's jaw clenched as he attempted to open his mouth, but I was plenty strong in Physicality, and today my efforts appeared to be holding just fine. Fury blazed in his eyes. He looked down, humming to himself, and shook his head with a snap and a crackle in the air. My muzzle shattered.

"Don't you dare—" he said with a rasp.

"Shut up," I snapped again with another burst of magic, and his lips smacked together. He glowered at me as he moved to free himself again.

I didn't know how long I could keep this up. The magic churning behind my collarbone was starting to burn and fray. I'd accumulated a lot simply by existing and being Rory Bloodstone, the unpredictable new-found scion, but I'd thrown all I could into each of these castings.

I drew in a breath to try another spell before he'd even broken through this one, and a shriek split the air from the direction of the pavilion.

My heart skipped a beat. More shouts and screams rose up in a wave, punctuated by a clatter of thumps and clangs. My gaze jerked to Malcolm, who'd just wrenched his mouth open again. "What did you *do*?"

To my surprise, he looked momentarily bewildered, staring in the direction of the pavilion where it lay out of our view beyond the hall. Then his expression molded back into his usual arrogant mask. "I haven't got a clue, Glinda. Didn't you realize? I only said I'd messed with the concert to get you to try me. Whoever's having their fun over there, it's got nothing to do with me. You'll have to blame some other villain."

A metallic-sounding crash made me wince. I believed him, if only because of that brief unguarded reaction—and because I couldn't imagine why he wouldn't be rubbing his triumph in my face if the chaos across the field *was* his doing.

I hesitated for just a second, long enough for a pained cry to pierce my ears, and then I smashed the wall I'd conjured around my body with a click of my tongue. The second the pressure left my body, I dashed along the path past the Killbrook Building. If Malcolm called after me, I didn't hear him.

A crowd of at least a hundred students and various teachers had gathered around the open pavilion at the far end of the field. They'd scattered now, some of them running back to the main buildings, some of them holding their ground and staring warily toward the stage. The stage where the orchestra set-up lay in a jumbled mess.

Instruments were strewn across the high wooden platform beneath the pavilion's arched roof, music stands tipped on their sides, chairs toppled. The performers lay sprawled between them. As I dashed over, I spotted one girl clutching her scraped elbow. A boy hissed as he moved his leg, his ankle twisted at an unnatural angle.

A familiar face emerged in the dispersing crowd—Imogen, her freckled face pale. I veered toward her. "What happened?" I said, breathless. "What's going on?"

She hugged herself. "Three bears," she said quietly. "They charged right past us and onto the stage. We could all guess they weren't really bears—you don't get ones that big around here anyway—but the Naries panicked."

Someone trying to top that bear-shifting prank Declan had told me about. My hands clenched at my sides. "Where'd the 'bears' go?"

If I found the mages who'd put on this performance… I'd find some way to make sure they never did it again, that was for sure.

"They charged off into the woods," Imogen said, and another thought raced through my head with a jolt of fear rather than anger.

"Where's Shelby?"

"I don't know. I saw—she was near the back—I think she might have fallen off the platform."

Oh, no. I took off again, heading around the back of the building.

Two students had taken the four-foot tumble onto the grass, alongside a couple of chairs. One, a boy, was picking himself up on wobbly legs. The other sat slumped with a hand pressed to her temple, her other arm tucked close to her chest. I didn't need to see her face to recognize Shelby's mousy brown ponytail.

One of the staff had already knelt down beside her. "People are coming from the health center right now," he reassured her as I came to a stop a few feet away.

"My arm," Shelby said raggedly with a sound like a swallowed sob. She shifted, and I realized her arm wasn't just tucked against her. It was bent wrong at the wrist, the joint already swelling and red.

A tear streaked down her face. She tightened her jaw. "I'll be okay," she insisted. "It's nothing. Nothing that bad." But I could tell she didn't believe that any more than I did.

CHAPTER TWENTY

Declan

I'd never really enjoyed sitting at my spot around the table of the pentacle of barons, but over the last several weeks, the meetings had become increasingly uncomfortable. Mainly because the other barons—and my aunt Ambrosia, whom I was stuck with here until I could be named full baron—were spending increasing amounts of time interrogating me.

They pretended it wasn't an interrogation, of course. Baron Nightwood, Malcolm's father, smiled the confident smile he'd passed on to his son as he asked one or another prodding question. Baron Stormhurst, Connar's mother, didn't ask anything at all, just made pointed statements framed by huffs of breath. Baron Killbrook, Jude's father, had a perpetual furrow in his forehead as if he were questioning me only out of well-meant concern.

The fifth chair, at the Bloodstone point of the pentacle, stood empty still. They hadn't wanted to bring Rory in for a meeting until they were sure they could count on her carrying the party line. And that was exactly why so much focus was turned on me.

"You've been seeing the girl twice a week for how long now?"

Baron Nightwood said, leaning back in his chair at a casual angle as if he didn't know the answer already. "I'd have expected more progress by now, Ashgrave."

"Not much good having a baron inside the university if he can't get done the things that need doing," Baron Stormhurst muttered.

Aunt Ambrosia shifted beside me, always eager for a chance to make me look bad. "He has taken on so much." She patted my arm with her cool hand. "Perhaps it's more than he's able to handle all at once."

"The Bloodstone scion has a defiant mind," I said, ignoring her remark and keeping my voice even. You couldn't show any emotion around these people if you didn't want them pouncing on it. I had never been so glad that I was the only one of the present barons who'd focused on Insight as a speciality. The others might have decades more experience than me, but my mental wall could keep out their habitual prodding.

As long as they never decided there was grounds for a real interrogation from the inside out, I was safe. I wouldn't be able to stand up to all three of them making a concentrated effort—and blocking them in that case could be considered as treasonous as whatever they'd accused me of.

So I had to make sure they had no reason to accuse me.

"It's taking time, but I've unsettled her with the information I've been able to pass on about the joymancers. I've seen the toll the other scions' efforts are taking on her. She's weakening."

Not really, not hardly, but I had seen bits of pain and worry in her mind here and there, so I could say the words genuinely enough.

"Her mentor has been ill and unable to advise her for quite a bit of the past month too," I added, watching the faces around me. "That loss of support has clearly put an additional strain on her."

None of them gave any indication that this was a surprise to them or that they knew more than I'd just told them.

Baron Killbrook shifted in his seat. What had Jude told him about *his* activities involving Rory, if anything? He didn't jump in to crow about how his son was pulling one over on the Bloodstone scion, so I supposed that was one more bit of proof that if Jude had some agenda beyond simple affection, it was only his own, not for us scions or the barons.

"You could pay her another visit if your son's efforts are failing in potency," Killbrook said to Nightwood. "You said your mere presence frightened her last time."

Nightwood cut him a dark glance. "From the gossip circulating around the school enough to reach many parents, we've gathered Malcolm's influence has had a rather large impact, actually. The girl has been giving the increasing impression of instability. Some of the families have encouraged attempts at wooing her anyway, but whatever social support she stood to gain in the aftermath of that assessment has greatly deteriorated."

I stayed silent. Rory could build her support back up. The exercises we'd gone through a few days ago should have strengthened her defenses even while unconscious. However the hell Malcolm was managing to affect her from across the building, his influence was going to diminish. Better if they thought it was the result of her own practice and research than my intervention, though.

That thought came with a sharp little pang and the memory of Rory challenging me that same day about my devotion to the barony. If she *had* been here and disagreed with something the others were talking about, she wouldn't have kept quiet. She'd have told them exactly what she thought of their smugly callous attitudes.

And then probably they'd have found a way to beat her down completely, despite her being the only Bloodstone left. I didn't have even that security. I was easily replaceable.

Still, in that moment, I missed her straightforward, no-nonsense approach. Maybe her priorities and loyalties weren't all the most sensible, but fuck, she knew how to take a stand.

"Besides," Nightwood added with a haughty air, "how would it look to the community if we spent our time negotiating with a teenager? Let the boys do their work, and when she's as wobbly as they can get her, we can bring her in and sort her the rest of the way out here."

Stormhurst nodded with a blunt grin. My stomach clenched, but I forced a smile as I tipped my head in supposed agreement.

I didn't know if I could save Rory and myself, but I'd do whatever I could to make sure she was strong enough not to be crushed when that day came. She deserved to take her place here as she was, ready to divide and conquer, lit up with determination to follow what she felt was right. She deserved the chance to come into her own without these jackals who were supposed to be our leaders tearing her apart.

Maybe I couldn't *have* her, but seeing her in the pentacle unbroken would make this job I'd taken on ten times more tolerable. I might even start looking forward to the meetings.

The discussion turned to a recent business venture that needed our approval, but tension lingered in the room, thick enough that it itched at my skin. I wasn't sure how much more time the other barons would give Rory. They were restless to get on with the plans they'd been making before I was around, the ones I was starting to suspect they weren't going to share with me at all until they believed they could browbeat me out of any complaints I raised four to one.

I left the meeting to a dreary spring day outside, warm but so overcast only thin sunlight penetrated the layer of gray clouds. After I'd sunk into the driver's seat of my car, I let out my breath fully for the first time since I'd walked into the pentacle building.

Like all the baronies, the Ashgrave estate never wanted for money. I could have had a chauffeur drive me to and from the meetings like the other barons generally did. I liked the feel of the steering wheel beneath my hands and the sense of control that came with revving the engine, though, especially afterward.

I had another tutoring session with Rory tonight. Another hour of tightrope walking between my various loyalties. Another hour of tamping down every other feeling her smiles and wry remarks stirred up in me. All the same, thinking about it, my pulse increased its tempo in anticipation. I couldn't deny I'd enjoy her presence even with the difficulties it brought.

Back on campus, I had a quick dinner and headed to the aides' office. I'd gotten there early, but Rory was already waiting by the door, her face drawn. My heart squeezed at the sight of her.

"Hey," I said carefully. There wasn't anything unprofessional about asking after a student's wellbeing when they looked so obviously distraught. "What's wrong?"

"Everything. This place. It's so—" She cut herself off with a sound of frustration. "I know *you* can't do anything about most of it. I just wanted to get on with the parts you can help with. If I'm too early—if you had something else you needed to get to first—"

"No, it's fine." I had been going to look through the archived records involving joymancers for another to add to the growing collection I'd been offering her—for background, for broadening understanding, for recognizing that those people she held in such high esteem *were murderers too*—but that could wait. "Come on in."

She strode past me when I opened the door. Rather than taking a seat at one of the tables, she paced from one end of the room to the other between them, her shoes tapping against the hardwood floor. A chill had crept into the room with the absence of sunlight. I flicked on the switch for the gas fireplace on the wall, and its faint warmth started to seep through the room with the wavering of the flames.

"He got in my head again," Rory said abruptly, coming to a halt. "Malcolm. He managed to mess with me, and I could hold him off but I couldn't completely *stop* him. If I had, if I'd been able to get over there in time like I meant to…" She exhaled in a rush. "I know he's your friend. I know you can't pick sides or whatever."

"Yes, I'm supposed to stay out of conflicts between students as long as no official rules are broken. That doesn't mean I *like* everything I see."

What had Malcolm done to her now? Despite all the confidence I'd had in her strength behind the report I'd given to the barons, she *did* look rattled, more than I'd seen in a while. The urge rose up in me to march right over to wherever Malcolm was and throttle him until he came up with some other strategy.

He kept doing this kind of thing because it was working, slowly but surely. It would keep working unless I could give her the tools to keep the essential parts of herself steady.

Rory made a dismissive gesture. "It doesn't matter anyway. I'm a scion. I'm going to need to know how to stop *everyone* from messing with me. That's what anybody here would say, right? I have to learn how to kick people out. I have to be able to cut off a persuasion spell if someone manages to sneak one in. There's got to be more you can teach me, more I can do."

"Of course there is." I stepped closer to her, holding up my hands as if she were a wild animal in a snare that might bite me even if I meant to free it. "Some of the techniques will be beyond me—things you'll be able to work on with Professor Sinleigh when you move up to having sessions with her, but I do know a few additional strategies you can try."

"All right." She shuddered as if shaking the tension out of her body. "Let's get to it then."

Rattled and frustrated but ready to leap to the challenge all the same. I girded myself against the twinge of desire that ran through me.

"Cutting off a spell that's already inside you is tricky," I said. "The most important factor to start with is a deepened awareness of your mind itself, so you can sense where the magic is working and interrupt it. Close your eyes, and see if you can shift your focus through the different areas in your head—the ones that activate when you breathe, when you move your hands or adjust your posture, when you focus on the tastes in your mouth or the sounds that reach your ears."

Rory let her eyelids drop, her fingers curling into her palms at her sides. After a few moments, her mouth pressed into a tight line.

"I can't sort it all out. I'm *thinking* too much. It's like the thoughts and feelings keep churning around getting in the way of everything else."

"That just means you have a fully functioning brain." I hesitated and let myself walk right up to her. This was what I'd have done for any other student. I just had to keep any of my own feelings out of it.

I rested my index fingers against her temples, just a light pressure. "Focus on my touch. Then spread your attention just a little farther into your mind from there. See what those parts light up to. Let the rest of the clutter fade into the background."

Her skin was warm and smooth beneath my fingertips. All of me warmed up standing this close to her. It took a conscious effort not to trail my gaze over the slant of her nose, the curve of her cheeks, down to those delicate pink lips that parted just slightly now.

"Okay," she said, her voice slow and distant. "I think I see what you mean. How do I go deeper than that?"

"Slide your awareness back." I eased my fingers across her head, into her soft hair. "Push the thoughts back with it. Can you do that?"

Her expression tensed with concentration. Then a little light came back into it. "Yeah. It feels easier when you put it like that. Not completely *easy*, but…" She opened her eyes, gazing into mine. "Thanks."

Her hand came up, probably intending to replicate the pressure point herself, but it ended up settling over mine. She hesitated and then let her fingers slip around my palm to give my hand a gentle squeeze of gratitude.

Her gaze darted down to *my* mouth, and in that moment she was barely shielded at all. I hardly needed to reach to absorb the thought at the front of her mind. She was thinking about kissing me. Wanting to kiss me, with a longing I could taste. It echoed through me, drawing out my own.

She didn't, though. Just as easily as I'd gleaned that first impulse, I felt her clamp down on it and hold herself back.

For my sake. Because I'd told her I couldn't, and she had too much honor to cross that line. Fuck, that only made me want her more.

She had more self-control than I did in that moment. I couldn't quite force myself to pull back from her. My other fingers came down to brush over her hair, the most innocent of caresses. Rory swallowed audibly, her eyes locking with mine again.

No one was here. No one would know if I gave in just this once. If I offered what Jude no doubt already had. Whatever the hell he was up to when it came to Rory, I didn't trust his intentions to be totally pure. Up until now, he'd gone through girls like daily specials.

If I showed her she could have me that way after all, maybe she wouldn't fall for him. Maybe it'd be just one more way I was protecting her.

I wanted to believe that, and that was the problem. I couldn't trust my judgment. I was just looking for excuses.

I lowered my head, not to bring my mouth to hers, but just to bow it next to her, my cheek brushing her temple where my fingers had rested a few minutes ago. My hands came down to rest on her shoulders.

"I can't," I said hoarsely.

"I know," Rory said. "I wouldn't—I wasn't..."

She didn't seem to know how to go on. Suddenly it seemed very important to make one thing clear, to let her know she wasn't alone.

"It's not just for me. What we're doing here—it's the only way I can protect you. I don't want anything else distracting me from that."

She nodded, just slightly, her hair grazing my face with its sweet smell. "Okay. Okay. Thank you."

She should wait to thank me until I'd actually succeeded.

CHAPTER TWENTY-ONE

Rory

When I came out of my bedroom the second morning after the concert, most of my dormmates were hanging out in the common room, eating breakfast or just chatting. All of them got a little quieter at my entrance, which was normal these days even though I'd managed to get through the past night with no nightmares at all. They all also directed their attention away from the bedroom door farther down the room—the one that had been Shelby's.

Someone had conjured a burst of rainbow glitter around two words in twinkling silver script. *Goodbye feeb!*

The words set my jaw on edge. The message wasn't for Shelby. The glowing writing was clearly magical, and no one here would have dared to break one of the school's few but particularly firm rules: Never let the Nary students witness anything they'd realize was magic.

But no one in this room had to worry about a Nary student seeing that display. Shelby had been sent home yesterday. With her fractured wrist, she wouldn't be able to complete the last few weeks of the term or the special summer session. Unless it healed unusually fast, she probably wouldn't be able to keep up with the other student musicians for months after that either.

Chances were, she wasn't coming back. A fact she'd clearly known from the agony written on her face as she'd left.

As soon as I'd heard about the decision, I'd gone to Ms. Grimsworth in protest. This was a school for mages, for fuck's sake. If I could conjure dragons out of the earth and ice out of the air, surely someone here could meld a broken bone back together. Shelby didn't have to know it'd ever been broken.

"It's against school policy," the headmistress had said, so calmly I'd wanted to scream. "The safety of our students and their ability to continue operating within the Nary world undetected is our first priority. Several other Nary students witnessed Miss Hughes' fall. Miss Hughes saw and felt for herself how badly her wrist was injured. There's too much chance of someone noticing signs of the supernatural at work if we attempted to simply wipe the fracture away."

"It's not fair," I'd said. "She worked so hard to be here, and she only fell because of a stupid prank she had nothing to do with."

Ms. Grimsworth had been unmovable. "We provide the Naries with opportunities and training beyond any they're likely to find elsewhere in exchange for the benefits they provide to the other students' training. She was lucky to have gotten as much instruction as she did here, free of tuition. I'm sure she'll find plenty of options open to her in the Nary world once she's recovered—naturally, without magical intervention."

Shelby wouldn't see it that way. She'd kept trudging to classes half delirious with fever because it'd mattered so much to her to keep her spot. I hadn't been able to figure out anything else I could do for her, though. Even if I'd wanted to risk healing her myself with whatever fallout might come from that, I had zero medical training. I might have made her arm even worse.

And now someone—most likely the angelic-faced, viper-temperamented girl whose lips had curled into a smirk at the dining table—had decided to rub that failure and my friendship with Shelby in my face. I'd have liked to stuff a shovelful of glitter down Victory's throat.

"You look a little sick," Cressida sniped from her seat next to Victory. "Another bad night for Princess Bloodstone?"

The nickname Connar had used affectionately and then in taunting grated on my nerves. If I was acting weird right now, it was because of the crap they'd done with the full intention of upsetting me.

I held my anger in check and glanced over at the two of them, keeping my tone perfectly neutral. "I'm fine. Just thinking about how pathetic it is to slap someone in the face and then mock them for their cheek being red."

Victory's gaze snapped to me at that comment. She stood up, flicking her auburn hair over her shoulder. "I don't think 'pathetic' is the kind of word you should be tossing at other people. You want to throw down? Make it a real challenge. I'm right here."

Did I want to get into a magical battle with the queen bee of Villain Academy at this particular moment? Not really. I had enough on my plate without escalating the tensions between us into full-out war. Anyway, it would annoy her more if I acted like I didn't care.

"I don't want to fight with you," I said as evenly as before. "I never wanted to fight in the first place."

She made a derisive sound and dropped back into her seat. "Because you know you'd never win."

That might have been true at first, but she didn't really have a clue how far my skills had developed. We hadn't had a real stand-off. That would probably happen eventually, the way she kept pushing. I'd be happy to surprise her when push came to shove.

Today, I just walked out of the dorm. I'd already eaten one of the muffins I'd been keeping in my bedroom away from anyone's spoiling spells, so at least I didn't have to worry about breakfast. Someone, maybe Cressida, snickered as I stepped out.

Had my refusal to fight looked weak? I couldn't find it in me to care about my social status when people were getting kicked out of school or possibly dying here.

I made it down to the first floor before it occurred to me that I didn't really know where I was going. I didn't have any classes until late in the afternoon. The sight of the library's vast bookshelves just made me feel more hopeless. Nothing I'd found in there had let me help anyone I'd wanted to save.

I wavered in the hall as a few students wandered by, debating my options. Then a familiar lanky figure emerged from the stairwell.

A grin stretched across Jude's face when he saw me. It was hard to remember, seeing the genuine pleasure in his expression, that there'd been a while when every smile he'd aimed my way had been sharp, mocking, or both.

I wasn't sure which was stranger: that or the answering warmth that lit up in me as he walked over.

His appreciation wasn't enough to wipe away my sense of futility, though. His grin faded as he took in my face. He slipped his hand around mine as easily as if we'd been holding hands from the start rather than barely having touched until a short while ago. "What's wrong?"

"What isn't might be an easier question to answer." I let out a strained chuckle. "I'm just… tired." Tired of this place. Tired of having to keep a strong front while the weight of all the things I had to grieve or worry about piled higher. I missed my parents, missed my real home, with an ache that radiated through my chest.

Jude cocked his head. "Are you up for a drive? I had something special planned for our last outing—since obviously you hardly require my instruction anymore."

"Until we switch to piano," I said.

Jude's fingers tightened for a second, and I remembered how startled, almost nervous, he'd looked when I'd walked in on him that night. For whatever reason, he kept his hobby secret.

I made a gesture as if zipping my lips. "Sorry. I think I could drive. Where are we going?" Jude had proven himself good at coming up with excellent distractions so far.

His grin came back. "My secret. I promise it's good enough to take your mind off just about anything."

He swung our hands together casually as we walked out to the garage. A few of the students we went by watched us for a little longer than just a passing glance, but Jude didn't show any sign of caring. I guessed he'd already made a big enough statement about where he stood when it came to me.

When we reached my car, he stopped and tugged me a little closer. My head came up automatically to meet his kiss—our first kiss since the ones in the piano room.

The heat of his mouth lit me up like a torch, but what really gripped my heart was the gentleness of the gesture, as if he felt he had to leave plenty of room for me to pull away in case I'd changed my mind about the whole kissing thing.

Whatever was forming between us felt as fragile to him as it did to me. It mattered to him to be careful with it. Somehow that reassured me in a way nothing he said could.

He drew back with a satisfied hum. "I could do that all day, but I did promise you we'd take this car somewhere beyond the garage."

"I'm expecting big things from this secret surprise," I said as I opened the driver's side door. "It'd better deliver after all this build-up."

He sprawled in the seat beside me. "What horrors should I expect if it doesn't?"

I arched an eyebrow at him. "I'm sure I could think of a few ways to express my disappointment."

He laughed. "Will I be frozen from head to toe this time, Ice Queen? I'm not worried. I keep my promises."

My pulse no longer sped up with anxiety when I eased the car out of its stall and drove out to the road into town. The motions were becoming automatic, the thrum of the engine more comforting than unnerving. The thought of driving somewhere completely on my own still made me a little uneasy, but maybe I'd start slow like I had with my drives with Jude. I could buy a lot more groceries at a time if I took the car into town.

The day was warm enough that we rolled down the windows. Jude leaned his arm partway out, the wind tussling his hair. "Do you want to tell me about any of the many things that are bothering you?"

He said it lightly but with enough gravity to make it clear he was asking honestly. I glanced over at him for a second as the shadows of the trees at the side of the road rippled over the car.

There was something different in his tone and in the general energy he gave off today. He'd pretty much always kept up a breezy, don't-give-a-shit demeanor when I was around, other than during the picnic when our conversation had turned briefly serious, but now… now he looked actually *relaxed*, in a way I hadn't realized that he wasn't before because I hadn't had the real thing to compare to. As if he didn't feel the need to keep up his usual frenetic pace and jokey attitude with me anymore.

My mind leapt back to that evening interlude in the piano room again—to the way he'd fallen so quickly into banter, the raw emotion I'd glimpsed vanishing beneath it as soon as he'd recovered from his surprise. If that wasn't how he acted when he was actually comfortable… how much of the joking and mockery was for his enjoyment and how much just a different sort of shield?

I didn't want to talk to him about Shelby. If I heard him call her a "feeb," I really might slam him with ice. His dismissive attitude about Naries was something we'd have to talk about eventually if this was going to become more than a little kissing here and there, but I wasn't in the mood to hash it out right now.

I could mention a different worry, though. "My mentor—Professor Banefield—has been really sick for a while now. No one seems to know exactly what's wrong, and I haven't been able to see him… He doesn't seem to be getting better."

Jude's forehead furrowed. "It's not often one of the professors is laid up for very long. Is there something you need to see him about?"

I also wasn't ready to tell him about my near-certainty that Banefield's sickness was part of some conspiracy against me. I shrugged. "I'm just worried about him. I was there when he first got sick. Maybe it's silly, but I feel like if I could talk with him, see how he's doing now, maybe I could help figure out what's going on."

"That sounds like the sort of thing you *would* think." Jude gave me a crooked smile. "But you're not thinking enough like a fearmancer. Someone told you you're not allowed to visit him? Who the fuck cares? If you can magic your way in without anyone realizing, that's your permission right there."

Oh. I… really *hadn't* thought about it that way, but he was completely right. That was how any other fearmancer would have looked at the situation. Rules didn't matter, only whether you could slip around them effectively.

"Those seem like extreme measures to take when I'm not sure what I'd be looking for… but we'll see," I said.

"Feel free to call on me if you need back-up," Jude said. "I do enjoy a good scheme."

We drove down the highway that we'd taken to our picnic spot until we'd gone about a half hour beyond that dirt track, and then took a turn to head farther south. Jude scanned the farms, forestland, and towns we passed rather than the street signs, as if watching for landmarks.

"Take a right here," he said after we passed a highway restaurant-slash-antiques shop. Five minutes later, he sent me left down a narrow but neatly bordered road through the thicker forest.

The road widened where it came to a wrought-iron gate in a high brick wall, the bars so close together I couldn't make out much other than a blur of green and brown on the other side. I eased us to a stop.

"Is this your family's place?" I said warily. The wall and the gate gave me the same vibe as the main buildings at the university—fearmancer tastes in architecture. Did Jude figure he was going to impress me showing me around whatever grand home his family owned? I didn't think I was ready for the meet-the-parents step.

Jude chuckled. "No, this is *your* place."

CHAPTER TWENTY-TWO

Rory

I blinked at Jude, thinking I'd misheard him. "My place?"

"The Bloodstones own about twenty-five acres here," he said, getting out of the car. "All behind that damned wall. Your parents didn't usually take visitors here—no one I've talked to has ever been on the property. The guys and I have always been curious what's in there. I mean, you've got a big foreboding stone mansion that was the main residence too, but we all have one of those."

I stepped out after him. "Is this trip for my benefit or for yours, then?" I teased, but my heart had skipped a beat with excitement along with my nerves. My first glimpse of the properties I'd inherited. The whole reason I'd wanted to drive in the first place. I didn't know how much poking around I'd be comfortable doing with Jude around, but still… Whether I liked the heritage I'd stumbled into or not, whatever lay beyond that wall was *mine.*

"Oh, I'll freely admit I'm looking forward to this as much as I hope you are." Jude's eyes glinted with anticipation. "If you touch the panel at the right side of the gate there, it should be spelled to open for any Bloodstone."

I walked up to it and set my hand on the warm metal. It tingled beneath my palm, and a lock thudded over somewhere I couldn't see. The gate swung open ahead of us. I found myself holding my breath as I entered.

The paved road narrowed again on the other side of the gate, leading to a wooden garage building that stood next to what by fearmancer standards must have amounted to a cottage, even though it was three times as big as my parents' place back in California. The whole thing was dark fine-grained wood: two sprawling stories beneath a tented roof with a gleaming weathervane spire shaped like a rearing horse and a broad deck stretching around the two sides that I could see.

The yard sloped down toward a glittering pond with a beach of what looked like crushed quartz directly in front of the house. Closer to us stood a prickly looking hedge with an arched doorway that had been coaxed out of the brambles. The whole property looked perfectly maintained, as if the owners had only just stepped out for the day.

"Will there be anyone else around?" I said with sudden apprehension. "Ms. Grimsworth said there were people looking after the properties… and I guess there's my grandparents."

Jude shook his head. "I asked around. No one due today. And any grandparents of yours still around don't have any claim on this place. Bloodstones only."

"Not much respect for in-laws, I guess?"

"Not when it comes to baron holdings. And especially not when they make asses of themselves." He shot me a sideways glance. "I don't know how much you've heard about your dad's parents, but I've heard *my* dad and grandfather complain about them. Apparently from the moment your mom took up with your dad, they've been pushing in, grasping at every bit of prestige they could reach for."

Lovely. "I'm glad I told Ms. Grimsworth I wasn't interested in a family visit, then."

"A smart move, I'd say. Now let's check this place out." Jude started toward the hedge with a clap of his hands. "Is this what I think... Hell yes." He spun around by the arched entrance, grinning. "You've got yourself a puzzle garden."

"Am I supposed to know what that is?" I ventured closer and made out another hedge beyond the first forming some kind of passage. Like a maze?

"There aren't many of them built because it takes a lot of magic." Jude peered inside. "Apparently there's a huge one just outside London. It's the same idea as a puzzle box, except expanded into an entire garden… They're works of art, really. You make your way between the hedges, and you'll come to doors and gates you can only open if you figure out the trick to the magic. Usually they're made with funnel shapes and conducting pieces."

He'd had me at "work of art." I still couldn't totally picture what he meant, but that just meant I had to see it with my own eyes. "Let's take a look at it then."

Just inside the archway, twinkling gravel like the quartz down by the pond rasped under my shoes. The hedge passage branched in two directions. Several feet to our left, the way was blocked by a wall of brightly blooming flowers that gave off a pungent fruity scent. To our right, strands of silver and bronze appeared to be woven into a barrier of hedge brambles, forming an intricate latticework between the dark green leaves.

"Petals or metal?" Jude said.

The metalwork had stirred the artist in me. I wanted to get a closer look just to see how the pieces had been fit together. "Metal," I said, walking over.

Up close, the pattern became clearer. The strands of metal formed a sort of flower themselves, with expanding rings of interlocking petals around a circular center. Silver and bronze wove together to form that center, holding a shape like a closed keyhole in the very middle.

I touched the smooth surface like I had the lock on the front gate, but the barrier didn't budge.

"It's going to take more than that to get through." Jude leaned forward to consider the piece. "The idea of these gardens is to keep your skills honed—and take a measure of your friends, if you let them at it. There's a trick to each of the puzzles: something you have to nudge with one of your skills. If you choose the wrong one or aim it wrong, the funnels and conductors will throw it right back at you with a zap."

"Funnels and conductors?"

He motioned to the pieces that fit together to form the flower's center. "Certain physical forms can work with magic to direct it, focus it, amplify it, without having any magic imbued in them at all. Some you'll learn to recognize because they're used often enough, but even if you meet an unfamiliar one, you can usually get a sense by carefully feeling it out… This bit here is going to concentrate any energy you send along it toward the narrow end, for example."

The part he was pointing at had a ridged hollow in its curved silver body, wider at one end than the other. I bent down to study it. The narrow end led to a gold piece that was dotted with little craters.

The magic at the base of my throat tingled. I could picture how energy might flow through one part and then disperse in a dozen directions as it hit those marks.

But maybe the "funnel" could direct a spell toward just one crater, and it would bounce the magic somewhere useful? I touched the pock-marked piece, and it turned at the press of my fingers. A little gap formed between it and another gold piece above it, revealing a small channel carved there. The arc of that piece carried it around to the keyhole spot.

"How do I know what kind of spell to cast?" I asked.

"I think there should be clues in the design—or sometimes the puzzle will make it obvious. I've never actually been in one of these before, only heard about them." He cocked his head. "Flowers are usually a symbol of persuasion. Do you want me to give it a shot so I'll take the zap if I'm wrong?"

"No, I'll try it." A weird sense of possessiveness had come over me. It was my garden, my puzzle. I adjusted the first gold piece until I was satisfied with the angle, and then I murmured a spell into the silver funnel. "*Open.*"

The energy leapt from my tongue, and the metal pieces shone. The cratered bit shivered. Then the plate covering the keyhole snapped up, and all the metal strands pulled apart to form an opening we could walk through.

"Never mind. You've clearly got this all in hand." Delight lit Jude's face as he followed me into the hedge passage beyond.

He caught me by the waist from behind and pressed a kiss to the crook of my neck. My body lit up in turn. I lifted my head to catch his lips, and he spun me to face him so he could deepen the kiss.

Standing there with his arms around me, a prickle of guilt wound through my gut. Just last night I'd stood almost this close to Declan—I'd wanted to kiss him almost as badly as I wanted to keep kissing Jude right now. Nothing could happen between Declan and me, but still…

I drew back just a few inches. "Jude," I said, "what are we doing here?"

He gave my forehead a quick peck with a smile. "I think the idea was taking your mind off your troubles."

"No, I mean *everything* we're doing. What are you looking for out of this? I know—I know how the inheritances work. That if we were going to be together, really together, long-term, you'd be giving up the barony."

His mouth trailed down to brush my cheek. "What's the need to think about that just yet? I'm nineteen. You don't have to worry about me proposing after a couple of dates. Right now, this is just… getting to know each other."

I swallowed hard. It was difficult to think clearly with him so close, the smell of him filling my lungs with a spicy zing like pepper and coriander. "But, if it's never going to be possible, what's the point of heading down that road?"

"Who said it's impossible? There are options, if that's where we end up." He pulled back for a second, his expression puzzled. "Are you *asking* me to make that kind of commitment right now?"

My face flushed. "No. I'm nowhere near ready for that either. I just—I guess I'm trying to figure out how seriously we're taking this. If it's just having fun together knowing it won't go anywhere—whether we're making any commitment at all… *Are* we dating? Is that what you're looking for? You mentioned other girls…"

I wasn't sure I'd made a whole lot of sense trying to get my thoughts in order, but Jude's expression relaxed. "I thought we could figure it out as we go. I'm definitely not taking anything off the table for the future. But all my attention is yours right now, Rory. There's no other girl I want."

The words stuck in my throat for a second before I pushed them out. "What if I'm not sure I can say the same thing about other guys?"

Jude's eyebrows rose. "Are you seriously considering any of the jackasses who're being shoved at you to make a grab at the barony's coattails?"

No, but I couldn't admit what had passed between me and Declan without putting the other scion at risk. "I don't know. I haven't been making out with anyone else or anything." Only thinking about it. "My world got turned upside down just a couple months ago. I'm still working out who *I* am, how I feel about things—about people... If I decide I'd like to kiss someone else, does that mean we're done? Or is that an acceptable part of 'figuring things out' if I'd still like to be kissing you too?"

My cheeks heated more with that question. Jude let out a rough breath and brought his hands to my face, his thumbs tracing over my burning skin.

"I can't ask you to be all in yet," he said. "I know that. If some other jerk catches your eye, you do what you need to do to be sure. If you do go all in with me, I want it to be because you want me more than anyone else, not because you're afraid to find out what you really want. And if it turns out you really want someone else more, then that'll be my fault for not convincing you I'm your best bet." He winked at me. "I just promise I'll be very convincing."

I had to laugh, my embarrassment fading. "You've already proven that."

Jude kissed me again, just long enough to leave me with a pang of yearning when he stopped. He glanced down the passage. "Shall we see what other wonders await?"

The metal theme continued farther into the puzzle garden. Around a bend, we came to a wall like an immense shield made of overlapping plates. Jude rubbed his hands together as he studied it. "Let me have this one?"

He was so eager for the challenge that now that I'd handled one myself, I didn't mind stepping back. "Be my guest."

He ran his fingers over the plates, finding a few that lifted up. After a few minutes' inspection, he knelt down and whispered beneath one. I caught a glimpse of a lick of smoke vanishing into the shadow beneath. Something whirred within the shield. Then it spiraled open so we could step through.

"I guess you measure up," I said, tucking my hand around his elbow.

Jude beamed down at me. "Let's see what else we can find. I was under the impression these gardens usually had special chambers you could gain access to as well as the main path."

I studied the hedges on either side of us as we walked on, and my gaze caught on a metallic gleam deeper within the brambles. I tugged Jude to a stop. "There's something here."

An intricate metal sculpture like a multi-faceted star hung behind the dense foliage. We peered at it together. Something about the shape struck me as just slightly off. The top point—it didn't extend quite as far as the others.

I hesitated and then whispered, "Grow," pushing a thread of my magic toward it. Seeing how I wanted the silver surface already there to stretch and lengthen, until it touched—

The point brushed a bramble just above it, and the entire section of hedge unfurled, the leaves and twigs pulling back into themselves. My breath caught at the sight on the other side.

I stepped tentatively into the secret room I'd opened up. It was still bordered by hedges, but the colorless leaves on the walls gleamed as if they were made of crystal. The branches between them shone gold. More gold arced over our heads forming a lace-like roof. And by the far wall stood a high crystal seat—a throne wide enough for two or three to sit on.

Jude let out a low whistle. "Fit for a queen. Especially an icy one. Come here, Your Highness."

He swung me onto the crystal throne so swiftly I lost my breath. A pleasant warmth seeped through the slick surface beneath me. Then all I felt was heat as Jude brought his mouth to mine.

The seat put me at the perfect height for us to kiss without him bending at all. My legs splayed instinctively to give him more room.

One of his hands settled on my thigh, staying there with a stroke of his thumb across my hip bone, the other tangling in my hair. His tongue teased between my lips, and I gave myself over to the pleasure racing through me.

We kissed, edging ever closer together until every nerve in my body was aware of the seam of his slacks grazing but not pressing against that particularly sensitive part of me. A giddy quiver traveled up through my core.

Jude traced a heated path across my jaw and over my neck. He stopped there with a swipe of his tongue and a nip of his teeth, and a gasp jolted out of me.

His hand slid up my body to cup my breast, and a different sort of jolt shot through me. The memory of my night with Connar on the cliff, the bliss of it wrenched through with the horror of his harsh words the next morning, flooded my head. My body tensed.

Jude stopped in an instant, his hand dropping to my waist, his eyes searching mine. A flicker of pain crossed his face before he schooled it calm again. "You're still scared of me."

I couldn't deny it. He wouldn't say that if he hadn't felt it, and my fear wouldn't have passed into him if he hadn't been partly responsible. I was afraid of giving myself over completely again, afraid of the harshness I'd already seen Jude was capable of.

"It's not just you," I said, to be fair. "The last time I was with someone else like this… things went badly."

Jude made an angry sound. "That asshole feeb? I can absolutely promise you I'll never treat you like you're *nothing*."

He knew from Insight class about my first boyfriend back home who'd ditched me and acted like I didn't exist after we'd slept together. Obviously word still hadn't gotten around about Connar and me. I didn't think I'd have wanted Jude to know about that anyway.

"I'm okay," I said. "But we don't need to rush anything, right?"

"Of course not." He tipped his head to nuzzle the side of my neck, his lips brushing my skin as he spoke. "What if we made this not about me at all? I solemnly swear to keep my dick in my pants today, even if you end up begging for it."

When I snorted, he straightened up with a smile. "I'm serious.

Would that take the fear out of it, if it was all about you? I can give and ask for nothing in return."

The promise in his voice made my skin tingle in anticipation. "That doesn't exactly seem fair."

"Sure it is. I was thinking too much about me when I was an asshole to you before. I know I'm not finished making that up to you."

Maybe it was fair then. My body leaned toward his of its own accord. "I suppose we could just… see how it goes."

His smile widened, and then he was kissing me again, tenderly but fervently. At the same time, he shifted backward so his hips no longer intruded on me quite so closely. Taking away that sense of impending expectations.

It was easier to let go when I knew he didn't expect me to open up to him completely. His fingers stroked over my breast again, but no panic sparked at their touch, only more heat. I gave a little growl and kissed him harder, and he rolled my nipple under his thumb with a pleased chuckle against my mouth.

He slipped his hand under my shirt to fondle me skin to skin, and my breath started to break apart between our kisses. Catching my lip between his teeth, he gave it a slight pinch that set off an even sharper flare of hunger, one that raced right down to my core.

Maybe I shouldn't have snorted at the idea of begging for him. An ache was building between my thighs with each skillful caress.

Jude returned his attentions to my neck, finding the sensitive spot that had made me gasp before. As my head tipped against the back of the throne, his hands dropped lower. One held my hip in place, and the other glided over my sex.

A whimper spilled from my lips. I couldn't stop myself from arching into his touch.

"I've got you," Jude murmured. "I can take you there."

My hips started to rock with abandon as he stroked me, first through my pants and then flicking open the clasp to cup me even more closely. His mouth came back to mine as his thumb swiveled over my clit, and I slung my arm around his neck as I kissed him back to try to counterbalance my growing shakiness. Pleasure spiked through me in waves as Jude's fingers delved deeper and curled right inside of me—one, then another.

"Good?" he asked breathlessly, and all I could manage was a stuttered gasp and a jerky nod. His fingers plunged deeper, all the way to a spot inside me that blazed with sudden bliss. Then I couldn't do more than cling to his shoulders and sway with him as he urged the flames higher and higher.

"Jude," I mumbled. "Oh!"

His voice came out ragged. "Rory, you're so fucking gorgeous. Fucking perfect."

He stroked that blissful spot inside even harder, and my orgasm burst through me like a firework. Jude captured my cry with his mouth. His hand kept rocking with me until the pleasure had burned through my body.

I sagged forward into his embrace, my head nestled against his chest, held by this boy I'd never have thought I could come to trust. This boy who'd offered me more in the last few weeks than anyone else at Villain Academy had been willing to.

"Was the outing sufficiently distracting?" Jude asked when we were on the road back to the university. The sun was still high overhead, only just starting to creep down with the waning of the June afternoon, but after exploring the puzzle garden and the rest of the grounds more thoroughly, we'd determined there was no food to be had in the Bloodstone country cottage. My stomach had already grumbled a couple of times in a demand for lunch.

"Absolutely." For a few hours, my mind had felt less like a hornets' nest and more like the placid pond beside the cottage. "I'd been wanting to check out my family's properties. Thank you for showing me the way out here."

"My pleasure." Jude sprawled back in the seat with a smirk that brought to mind all the pleasure he'd conjured in me this morning. "Any time you want to get out of town, I'm your man."

"I'll keep that in mind. It's gotten kind of crazy on campus with all the competing for credits."

"Everyone's got to support their league. I see Insight has been rising in the rankings. Apparently you've had a productive influence there. I expect Illusion can still rule the day, though. I don't plan on serving anyone a feast this term."

The members of the winning league of each term's competition got to eat a celebratory banquet prepared and served by the losers—who had to do a good job of it, or they'd get in trouble with the staff who were partaking too. There was a board up in Killbrook Hall regularly updated with the recent credit additions, but I hadn't checked it recently. I really didn't give a crap whether I ended up in the kitchen or at the feasting table.

"It's ridiculous," I said. "I guess I shouldn't be surprised by how far people are going, but I still think it's too much."

"It's just one more way to practice our skills. Why do you think the teachers encourage it?" Jude tipped his head to the sunlight with a satisfied expression. "You've got to admit that illusion during the concert was pretty spectacular, at least."

Something that was nothing like hunger twisted my stomach. "Illusion?"

"You know, rampaging bears and all. I thought it was a pretty spectacular way to top that last stunt nobody would stop going on about. It's no easy feat getting *three* bears that size moving independently and detailed enough that no one would suspect they're not the real thing."

My grip on the steering wheel wobbled. I'd assumed the bears had been shape-shifting students, but there was no reason they couldn't have been an illusion. I hadn't heard the credit called. But more importantly… "And you'd only know that if you were the one who cast it."

"Hey, I'm not looking for an ego stroke. We all have to do our part. It just so happens I could contribute a large part. The Illusion league is clearly the one to beat."

He was talking about it so breezily, as if it'd been nothing but a lark. My gut clenched tighter. "People got *hurt* because of that stunt."

Jude shrugged, glancing over at me with his brow knit. "A couple of Naries got bruised up a bit. No big deal. If they'd kept their cool, they'd have been fine. I couldn't let the things really hurt them—any injuries they caused directly would have vanished with the rest of the illusion."

"There were plenty of injuries caused indirectly! They had no idea the bears weren't real. And my friend didn't just get bruised. She broke her wrist—she had to leave the school because she can't play her cello for who knows how long."

Jude paused, watching me. "Are you really this worked up about a feeb? They know the school is going to be tough. It comes with the territory. The profs make sure they get a good bang for their buck, especially considering they're not paying for anything. If she hadn't panicked, she'd still be here."

"If you hadn't made her think rampaging bears were charging at her, she'd still be here." I inhaled sharply, trying to keep my voice from shaking. I could stay calm. If I just put it the right way, he had to get it. "Do you really not see how that's a problem?"

"Are you really getting angry at me for doing an amazing job at exactly what we're supposed to be learning how to do? That was the largest and most complex illusion I've pulled off in my life. I'd like to see anyone else top it in the next ten years."

"It's got nothing to do with that. What part of this person being my friend do you not understand? It doesn't matter whether she was a Nary or not."

Jude had bristled. His voice came out scoffing. "Of course it does. They're not at Blood U for us to make friends with them. They're there for target practice and forcing stealth. How can you be 'friends' with someone you can't tell the most basic thing about yourself to?"

My calm frayed. "By realizing there are a whole lot of other things that matter about people. How can *you* go around breaking people's bones and ruining their lives and not care?"

"I didn't hurt any of them on purpose! And that's the whole reason the staff bring them in—so we can use them. I'm sure she learned plenty from the experience."

He said the last bit so bitingly flippant that my stomach lurched right up toward my throat. I jerked the car over to the gravel shoulder and skidded to a halt just in time to throw open the door and vomit what was left of my breakfast onto the asphalt.

For a few seconds afterward, I just stared at the pale splatter on the dark pavement, my mouth sour and my head spinning. The guy saying these awful things was the guy I'd bantered and laughed with for the last few weeks. The guy I'd kissed, the guy I'd let touch me in the most intimate way just a couple hours ago…

He'd started being nice to me. That hadn't changed who he was to everyone else. I simply hadn't let myself think about it all that deeply.

He didn't give a shit that his stupid prank had cost Shelby her dream. He didn't even see her as a human being with a right to have those dreams. She and all the billions of Naries that made up the rest of the world had no rights at all to him.

"Rory?" Jude said, his tone abruptly uncertain.

I straightened up, wiping my mouth, and found I didn't even want to look at him. "Get out," I said as I yanked my own door closed again.

Jude stared at me at the edge of my vision. "What?"

I forced myself to turn toward him then. "*Get out of the fucking car.*"

I hadn't meant to hit him with a spell. I wouldn't have expected it to work even if I had meant to cast magic at him. But either his mental shields had faltered in his confusion or my anger had driven my persuasive magic right through them, because the second my voice crackled through the air, Jude groped for the door handle automatically. He swore as he stepped out onto the gravel, obviously compelled beyond his control. I leaned over to pull the door shut and locked it.

Jude grabbed the edge of the open window. Fear shuddered through me from him, but the whitening of his face looked as furious as it did horrified. "What the hell are you doing? *This* is ridiculous, Rory."

"No," I said. "What was really ridiculous was forgetting that you'd already shown me exactly who you are. Let go of the car."

"You can't just leave me on the side of the road!"

"We're less than ten miles from campus. You were just telling me what a great mage you are—I'm sure you can figure out a way to make it back there. Let go of the car *now*, or you might end up with a few broken bones too. But I guess that's no big deal, right?" I tugged the gear shift from park into drive.

Jude jerked his hand back. "Rory," he started again, but I didn't wait to hear how he'd try to justify himself next. With my gut still roiling and my eyes burning, I hit the gas and tore down the road alone.

CHAPTER TWENTY-THREE

Rory

The voice echoed up from below as I climbed the stairs to the staff wing of Killbrook Hall. "It was awesome! He had this whole scheme planned out to transform a bunch of stuff, but it was all right there at the front of his mind, easy pickings. I pulled the rug out from under him in just a couple seconds."

"I think Insight really has a chance this term," someone said in answer.

The voices faded away when I headed down the hall, but they left me feeling nearly as queasy as when I'd kicked Jude out of my car two days ago.

It was still more than a week before the winner of the league competition would be announced, and all the students would just keep ramping up their efforts until then. And after that, the process would start all over again. Maybe my strategy of interrupting planned stunts was helping mitigate the damage a little, but at this point I just wished there was no such thing as credit in the first place.

Declan wasn't part of the competition, at least, having to stick to observing because of his teacher's aide position. I walked into the aide's office, and he got up from the table where he'd been paging through a book. But at the sight of his expression warming with a small smile of welcome I could tell he was restraining from getting any larger, I found it suddenly hard to smile back.

Jude had helped me, warmed me up with affection that might have been genuine… and I'd let that stop me from seeing or talking about how he was treating everyone around me.

How much did I really know about Declan Ashgrave and his views beyond the few subjects we'd talked about? He probably saw Naries as just as "feeble" as the other fearmancers. Who knew how many pranks he'd been part of before he'd taken this gig?

It wasn't just my heart I needed to be careful with here. It was the safety of everyone else I'd known and cared about or at least respected beyond the boundaries of this campus.

A couple of the other aides were standing off to one side of the room in conversation, so I couldn't say half of what I wanted to yet. "Should we pick up where we left off last time?" Declan asked, and I nodded, and for the first twenty minutes I tried to train all my attention on magical techniques and not on the motives and feelings of the guy leading me through them.

Declan was obviously wary of being overheard too. He carried on as if everything was fine, even when I wavered a few times during the exercises, but his posture drew straighter when his coworkers headed out the door. The leash I'd kept on my tongue loosened at the same time.

"Is everything all right?" he said. "You're having more trouble focusing than usual."

"I've got a lot on my mind." I hesitated and then just spat it out. "Have you hurt people?"

His eyes widened. "What?"

I swiped my hand across the table top. "You were with the blacksuits when they killed my parents. Maybe you've gone on other missions with them where you didn't stand back. You were at this school for years before you had any rules about not picking sides—and that still doesn't apply to the Naries, right? Have people gotten hurt because of the things you've done, accidentally or on purpose, as far as you know? I don't think it's that hard a question."

Declan considered me in silence for a moment. My defenses stayed firmly in place, but he'd shown before he could put the pieces together without looking right inside my head. "This is about Jude and the thing with the bears, isn't it?" he said. "The Nary girl who had to be sent home—she was from your dorm."

"She was my friend," I said tightly, daring him to object. "The *only* friend I've made here who's never hurt me, I should mention." Which he should have already known if he'd heard about my falling out with Jude straight from the source. "Did you know it was Jude's spell? Did he tell you he was going to do that?"

Declan shook his head. "It was easy to guess after the fact. I don't know any other student here who could have cast an illusion that complex."

"Fine. It was a brilliant spell, etc. etc. I've already told Jude exactly what I think about it. We're talking about *you* now."

"Okay." Declan inhaled slowly. "I've never done anything with the blacksuits other than that one mission. They only had me along because it was you—because of the similarities in our past. Beyond that… I can't tell you I've never caused anyone even a little pain, Rory. Can *you* say that, even in the short time you've been here? Striking fear in other people is how we operate. I can say that I've always tried to act in ways that won't do any lasting damage."

"What does that mean?"

"To the best of my knowledge, I've never outright traumatized someone, and I've definitely never intended to. I don't believe I've caused any physical injuries either. Scaring other fearmancers, within limits, is another way of teaching them how to handle themselves when they graduate and have to compete with mages who have far more experience."

My chin came up. "And the Nary students?"

"I don't target Naries," he said. "I think it's good that we have them here to prepare us for moving among them in the wider world, but tripping them up doesn't seem fair."

I studied him with a frown. Did he mean that, or was he just saying it because he knew it was what I'd want to hear? "Everyone else seems to think it's fair. What makes you so different?"

He paused, and a flicker of uneasiness passed from him to me. He was nervous about talking about this—about what I might do with the information? About what I'd make of it? I braced myself.

"I don't think I am so different," he said quietly. "I know my family isn't the only one that's started to feel this way. It's the way my father brought my brother and me up to believe, and from what he's said and the comments I've heard from the barons, my mother had similar feelings. There's always been jockeying for power and manipulation, but the kinds of aggressive harm a lot of the families are carrying out and encouraging… It's not necessary. It gives the joymancers an excuse to come down on us, and it puts us at risk by weakening our own bonds and getting us into precarious situations with the Nary population. We should be better, smarter, than being malicious just for the sake of it."

"So, you think we should be nicer to everyone for strategic reasons."

Declan held my gaze. "That's the best case I can make for it that anyone here is likely to listen to… which they're still not very likely to. If the other barons heard me say that, I could be accused of treason. I don't enjoy seeing people in pain. I don't want to ruin people's lives. That's my personal moral compass, where *I* draw the line, not an argument."

And yet it was the part that mattered most to me. "But you don't draw the line enough to stick up for me when I say anything like that to the other scions," I had to point out.

He gave me a crooked smile. "Did you miss the part about treason? I trust the guys more than I trust their parents, but they don't really know—they haven't seen— I can't be sure they wouldn't say something that would shatter everything I've worked for. And just because I don't enjoy pain, that doesn't mean I don't understand it can be necessary. This is how the world you were born into works, Rory. You were never going to be ready for it if you didn't have to face it."

I let out my breath in a huff. "I'm starting to get very tired of people deciding what's good for me. If all that is true, though, I'm really sorry for all of us that you lost your mom. If the joymancers had known she was pushing for peace…"

"That wouldn't have stopped them. They wouldn't have believed it. We're all villains in their eyes, believe me." He reached into his bag and pulled out a few folded papers I recognized as another report. I had three of them now stashed in the back of my wardrobe, so many words and images I didn't *want* to believe.

When I got out of here, when I could go back to the Conclave and prove I was better than they'd expected, maybe I could get a few answers from them too. Some of the fearmancer records *had* to be biased, but… the joymancers could have gone too far too.

Still, even the worst incidents the blacksuits pinned on the joymancers didn't compare to the attitudes my fellow students put on display every day here.

"Why are you giving me that?" I said abruptly. "What's the strategy there? Are you actually trying to help me by showing me all that stuff, or is this part of some plan Malcolm or your baron colleagues or whoever came up with? I'm *never* going to hate the parents who raised me, if that's the end goal."

A flicker of guilt crossed Declan's face. My hands clenched.

"You need to know the magical world isn't as simple as good guys and bad guys," he started, but I was already shoving my chair back to stand up.

"Why? Who says I have to know right now? Don't lie to me. *Everyone* here always has some other agenda—that much I'm figuring out."

"Rory." He got up to follow me.

I wasn't sure I could stand to hear more right now. I headed for the door, and Declan caught my hand partway across the room. When I glanced back at him, there was so much turmoil in his bright hazel eyes that my feet stalled.

"I'm doing my best," he said, his voice rough. "I'm trying to prepare you for everything that's going to be thrown at you. Sometimes that goal is going to line up with something someone else wants, and sometimes I have to make… concessions, but I'm not in this to hurt *you.* I don't want to see you broken. I want you strong enough to stand up with me in the pentacle of barons when there are hard decisions being made."

"I'm just a tool, then—a future ally you'll want to use."

"*No*." He tugged me closer, and my heart stuttered with the impression that he might try to kiss me again. Instead, he just tipped his head close to mine, dropping his voice even lower than before. "I've been as much of a shield for you from the people who *do* want to use you as I can without screwing us both over. Even telling you that could be a mistake. The barons are the most powerful mages alive, Rory. You don't fuck with them unless you want to end up with your head on a pike. But I am anyway, because the alternative is purposefully screwing you over, and I do have a goddamned line."

Strain radiated through every word he spoke. A tremor passed through his hand into me. My throat constricted as I squeezed his fingers. I'd thought I was carrying a lot of weight, but the pressures I'd felt were nothing compared to the tension in Declan's voice.

"I didn't know," I said. "You didn't *say* anything."

"The less I tell you about it, the less chance they'll pick up on it, one way or another. You're not the only one I have to look out for."

Not just himself, but his brother too. I swallowed hard. He was shielding both of us with all he had, even though those goals had to be in nearly direct opposition.

"Okay," I said quietly.

He pulled back, releasing my hand, and grabbed the report off the table. "Will you at least take this? Throw it in the garbage as soon as you get back to your room if that's what you want. At least then I can say I gave it to you."

I took the papers and shoved them into my purse. I didn't know what else to say in the face of the confession he'd just made. Maybe it was better to not say anything at all.

"Thank you… for the tutoring," I ventured.

The smile he gave me looked exhausted. "You're welcome. Keep those mental walls strong."

I didn't throw the report in the garbage. As soon as I was back in my room, I flopped on my bed and leafed through the papers. What other catastrophe had the joymancers supposedly caused?

This one wasn't as large scale as the others. It was personal. No one had died. No one had even been injured, at least not in a physical way. But there was a cruelty to the account that made me feel more sick than any of the others had.

Deborah scurried up to join me. *What now, sweetheart?*

"Another report on the joymancers. This one says they messed with a fearmancer they didn't like by forcing him and his wife apart. According to the blacksuits who investigated, anyway, someone cast a spell so that if either of them expressed affection for the other, they'd get violently ill. No one could figure out how to break the spell, so they just couldn't be together."

As I summarized it aloud, something sparked in my head. A spell that could trigger an illness only during certain actions…

That sounds more like a fearmancer spell than a joymancer one, Deborah said, but she'd hesitated first. I glanced down at her small body next to my arm.

"You've heard of something like this being done before."

Only for the good of the people involved, she protested. *And not so severe—no physical effects. There are times when we've implemented a repulsion in cases of unrequited love that was becoming harmful or other sorts of partners who always ended up in trouble if they associated with each other. Sometimes a bad relationship or friendship can be intoxicating, and those involved need a little help to break the habits. It doesn't come up very often.*

Often enough that she'd known about it. "You don't think… It sounds almost like what's happened to my mentor when he's tried to talk to me. Could a *joymancer* have done something to him?"

Deborah made a doubtful sound in my head. *How would a joymancer find him or know he had anything to do with you? Do you think he'd have gone to them of his own accord?*

No. I couldn't imagine any mage here risking the security of the school like that. And Banefield had seemed worked up about threats I was facing right now, while I was hidden away here where the joymancers couldn't reach me.

But that didn't mean a fearmancer couldn't have learned a trick or two from the joymancer technique in this report—if it hadn't been a fearmancer spell in the first place and the report a lie.

"How did those spells work?" I asked. "How did they get the magic to stay on the person so long? They wouldn't follow them around recasting it over and over."

No. There'd be a mark placed on the body somewhere, innocuous but designed to contain the spell.

A mark. That was something I could prove. I got up and shoved the report out of sight.

What are you going to do? Deborah asked.

"I'm going to see if I can finally figure out what's making my mentor sick."

I might object to Jude's attitude about a lot of things, but he'd given me one good piece of advice. A locked door and the headmistress's refusal didn't have to stop me. I waited until a couple students had left the teaching staff hallway in Killbrook Hall, and then I went to Professor Banefield's door and knocked, just in case.

No one answered. I waited a full minute, my ears perked for any sound on the other side of the door. Then I whispered a word to the doorknob, picturing the lock shifting to the side. Magic prickled up through my chest, and the door clicked open at the twist of my fingers.

The office on the other side was dark, only a faint glow seeping around the drawn curtain. I crossed the room to the door on the other side that led into Banefield's private quarters, disengaged that lock too, and slipped inside.

The apartment I found myself in looked equally gloomy. Shadows slanted across an old-fashioned living room set and an open-concept kitchen, the smell of stale bread lacing the air. I followed the rasps of breath to the bedroom.

It was brighter in there, the heavy curtain pulled back leaving only a gauzy one beneath in place. My mentor lay sprawled in his four-poster bed, the covers off other than where they were tangled around his midsection, fresh sweat beading on his flushed face. The air held the lingering tang of vomit.

His eyelids twitched but stayed closed. I hoped his dreams weren't too troubled.

He looked thinner than he had the last time I'd seen him, a couple weeks ago. His bent elbow stuck out with a knoblike shape that didn't seem right. How much had the health center staff been able to get him to eat?

I shifted on my feet. I was here now, but where did I start? The thought of peeling the sheets off him to examine his whole body for some sort of mark made me balk.

As I hesitated, his hand jerked lower to scratch at his knee. A memory sparked. Deborah had said he'd done that a few times while she'd observed him. Because something there was niggling at him, maybe.

I crept to the side of the bed and grasped the ankle of Banefield's pajama bottoms carefully. Inch by inch, I eased the fabric up over his calf. He was so deep in the fog of his illness, he didn't even stir at the movement. When I'd uncovered his knee, I stopped, studying the skin there.

Nothing looked obviously magical. Some reddish hairs, a nick of a scar, and a small brown mole protruding right in the middle of his inner knee.

When I focused on the mole, a quiver of energy passed through me. Was there magic in it right now, working on him, keeping him sick like this? If I could tell, why the hell hadn't the health center mages done anything about it?

But then, no one had been able to help the couple in the report I'd read. A strong enough spell might be nearly impossible to break.

I had to try. Whatever the spell was, it had reacted to *me*—it was punishing him for talking to me. Maybe that would make the difference. If I could simply disperse the structure that held the spell…

I aimed all my attention on the mole. "Shrink," I said, picturing it shriveling up into nothing.

Magic tingled over my tongue, but the mole didn't budge. I tried again. "Disintegrate." And again. "Dissolve." And again. "Vanish."

I worked through a few dozen words and angles, leaning closer and stepping farther away, hovering my fingers over the spot as if that might help. The mole didn't so much as shiver.

I might not be trained in medical arts, but I should be able to have some physical effect, even if it was only superficial. The fact that the spot wouldn't change at all only reinforced my certainty that it was made of magic. A toxic magic that was draining the life out of my mentor.

A magic that no one who'd treated him had been able to cure. Did the doctors plan on just letting him waste away until he died?

I couldn't let that happen… but I'd just used up all the ideas I had. I didn't have the faintest clue how to save him.

CHAPTER TWENTY-FOUR

Malcolm

When I came down into the scion lounge, Jude was slouched on the sofa, a glass half-full of amber liquid in his hand. Even though he'd thrown my concern back in my face the last time we'd really talked and it'd been a couple years since I last saw him go overboard with the booze, I took a quick scan of the room for empty glasses or bottles that appeared significantly drained since I was last down here. There weren't any.

"Shut up," Jude said pre-emptively. He didn't look at me, but he didn't slur either, which suggested he was sober enough that I could lay into him instead of saving him from his stupid-ass self.

I ambled over to lean on the back of the couch at the opposite end from him. "Shut up about what, exactly? The fact that *she* hit and split on you?"

He glared at me then, with enough ire that I could tell I'd hit decently close to the mark. I didn't know exactly how far he'd gotten with our Bloodstone scion or what had led to him needing to call up Connar for a ride home a few days back, but from the little Connar had gathered and the way Jude had been skulking around since then it wasn't hard to figure out that something had gone sour between him and her.

"Self-righteous feeb-loving fucking bitch," he muttered, and downed the rest of his glass. He jabbed a finger at me with enough of a wobble to betray that he'd definitely had at least one other drink before that one. "Which doesn't change the fact that you're a fucking asshole."

"I don't remember claiming otherwise," I said. "Takes one to know one, doesn't it? What did you do that ticked her off?"

"It wasn't— I was only—" He smacked his glass down on the side table and got up. "I'm not discussing it with you."

He strode out of the room, brushing past Connar, who'd just come down, without a word. The Stormhurst scion glanced after him and then at me.

"He's still in a mood, huh?"

"As only Jude knows how to be." I went over to the bar cabinet to pour a drink of my own. "I don't know what he was thinking going after her in the first place. Anyone could have told him that wasn't going to end well."

And yet somehow without even being here, Rory's presence had wormed into this room and drawn fault lines through the bonds we'd spent over a decade forming. My fingers tightened around my glass.

Jude would get over it. He'd have to get over it. All the shit he'd said the other day—he couldn't really dismiss everything we'd survived together like that. She'd gotten into his head somehow, or he'd been peeved about something else. We'd still be here when he finished tending to his wounded ego. We'd all had plenty of practice at forgetting the things he said when he let his tongue right off its leash.

Connar's mouth had flattened into a pained line.

"He'll come around," I said to reassure him. "Faster if we can finally knock her off that goddamned high horse." Bring the Bloodstone scion to heel, solidify the pentacle of scions, prove to my father that some prissy joymancer-raised novice couldn't get the better of me—it shouldn't have taken this long. She was cracking, but she still wouldn't break.

My back prickled with the memory of the disappointment that had loomed large in my father's voice the last time we'd spoken on the phone—and with the scars etched in my skin from his past judgments and lessons. I was not going to let Rory make me look like a fool. "You've still been throwing her off in class like we've talked about, right?"

"When I can work it in without being noticed." Connar folded his arms over his chest, his gaze dropping to the floor. "It's harder to make sure she can't tell there's outside interference as she gets better—and if the professor catches me, I'll get in shit too."

I knuckled his arm. "Live a little. Take a few risks. You can run circles around her. Maybe we can find another way for you to shake her up too. Sudden limb transformation. Shift the ground right under her. She can block off her mind, but she hasn't got full-body armor."

"That doesn't sound so subtle to me."

"Maybe we went too far in the opposite direction. Let's just get this thing done." I clapped my hands together, trying to shake off the jittery edge of the tension that had wound through me. This had gone on too long, this stupid feud, and not just for me. It had fractured the four of us too much. What was the point in being scions if we couldn't hold each other strong? "She has to be willing to stand up for us before we can stand up for her. That's the only way this can work."

Connar hesitated. "I'm not—" he started with a grim expression.

I waved off his worries before he had to say them. "Don't you think for one second you can't keep up with her. We'll all push together, and she'll topple. Let me think on it, and in the next couple days, we'll have a solid plan. In the meantime, just keep picking at her any opportunity you see. I know I can count on you for that."

"Of course," Connar said. "Whatever you need."

He left, which seemed a little odd considering he'd only just come down, but maybe he'd simply been looking for reassurance that we were on the right track. I wandered restlessly through the lounge as I finished my drink, but the emptiness of the space and everything I had left to accomplish ate at me.

It was just about time to let Shadow out of the kennel. I might as well head over there now.

Nothing looked particularly out of the ordinary on the way out to the little wooden building at the edge of the east field. I stepped inside, my mind already skipping ahead to watching my familiar bound joyfully into the woods, and froze at the sound of a human voice.

I was the only one with a large enough familiar to require the use of the kennel this year. No one else should have been in here.

"Oooh, you think you're fierce, do you?" the voice said in a teasing tone, with a scuffing of feet against the floor and a rasp that I knew was my wolf's claws. He let out a low growl, but not his threatening one—the eager one that egged you on.

That wasn't the problem. The problem was I knew the voice who'd spoken to him.

I marched over to the kennel stall and yanked the door open.

The heir of Bloodstone was standing in the middle of the large concrete space, her back to me, her hands clamped around a short length of knotted rope with which she was in the middle of a tug-of-war with Shadow. Her head jerked around at the squeak of the hinges with a tumble of her dark brown waves. Shadow dropped his end of the rope and bowed down with glinting eyes in a wolfish request that I join their play.

My gaze shot back to Rory. "What the fuck are you doing with my familiar?" I snapped, every muscle in my body tensed.

Rory turned to face me, the rope toy—which I'd never seen before; she must have brought it with her—still dangling from her hand. Her stance had stiffened, but she raised one shoulder in a careless shrug. "What does it look like? He was bored. I figured I'd keep him company when I had a moment."

The lift of her chin and the intentness of her deep blue eyes dared me to complain. I had outright *kidnapped* her familiar not that long ago, a fact I doubted she'd ever forget. If I freaked out over her entertaining mine, I'd only look like a hypocritical idiot. I reined in my emotions.

All of my emotions. Alongside the instinctive alarm, part of me couldn't help appreciating the fire and steel that radiated from her stance. Every ounce of my training, both formal and informal, had prepared me to welcome an associate like this: fierce but controlled, quick-tongued and quick-witted, strong down to the core. How could she be everything a scion was supposed to be and yet still hate the rest of our guts?

She should be with us, not against us. I felt it down to my bones.

She should be with *me*.

I shoved aside that thought as quickly as it rose up and snapped my fingers by my side. Shadow came trotting over with the same wolfish grin as if to say this was the best thing that had ever happened to him, and wasn't I just as pleased as he was?

I gave him a tight smile and scratched between his ears. Didn't he remember pouncing on this girl a couple months ago?

"Shadow," I said, pointing at Rory, "we need to remind her who's in charge here. Take her down."

Rory's posture went even more rigid, but she held her ground. Shadow took a step toward her, but instead of lunging like he should have and knocking her over, he glanced back at me with an uncertain expression, asking if I was really sure about this.

For Christ's sake, how long had she been making friendly with him that he'd ignore a direct command?

Or maybe he could read my own mixed feelings about this girl. The familiar connection ran deep.

"It's all right, Shadow," Rory said in a gently cajoling tone that brought my hackles up even as it tingled over my skin. My wolf's ears swiveled right back to her, and his head came up as he watched her avidly. "You need to push me around to make him happy? Go ahead. I'll be fine." She held up her hands in offering.

Just when I'd thought this situation couldn't make me look any less effectual. Thank all that was holy we didn't have any witnesses.

"Never mind," I muttered. I could make my familiar follow the order, but it'd disturb him more than seemed worth it. I wanted to set her off balance, not torture him, and she wasn't the slightest bit afraid. Pushing the stall door wider, I stepped back to make room for Shadow to trot past. "Ready for freedom?"

My wolf didn't need any more encouragement than that to wheel around and lope out of the stall. The kennel door still stood ajar. He slipped out in a blur of dark fur.

"Why do you keep him shut up in here at all?" Rory tossed the rope toy to the side of the stall where his sleep blanket was. "It doesn't seem right for a wolf."

"I know it doesn't," I said tersely. "The staff are concerned about him roaming around during main school hours when the students are walking to and from classes. If you have a problem with that, you can take it up with Ms. Grimsworth, although even I couldn't persuade her, so good luck."

Rory had the decency to look a bit startled. "Oh. I didn't realize."

"I'd leave him at home where he can run free as much as he wants, but he'd be miserable that far apart from me," I added. I wouldn't feel that great about it either. The familiar bond started to gnaw at you if you were separated from your animal by a lot of distance for very long. "Whatever you've been doing here, you can stop it now." I motioned for her to get out too. "You made your point. I haven't even looked at your familiar in weeks. Leave mine alone."

She crossed her arms over her chest. "I think he'd rather I came back. What are you so worried will happen if I keep coming by?"

"I'm not *worried*. I just don't want you near him." Near the one living being in the world that had a direct line to my mind, although I wasn't going to emphasize that point for her. On the off-chance that she *hadn't* already considered that factor, I didn't want to put the idea in her head. "You know it's never fun for you when I have to make you do what I say."

She just gazed back at me with the calm defiance that rankled me all over again even as—damn it—it turned me on. "I don't think it's ended up being much fun for you either."

My jaw clenched. "If you really want me to show you I have what it takes to smash your defenses—"

She held up her hands again and walked past me, having to step close enough on her way into the outer hall that a whiff of a scent sweet as toffee reached my nose. The thought of Jude with his hands on her, with his mouth on her, and God knew what else sent a sudden flare of fury through me. Then Rory turned to meet my gaze, and there was something so unexpectedly vulnerable in her expression that my jealousy deflated.

"Do we really have to keep doing this?" she said. "The sniping at each other and the trying to get the upper hand? I don't like you, and you don't like me—so what? Can't we leave it alone and just ignore each other until we're done here?"

I don't like you, and you don't like me. The certainty with which she said that came with a jab to my gut. She had no fucking idea. As if I could ever ignore her.

"And then what?" I said. "You're stuck with me, Glinda. We're meant to work together until we retire decades and decades from now. Better we sort out our differences now."

"Is that what this is?" She shook her head in disbelief. "Let's just assume we'll tolerate each other's presences when we have to, then. It's probably going to be easier if we haven't been fighting the whole time before."

"You've got to know there's no chance of that. If I go easy on you now, then you win. I'm not going to look like a weakling so that you can have a little peace and quiet."

"But it's okay for me to look weak, if I finally give in and do what you want?"

I exhaled roughly. "What do you think? You have excuses. People hardly know you. You'll have tons of time to recover the respect you need. Hell, we'll *help* you get it back." But I—I had so much more to lose and so much farther to fall. Our peers here might never look at me the same way again. My father might never gain the confidence in me that I'd sweat and bled to gain.

She was smart—didn't she get how this worked?

For a few seconds, she just studied me. Was she really considering giving up just to put an end to the conflict between us?

I had the urge to offer her something to smooth the way, but what the hell did I have? Maybe there'd been a time when I could have turned the tension between us around the way Jude had, insomuch as he had before he'd fucked that up, but I knew without trying that I'd gone too far to have a chance now. The girl in front of me was *never* going to believe a friendly gesture from me until we'd beaten her down enough that she was begging for it.

The thought shouldn't have twisted my stomach the way it did. I couldn't even tell her I wished it was over too.

The moment dragged too long. I squared my shoulders, drawing another biting comment onto my tongue—and Rory ended the moment.

"Then it's going to be how it's going to be," she said, and walked away without waiting to hear how I'd have responded.

CHAPTER TWENTY-FIVE

Rory

My nerves twitched as I walked out to the garage, even though there was nothing to worry about. The discomfort was partly because of all my memories of meeting Jude there, now clouded by all the reasons I had to regret allowing those moments to happen, but it was also because I wasn't sure whether the guy I'd invited today would turn up. I couldn't tell which made me more nervous: the possibility that he'd be there or the possibility that he wouldn't.

When I came around the aisle to my parking spot and saw Declan waiting in the dim light, my heart leapt with an exhilaration that was only partly anxiety. Plenty of relief was mixed in there as well, along with other feelings it was safer not to look at too closely.

He swept a few stray strands of his black hair back from his face, his stance wary as he watched me approach. His gaze flicked from side to side to confirm no one else was around. It'd be hard to excuse this get-together as a tutoring session.

"What's this about, Rory?" he said when I reached him.

"I'll explain in a second. Hold on."

I scooted past him, more aware than I liked of the warmth of his slim body, and stood by the nearest window. "Hold the image," I murmured, willing some of my magic into the glass to fix the view of the empty passenger seat, ignoring the driver's seat where I'd be sitting. The spell came easily enough after the practice I'd had obscuring Deborah's hiding spots. I moved around the car, repeating the spell on all the windows, freezing for a second at the sound of an engine above.

Declan ducked down between my car and the neighboring one as a BMW cruised by. I finished my casting. When the other car had pulled out of the garage, he straightened up again, his mouth twisting.

Before he could argue, I motioned to the passenger door. "Get in. Let me make sure the illusion worked."

"Rory…"

"I promise I have a good reason. Go on."

He gave me a bemused look, but he climbed in. When he closed the door, he might as well have vanished from existence. I circled the car again, but the seat looked perfectly vacant from every angle. With a rush of relief, I got in on the driver's side.

"No one will see you're in here," I said. "If you want, on the way back I can drop you off in town and you can walk the rest of the way to campus, so there's even less chance of anyone realizing we went off together."

"On the way back from where? What's this all about?"

I looked at him, sitting where Jude so often had but with such a different presence—reserved and thoughtful and far more serious. His bright hazel eyes held mine with a glimmer of the longing I'd so often watched him squash. So many responsibilities and emotions he was juggling, and *my* presence in his life had made his so much more difficult.

"You've helped me so much, the last couple months," I said. "I didn't even realize how much until the other day… I didn't even think about the pressure you must be getting from the barons on top of everything else." My brief encounter with Malcolm's dad, Baron Nightwood, had made it clear that they didn't approve of my attitudes any more than the younger generation did.

"I want to take a trip out to one of my family properties that's near here," I went on. "I'd rather not drive alone. And I figured you might appreciate taking a break somewhere without having to worry about who might be watching or judging you. I've made sure the maintenance staff won't come by today. There won't be anyone else around. I'll do my thing, and you can just… chill out. Or you can say no and get out of the car. I'm not going to kidnap you."

Declan gave a laugh that sounded a little startled at that last remark. Maybe because the last time we'd taken a car trip of sorts together, the blacksuits he'd been with had technically kidnapped *me*. He ran his hand through his hair again, his gaze sliding to the windshield as he considered.

"It'll definitely be just us?" he said.

"The place is incredibly secluded. No neighbors around to see who goes in, and no one's going to get inside unless I let them."

He sank a little deeper into his seat. "All right. Maybe I *could* use a break. It doesn't sound like it'll hurt anything, anyway. And you're getting to practice your Illusion skills." He smiled wryly, but his expression softened when he looked at me again. "Thank you."

The flutter that look provoked in my chest was definitely not worth paying attention to. "Thank *you*," I said jokingly. "Today you can be my shield against having a panic attack in the middle of some country road."

I drove out of the garage and onto the road, pleased to find that whatever complaints I could make about Jude, his instruction in the car had left me reasonably confident. Declan watched without comment as I navigated the turns in town.

"You don't look like you need much help with this," he said.

"I've only ever driven about ten miles on my own," I said. "And that was fueled by being extremely pissed off at Jude. It's easier to feel secure knowing there's someone else here in case I run into some situation I haven't encountered yet."

"Not likely to be much trouble on these roads. Just don't go driving into New York City."

"Yeah." My thoughts leapt back to the story Imogen had told me about Professor Banefield's wife. I couldn't do anything about that loss, but there was still a chance I could make sure my mentor didn't lose his own life. And maybe the answer would be somewhere in my parents' former home.

Jude had said they never had company over there. That'd make it an ideal place for hiding information they didn't want their enemies knowing about. Ms. Grimsworth had mentioned my grandfather Bloodstone packing things up for storage, which I'd determined meant it'd be off in Maine at the primary family home, but I had to at least check.

The shade of the scattered trees along the side of the road slipped over us. Another, smaller smile curved Declan's lips. "You know, this is how it should be. How it's supposed to be. The scions looking out for each other, supporting each other, as we need it… It's how the four of us have been since we were kids. I know you've had your problems with, well, all of us, but if we can get through this—and Malcolm can get over his vendetta—you have a family here."

A lump clogged my throat. "My family was murdered." *By your people.*

"I know," Declan said quickly. "I didn't mean—obviously it's not the same. But it's something. You don't have any other Bloodstones to rely on while you're figuring things out. I don't think you'd be in the same kind of danger if you did. We can fill that gap, is all I'm saying."

I had trouble imagining the other guys expressing the same sentiment, but I believed he meant it. "Is that why you've helped me even though it puts *you* in danger? Because you've decided I'm family?"

"In a way." He paused. "You remind me of all the things I'd like to do and say if I didn't feel my position was so precarious. Maybe it makes me a coward that it's easier for me to ensure you can keep doing and saying all that stuff rather than making a bigger stand myself, but… it's something."

"I wouldn't expect you to risk yourself or your brother for me," I said. It wasn't as if there weren't things I'd kept to myself rather than risk admitting them to the wrong person. My whole plan to bring Bloodstone University down, for example. "He's your real family."

"I don't think the bond of the scions is any less real. It's just different."

"I guess most families don't have to suppress the desire to kiss each other."

I'd spoken without really thinking that comment through, but Declan just laughed. "There is that. Not that it's been much of a problem until recently. You… have added an interesting dynamic showing up all of a sudden, let's just say. I'd suggest looking farther afield when it comes to the kissing thing, though. Plenty of eligible bachelors beyond the pentacle of scions."

Considering that I'd kissed three out of four in the last two months, that comment seemed fair. Heat crept up my neck. "I guess the thing is that with everyone else I have to worry about what they really want from me. So far the guys who've tried to chat me up—or worse—only seemed to care that I'm a scion and not about me as a person. At least with you or Jude or… whoever, I know I'm not just a step up the social ladder."

"But on the other hand, anything you have with us can't lead all that far."

"Maybe that's okay. We're in college. Isn't that supposed to be the time for experimenting and figuring out what you want without worrying about making big commitments?" I hesitated, and my voice dropped. "I don't really trust anyone at Blood U yet. But maybe the fact that I can't have a real future with any of you makes you safe in that one area. Just mutual attraction, no expectations."

Declan wet his lips. "You know, today, it can't be—"

"I know," I said. "I wasn't thinking—that wasn't the idea. I really did just want to do something nice for you, as foreign a concept as that might be in fearmancer circles."

"Sorry. I know I didn't need to say that." He looked over at me. "You might have shaken things up, and obviously the clash hasn't been easy on you, but I think we're lucky to have you the way you are."

I let myself glance away from the road for a second to meet his eyes. The honest appreciation there set off a whole lot more than a flutter inside me.

Maybe that was okay. He was the safest one of all, really, because he didn't *want* to want me. If anything ever happened between us, it'd be desire, pure and simple, not some other goal he thought he could use me for.

He reached for the radio, breaking the moment. "Do you mind?"

"No, go ahead."

He found a local station playing jangly pop music that I wouldn't have thought was his thing, but it reminded me of the songs I'd have listened to back home, three months and a lifetime ago. At least it was a pleasant memory of times past for once. The buoyant beats filled the car the rest of the way to the cottage.

There was no sign of anyone on or around the driveway, as expected. I'd gotten the contact information for the company that had been overseeing my family's properties from Ms. Grimsworth to ensure we had no interruptions today. As a secondary measure, just in case, I cast a little magic toward the gate's panel as I pressed my hand to it. "No one but me."

Energy shivered through the warm metal. As long as that spell lasted, it should reject any other attempts to open it.

On the other side, Declan exhaled slowly as he took in the grounds and the buildings, his shoulders relaxing with the clang of the closing gate in a way they hadn't quite while we were in the car. The sun beamed over us, glinting off the pond and turning the green of the yard and the hedges even richer. His family must have places just as nice, but I could tell he liked it.

I headed over to the house intending to begin my search, and he followed.

"What exactly are you up to here?" he asked. "This isn't just a break for you."

"No. Mostly I'm just trying to learn more about my family and what they did before my parents died. This seems like a good place to start." I didn't want to go into more detail about my hopes of helping Professor Banefield. I might trust Declan not to be involved with that plot, but he still had to report back to the other barons somehow or other, and who knew how they might be tangled up in this mess. "Feel free to take a walk around the grounds or find somewhere to just lounge around or whatever. Just enjoy having nothing to worry about for a little while."

Declan looked as if he wasn't really sure what to do with himself if he didn't have some pressing issue to deal with, but he nodded to me and meandered on toward the pond. I stepped into the house and started a much more intensive investigation than I'd felt comfortable getting into while Jude was around.

The great room on the main floor had a ceiling two stories high and a view from its picture windows down to the pond, but not a whole lot to look through. Somehow I didn't think my parents had hidden secret documents under the leather couch. Branching off from there, though, was a room that appeared to be a study, with bookcases filling two of the walls and a big oak desk by the window.

I'd only glanced in there with Jude. Today, I marched right in and got to work.

Every book on the shelves—some of them old novels, some volumes of magical theory, some more mundane business and legal reference texts—I slid out and flipped through in case anything had been secreted away inside. Then I started on the desk drawers.

The ones on the left side only held basic items like pens and paperclips, blank notepads not yet used, an old personal phone book that looked as if it hadn't been opened in decades. The yellowed pages crackled and started to tear as I flipped through it. Other than a few last names from the baron families, I didn't recognize anyone in there. I slipped it into my purse in case it'd come in handy later.

The drawers on the right side were locked. I fiddled with them for a while, testing my magic against each one, shivering with the deterring jab of the spells on them. Finally, my fingers managed to press the right spot with the right nudge of magic on the top drawer. It opened to reveal what first looked like just a bunch of scrap papers. I dug through them, and my fingers brushed a leather surface toward the back.

I pulled out a small leather-bound journal. The first page showed a list of notations—names, dates, jotted notes about the topics of meetings or phone calls.

I paged through, again checking for any familiar names. Whether it'd been my birth mother or father who'd kept this record, they'd been in touch with Ms. Grimsworth a few times in the year before their death. The name Crowford came up once, but I didn't know my Persuasion professor's first initial to be sure this was him and not some other member of his family. The information was all dry facts, no hint at how the writer had felt about any of the interactions noted.

After several unsuccessful attempts at the other drawers, I gave up for the time being. My stomach was starting to gurgle. I checked the fridge and found the fruit and premade sandwiches I'd asked the maintenance workers to drop off on their last visit. Digging into a peach, I went out to find Declan and see if he wanted anything to eat.

I almost didn't see him stretched out on the padded lounger on the deck. His arms lay loosely folded over his chest, his head tilted against the cushion as he dozed in the warmth of the sun. His lips had parted just enough to emphasize their soft cupid's bow shape.

My heart twinged. I guessed he really had needed a chance to properly relax. More strain than I'd realized was there had faded from his expression, leaving it completely at peace. An image popped into my head of waking up next to that striking face, of pressing my mouth to his, with a rush of heat I had to shake off.

In some ways, he really was as caught in his circumstances as I was. He didn't want the barony. He didn't agree with half the stuff he saw around him.

When I got out of here, when I could send the joymancers to topple the university and anything else it led them to, I'd tell them to make sure the Ashgraves stayed safe. Maybe the fearmancer world wouldn't be half so terrifying if all the barons had been like him.

The upstairs of the cottage held four bedrooms and a bathroom. Two of the bedrooms contained no personal items at all, so I figured they were guest rooms, presumably not used very often in my parents' day. The next one held a crib and a changing table.

Last time, I'd glanced in there briefly, Jude had made a joke, and I'd walked on before the implications had really sunk in. Now, my fingers tightened where I'd grasped the doorframe.

This had been my bedroom. I didn't have the slightest memory of it, but it couldn't have belonged to anyone else.

For the first two years of my life, when we'd been here, I'd slept in that crib. My birth parents had changed me on that table. I'd watched that silver star mobile spin as I drifted off to sleep. I'd played with the stuffed animals sitting in their wicker basket next to the wardrobe.

I drifted over to the crib and looked into it. The sheet was neatly tucked, the furniture free of dust—the cleaner kept the place spic and span. Not a hair or a crease remained of my long-ago presence here. But just the sight of the room brought the idea of the family before the one I remembered crashing home.

I *had* had other parents, parents who'd set up this room for me, parents who'd cared for me. Parents who might very well have loved me, even if I found it hard to associate those tender emotions with fearmancers.

I shivered and backed away, leaving the haunted sensation behind as I moved to the last bedroom.

Just outside it, a framed photograph hung on the wall. My birth parents stood in a formal embrace in front of a marble wall. My mother in her deep blue gown looked like a slightly older version of me, with eyes a little closer set and dark chestnut waves that tumbled all the way to her waist. My father stood half a foot taller, broad-shouldered but narrow in his face, his hair a lighter brown both on his head and the neat beard on his pointy jaw.

They were posed the way you often saw in wedding photos, but their clothing didn't fit—unless fearmancers had different traditions. I tore my gaze away and went on into the room.

It was clearly the master. A king-sized bed with a mahogany sleigh frame dominated one half of the room, the other holding a dressing area with wardrobe, vanity, and a couple of armchairs. Like the rest of the house, the room was spotlessly clean, the air carrying a faintly citrusy scent.

I started with the wardrobe, hoping my search upstairs wouldn't be totally fruitless. The top shelf held a box that proved to be full of dry pressed leaves—who had collected those?

Groping as far as I could, my hand came to rest on a large clothbound book shoved right to the back. An old photo album, I realized as I tugged it out. The dates written on the cover showed a span of six years that ended a few years before my birth.

I sat down on the floor with the album and leaned against the wardrobe as I paged through it. My birth parents featured in most of the photographs, one or both of them. It started in their university days. There they were with a few other kids in their late teens standing on the green with Nightwood Tower in the background. There was my mother lounging on the dock with a friend, a big but elegant sunhat shading her eyes.

This wouldn't tell me who their enemies were, but it might give me a better idea who my allies in the wider world should be.

I turned another page, and came face to face with a couple more familiar figures. The golden-haired guy with his hand on my mother's shoulder was the spitting image of Malcolm, if maybe a tiny bit wider in the jaw and a tad more smoldering with his gaze. His dad, no doubt. And next to him stood a willowy woman with Declan's smooth black hair and pensive eyes. She looked a little stiff, as if she hadn't wanted to be in the picture.

The creak of the floor brought my head up. Declan stood in the doorway, his face still a little languid from his sleep, his hair windblown.

"Sorry," he said. "I didn't mean to startle you. Have you found what you were hoping to?"

"I'm still figuring that out. I've found more than I had before, anyway. Have a good nap?"

He laughed with an embarrassed flush that only made him more attractive. "I didn't mean to drift off."

"It's fine. You must have needed it. I'm glad my mission succeeded." I grinned at him.

Something about his gaze felt more intense than usual, but maybe it was only the effect of that recent sleep. He took another step into the room—still several feet away, but my skin tingled with awareness of him anyway. "Is there any way I can help?"

I wagged a finger at him. "*You* are on strict orders not to do any work for what I'm starting to think is the first time in your entire life."

This time his laugh came easier. "That might not be a total exaggeration."

As I continued perusing the photo album, he wandered through the room. He drifted into the hall for a few minutes to consider the picture of my parents and then moved to the bedroom window to take in the view. Every now and then, I felt his gaze come to rest on me again, but he didn't say anything. He didn't seem to want to venture off on his own again either.

None of the photographs were labeled. Once they moved beyond the university years, I didn't recognize most of the places in them, let alone the people other than my birth parents. I set the album over by the door to take with me back to campus and hopefully do some cross-referencing—maybe I could get Declan to look through it on the drive home, come to think of it, when I released him from total relaxation.

One more glance through the wardrobe turned up nothing. I opened the vanity drawers and found them empty. With a huff of breath, I set my hands on my hips.

"Well, maybe I'm going to have to do some relaxing now too. I think I've run out of places to search."

Declan turned to face me. "You haven't exactly had the most peaceful time of it the last few months. You've got to deserve some down time as much as I do."

"There's just… so much I need to take care of, as soon as I can." I grimaced. "Okay, now I probably sound like you too."

He chuckled and ambled closer, and that impression of intensity tickled through me again. "Yes, you do. Why do you think I like you so much?"

"I was hoping it was my brilliant wits and irrepressible spirit."

"Those too." He raised his hand to touch my cheek, and my pulse stuttered with desire. I expected him to pull back again, to let the moment pass, but instead he leaned in, so slowly my heart thumped faster and faster, until I felt like I'd die if he didn't kiss me.

And then he did.

CHAPTER TWENTY-SIX

Rory

This kiss wasn't at all like the one Declan had sprung on me in the library repair room, sudden and demanding. His lips brushed mine before catching my mouth more fully, the gentle motion setting off eager quivers all through my nerves. Even as I kissed him back, there was a tentativeness to the way he met my lips, as if he half anticipated the world to blow up with this transgression.

When it didn't, he tugged me closer, his fingers coming to rest by the crook of my jaw. He kissed me again, a real kiss, all determined longing, so heated I started to melt. His other arm looped around my back to hold me steady.

It was over way too soon. He drew back, leaving his arm around my waist, his hand at the side of my cheek. The tip of his nose grazed mine.

"Rory?"

I wasn't sure what he was asking me. He had to be able to tell from my response to the kiss that I had no objections. Well, maybe just a possible one.

"I thought you said we couldn't do this."

"I thought we couldn't do it." His breath had turned a bit shaky. It scorched my skin. "But being here, thinking about everything you'd said, finally having a chance to step back from all the stress hanging over me… Maybe I have a better chance of keeping it together and keeping us both out of trouble if I can let some of those feelings out while we're someplace safe. Maybe the fact that I want you won't eat at me so much if I can remember what it's like to have you."

I touched his chest and ran my hand down his slim but solid torso. "Are you sure?"

"No. Maybe I'm just kidding myself into giving in. I don't know. We still—we still can't be close after we leave here, as long as I'm an aide. And we still can't really *be* together in the long run. If that makes it too hard for you, we can stop right now. You just have to say it. I only want this if you do too."

No strings attached. No promises made. Nothing to figure out or wait and see about. After the messes of the last two guys I'd hooked up with, what Declan was offering felt perfectly simple. I'd been holding in the fire that kindled whenever he was around so long, it seemed to sear over my tongue as I answered.

"I do. I want you."

He didn't need any more answer than that. His mouth collided with mine again, his dry cedary scent washing over me, and I gripped his shirt, tucking my other hand around the back of his neck. His silky hair tickled my fingers. His lips slid against mine, finding a deeper angle, and the fire inside me spread through every inch of my body.

We were really doing this—me and Declan Ashgrave. After all those weeks of restrained desires, he was giving himself over to me. Putting his livelihood, his security, and his family's future in my hands. So much trust, so much more than I could imagine having in anyone right now. My heart swelled with more emotion than I'd thought it could contain.

Declan walked me backwards one step, and then another, until my legs bumped the side of the bed. He reined in the urgency of his kisses, drawing the next one out long and slow, his tongue teasing over the seam of my lips. He pressed another kiss to the edge of my jaw and charted a path along the sensitive skin there all the way to my ear.

"This might be the only time we get to do this," he murmured. "So I'm going to take my time. I want to remember all of it."

"I'm not going to argue with that." I stroked my fingers up his neck into his hair. He let out a tight hungry sound and reclaimed my lips.

Between kisses, I started unbuttoning his shirt. When I'd made it halfway down, Declan drew back for just long enough to pull it up over his head, rumpling his hair even more. He looked younger like this, flushed and eager, more like he really was only a couple years older than me and less like the professional persona he put on so often. I liked it.

Compact muscles lined his slim body. I traced my fingers over them, and he tipped my head into another kiss. His tongue teased over mine and twined around it. I kissed him back harder.

When it felt as if he must have explored every inch of my mouth and my nerves were singing with need, he eased me onto the bed, following me as I scooted farther across the mattress to make room. His fingers slipped along my waist to grasp the hem of my blouse. I raised my arms in case he needed a definite invitation. With a crook of his lips, he tugged off the shirt and dropped his head to kiss my shoulder. My collarbone. The swell of my breast just above my bra.

My necklace with the glass dragon charm, its base broken from when Malcolm had forced me to smash the others, slid across my chest. Declan paused over it with a hint of a wince, maybe at the same memory. He kissed my skin just beneath it and eased it to the side to rest on the pillow.

His fingers traced heat over my shoulders as he eased down the straps of my bra. He tucked his hand beneath one of the loosened cups with careful attention, stroking the soft curve and then sliding over the peak. My nipple pebbled instantly. When he rolled his thumb over it again, pleasure rippled through me and jolted a gasp from my throat.

He unclasped my bra, and I pulled him down for another kiss as he brought both hands to my breasts. My breath broke as he fondled them at the same time. I gripped his shoulders, massaging the taut muscles there.

Declan bowed his head over mine, watching my expression as he teased me, softly and then with a squeeze that provoked a shock of pleasure. I pressed my head back into the pillow with a whimper.

"Is that what you like best?" he said in a lightly teasing tone. He pinched my nipple carefully between his thumb and forefinger, and my back arched off the bed with the rush of sensation.

"Feel free to keep doing that," I replied raggedly.

He repeated the gesture a few more times until I was squirming with the tension building between my legs. Then he set to work with his mouth. His lips closed around one peak with a forceful flick of his tongue, and a sound that was half moan, half growl wrenched out of me.

I wanted to be the one taking. Calling the shots, leading the way. I was a fucking scion, wasn't I?

The pleasure we were stoking between us was mine as much as his. I would own it, and whatever happened after happened.

I would not regret *this.* I would make it exactly what I needed it to be.

For another minute, I trembled under Declan as he worked more bliss through my chest. When the need burning in me flared higher, I ran my hand down to his stomach and pushed. He eased away, checking my face with a flicker of concern, and I shoved him right over onto his back.

A smile curled his lips as I straddled him. I trailed my fingers up and down his torso, and he pulled me in for a kiss. My body rocked against him instinctively, flaming hotter at the solid length that met my core through our pants.

Declan groaned. He gripped my ass, encouraging the motion.

The friction between us left my head spinning. Fuck taking our time. I fumbled with the fly on his slacks, and he popped open the button on my jeans in turn. Before he tugged them down, he stroked his hand between my legs, earning him another gasp. We wriggled out of our pants between more hasty kisses.

I teased my fingers over the bulge in his boxers, and Declan tipped his head back with an inarticulate sound. I'd never really explored a guy's body this intimately before. The rush of my longing eased back as I caressed and then gripped his erection through the fabric. Declan stroked my breasts in turn, his eyes glazing each time I swiveled my thumb over the head of his cock.

"That feels so fucking good," he rasped. "God, Rory."

Something deep and distant twisted inside me, sharply enough that I couldn't ignore it. I leaned closer to him. "No regrets?"

His gaze cleared as he looked back into my eyes. "No regrets," he said firmly.

I yanked his boxers down, and he kicked them the rest of the way off. The smooth hardness of him felt even more thrilling skin to skin. I had the urge to kiss him there, to take him into my mouth, but I was getting too impatient for that. My panties were damp, my sex aching.

Declan pushed himself upright and helped me squirm out of my panties. He stayed there, sitting up to meet me, as I lowered myself over him. We kissed, his cock sliding against my clit, and my teeth grazed his lip with my whimper.

"Hold on," he murmured. "Let me..." He spoke a couple of casting words, his fingertips gliding between my thighs, and a similar protective tingling to the one Connar had provoked rippled up through me.

I drew him to me and sank down so his cock pushed inside me. Declan's breath caught, and I gripped his shoulder tightly as he filled me. A sudden swell of emotion nearly overwhelmed me.

Maybe there'd been no going back from the first moment I'd accepted his kiss, but in this moment, we couldn't have been any closer. He was offering up so much power to me that it left me breathless.

I cupped his face and kissed him with all the tenderness I had in me. With a shift of my hips and a rush of bliss inside me, our lips parted with a shared gasp. I flexed my thighs, pumping up and down over him, while Declan braced his hand against the mattress to hold himself with me. His other hand traveled over my side, stroked my breast, tangled in my hair as we kissed again, roughly now.

With each roll of his hips, each thrust to meet me, the pleasure building inside me soared higher. I bucked harder, faster, letting my body sway backward. Declan wrapped his arm around me and caught my nipple in his mouth, and that extra spark of ecstasy set off the final chain reaction.

I clenched around him with a cry I couldn't hold in, and my release blazed through me in a wave of fire. Declan let out a choked sound and plunged into me even more deeply. The sear of his cock sent me spiraling higher. He came with a groan against my shoulder, flooding me with fresh heat.

Declan tugged me to him, but not for a kiss, just to rest my cheek against his as my breath evened out again. I let myself relax into his embrace.

"I—" he started, and caught himself.

"What?"

He shook his head. "Never mind. Nothing important."

When I pulled back to look him in the eyes, he gave me a bittersweet smile. "I promise, it's not anything you have to worry about. It'd only make letting go of this when we leave here harder."

We snuggled together on the bed for a while, and then I dragged Declan downstairs for a late lunch he absolutely needed, sitting with my knee resting against his beneath the table. Drawing out the contact for as long as I could until I couldn't have it anymore.

When we finally headed out, I found myself taking his hand as we walked toward the gate. He twined his fingers with mine. I pressed my other hand to the panel to open the gate. It swung open—and my heart stopped at the sight of another car parked behind mine.

I dropped Declan's hand, but not fast enough that I was sure the two strangers standing by the second car hadn't noticed.

"Persephone!" the woman said in a gasp of a voice, and hustled over, her silver-white curls swaying around her broad face. The man, his short-cropped hair pure white, approached more cautiously, his broad shoulders and contrasting narrow face striking a chord of recognition in me.

I took a step back before the woman got all the way to me, tensing at the thought that she might try to hug me. She halted with a disappointed expression. "You don't know us at all, do you? How could you, you were so little? I told that headmistress at the university we should be allowed in to see you—"

"You're my grandparents," I broke in as the pieces clicked. My father's parents. "What are you doing here?"

"We keep in touch with the Bloodstone staff," my grandfather said in a more even tone. "They mentioned you were coming out here today. It seemed like an ideal time to introduce—or rather, re-introduce—ourselves."

"We knocked on the gate a few times, but I suppose the house is so far away, it's difficult to hear. You'll really need to get a new intercom system set up now that you're back." My grandmother peered at me, still looking like she was judging how she could finagle a hug out of me. "We have so much to talk about. You're all we have left."

That felt like an awful lot of pressure from two people that as far as I could remember I'd only just met. I was sharply aware of Declan standing tensed beside me, of the way they'd seen us coming out together. Of the fact that they'd seen us together here at all. And clearly Jude's account hadn't exaggerated their pushiness. The hairs on the back of my neck rose.

"I—I'm sorry," I said. "I really don't remember you. It's been a big adjustment, and I've been taking things one step at the time. Right now I need to get back to school. Maybe we could arrange a time for us to grab lunch together in town and talk, or something like that?"

My body balked at the idea, but I had to offer them something so we could get out of here. And they *were* family. I could give them a chance, even if their showing up here like this rubbed me completely the wrong way, just in case there was more to them than a regular fearmancer would recognize.

My grandmother's face fell. Her husband grasped her shoulder. "Of course you have your own plans. We'd only like to make the transition smoother in whatever ways we can. Let me give you my phone number so we can arrange that lunch."

As he jotted the number down on a slip of paper he retrieved from his pocket, my grandmother peered at Declan with sudden interest.

"Ah!" she said as if she'd solved a difficult puzzle. "You're the Ashgrave boy, aren't you? There's a lot of your mother in you."

"Thank you," Declan said, not quite able to smooth all the tension from his voice.

Her pale little eyes flitted between us. A knowing smile crossed her face. “The adventures of youth. I remember them well. You be good to her and don’t promise anything you can’t follow through on.”

“We’re not—It’s not like that,” Declan said.

Her eyes twinkled with even more curiosity. “Oh, is it not? This is a rather long way to come from the university for just a friendly romp. If you want to keep your adventuring quiet, you don’t have to worry. We can keep it to ourselves.” She winked at me.

Oh, fuck. I had no idea whether we could trust her, but every instinct told me no.

To my limited relief, when my grandfather handed over the phone number, my grandmother drew back beside him. “If you’re sure we can’t talk more now…”

“I have a tutoring session,” I lied. “I’m almost late as it is. I’ve had a lot of catching up to do, of course.”

“Of course,” my grandfather said, but his face momentarily darkened, and for the first time I got the sense that he wasn’t all that pleased with how their impromptu visit had turned out either. “It was a gamble, dropping in like this. It was good just to see you.”

They got back into their car, turned it around, and headed back down the drive. I waited until they were out of sight before I slumped into the driver’s seat of the Lexus. My hand shook when I pushed in the key. Declan said nothing.

If I’d just driven the car right up to the garage after I’d opened the gate—but that might have been worse. They might have spotted it through the bars and stuck around anyway, and I’d still have had to stop to talk, and they’d probably have noticed both Declan and the spell meant to hide him. Then it would have been even more obvious how secret we were trying to keep this excursion.

My thoughts tumbled around in my head as if they were caught in a clothes dryer as I aimed the car toward the university. I couldn’t help searching for something different I could have said, something better. A growing horror filled the pit of my stomach with each passing minute that Declan didn’t speak.

If they said something to the wrong person, my risky plan could completely screw him over. Why hadn’t I left well enough alone? We’d been fine the way things were. No regrets—ha. He was going to regret ever speaking to me. Any lingering pleasure from our coming together had soured.

"I've taught you just about everything I can anyway," Declan said abruptly. "I'll talk to Professor Sinleigh tomorrow about starting up those advanced sessions she promised you."

Now that he was speaking, my stomach only squeezed tighter into a ball of misery. "Okay."

"It'll be better if we don't even talk for a while, just to offset anything your grandparents might say. That shouldn't be hard once we're done with the tutoring."

"It shouldn't," I agreed. My hands gripped the wheel harder. "I'm sorry. I know I shouldn't have—I dragged you out there. It's my fault. I—"

"No. Rory—" Declan motioned to the side of the road. "Pull over. We can't talk properly when you have to focus on driving."

I did as he asked, braced for the anger that had to be coming. He'd snapped at me just for the fact that he'd lost control and kissed me that day in the library. This was a gazillion times worse. This time I really had fucked up.

As soon as I put the car into park, Declan set his hand over mine. When I met his eyes, his expression was solemn, nothing worse.

"I'm not saying these things because I'm upset at you," he said. "I'm not saying them because I don't *want* to see you. It's not your fault. You couldn't have known they'd come nosing around."

"I was still taking a chance, asking you to come out here. It was my idea."

"And I went along with it—I decided to take that chance. That's on me. Inviting me out here, giving me that space to really breathe and think, is the nicest thing anyone's done for me in ages. Okay?"

I sucked in a shaky breath. "Do you think they'll stay quiet about seeing us together? Would they even know that you're not supposed to—that you're an aide and all?"

"I don't know," Declan said. "But if word gets back to the university staff, it won't matter whether they knew how much shit I'd be in." He rubbed his hand over his face. "So that's why we have to make everything look totally professional and distant now. Maybe if someone hears what seems like just a rumor, they'll look at how we are with each other on campus and dismiss it. That's the best we can hope for."

"Yeah," I said quietly. I'd known we weren't going to keep anything like that brief intimacy after we left the cottage, but I'd thought I'd still have him in the ways I'd had him before.

Declan squeezed my hand. "I'll still do what I can to help you. It'll be harder, but—I'm not abandoning you."

"Okay." I couldn't seem to say more than that. I was afraid that if I did, the burn forming behind my eyes would spill over into tears. I couldn't cry over this. Over a relationship that had barely even existed in the first place. It was just the shock and the suddenness of the threat catching up with me.

"Hey." Declan let go of my hand to brush a few strands of my hair behind my ear. "I can't say I don't regret anything, but I've still got no regrets about what we did together."

"Are you sure?"

"Best day of my life, if we leave out the way it ended."

"That's kind of an important part."

"And I'll deal with it, because it's mine to deal with." He hesitated. His voice softened. "Come here? One last kiss, before we're all the way back to reality?"

My body shifted toward him automatically, my head tilting. He kissed me with a lingering desire that brought the flutter back into my chest and dulled the edges of my anguish.

I didn't know if everything would be okay, but with that, I at least believed that he didn't blame me. That we were okay.

I just couldn't believe that fact would be enough to shield *him* if the rest of the world came at him.

CHAPTER TWENTY-SEVEN

Rory

The voice slid into my sleep, winding through the last fragments of a dream. "*Wake up.*"

My eyes popped open to my dim bedroom, morning sunlight seeping from around the curtain. My body had curled tight defensively beneath the covers while I slept. A sharp smoky smell filled my nose and seared down into my lungs.

I jerked upright, searching for the source of the scent, half-expecting to find my room on fire. But it wasn't flames that shifted along the walls. Before my eyes, the shadows of the furniture thickened against the fainter darkness.

They crawled along the walls and lunged toward the bed, maws forming in their wavering forms. One that looked like a snake sank its fangs into my foot through the sheet with a bolt of pain. I bit my lip trying to swallow a yelp as I scrambled back on the mattress, my pulse thudding so loud it seemed to echo through my head.

This wasn't real. It couldn't be real. I closed my eyes, shook my head, and looked again. The shadowy creatures loomed larger around me. And then the bed began to move.

It shuddered under me and hitched upward as if flying off the floor. The shadows clotted. The front of the wardrobe on the far wall sagged as if melting; the curtain billowed into the shape of a demonic face like the one that guy had conjured weeks ago in class.

Not real. Not real. I hugged my knees and buried my face against them, my breath coming ragged. But it wasn't enough not to look. The shadows nipped at my skin with icy mouths, alternately scraping me raw and pricking me with pain. An eerie groan filled the room, and then a hissing sound rose up, like bubbling acid eating away at something nearby. Through all that, the bed continued to sway beneath me.

I yanked my mental shields around my mind as tightly as I could, but that changed nothing. However much this was coming from inside my head, it was a seed already planted. And triggered. *Wake up*. It must have been Malcolm who'd done this. He'd sent his voice to me from wherever he was. How could I shut him out if he could hit me anytime he wanted without any warning?

I tried to dig inside my head for that malicious influence and rip it out, but my thoughts kept scattering with the horrible sensations around me. The nips and the noise and the sickening rocking carrying on and on. I clutched my knees tighter. A sound like a choked breath reached my ears, and every muscle in my body stiffened.

It was the gurgle of Mom's throat being severed. I'd heard it enough times in my dreams and in the desensitization sessions since to recognize it even without seeing anything. The thump of her body lolling, the fleshy tearing of the magic that had carved into Dad's chest…

I clapped my hands over my ears, but they couldn't shut out the sounds. I had the feeling if I let myself look, I'd see their bodies slumped right here in the room with me. A bloody metallic smell laced the air in place of the previous smoke.

Tears welled up behind my closed eyelids. I clenched my teeth against a scream.

Was it really worth it, keeping up this battle, having to endure this horror just on principle? Malcolm was never going to back down as long as I kept resisting. All I'd have to do was lie and pretend I'd seen the light, make a little show of surrender, and he'd end his campaign of torment. Maybe everyone who'd hassled me would leave me alone if he took me into his good graces, Victory and her crew included.

He *would* take me in. He'd meant what he'd said in the kennel the other day, just like Declan had meant what he'd said about the scions being their own sort of family. If I bent to Malcolm's will, they'd welcome me into their circle. It would be so fucking *easy*.

The thought filled my head for a moment with a twinge of temptation, and then a deeper nausea swelled to overwhelm it.

No. *No*. I was not going to give in to a sadistic asshole who believed provoking someone's worst nightmares out of them was a reasonable approach to getting his way. I was not going to let every other student at that school become even more convinced that torture was the path to victory. Fuck *no*.

The tears trickled down my cheeks. The chaos around me raged on for longer than I could keep track of. I pulled back as deep into my mind as I could go, focusing on my brightest memories: my first trip to the Museum of Contemporary Art in L.A. with my parents on my thirteenth birthday. Splashing through the waves with them at the local beach as a kid. The first moment I'd really felt and controlled my magic, known how much power I could wield. The way Declan had looked at me two days ago just before he'd kissed me.

Eventually I became aware of a small furry body against my hip and the quiet and stillness all around me.

Are you back? Deborah asked tentatively. *Are you okay, sweetheart?*

I swallowed thickly and swiped at my damp cheeks. "Yeah," I whispered. "I'm okay enough now that it's over."

My dormmates were moving around in the common room getting ready for the day. I stood up on shaky legs and peeked out just long enough to confirm that Malcolm wasn't hanging out there among them. Victory and her friends were sitting on one of the sofas, only the backs of their heads visible over the top, paying no attention to my room at all.

I ran all through the building when I saw the state you were in, Deborah said, her voice reaching me more faintly because she wasn't touching me. *I didn't see anyone actively casting, just like before.*

Of course not. That would be too easy. I went to my window and yanked the curtain aside.

When I pushed it open, I could lean out into the warming air and get a good look at the grounds below. A few students were already heading to the Stormhurst building, and a couple were standing by the lake, but none of the scions were among them. The area near my side of Ashgrave Hall was vacant.

Frowning, I turned my attention to the building itself. Malcolm was reaching me *somehow*. He lived in the dorms here too—Deborah had determined on an earlier foray that his room was the one at the opposite end of the building on the same floor as mine. My gaze traveled over that side of the building.

The stone wall looked the same as it always had. When I'd studied it before, nothing had stuck out as concerning, but now my eyes halted on a small knob-like protrusion near the window closest to mine, belonging to one of the girls in my dorm.

The object was hard to make out from some twenty feet away—I must have seen it before and assumed it was just a normal part of the design. I would have again now if something about the shape of it hadn't triggered a prickle of recognition.

The curve of it, the impression of a hollow, gave the same impression as at least one of the pieces I'd had to work with in the puzzle garden the other day.

From watching the other girls come and go, I was pretty sure that room belonged to Cressida. It wasn't hard to imagine Malcolm managing to get in there for long enough to fix something to the wall outside. If he'd told her he was going to screw me over, she'd probably have given him an all-access pass.

She wasn't going to give *me* a pass to march into her room and get a closer look. I studied the ridges of limestone that formed the rest of the building. "Deborah?" I murmured.

My familiar darted across the floor to me, and I scooped her up to hold her by the window ledge where she could see outside. "Over there by the next window, there's something sticking out of the stone that I think might have magic in it—or be built for conducting magic somehow. Do you think you could handle the climb over there to check it out?"

Deborah considered. *With that groove there, it shouldn't be too much trouble. I'll go slowly.*

She hopped off my hand onto the sill and picked her way onto the thickest ridge of stone that ran along the side of the building. I watched, braced and starkly aware of the five story drop below, as she scurried along it toward the protrusion.

It only took her a minute to reach it. She climbed a little higher to sniff the shape, and a little shiver passed through her body. She darted back to me twice as fast as she'd gone.

It's had magic in it recently, she said as she scrambled inside. *It's built to store and amplify spells, as far as I can tell from the shape of it. We use pieces like that in our joymancy work too.*

Store and amplify spells. Amplify them enough that they could reach me in my bedroom without any more targeting than that? My queasiness returned, but a punch of resolve came with it.

"No one's going to be using that piece anymore," I said. "Come here?"

She let me scoop her into my hand, and I kept her tucked out of sight against my pajama shirt as I stepped into the common room. I didn't look at the other girls, didn't show any sign at all that I was about to infringe on anyone's privacy, just marched right over to Cressida's door as if I had every right to head straight in.

She hadn't bothered with a locking spell while she was right there in the common room. A small smile caught my lips as the doorknob turned in my grasp. "Hey!" a startled voice called out behind me, but I was already striding inside.

I dashed to her already-open window through a mist of lily-and-musk perfume and leaned out. The sculpted stone fixture was just within arm's reach. I grabbed it, yanked, twisted, and yanked again with a mutter of magical encouragement. It popped off the wall so abruptly I nearly tumbled right out the window.

I caught myself and yanked myself back into the room, shoving the fixture into the pajama pants pocket I'd never realized I'd be this relieved to have. Just in time, because a second later, Cressida burst into her bedroom.

"Get the fuck out of my room," she said in a taut voice. "What are you doing?"

"I'm so sorry," I said with an apologetic shrug as I headed over to the door, and held up my hand to reveal Deborah. "My familiar went roaming around farther than she should have. I was just getting her out of here before she disturbed you."

"Like I'd be scared of a stupid mouse," she sneered, but a little wariness had come into her eyes—in memory of the last time she'd been part of a plot involving my familiar, no doubt. "*I* didn't put her in here."

"Oh, I know! I think she just got turned around and lost her way. It's all good now. I'll make sure it doesn't happen again."

"You do that," Cressida said to my back as I crossed the common area to my bedroom, but she sounded more apprehensive than angry now.

If I was lucky, she didn't have anything to do with Malcolm's scheme other than letting him into her room. There was a decent chance she didn't know what he'd placed just outside her window or what spell-casting he'd done, considering he'd been secretive about it even with Jude. But I wasn't going to count on luck. As soon as my door had closed behind me, I set down Deborah and pulled out the stone fixture to examine it.

It did have similarities to pieces in the maze. I ran my thumb over the smooth surface, and a jolt of recognition shot through my head.

I'd had the feeling of holding this object in my hands before—no, of holding it in *Malcolm's* hands when I'd dipped inside his head that day in Persuasion class. This was one of the impressions I'd glimpsed. I just hadn't had any way of understanding it until now.

Maybe I couldn't prove it, but he'd definitely been the one who'd put this thing in place.

My jaw clenched as I considered how a spell would flow through the piece. Deborah had said it'd had magic in it *recently*, but I wasn't sure how accurate her magical senses were inside that mouse body.

Were there more spells waiting to mess with me inside the thing right now?

If there were, how the hell did I get them out? In the puzzle maze, I'd needed to apply my own magic to the pieces' natural functions. This was a different problem altogether.

I hesitated for a moment before getting up. I had one person nearby who might be able to answer that.

This time, the two girls still in the common room looked my way the second I came out. I suspected Victory and Sinclair had joined Cressida in her room to check whether I'd done more in there than I'd claimed. Well, then they couldn't interfere with what I was doing now. I rapped my hand against Imogen's door.

She opened it with hair damp and mussed from a recent toweling. Her stance tensed. "Rory? I—"

"I need to talk to you," I said firmly. "Now. You owe me." I didn't care how uncertain she was about continuing our friendship—I wasn't looking for friendship. I was looking for a Physicality specialist.

Guilt flashed across her face, and she stepped back to let me in. Even if my weirdness over the last several weeks had made her cautious, she recognized she had a lot to make up for. Good.

"Congrats on the league win," she said as she closed the door.

My mind was so far elsewhere that it took me a second to process her words. They still didn't quite click. "What?"

"Insight won. It was announced last night. Didn't you hear?" Her mouth twisted wryly. "I'll be helping serve all of you people a big fancy dinner tomorrow."

Last night I'd been reeling from my encounter with my grandparents and the damage they might do to Declan. I wasn't surprised I missed the news. I couldn't summon much enthusiasm over the win. "I guess I was too caught up in studying. That's great. But that's not—" I held out the stone fixture. "Do you know what this is?"

Imogen took it from me and turned it over in her hands. "It's a conducting piece with a holding pocket." She glanced at me. "Do *you* know what that means?"

I nodded. "I've got the gist. Can you tell if it's 'holding' anything right now?"

She peered at it more intently, mouthing a few words under her breath. After a minute, she lowered the piece with a long exhale. The effort had left her face drawn. "There's a little something in there. Not much. I can't tell what the function is."

"You know how to stop this thing from working, though, don't you? That's got to be a Physicality thing—it's all about the physical structure."

"It is," Imogen agreed. "That's how pieces like this work. I could tell you approximately how to *make* something like this. But the way they're constructed, the magical resonance contained in the design—these pieces resist any attempts to reshape or unshape them like crazy. *Maybe* one of the professors would be able to break the symmetry, but I'm not even sure about that. I definitely can't."

In that case, I didn't have much hope. I sucked my lower lip under my teeth in contemplation. "So there's nothing anyone can do to break one of these?"

"I didn't say that, although the other way is still pretty tricky." Imogen looked at the piece, her wry smile returning. "You can't brute force this thing into changing, so you've got to come at it from a different angle that it's not built for. With Insight aimed right, you could probably get a gist of any spells inside it. And I've heard of people 'persuading' the resonance to shift to throw the structure's natural capacity off. If you're strong enough. Those aren't my areas—I wouldn't have a chance. You, though…" She handed it back to me with a curious expression.

I had all four strengths. A quiver that was almost giddy ran through me. I focused my gaze on the holding side of the conducting piece and whispered my Insight casting word, too quiet for Imogen to hear.

It didn't feel like falling into someone's head. Only a piece of me seemed to tumble forward, with just a flicker of sensation meeting me in response from deep inside—a sensation that delved and burrowed with a prickling of hooked claws. I didn't like that at all. It definitely wasn't anything I wanted aimed at me, whatever exactly the spell was.

Could I persuade it out? Or persuade the form of the piece to alter so it couldn't hold the spell or conduct it anymore? I knit my brow as I inspected the structure again. The connection between the holding area and the amplifying part—that seemed like the key. If I could shift it even a little…

I pulled more magic onto my tongue and trained my attention on that area. "*Bend*," I ordered it, tasting the shape of the channel with the word.

I got no sense of it budging. Maybe I was focusing too much on the physical aspect still. Imogen had said to persuade the "resonance" of the thing. The way the shape mimicked the flow of cast magic.

"*Come out*," I tried again, thinking instead of that flow, the way the energy would bend with the structure. Nothing. I grimaced, my voice rising just a bit. "*Let* go."

A twitch passed from the stone into my hand. My heart lifted. I peered into the channel and spotted a tiny crack that had opened up in the middle of it.

Imogen let out a breathless laugh. "You did it. It won't work anymore like that—not unless someone else persuades it whole again, I guess."

Or Malcolm stuck another conducting piece in place. But the hitch of Imogen's breath had jerked my mind in a totally different direction with a rush of hope.

"Imogen," I said, "if I could persuade something like this to stop working… That strategy could apply to any physical form, right?"

"Any physical form created to conduct magic, anyway," she said. "The more intricate and condensed the form is, the harder it'd be to shift it, though. Why?"

I turned toward the door, my heart thumping faster. "I'll tell you later. Thanks for your help."

I had a life to save.

CHAPTER TWENTY-EIGHT

Connar

The last place I expected to see Jude going into was the junior cafeteria. I stopped in my tracks on my way through Killbrook Hall after my monthly check-in with my mentor, blinking a few times before I convinced myself that it really had been his lanky form slipping through the doorway few seniors ventured through under regular circumstances. There wasn't anyone else on campus with that dark red hair. It'd have been pretty hard for me to confuse someone else for him.

What was he up to? A tug of uneasy curiosity drew me to the doorway.

It was early afternoon, a little late for lunch. Only a few clusters of the younger students still sat around the wooden tables that filled the room. Tomorrow evening, those tables would be draped with fancy fabric and the sconces on the burgundy walls would be lit for the league competition banquet. Right now, the place looked unimpressive in the muted daylight that glowed through the windows. The meaty smell of whatever the staff had served for lunch hung in the air.

Jude had seated himself at the end of a table right next to one of the bunches of students. Not just any students either, I noted after a moment. Gold leaf pins glinted on all their shirt collars. They were Naries. What did he want with them?

Not much, as far as I could tell from simply observing. He pulled out a book and turned the pages absently, occasionally glancing up in the general direction of the Naries' table next to him. They chattered on without giving him much mind. Out of all the students here at Blood U, they had the least idea why he was anyone to be wary of.

After a few minutes just standing there in the doorway watching, I started to feel conspicuous. The puzzle in front of me still niggled at me, though. I pushed myself on into the room.

Jude's gaze shot to me with a startled twitch of his expression when I sat down across from him. He frowned. "What the hell are you doing here?" he said quietly, but there was no real venom in his voice, only mild irritation.

"Finding out what the hell *you're* doing here," I said. "What's going on? What's important about them?"

His shoulders came up as he slid farther down the bench so we were less likely to be overheard by the Naries. "Nothing. I just wondered."

I followed him, still confused. "Wondered *what*?"

Jude turned his frown toward his book rather than me. "What they even have to talk about. What *they* think is important. How someone could find their company appealing. I don't know."

Someone, huh? That last bit clued me in. "This is about—"

His gaze jerked back up. "Don't. We aren't talking about that." Then he looked toward the table of Naries, his brow knitting as if he found them as puzzling as I found his sudden interest in them.

What had Rory said to him when they'd had their fight anyway? He obviously wasn't going to tell me, but it was also obviously eating at him.

That question had niggled at me all the way down to my gut from the moment I'd picked him up on the side of the road, maybe because I had the most direct experience with having failed her. But he'd probably called me because he'd known I was less likely to keep prodding him about it than Malcolm or Declan. I wasn't going to hassle him when he was so clearly unsettled.

I wasn't sure I was any less conspicuous sitting here, and Jude hardly wanted my help with anything. "Well, good luck with it," I said, getting up. Malcolm had asked me to meet him in the lounge in a few minutes anyway.

Our private room below the library had always offered a bit of an escape—not as much as my cliff spot, but a place where I didn't have to be quite as aware of the fears and suspicions I provoked in everyone on campus. Normally, relief would have washed over me as I descended the stairs. Today, the tension in my gut clenched tighter.

I couldn't remember us ever arguing the way Malcolm and Jude had before. Declan had barely come down at all in the last few weeks, and I wasn't sure I could blame him. A deeper apprehension coursed through my body as I sat myself down to wait for Malcolm, to find out what he was planning now.

He came down a few minutes later with an energy about him that was eager but brittle. I didn't need any Insight spell to tell me something had frustrated him and he didn't intend to take it lying down.

"Good," he said, seeing me. "I've got it all figured out. We don't need anyone else—the two of us can build off each other's spells just fine."

I shifted forward on the couch, ignoring the jab of tension that comment gave me. "What have you figured out?"

He walked from one end of the room to the other, his eyes intent but distant as if picturing something a long ways away. "We're going to knock her down hard with the whole school as an audience. The league banquet is the perfect opportunity. The girls in her dorm already think she's going bonkers. Victory and the others have been spreading that gossip, and probably some of the others too. Everyone's primed."

The jab turned into a dull ache that filled my entire abdomen. "Primed for us to do what?"

"To show just how out-of-control the star pupil has become in her insistence on going it alone. You can kick things off. Mess with her food or her drink, make her seat shift under her, whatever else you can think of that'll unnerve her but not be too noticeable to anyone else. While she's thrown off by that, I'll slide in there and take care of the rest. If she still isn't ready to bow to us, then I'll just make her do it."

The vehemence in his voice had taken on an almost frantic edge. My body tensed. Malcolm didn't let himself get overly caught up in anything—not usually. He observed and he made his moves with cool confidence. I didn't see that cool right now, and I wasn't so sure about the confidence either.

"Do you really think this is the best approach?" I ventured. "The banquet is sort of sacred. All the professors will be there too."

"That just makes it better. Let them watch too. We'll be ruling over all of them when the old guard retires—they should know what happens to anyone who challenges us." He spun on me. "Come on, Connar. I need you with me on this. We're so close."

If we were, I didn't think he'd have that wildness in his expression. I hesitated, and all the doubts that had been churning inside me since the moment I'd turned on Rory collided with a lurch of my pulse.

I trusted Malcolm. I'd have been willing to lay down my life for him if need be. But I didn't believe he was right about this, about her. And even though I'd called him my best friend and given him that trust, I was fucking *terrified* to tell him that.

That wasn't right, was it? We were all scions, no matter how we'd come into that title. My opinion should at least matter enough for him to care without brushing off everything I said. He expected me to follow his lead and do whatever he asked simply because he said so as part of the loyalty between us, even though I'd never have pushed him the same way.

Rory had never pushed me. Even knowing how close I was with Malcolm, even when she'd been willing to open up to me, she'd never once asked me to so much as speak up on her behalf, let alone come right over to her side of the fight. When we'd talked the other day, despite all the anger I'd seen in her, she hadn't thrown my past in my face; she hadn't demanded anything other than that I leave her alone.

She'd only ever wanted me to be myself, to follow what mattered to me, whatever that happened to be. Wasn't *that* some kind of loyalty, one I could hardly say I'd earned? My hand closed around the memory of the dragon she'd made for me where it had once pressed against my palm.

I hope you don't forget that you're you *too*, she'd said when she'd given it to me. *At least some of the time, that's got to come first.*

If it didn't come first now, then it probably never would.

"Connar," Malcolm started again in his cajoling tone.

I stood up before he could go on. My entire chest had constricted into one big knot, but I propelled out the word. "No."

Malcolm blinked at me, momentarily speechless. "Excuse me?"

I crossed my arms. "No, I'm not going to mess with Rory during the banquet. I think we've done enough. She's still standing because she's strong enough to deserve to. *I'm* done with this."

His eyes flashed. "What the fuck is wrong with you? We've got her; we just have to—"

"*No.*" My voice came out louder than I'd expected, loud enough to cut him off completely. A strange exhilaration washed over me despite the ache inside.

I could make this choice. I wasn't even betraying him, no matter how he was going to see it. I was making this stand because it was better for *all* of us. "And if you try to hassle her tomorrow night, I'll step in. You want her in the circle? Find another way."

For a few seconds, we just stared at each other. Malcolm's jaw worked. "I have *always* had your back—"

"And I've always had yours. That's why I'm saying no, just this once. You're taking this whole thing too far. This isn't you."

"Don't you *dare* tell me who I am or what I'm capable of," he snapped. "You—She—" He shook his head, his entire posture rigid. "Fine. That's how you want things to be? Or maybe that's how *she* wants things to be. You think she's so above all this? When you get your head on straight, you'll see how she's breaking us apart. Until then, get the fuck out of here."

I wouldn't have wanted to stay anyway. As I headed up the stairs, the clenching inside me started to release—and a new weight settled over me.

As far as I could see right now, it wasn't Rory breaking up the pentacle of scions. Malcolm was doing that all by himself.

CHAPTER TWENTY-NINE

Rory

I kept a careful distance from the cafeteria where the banquet would be held as I hurried to the staff wing of Killbrook Hall. Clinks and thumps carried through the doorway as the members of the other leagues set up the décor. The smells of roast pork and caramelized onions and all sorts of other deliciousness drifted from the kitchen. My mouth might have watered if it wasn't parched dry in anticipation of the spell I was about to attempt.

I'd waited until not long before the feast was supposed to begin so I could be sure any staff not teaching classes right now would be downstairs supervising the preparations. The hall of offices was empty and silent. I set my feet softly on the carpet on my way to Professor Banefield's door just in case someone had lingered after all.

The door opened with my whispered spell, even easier now with practice. I slipped through his office and ventured into his apartment on the other side.

The smells of sickness had spread from his bedroom, even though I had to assume the health center staff who'd been coming to look after him must have been doing their best to keep things clean. Stale sweat, dried vomit, and something like rotting fruit mixed together in a sour cocktail that faintly laced the air. It got stronger as I reached Banefield's bedroom, enough that my stomach turned.

In the thin late afternoon light drifting through the window, his broad body looked even more diminished than it had when I'd been here only a week ago. The sheet had fallen off him and his undershirt had ridden up, showing the lines of ribs protruding from his side, shallower and then deeper with his erratic breathing. His hair no longer stood up in its usual tufts but clung damply to his scalp.

This was my fault. Whoever had attacked him had done it to hurt me, to stop him from helping me. So I'd better be able to make it right.

I sat down carefully on the edge of the bed by his sprawled legs. I'd spent all of my time between classes and meals for the last two days reading any information I could find in the library about using persuasion to influence physical objects. There wasn't a lot of it, and most of it related to the sculpted pieces like the one I'd found on the wall outside our dorm, expanding on what Imogen had told me. I knew a little more than I had yesterday morning, at least.

Had the health center doctors even considered this approach? Had they realized the mole was the likely source of my mentor's illness in the first place? It didn't seem right that I might have figured out a solution where they hadn't… but then, it was possible they hadn't looked all that hard once they'd realized it was almost certainly a magical attack.

It was possible they'd realized that whoever could conduct an attack like this could strike them down as well, and decided it was better to let Banefield's illness run its course.

I might face consequences from our enemies if I cured him, but at least I could face them with his help. If I could convince the mole to give up its magical resonance, he'd be able to tell me who our enemies were, maybe even how to protect ourselves from another attack. Or how to fight back.

As I tugged up his pajama pant leg like I had before, Banefield stirred. I froze, distinctly aware of how inappropriate it was for me to be sitting on a professor's bed while he slept, partly undressing him.

Banefield's head turned. His eyelids stuttered and opened just a crack. His voice was a weak croak. "Rory?"

"I'm going to try to make you better," I said quickly. "I know someone's placed a spell on you. I think I might be able to remove it. Will you let me try?"

He peered at me a moment longer before his gaze wandered off as if he hadn't heard me. His eyelids closed completely. A hacking cough sputtered out of him, and then he lay still.

Well, he hadn't made any attempt to stop me. I guessed that was as close to permission as I was going to get.

No sound but his breathing emitted from his chest as I uncovered his knee. Peering at the mole more closely than before, my pulse skipped a beat. I hadn't studied it that intently before, assuming it was meant to look like any mole. It… almost appeared to have a magically attuned shape to it, like a tiny version of one of those conducting pieces, only made out of flesh instead of metal or stone. The tiny dimple here, the barely visible ridge there.

Of course. That made perfect sense, didn't it? How else could the person who'd cast the spell have been sure the mole would hold its energy until it needed to activate? They'd built a conducting structure right on his body. Maybe it amplified the effects too, or some other awful function I hadn't encountered yet.

Imogen's words came back to me. *The more intricate and condensed the form is, the harder it'd be to shift it.* I'd better get started.

"I was going to have a daughter," Banefield mumbled, so low I wasn't sure I'd heard him right. His eyes stayed closed.

"What?" I said quietly, not wanting to disturb him if he was simply talking in his sleep.

"She was pregnant. Amara was. Twenty-two weeks, with our little girl. And they—they—" Another cough rattled out of him.

I rested my hand on his calf as if that might comfort him, my heart wrenching. "It's okay. You don't have to talk about it."

He rambled on in the same mumbled, wavering voice. "They didn't call. They didn't do anything they should have. Stupid bloody feebs." His chest hitched. "They—she— But you. You would have forgiven them."

"I don't know. I don't know anything about it, really." I sure as hell wasn't going to blame him for being mad about his wife and their unborn child dying.

"You would," he said, with more firmness than before. "You would. Because you let yourself see." He trailed off for a long enough moment that I thought he was done. Then he added, "She would have been like you, I want to think. If my daughter had come. That's what — If I hadn't— She would have seen too."

For a second, I couldn't breathe, my throat was so constricted. I didn't totally understand what he was saying, but the gist was clear enough. "I'm sure she'd have tried to save you," I said. "So that's what I'm going to do too. Just rest for now, and I'll do my best."

I touched the mole lightly, fighting a cringe, letting my fingertip absorb the shape of it. A faint pulse of energy tickled my skin. I focused on the feel of it and the image of it in my mind, the toxic spell contained in a sort of chamber I could picture inside it, and rolled magic off my tongue with the command that had worked on Malcolm's stone. "*Let go.*"

I didn't sense any change from the form beneath my finger. Banefield's head twitched. "No. If you— They'll— I can't stop them."

"Maybe I can," I said in the most soothing voice I could summon. "It's okay." Please let it be okay.

It wasn't the structure but the energy its shape resonated with that I had to focus on. I couldn't forget that, even as the prickling pulse sent a queasy shiver through me. The tiny strands of a spell wound through the nub of constructed flesh—I could speak to them too.

"*Let go,*" I murmured again. The energy didn't so much as tremble. Fuck. Okay, on to the untested strategies.

Think about the purpose of the spell and its container. What was the right direction to untangle it from its target? Was the sickening spell leaching my mentor's health away from him or leaking poison into him?

No matter what I did, he couldn't get much worse off. I squared my shoulders and aimed my attention at the mole again. "*Release.*" Nothing. "*Pull back.*" Still nothing. "*Snap.*"

Sweat was beading on the back of my neck now. I was throwing all my effort into each casting, and they seemed to just bounce off the thing.

"No," Banefield muttered again into his pillow.

Could I take the spell into me? "*Come here*," I said to the fizz of energy. No luck.

Frustration gripped me. What if I just wasn't powerful enough? I only had three months of training. No matter how many strengths I had, they couldn't counterbalance all the time I'd missed when I should have been honing these skills.

Damn it. I was not going to let him die. I just was *not*.

The anger that came with that thought jolted through the magic coiled behind my collarbone. Without letting myself second-guess the impulse, I hurled it into my next command. "*Get out!*"

The pulse of energy jumped against my skin with a pinching pressure that faded in an instant. Beneath my fingertip, the mole deflated. As I jerked my hand back, it settled into a patch more like dark freckle. Banefield dragged in a heave of a breath.

My jaw went slack. I'd done it. I'd really managed to pull it off. Would he simply get better now on his own, or—

Banefield lunged upright so suddenly I startled in surprise, falling off the edge of the bed. His eyes popped open, ruddy with blood vessels crisscrossing the whites, and his hands snapped around the spot where I'd been sitting an instant before. A strained growl broke from his lips.

What the hell?

I scrambled backward and onto my feet. My mentor lurched out of the bed at the same time. Another angry, wordless sound escaped him. "Go!" he spat out, and threw himself at me.

I dashed out of the bedroom, my thoughts scattering in my bewilderment. Banefield charged after me with more speed than I'd have thought his wasted body could achieve. His hand shot out and clamped around my wrist. He wrenched me around with a heave so vicious that pain lanced through my shoulder cap.

"No!" he shouted, but I didn't think he was talking to me. He propelled himself toward the kitchen, dragging me with him. His fingers dug in deeper, and his other arm whipped toward me. I ducked just a second before his fist would have clocked me in the head.

"*Stop*," I said, tossing a persuasive casting into my words instinctively. "*Let go of me.*"

The magic bounced off the solid surface of his mental shields.

"I can't," he rasped, and flung himself at the kitchen island. "A failsafe— They wanted to be sure— It's too deep in me. There's no way."

"If there's something *I* can do to stop this, tell me," I said, with a yelp as he twisted my wrist.

He was panting now. His free hand jerked toward me again, and he managed to slam it into the side of the island instead, hard enough that I thought I heard the crack of bone. Even in his agonizing grasp, I winced for him.

All at once, he hauled me past him, sending me hurtling to the end of the kitchen. My ribs smacked into the edge of the counter, but Banefield's grip snapped. He plunged his hand into the drawer he'd just opened.

"I'm supposed to crush the magic out of you," he said raggedly. "It won't let go of me until I do. They wanted you helpless. They want— they wanted to make sure you never trust anyone who'd help you again. Don't let it work. Don't let it *work*. There'll be people who'll mean it. There'll be people on your side."

"*Who* did this?" I spun around and ran for the living room, but Banefield was faster. His punch rammed into my gut, knocking the air out of me.

"Fuck," he sputtered as I doubled over with a gasp. "The older barons, the other reapers with them. The cancer in the fearmancers." He fumbled across the island and snatched up a butcher's knife from the block there. As he swung it toward me, I wrenched away from him with a burst of panic.

His arm kept swinging, all the way back to his own body. He plunged the knife straight into his chest.

"Professor!" I cried.

He slumped, blood spilling from around the blade into his

undershirt and streaking over his skin. I dropped down beside him. His breath came with a wet rasp.

"I'm sorry," I said, choking on the words. "I don't know what to do."

"Only way to stop them," he mumbled, his head rolling back to stare at the ceiling. Blood flecked his lips. "Only way. You need it. Stop the cancer. Maybe you can cure that too. If you go—"

The last word cut off with a seize of his body. His hand snatched after mine. He caught it as I yanked myself backward, clutching tight… and then going limp with the rest of his body as the light faded from his eyes.

"Professor Banefield?" My voice came out so hoarse I'm not sure he'd have recognized his name even if he'd been conscious to hear it.

He gazed blankly upward. Blood seeped into a puddle on the floor beneath him. I squeezed his hand as if that could jolt him back to life, and a solid shape pressed against my palm.

My fingers curled around it instinctively. I shoved myself to my feet and sprinted to the door. Maybe there was still a chance—maybe if a doctor got to him quickly enough—

But even as I burst into the hall with a cry of "Help!" bursting from my throat, an ache of loss was already spreading through me from head to toe.

I'd saved him, and then he'd saved me from himself. From the barons… From the "reapers"?

How many enemies did I have in this world—and just how much blood were they willing to spill to get to me?

I couldn't think through the blaring of grief and horror in my head. All I could do was shout, "Help!" again as I raced down the hall.

CHAPTER THIRTY

Rory

Not long after I'd dropped into the armchair in Ms. Grimsworth's office, I'd started shaking. When she came back into the room after doing whatever she'd needed to do to handle Professor Banefield's death, I hadn't stopped. My hands stayed clenched tight on my lap as I looked up at her.

The tensing of her expression told enough of the story before she even opened her mouth. "I'm afraid there was nothing any of us could do for him."

I swallowed the lump that had crawled up my throat and hugged myself. Tears seared in the back of my eyes, but somehow they hadn't spilled out yet. My head was whirling.

Ms. Grimsworth's gaze dropped to my right arm. To the purpling bruises in the shape of Banefield's fingers where my mentor's hand had clamped around my wrist. The twinge at my side when I adjusted my position told me my ribs were probably bruised too, from when he'd thrown me against the counter.

He'd been trying to get me away from him right then, not trying to hurt me. I'd replayed the episode a hundred times in my head, and that was the conclusion I'd come to. There'd been another spell—a "failsafe," he'd said—that had activated when I'd destroyed the mole that held the one making him sick. Some kind of persuasion magic, I had to guess.

It had forced him to attack me against his will, but he'd fought against the spell as well as he could. I was pretty sure when he'd told me "no" while I was working at curing him, he'd been trying to warn me, knowing what would come. He'd done everything he could not to fulfill its purpose: to crush the magic out of me, however exactly that worked.

Should I have left him alone, not tried to cure him? It was hard to believe that. In another week or two, he'd have wasted away completely. The health center staff hadn't done anything useful for him. Either way, he'd have been dead.

This way was just more horrifying.

Ms. Grimsworth propped her thin frame against the edge of her desk rather than sitting behind it. "I can only imagine how distressing the experience you just had was, Miss Bloodstone. Can you tell me again, as thoroughly as possible, exactly what happened?"

I sucked in a breath. When I'd banged on her door and found her, mercifully, still inside, I'd babbled a fractured account of Banefield's death, and she'd ushered me in here before rushing off. Now I had to decide what it was safe to tell her.

She looked shaken by what she'd seen, but how much could I trust that impression? She wasn't a baron, but she could have been under their sway. She could be associated with whoever or whatever the "reapers" Banefield had mentioned were.

He'd given his life to save me. I had to make sure I didn't stupidly throw my own away before his body had even stopped bleeding.

"I've been reading up on healing spells in the library," I said, which was a version of the truth. "Maybe it sounds silly, but I wanted to see if I could do anything for Professor Banefield. He's looked out for me since I first got here… I used magic to get into his quarters, and I tried a couple of the spells, and nothing seemed to happen. Then all of a sudden he attacked me."

I rubbed my wrist. "I have no idea what was going on. He seemed delusional. He almost stabbed me with that knife, but when I dodged, he stabbed himself instead."

The headmistress's lips pursed. "I would say that sounds ridiculous, but our analysis confirms that he delivered the blow himself. Did he say anything to you during this attack? Any indication as to what provoked it?"

I shook my head. Better no one knew how much he'd managed to warn me. Better my enemies thought I was still totally ignorant. "He was mumbling and muttering, but I could hardly make out any of the words. I have no idea whether he understood who I was, even. He said something about a daughter… That's the only part I remember catching. It all happened so fast, and I was so shocked…"

"Of course," Ms. Grimsworth said, in a tone that I suspected was meant to be reassuring but that only came out as dour. "Of course you were. I hope you can see now why we restrict visitors in cases like this where we're uncertain of the illness—we can't predict how the patient will behave."

I hung my head. She sighed. "I expect that isn't a rule you'll ignore again. And your desire to contribute to Professor Banefield's healing was admirable if highly misguided. Clearly his illness was even more serious than we thought, affecting his mind as well as his body. Do you recall the specific spells you attempted?"

I tossed out a couple of the common ones I'd seen in my research, which seemed to satisfy her enough. "I can't imagine it was anything specific about you that provoked the attack," she said. "If you hadn't come, most likely it would have been the nurse who checked in on him in the morning. Don't make this any harder on yourself by feeling responsible."

"I know," I said quietly. I wasn't responsible for how the spell had made him act. I was only responsible for making him a target in the first place.

Ms. Grimsworth straightened up, brushing her hands together. "The health center may have more questions for you in the morning, but for now I think you've had enough. Let me see your arm."

She made a quick motion toward my bruised wrist. I held it

toward her awkwardly, and she murmured a word under her breath with a swiping motion of her fingers.

Before my eyes, the bruise shimmered away, leaving only unblemished skin. I touched it instinctively and winced at the soreness that remained.

"It's still bruised," Ms. Grimsworth said. "The healing arts aren't my area of expertise. I cast an illusion over it so no one should notice anything's amiss tonight."

"Tonight?" I repeated.

"At the banquet. You'd better go on down there now."

Just the word "banquet" made my stomach lurch in refusal. "*What?*" I said, wondering if I'd misheard.

The headmistress nodded, gesturing me to my feet. "The food will be served in just a few minutes. Not having their scion there will dull the celebration for the Insight league. You'll be surrounded by friends and festivities rather than left alone with your thoughts. Let the festivities distract you, take comfort in the company, and if it begins to wear on you, then make your excuses and leave. We can't let this tragedy ripple even farther through the school."

All I wanted to do was crawl into bed. My body balked. "I—"

"I can escort you down to the dining room if that would make it easier."

No, having Ms. Grimsworth march me down there would be even worse. I could manage the walk. I could stay five minutes, anyway, if that was my duty as scion tonight.

Put on a brave face. If my enemies were watching, let them think I hadn't been that fazed. When I thought of it that way, the idea sat a little more easily.

"That's all right," I said, forcing myself to stand. "I can manage."

My shaking had subsided as we'd talked, but the shock still clung to me like a layer of gauze that hazed my mind. The floor felt far away beneath my feet. Outside Ms. Grimsworth's office, the silence in the hall blared.

I tightened my jaw and kept walking, one foot at a time, out to the staircase and down and along the shorter hall to the front wing.

I'd just reached that space when a brawny figure moved into view at the far end. The light from the flames in the sconces wavered across Connar's chiseled face.

My legs locked. I couldn't deal with him, not now, not on top of everything else this awful evening had thrown at me.

He didn't come too close, just caught my gaze and held out his hand. A metal figurine gleamed in his grasp—a dragon, almost identical to the one I'd made for him. I stared at it.

"You said I had to make it myself," Connar said. "I'm going to be that guy."

He extended his arm a little farther. When I looked at him blankly, he brought his hand back to his side and slid the dragon into his pocket. It occurred to me only then that he'd been offering it to me as a sort of gift. Like I'd offered the one I'd made to him.

"It's just the beginning," he added with a pained smile. "I know it's hardly enough on its own."

He turned and left me even more shell-shocked than I'd been a minute ago, which I wouldn't have thought was possible. What had he expected me to say?

Warm lights and music trickled from the doorway beyond the hall. I stepped inside warily, and a girl from the Insight league grabbed my elbow, so abruptly I had to restrain a flinch. She beamed at me. "About time you made it. Come on—you've got the best seat in the house."

The tables throughout the room had been laid out with gleaming gold-embroidered tablecloths. Sconces glowed all around me. The crystal chandeliers overhead swayed and tinkled with the music.

One table at the front of the room was set perpendicular to the others. A few of the senior Insight league members were already sitting there, including the guy who'd led the meeting last month, and… Declan. The empty chair in the middle next to him was obviously meant for me.

I let the girl guide me over and sank into the chair, tucking my hands under the table. Declan gave me a quick glance and a quicker nod in greeting, the distant politeness of two people who'd never really talked, let alone fucked.

Chatter carried from around the tables ahead of us. Not a single person here had any idea that a man had just stabbed himself to death upstairs.

The door at the other end of the room opened, and our servers filed into the room, carrying the platters that held our feast. The other leagues had dressed in black pants and white shirts for the occasion. I might have found it mildly amusing if the circumstances had been different.

Three particularly familiar figures made their way to our head table. Apparently the rule was that scions served scions.

Jude reached us first. He set down a platter of carved pork near my plate with a mocking little bow. "For Your Highness," he said in his flippant tone. "May the food be tasty enough to wash away all memory of my sins."

The smell of the meat made my stomach churn. I couldn't find the wherewithal to come up with an answer to his remark. My gaze slid to Connar, who'd just set down a platter of asparagus and pine nuts near Declan. He was watching me, a flicker of concern crossing his face. Between how I must look now and how I'd responded to him in the hall—or rather, not responded—it couldn't be hard for him to pick up on the fact that something was wrong.

He hesitated, opening his mouth, and my hand clenched tighter on my lap as I rested the other on the table. I gave a curt shake of my head. There was nothing I wanted to talk about here, and nothing I wanted to talk about with him, whatever sins he intended to make up for. Not right now with the moments in Banefield's room still so fresh in my head.

As the two of them veered away, Malcolm set down the platter he'd been carrying—skewers of garlic grilled shrimp—between Declan and me. He met my eyes with a glower, his posture radiating displeasure. I looked right back at him, refusing to cower despite the implicit threat in his gaze.

We weren't done? Fine. I might be shaken, but I had so much fight left in me.

He swiveled on his heel and stalked away. Beneath the table, I uncurled my fingers just slightly. Just enough to run my thumb over the warmed metal of the object Banefield had pressed into my hand as he'd died. A little silver key.

He must have grabbed it from the drawer—it must have been why he'd wrenched himself over to the kitchen despite the spell's compulsion. He'd given every last bit of will he had to placing it in my grasp. I'd thought he might be the key to navigating the treacheries of the fearmancer world, and he'd turned out to have a completely literal one for me.

The spell had taken him over before he could tell me where to use it, but that was all right. I'd mourn tonight, and tomorrow I'd start searching for the lock that matched it. Whatever this key opened up, he'd believed I needed it. To heal the cancer he saw among the fearmancers? Maybe.

Or maybe I'd just burn this whole place to the ground.

VILE SORCERY - BONUS SCENE

Ever wonder what went through Jude's mind when Rory left him on the side of the road in Chapter 22, and how he came around to deciding he had to win her back? This bonus scene gives you the chance to find out…

Jude

Rory sat up, wiping her mouth. She didn't even look at me as she yanked the driver's side door of her Lexus shut. "Get out."

"What?" I didn't know what else to say. Didn't know how this perfect outing had somehow turned on its head in the space of a few minute's conversation. Didn't have the slightest clue why the heir of Bloodstone was suddenly so damned angry with me—over a *feeb*, of all the things.

She'd just puked on the asphalt. Even if I didn't understand what she was feeling, she was clearly feeling it very strongly.

She turned her gaze on me then, those dark blue eyes so searingly intense I wouldn't have been surprised to feel my skin turning crispy. "*Get out of the fucking car.*"

Persuasive magic wound through her taut voice and smacked straight into my skull. I'd lowered my defenses over the past few hours with her, had relaxed enough that I'd let my mental shields slide, and my distraction over the argument hadn't helped matters. Whatever protections I'd had left shattered in an instant.

The spell, as potent as anything I'd imagine Malcolm the Persuasion expert could have cast, gripped my limbs. My hand jerked on the door handle beside me. I sputtered a curse, but that didn't stop my legs from heaving me out onto the gravel on the side of the road.

The instant I'd stepped out, Rory yanked my door shut again. I heard the click of the lock through the open window. My hand snatched out through instinct rather than magical compulsion this time, gripping the edge of the window frame. "What the hell are you doing? *This* is ridiculous, Rory."

She glared back at me, so far from the glowing angel I'd brought to a breathless climax earlier this afternoon that my stomach ached. If she was an angel now, it was an avenging one—but in what universe did I deserve to be on the other end of that righteous wrath?

"No," she said tersely. "What was really ridiculous was forgetting that you'd already shown me exactly who you are. Let go of the car."

And what, let her drive off without me? Was she fucking kidding me? "You can't just leave me on the side of the road!" I protested.

"We're less than ten miles from campus. You were just telling me what a great mage you are—I'm sure you can figure out a way to make it back there. Let go of the car *now*, or you might end up with a few broken bones too. But I guess that's no big deal, right?"

The steel in her voice and her crank of the gear shift turned my gut into ice. She really meant it.

I jerked my hand off the door as if it'd burned me. "Rory," I said, scrambling for the right quip or plea to turn this absurd catastrophe around, but she'd already hit the gas. The Lexus roared away from me, racing off along the highway like a streak of silver.

She'd really done it. A few weeks ago she hadn't even known how to drive that car around the school parking lot, a deficit *I'd* rectified for her, and now she'd gone and stranded me in the middle of nowhere.

Fucking bitch.

I couldn't manage to put the full force of my rancor into the insult, even in my head where no one could hear, least of all her. The ache in my stomach was creeping up through my chest.

I'd been so close. So close to winning her trust. So close to baring my goddamned soul. And over one stupid prank—a prank that'd a glorious culmination of all the skill and talent I'd been cultivating for years, thank you very much—she'd pushed me right out of her life and tossed me to the curb like she was putting the trash out.

It wouldn't have rankled so badly if I wasn't already intimately familiar with that sensation.

I closed my eyes, willing down the nearly dizzying urge to douse the venomous mix of hurt and fury churning inside me with as much alcohol as I could get my hands on. It wasn't as if there were any alcoholic beverages in a several-mile radius anyway.

When the other guys heard about this—when *Malcolm* heard about this—

A strangled sound escaped my lips. I clenched my hands at my sides until my fingernails stung my palms. A warm breeze gusted over me, flecking dirt against my skin, but not a single car passed by.

I'm sure you can figure out a way to make it back, Rory had said, but I couldn't exactly conjure myself a car, could I? A very nice illusion of one, sure, but it wouldn't carry me to campus.

I was going to have to call one of the guys. Muttering a few more curses, I pulled out my phone. After a quick glance at my contacts list and a brief grinding of my teeth, I tapped out a text to Connar.

After a couple of back-and-forths in which I did my best not to take my rancor out on him, I had a ride. The Stormhurst scion pulled up on the other side of the road less than twenty minutes later. He must have gone straight to the garage the second we'd stopped talking. He hadn't dicked around about coming to get me—I'd give him a little credit for that.

As I stalked over to the passenger door, he shot me a puzzled look through the windshield. "What are you doing all the way out here?"

I slumped into the seat. An edge of sarcasm crept into my voice. "I took a little walk to stretch my legs. I decided to conjure myself some wings and flew too close to the sun. What do you *think*?"

He started the engine and pulled the car around in a U-ey, but he was still frowning. "I have no idea. If something's going on that the rest of the scions should be looped in on—"

"It's nothing to do with the scions," I snapped. "My original ride kicked me out of the car, okay? I have no interest in saying anything else about it."

He let the rumble of the engine fill the silence for a minute or so. Then, because even Connar had some brains to him, he said, "You were out with Rory."

What was the point in denying it? "Did you miss the part where I said I didn't want to talk about it?" I asked, sinking deeper into the seat.

Malcolm would have badgered me until I spat out some more details just to get him off my back. Declan would have studied me with that insight-trained gaze of us and deduced half of what I wasn't saying. Good old Connar managed to take the hint and shut up for the whole rest of the drive. By the time he pulled into the garage, I was grateful enough of that in spite of the sour emotions still eating at my insides to offer him a brusque "Thank you" before I sprang out of the car and stalked away.

Days later, it still didn't make any sense. I sat in the junior cafeteria—a room I'd never entered except for special banquets in my entire time at Blood U—leafing through the book I wasn't really reading, and not a single thing the Nary students at the table next to mine said illuminated me as to why the heir of Bloodstone would be so enamored with them. Frankly, the feebs were boring as fuck. All they talked about were their classes and some TV show that sounded inane.

So what if that one dormmate of Rory's had lost her spot here? If Rory thought the way we treated the Naries was so horrible, then she should be happy the girl was out of our reach. The feeb clearly hadn't been made of very strong stuff if she'd managed to break bones in her panic. My illusion wasn't what had hurt her.

All of that was true, but when I left the cafeteria, the uneasy restlessness that'd dogged me since our trip to the Bloodstone property followed. I wandered through the building named after my father's family, out across the green, and up the many flights of stairs in Nightwood Tower to the piano room.

Normally, that space was a sanctuary from the rest of campus. I rested my fingers on the keys and let my attention flow into the latest piece I'd been perfecting, with a smidge of satisfaction at how pissed off Baron Killbrook would be if he ever found out I'd taken up this hobby and why. But while I found the notes easily enough, the music didn't stir the usual sense of peace. When I finished, I felt just as hollow as when I'd started.

The ghost of Rory's presence lingered beside me. I could almost feel the warmth of her body from when she'd sat there gamely playing the chords I'd modeled for her, watching me noodle away on the rest of the keys with genuine admiration. And then—the way she'd leaned into my kiss, the eager hitch of her breath—

I slid the fall down over the keys and rested my elbows on it, tipping my face into my hands. I'd allowed her into nearly every part of my life—I'd gone out of my way to cajole her into joining me—and now she was still here even though she wasn't in the way that counted most. Nice work, Jude.

When I meandered back downstairs, the chatter among the other students had taken on an excited edge. I caught the phrase "league results" and rolled my eyes. Time to find out whether I'd be serving Malcolm or Connar at the competition banquet. I'd put in a good effort for team Illusion, but I knew we hadn't pulled off that great a showing.

My trek took me back to Killbrook Hall. A gleaming announcement message had been conjured on the wall in the main entrance room. The students drifting away from it looked more puzzled than celebratory, except for one junior who took a glance and let out a whoop.

Seeing a scion approaching, the crowd parted for me. I walked right up to the glowing letters and halted with a bark of a laugh.

Congratulations to Insight on their league win!

Insight had won? Had hell frozen over as well? They'd never come out on top for a term in my memory. Declan must be beside himself, as gleeful as that stuffed shirt ever let himself get. Had *he* orchestrated some new strategy that'd—

Understanding cut off that bemused question, hitting me like a spear of light straight through my core.

No, it wouldn't have been Declan. If he'd been going to pull off a win for his league, he'd have done it ages ago. But Rory had declared herself for Insight. Rory was the new ingredient in the mix. She must have been the one who'd shifted the tide.

Maybe I should have felt at least a twinge of irritation that the Bloodstone scion had found another way to best us. Instead, a strange glow of awe and pride lit up in my chest.

Of course she had. That was Rory Bloodstone for you.

That was *my* Rory.

I stepped back to make room for the other curious students. A small smile had curved my lips. The glow filled that hollow inside me, and my restlessness fell away beneath a rush of resolve.

No, I still couldn't make any sense of why she'd turned on me the way she had. I wasn't any happier about the way she'd cast me off either. But I'd just have to deal with that discomfort, because the delight of having her meant so much more.

For a little while, that girl had cared about me. Trusted me. Wanted me. If I'd earned that much from her once, I could do it again.

I *had* to do it, because the alternative was going back to this awful nothingness I hadn't realized was quite so empty until she'd shown me how much different I could feel.

I strode out of the building, buoyed on the swell of determination. Whatever it took, whatever it required of me, I would win her back.

SINISTER WIZARDRY

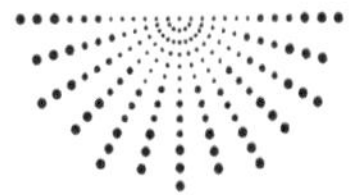

ROYALS OF VILLAIN ACADEMY #3

CHAPTER ONE

Rory

The main Bloodstone residence couldn't have been more different from the family home I'd done most of my growing up in. I'd heard the building described as a "big foreboding stone mansion," and that was right on the mark. It loomed over the forested Maine landscape—not so much manor house or castle like the buildings back on campus, but more a fortress of weathered limestone. The windows I could see, narrow and arched, held only darkness. I half expected to catch a glimpse of a medieval warrior standing by one with a crossbow at the ready.

I'd never missed my bright and airy house in California more.

The pang of homesickness and grief echoed through me as I peered through the car window. My hand rose instinctively to the glass dragon charm on the silver chain around my neck—the last remnant from a bracelet made up of years of birthday gifts.

The chauffeur, on staff with the company that had been tending to the Bloodstone properties since my birth parents' death and my disappearance, drove us past the stretch of mossy stone wall and came up on the wrought-iron gate. Someone had clearly been waiting for us.

He didn't make any movement, but a second later the gate whirred open to admit us.

The chauffeur cleared his throat as he pulled into the property. "Your grandfather—the former baron—left strict instructions for the care of this property before his death. Everyone who's worked here was carefully vetted. But if you have any concerns about the valuables, there's a list at the bank of what should be present. Your grandfather packed away the more personal items in a locked room in the basement that no one has touched at all. That's the third key on the ring they gave you." He made a sideways nod in my direction.

"Got it," I said, and touched the side of my purse where I'd tucked that keyring away.

As one of the ruling entities among the fearmancers, my birth family had several properties across the Northeast, but this was the oldest and the largest. I was still getting used to the fact that I'd gone from owning not much more than some clothes and art supplies to having an immense bank account and extensive real estate.

Of course, if I could have reversed the trade and gotten back my *real* family, I'd have taken that deal in an instant. I didn't know a lot about my birth family, since I'd only been two when my parents had been killed, but I knew enough to make a few basic judgments. The fearmancer authorities had viciously murdered the people I thought of as Mom and Dad in front of me. The heirs of the other ruling families and a whole lot of the other young fearmancers had made my life hell when I'd first arrived at the fearmancer university to learn how to use my powers.

And just a few days ago, I'd watched one of the few professors who'd seemed to give a damn about me fatally stab himself to cut off the effects of a spell compelling him to attack me. A spell he'd told me had been cast by the older barons as well as "the reapers," whatever that meant.

The mages who ruled over fearmancer society, the ones I was supposed to rule alongside when I finished my education, had attempted to batter my magic out of me. That was the world I'd been thrown back into—a world where fear meant might, and might ruled over any ideas of human decency. I'd seen enough to realize the joymancers I'd left behind in California weren't perfect, but at least they didn't thrive on violence and destruction. Powering your magic through happiness made for very different attitudes than powering it through terror did.

The car pulled to a stop in the curve of the drive just outside the imposing front door. "The staff inside will show you around," the chauffeur said. "They'll be glad to have a Bloodstone in residence again. The work's more fulfilling when there's someone to appreciate it." He shot me a quick smile.

"Thank you for the drive." I bobbed my head in return and eased the car door open. It might be summer now, but the Maine air wafted damp and a little cool around me, the sun partly blotted by thin gray clouds. The clover scent that reached my nose was pleasant enough, at least. I dragged in a deep breath of it and started up the steps.

My mouse familiar dug her claws a little more deeply into the shoulder of my blouse. Her small white head swiveled as she took in our new accommodations, and her dry voice trickled into my head. *Plenty of atmosphere, I'll give it that.*

Most mages' familiars couldn't outright talk to them, only pass on vague impressions through the magical bond. Deborah wasn't just a mouse, though. The Enclave that ruled over the joymancers had arranged for the spirit of one of their mages, a woman who'd been dying of cancer, to be placed into the animal's body.

The opportunity had meant a second life for her—and a way for them to monitor me. The more of the story I'd managed to get out of her, the more it'd become clear that the joymancers had been very worried about my fear-based powers emerging despite the steps they'd taken to suppress them.

I couldn't reply to her telepathically, unfortunately, and saying much to her out loud wasn't a good idea in front of witnesses. The fearmancers had no idea I'd brought one of their enemies into their midst in mouse form, and if they found out, I had no doubt Deborah's second life would be cut much shorter than her first had.

The door to the mansion opened just as I reached the top step. A middle-aged woman beamed at me. She welcomed me in with a sweep of her arm, her black hair, piled high on her head, gleaming with a purple tint.

"Welcome home, Miss Bloodstone," she said in a measured but friendly voice. "I'm Eloise, the house manager. I'll see to it that everything remains in order during your stay."

"Thanks," I said, and then anything I might have added was lost with my breath as I took in the vast front hall on the other side of the doorway.

A brocade rug covered the tiled floor, and another ran up the grand staircase ahead of me. Oil paintings with gilded frames hung on the walls between mahogany side tables with porcelain vases and bejeweled boxes. A young woman in a maid uniform was just setting a bouquet of lilies into one of the vases. A faint perfume drifted off them. The space was airier than I'd have expected from its imposing exterior.

I must have spent a lot of time here in the first two years of my life. I didn't have the faintest memory of any of it. Eloise had welcomed me home, but this didn't feel like home at all, more like a well-kept museum dedicated to strangers. What did any of this tell me about my birth parents other than they'd had old-money aesthetic tastes like most other fearmancers seemed to?

Maybe I'd get a better sense of them going through these "personal" items my grandfather Bloodstone had apparently stashed away.

The shifting of Deborah's body on my shoulder reminded me of one thing I needed to have "in order" from the start. I caught the house manager's eye and motioned to the mouse.

"This is my familiar," I said. "I'd like to give her free run of the property while we're here. All the staff need to know to be careful of her."

If Eloise thought it was strange for a fearmancer to have a mouse for a familiar rather than the predatory animals that most preferred, she didn't let it show. "Absolutely, I'll make that exceptionally clear to everyone on staff."

She led me through the ground floor, which included a sitting room, a music room, a ballroom, a parlor, a dining room that could have accommodated fifty people, and then the kitchen, which was unexpectedly open and modern-looking compared to the rest of the furnishings, if still at least a decade out of date. My grandfather Bloodstone would still have lived here until his death, presumably. I guessed the family had appreciated modern amenities over style where it mattered most.

A skinny man with angular limbs and a round head that made me think of a grasshopper was perched on a stool by one of the gleaming counters. He hopped up at our arrival.

"This is Claude, your chef," Eloise said.

The man offered me a little bow. "At your service. Perhaps you could tell me what you'd be interested in having for your meals today? We have enough ingredients on hand to manage a simple lunch, but if you wanted anything more complicated—for dinner as well—it would be good to know ahead of time so I can get everything I need."

My mind went blank. I'd known a lot of my classmates had family chefs preparing and sending their school meals, but I'd been managing to feed myself just fine, and I'd assumed it'd be the same here. "I, um… I hadn't given it much thought. I'm not very picky. Would it be a problem if I said you can make whatever you think would taste good?"

He blinked, and then the corners of his mouth curled upward. "It would be my pleasure. If you do think of anything in particular you'd like during your time here, don't hesitate to make a request, of course."

I wasn't sure how long I was going to be here. Bloodstone University—or Villain Academy, as the joymancers called it, which was a pretty accurate nickname—was closed for two weeks, but then it would open again for an optional summer term. I'd gathered that only the senior students attended, and usually only the stronger talents among those, to compete in some sort of special project.

I didn't like the idea of spending any more time on campus, surrounded by peers who mostly saw me as either a tool or a target, but I'd accomplish a lot more there than I could here. My mentor, Professor Banefield, had given me a key just before he'd died, one that mattered a lot more to me than any on the ring in my purse. He'd seemed to think it would lead me to something that would help me against my enemies.

My hand came to rest on my purse, where I'd stashed that key too. I needed to figure out what the hell it opened… and I also needed to continue finding out everything I could about the school so I'd be able to see through my plan to bring the place down.

Bloodstone University taught young fearmancers to turn into the sadistic murderers so many of the adults were. Deborah had told me the joymancers had been trying to put a stop to those teachings for years, but the wards had stopped them from even locating the university. If I could bring them the information they needed to tackle that part of fearmancer society, they'd *have* to see that my magic didn't mean I'd turn out as cruel as my heritage would suggest. I'd get vengeance for Mom and Dad and for Professor Banefield, and I'd be able to return to my real home.

And with my enemies ramping up their efforts to take *me* down, I might not have much time left to accomplish that.

Upstairs, Eloise showed me to the master bedroom, my childhood bedroom, and several guest rooms. Even my birth parents' most private space didn't give much sense of who they'd been as people. A framed photograph of the two of them hung on the wall—the woman dark-haired and eyed like me with an elegant bearing, the man a little lighter in coloring and slightly awkward in his tallness—but everything else was more posh, old-fashioned furniture and antiques.

The room with the crib had been stripped of all but a few well-preserved stuffed animals and basic furniture. I tried to imagine the man and woman from the photograph moving through this space, tending to and playing with a younger version of me. No memories stirred. I couldn't even bring them to life in my mind.

Both places left my skin prickling with discomfort. I picked a guest bedroom somewhat at random and told Eloise, "I think I'll sleep in here. I don't want to disturb my parents' room yet."

She nodded as if she understood. I reached for my purse again, thinking of the chauffeur's comment about other rooms I hadn't yet seen. "I was told there's a storage room in the basement with the things my grandfather wanted to keep particularly secure. Can you show me where that is?"

If I was going to unravel any mysteries within my former home, I might as well get started now.

"Of course," Eloise said. "Right this way."

CHAPTER TWO

Rory

The Bloodstones certainly had a lot of things they wanted to hide away, Deborah remarked from where she was perched on my knee.

I sighed and shoved aside the plastic bin I'd been sorting through. "I'm not sure it's so much hiding as normal security. Even regular Naries don't want people they don't know digging through their financial records."

That was mostly what I'd found in the basement storage room across the last two days—bins and bins of receipts and invoices and statements, most of which didn't look especially significant to me. I'd looked at every bit of paper in those things, though, and there were dozens more boxes in the large room around me. It was brightly lit, at least, with beaming florescent bulbs across the ceiling, but the artificial brightness and the extra layer of chill in the air didn't let me forget I was underground.

Looking at the stacks I still hadn't touched, my heart sank. I forced myself to reach for another box.

This one was on the smaller side, and the contents jostled in a way that didn't sound at all papery when I lifted it. Maybe I'd get a change of pace. I set it on the floor, popped off the lid, and froze.

I'd unearthed a box of baby memorabilia. A tiny gold-cast shoe sat right at the top—the rich people equivalent of bronzing? Underneath it lay lacy dresses that couldn't have fit any child older than an infant, a board book that appeared to have teeth marks around the edge, a plastic bag with a lock of dark brown hair… My hair, obviously.

My chest clenched. My birth parents had kept all this stuff after I'd grown into a toddler. I couldn't have asked for clearer evidence that whatever they'd been like, whatever fearmancer horrors they'd been party to, they'd seen me as more than a necessary heir. They'd loved me.

I didn't know what to do with that knowledge, especially with it staring me in the face so blatantly.

Lorelei? Deborah said tentatively.

Before I could find the wherewithal to answer her, footsteps tapped down the hall outside the storage room. They paused before they reached the doorway, respectful of the private nature of the room. Eloise's voice carried to me.

"Miss Bloodstone, there's someone here to see you. A Lillian Ravenguard from the blacksuits. She says she's hoping the two of you can have a word."

Someone from the blacksuits? My body went rigid. The blacksuits were the fearmancer version of law enforcement. It'd been blacksuits who'd stormed into Mom and Dad's house and killed them in front of me. What did this woman want to talk to me about now?

The obvious answer came to me a second later: Professor Banefield's murder. If they'd even figured out it was a murder and not simply a delusion brought on by a natural illness. I didn't trust these people not to be under the barons' thumbs, but maybe I'd learn something useful from her. I got up, scooping Deborah into my hand.

"Okay, I'll come up," I said. "You can let her in."

"I'll show her to the sitting room."

I think I'd better keep my distance from this guest of yours, my familiar said as Eloise bustled off. *We don't know how finely honed her skills are. I'll find a covert place to watch from.*

"Good thinking," I said. A blacksuit was a lot more likely to ask questions about my familiar than my family's hired staff was.

When I reached the top of the stairs, I set Deborah down so she could scurry to a safe vantage point and headed into the sitting room myself. I still hadn't figured out how it was any different in purpose from the parlor. Eloise escorted my visitor in a moment later.

The woman who strode into the room was tall, broad-shouldered, and well-muscled but with enough poise to give a svelte impression over her toughness. With her short, silver-flecked tawny hair and wide-set eyes, she made me think of a lioness on the prowl. She wasn't wearing the usual black outfit of her job but fitted jeans and a modest silk blouse.

"Persephone," she said in a commanding voice that rolled through the room. "It's so good to finally see you again."

Again? "I, er— I'm actually going by Rory," I said quickly. "It's the name I grew up with. Whenever anyone mentions 'Persephone' I feel like they're talking about someone else."

The woman paused and then nodded, studying me with what felt like professional precision. Then she smiled with more warmth than I'd been prepared for. "I'm sorry. I'm sure this has all been overwhelming for you. I'm hoping I can help make the transition easier. Your mother and I were good friends—I did everything I could to locate you so we could bring you back. If I hadn't been on assignment overseas at the time, I'd have been there to retrieve you."

I restrained a shudder at the memory of my bloody "retrieval." So, this wasn't an official visit after all. I groped for something to say as I sat down on one of the stiff armchairs. Was I supposed to thank her for her contribution to wrenching me from the life I'd loved and the slaughter of my parents?

"Thank you for coming by," I settled on. I could say that without wincing. "Was there anything specific you wanted to talk about, Ms. Ravenguard?"

She made a dismissive wave as she sat across from me. "Please, you can call me Lillian. I just wanted to see how you've been doing. Have you been coping with the changes all right? Is there anything you're still confused about?"

How so many of you can be such total assholes and not even seem to realize it? I thought, and bit my tongue. Not all of the fearmancers were awful all of the time, and so far this one was being kind.

"Not really," I said. "I mean, it's kind of weird… I don't remember any of this." I motioned to the house around me. "I still don't have a very good sense of what my family was like. But I think I'm getting along pretty well with everything at school. That seems to be what's most important right now." *That, and making sure the other royal families don't destroy me.*

Lillian made a humming sound. "Of course. I think I might have…" Her gaze sharpened. "You must still be shaken by what happened with your mentor at the university. I can assure you that the blacksuits are working hard on that case to determine why his illness caused him to take his life in that way—and to ensure any contagion doesn't spread."

I could have told them it wasn't a contagion but a purposeful spell, if I'd trusted any of them enough to relay what Banefield had told me. I didn't trust them, though—not even this woman in front of me. I'd known her for all of five minutes, no matter how much presence she claimed to have had in my family's life before.

"That's good to hear," I said. "It was horrible. He was a good mentor—he helped me a lot in adjusting."

"No matter how long it takes, we always get to the bottom of a situation eventually," Lillian said.

I found that a little hard to believe given the number of crimes I'd already heard of fearmancers getting away with, but I wasn't going to argue with her.

She switched topics with a smooth grace, mentioning a few shops, restaurants, and other attractions nearby I might want to visit while I was home, and I replied as well as I could. She must have sensed my uncertainty about the whole conversation, because she didn't try to sustain it very long.

"The main reason I stopped by was to let you know you can call on me at any time, anything you need," she said, scooting forward on her chair. She handed me a business card with her name, phone number, and email address in stark print. "If you don't get me, you'll get my assistant, Maggie, who can connect you to me right away if necessary. Don't hesitate to get in touch. I mean it. Your mother was my best friend, and watching over you is the best way I can honor her memory."

The vehemence in her voice sent a pang through me, a longing to be able to believe and trust in someone who'd say that. My fingers closed around the card. "Thank you. It means a lot."

"It's no problem at all. I can already tell you've grown up to be an impressive young woman."

After Eloise had shown Lillian out, I went up to my room to save her number in my phone. It definitely couldn't hurt to have a blacksuit on call just in case, right? Maybe she'd end up being on my side like Professor Banefield had.

I'd just added her into my contacts when the phone rang in my hand. The number that came up on the screen was Jude Killbrook's.

My pulse hiccupped. For a second, I sat there frozen.

Jude was one of my fellow scions, heir to the Killbrook barony. He'd also been one of my main tormenters when I'd first arrived at the school, but after I'd proven my magical abilities, he'd appeared to have a change of heart. He'd put a hell of a lot of effort into making amends and winning me over, and I had to admit it'd worked… until I'd gotten a chilling reminder of how strategic his kindness could be.

He'd been sweet to me, sure, but at the same time he'd happily been planning pranks to torment the nonmagical—Nary—students the university took in on scholarship. The most recent of those tricks had ended with my dormmate and friend Shelby fracturing her wrist and losing the spot in the music department that had meant everything to her.

Jude hadn't even felt bad about destroying her dream. He'd tried to justify it—he'd expected me to be *impressed* by his stunt.

Remembering the last real conversation we'd had, which had ended with me forcing him out of my car and leaving him on the side of the road, sent a twist of nausea through my gut. That'd been a couple weeks ago though, and I hadn't really talked to him since. I should probably at least find out what he wanted.

I raised the phone to my ear. "Hello?" I said warily.

"Hello, Ice Queen," Jude said in his usual languidly wry tone. "You're having quite the busy social life at the family home, aren't you?"

"What are you talking about?"

"I was just coming up on the place, and there's someone leaving. Who've you been entertaining already?"

"I don't think that's any of your business," I said automatically, and then the rest of what he'd said caught up. "You were just coming up on *what* place?"

Jude chuckled. "The Bloodstone mansion, Rory. I'm right outside the gate. Will you let me in so we can talk? I promise not to bite unless you ask nicely."

I rolled my eyes, but at the same time I was springing to my feet. I hurried across the hall to one of the rooms with a view of the front yard.

Indeed, a red Mercedes was parked beyond the wrought-iron bars. As I watched, Jude's lanky figure emerged from the driver's side. He shut the door and propped himself against it, looking toward the house, the sunlight gleaming off his dark copper hair. I was standing far enough back that I doubted he could see me, but he must have suspected I'd come take a look, because he aimed a cheeky wave toward the house.

Did he figure if he ignored our argument for long enough, the conflict would disappear?

"What, you just happened to be in the neighborhood?" I said. Was the Killbrook home in Maine too?

He shrugged. "You could say that, only I took about a four-hour detour to get into the neighborhood. It was a very scenic drive. Although the only thing I'm really interested in seeing is you."

He did know how to lay on the charm. And, fuck, he'd driven four hours just to pay me this visit without any idea of how I'd respond?

"You really should have called *before* you headed over."

"Ah, but it's much harder to turn me away when I'm already here, isn't it?" He grinned wide enough that I could see the flash of his teeth. "Come on, Rory. I'm not asking for much. Just to talk for a bit face to face."

"I'm not sure that's a good idea," I said. Especially since his cajoling was already working its way under my skin.

The times I'd spent with Jude before we'd fallen out had been among the few bright spots in my new life. He'd made me laugh. His kiss, his touch, had lit me up from the inside out. He'd expressed such unwavering devotion—and proven it in front of the other students—that I couldn't believe it'd been a sham or that he'd had any part in his father's plans as baron. He'd had way too many chances where he could have hurt me but hadn't.

Maybe now that he'd had some time to think over what I'd said…

"You know I can make it good," he teased, and then his voice turned more serious. "I'm sorry about what happened, all right? I didn't set out to hurt anyone, and if I'd known that Nary was your friend, I'd have been a lot more careful of her—I swear it."

The hope that had been rising inside me snapped away in an instant. I swallowed thickly. With those few words, he'd put the problem on full display.

"You still don't get it," I said. "That's not the point. It shouldn't matter whether any of them are my friends or not. If I hadn't known who she was, it'd still be a horrible thing to leave her injured and cost her the spot at school over some stupid prank."

"It's not as if I did that on purpose. We can't tiptoe around them all the time."

"There's a big difference between tiptoeing around them and just avoiding pointless pranks that'll totally freak them out," I said before he could keep going. My stomach was full-out churning now. "I don't want to talk about this anymore. We obviously think about it too differently."

"Rory, please…"

I closed my eyes and gathered my resolve. "Look, I'm not furious with you like I was before. I understand that you didn't think you were doing anything wrong. But I can't trust someone who has such a different perspective on… well, everything. When we're back at school, we can be classmates and colleagues, but that's it. That's as far as it can go. All right?"

He was silent for a moment. "You're really not letting me in."

“No. I’m sorry about the drive.”

“Well, that was my own damn fault, wasn’t it?” He laughed, a little tightly. Then his tone relaxed again. “It’s fine. I’ll try again another day, another way.”

I trusted he meant *that*, regardless of my other doubts. A question tumbled out. “Why does being with me matter so much to you? You know we can never have anything serious.”

I was the last living Bloodstone. Any guy I married, on the off-chance I stuck around here long enough for that to happen, would automatically become a Bloodstone too. Jude and I couldn’t have a real future together, even if his attitudes had lined up with mine, unless he gave up the barony. I wasn't sure he even could—if there was anyone to inherit it in his place. He didn’t have any siblings.

“Don’t you worry about that,” Jude said without missing a beat. “I will find a way to convince you to give me another chance, I promise you. Just wait and see.”

CHAPTER THREE

Declan

Malcolm leaned back in the lounge chair, rotating his beer bottle lazily between his fingers. "You know," he said, "this isn't bad at all."

The July sun beamed over the back deck with just enough heat to be pleasant but not searing, and the breeze rustled through the trees that framed the lawn beyond. It was a perfect summer day, really.

Some of the prominent fearmancers looked a little horrified when they first saw the large modern sunroom and wooden deck Dad had arranged to be built off the back of the old Ashgrave mansion. If I looked at it with an outsider's eye, I could admit the addition did clash with the stone walls and gothic styling of the rest of the place. But it was around back where only family and guests saw it, and I'd take the enjoyment of it over maintaining appearances any day.

I downed a gulp from my beer. "I'm glad you could come over. It seems like a shame to have this spot and no one to hang out with back here."

The deck had gone in last summer, and all four of us scions had gotten together a couple times back then to relax and shoot the breeze. Considering how tense things had become between Malcolm and the other two, I'd figured a group hang-out wasn't the best move right now.

Besides, I'd wanted the chance to talk to each of them one-on-one. There were some subjects sensitive enough that it was hard enough feeling my way to a real answer without an audience.

I'd talked to Connar and Jude earlier this week. It'd been obvious pretty quickly that neither of them had any information about what the barons were up to beyond what I knew. But then, Jude had always seemed antagonistic toward his dad, and Connar avoided talking about his mother as much as possible, so I didn't think much political gossip got passed around in their homes.

Malcolm, on the other hand, had been doing his best to follow his father's footsteps and become part of the most senior baron's plans for as long as I'd known him.

"You're going back for the summer project?" I said, to shoot the breeze a little more before I got to the subject that really mattered to me.

Malcolm snorted, because it *was* a rather stupid question. "We've got a reputation to maintain, don't we? Can't look like we're shirking the chance for extra practice." He cracked his knuckles. "I wonder which of the profs got to pick the assignment this time. Hopefully it'll be better than Sinleigh's lame project last year."

I let that jab slide past me. *I'd* won last year's summer competition, partly because Professor Sinleigh had naturally picked a task that revolved around Insight. Which was also Malcolm's weakest area of magic. Malcolm's comment had been said casually enough, though—only a bit of mild posturing to remind me that he considered himself king of the scions even if I was nearly full baron now. I was used to that.

"I can't compete since I'm an aide now, so you'll have it a little easier," I said, giving him a light kick to the ankle.

He laughed and shook his head, relaxing into his chair. Malcolm held onto his authority rigidly with most fearmancers, but he liked it when the three of us pushed back. He'd never said it in so many words, but I got the impression it made him feel better to think he'd be ruling alongside friends he could also consider equals.

Of course, even scions could push back too much. I didn't even know exactly what line Jude or Connar had crossed, but they'd clearly pissed him off somehow or other. One of the—increasingly many—downsides of the teacher's aide gig was how much less time I'd been able to spend with the other guys at school.

"I suppose there's Rory to contend with this year, though," I added.

Malcolm's shoulders tensed just slightly, but he kept the same nonchalant tone. "I'd imagine five years of practice with three strengths will still beat out three months of practice with four."

It wasn't all about magical power, though. Even when there were scions attending the university like now, the records I'd seen indicated that regular students still won at least half of the time. Any good project included a bunch of plain old strategizing.

"She might have some trouble focusing anyway," I said. "The professor who died—did you know he was her mentor?"

Malcolm's head jerked around at that. He could keep a good poker face, but I didn't think he was a good enough actor to fake that startled response. "Seriously?"

I nodded. "I've been wondering if that fact isn't at least part of the reason he's dead now."

"Everyone's saying he had some awful illness."

"Well, it's not as if magic can't make someone sick. How many illnesses do you know that'd make someone stab himself?"

"So you think… someone might have killed him. Because it'd hurt her. Who—" Malcolm stiffened much more obviously than before, straightening up in his chair. His eyes darkened. "If you're trying to hint that *I* would have resorted to—to murdering a fucking professor just to make a point, then—"

"Hey!" I raised my hands, cutting him off before he could go any further. I couldn't blame Malcolm for getting upset about the possible insinuation, but an angry Malcolm Nightwood was pretty unnerving to be around. "That's not what I was implying, not at all. I know you're not a psychopath."

His dad I was less sure of. The barons hadn't mentioned Professor Banefield's death at our most recent meeting, but there was plenty they didn't bother to loop me in on. They hadn't made any secret of the fact that they wanted Rory as helpless as they could get her so they could mold her to their whims—for some higher purpose they also hadn't shared with me. A bad sign, since it meant that purpose was probably something I'd disagree with.

Malcolm's shoulders came down, but his expression stayed stormy. "Then you think someone *else* had a big enough beef with Glinda the Good Witch to start offing her support system? It's one thing to duel it out with someone you have an issue with directly. Going around killing random bystanders… that's just wanton brutality. Why the hell would anyone come down on her that hard?"

"I'm not sure," I said carefully. I wasn't supposed to reveal anything that was discussed in the baron meetings with anyone outside that pentacle, and I didn't really *want* to place the burden of all the things I'd learned about the other scions' parents on their shoulders yet. I'd had to grow up way too fast out of necessity. No need to drag them along with me before they were ready. "That's what I'm trying to figure out. You've been pretty… focused on her since she turned up. Have you seen anything odd?"

Malcolm frowned. He appeared to give the question genuine thought. "Nothing anywhere near murderous," he said. "For fuck's sake. Are you *sure* it wasn't some other kind of feud that had nothing to do with her? Who knows what this Banefield guy got up to. Everyone says he cracked up a little after his wife died."

I hadn't heard anyone say that, so I'd be willing to bet "everyone" in this case was Malcolm's parents. Interesting. A broken mage was easier to use than a strong one. But Malcolm wasn't showing any sign of knowing about this specific plan. Time to let it drop.

"I was just speculating," I said with a wave of my hand. "You're right—it could be something totally unrelated. It could even have been a natural illness after all. Still hard for her, though." I paused and couldn't help adding, "Maybe it's not the best time to keep going at her the way you have been, while she's recovering from that? She had to watch him die—I think we could cut her a break."

Malcolm's mouth shifted into a grimace. "She's the one who made the rules here. She's the one who threw our generosity in our faces. I've just been re-establishing the status quo."

"It has been going on for quite a while."

"I *tried* to give her a way out, and she wouldn't take it." He took a swig from his beer and glowered at the trees. "If she wants to survive in this society, she's got to learn that decisions have consequences."

I was pretty sure Rory had already figured that out. It wasn't a lack of learning—it was that she was just as stubborn as Malcolm was and just as dedicated to her own principles.

But after his refusal, a brooding expression came over the Nightwood scion's face, as if maybe he was thinking through what I'd said in a little more depth after all. I decided to leave it there for now.

Malcolm wasn't any real threat to Rory, not compared to the barons and whoever else they might have roped into their scheming.

We chatted some more and one of the staff brought us lunch out on the deck, and then we whiled away a good part of the afternoon playing a magically-modified version of basketball Malcolm had invented some ten years ago. It wasn't quite the same with just the two of us, but my brother and one of his friends ended up joining in. There was a relief in just goofing around without thinking about all the pressures looming over me.

After Malcolm and my brother's friend left, Noah sat down on the front steps next to me with a satisfied sigh. He'd stopped getting taller a few years ago, topping out at just an inch shorter than me, but every time he came home from the fearmancer college in Paris, he seemed to have aged at least a year. He was only seventeen still, but it was getting harder to see him as a kid.

He still needed his big brother's protection, though. I was the only thing standing between him and our aunt's ambitions for the barony. Get rid of me and then him, and the authority would be all Aunt Ambrosia's.

"That was fun," he said, swiping his sweat-damp hair away from his eyes. "We should do that more often."

"Yeah." Guilt pinched my gut. "I guess I haven't been able to hang out as much as we used to lately, huh?"

He elbowed me teasingly. "I know you've got all your important baron stuff to take care of. Just don't get too self-important."

I had to laugh. "It's a period of transition," I said. "Things should settle down once I'm finished with school and can focus just on the barony." At least I damn well hoped they would.

"Like I said, it's okay. I'm not some little kid who's going to expect you to drop everything the second I'm back home."

"You're liking the school over there still?" I asked.

"Oh, yeah. It's great. The fearmancers over there seem a little more… relaxed than people here. And I get to be an exotic foreign student." He waggled his eyebrows.

"Be sure to use those powers for good and not evil," I teased.

He gave me a mock salute and then turned his gaze toward the driveway. "I was actually going to ask you… I know the plan was that I'd start attending Blood U once you graduated, but I think I'd like to go all the way through in Paris, if that's okay. I realize I don't know how expensive it is or whatever…"

"Hey, we can afford it. The money's no issue." I studied him with an affectionate twinge. I'd hoped sending him to school overseas would help broaden his horizons even if Dad and I weren't there as much for guidance. It'd worked—and he was hungry for more. "You get your education wherever you're happiest, Noah. That's what matters the most to me."

Maybe there was a bit of envy in that twinge too. I hadn't let myself stray very far from my territory here out of fear of what moves Aunt Ambrosia or the older barons might make if I were an ocean away for any significant length of time, but I couldn't deny that part of me itched to see more of the world. To experience more of the people and cultures in it, outside this often suffocating cycle of struggles for domination.

That sacrifice was made worth it by the relieved smile Noah shot me. I stayed here and shouldered the responsibilities of our family name so he could have some kind of freedom.

His smile turned a little sly. "So, what's new with the pentacle of barons? Any unexpected new power plays or big events in the works?"

Noah had always been curious about the work of the barony—

more than I really preferred. He wouldn't have been half as enthusiastic if he'd had any idea what it really involved or how much danger came with it.

"You know I can't talk about anything that's not already public knowledge," I said.

"Hey, I can keep a secret! I've got to be ready as next in line, right?" He gave me another teasing jab of his elbow with no idea how sharply that remark hit me right through the chest. God forbid it ever came to that.

Before I had to answer, Dad appeared at the door, his brow furrowed.

"Declan," he said. "Someone's called for you on the home line. They wouldn't tell me what it's about."

That was odd. I conducted all my business, both barony- and school-related, through my own phone. I headed in, with a sudden leap of my heart that it might somehow be Rory.

My heart shouldn't be leaping about anything to do with Rory, even if she was the fiercest and yet the most compassionate girl I'd ever met. Even if the one intimate afternoon we'd indulged in had become my favorite memory.

I couldn't be with her without dumping the responsibilities of the barony on Noah's shoulders. If anyone found out she and I had slept together while I was working as an aide and she was a student, my position would come into question regardless. So that moment had to stay just a fond memory, and it was hands and heart off from here on.

Especially because the two of us weren't the only people who remembered what had happened between us.

"Mr. Ashgrave," a voice cooed over the line when I picked up the phone. "It's Stella Evergrist. We met recently at my granddaughter's country home."

Every inch of my body tensed. By the most awful luck, Rory's paternal grandparents had caught us leaving her country property together. They hadn't seen anything *that* incriminating, but I had been holding Rory's hand, and we had come all the way out there just the two of us… It'd been obvious they assumed something more than friendly was going on.

"Yes," I said evenly. "I remember. What can I help you with, Mrs. Evergrist?"

"Oh, mostly I just wondered if Persephone is there. The two of you did seem quite close, and we haven't heard from her as soon as we were hoping."

It wasn't difficult to figure out why. They'd tried to glom onto Rory from the first second they'd seen her, without any apparent sense of the fact that to her they were strangers—and horribly pushy ones at that. I'd heard the other barons make occasional disparaging remarks about the family that had most recently mingled with the Bloodstones. The Evergrists were known for being grasping and power-hungry with little self-moderation. Not a pleasant combination.

"I'm afraid Rory and I aren't actually in frequent contact," I said. "Our trip to her property was a one-time occasion, something she needed help with out there. I haven't seen her since school let out."

Mrs. Evergrist let out a soft guffaw that told me she hadn't bought into my lie in the slightest. Well, it'd been worth a try. "Now, now," she said. "I understand why you're so cautious. Got yourself set up as a teacher's aide, they tell me. Can't have it getting out if you've taken a student too far under your wing, hmmm?"

I kept my voice as emotionless as possible. "I can't say I know what you're talking about, Mrs. Evergrist."

"No, of course not. Well, when you do talk to Rory again, remind her that we're dearly looking forward to reconnecting. Oh, and there was one other thing."

I braced myself. "Yes?"

The wheedling note came back into her voice. "My husband and I have an interest in a business venture that's been put before the pentacle. It should come up for consideration soon… I hope, in recognition for our discretion, you'll help nudge it along?"

Shit. There it was. I lowered my head, my jaw clenching at the blatant blackmail.

I couldn't completely shut her down. If I could keep her thinking I was playing along until I finished the aide gig—it'd just be a few more months—the situation would be much less precarious. The consequences wouldn't be as harsh if they made a claim after I no longer had authority over any students anyway.

"I'll see what I can do," I said.

As she babbled on about the details of the venture, Dad and Noah meandered down the hall past the sitting room where I was taking the call. Noah was gesturing wildly with the story he was telling, and Dad was chuckling, glowing with fatherly joy. My stomach knotted.

If I was under threat, then they were too, just as much. I *had* to play this right, or I could be screwing over my entire family.

CHAPTER FOUR

Rory

"The bitch of Bloodstone returns," Victory Blighthaven said in an undertone the moment I walked into the dorm. She was standing by the dining table with her besties, Cressida and Sinclair. The queen bee of Villain Academy looked as pretty and polished as ever, her auburn hair falling in sculpted waves and her silk summer dress perfectly tailored to her hourglass figure, but her personality clearly hadn't gotten any less ugly.

I'd spent most of the last few months ignoring Victory's jabs. Her dislike seemed incredibly petty, based mainly on the fact that the administration had given me the corner bedroom with a view that she'd once claimed—and that she adored Malcolm Nightwood and I very openly did not. I'd had bigger things to worry about, like mages who'd outright kill to screw with me. But as I tugged the strap of my purse higher on my shoulder, I found I'd completely run out of fucks when it came to keeping the peace.

The rulers of the fearmancer world were out to destroy me. If Victory thought I was going to be scared of *her*, she could forget it.

"Takes one to know one," I said breezily, and headed across the room without waiting for her reaction. From the corner of my eye, I saw her expression darken.

"You know," she said with forced sweetness, "it's just you, the three of us, and your good friend Imogen here for the summer. Keep that in mind before you start picking fights."

Sinclair, who'd been especially pissed off at me ever since Jude had declared his affection for me, let out a sharp snicker. Cressida tossed the tail of her ever-present French braid over her shoulder.

Oh, wonderful. Imogen and I *had* been becoming good friends until Victory had manipulated her into betraying me. Since then, I'd held her at a wary distance. None of the other girls in our dorm had ever stood up for me against Victory and her crew, but they'd at least been a small moderating influence. I had to assume there were things Victory wouldn't have openly said or done in front of them. Now I didn't even have that buffer.

"Thanks for the heads up," I said. As I reached my bedroom, my gaze slid down the line of doors to the one that had been Shelby's. A lump of guilt rose in my throat.

She might have been the dorm's one Nary student, but Shelby had been the only person at Blood U I could still call a real friend, even if I hadn't been able to talk to her about the magical side of my existence. The Naries were brought into the university so the mage students got practice at being careful with their magical practice in regular society—and to give them easy targets for stirring up fear. But Shelby had loved it here despite the bullying she'd faced. She'd keep going to classes even when she was falling over with a fever. The opportunities she'd get with her musical career after finishing the program mattered that much to her.

And with one stupid trick, Jude had stolen the future she'd dreamed of away from her. If I hadn't been distracted by Malcolm's harassment, maybe I could have helped her, stopped her injury from happening…

So many things to look forward to being back on campus. I restrained a grimace and went into my room, shutting the door firmly behind me. Who knew how many new dangers might be lurking around me this term?

Deborah crept out from where she'd been hiding beneath my hair at the back of my neck. I let her run down my arm to hop onto the bedspread. *So lovely to be back*, she said in a tone dry as dust.

"No kidding," I murmured.

Nothing in my room appeared to have changed during the last two weeks. The cleaning staff must have come through, their efforts leaving a faint lemony scent in the air. Between the double bed, the wardrobe, and the desk and chair set by the window, the space was pretty full. Beyond the window stretched the north end of campus, across the green and the wilder fields to the glinting water of the lake.

I tugged the window open to let in the warm breeze and sat on the edge of the bed. Deborah set her front paws on my leg.

What's the plan now?

"I have to find out what this summer project is about and work around that," I said. "There's an assembly in about half an hour that's supposed to explain it. Then I've got to figure out some way to uncover what Professor Banefield wanted to tell me."

You be careful, Lorelei. I don't trust a single person in this place. They've shown just how vicious they're willing to be. I'll keep watch around your dorm as well as I can—and you let me know if there are any other ways I can help.

"Thank you." I stroked a finger over her fur.

I didn't feel entirely safe even in my bedroom, knowing Victory and company were hanging around on the other side of the door. I flopped down on the bed to relax for a few minutes, but then restlessness had me back on my feet. A little meander around outside would give me some idea who'd come back for the summer session, anyway.

I cast my protective wards before I even opened the door, not wanting to give Victory any chance to observe my strategies. Magic tickled up from behind my collarbone, gathered there from my walk through the forest after the chauffeur had dropped me off in town and from the few students I'd encountered on my way to the dorm building who gave off jolts of fear just at the sight of the newest scion. I still didn't exactly *like* the idea that my mere presence could inspire terror, but it did come in handy for building up my power.

Victory's trio kept murmuring and giggling amongst themselves when I came out. They weren't quite finished with me, though. I caught the extra shine on the floor ahead of me a split-second before my shoe came down on the conjured slickness. I stiffened my leg just in time that I only wobbled a little. Without a backward glance, I dodged the rest of the spot meant to toss me on my ass and strode out.

Nice try, sorry to disappoint.

The area of trimmed grass between the university's three main buildings—Killbrook Hall, which held the junior residences and the staff quarters; Ashgrave Hall, home to the senior dorms and the library; and Nightwood Tower, with all the classrooms—was definitely emptier than usual. Normally during class hours, there might have been dozens of students and teachers ambling across it and more in view farther afield.

But the junior fearmancers didn't take part in the summer session at all, and I'd heard only about half of the seniors attended. A handful were already setting off toward the Stormhurst Building closer to the lake, where the assembly was being held, and a few small clusters stood around the fringes of the green catching up after their time away. I didn't see anyone I knew all that well. No one I could be sure wasn't a threat, but no one who definitely *was* either.

Too bad it couldn't have stayed that way. I was just starting toward the Stormhurst Building at a leisurely pace when an all-too-familiar voice rang out.

"Couldn't wait to leap back into the fray, huh, Glinda?"

Malcolm Nightwood had just come around Killbrook Hall, his posture confident, his tone cocky. As often before, I was struck by the unfairness that a guy who could be such an asshole was so stunning to look at. His golden-brown hair with its hint of curl framed his face perfectly, his features such a perfect mix of sly and sweet that I'd thought of him as a divine devil when I'd first seen him.

The conversations around the green quieted at his arrival. The scions ruled this school, and Malcolm had set himself up as king of the scions.

I tensed as he approached, focusing twice as much magic on my mental shields. Malcolm's primary strength was Persuasion, and he'd gotten a lot of mileage out of inflicting that talent on me. I'd been getting better at shutting him out of my head, though.

How complicit in the barons' plans was he? It'd seemed like he and his dad were pretty tight.

"I was under the impression participating in the summer project was a matter of honor," I said with forced calm.

"Not much honor in it if you've got no hope of winning," Malcolm replied.

"I wouldn't count me out yet. I led my league to a win, didn't I?"

He made a scoffing sound, but it *had* been my approach that had allowed the Insight league to come out on top in last term's competition. Each student joined a league when they discovered or decided on their main area of magic, and the professors assigned credit throughout each full term based on spells cast in that area. The league with the most credit at the end of the term got to have the other three leagues cook and serve them an epic feast. Insight, not being a particularly flashy sort of magic, rarely won.

"You won't have a whole team behind you this time," Malcolm said. The remark didn't sound as threatening as I'd have expected the heir of Nightwood to make it. He was studying me, but his attention felt less aggressive than I was used to from him, as if he was evaluating me in a broader way rather than simply as a target.

Of course, I didn't want this guy evaluating me in any way at all. Any weaknesses he thought he'd spotted, it was fearmancer nature to exploit—and Malcolm seemed to enjoy exploiting weaknesses as often as he could. He'd messed with me way too many times and in too many horrible ways in the past for me to patiently wait around to find out what he was up to now.

"I'll remind you of that when you're eating my dust," I shot back. "For now, how about you make things easier for yourself and just fuck off."

I spun on my heel, hearing his sharp intake of breath behind me, half hoping that might be the end of it for now but knowing it probably wouldn't be. A second later, he spat out one of his casting words.

Advanced mages made up strings of syllables or contradictory phrases to direct their spells so that their target and anyone observing wouldn't be able to anticipate the effect. I knew exactly what Malcolm had tried to throw at me in an instant, though. He'd hurled a general insight spell at me like a spear aimed straight at my mental shields.

I hadn't been prepared for him to try insight. The wall around my mind could fend off a fair bit of magic in general, but I'd been focusing on the idea of preventing persuasive castings. The sharp edge of Malcolm's spell split a small crack in the barrier that made me wince. I murmured under my breath to tighten the layer of protection against that kind of intrusion.

Which was exactly what the Nightwood scion must have wanted. The second I'd shifted my focus, he threw out another comment, this one with the eerie lilt of magical compulsion.

"*Stop walking.*"

The persuasion spell pierced through my momentarily scattered defenses like a needle, finding the tiniest gap to stab into my brain. My feet jarred to a halt under me. Shit.

I heaved power into my shields. He'd only told me to stop. I wasn't letting him get in another command.

"Nice try," I said. "That's as much as you're going to get. And you know what, I bet I can make it to the Stormhurst Building without doing any walking at all."

Malcolm let out a quiet growl. "Lift," I murmured to my feet, and with a jerk I propelled myself an inch off the ground. "Float."

It took enough energy that sweat started to trickle down my back, but I drifted slowly along the path the way I'd meant to go.

"*Come back here*," Malcolm ordered, but the persuasion spell bounced off my defenses this time. His feet thumped against the path as he strode after me. He tossed out another nonsensical casting word —and an invisible wall slammed my shoulder, spinning me around. We were switching to Physicality now, were we?

I glared at him as I caught my balance and opened my mouth to shatter the force that had hit me—and a brawny figure hurtled into my field of view, straight toward Malcolm.

"Leave her *alone*," Connar Stormhurst barked, and shoved the guy he'd once called his best friend so hard Malcolm stumbled right off the path.

Malcolm whipped around. "What the fuck are you doing?" he snapped, staring at the Stormhurst scion. His face had flushed to an angry red hue.

I was staring at Connar too. The most physically intimidating of the scions had also proven to be the kindest for a little while. Connar and I had ended up bonding—in, er, ways both emotional and physical—during secret talks in his favorite clifftop spot away from the rest of campus. But he'd proven where his real loyalties lay by tearing me down on Malcolm's behalf not long after.

He'd said something to me about making up for it the last time I'd seen him, the night of the League feast. I'd been shell-shocked from Professor Banefield's murder, so my memory of that moment was blurry. I hadn't really considered whether or how he'd follow through on that promise.

Apparently he'd meant it—even more than I'd have imagined. He stepped between Malcolm and me, glowering at his friend, his entire muscular frame tensed. I'd seen him come at people who threatened the other scions before, but I'd never seen him turn physical aggression on anyone within the pentacle.

Neither had anyone else, from the expressions our spectators around the green were sporting. I had a feeling every mage on campus would hear about this confrontation by the end of the day.

"You've been waging this war long enough," Connar said to Malcolm. "It's time for it to stop. And since you didn't listen to me when I told you that, I'll just have to *make* you stop."

The spell that had pushed me around had faded. As I let my feet touch the ground, I realized the effect of Malcolm's persuasive spell had wisped away too. He might have been able to jab it through my shields, but not very deeply. I shifted my feet, and they moved just fine.

"I'm okay," I said cautiously. "I just want to get to the assembly."

Connar eased over to stand beside me. Malcolm stepped back onto the path, rage and betrayal etched all over his face. "I've been there for you through *everything*," he started.

"Right," Connar said before he could go on. "Because that's what we're supposed to do—look out for the other scions. Not tear them down. The pentacle shouldn't be divided, and it's not Rory who's dividing us. It's *you*."

He turned to me. "Let's go."

I nodded, a little stunned, and we turned our backs on Malcolm, who for once in his life was completely speechless. But as I set off for the Stormhurst Building, I couldn't help wondering if what Connar had just done had ended the war—or pushed it to an entirely new level.

CHAPTER FIVE

Rory

My altercation with Malcolm had sapped away most of the time before the assembly. Now that there was no spectacle to watch, a whole bunch of students were making their way to the Stormhurst Building. Connar walked steadily beside me, his jaw still tight, the muscles in his arms flexed.

I had no idea what to say to him. The history between us had gotten so messy.

"Thank you." That seemed like a reasonable place to start. But I also had to add, "You didn't have to jump in. I can handle Malcolm."

"I know," Connar said in his low voice, which was no longer taut with anger. "But I meant what I said. This feud has gone on too long, and I know you never wanted a war in the first place. Malcolm's just..." He sighed. "Maybe if enough of us put our foot down, it'll snap him out of the mindset he's gotten into."

He paused and ducked his head. "I'm sorry. I should have spoken up to him sooner—I obviously never should have lashed out at you the way I did. All I can say is... he has been there for me in an awful lot of ways for an awfully long time, and I'd gotten into the habit of trusting his judgment over my own. I didn't want to be the kind of guy who'd betray his best friend. I don't think I *am*, though. He needs to hear this. He needs to know it's gotten to be too much."

The pain in his expression made my chest ache in spite of everything. "Well, I'm still not happy about how horrible you were to me, and I wish you'd had this change of heart sooner, but… I am glad that you're seeing things that way now."

"I'm sure it'll take time for you to trust me again," he said. "I don't want to be pushy. You should just know that I'm on your side, officially." He glanced around at our fellow students, many of whom were continuing to shoot curious glances our way. "And very publicly, apparently. If you ever do feel you can turn to me and need to, I'll be there."

"Okay," I said, with a little relief that he wasn't pressing me to sort out my feelings or grant full forgiveness right this second. "I'll keep that in mind. And, just so you know, I really did mean that 'Thank you.' I get that it must be hard to stand up to him after being friends that long."

Imogen waved to me as I came into the gym where the assembly was being held, and as I headed over, Connar drifted away. He was keeping his word about giving me space, at least.

The forty or so students already in the space were buzzing with anticipatory chatter. I spotted Declan standing with several of the professors and a few other teacher's aides by the small platform that'd been set up, but he wasn't looking my way. I swallowed hard.

Things had gotten messy between him and me too, and that was mostly my fault. The trip to my family's country property near here should have been just a brief interlude away from the pressures of the school and everything else he was dealing with. A thank you for everything he'd been doing to protect me from larger forces that wanted to manipulate me behind the scenes—and, as it'd turned out, a chance to act on the attraction we'd held in check up until then.

And now that moment of indulgence could screw up everything he'd worked for. He'd helped me so much, but he had to keep his distance from here on. *I* had to make sure I didn't show our relationship had become anything beyond student and aide. I owed him that much.

"Do you have any idea what the project is going to be?" I asked Imogen as I came up beside her.

She shook her head, one of her usual silver clips flashing in her blond hair—a sparrow today. "No idea. They never let anything slip until the official announcement. Oh, there's Ms. Grimsworth. She'll deliver the news."

She rocked on her feet in anticipation. A few last students trickled in after the headmistress's entrance, a familiar head of floppy copper hair among them. I tensed at the sight of Jude, wondering if he was planning on making good on his promise to find some way to win me over before the assembly started, but before he'd looked my way, Ms. Grimsworth had gone up to the podium and picked up the microphone.

"Hello to our senior students who are participating in this year's summer project," she said in her cool voice. She looked prim as ever in her navy dress suit with her graying hair pulled into its tight coil at the back of her head. Her beady eyes skimmed over the crowd in the gym. "I know you're all eager to get started, so I won't keep you waiting. This year's project was proposed by Professor Crowford, although I expect it will involve many talents other than Persuasion."

The Persuasion professor tipped his head to her where he was standing by the edge of the platform with the other teachers. I thought the black streaks in his silver hair had gotten thinner since the last time I'd seen him.

Ms. Grimsworth leaned over the podium. "We'll have fifteen Nary students on campus for the summer session. Each of you will be assigned one as your target. You must come up with a specific outcome you wish to achieve with that student—an action you'd like to see them take, a habit formed—the larger and harder the impact earning you a higher score, naturally. Over the course of the next six weeks, you'll attempt to sway your target along your chosen course."

What? A wave of cold horror swept through me. It was bad enough that the administration brought in the nonmagical students to be used in more subtle ways without them knowing, but to instruct us to actively set out to alter their lives in some major way…

The headmistress wasn't even finished. "As you can probably determine, there are many more of you than there are Nary students. Your target will have three or perhaps even four other mages also trying to influence their behavior. If your opponents are careful, you won't even know who you're competing against. So you will not only need to affect your target if you wish to win, but offset the effects of other magic as well."

I glanced at Imogen, but she appeared to be taking this assignment in stride. Of course, she'd always been a little hesitant about including Shelby in any friendly activities. To her—to everyone in the room other than me, by the looks of things—there was nothing odd about this proposal at all.

"Throughout all this, you must remember the policies of Bloodstone University," Ms. Grimsworth added. "If you are careless enough that your target or any other Nary realizes that you're working a supernatural influence on them, you'll be immediately disqualified. Slow and steady will win the day here. Now come up and receive your assigned student."

She read out our names one by one, in alphabetical order by last name. That meant I was the third student called. Professor Crowford had stepped up in front of the podium to distribute the envelopes. He gave me a small smile as he handed mine to me. "I hope to see great things from you during your first summer project, Miss Bloodstone."

Apparently the disgust twisting my stomach wasn't printed all over my face. I slipped away to the wall and opened my envelope.

"My" Nary was a senior student in the architecture program, which I hadn't even known was one of the scholarship offerings. Benjamin Alvarez, twenty years old, with a shock of black hair and an intent expression in the photograph that came with the brief information sheet, which also told me he was staying in dorm A4. The second paper held his class schedule for the summer. The other blanks in my knowledge about him, I guessed I was supposed to fill in myself.

I scanned the gym as others went up to grab their envelopes. At least two other students had also been assigned Benjamin. What were they going to try to change about him?

What was *I* going to do to him?

The queasiness in my belly expanded. Would it be enough just to set out to stop him from being affected by any other magic? I should be able to manage that if I worked hard enough.

That wouldn't help the fourteen other Naries my fellow fearmancers would be bending to their will, though.

The last of the envelopes must have been handed out. Ms. Grimsworth started talking again.

"The Nary students will be arriving tomorrow. By the end of that day, you must turn in a paper with your mission statement, which I will hold onto. This allows us to confirm that whatever effects you achieve line up with your goals. And of course, there's the matter of the prize. As usual, the winner can request any object in their possession to be enchanted to the purpose of their choice by the professor of their choice. You could have one of these experts' skills at your disposal. Let's see who's up to the challenge. May the best mage win!"

It took a moment after I knocked on Ms. Grimsworth's office door before the headmistress answered. She peered at me, her expression puzzled before she schooled it to be impassive. I guessed she hadn't expected anyone to come calling quite this soon after the assembly. I'd let my feelings stew for about twenty minutes and then been unable to do anything other than march over here.

"Miss Bloodstone," she said. "Come in. Is there something I can help you with?"

I eased inside and waited until she'd shut the door. Nothing was burning on the shelves that lined her office walls, but a powdery whiff of incense smoke lingered in the air. I shifted on my feet on the thick rug.

"I hope so," I said. "I—I wanted to raise an objection to the focus of the summer project."

The headmistress's eyebrows jumped up. "And what objection is that?"

I clasped my hands together in front of me to stop them from fidgeting. "The Nary students come here without realizing anyone might be using magic on them. I already have a problem with the pranks and so on that get played on them during the rest of the school year. But this is encouraging us to yank them around and change them to our whims… It just isn't *right*."

"Mages have always needed to manipulate the nonmagical population in order to maneuver around them."

"But this isn't for survival," I protested. "This is going out of our way to treat them like puppets. Isn't that the opposite of learning how to live productively alongside them?"

Ms. Grimsworth's mouth had tightened. "I believe this assignment will actually stretch all of our students' abilities in that area—to help you learn the limits of how far you can extend your magic without tipping off the Naries to a supernatural presence."

"But—"

"Miss Bloodstone," she said firmly. "The project has already been decided. The professors take turns choosing on the content, and Professor Crowford's submission meets our guidelines. I don't expect the Nary students will come to any major harm. If they do, then please make that known to me. In the meantime, you may approach the project however you'd like, but the project itself stands."

She wasn't budging. I wasn't sure how much hope I'd really had that she would, but my spirits deflated anyway.

"Is that all?" she asked.

I couldn't think of any argument that would overcome her last statement. "Yes. But I might be back."

Did the corner of her mouth twitch upward just for a second? I might have imagined that. "And if you do, I'll be happy to hear your further concerns." She paused. "Have you been well during your break? I understand it may have taken some time to recover from recent… events."

From watching my former mentor stab himself to death in front of me? Yeah, that had been an event all right. I suppressed a cringe.

"I'm still upset about what happened, obviously," I said. "But I don't think it'll get in the way of my work here. I suppose... Professor Viceport is still my mentor now?"

I'd have rejoiced if the headmistress had corrected me. Viceport, whose specialty was Physicality, held some kind of a grudge against me that I hadn't figured out, other than she seemed to dislike the fact that I was a Bloodstone at all.

But Ms. Grimsworth was nodding. "You'll continue to meet with her once a week to discuss any concerns. We'll be distributing the new schedules later today. Classes continue during the summer in a modified form to directly tackle aspects of your project."

Wonderful. I managed not to groan and made my escape.

In the hall, I tipped my head back against the wall and closed my eyes to gather myself. Okay, so it didn't appear I could get this project cancelled. I'd just have to think until I came up with a strategy I could live with.

And if it was a strategy that would win me that prize, even better. There were a heck of a lot of uses I could think of for an object enchanted by one of the experts on staff—many of which could end up making the difference between whether I survived my time here or not.

CHAPTER SIX

Jude

My Nary target was a slip of a girl who wandered around campus in frilly dresses with hair that looked as if it hadn't been brushed since she got up. According to my project package, she was sixteen, but she didn't look much older than twelve. She basically embodied the word "feeb."

I couldn't say I felt any burning desire to make her acquaintance, but a certain amount of pity stirred as I watched her meander toward Killbrook Hall. It wasn't hard to imagine why Rory had been peeved about this assignment.

From the glimpse I'd caught of her face as Ms. Grimsworth had announced it, maybe "infuriated" was a more accurate word. It was a good thing I didn't really give a shit about winning this competition, because I sure as hell couldn't put in a solid effort without making the Bloodstone scion even more pissed off with me.

So I'd throw this game. No big deal. I cared a lot more about getting back into Rory's good graces than pleasing the professors. She was probably already coming up with some scheme to turn this project around. I'd give her a little longer for her initial fury to cool off, and then I'd come around offering my assistance, and we'd see if that didn't gain me some ground.

Just as the feeb disappeared into the hall bearing my family's name, Connar came ambling out. At the sight of my fellow scion, a prickle ran down my back. I had a few things to say to him right now.

I caught up with him halfway across the green and fell into step beside him, our footsteps rapping against the ground together, my slim shadow looking rather feeble itself next to his bulky one in the warm mid-morning sunlight.

"Mr. Stormhurst," I said with forced brightness. "I hear you've set yourself up as our Bloodstone scion's white knight."

Connar's expression twitched, but he had to have realized that a display that public would get talked about. He drew his chin up, his mouth firming. "She doesn't need a 'knight,' but it was about time someone stood up for the pentacle."

I guffawed. "Oh, this is all about scion solidarity, is it? And not at all because you'll champion your way into her bed?"

I hadn't really been sure whether attraction factored into Connar's motives, but the faint flush that crept up his neck gave me all the confirmation I needed. The guy could be a blockhead, but he had *eyes*. Rory was gorgeous no matter how you felt about her attitude, although personally it was her spirit I liked best. Even if her stubbornness was making achieving my aims difficult at the moment.

"That's not the point," Connar said. "She might not want anything like that after the way I treated her. And if she does, then it won't be any of your business, will it?"

"I just thought you might have forgotten that you can't offer her much of anything. Seeing as you're the only remaining Stormhurst heir, thanks to various violent takeovers."

That might have been a lower blow than was absolutely necessary. Some of that violence had come from the guy beside me. Connar's stance tensed, and his voice came out just barely above a growl. "That isn't how I wanted things to be. And *you* are in pretty much the same position, but that didn't stop you from chasing after her last term, did it? You weren't what she wanted, though, it seems like. Whatever she does now, it's up to her, not either of us."

"Of course," I said, letting my tone lighten again. I didn't really want Connar pissed off at me too. He was not a guy whose bad side you wanted to get on—and it actually did take quite a bit for him to hold a grudge, to be fair. He just needed to realize he couldn't expect to slide right into Rory's heart easy as pie. "But I intend to make her choice very easy. So don't get your hopes up."

I veered off as he reached Nightwood Tower, where he must have had class. I wasn't due anywhere until the afternoon, so I meandered vaguely in the direction of the lake, turning over possible grand gestures in my mind.

Driving all the way over to pay her a visit hadn't swayed her. Well, it might have if I hadn't somehow said the absolute wrong thing all over again. Just showing up on her doorstep now and saying I wanted to help might not cut it.

I could do better than that anyway. Scheming was my forte. How could we best turn this project on its head with maximum enjoyment along the way? If I came to her with a plan already worked out, or even in motion…

My mind was spinning through the possibilities so intently I almost ignored the jangle of my ringtone. It cut through my concentration, though—and there was a *tiny* chance it could be Rory, taking me up on my promise to win her over of her own accord. I fished the phone out of my pocket and grimaced when I saw it was my home line.

"Hi, Mom," I said when I picked up, because my father never called me. He barely spoke to me when I was in the same room as him, let alone a whole state away.

"Darling," my mother said, in a simpering tone that set my nerves on edge in an instant. It was the voice she used on my father when she had to give him news she expected him to react badly to—her walking-on-eggshells voice, I'd always thought of it as. She generally hadn't felt the need to use it on me. "How are you doing?"

"About the same as before I left home two days ago," I said breezily, staying wary underneath. "We got our summer project. Lots of work ahead. The usual crowd came for the session. Not much else to report."

"Well, at least there hasn't been any trouble." She let out a twitter of a laugh, which also sounded nervous. What the fuck was going on? Had Dad made a big to-do about something to do with me, and she was looking for me to smooth things over with him, as if it were my fault?

"Did you expect there to be trouble?" I asked. "What are you calling about, Mom?"

"Oh, I just—I would have told you while you were here, but there's so much uncertainty, especially at my age—I didn't want to bring it up until we were sure everything was progressing as it should, and now you might not be home for over a month..."

All her rambling was only making my skin tighten more. "*What* are you going to tell me?" I said. "You don't have to explain all that other stuff." *Just spit it out.* Before I broke the phone with how hard I was gripping it.

She sucked in a breath and gave another twittering laugh. "I'm sure this will be a surprise—it was to us—but we are so happy. You're going to have a little sister."

I stopped dead in my tracks where I'd still been moseying along the path, my heart plummeting to my stomach. One sharp word slipped out before I could control my reaction. "*What*?"

"I'm three months along now. We just got the results from genetics testing to make sure she's healthy—and the report gave us the gender too. Isn't it wonderful? Not that you weren't enough, of course, never think that, but we always did hope for two, and for it to happen after all this time…" Her laugh sounded genuinely joyful now. "Honestly I've had trouble believing it."

The strength in my legs wavered. I'd have leaned against something if I hadn't been in the middle of a damned field. Instead I let myself lower to the grass a few feet from the path. My heart still seemed to be pummeling my stomach with its thudding beat. The world around me had numbed.

"I guess Dad must be happy too," I managed to say. There was no way I could ask the question I really wanted to—but I already knew the answer to that, didn't I? I'd heard the way he talked about me. This pregnancy wouldn't have happened unless it was the way he'd have wanted. The way he'd wanted all along.

Fuck, fuck, fuck. I was screwed. Completely and utterly screwed, so much more than even before.

But Mom had no idea I knew about any of that. She babbled on about her due date in the new year and possible names and, like a knife to my chest, how thrilled Dad was, yes, completely.

As her voice washed over me, I thought back to the last two weeks at home. Dad had been his usual standoffish self… but I *had* thought once or twice that he'd seemed more affectionate toward her than he usually was, hadn't I? And maybe her spirits had been slightly more buoyant. The first signs had been there. I just never would have put the pieces together like this. She'd turned forty-five this year.

But it happened, especially when you had fearmancer doctors using magic to help things along. After all this fucking time…

I registered that she'd paused, presumably waiting for me to say something a little more meaningful than, "Huh," or "Great." I fumbled for my words. Generally I was rather good with them. At this particular moment, they careened around my head in total chaos.

If I gave away what I knew, I'd be in even deeper shit than I already was. I had to react like she'd expect me to.

"I'm so happy for you," I said, injecting as much warmth into my voice as I could summon. "And I'm looking forward to meeting her."

After I hung up, my hand dropped to my lap. I couldn't find the wherewithal to even return my phone to my pocket. I could barely focus on the scenery ahead of me as anything more than a greenish blur.

Six months. I'd thought I'd have years, maybe even decades, but now it was six months until my life completely imploded.

CHAPTER SEVEN

Rory

Benjamin Alvarez and his friends had obviously gotten wise during their years at Blood U. The four architecture students who were studying here over the summer had come onto the field behind Ashgrave Hall to work on sketches, and they positioned themselves back-to-back in a rough circle. As far as I could tell, it made conversation awkward, but it also meant no harassing fearmancer could sneak up on them.

Which meant that spying on them was a little tricky as well. I'd spotted them when I'd come out of the kennel farther up the field, after paying Malcolm's familiar a little visit. The Nightwood scion might have warned me off from Shadow, but the eager lift of the wolf's head when it'd heard my voice had been enough confirmation that in its opinion, I was perfectly welcome.

When I'd seen Benjamin with the others, I'd wandered into the forest that bordered the campus grounds and picked my way along through the cool shadows until I was as close as I could get while staying concealed. I'd still had to brainstorm my way into working out a sound amplifying spell so I could hear what the Naries were saying.

It was halfway through the afternoon, and I still wasn't sure what I was submitting as my project goal. Maybe my subject would give me some inspiration.

So far they hadn't talked very much, just brief comments of encouragement when one or another had shown off a sketch. Watching them, my fingers itched to create something myself. Back home, I'd sketched and then transformed those images into little sculptures all the time. Now, with magic, I could do way more way faster. I just hadn't had much time or energy to exercise my artistic side.

One of the two girls had brought a plastic grocery bag out with her. She'd been eating an apple when I'd first spotted them. Then she'd gnawed through a granola bar. Now she'd moved on to mini powdered donuts that required her to regularly wipe her fingers on the grass before she started drawing again.

As she started on her third of those, the other girl glanced over at her with a frown. "Are you okay?" she said, her voice turned tinny by my spell as it traveled to my ears. "We just had lunch a couple hours ago. Are you that hungry still?"

The girl's hand paused halfway to her mouth, and her cheeks reddened. "I know. I just—my stomach keeps feeling empty. I should probably stop now." She gulped down the rest of the donut and nudged the bag farther away.

My gut twisted. She didn't look like someone who regularly overate—she was pretty slim, really. And her friend obviously wasn't used to her snacking that much. I lifted my gaze to scan the area around the field.

My eyes caught on a figure propped against the side of Ashgrave Hall, mostly hidden in the building's shade. I couldn't recognize the guy at that distance—he wasn't anyone I knew well—but I could tell from his slick clothes that he was almost certainly a fearmancer, not another Nary. And I'd be willing to wager half the Bloodstone properties that he'd already picked his goal for his summer project target. He was trying to make her stuff herself… so she'd get fat? *That* was his big plan?

The girl was glancing at the grocery bag again, hunger pangs apparently still bothering her. I set my jaw and murmured a warding spell that I directed her way. It would cut off any magic flowing toward her, at least for now.

After a moment, the tension in her face relaxed. She went back to her sketching, no more longing looks at her snack stash.

I got a little relief from seeing that, if not much satisfaction. I'd protected her for now, but I couldn't follow every Nary on campus around, warding them constantly as my magic faded. It wasn't all that easy to cast a long-term spell on a living being to begin with.

Benjamin held up his latest sketch of a sweeping modern structure, and an idea tickled up from the back of my head. I couldn't make all of campus safe for the Naries, and none of it was really safe for them right now. Their dorms were shared with several fearmancers, and they had no magic to lock their bedroom doors.

What if they had a space here that was just for them, like we mages had the warded areas the Naries weren't allowed to know even existed? A building they could retreat to if the other students' aggression got to be too much. One spot would be much easier to ward. And I'd be playing to the strengths of my "target."

The inspiration came with an exhilarated rush. I watched the group for a few minutes longer as more and more pieces clicked into place in my mind, and then I hustled across the field, giving them a wide berth, so I could get writing.

When I came into my dorm room, Victory and Sinclair were lounging on one of the couches. Imogen was just clearing her dishes from the table after a late lunch. My nemesis ignored me, but Imogen caught my eye as I crossed the room and pulled a quick grimace that served as a warning.

The girls had been up to something. I braced myself as I opened my bedroom door.

For the first few seconds, I just blinked, my mind taking a moment to process the scene in front of me. They'd… turned all of my furniture upside down. The desk wouldn't have been that hard, but the bed tipped at an angle from its thick wooden headboard, the wardrobe with its knobby feet sticking up by the ceiling—that would have taken some effort. And I didn't want to think about the mess my clothes would be in when I managed to right it.

It'd have taken even more effort to break through the protections I'd cast on my door. I'd put a lot of energy into them... but Victory was one of the top students here at Villain Academy, and she'd had at least one helper. How long had they spent on this prank?

I didn't have time to worry about that. I closed the door without giving the girls the enjoyment of seeing my reaction and heaved the desk and chair over with just a quick punch of magic for help. I'd fix the rest later. Right now I needed to get this project statement written.

But as I sat at the desk with my back to my upside-down bed, the uncomfortable sense crept over me that even *I*, scion and nearly baron, didn't have any place on campus I could really call safe. I didn't even know who I could count on and who I needed to protect myself from.

Well, that wasn't entirely true. There was one person I was sure of. I'd just have to draw on some of that creativity of mine if I wanted to talk to him again.

By daylight, this plan had seemed pretty solid—and a little amusing too. Now, as I peered out my bedroom window toward the one below through the darkness just before midnight, I was starting to feel it might be full-out ridiculous.

It'd been the best option I could come up with, though. I'd be leaving no evidence like a text or a phone call would. There should be no chance of being interrupted in that one private space. I knew I could cast an illusion strong enough to hide a person.

Just go for it, I told myself as the cooling night air washed over me. I had to do something. If there was anything I was becoming convinced of by my time here at Blood U, it was that I wasn't likely to survive fearmancer society very long if I tried to go it alone.

I tested the length of hunting rope I'd been able to buy at a store in town. It held firm where I'd tied a knot to the leg of my now right-side-up bed, doubly secured with magic. I looked down the building toward the open window below mine again and murmured the words to reinforce the illusion I'd already cast. No one looking this way should see anything other than empty windows and a blank wall.

Clutching the rope, I clambered out the window. The taut material bit into my palms as I adjusted my weight so I was balancing between my grip on the rope and my feet braced against the stone wall. Then, with a shaky breath, I started walking my way down. I kept one hand tight around the rope at any given moment, moving one and then the other.

There was a five-story drop below me. I wasn't sure any mage had enough magic to heal me if I fell.

An ache spread through my fingers and then across my shoulders. My heel hit the window frame a moment later. It hadn't been that far a climb.

This was the tricky part, though. I eased myself to the left of the window and descended until I was level with it. Then I took a little jump and swung right through, tugging the rope with me.

Thankfully, the furniture layout in all the dorm rooms was essentially the same. I landed on a desk identical to my own, scattering a few papers that'd been left on it. At the thump of my arrival, the form under the bed covers jerked and shoved into a sitting position.

Declan squinted at me in the darkness of the room, his defensive posture relaxing as he recognized me. He didn't look exactly happy, though.

"What are you *doing*?" he said in an urgent whisper.

"Sorry." I slid off the side of the desk to plant my feet on the floor as quietly as I could. "Cast one of those silence spells?"

I knew he could manage it—he'd done it once before when he'd ended up stuck in my bedroom above while Victory and her cronies chatted outside. The Ashgrave scion's brow stayed furrowed, but he said something with a wave of his hand and let out a sigh.

He ran a hand through his black hair, the smooth strands adorably rumpled from his interrupted sleep. The whole room smelled like him —that warm and dryly sweet scent like cedar wood. My pounding heart started to slow as I soaked it in.

"Okay," he said, still quietly but no longer at a whisper. "Now are you going to tell me what you're doing here?"

I ducked to pick up the papers I'd scattered and set them back on the desk. "You don't have to worry. I cast an illusion spell so no one would see me coming down. It just—I needed to talk to you, and it was the only way I could think of that seemed totally, er, covert."

His eyebrows arched slightly. "Well, it was definitely that."

I shot him a mock glower for the teasing note in his voice, but my gaze couldn't help dropping over the slim but solid muscles that defined his bare chest. The covers were pooled on his lap—I couldn't tell whether he slept in pajama pants or boxers or… maybe totally naked?

A weird but giddy little thrill raced through me. When I raised my eyes to meet Declan's again, even in the dim moonlight, I could see the smolder that had lit there. And suddenly there was one thing that I absolutely had to do before we got to the talking part.

I stepped around the desk to the edge of the bed and leaned in, my hand rising to his cheek. I was half afraid Declan would pull away, but he shifted forward to catch my mouth with his. His fingers slipped into my hair, tracing trails of pleasure over my scalp as we kissed, and God, I wished we didn't ever have to stop. Why couldn't my life be just this?

When he did draw back, it was only a couple inches, his hand falling to my shoulder. His voice came out a little hoarse. "You know I don't like having to act as distant as I've been with you. If I could stand right there by your side—but with everything that's at stake—"

Affection for him, for everything he was trying to do and how hard he fought to hold it together, squeezed my chest. "I do know," I said. "Why do you think I went to all these lengths to arrange the stealthiest possible meeting?"

He laughed under his breath, and then he was tugging me to him again. He kissed me so hard my knees wobbled with the rush of pleasure. When he let me go, it took me a moment to catch my breath.

"I'm sorry," he said. "We shouldn't even— We *definitely* can't do anything else. Even this room isn't totally secure from intrusion."

Yes, there were more compromising positions that would be much harder to explain away than me simply being in his room. "Of course," I said. "But you don't have to apologize."

Before I ended up kissing him again, I sat down on the bed a few feet away, leaving what felt like a reasonable space. Declan scooted closer to the edge so that I only had to turn partway to look at him. "What's going on?" he said. "It must have been pretty important for you to go to all those lengths."

He had that lightly teasing tone again, but what I could see of his expression was serious. I swallowed hard. I had no doubt that I'd come to the right person, but discussing this still wasn't going to be fun.

"You heard what happened to Professor Banefield," I said.

Declan's mouth twisted. "He attacked you and then stabbed himself in some kind of delirium from his illness. Although I've been assuming there's more to the story than that."

"Yeah. That's just the official version. I didn't know how much to tell anyone else. I didn't know who I could trust." I looked down at my lap. "Someone made him sick—magically. I know because I was able to dispel the curse. But they left a failsafe in, one that meant he'd try to hurt me, to make it so I couldn't use my magic anymore. He killed himself to stop himself from doing that."

Declan sucked in a sharp breath. "God." He reached for my hand, and I let him twine his fingers with mine. His grip steadied me. "Did you find out anything about who cast those spells?"

I nodded. "He managed to tell me a little. He said… He said it was the older barons and someone called 'the reapers'."

"The barons." Declan's voice darkened. "I wondered, but they haven't said anything to me. They haven't even hinted… I knew they'd been making plans without looping me in. They don't totally trust me. Fuck." He paused. "And… the reapers?"

"That doesn't mean anything to you?" I asked. "I have no idea what he meant. And I didn't get a chance to ask for clarification."

"No. I've never heard anyone use that term to refer to anyone in the community. But I can do some digging and see if I can turn anything up. It's hard to keep something totally secret from a person who knows what they're looking for." He squeezed my hand tighter, and his expression shifted. "Speaking of which… your grandparents called on me."

Shit. I stiffened. "What did they say?"

"Well, they seemed upset that you hadn't gotten in touch with them yet, so it might be a good idea to do that soon if you can bear it. They made insinuations about our relationship—which of course I denied as blandly as I could—and then prodded me about helping them with some business deal that's being put to the barons."

"I'm so sorry."

"Not your fault. I can handle them."

"But anything I can do to convince them they've got nothing to hold over your head, the better." I bit my lip. "I'll give it my best shot. What do you think I should do about— We might not know who these 'reapers' are, but the barons aren't a secret. Is there something I should watch out for, some way I can defend myself better?"

Declan frowned. "I don't know. They shouldn't be meddling like this in the first place. If we had solid proof, it could cost whoever cast the spell or gave the order the barony. But that's exactly why they'll have been incredibly careful. It's impressive Professor Banefield was able to tell you as much as he did."

My poor mentor. "He did his best. He gave me a key, too, that he implied would lead somewhere important, but I have no idea what it's for."

"I can't help you there, but if you can find it, it might help a lot. I can pay extra attention to the barons' activities. It'd be hard for them to come onto campus without anyone noticing."

"They got to Banefield when he took a trip off-campus, I think," I said.

"That makes sense. So I'd be extra careful of any staff if you find out they've taken time off—or anyone new on campus who you haven't seen around before. And just watch for changes in behavior in general. That's where your skill in Insight will help you the most." He grazed his fingertips over my temple. "I'll keep an eye on the staff and students too. Between the two of us, hopefully we can pick up on any ill intentions before it turns serious."

I could take a little comfort from that solidarity, anyway. "Do you think—if the other barons haven't even told *you* what they're doing, will they have mentioned it to the other scions?"

The emphatic shake of Declan's head put that one worry to rest. "I talked with each of them to feel them out during the break. I can't promise they'll all be on good behavior, but everything I saw convinced me that none of them had a clue about a plot among the barons. They didn't even realize the professor who died had any connection to you."

"Well, I guess that's something." I groaned. "It's so hard not knowing who to trust."

"Hey." He waited until I met his eyes again. "I might not be able to offer you very much, but I can offer you this: I'll have your back in every way I can, no matter what happens. You can trust in that. I don't want to be standing in the pentacle of barons unless you're going to be standing there beside me."

My throat tightened as I smiled back at him, closing around the one secret I couldn't reveal even to him: that I didn't intend to stay among fearmancers long enough to take on the barony in the first place. But either way, I did still have to survive first.

I clasped his hand. "Let's hope we make it that far, then."

CHAPTER EIGHT

Rory

Malcolm must have been waiting for me to come down from my dorm. As I stepped out of the stairwell into the hall, he peeled himself off the wall across from me, his dark brown eyes fixed on me with a cool glower.

"Bloodstone," he said, "we need to talk."

I tensed automatically from head to toe—shields up, casting words at the ready, alert to any move he might make. But apparently he really did just want to talk. He tipped his golden head toward the far end of the hall and started ambling over as if he expected me to follow him.

I did, just a short ways, keeping a careful distance and trying to figure out what he was leading me to. I came around the bend to see him reaching for the door to the scions' basement lounge, and stopped in my tracks.

"If you want to talk, we can talk up here," I said. I had no interest at all in being alone in an enclosed space with this guy.

He stopped and folded his arms over his chest. He might not have been quite as brawny as Connar, but the pose still highlighted the ample muscle in his chest and arms. "I think it's best to keep scion business between scions, don't you think?"

I couldn't hold back my laugh. "Oh, like you've kept your issues with me so very private in the past? What's different this time? Are you starting to realize that you don't actually come off looking as impressive as you assumed you would when you try to push me around?"

His jaw tightened, and he took a step toward me. His gaze darted across the hallway and came back to rest on me. This end of the hall was decently secluded. If I yelled, there were plenty of people in the library and coming and going from the dorms who'd have heard, but speaking at normal volume, we wouldn't draw any notice.

Maybe I didn't want to be totally alone with the Nightwood scion, but I wasn't itching for an audience either. Having spectators seemed to add extra fuel to Malcolm's spite.

"I thought you were so big on conscience, Glinda," he said, his voice searingly cold. "Now seducing my friends so you can use them against me is fair play in your book?"

I blinked at him. "'Seducing' your friends? Excuse me? Who exactly are you talking about?"

"Connar didn't get it into his head to come to your rescue out of nowhere. He wouldn't throw away more than a decade of friendship over some girl out of nowhere. You might have picked insight, but somehow I suspect you've been honing your persuasive skills as well."

For a second I could only sputter, my throat was so choked with indignation. "Are you fucking kidding me? Maybe he just happens to think that you're wrong without any outside influence at all. I didn't even *ask* him to do anything, let alone magic him into jumping in."

Malcolm's glower came back. "Do you really expect me to believe that, especially when you've somehow convinced Jude to trot at your heels for weeks now too?"

I just about exploded then, but the murmur of voices carrying from around the bend brought me back to caution just in time. I schooled my voice as low as I could without diminishing the bite of anger. "I didn't *want* Jude's attentions. I've been telling him to leave me alone. You know, you really should spend some time paying attention to what's actually going on around you instead of making up stories in your head. I'm not the villain in this story to *anyone* but you."

"I can see perfectly fine," he snapped, his hands dropping to his sides as he shifted closer. His gaze didn't leave my face for a second. "And if you think casting a couple of love spells is going to make me go easier on you—"

"I didn't cast any spells," I shot back. "And you know what? Even if I was happily welcoming every guy in this school into my life and, hell, into my bed, it wouldn't be any of your business. Or do you think being king of the school means you get to decide who your friends date too?"

Malcolm's jaw clenched. "It's not dating if you're brainwashing them into it." But even though the words came out taut, I caught a flicker of some emotion other than anger in his devilishly divine face. Something that had come out when I'd mentioned taking guys into my bed. Something as hot and hungry as the way Declan had looked at me when I'd appeared at *his* bedside last night.

I'd have expected to recoil at the idea that Malcolm had any interest in me that way. Instead, the recognition sent a triumphant shiver through me. The magic that coiled behind my collarbone, born of others' fears and weaknesses, hummed in harmony.

There was a chink in Malcolm's armor. There was a way of dueling that I hadn't tried yet, one where I now knew I had the upper hand. Maybe a way to stop us going in more and more of these stupid vicious circles and put him off from hassling me for good.

And fuck, it would feel so good to win one real victory here.

I didn't question the impulse. It rose up in me like an instinct I'd always had, and I let it propel me forward. Close enough to jab my finger against Malcolm's well-built chest and watch the spark light in the back of his eyes.

"You know what?" My voice fell into a silkily cool murmur I hadn't known I had in me. "I don't think even you really believe all these stories about me working voodoo on your friends. I think you're just jealous that I'd even consider giving them the time of day when I can't imagine ever wanting anything to do with *you*."

Malcolm's stance went rigid. "What the fuck are you talking about? That's the last thing I—"

"No?" I said, cutting him off, and bobbed up the last short distance between us to brush my lips against his.

At least, it was supposed to be just a brush, the faintest whisper of a kiss to kindle a reaction. But oh boy, did he react. The second my mouth grazed his, he caught my jaw and tugged me closer, turning the kiss into a branding.

It wouldn't have mattered. He was proving me right. The problem was in an instant I wasn't so sure I had the upper hand here after all. The heat of his mouth blazed through me right down to my toes—fuck, the guy knew how to kiss—and a whole lot of other parts of me woke up with tingling attention.

I didn't *want* to want him, but apparently a significant portion of me did despite myself.

I jerked back, willing my breath to stay calm and the flush to retreat from my cheeks. With what remained of my composure, I managed to swipe the back of my hand across my mouth as if the kiss had been so distasteful I couldn't wait to wipe all trace of it away. Malcolm stared at me, his gaze outright scorching now, his stance momentarily hesitant.

Thank God for that brief hesitation. "I think I've made my point," I said with all the tartness I could summon from the whirl of emotions racing through me, and strode off before he might try to pay me back in kind.

What the fuck had I been thinking?

It was over. I'd kept up my front of being unaffected. The gambit might have worked, regardless of how I'd felt about it. No matter what else he felt about me, Malcolm wanted me, and he knew I knew it. That meant I had one thing over him I hadn't had before.

I could at least be thankful that my summer project target was predictable. Benjamin and his three architecture program friends took to what appeared to be their favorite spot in the field nearly every day in the early afternoon and stayed there for a couple hours as long as the weather was pleasant. Today, no one was lurking beside Ashgrave Hall watching them—until I took up that post myself, anyway.

Naries didn't have any mental shields, with no magic to generate them and no knowledge that they'd need to. I guessed that was part of what made them such appealing targets in general. I fixed my eyes on Benjamin's forehead from across the field and murmured my casting word for a general insight spell—the word that honored the family that had raised me to care about how others saw the world: "Franco."

I didn't want to delve too far. Benjamin Alvarez deserved as much privacy as anyone. But I needed to figure out the best way to motivate him toward my goal, which I suspected he'd have had as a goal of his own if he'd been given reason to think it might be possible.

I'd just have to give him that reason.

Impressions flitted through my senses. Insight wasn't a direct ask-and-answer situation even when you asked a specific question. You caught a glimpse of this and that inside the person's head and had to construct the meaning out of that.

Benjamin enjoyed the warmth of the sun and the soft cushion of grass beneath him. Pride rippled through his evaluation of the sketch he'd been working on—it was a building he was hoping he'd get to renovate someday back in his home town, wherever that was. I pushed a little deeper, sharpening my mind with thoughts of this school, of the potential hostilities of the other students.

Ah, there it was.

I caught a whiff of frustration in a memory of some guys jostling past him, skewing the line of his pencil. A general sense of always being watched. Unnerving pranks like all the writing instruments abruptly disappearing from his room. He rose above the tensions of the university pretty well, but the need for constant vigilance wore at him. I could relate to that feeling.

He wasn't going to need much persuading at all. He just needed to believe in the possibility enough to pursue it.

"*Look around,*" I whispered, aiming a waft of magic tinged with compulsion toward him. "*Look at all that space. There'd be room for a small building right here. The professor would be impressed if you proposed a project that hands-on. A clubhouse for the scholarship students. Why shouldn't you have your own space, especially if you can build it yourself?*"

Benjamin's head had come up. He gazed around him, and inspiration brightened his face. I had to smile. Beautiful. Of course, he'd be more likely to move forward if he had some concrete support.

"*Tell the others about it. They'll see what an awesome idea it is.*"

He turned and started talking to his friends with an animated gesture toward the field. A look of doubt came over one of the girls' faces, and I aimed another wisp of persuasion her way. "*You can make this happen if you campaign for it together. Just stand firm and draw your proposal up well.*"

Within a few minutes, the group was chattering away with excitement I could hear from where I was standing even if I couldn't make out their voices. I leaned back with a wash of relief and satisfaction.

The funny thing was, as large-scale as my plan was, it might be easier to pull off than what many of my peers would be attempting. They all wanted to push the Naries against their natural inclinations, to show how they could mess with them and lead them astray. I was giving them a task that appealed to them. I could nudge them along rather than drag them.

The hard part was going to be keeping them on track once my competitors figured out what path I'd set them on.

Footsteps rasped across the pavement, and I glanced around. Connar stopped a few feet away from me, glancing past me to the cluster of Naries and then meeting my eyes. He offered me a small but warm smile. "Getting a quick start on your summer project?"

My hackles came up instinctively, even though there hadn't been anything threatening in his tone. I tried to exhale my nerves, but I stayed wary as I answered lightly. "If I was, I wouldn't be supposed to tell you, would I?"

He chuckled. "No, I guess not. I'll be interested to see what you do come up with, though."

I gave him a more intent look with a hitch of my pulse. "What are *you* planning to do to your Nary?"

"That's my secret too, isn't it?" he said, but his smile faded as he took in my expression. "I'm not aiming for anything big. Just enough that I can say I tried. The skills this assignment is going to take aren't really my forte." He paused. "And it's a little cruel, isn't it—setting out to push them around when they've got no way of defending themselves?"

"Yeah." I relaxed a little at those words and checked the time on my phone. "I've got to get to a seminar."

"I'll walk with you to the Tower? I have a Desensitization session." He made a slight grimace. What fears did that chamber throw in the Stormhurst scion's face?

I couldn't see how it would hurt to just walk with him. "Okay," I said. But we'd only taken a few steps across the green when I tensed up all over again—not because of Connar, but because of the lanky figure who'd emerged from Nightwood Tower to stride toward us.

Jude's gaze took the two of us in with a flick of his dark green eyes. I expected some kind of flirty comment or ribbing remark, but instead his expression soured in a way I'd never seen before. My body instinctively braced even more.

A response which mustn't have been lost on him. "You don't need to worry about me," he said to me in an unusually flat voice as he reached us. "I'm not going to make any demands on your precious time today."

Where had that bitterness come from all of a sudden? I opened my mouth, searching for an appropriate reply, but Jude's attention had already shifted to Connar. "Enjoy it while it lasts. It's not as if it's likely to for very long."

He marched on past us with such a grim smolder that I couldn't help staring over my shoulder at him as he disappeared into the hall behind us.

"What's going on with him?" I said.

Connar was peering after Jude too, his brow knit. "I don't know," he said. "Usually even when he's pissed off, he manages to sound a lot more energetic while he's ripping into you. I don't know if I've ever seen him quite that… deflated." He shook his head. "Whatever bad moods he gets into, he usually snaps out of them pretty fast, though."

I hoped that was the case with this one, rather than it being some kind of omen of worse to come.

CHAPTER NINE

Malcolm

My dad had a way of expressing disapproval with nothing more than the way he drew in his breath, like he did right now when the nachos I'd ordered while I was waiting for him arrived at our booth in the back of the bar. The nachos were as posh as the gleaming modern space itself—they had fresh crab meat on them, for fuck's sake—and they were the best food the place made, but no doubt Dad could only think "feeb food" when he looked at them.

"You're welcome to some," I said as I grabbed a cheese-and-crab laden chip. There was no way he'd touch the stuff, but he'd probably be even more irritated if I didn't offer than he was by my order in the first place.

"I've already lunched, thank you," he said in his usual cool tone, and took a measured sip from his Old Fashioned.

I wasn't sure what this meeting was about. He'd been working on some sort of business not far from the university and texted me to suggest an early afternoon drink in town. It couldn't be simply that he wanted to pass on instructions or criticism. The former he'd have handled by phone, and the latter he'd never have done in public.

Whatever was on his mind, it was important enough that he wanted to judge my response in person. That probably didn't bode well.

A Nightwood never let discomfort show. Or impatience. I took another chip, this one with ample salty avocado, and pretended I wasn't concerned about anything other than the crunch and the flavors mingling in my mouth.

They always had the air conditioning turned a little too high in this place. I'd worn a thin shirt today in consideration of the summer heat, and now I was fucking cold, but I couldn't let that show either.

Dad said a word and raised his hand, and I knew he'd cast a shell of privacy around our booth. The staff and other patrons wouldn't hear our conversation.

"You've made far less progress with the Bloodstone scion than you promised us," he said.

My back tensed automatically. I finished chewing and swallowed, but the mouthful sank like a lump of stone into my stomach.

"I've landed plenty of blows," I said. "She just keeps bouncing back from them. Growing up with joymancers and feebs obviously didn't dull the Bloodstone spirit all that much. The pressure will still be adding up. She'll crack eventually." I paused, glad I could observe *his* response to this comment face-to-face. "Especially now that her original mentor situation imploded in epic fashion."

If Dad had anything to do with or knew anything suspicious about Professor Banefield's violent demise, he didn't show it. His face stayed in that mildly bored expression that was at least better than his chillingly angry expression or his delightedly vindictive expression. Declan *could* be wrong about there being anything to the death other than a natural if potent illness.

But, as irritating as this fact could be, if Declan was confident enough in a theory to put it forward, he was generally right. The guy was nothing if not conscientious. And Dad could bluff with the best of them. So I really didn't know anything more about the professor's death now than I had before.

I'd have liked to think my parents were above murdering bystanders to get their way, especially when they'd supposedly been allowing me to make a go at their goals. Their methods might have been harsh, but there'd always been a clear if cold logic to the lessons they'd taught me. A Nightwood should have more honor than to slaughter respected members of the community because a foe proved a little difficult to tackle head-to-head.

Did Mom and Dad uphold those values to the letter, though? I couldn't say I believed that with total certainty. Rory was a pain in my ass and a threat to the balance of power at school, sure. To Dad, she was the final piece in a full pentacle, the one sticking point before the barons could do… whatever exactly they were so keen to get done. He didn't discuss policy with me.

He'd let me know when he felt I'd earned that right.

"I think you've had plenty of opportunity to make use of your own resources," he said now. "In some ways, you may have inadvertently encouraged her resilience. From here on, I think it's better if you don't associate with her at all, at least until she's had the necessary attitude adjustment."

I couldn't stop myself from staring at him for a second as he took another sip from his glass. "You want me to completely back off? To let her do whatever the hell she wants?"

Dad's eyes narrowed a smidge. "I trust you can handle the change in a way that doesn't diminish your standing."

You'd better handle it that way, his tone said, *or there'll be hell to pay when you're next home.*

"Whatever you've got planned, I can at least assist," I said. "I'm right there on campus—it doesn't make sense for me to—"

"We'll decide what's most sensible. And right now we have our next steps well in hand with no additional involvement necessary. Your observations may still be valuable, but that's all I want from you. Understood?"

Anger flared in my chest, sharp and searing. *I'd* been the one dealing with Rory's stubborn defiance from the moment she stepped onto campus. I'd nearly had her on her knees at least once. He'd talked to her all of once for five minutes and he thought he could judge how to tackle her better than I could? He thought he could accuse me of making things *worse*? What the hell would he have done differently?

"If that's what you think is best." I bit back that frustration and dug into my nachos instead. I'd done every goddamn thing he could have asked of me, and he—

With reflexes honed from two decades of vicious little tests, I registered the weirdly brittle texture between my teeth just as the first faint prick of pain echoed through my tongue. All my attention narrowed down to the sensations inside my mouth. Yep. Right there. Without my even noticing the spell, he'd conjured a sliver of glass into my lunch.

I kept my face impassive as I shifted the food carefully and raised my napkin to my lips. I didn't even look at the shard as I spat it into the cloth. A metallic hint of blood flavored the rest of my mouthful.

Dad didn't say anything, so he must have been satisfied with how unfazed I'd appeared. He threw back the last of his drink and stood up. "I know I can count on you. There'll be plenty more responsibilities ahead if all goes well."

I allowed myself a brief glower at his retreating back. He counted on me to do shit-all, as far as I could tell.

The plate in front of me no longer looked particularly appealing. That sliver of glass might be a one-off—or he might have laced the whole heap of nachos with them to express his displeasure with my meal choice. I debated for a second and then gestured for the bill.

The walk back to campus didn't do anything to burn off the prickling energy churning inside me as if I'd swallowed a whole plateful of glass shards. I kept going, past the main buildings to the kennel where my familiar was cooped up during class hours, as usual.

Shadow perked up at my entrance, his feet pattering against the floor as he bounded to the stall door. I stepped inside and sat down with my back against the wall, and he pushed right against me. With a pleased huff of breath, he nuzzled my shoulder.

I scratched his favorite spot behind his ears and breathed in his warm wolfy smell. It wasn't quite as comforting as it'd been when I was only twelve and I'd had a whole lot less weighing on my shoulders, but it still took the edge off.

I knew who I was. I knew what I was capable of, even if Dad didn't. Fuck him and the rest of the barons.

Not that even Shadow completely had my back when it came to Rory. He'd turned traitor thanks to her softening-up routine too. If she'd outright attacked me, he'd have defended me, but a wolf didn't understand the more subtle ways a person could pick away at your defenses.

I'd told her to stay the hell away from him, but she obviously hadn't listened. A ball lay in the corner that I hadn't brought for Shadow to play with. I glared at it, trying to summon more fury, but it was hard to be really angry about *that* with my familiar fawning over me showing just how hungry for attention he got in here. Maybe she was only visiting him to mess with me, but he did get something good out of it.

That was becoming a common theme. As Shadow flopped down on the floor next to me, his head resting on my knee at the perfect angle for more ear scratches, my mind skipped back to that moment in the hall a few days ago. To the perfect sweet press of Rory's lips against mine. My heart thumped faster just remembering it.

I didn't think she'd been trying to soften me up with that. No, she'd been using it as one more ploy in our escalating feud. But damn, it *had* been good. To feel all the fierceness in her body radiating into me, to absorb some of that fire…

She'd made a show of dismissing the kiss, but I'd been with enough girls to get a read on when someone was into the moment and when it was time to ease back. For just a second before Rory had yanked herself away, she'd leaned into me. It'd been good for her too, even if she didn't like that she'd liked it.

I wet my lips, and a slow smile crept across my face. Dad didn't know what the fuck he was getting into, trying to break Rory down. I could step back from my other tactics, but she'd just opened up a whole new avenue of competition. There were so many ways I could throw her off without doing anything you could call harm, and I'd enjoy it a hell of a lot more than any skirmish we'd gotten into before.

I still ruled here at Blood U, and no one—not my dad, not Rory, not my traitor friends—was going to stop me from living that role to the fullest.

CHAPTER TEN

Rory

In some ways, the reduced student population during the summer was nice. There were fewer random seniors around to either try to take a jab at me or try to hit on me, both attempts to boost their own standing. More chance I'd get a little welcome solitude in my dorm room. Only half as many witnesses to any noise I made in the grips of the nightmares that still haunted me—not magically induced now, but still painful, with Professor Banefield's death taking a spot amid the reruns of my parents' murders.

On the other hand, fewer students meant I saw more of the same people in our sporadic classes. My current Physicality workshop included not just Connar but Victory and Cressida as well.

I'd chosen a spot in the front corner, and now I was regretting that. My two dormmates' murmurs and giggles from a couple rows behind me made my nerves jitter on high alert, but I couldn't see what they might be up to. With Professor Viceport gliding back and forth at the front of the room, eyeing my work with particular critical attention, I couldn't afford to let myself be distracted anyway.

All our classes during the summer session revolved around our project, and today Viceport had us focusing on conjuring scents. "Smell is a powerful but often overlooked sense," she'd said at the start of class. "It can provoke powerful emotions in an instant, draw a person in or repel them away. When you're directing your target, you may find it an incredibly useful tool."

We were actually working two different skills, though. So that we—and she—could evaluate our own conjured scents accurately, we'd first needed to construct a bubble of magic around us that would hold our work in and prevent mingling. Thankfully I had plenty of experience generating walls and other barriers at this point. Not that I'd ever thank Malcolm for that.

At the moment, we were supposed to be pulling together a scent that we felt would calm our target and make them more open to suggestion. The idea turned my stomach, but as long as no one was going to force me to use this skill on my Nary, I could go along with the assignment here.

I'd tried merging lavender, which was supposed to be relaxing, with a sort of fresh-baked cookies smell that brought an ache into my chest remembering that scent in my parents' kitchen. When I'd been a kid, I'd have found it comforting.

Viceport was making her way toward me now, stopping at the desk two over from mine to lean into that student's bubble. I drew in a breath and urged a little more buttery doughy scent into the mix.

A tingling sensation shot past my ear, and all at once the smell I'd conjured turned sour and rancid, as if the cookies had gone moldy. My stomach lurched, and I diffused the odor as well as I could. I didn't want to send it flying out into the rest of the air for the professor to notice. Not that I had much time to come up with something different to offer her now. She was just moving to my neighbor's desk.

A faint snicker behind me told me exactly who I could thank for the disruption, if I couldn't have already guessed. I gritted my teeth as I worked more of the stench out of the air.

I'd had enough of taking the high road. I wasn't going to stoop to Victory's level and launch unprovoked attacks, but she could damn well find out that if she took a shot at me, it'd rebound right back at her.

I condensed what remained of the smell into a compact spear of air. With a quick glance over my shoulder, I confirmed exactly where Victory was sitting. "Pierce," I murmured, and whipped the stench toward its creator with a flick of my hand.

I didn't have a whole lot of experience trying to sabotage people, so maybe I tossed it Victory's way a little more forcefully than was necessary. I knew it'd hit the mark, at least, from her startled but furious gasp. Her clothes rustled as if she were wiping at them—had I sent the smell right onto *her* instead of just into her bubble?

The corner of my mouth twitched with a smile I couldn't restrain. That should make her think again if she felt like screwing with my magic, anyway.

I scrambled to recreate my original scent as Professor Viceport nodded to my neighbor and offered a couple of suggestions. The lavender prickled my nose a little more pungently than I'd have preferred, and the sweetness of the cookie scent overwhelmed the doughy aspect that I liked best, but at least I had an approximation of what I'd been going for when Viceport stopped in front of me.

"Ready, Miss Bloodstone?" she said in the icy voice that only I seemed to receive. Her pale eyes, equally cold, peered at me from behind the rectangular panes of her glasses. Between that, her wispy ash-blond pixie cut, and her skinny but elegant frame, she fit the "Ice Queen" nickname a whole lot better than I ever had.

"It still needs some refining," I said, "but you'll get the general idea."

I started to speak to adjust the bubble so she could take a sniff inside—and another tingle raced past me, this one ten times as violent as before. I didn't have a chance to so much as flinch before my shell of magic burst apart with a force that smacked my face. And Viceport's too, from her wince. The scent I'd conjured dissipated in an instant.

"Miss Bloodstone," Professor Viceport said sharply, raising her chin and peering down her nose at me. "I expect a mage of your supposed caliber to maintain far better control over your conjurings. Have you learned *nothing* in the last three months?"

My hand clenched on the desktop. I forced my voice to stay even. "There wasn't a flaw in my conjuring. Someone else shattered it."

She sniffed. "Come now, you should at least be above blaming others for your own failings. Although perhaps I shouldn't be surprised."

What was *that* supposed to mean? I held my frustration in by a fraying thread of self-control. "I'm simply telling you the truth. It isn't as if sabotaging other students is an uncommon occurrence around here, is it?" It wasn't that she couldn't believe someone would have done it, only that she'd rather blame me.

"I'm sure all of your classmates are currently fully occupied with their own work. You must admit you've had plenty of struggles in the past. Now—"

A low voice interrupted from the other side of the room. "Rory's telling the truth. I saw Victory cast something at her."

My head jerked around at the same time Viceport's did. We both stared at Connar. He looked back at us, his expression tense even though his tone had been matter-of-fact.

Victory had turned to look at him too, although *her* eyes were narrowed into a glare. Beside her, Cressida's face had turned pink with a nervous flush. They obviously hadn't expected to be taking on two scions today.

"Professor Viceport," my nemesis said quickly in her most honeyed voice, "I think Connar must have misinterpreted what he saw of my casting—"

Connar shifted his already impressive form taller in his seat. "I'm the most skilled Physicality mage out of all the students at Blood U," he said firmly. "I know how to tell what I'm looking at."

Viceport's mouth twisted as if she resented having to address this new development at all. She sighed.

"Well," she said, "I can't give credit to anyone, since it appears you all bungled what you meant to do." Her gaze slid back to me. "Even if your fellow students decide to interfere, it's up to you to keep your castings solid. I'll evaluate your performance in this exercise based on past demonstrations."

A whole lot of which I'd struggled with for reasons I didn't totally understand. But I didn't see how else I could argue with her. At least Victory wasn't getting any praise for getting caught in her trick.

I thought that would be the end of it, but Connar spoke up again, his voice quieter but still grave enough to command attention. "There's actually something else I need to talk to you about, Professor. After class lets out."

Victory and Cressida shot wary glances Connar's way as they gathered their things to go at the end of the workshop, but he didn't acknowledge them in the slightest. Whatever he had to talk to Professor Viceport about, they were obviously worried it might have to do with them… but they couldn't defend themselves without admitting they'd done something that needed defending. After a moment, they filed out of the room with the rest of the class.

I grabbed my purse, planning to follow—very carefully, in case of potential ambush on the stairs—but Connar motioned to me as he went to the professor's desk. His expression wasn't just grim but a little green now. Whatever he was going to talk about, he didn't feel good about it.

"You should hear this too," he said.

Viceport folded her hands together where she was standing behind her desk, her lips pursing. "What is this about, Mr. Stormhurst? I don't think there's anything more to be discussed regarding today's performances."

"It's not about today." Connar inhaled sharply. "You've gotten a skewed impression of Rory's abilities in Physicality not just today but for the last two months. I've been intermittently… interfering with her conjurings. Weakening them, making them disperse. I know protecting our castings is an important skill too, but I think you can agree that expecting a student just learning how to control her abilities to protect herself from the top student in that area is above and beyond."

My whole body had chilled. It took me a second before I could force out the words. "You were throwing off my spells, all that time…?" He'd done it so subtly I'd never even suspected someone else's magic had meddled with mine.

Now he looked even more sick. "I stopped a couple of weeks before the end of term. I shouldn't have—it's complicated." He fixed his gaze on Professor Viceport. "The successful castings that Rory has managed are reflective of her true abilities, not the others. I regret interfering, and I think she should be judged based on her actual talent. That's why I'm telling you."

Viceport had gone a bit paler even than usual. She pinched her nose just below the bridge of her glasses as if she had a headache. "All right," she said. "Thank you for your candor, Mr. Stormhurst. Credit to Physicality for carrying out your intentions in a way neither I nor Miss Bloodstone clearly caught on to. I'll keep this information in mind as we proceed."

I wasn't even surprised anymore that she didn't offer any punishment or even a chiding word. Blood U encouraged its students to be cutthroat. Any of the professors, even Banefield, would have said it was my job to learn how to defend myself. But Connar's admission still left me numb, as if I hadn't already known he'd made himself my enemy.

Viceport appeared to be done with us, so I hurried on out of the room. Connar didn't have any trouble catching up, though.

"Rory," he said, following me down the stairs, "I'm sorry. That's *why* I told her—why I wanted you to hear it too. I know I can't make up for everything unless you know everything I've done."

I walked on without looking back at him. "If you expect kudos just for owning up to doing something shitty—"

"I don't." He swallowed audibly. "I'm trying to do the right thing—that's all I've ever been doing. I honestly thought I was doing the right thing before. All I can tell you is how sorry I am and how stupid I feel for not listening to my gut sooner. And that's it. There's nothing else I did to trip you up that you don't know about it. I felt like shit the whole time I was doing even that much."

"So why the fuck did you do it?" I spun on him at the next landing. "I still don't understand that. Did Malcolm ask you to attack my work?"

The guilty tightening of his mouth told me enough.

"Oh," I said. "And of course you had to go along with it because he's such a good friend."

"He is," Connar said. "When he isn't being a jackass, anyway, which is actually most of the time, as hard as that might be for you to believe. But he's wrong about this—he's wrong about you—and I've told him that, more times than just the other day. I'll keep telling him until he sees it." He paused. "I can make up for screwing up your castings directly—if you want any extra tutoring—I can teach you the best tricks I've learned over the years…"

The hope that crept across his face with the offer made my insides ache all over again. "Let me see," I said abruptly.

He blinked at me. "See what?"

"That you're telling the truth. That this isn't another way to mess with me. Let me use insight on you."

I'd done it once before, skimming the surface of his mind, without him even knowing it. But I wanted full access right now—and I also wanted to see how he'd react to the request.

He hesitated, as I guessed anyone would when asked to open up the contents of their head for someone else to rummage through. Then he nodded. "Go ahead. Look as much as you want. I owe you that."

He came down the last step to stand on the landing next to me. I fixed my gaze on his forehead, tamping down on my awareness of his presence, his body, so close to mine.

"Franco," I murmured.

Connar had taken down any walls he normally kept up. I tumbled straight into the whirl of impressions. A pang of guilt raced through my awareness, followed by a burn of shame, a flicker of Malcolm's furious face in the scions' lounge, a wave of loss as I'd crumbled the dragon figurine I'd made for Connar in his hand. Over it all was the stark sear of desperation and longing as he looked at me right now, wanting so badly for me to recognize his repentance.

The force of all those emotions squeezed the breath from my lungs. I pulled myself back out with a gulp of air. Connar watched me, waiting, his hand closed tight around the railing.

He *was* sorry. I believed that now without a doubt. But he'd also honestly thought that tearing me down was a reasonable expression of loyalty not that long ago. The regret he felt today wasn't necessarily permanent.

"Okay," I said. "Apology accepted. Forgiveness might take a little longer. So will deciding whether to trust you with that extra help."

"Of course," Connar said with obvious relief. "Take all the time you need."

He dipped his head to me and continued on down the stairs, giving me space as well. I watched him disappear around the bend, somehow feeling even more uncertain than I had before.

CHAPTER ELEVEN

Rory

I might not be looking to continue my romance with Jude, but he had taught me some useful things during our brief friendship-and-more. One of those was not to worry about breaking the rules so much as ensuring I didn't get caught. So I watched the hall that held the teaching staff's quarters carefully as I magically sprung the lock on Professor Banefield's office door, but I didn't hesitate before stepping inside.

It'd been nearly a month since his death, but the maintenance staff had left the room pretty much as it'd always been. I'd heard that Ms. Grimsworth was having trouble tracking down his next of kin. The new junior Insight professor she'd brought on had taken a different, vacant office.

As my gaze traveled over the familiar bookshelves and the desk where I'd so often sat across from my mentor, my heart squeezed. The air smelt a little stale and the space was dim with the curtain mostly pulled over the small window, but something of Banefield's upbeat demeanor still lingered.

He'd been the only authority figure at the school who'd been anything like warm with me. Maybe I hadn't agreed with his attitudes about Naries—the same ones so many other fearmancers shared—but he'd been willing to listen to my arguments. He'd seemed to really consider them. He'd talked me through so many of my worries and my struggles with my magic.

And when push came to shove, he'd put his whole life on the line to save me.

I dragged in a breath past the heaviness in my chest and began my circuit of the room. Every book, every container on the shelves, I needed to check for some spot, obvious or hidden, where the key he'd placed in my hand might fit. It didn't seem likely that he'd been keeping whatever he wanted me to find right here, or he'd have handed it straight to me, but I didn't have much else to go on.

The office didn't turn up anything. There were a couple of drawers with keyholes on the desk, but one of them was already unlocked and the other one didn't accept my key. I walked over to the far door that led into the professor's private quarters, the weight inside me getting heavier.

The last time I'd been in those rooms, I'd cured Professor Banefield of his cursed illness—and then he'd tried to destroy my magic. Instead he'd ended up gouging his own heart.

I braced myself as I murmured the unlocking spell and eased the door open. The hall on the other side was equally dim. But the maintenance staff had clearly come through here to do some basic clean-up. Only a hint of the sickly sweat smell from his long sickness remained in the air. The tiled floor in the kitchen shone pale beige, no trace of his blood remaining. Even in his bedroom, where he'd lain in a stupor for weeks, the bed had been made with clean sheets tucked neatly around the mattress.

I wouldn't have wanted to see the mess, but this sanitized space left my skin creeping. It was as if Banefield's final days and selfless sacrifice had been completely erased. You wouldn't have known anyone had existed in this space at all recently.

Walking into the kitchen made my wrist twinge where Banefield had gripped it so hard he'd bruised me. I shoved the memories aside and forced myself to focus on my search. I needed to find *something* to give me a direction. Otherwise that sacrifice of his wouldn't have accomplished half of what he'd wanted it to.

I didn't discover any secret safes or secured cupboards. My spirits had sunk by the time I reached the last focus of my search, the living room. No unexpected objects lay behind the sofa or the armchairs. The side tables had no compartments, and the drawer on the oak coffee table opened at my tug. All it held were a few papers.

With a looming sense of hopelessness, I sifted through them. My hand paused over an envelope. I drew it out.

The envelope and the papers inside didn't offer any specific clues. They appeared to be a letter from a friend or colleague about some area of magical study Banefield had been researching—nothing to do with me, as the date at the top was from before I'd even arrived here. But they gave me something else that might be even better.

The letter hadn't been sent to Professor Banefield here at the university. The writing on the envelope was an address in a town I didn't recognize somewhere else in New York state.

Of course Banefield had his own home apart from here. A place he might have felt was more secure from the people who'd wished me and him harm?

I took a picture of the address with my phone. As soon as I had the chance to take a road trip out there, I'd have to find out whether that place held the answers I needed.

As I took my seat for my morning Persuasion seminar a couple days later, I found myself eyeing Professor Crowford's lightly lined face more warily than in the past. I couldn't have said I'd been especially fond of him before, even though he'd intervened a couple of times to save me from potential embarrassment when Malcolm and I had faced off. The professor always kept a suavely detached air as if he saw our squabbles and other classroom activities as a mild amusement rather than anything serious.

The summer project he'd chosen made me rethink my neutral opinion of him. He wasn't just dismissive of the Naries like every fearmancer I'd talked to other than Declan was—he'd thought it'd be a good idea to encourage the entire student body to manipulate them way beyond what normally happened here. There was a particularly cruel, callous side hiding under those fading good looks.

I was distracted from my analysis by Malcolm's arrival. The Nightwood scion didn't look at me as he sauntered across the room to claim the seat at the other end of the row, but my whole body sprang into extra alertness. Persuasion was his specialty, and he did enjoy using it on me.

And he still hadn't done anything to get back at me for that kiss I'd intended in mockery the other day.

A couple more students filed in, leaving one empty desk at the back. Professor Crowford considered it and then the doorway, and seemed to decide whoever hadn't yet arrived shouldn't hold up class. He stepped around his desk and clapped his hands authoritatively.

"All right, let's get down to business. Since I set you off on your project this summer, I suppose I'd better supply you with some innovative strategies for accomplishing your goals. One thing I want you to keep in mind is that while we most often focus on using persuasive spells to direct the *actions* of others, they can be equally powerful in directing thoughts and emotions. For a more subtle change in behavior, that's where you'll want to at least start."

He went on to describe a trick for provoking a mild emotion in your target using your own memories as a sort of fuel. I found myself listening intently despite my qualms about the project, because hell, I still needed to do some persuading, even if it was with good intentions.

Benjamin had seemed pretty excited about the clubhouse idea the few times I'd encouraged his discussions with the others along as they'd worked out their design proposal, but you never knew when doubts might set in. Especially since there were at least a couple other mages who'd be pushing him in different directions.

A faint warmth brushed over my left knee. I glanced down automatically, my leg stiffening, but… nothing was there. My pant leg looked perfectly normal.

But as I watched, the sensation returned. If I hadn't been looking right at my knee, I'd have sworn someone had teased their fingers across it and then, slowly, softly, settled their hand just above it. It wasn't an especially intimate touch, and the carefulness of it stopped me from leaping out of my chair in response. It held there, a spot of gentle warmth in a gesture that could have been comforting if it hadn't been so bizarre and unexpected.

My gaze jerked up with a sudden suspicion. Past the student sitting between us, Malcolm was watching Professor Crowford with apparently rapt attention. But his right hand was resting on his desk with the fingers slightly curved as if cupped around something about the size of a knee.

A person's hand could have fallen into that position by coincidence, but as I watched, he glided his thumb a few inches through the air. A teasing pressure traced over the outside of my leg.

Fuck. He must have cast some sort of illusion spell to make me feel the movements of his hand as if he were touching me. To pay me back for the kiss? To try to distract me from the lesson? To make some other point about how I'd react?

Probably all three of those at once.

I just had to ignore it. A slight warmth on my knee—no big deal. If I *didn't* react, then I'd have won.

I focused my attention back on the professor's lecture. It should have been easy to tune out Malcolm's current gambit. The sensation wasn't that intrusive.

But his fingers moved again, a breath of a caress that grazed my skin through the fabric of my pants, and a quiver of heat shot up my leg. Just for a second, the kiss came back to me—the searing determination with which he'd kissed me back, the jolt of pleasure he'd managed to summon with one skillful shift of his mouth.

I didn't want him touching me, not even through an illusion. He was the last person in the world I wanted anywhere near me. So why did any part of me recognize that the stroke of his fingertips felt good?

Why the hell was I sitting here and taking this? I'd thrown Victory's spell back in her face a couple days ago, and I could do the same to Malcolm. It didn't matter how much he could affect me when I already knew I could affect him more.

I sorted through my thoughts for the right phrase, the right way of shaping my intention from my hand into an illusionary touch only he would notice. "Like a ghost, feel my touch," I whispered, so quietly the words were barely more than a warble of my breath. I drew my fingertips across the top of my desk, watching Malcolm from the corner of my eye. Imagining those lines traced across his back from shoulder blade to shoulder blade.

His stance twitched. I pretended not to see him glance toward me, but I let a smile curl my lips. He'd figured he was going to be the master of this game, did he? Let's see how well *he* could follow Professor Crowford's lecture now.

I eased my hand toward me as if down his spine. Malcolm was sitting perfectly still now. Fingers stroked over my knee once more, a little more insistently—and then that presence disappeared.

I stilled my hand. If he was giving up, I'd end this now.

But I should have known he wasn't done. A moment later, those ghostly fingers grazed my cheek. They reached my ear and then glided down along my jawline with such a tender caress my heart thumped.

Fuck, no. I closed my eyes to steady myself, trying to tune back into what Professor Crowford was saying, and skimmed my own hand upward. All the way up Malcolm's neck to splay over the sensitive scalp at the back of his head.

Malcolm covered the start of a sound with a forced cough. His posture drew straighter. I'd hit a provocative spot, clearly, because his touch faded away again. Before he could resume his attentions, I eased my fingers around in a slow circle, trailing sensation over his skin. I honestly had no idea what Crowford was talking about now, but if I could convince Malcolm there was no way this tactic was playing out in his favor—

"Hello, good people of Persuasion!" a forcefully flat voice said from the doorway. Jude ambled into the classroom, his face flushed and his eyes a little glassy. He took his next step with a wobble. "Sorry I'm late. I hope you all managed that short while without me."

Professor Crowford stared at the Killbrook scion, and his nose wrinkled slightly. "Mr. Killbrook," he said, "have you been drinking?"

"Maybe a little. Just a little. I think I'm owed that much." Jude swung around, swayed, and fixated on the empty seat at the back. "There we go. I've found my place."

Crowford caught the scion's arm before he could really set off. He leaned close to say something I couldn't hear, but Jude shoved away from him with a scoffing sound. "Excuse me! I have a right to an education. *Every* fearmancer has a right to that. Don't you damn well tell me what classes I can go to."

The professor's mouth tightened. "You can come to all the classes you like if you're in fit condition to participate," he said. "We can try again next week."

"Next week?" Jude sputtered. "What the hell kind of—"

"*Go back to your dorm room and drink plenty of water*," Crowford said in a slightly singsong tone I recognized as a casting.

Clearly Jude didn't have much in the way of mental defenses while alcohol was addling his brain. He spat out a few curses, but he also spun toward the door and sashayed back out.

Malcolm sprang to his feet. "Maybe I should make sure he gets to his room okay?"

Crowford shook his head. "Don't let Mr. Killbrook's foibles disrupt your own learning, as admirable as your concern for your friend is. I don't think he's in any real danger."

Malcolm lowered himself back into his seat slowly. When I looked at him, I saw the same confusion and worry on his face as were whirling inside me. He didn't know what to make of this performance any more than Connar had been prepared for Jude's dark comments on the green the other day.

If even the guys who knew Jude best had no idea what was wrong with him… it had to be pretty fucking wrong, didn't it?

CHAPTER TWELVE

Rory

I had to give my Nary credit for initiative. Benjamin had done his own research into school policies and figured out almost everything he needed to know to convince the headmistress to let his group go ahead with their construction proposal. I'd contrived for one last bit of obscure school procedure to land in his lap yesterday. Now I just had to make sure he didn't lose his confidence.

Right now he was standing with a couple of his friends in the main fore-room of Killbrook Hall, five minutes shy of their scheduled meeting with Ms. Grimsworth. Benjamin had already paced across the middle of the room several times, his shoulders up and his eyes a little wide. The scrape of his anxious footsteps echoed against the high ceiling.

None of these students had gotten the best reception from the fearmancer staff in the past. While the teachers might not outright bully them like so many of the mage students did, their disdain couldn't be hard to pick up on.

"Maybe we should reschedule until we've reworked the drawings again," he said, his voice carrying to me faintly where I was sitting on one of the hard, elaborately carved mahogany benches near the front door. "If they're going to go for this, everything has to be *perfect.*"

I flipped a page in the book I was theoretically studying and thought back to my own moments of assurance in the face of uncertainty over the last few months. I'd managed to pick up some strategies from that Persuasion seminar a couple days ago, despite Malcolm's efforts at distraction. With an exhalation, I cast a stream of bolstering energy his way. "*You can do this. You're ready. Show the headmistress that.*"

"If you really think so…" the girl beside Benjamin said with a frown, looking down at the portfolio she was carrying.

Benjamin paused, and his chin came up a smidge. "No. We've done a ton of work. It should be enough, right? And if Ms. Grimsworth tells us it's not, then we'll have a better idea where the plan isn't strong enough."

The other two brightened, and they set off toward the staff wing. I sank back on the bench in relief, hoping my encouragement had been enough to get them through their meeting.

I wasn't only in the hall to keep an eye on my Nary. Yesterday I'd heard from the assistant of that blacksuit friend of my mother's, Lillian Ravenguard, asking if there was a good time for her to drop by. Apparently Lillian had found a few things she'd wanted to pass on to me, and she'd prefer the delivery happened in person. Since I'd known I'd be here to see Benjamin off anyway, I'd asked the assistant to meet me here a little after his meeting time.

The young woman who slipped into the hall a few minutes later had a presence about as far from her employer's as you could get. If Lillian was a tough lioness, then her assistant was a cuddly kitten. Silky waves of chocolate-brown hair framed her rounded face, and a pink summer dress floated around her petite frame. She caught sight of me and headed over with an energy so upbeat I half expected her to start skipping.

"You must be Rory," she said in an equally sunny voice. "Magnolia Duskland—but everyone calls me Maggie. It's great to meet you. Lillian would have come herself, but her work keeps her awfully busy."

"That's okay," I said, getting up to receive an enthusiastic shake of my hand. I didn't meet many fearmancers who were quite this… cheerful. As I sat back down on the bench and she joined me, I found I had no idea what else to say.

Thankfully Maggie had no problem diving right into the matter at hand. She dug a cloth bag out of her expansive purse and handed it to me. "Lillian said you mentioned you were feeling a little disconnected from your parents. She found some old letters and videos and that sort of thing that she thought might help you get to know your mom better. The digital media is all pre-loaded onto a phone in there to make everything easy."

I hadn't been expecting anything like this. Cautiously, I peered inside the bag. There was a phone, all right, and sheaf of pages filled with handwriting, and a couple of folders I couldn't make out the contents of yet. A strange shiver ran through my gut, one that might have been excitement or apprehension or both.

"Thank you," I said. "And please thank Lillian for me too. I really —I don't remember anything from the first couple years of my life— it'll be good to have some more context."

If Maggie had been waiting for a more effusive response, she didn't show it. "She wants to help you adjust however she can," she said. "She also asked me to remind you that you can reach out to her—and me, of course—any time. Oh, there's a letter from her in there too, explaining why she picked all the different materials, what she thinks is important about them."

"Perfect." Did Maggie expect me to start going through this stuff right here in front of her?

Before I had to decide whether I should politely end the visit somehow or try to act like more of a host, the assistant was springing up again. "I'm sure you're looking forward to checking all of that out. I won't keep you from that! I hope you find what you're looking for in there."

She gave me a quick look up and down as if evaluating me somehow, but her smile never dropped. Then she was vanishing out the front door as quickly as she'd arrived.

When I shuffled the contents of the bag around, I could squeeze it into my own purse. I definitely didn't want to delve into my family history here where any student or teacher could walk by. Hugging my purse close to my side, my pulse thumping away, I set off for the dorms.

As I crossed the green, my gaze caught on a broad figure beyond Ashgrave Hall. Connar was crossing the field toward the surrounding forest with a purposeful air that seemed odd for someone just planning on taking a stroll through the woods. I hesitated, watching him, my lingering doubts stirring.

It wasn't so strange that I'd want to know where he was going, was it? He'd messed with me in more ways than I'd even guessed, and breaking from Malcolm's orders obviously hadn't been easy for him. I was just making sure his loyalties weren't leading him in unfriendly directions again.

I came around the building, waited until Connar had stepped between the trees, and then hurried after him. By the time I reached the edge of the forest, I couldn't make out his brawny form, but here and there the crackle of someone moving through the underbrush reached me. I set off after that sound, placing my feet carefully so I didn't make much noise of my own.

I'd walked maybe twenty feet into the woods when an overwhelming rush of emotion hit me. What was I doing out here? I had things to take care of back on campus. If I didn't get on with that—

My feet had already carried me back in sight of the field before my thoughts cleared enough for me to realize what had happened. I didn't actually have any urgent business to get on with. There must have been a ward in the forest, a spell that had compelled me away. Why the hell would anyone do *that* unless they were trying to hide questionable activity?

I crept back through the forest even more warily this time. The sounds of Connar's passage had faded away completely. If I stayed alert for the first jab of the ward's effect, maybe I could—

Another jolt of emotion hit me, this one more fearful. My legs scrambled back from the unknown threat of their own accord.

I clamped down on the panic racing through me and tried to force myself to walk on through it, but my mind went blank. The next thing I knew, I was standing at the edge of the field again.

Shit. That must be quite the ward. I didn't think even one of the scions could have cast something like that in the short head start Connar had gotten on me. What was out there? I didn't remember getting redirected during any ramble through the woods before, but I wasn't sure I'd ever explored that particular section.

I wavered for a minute, but I hadn't been prepared to tackle a deflection that strong, and at this point Connar could have gone anywhere in the deeper forest. Even if I managed to break the ward—and that didn't set off some sort of magical backlash—I'd probably never figure out where he'd been headed. With a grimace, I turned back toward Ashgrave Hall instead.

My dorm's common room was empty. Some of the tension I carried around in me whenever I was out around campus released, but my hackles rose again at the scrabble of claws on the other side of my bedroom door. A scrabble much heavier than anything Deborah would have produced.

I mumbled a few hasty words to disable my deterrent spells and shoved the door open. A cream-and-chocolate-brown shape was just disappearing around the side of my bed. I dashed around the frame to find a slender, glossy-furred Siamese cat prowling alongside my desk.

Thank goodness, Deborah's voice reached me, reedy across the distance from wherever she was hiding. *That beast got in here ages ago, and it's been looking to pounce on me ever since.*

The door to my wardrobe stood ajar, as if the cat had tugged it open in its search. My teeth gritted. Wary of its claws, I grabbed the spare blanket off the top of the wardrobe and stalked after the cat. It spun on me with a hiss, and I pounced on *it* with the blanket at the ready.

The cat wriggled and spat as I lugged it out of my bedroom, but it couldn't fight through the blanket. I'd stopped in the middle of the common room, not sure what to do with the creature next, and Imogen came in. She took in me and the churning blanket I had clutched in my arms, her eyebrows rising.

"I don't suppose you know who a Siamese cat would belong to?" I said.

She winced. "That would be Victory. He's her familiar."

Of course it'd been Victory. Frustration bubbled up inside me. "Well, *somehow* he ended up in my room hunting *my* familiar. Unless he's learned to cast magic on his own, I'm pretty sure that wasn't an accident."

I marched over to Victory's bedroom door and squeezed one arm tighter around the cat while I tested her security spells. Oh, she figured that combination was enough to keep people out, did she? One of the two impressions with its cold sear through my stomach reminded me of a structure in the Bloodstone puzzle garden that I'd worked part of my way through with Jude weeks ago. I had experience my nemesis hadn't been prepared for.

I drew back a step so the repulsive effects didn't dig into my mind so deeply and started to talk my way through a counteractive casting under my breath. Imogen watched in silence. The cat kept squirming, but my anger sharpened my concentration. I spoke a little more forcefully with a jerk of my free hand, and the spells on the door fell away.

Ha. I strode inside, taking in the fluffy lilac-purple duvet and the matching lace curtains over Victory's much smaller window, the computer and library books positioned neatly on her desk, the tart perfume scent that lingered in the air. That last observation sparked an idea. Victory had wanted to inflict the downsides of a cat on me? I could remind her of another of those.

With a murmur and another twitch of my fingers, I summoned traces of water, ammonia, and other chemicals from my surroundings. Then I propelled the mix onto Victory's lovely bedspread. The purple darkened with a splotch that spread across most of the bed, and the stench of cat urine choked every other scent in the room. I dropped her familiar out of the blanket and quickly shut the door.

Imogen stared at me. "She's going to be *furious*."

"If she doesn't want cat piss in her room, maybe she shouldn't keep a familiar so poorly trained it goes roaming around in other people's private spaces," I said. "You don't have to mention that I did it."

"I wouldn't," Imogen said quickly. "But you know she's going to figure it out."

I shrugged. I was so done with caring how Victory felt about anything. She hated me no matter what I did, so why the hell not make it cost her? "I'll survive. And maybe eventually she'll figure out she's better off leaving me alone."

I went back into my bedroom, shut the door, and flopped down on the bed. It was only mid-afternoon, but I was already ready for this day to be done.

The covers quivered as Deborah scrambled up to join me. She nestled herself next to my hand. *Thank you. That horrible thing took me by surprise. It's a good thing I was close enough to one of my nooks in the wall to escape.*

"Be extra careful from now on if I'm not here," I said. "Who knows what she's going to try next."

Already planning on it. She nuzzled my fingers. *What did that blacksuit assistant have to say?*

After everything, I'd almost forgotten why I'd come back to my room in the first place. I sat up, setting Deborah on my knee as I crossed my legs, and tugged open my purse. "Some stuff to do with my mother—my birth mother. I made a random remark about not knowing much about my Bloodstone parents, and I guess she figured it'd be helpful."

Even though it was hard to think of anyone except the parents I remembered, the joymancers who'd raised me nearly my entire life, as family, I had to admit I was kind of curious. I'd gotten a brief glimpse into my birth parents' lives from a photo album I'd found at their country property nearby, but it hadn't come with much context.

The phone was loaded not just with videos but also photos and music, what Lillian said in her note had been some of my mother's favorite artists. I went to the videos first. They were grainy, the low quality you must have gotten with casual cameras a couple decades ago, but I could make out the action well enough. I held the screen where Deborah could see it too.

The first one was from a birthday celebration—someone's twenty-first. My birth mother, her dark brown hair just a little longer than mine was right now and her make-up done with professional polish, clinked glasses with a man I recognized as my father from the photos I'd seen, a younger version of Lillian, and another guy sitting with them. "Let's see who's not afraid to do another round of shots," she called out to laughter around the room.

That one reminded me uncomfortably of the fearmancer parties I'd navigated here, but the next video showed my mother in a garden I recognized as that country property, her dress still tailored but more casual, her smile bright as she motioned to whoever was holding the camera. "Just watch this!"

She spread her hands a few feet above a bare patch of ground. The soil trembled, and a sprout poked its way through. She urged the conjured plant up until it stood at her knee height, a vibrant blue flower opening at the peak of its stem.

"I wonder if Physicality was her focus," I said. Watching her brought a tingle of recognition into my chest—the joy that came with creation. She'd felt it too.

Deborah made a humphing sound inside my head. *Of course this friend would send all the happy videos. I'm sure plenty of death and destruction was edited out.*

"We don't actually know that my birth parents ever hurt anyone," I said. "Badly, anyway." Being a fearmancer meant you pretty much had to cause some distress on a regular basis to fuel your magic. We *did* know that some joymancers had been horribly violent toward my birth parents, so it wasn't as if the capacity for violence didn't exist on the other side. I'd seen the report on their deaths, photos and all—I was never going to get the images of those burnt bodies out of my head.

Violence wasn't what I wanted for this place when I brought it down. All the sick practices and the sadistic behavior the fearmancers encouraged needed to stop, but I didn't want anyone slaughtered.

The next video made my chest clench up. It was my mother in bed with an infant clasped tightly to her chest. An infant who must have been me. My mother's hair was mussed and her face weary, but that didn't diminish the happiness that shone through her expression.

"Say hi to Auntie Lillian," she said in a teasing voice, turning me toward the camera. Then she pulled me back to her to kiss the top of my head.

An unexpected burn formed behind my eyes. For the very first time, looking at the woman I couldn't remember, some part of me responded with a pang that said, *Mom.*

Lorelei? Deborah said. *Are you sure you want to watch this—that it isn't just going to upset you?*

"It's fine," I said with a rasp. "I want to know." Maybe this was only the good-parts version of my mother's life, but… it meant something that there had been good parts.

It meant something that I'd lost the love I could see so clearly on the phone's screen.

CHAPTER THIRTEEN

Connar

I was so focused on the event to come that I think Rory must have called my name at least twice before I heard her. I stopped where I'd just stepped into the woods around campus and turned with a mix of delight and concern. Delight that she was seeking me out at all, and concern about what might have made her feel she needed to.

She came to a stop by the first trees, her deep blue gaze serious as she studied me. She might have been even more wary now than the first time she'd stumbled on my clearing on the cliff over the lake. The thought made my stomach twist.

It was my fault. I'd betrayed her, not just once but over and over. That kind of wound could take a long time to heal.

"Where are you going?" she said abruptly. The warm breeze tickled past me and ruffled the dark waves of her hair. The leaves hissed together overhead.

For some reason it hadn't occurred to me that she'd come to ask about my plans rather than to tell me something. My tongue stumbled. "I—what?"

She folded her arms over her chest. "Where are you *going*? I saw you head off this way a few days ago, and when I went after you, some super powerful ward shoved me back. What's out here?"

Ah. Maybe I should have been amused that she hadn't picked up on my trips into the forest sooner. A small part of me balked, but at the same time, my spirits lifted. This could be one more way for me to show her how open I'd be with her now—how much of my life I was willing to trust her with. And that might help her trust me more in turn.

If I didn't terrify her, that was.

I beckoned for her to join me. "It's nothing illicit. The wards are to make sure no Naries stumble on the spot—and some of us like to be sure of privacy in general."

"Privacy for what?" she said, but she eased after me without hesitation. I had to remember that Rory didn't terrify easily.

"Shifting." My gaze veered away from her as I said the word. I was proud of my talent, make no mistake there, but it wasn't something I generally talked about. Not many students had enough control over their powers to perform a full shift, and those who couldn't sometimes got a little weird about those who could. "There's a clearing set up out here for those of us who are capable of performing that magic, so that we can practice without being disturbed. Easier to keep the transformations hidden when we have a spot off in the woods."

"Oh," Rory said, sounding a little startled. "That makes sense. I didn't even realize." She paused and glanced over at me. "If you'd rather I wasn't there, I don't have to tag along. I'm sorry about the questions. There are just so many secret agendas at this place, I can't help wondering when I see something odd."

And that right there was what had made me fall for this girl. She had every reason to be suspicious of me, but the second she'd recognized that I wasn't doing anything shady at this specific moment, she'd apologized and offered me whatever space *I* needed. She cared that much even after what I'd done to her. It just came naturally to her.

My throat tightened. I had to be able to pay her back for all the kindness she'd shown me, so much of which I'd thrown in her face before.

I stopped by the main ward. "Do you want to see me shift? I don't really show off the skill very much, but… I don't mind you watching. You might even appreciate my second form more than most do."

Curiosity lit in her eyes. "What do you shift into?"

I couldn't help grinning at her. "Come along, and you'll find out."

She made a face at me, but she came. When she'd passed the ward, I spoke a few words to activate it. It'd set off a chain reaction effect through other wards placed around the shifting grounds to create a ring of protection.

The clearing was only a few minutes' walk farther. Sunlight streamed down into the open circle amid the trees, nearly a hundred metres in diameter. I soaked in its heat, letting the sensation loosen my muscles and melt away any worries I had. To perform the shifting magic, I couldn't be at all distracted—one of the other reasons we took so much care to make sure we weren't disturbed.

Rory sat down with her back against a tree trunk at the edge of the clearing. Under her thoughtful gaze, another potential problem occurred to me. A sharper heat crept up my neck.

"I, ah, normally would get undressed for the transformation. I *can* shift clothes too, but it's harder and not entirely pleasant…"

Rory blinked at me, and her cheeks pinked slightly. "Er. Well. I guess I have already seen all you've got to offer." One eyebrow quirked up.

Sure, I'd been naked with her that once before, but we'd been naked *together*, not her watching me in a sort of performance. I debated with myself and then said, "I think I'll maintain a *little* modesty."

She laughed, and that reassured me enough that I started unbuttoning my shirt. I pulled it off, folded it, then made short work of my shoes, socks, and pants. The boxers could stay on. I didn't need to put everything on display, and one piece of fabric wouldn't be too hard to work with.

With the fresh air teasing over my chest and legs, I was abruptly aware of the picture I presented. Of how most other people reacted to my strength. Rory had trusted me to be gentle before. Did she still see that capacity in me, or only the brutality this body could inflict?

A fresh jolt of uncertainty shot through me, but I'd committed now. It'd be worse if I asked her to leave after inviting her here. I had to believe… that she'd see what this form really meant to me, the way she'd seen something good in me before.

It was strength, yes, but not the brutal kind. The power to protect, the power to rise above.

I dragged in a breath and lowered my head. When I spoke my casting word, the magic in my chest flared. I focused on its spread through my limbs and over my back, the burn of it up over my face.

With each wave of searing sensation, my muscles and bones stretched and expanded. The sinews ached with the now-familiar process. My jaw extended; my eyes moved farther apart. More heat burst in my back as new limbs sprouted, wings rising and unfurling with the breeze tingling over their surface.

My body shuddered and settled into its new shape. I peered down at Rory from twice my previous height, my clawed feet braced against the ground and my wings spread on either side of me. She stared up at me, her jaw gone slack.

I knew what she was seeing because I'd had to picture this form inch by inch for months before I'd been able to complete the shift. I knew it as well as my human reflection in the mirror.

A dragon stood before her, far more alive than the little sculpture she'd conjured, ruddy scales dappled with orange running along my throat and belly, purple across my wings. I didn't dare move, my dragon heart thudding as I waited for the rest of her reaction.

Her mouth snapped shut. Her eyes were still wide, but a small smile crept across her lips, growing more with each passing second. "And you asked me if I liked dragons," she said, her voice awed and amused and not terrified at all. Her hand rose to the neckline of her blouse, where the chain that held her glass dragon charm disappeared behind the fabric.

A dragon couldn't really smile—and if I tried, it'd look more like I was baring my many impressive teeth. I could put on more of a show for her, though. I came out here not just to keep up my shifting practice but to work out my body in ways I couldn't in human form.

I took a few broad steps backward and to the side, and then

sprang toward the other end of the clearing. My wings caught on the breeze with a massive flap. I glided up to the level of the treetops and circled around, pulling off a roll I probably wouldn't have bothered with if I hadn't had an audience. Rory whooped in encouragement.

Bringing her here had been right. I should have known that for sure from the start. Even after she'd been angry with me, it'd only been for what I'd actually done, not for any vicious potential she imagined in me like even Declan and Jude clearly did sometimes.

I flew several circuits of the clearing until the first prickling started to spread over my skin. I could have fought against it and held the shift for several minutes longer, but the warning sensation would only escalate from discomfort to actual pain. Rory had gotten a good show already.

I came back to earth and rolled my joints a few times before I released the magic. That first moment, when my body collapsed in on itself, always sparked a flicker of panic before I caught my balance and control. I contracted the rest of the way into my natural form as easily as breathing.

Rory's face was still lit with wonder. "My mentor told me people could shift a lot larger than their human bodies, but it never occurred to me—I didn't think—" She laughed again. "That was amazing."

"Not horrifying?" I said in what I meant to be a teasing tone, but maybe some other emotion leaked into it.

Her expression turned more serious as she watched me pull my clothes back on. "Not at all. Anyone who thinks you're horrifying like that needs to have their eyes checked." She glanced around the clearing. "This isn't much space for you. Do you ever get to really fly?"

"Back at the main Stormhurst home, there's a hilly area where I can cruise around without worrying about being seen."

"I'm glad you have somewhere." Her voice softened. "Thank you for letting me see."

"Now you know all my secrets," I said with a crooked smile. I sat down a few feet away from her, my feet still bare in the soft grass. After a shift, it was nice to take a little while to linger here until the dragon impressions completely faded away.

At the tensing of her mouth, I regretted that flippant comment instantly.

"Not all of them," she said in the same quiet tone. "Connar… Will you tell me what happened with your brother? I want to hear it from you, not go by rumors."

Of course she did. And asking this couldn't have been more fair of her. Still, I closed my eyes against the rush of guilt that rose up even at the mention of Holden.

I'd told myself I wanted to show her how open I could be. How could she ever trust me completely if I wouldn't own up to the past horrors I'd inflicted? If the truth meant she never trusted me at all, then that was my own damn fault.

She'd seen the beauty in my dragon, but there wasn't anything pretty in this story.

"What do you already know?" I asked. My voice came out raw.

"What I *heard* is that you have a twin brother, and the two of you had some kind of… fight, and he never ended up coming to the university."

"That's all true." I forced myself to look at her. I deserved to see her reaction as it played out in the moment. "I have a twin brother named Holden. Non-identical, not that you'd ever need to worry about confusing us these days." I exhaled shakily. "It was always going to be a complicated situation. The inheritance of the barony is usually decided by seniority, but when you're only a couple of minutes apart, that's not considered enough of a deciding factor."

Rory knit her brow. "So you were expected to fight it out?"

"Not exactly. Even with siblings who are farther apart in age, occasionally the older one abdicates because they don't really want to rule, or they feel their younger sibling will do a better job… We should have had lots of time to decide. I don't think either of us was really in any position to hash it out before we'd even come into our magic, and it's going to be more than fifteen years still before my mother ages out and anyone needs to take over."

My fingers twisted into a patch of grass. The violence had been so stupid, stupid and pointless.

Rory watched me quietly until I was ready to continue.

"My parents… are very competitive," I said. "If you've heard about my brother, you've probably also heard that my mother wasn't the original heir to the Stormhurst barony either. She grabbed it from my uncle."

Rory inclined her head. "That part did get mentioned too."

"I guess it must have really gnawed at them, the two of us having equal claim—not knowing who the real heir was. They wanted to know who was stronger as soon as possible. Or maybe they just enjoyed jerking us around… Anyway, pretty much from the moment my mother took over the barony, she and my father started pushing Holden and me into conflicts. Setting up little competitions where only one of us could get a reward. Punishing both of us if one of us made a mistake. Showering one of us with attention while completely ignoring the other one day, and switching it up the next. Having a brother started to feel like a punishment in itself."

"That's awful," Rory said. Her eyes had widened again, but not with any kind of awe this time.

"There are worse parents. I'm not sure I'd have been better off with Malcolm's, for example." I grimaced. "But, even with all that, my brother and I didn't really want to fight with each other. We knew our parents were the real ones at fault. And they hated that we didn't hate each other. So as it got closer to our fifteenth birthdays when our magic would show up soon, they kept ramping up their efforts."

I had to pause for a second to brace myself against the memories. "In the end, they shut us in the attic together. It's like a greenhouse up there in the summer, and they didn't turn on the air conditioning. They barely gave us any food or water, and what they did give us always tasted funny…" My impressions of that time were hazy, a mass of sweat and dizziness and a hollow stomach, powdery sensation on my tongue, buzzing in my brain. "They told us neither of us could come down until the other *couldn't* come down."

I'd thought Rory would recoil as I told the story. Instead, she eased across the grass to clasp my hand. The compassion in that contact wrenched at me.

"I think we'd been up there maybe a week when it happened," I said, willing my voice not to falter. "They'd been messing with our sleep too, conjured noises at random intervals to startle us awake. And that night—or maybe it was day, my mind was pretty jumbled by then—I heard Holden's voice shouting me awake every time I started to drift off. I was so fucking tired and starving and dizzy with the heat… I snapped. I don't remember what I was thinking; I just remember hitting him, so hard, as hard as I could so that he would just stop. So that it would all stop."

My throat closed up. The hand Rory wasn't holding had clenched against the grass.

"I broke his back," I forced myself to say. "And fractured his skull. He's paralyzed from the waist down, and the brain injury—he's still in there, but he can hardly communicate, can't get his words out well enough to do much in the way of casting. Which is why there wasn't any point in him coming here. But I can't say that I feel like I won."

"Of course you don't," Rory burst out. "Your parents—Christ—they tortured you until you broke, like anyone would if they were beaten up enough."

I swallowed hard. "Yeah, but I broke first. He never came at *me*."

"Connar…" She squeezed my hand so tightly the bones ached. "I still don't think you're a horrible person. *They're* the horrible ones. I can't even—to put your own kids through that—" She let out a wordless sound of fury. As if I were worthy of defending.

It occurred to me that I did owe someone else one more thing. "You should know," I said, "even after that, Malcolm never treated me any differently. Declan and Jude—well, they'd been wary from the moment my mom stole the position, and that just made it worse. And everyone at school, when I got here, just knew that I'd beaten my brother to a pulp to claim scionhood, so they kept their distance. Malcolm was the only person who made being here bearable. Who made me think maybe I could move past that. The last thing I ever wanted to do was turn on him too."

Rory got what I was saying. "When you put it that way, I can see why you'd have picked him over me. Not that you had to go that *far*—"

"I know. I panicked and I overcompensated and—there's no excuse. I was awful to you. I just wanted you to know it wasn't blind loyalty. Malcolm really has been there for me when no one else was. I just hope he can snap out of this furor he's gotten into now, because it's not good for any of us."

"No." Rory looked down at our joined hands. Her jaw worked, and she raised her eyes to meet mine again. "But I want you to know that I'll never be like that. I'll *never* expect you to hurt anyone else, to betray anyone, on my behalf. You decide what you do on your own. I just ask that you don't hurt *me*."

For the first time since she'd brought up my brother, I felt capable of a smile, if only a small one. "Yeah," I said, gazing back at her with a hum around my heart like nothing I'd ever felt before. "I think I can manage that."

CHAPTER FOURTEEN

Rory

"Well, now, I suppose we can order anything on this menu without it being a hardship to your accounts," my grandmother said with a twitter and a fluff of her silver-white curls. The laugh was supposed to tell me she was only teasing, I thought, but the ravenous gleam in her pale little eyes told a different story.

How had Jude described my paternal grandparents? "Grasping" was the word that came to mind first, maybe because I'd seen plenty of evidence of that just in the first five minutes of this lunch I'd reluctantly arranged. My grandmother had immediately vetoed the nice but casual restaurant I'd picked because I liked the food in favor of one of the town's few posh offerings. While my grandfather was more subtle, he'd already made an inquiry about the Bloodstone collection of vehicles hinting that I couldn't possibly need all of them and should gift one to him.

I'd have been happy to hand over a car or three if it meant the senior Evergrists would have gone away and never hassled me or Declan again, but I had the feeling they'd be like a toddler handed a cookie to soothe a tantrum. As soon as you gave in once, they'd come back kicking and screaming for another even more insistently than before.

Thankfully, the Bloodstone accounts *could* handle the entire menu with no trouble at all, so I pretended I'd only heard the comment as a joke. "Order whatever you like," I said, and picked out a Cobb salad for myself. I could get through that and therefore this lunch pretty fast.

It was hard to imagine what kind of son these people might have raised. If he'd been anything like them, it was even harder to imagine what my mother, as the heir of Bloodstone, would have seen in him beyond the grasping for power. But then, people didn't always follow in their parents' footsteps. Connar was clearly nowhere near the monster his parents had tried to bully him into being.

The memory of that recent conversation brought a fresh ache of sympathy into my chest. God, to be raised by people like that—to be brutalized and battered into brutalizing in turn… I restrained a shudder.

I wanted to think that my birth parents hadn't been anything like that. That if I *had* been raised by them, my life wouldn't have been horrific. But… I really didn't know, did I? How a mother responded to a newborn might be very different from how she'd act as that kid grew up, as the expectations grew. From the pictures in their photo album, my Bloodstone mother had been friendly with Malcolm's dad, who was his own brand of asshole.

And she'd also connected herself to the two people sitting across from me, who turned on the viciousness in their falsely sweet way the second after our meals arrived.

"So," my grandmother said with a sharp smile as she speared a piece of her pasta, "you've become quite fond of that Ashgrave boy, have you?"

My fingers tightened around my fork instinctively. I kept my expression and my tone as blasé as I could manage. "Well, you know, he's a fellow scion. It's good for us to get along."

My grandfather cleared his throat. "It looked as though you were more than 'getting along'."

Declan had stonewalled them, so they were looking to get some telling admission from me. Fuck that. I smiled back at them, my mind leaping to a possible diversion. "Oh, at the country property? That was more like a study break. I've had a lot of catching up on my magical practice to do, as I'm sure you can imagine, and sometimes it's hard to concentrate on campus. I've actually found I'm enjoying the company of the other scions more when I'm not studying."

That wasn't the direction they'd wanted to steer me in, but my grandmother's gaze lit up eagerly anyway. She just loved gossip, no matter what information she was getting. "Oh, really," she said in a cajoling tone. "I suppose they are all a fine lot of gentlemen."

Gentlemen was probably not the word I'd have used for all the scions, but I could go with that.

I set my face in a dreamy expression. "They are. Jude can be so charming—and Connar… There's something about a guy that physically powerful…" I shook my head as if in bemusement, although my mind had slipped back to the awe-inspiring form he'd shifted into the other day. That dragon—I couldn't have drawn or sculpted anything so vibrantly spectacular. "The hard part is deciding who I want to focus on. But I guess there's nothing wrong with playing the field, right?"

"Of course not," my grandmother said, but she looked a tad disgruntled. Me dallying with those two scions didn't give her any blackmail material. She obviously hadn't let go of her main goal, though, because a few bites later, she remarked, "The Ashgrave boy should be more careful about appearances. I don't think it'd do for him to seem to be getting too close to a student he's supposed to be helping teach, scion or not."

"I'm sure he's well aware of that concern," I said, resisting the urge to grit my teeth.

My grandparents prattled on about this thing and that—what I should do with the Bloodstone properties, how much they'd like visiting access to one of them, various possessions of my father's they wondered pointedly about—until our plates were cleared. I couldn't summon the bill fast enough. I'd thought I'd make my escape then, but as we stepped out of the restaurant, my grandmother grabbed my elbow and tugged me in the opposite direction from the road to campus.

"It's been so long since we had you with us, we must extend the visit a little longer. We can have a stroll and window-shop."

Somehow I suspected "window-shopping" was going to turn into "make noises about how lovely it'd be if Rory bought one thing or another for us." And even if it didn't, I had zero desire to spend one minute longer in the company of these people, family or not.

"I actually have to get back to school for class," I said. The class in question wasn't for another hour and a half, but they didn't know that.

"Oh, what are they going to say if you miss one? You're the Bloodstone scion! You deserve to enjoy some freedom."

Walking around with her clutching my arm wasn't exactly what I'd consider freedom. I suppressed a wince as her fingers dug in tighter, groping for a way to refuse more firmly without totally pissing her off —because Lord only knew how she'd retaliate against me or Declan then—and of all people, Professor Viceport came ambling down the street toward us.

I tensed automatically, expecting my difficulties to multiply, but my new mentor glanced over the three of us, and something shifted in her reserved expression. She strode right up to us.

"Miss Bloodstone," she said. "I believe you're wanted on campus, as soon as you can get there. A concern about your project."

She put a slight emphasis on that last word and gave me a meaningful look. I stared back at her, only fully comprehending when she turned her gaze on my grandparents with a tight slant of her lips.

I'd finally found someone the Physicality professor liked even less than she liked me. She must have recognized my discomfort, and she was offering me an escape route.

"I'd better get on that right away," I said gratefully, extricating my arm from my grandmother. "So sorry to run, but my summer project has a tricky balance to maintain. The whole thing could end up ruined."

"But—" my grandmother started.

Professor Viceport interrupted her with a curt little cough. "Miss

Bloodstone's education must be a high priority to her family, I'm sure, considering the time she's lost from it."

My grandmother snapped her mouth shut. My grandfather, at least, looked chagrinned. "Of course," he said to me. "You do us proud now."

Gladly. "I'm sure we'll talk again," I said. I couldn't quite bear to add a "soon" to the end of that sentence. With a brisk wave, I hurried away.

The afternoon class I actually needed to attend had been labeled as Illusion, but when I looked at my schedule again as I got ready to leave, I noticed the location wasn't a classroom but someplace called "Casting Grounds." Where the hell was that?

To my relief, when I set off to figure that out, I ran into Imogen on the green. "Hey," I said. "Can you tell me where the Casting Grounds are?"

"I can show you," Imogen said with a quick smile. "I'm heading there too. Looks like we're learning by example today if they're calling everyone out there. It's a clearing in the west woods not too far from the lake for larger scale practice in conjuring and illusions."

She led me past Nightwood Tower and across the west field to the woods. When we reached the clearing after about a ten-minute walk through the forest, it turned out to look pretty much the same as the Shifting Grounds where Connar had shown me his mythic transformation: a wide circle of trimmed grass framed by trees on all sides. I guessed there had to be wards up here too, preventing Naries from wandering out this way when we were working magic.

As Imogen had suggested, it looked like all the fearmancer students currently on campus had been called to this lesson. A few dozen students already stood along the edge of the clearing. Professor Burnbuck, who'd taught my Illusion seminars so far, was poised in the middle of the grassy space with a woman whose name I didn't know but who was probably the junior Illusion instructor.

"Come around, spread out," the woman said with a sweeping

gesture. "No need to cluster together. We want you all to have a good view."

"What's happening?" one of the other students asked.

"Some of our most advanced students will be giving a demonstration in the full capabilities of illusionary magic," Professor Burnbuck said with a tip of his head toward a few figures gathered at the far end of the clearing.

I drifted away from Imogen, studying that bunch. Jude wasn't with the group or anywhere else around the clearing that I could make out. Surely he should be part of this demonstration? I might not have appreciated his prank with the illusionary bears last term, but there was no mistaking he had plenty of skill in that area. As scion, he was probably the best in the school, just like Connar was in Physicality.

Was he off somewhere getting drunk again? Or getting into some other kind of trouble? My stomach clenched at the thought.

The rest of the students must have arrived. As Professor Burnbuck began his introductions, I spotted Victory and her crew across the clearing from me, Victory shooting me a narrow look before turning her attention to the professor.

The first advanced student stepped forward to show off his skills. I stepped closer to the trees as he sent a streak of light singing around the clearing—and nearly bumped into someone I hadn't heard coming up behind me.

"Careful there." Malcolm's voice came out smooth and quiet. He set his hand on my waist as if to steady me as I caught my balance, but it lingered there. His thumb traced a line up over my side like he'd caressed my leg through his magic the other day, and a flicker of warmth I didn't like at all raced over my skin.

"Sorry," I said flatly. "You can let go of me now."

"Are you sure that's what you want? I think you like this." He teased all of his fingers over my side with a slow stroke, pulling them together and then splaying them.

So we were ramping up the game, were we? For a second I was torn between pulling away from him and pushing back, but the second impulse won. Walking away was backing down, wasn't it?

Even if I liked the sensation a little, he wanted this more than I did. That gave me the power.

I eased backward half a step so my body came to rest against his. The faint hitch of his chest at the contact brought a smile to my lips. "Are you sure *you* don't like it too much? I'm not the one getting hot and bothered." Just… warm and slightly distracted.

There was a moment when I thought Malcolm might be the one to back down. Then his hand clasped my waist a little more firmly. "Usually it's the people who play with fire who get burned."

"Hmm. So your mistake is assuming that you're the fire in this equation when it's actually me."

I adjusted my stance just a smidge, just enough to create a bit of friction between us as I moved. Malcolm's hand slid to my hip, his voice rough when he spoke next.

"Not so good anymore, are you, Glinda?"

"I guess that depends on your definition of 'good'."

The glide of his thumb over my hipbone sent a deeper flare of heat to my core. I concentrated all my attention on the display the first advanced student was just wrapping up, willing my body's reactions to fade into the background.

It was kind of ridiculous, wasn't it? My grandparents had been all caught up in the idea of me with Declan, and I'd fed them that story about bouncing between Jude and Connar, but I'd been more physically intimate with the guy behind me than any of those three in the last couple weeks.

That thought might have given me more pause, except as the student giving the first demonstration stepped back, Victory made an odd gesture with her hand. My back stiffened in recognition that she was casting before I even saw what she'd produced. Then my entire body froze.

She was playing with illusions too. A white mouse shimmered into being in the middle of the clearing between us, floating in mid-air—larger than Deborah was so people could see it from the fringes, but I had no doubt it was my familiar she intended to represent.

In that moment, I forgot Malcolm completely. I sucked in a

breath, and the mouse's body began to tear apart limb by limb. It shuddered and spasmed as one leg wrenched off its abdomen, then another, then the chest flayed open with a spurt of blood—

My stomach heaved. I had to clamp my mouth shut to avoid spewing half-digested Cobb salad all over the grass. Across the clearing, a triumphant grin had curved Victory's lips.

She still hadn't learned her lesson.

I balled up all my horror at her display and whipped a surge of energy toward the illusionary mouse with a tautly whispered word. My magic flung the image straight at her, so abruptly she had no time to dodge.

The white ball of fur exploded in a burst of far more blood than any mouse's body could really contain, splattering Victory's face and blouse.

It wasn't real gore of course, any more than the mouse had really been Deborah. But I'd thrown a metallic stink and the tacky feel of congealing blood into my casting, and she'd be experiencing all of that as if it were real. With a yelp of dismay, she swiped at her face and arms—but she couldn't dislodge an illusion like that.

She caught my gaze from across the clearing, looking twice as fierce with red streaked across her forehead and cheeks. I didn't have to find out what she'd have tried to do to me next, though, because Professor Burnbuck lifted his voice right then.

"Thank you for the additional demonstration, but I'd appreciate it if we could get back to the ones planned now."

He shot a firm glance Victory's way. I wasn't sure he'd even realized who she'd been sparring with. She took a step back and then faded farther out of sight between the trees, presumably to dispel my illusion.

Malcolm leaned close enough that his breath spilled warm over my hair, bringing me back into tingling awareness of his presence. "Not so nice at all, Bloodstone. You do have that fearmancer viciousness in you somewhere, don't you?"

His voice held a smolder hotter than before, as if watching me lash out had turned him on. The heat of it sank right into me. "Maybe you should keep that in mind when you're trying to mess with me," I shot back.

"Mmm. I don't mind if you pay me back for this kind of messing around." His mouth grazed the back of my head. His fingers caressed my hip again, and the heat he'd provoked in me pooled between my thighs.

"Oh, yeah?" I made myself turn to look up at him. I'd known how I meant to end this, but the hunger in his gaze stopped me for a second, radiating into me.

I remembered that one kiss. I remembered how good it had felt. An echo of the sensation tingled over my lips.

Malcolm was obviously thinking along similar lines. His head dipped down, and I snapped out of that momentary daze. He'd just given me the perfect opening.

"What if I pay you back by leaving you hanging?" I said, and slipped out of his grasp just before his mouth could catch mine. I walked off along the edge of the clearing behind the other gathered students, not gratifying him with so much as a backward glance. As if nothing we'd just done had any impact on me at all.

It had, though, in ways I hadn't even expected. Simply walking away from him sent a weird thrill through me even hotter than what his touch had stirred. My nerves were humming with it.

It turned *me* on, knowing I could provoke that hunger in him and leave him wanting.

I came to a stop several feet away from him to focus on the demonstration again, but that sudden piece of understanding settled inside me with an uncomfortable jab. What did it say about me if I could enjoy jerking someone around like that, even someone who'd jerked me around as much as Malcolm had before? How much of the predatory fearmancer instinct was innate, something waking up inside me rather than something I'd escaped when the joymancers had taken me?

Had my birth mother even liked my dad… or had he simply been useful to her in some way I couldn't comprehend yet? Maybe I was following *her* footsteps in ways that never would have occurred to me.

A sour flavor filled my mouth. I made myself raise my chin as I listened to the next planned illusion with its swell of music.

I didn't have to be as cruel as most of the fearmancers I'd met could be. I didn't have to be as calculating. But if I had the instincts to fend for myself in a community full of predators… was it really so wrong to use them?

CHAPTER FIFTEEN

Rory

I wasn't so naïve as to think that my take on the summer project would go undisturbed. After some research in the library, I'd constructed a spell that I'd attached to the soil around Benjamin's chosen building site that should send a jolt of magic my way if anyone expended much of their own magical energy there. I'd had to bolster the spell's power a couple times a day to make sure it stayed effective, but the time and effort I'd put in proved to be worth it when the first jolt hit me just as I was rinsing my dinner dishes.

The signal shivered up my spine, and I nearly dropped the plate I was holding. I set it down on the other, unrinsed dishes that my dormmates had left behind—I still couldn't quite bear to leave all the work to the maintenance staff—and headed straight out the door, wiping my wet hands on my pants.

I took the stairs at a swift pace, my shoes clattering against the hard surface, but I could tell something had already gone wrong as I came around the outside of the building. Someone was talking in a raised, anxious voice.

Benjamin and his three friends from the architecture program were standing by the site. Earlier today, the maintenance staff they'd been allowed to rope into their plans had prepped that spot for the foundation of their scholarship clubhouse. The smell of freshly dug earth reached my nose on the breeze.

One of the girls was flinging her arm toward the cleared and flattened ground. "It's going to look awful," she was saying. "This whole idea was stupid."

"Come on," Benjamin said. "We've gotten so much done—we got the whole ball rolling. We can't stop now. I still think it's going to be great. You did awesome work on it, Cassie."

She shook her head before he'd even finished speaking. "It's taking up so much time too. I have—I have other things to get done."

Other things like whatever her various assigned fearmancers had planned? I set my jaw, staying where I was. In the fading evening light, no one was likely to notice me there beside the building. If I walked closer, onto the field, they might get nervous and scatter. None of them knew I was on their side.

Benjamin was my official "target," but I hadn't heard anyone say we couldn't cast magic on other Naries too. I trained my eyes on Cassie and gathered the energy thrumming at the base of my throat.

"*You remember how great it would be to have a place where the regular students can't hassle you. Think about all the work you've put in. You're just feeling a little overwhelmed. You really do want to see this through.*"

As I watched, she hesitated. Then she swiped her hand across her mouth. My persuasion might have swayed her thinking, but she wasn't expressing those new thoughts to her friends.

"The staff don't really want to help us either," she said after a moment. "We're architects—and not even real ones yet—not builders. If they're going to take forever…"

Had my classmates been messing with the maintenance workers too? I made a mental note to stop by while the three guys I'd seen handling this project were out here tomorrow. But in the meantime…

My gaze slid over to where a few other students, also with the gold leaf pins that marked them as Naries, had wandered onto the field nearby. The more support my bunch had, the harder it'd be for anyone else to shake them from their goals.

"*Ask what they're doing*," I murmured, training my attention on the nearest guy, and then shifted my focus to Benjamin. "*Tell them the truth.*"

As the one guy asked and the other explained their plan for the clubhouse where they could relax without worrying about harassment from the rest of the student body, satisfaction unfurled in my chest. I shouldn't get complacent, though. While the other Naries exclaimed over what a great idea the building was, I whispered a few more lines to shape my warding spell across that distance.

I thought I could get it to not just warn me about magic being cast, but deflect at least some of that energy. It wouldn't protect the Naries all over campus, but it'd shelter them a bit while they were joining the work out here.

Cassie had brightened with the other students' enthusiasm. It looked as though I'd kept them on track. I drew back around the building, meaning to head back up, but as I reached the green I caught a flash of copper hair as a lanky form stalked into Nightwood Tower.

Where was Jude going? There weren't any classes this late.

He must be heading up to the piano room. That was the place I'd seen him retreat to after Malcolm had torn him a new one for expressing his interest in me last term. I didn't think he turned to his music when he was in a cheerful mood.

I wavered for all of half a second, and then I hurried after him. Whatever had gotten into Jude, it clearly wasn't getting out again easily. I'd taken a chance confronting Connar the other day, and that had worked out just fine. Maybe I could figure out what Jude's problem was just as quickly.

At the very least, I wanted to try. Maybe I was angry about the way he'd treated the Naries and his lack of remorse, maybe I couldn't see us being anything more than colleagues, but I was allowed to worry about a colleague who was going off the rails. I didn't wish misery on Jude. He might have messed up priorities, but I didn't think he was an awful human being. If there was something making him miserable that I could help with… I'd do what I could.

This time, I was far enough behind that I didn't need to use any magic to disguise my approach. I knew where I'd find him without trailing close behind.

After more than three months of tramping up and down the tower's stairs, I managed to make it to the piano room on its high floor without getting winded. I stopped outside, leaning close, and a clang of aggressively played keys reached my ears. Yeah, he didn't sound happy at all.

I nudged open the door. Jude's hands jerked to a halt where they'd been moving over the keys. He stared at me for a second, his expression tight with an emotion I couldn't read. Then he said, flat and dark, "Get out."

"No." I shut the door behind me. "Whatever's going on, I think you should talk to someone about it. Drinking, skipping classes, and being a jerk to everyone around you clearly isn't fixing anything."

"And you think you can fix it?" He let out a hollow chuckle. "Let it go, Rory. You didn't want me anyway."

"So I'm only allowed to care what happens to you if I'm also willing to date you?" I came over to the side of the piano. Jude studiously kept his gaze on the instrument. A chill tickled through me with a sudden thought—what if he'd found out something to do with *me*? That was, something to do with whatever malicious plots were still going on around me. Something that disturbed him but that he didn't believe he could fight against, so he was shutting me out.

His father was a baron, after all. Jude might not have known much when Declan had talked to him, but that could have changed.

"Look," I said, "you're going to tell me, or I'm going to pick it out of your brain. I'd rather it didn't come to that. You know I wouldn't ask so I could hurt you, Jude. Please."

He shifted his gaze back to me then, his dark green eyes steely. "You can try to take a peek in there, but I don't think you'll get very far. I've got plenty of strength in Insight."

I had actually thought I'd turn to my chosen area of magic. But in the face of his defiance, the memory swam up of how Malcolm had turned the tables on me my first day back. While I'd been shielding myself against insight magic, I'd left chinks where a persuasive spell could slip through.

Jude wouldn't expect persuasion from me. I'd been getting a lot of practice with the summer project, though. "We'll see about that," I said, and focused on his head, willing a surge of magic up my throat and onto my tongue. I shot out the spell with all the power I had in me. "*Tell me what's been bothering you.*"

I felt the spell pierce through and saw its success in the flicker of Jude's eyes. The color drained from his face even as his mouth opened by my compulsion. "Rory, don't— I found out my parents are expecting."

"Expecting…"

"A baby."

"Your mom's pregnant?" I said, puzzled. "What's so horrible about that?" He'd never seemed close enough to his parents to be devastated over the arrival of a sibling who'd take up some of their attention.

My spell was still wriggling around in his mind. He knew he hadn't given the full explanation. His jaw clenched for a second before the words wrenched out. "They don't need me anymore."

"What are you talking about? You'll still be the senior heir." Connar's explanation of the barons' system of inheritance was fresh in my mind. "You don't even know what this kid will turn out like. Will they even be old enough that your dad could make them baron when he's got to step down?"

"It doesn't matter." Jude's shoulders sagged. All at once he looked utterly hopeless, as if he couldn't see any point in even fighting this conversation anymore. He turned to the piano and gazed blankly at it. "They have a real Killbrook heir now. Out goes the fake one with the trash."

"The fake one," I repeated, staring at him. None of this made sense. Was he speaking metaphorically? "How could you be—I don't understand."

"Are you really going to make me spell it out?"

My throat tightened thinking of how I'd forced this confession out of him. I'd had no idea it'd be something this fraught, something that clearly had nothing to do with me and my security at all.

"No," I said quietly. "I'm sorry. I'll go if you want me to. But do you really think you'll feel better if you send me off with nothing to do but speculate?"

He considered that for a long moment. Then he tugged out the keyboard guard to cover the keys and set his elbows on it, tipping his head into his hands.

"I'm not my father's son," he said in a rough voice. "I'm not a Killbrook."

My jaw went slack. "*What?* How… Why…?" My mind couldn't wrap around that idea to figure out the question I most wanted to ask.

Jude sort of answered all of them. "It was some stupid plan… They tried to have a kid for years and nothing worked, and Dad must have gotten scared about his younger brother getting ambitions if he wasn't continuing the family line, so he and my mother arranged—I don't think she even *wanted* to; it was all for him—that she would get pregnant with some other man, and they'd say the kid was theirs. It worked. That's me."

Holy fuck. My legs wobbled. I sat down on the edge of the bench, leaving as much space as I could between Jude and me. "How did you find out?" I ventured.

He sighed. "I overheard them arguing about it when they thought I was someplace else. My dad… has basically regretted it from the start. For twelve years, I had no idea why he acted like he couldn't stand me, and then—and then I find out it's all his fault in the first place—" He ran a hand over his face. "They don't know I know. I've wanted to scream it in his face so many times… but I have no idea what he'd do with me if he realized the secret's out."

"And this new baby…?"

"Means they don't need me, like I said. It was always going to come out eventually. There's a ceremony when you take the barony. But I had years and years to go yet. Now, as soon as that kid is born… He's going to want to cover up his lie. It's basically plotting treason."

Something clicked in my head through the swell of horror I was feeling on his behalf. I paused, but it gnawed at me too insistently for me to set it aside.

"Is that why you started wooing me? You figured you could ditch the barony that wasn't really yours, but stay part of the circle by marrying me?"

"I don't give a flying fuck about the barony," Jude said. "I just… Like I said, the truth was going to come out, one way or another. And you're the only mage I'd ever met who I didn't think would care. You think it's all bullshit too. And you've got the balls to say so. Why the hell wouldn't I like you? The ridiculous thing is it took me so long to realize how fantastic you are."

The flattery wasn't enough to dissuade me. "If you didn't think I'd care, why didn't you just tell me to begin with?"

"I was going to. When things got serious, I'd have told you. But then… shit went down. You got kind of judgy." He glanced at me sideways, his forehead still propped on his hands. "I wasn't going to start spilling secrets when you'd hardly talk to me."

"Jude…" With the distress he was obviously in, I couldn't bring myself to be annoyed by the way he'd described the situation. "I had no idea you had something like this weighing on you."

"Would you have been less pissed off at me if you had?" He shrugged. "I didn't know about the baby factor until a couple weeks ago. The rest is old news. You didn't want us to be anything other than colleagues—well, I'm not even that. I'm a lie. A con. I'm fucking *treason*."

"No," I said with a rush of vehemence. I scooted over on the bench to clasp Jude's shoulder. "Your father lied. Your father conned people. You had no say in it. I—I might get 'judgy', but it's never going to be about who your parents are or what *they* did or what position you're supposed to inherit."

"No? It doesn't even matter that I'm a weaker mage than everyone thinks? My father arranged to be on campus to skew the assessment results. I've only got two strengths, not three."

I let out a sputter of a laugh. "Who the fuck cares? Jude, you could be a *Nary* and that'd still have shit-all to do with whether I want to be your friend or—or whatever else. All that matters to me is what you do and what you believe."

He raised his head, his gaze holding mine, a furrow creasing his forehead. "You really mean that, don't you?" he said after a moment.

"Of course I do. It's part of how fantastic I am." I pushed my mouth into a smile to go with the weak joke.

Jude just blinked at me. His eyes had widened, his pupils dilating. Then he gave a breathless laugh and wrapped his arms around me in a tight embrace.

"Yes, it is," he mumbled into my hair. "You *are* fucking fantastic. Apparently I still hadn't really realized it."

I hugged him back, abruptly choked up. "You know this doesn't mean—I still don't think us being a couple is a good idea—"

"I know," he said. "I promise I'm not angling for that. Can I just… hold onto you for a little while?"

"Yeah," I said, bowing my head next to his. "I can give you that." And I sure as hell wasn't letting his father or anyone else get rid of him. Maybe if I could figure out how to take this place down before it came to that—there could be some sort of asylum for people like him who needed it—

But that was a long ways away still. Right now all I knew for sure was my heart was aching for the guy in my arms and all the pain he'd been enduring behind the jokes and the smirks. Even if I couldn't see any solid future with him, I didn't really want to let him go.

CHAPTER SIXTEEN

Rory

Imogen let out a huff as we left the tower after a class, the hot July air smacking us in the face. She swiped at the sweat that had instantly started beading on her forehead.

"You know what we need?" she announced. "A swim. Let's go down to the lake."

Even thinking about the water gave me a rush of relief. "Sounds perfect."

We grabbed our swimsuits and towels and went down to the shore. We hadn't been the only ones with this bright idea. A few senior girls I didn't know particularly well were drifting around just past the boathouse. I set my towel down at the end of the dock, eyed the rippling water, and decided to take it in one jump.

The flood of cool rushing over my skin was delicious. I surfaced with a laugh and floated on my back while Imogen entered more tentatively by climbing down the ladder. She took the last short distance with a little leap and a gasp that turned into a grin.

The water warbled around me, and the sun beamed over my skin wherever my modest bikini didn't cover it. I glided along with a light kick, soaking all the sensations in. A few parts of Villain Academy were awfully nice, I had to admit.

Imogen cruised past me, and I turned to swim after her farther across the lake. As far as I could see, dense forest stretched along the rise and fall of the rocky shoreline. I couldn't make out any cottages or other buildings. The lake was huge, but apparently we had it all to ourselves.

As we headed back toward the shallower water, a pleasant burn forming in my arms and legs with the exercise, another group came ambling down to the shoreline. A couple of guys I'd seen playing football with Connar before… and Malcolm, unmistakeable from the golden gleam of his hair. My pulse stuttered.

I had the impulse to make straight for the dock and get the hell out of there, but I summoned my resolve instead. I was just as much a scion as he was—and *any* student had a right to enjoy the lake. Why should I let his presence chase me off? I'd even kept the upper hand the last few times we'd sparred in the interesting new form of combat we'd found ourselves engaged in.

And if it was hard not to notice his impressively muscled chest as he pulled off his T-shirt and strode into the water, this was the perfect opportunity to work on that.

Imogen had noticed the new arrivals too. She glanced over at me as we came to a stop a few feet from the dock. I made a face to her as if to say, *Not happy about it, but what can you do?* and started treading water.

"How's your summer project going?" I asked. I wasn't sure which Nary student Imogen had been assigned to or what her plans for the kid were, and to some extent I hadn't really wanted to know. She was the only even sort-of friend I had here at the moment. But it was probably better to know just how malicious she could be toward the Naries than to bury my head in the sand.

"Oh, I don't know," she said with a bit of a groan. "I didn't know what to pick as a goal, and what I went with is so low key I don't think anyone will be impressed." She dropped her voice, mindful of the fact that one of her competitors might be among our fellow swimmers. "I got one of the music program girls. I'm just encouraging her to listen to and then learn how to play songs by one of my favorite bands. It seemed like something I could pull off."

And not particularly harmful. The tension that had gripped my gut as I'd asked released. "You're expanding her musical horizons," I said with a smile.

"Yeah. I know I'm not going to win—there's never really any chance of that. I only come because my dad's got to be on the grounds during the summer anyway, and maybe the extra work will help improve my skills."

The lake's currents had been shifting around me the whole time, but right then one seemed to condense, teasing around my bare torso like a tracing of soft fingers. My skin tingled, and I caught myself just before my gaze jerked toward Malcolm.

Who else could it be? I didn't have to give him the satisfaction of showing I'd noticed his efforts.

He and his friends had stayed where they could stand on the lake bottom, the water up to their shoulders, with shouts and laughter as they tossed what looked like a frisbee conjured out of water between them. Malcolm had his back to me at the moment, but I guessed he'd gotten a clear enough sense of where I was before he'd taken his current position.

I paddled a little farther out, where I could also more easily keep an eye on him without being obvious about it. With a casting word I hid in an exhalation, I swiveled my hand by my side under the water. We'd see how well *he* could concentrate with currents caressing across his chest.

"How about you?" Imogen asked as she drifted after me. "Are you happy with your progress? We're already almost halfway through."

I thought of the foundation I'd seen laid out this morning, ready for the rest of the building to commence. The staff on the job might be working slowly, but the clubhouse was coming together piece by piece. "I think it's going well. I'll tell you the details when it's done."

She arched her eyebrows, and I wondered if she could already guess that I might be responsible for the activity on the field.

Malcolm hadn't shown any sign of reacting, although his spell was still licking across my belly. I drew my fingers down through the water to send my spell stroking over the planes of his own abdomen, just as the conjured disc soared toward him.

Malcolm's arms twitched, and the watery frisbee flew past his reaching hands. I suppressed a triumphant smile.

He must have redirected his own spell in retaliation, because a few seconds later, it flowed up my front, over the fabric of my bikini. The caressing sensation swept across the curves of my breasts and kissed my nipples with a jolt of pleasure that made me gasp.

Imogen knit her brow. "Are you okay?"

Fuck. I hoped he hadn't heard that sound. "Yeah," I said, fighting to keep my voice steady as the current stroked over my breasts again. "I think a fish brushed my foot. Silly thing to get startled by."

Despite the cool of the water, a flush was rising in my cheeks. Nope, if Malcolm thought he was winning this battle, he could forget about it. Without letting myself second-guess the idea, I raked my fingers even farther down.

Even from some twenty feet away, I heard Malcolm's breath catch as the current would have flowed over his groin. The throw he'd been about to make went wide and crashed into the water.

His friend shook his head with a chuckle and conjured a new disc. "You're off your game today, Nightwood."

I'd braced myself, but I still wasn't quite prepared for the rush of heat as the current shifted against me again. It slid over me until it reached my thighs and trailed over then just below the spot where they joined. An ache formed there, begging to be satisfied, even as I kicked my legs to try to disrupt the spell or at least distract myself from its effects.

I curled my fingers into a cupped shape, and Malcolm let out a sudden cough that might have been disguising a groan. The water flicked right up over my clit, and I closed my eyes with a clench of my jaw to hold back a whimper.

"Rory?" Imogen said tentatively.

"A little dizzy," I managed to answer. "Must be an aftereffect of the heat."

"Do you want to get out?"

Before I had to answer, the purposeful current fell away, leaving only a faint echoing of sensation in its wake. When I opened my eyes, Malcolm was motioning the other guys out of the lake. "I'm cooled off now. Let's find something more interesting to do."

He was giving up. I'd won again. This victory didn't feel all that sweet, though. An unsettling heat was still coursing through my body.

He wrapped his towel around his waist awfully quickly, I noticed. As soon as the guys were well on their way, I pushed myself toward the dock. "I think that's enough for me."

Imogen climbed out after me. I tugged my towel around myself, but it didn't mute the tingling of my nerves. Malcolm and the guys had stopped halfway to the Stormhurst Building. My body balked at the idea of walking past him feeling this exposed.

Imogen started off, and I hesitated at the end of the dock. "You know, I left something in the boathouse the other day. You go on ahead."

"Okay." Her glance was curious, but even if she suspected there was more I wasn't saying, she wasn't going to push the boundaries of our tentative friendship by hassling me about it. She walked on, and I ducked into the dark interior of the boathouse.

By the far side, a motorboat bobbed in the water with a faint squeak of the cables that held it partly suspended. In the stall near me, a couple of kayaks floated. A canoe was propped on the wooden aisle that ran between the two stalls. Lifejackets hung from hooks along the wall over a rack of paddles.

I leaned against the rack, pulling my towel tighter around me. Humid air and the smell of damp pine wood enveloped me. I just needed a few minutes to gather my composure and shake off the effects of Malcolm's teasing.

My pulse had only just started to even out when the boathouse door swung open and Malcolm barrelled in.

"You," was all he said, his voice a rasp, and then he'd reached me, catching my chin to tip my mouth toward his.

I should have pushed him away. I shouldn't have liked it. But every inch of my body sang out in relief with the crash of the kiss.

My mind went blank with the rush of need. My fingers tangled in his cropped curls, digging in tight, my other hand sliding down his bare chest. He groaned against my lips. His hand caught my thigh. My towel dropped to the floor as he lifted me onto the paddle rack.

My legs splayed around his waist. His mouth trailed along my jaw and to the side of my neck with scorching heat. "We can fight more later," he muttered against my skin. "Right now—you've been driving me fucking crazy."

I couldn't find the wherewithal to disagree. The flames we'd been kindling between us blazed through me, and every press of his lips sent them flaring higher. It didn't mean anything other than getting a release.

"I've been driving *you* crazy?" I couldn't help shooting back. Other than that first kiss, he'd been the one lighting the first sparks. I'd have left him alone if he hadn't kept working magic on me.

But I couldn't point that out, because Malcolm was tugging down the strap of my top. His mouth closed over the peak of my breast with a shock of pleasure ten times as intense as anything I'd experienced in the water. I gasped and tipped my head back against the padding of a life jacket.

After a rough swipe of his tongue, the Nightwood scion leaned in to claim my lips again, his hand rising to continue his attentions on my breast. His body pressed against mine, still damp from the lake but even hotter than my own felt. His breath seared over my cheek. "God, I can't wait to be inside you."

Those words cut through my haze of pleasure like a butcher's knife. My back tensed, and my thoughts tumbled back into sharper clarity.

This was Malcolm Nightwood—my tormenter, my enemy. I'd spent the last few months doing everything I could to keep him out of me. I didn't want him penetrating my body any more than I'd wanted him delving into my mind. The idea sent a chill through me that washed away all the heat of the moment.

I yanked myself away from Malcolm, stumbling as my feet hit the floor. Before I could make it more than a couple of steps, he caught my wrist with a chuckle.

"Where do you think you're going? I think we've had enough of a chase."

He tugged me around, and I pulled against him. My feet slipped on the wet boards. Malcolm's grasp slowed my fall, but my ass still hit the floor. He bent over me, kissing the crook of my jaw, one hand cradling the back of my head as the other ran down my body. The strength radiating from his well-built form as it loomed over me set off a flash of panic.

"Get off," I snapped.

He chuckled again. "We're nowhere near finished."

I smacked at him, and he snatched my wrist before the blow landed. A fresh wave of fear raced through me. It must have coursed into Malcolm, since he was the one who'd caused it, but he brought his mouth to the side of my neck without any sign of caring. My pulse stuttered.

"So you're going to *rape* me?" I said, and spat out a word full of magic. "Off!"

He was already recoiling when the wallop of energy slammed into him. It threw him not just off of me but staggering a few feet back. I scrambled up into a sitting position, pulling my knees up defensively and hauling my bikini top back into place.

Malcolm was staring at me, his chest heaving. "I—You *wanted* this."

He took a step back toward me, and I flinched. He must have been able to feel the shudder of my anxiety as well as seeing it. He froze, his stance going rigid.

"Not with you," I said, not quite able to smooth the quaver from my voice. "Not like that."

A waft of answering fear flowed into my chest. Fear of what I'd do next? Fear of what *he'd* almost done?

His expression had stiffened too. "I didn't mean—" he started in an uncertain tone, and then his jaw clenched. "*You're* the one who started this."

That was a fair point. I pulled myself onto my feet, groping for my towel. The feel of the thick fabric draped around my shoulders steadied me.

"I did," I said. "And I'm sorry I did. So now I'm stopping it. Don't touch me again, in any way, or I'll break every bone in your hands. Are we clear?"

He opened his mouth and closed it again. His face had paled and flushed at the same time, turning it blotchy. "I wouldn't have forced you," he said finally, his voice ragged. "Just so we're clear on *that.* I thought you were into it. I thought it was all more messing around."

My teeth gritted. "Then you weren't paying enough attention. I was fucking terrified." And he had no real excuse for not being perfectly aware of that other than he'd ignored the emotion because he'd been too caught up in his own desires.

Which he knew just as well as I did. He took another step, away from me this time, with an audible swallow. I couldn't see that there was anything else to say here. Hugging my towel around me, I hurried out of the building.

I made it most of the way to Ashgrave Hall without running into anyone. But when I reached the green, Declan was just crossing it, heading toward me. He stopped in his tracks at the sight of me, the worry that flashed across his face enough to tell me how out of sorts I must look.

"What happened?" he said, marching over. "Are you all right, Rory?"

There'd been a time, early on in my education here, when he'd asked a question like that and I'd thrown it back in his face because I'd known he wouldn't help me. Now, I could see the determination to defend me all through his posture, gleaming in his eyes. It made my throat close up.

He wasn't supposed to be defending me. He was supposed to be pretending he barely cared about me at all. I could ruin his life because of all the impulses I'd given into just as easily as I'd set Malcolm and me on that path toward near disaster.

There were a lot of problems here at Blood U, but I couldn't say I had no part in them.

I dragged in a breath. "I'll be okay. Really. Thank you. I'm sure you've got more important things to worry about."

Declan's jaw worked, but he schooled his expression to be more detached at the same time. "If you change your mind—"

"I know." I managed a small smile that seemed to convince him. He hesitated for a second longer and then continued the way he'd been going. I dashed the rest of the way into the shelter of the dorm building with a lump of guilt expanding through my stomach.

CHAPTER SEVENTEEN

Rory

The cry rang out loud enough that it pierced my closed window and reached my ears through the hum of the air conditioning system. I jumped up from my bed where I'd been flipping through a magical text from the library and leaned close to the glass. From that angle, I couldn't make out the cause of the disturbance. A few students on the ground nearby had turned to look at something out of my view—something to the east. Where the clubhouse was being built.

My heart lurched. The spells I'd laid down hadn't given me any warning, but I knew better than to count on them to work perfectly. I dashed out the door and down the stairs, wishing for the thousandth time that the school administration had invested in elevators.

The second I came around the building, I knew my fears had been right. Several students were gathering around the construction area where the framework had just started to go up. I spotted Benjamin and a couple of his friends among them, his shoulders tight as he gestured toward the site with jerky motions. I hesitated and then let myself drift over for a closer look.

Lots of people had heard that cry. I wasn't the only one who'd come by to see what the fuss was. My presence wouldn't be too conspicuous.

As I approached, my spirits sank even lower. The boards that had gone up over the last few days lay splintered and ragged across the ground. A large stone, practically a boulder, lay in their midst, as if it had caused all that damage smashing through from who knew where.

That wasn't how it had happened at all, of course. Someone had destroyed the frame purposefully like magic, leaving that boulder to give the Naries a plausible if unexpected explanation.

Beneath the scattered boards, the concrete foundation was split with cracks, some as wide as my thumb. I winced inwardly at the sight of them. Shit. That whole slab would probably have to be dug up and laid all over again. Were the Naries supposed to believe the randomly falling rock had smashed the cement hard enough to cause all that damage too? A few damp spots gleamed on the cement in the mid-morning light—maybe they were supposed to think a sudden swelling of groundwater had contributed?

It didn't really matter what they believed. Either way, so much of the progress they'd made on the building was ruined.

One of the girls from the architecture program was sputtering angrily, and the other boy offered her a hug, looking like he needed one too. Benjamin picked his way around the site, shaking his head, his expression stormy. From where I stood several feet away, I murmured a few words to test the wards I'd put up. They didn't respond to my magic at all. Whoever had done this had picked them apart first, so carefully the spells hadn't triggered.

A couple of the other Naries who'd been helping the architecture students had joined the onlookers. "What the hell are we going to do now?" one of them moaned.

Watching them in their obvious distress, my stomach knotted. In some ways, this was my fault. I'd come up with this idea; I'd decided I could beat all the other fearmancers in the school, direct not one but several Naries, and create some sort of permanent haven for them. I'd only had a few months to get a handle on my magic. Maybe I'd taken on too much, gotten in over my head…

It wouldn't be the first time I'd gone careening way over a line I should never have crossed. The thought of Malcolm in the boathouse two days ago, the way I'd *welcomed* his passion when he'd first come in, made my stomach turn.

I'd pushed these people so far for my goals, and now they were devastated, and I couldn't even step in and tell them I had their backs. I couldn't even promise, openly or not, that I'd make sure they could see this endeavor through. It could be I'd pumped them up for nothing but a whole lot of failure.

The doubts stole my breath. I backed up a step. Should I just let it go now? I obviously couldn't protect this project the way I needed to in order to ensure they ever finished the building…

But as I grappled with the idea of retreating, Benjamin stepped toward the others. "We can't let them take this away from us," he said, his voice raw.

The other guy from his class stared at him. "You think it was—?"

"I think those assholes had something to do with it. They can't stand the thought that we'd have our own place. That's why we needed this so fucking much." He kicked at the grass in a futile gesture.

"So, what can we do about it?" the girl said, swiping at her eyes. Tear tracks glinted on her cheeks. "I don't want to give up. I wanted this to work so badly. But… look at it."

I swallowed hard, watching them. I could see how much this project had come to mean to them on every face, in every stance. Maybe it'd been my idea, maybe I'd nudged them into taking it on, but the pain they were feeling right now, I hadn't conjured. They were upset because having this safe place amid the hostility they faced here truly mattered that much to them.

I drew up my chin. I'd dangled that hope in front of them. I'd gotten them this far. It might have been crazily ambitious of me, but I was the goddamned heir of Bloodstone, powerful in all four domains of magic, and I would *make* this thing work. Because I owed them. Because it was the one really good thing I'd started to do here.

Just let the other fearmancers try to stop me.

I walked back to the central buildings, but once I reached them I found a spot on my own and turned to watch the Naries again. "*It's just a setback, that's all,*" I said under my breath, focusing on Benjamin. "*You know you've got enough time to start over. You can start clearing away the wrecked pieces right now. The workers will start over—they're committed.*"

Or at least, they would be after I'd worked some persuasive magic on them too.

First, though, I had to rebuild my protections—and build them better—so no one shattered the building efforts all over again. I nibbled at my lower lip, thinking over the various strategies I'd read about in my research over the last few weeks. The one I'd used had seemed like the best option. Was there something I could add to it?

Maybe I just had to re-power the spells more often? If it'd help keep this site secure, I'd set an alarm to get out there in the middle of the night as well as however many times it took during the day.

The Naries had started lugging the boards off of the cracked base, tossing them into a heap to the side of the site. Obviously Benjamin had passed on the inspiration I'd sent into his head. I eased closer again, giving the site a wide berth but studying the grassy landscape around it as I considered the possibilities.

Footsteps whispered through the grass toward me. I looked up to see Connar coming to join me, his hands slung in the pockets of his slacks, his face set in that cautiously hopeful expression it often had around me these days. After his openness with me out at the Shifting Grounds, his presence didn't make me tense up anymore. Right now I needed to strategize, not talk, though.

As Connar had apparently already figured out. He stopped beside me, took in the clubhouse site and the field around it, and glanced my way. "So this is your take on the summer project, huh?"

"Is it that obvious?" I said, a little warmth creeping into my cheeks. I'd been *trying* to keep my involvement secret, but I couldn't say that subterfuge was necessarily one of my strong points.

He chuckled softly. "Knowing you, I could make an educated guess. I think a lot of other people are starting to catch on, though, because of the scale and the direction you're going in. There aren't many students here who'd come up with an idea this ambitious that'll make it *harder* for anyone to harass the Naries."

"Which is exactly why they need a place where no one can," I muttered, and let out a sigh. All right, so the cat was out of the bag. Connar didn't sound as if he was bothered by the direction I'd taken. He had offered to help me with my magic before. With Physicality, though—I wasn't sure that was the angle I needed to take here. My previous protective spells had been a mix of illusion and persuasion.

"I need to figure out how to stop the others from wrecking this all over again," I went on with a subtle tip of my head toward the demolished structure. "I had wards up to warn me about magic being cast and to try to drive people away, but they didn't work well enough, obviously."

Connar nodded and wet his lips. "Do you… want some help?"

His uncertainty about how I'd respond to his offer sent a twinge of affection through me. "Sure. If you've got ideas, I'm happy to hear them. And if you don't mind supporting someone else's bid for the win."

He gave me a crooked smile. "Somehow I don't think seeing this thing built is about winning the contest for you. And even if it was, I'd rather see you take it. How did you handle your original wards?"

He listened thoughtfully as I explained the pieces I'd brought together and my reasoning, with a hum here and a nod there. When I finished, he turned and motioned for me to follow him. "Come on."

"Where are we going?"

"Just to the forest. It'll be easier to find what we're looking for there." He walked a few paces past the first trees and then scanned the ground. After a moment, he bent by a jutting root and picked up a rock about the size of his palm. "That's got a good heft. Look for more like that or even a little bigger. If you want something to act as an anchor, it works better if it's got some literal weight to it."

"An anchor?" I repeated, brushing the dirt off the rock and dropping it into my purse.

"You've been fixing your spells to the ground in general," Connar said, moving on with his search. "That works, but the energy tends to disperse faster when it's not tied to a specific object. And you can concentrate the magic for a stronger effect when you have a concrete thing you're imbuing. We can even reshape them so they'll conduct the energy more effectively."

That fit with some of what I'd read. A powerful mage could imbue the right object with a spell that could last centuries, like my puzzle garden. But—

"I just figured it'd be a lot easier for someone to displace them, if they can spot the object I've tied the spell to. Having the magic spread across the ground makes it harder to target a counterspell." I crouched to pick up a rock.

"True. But I think you can get around that. Embed a few of them in the dirt right before they pour the concrete again, for example. No one will be able to dig them out easily then, but you'll know where they are if you need to boost the spells."

"Right. I should have thought of that." They'd just been nowhere near the concrete pouring stage when I'd first set up my wards.

"You're new at this," Connar said calmly. "You'll get a better handle on what works best for any given situation as you gain more experience."

"As people keep telling me. I guess it's pretty obvious how far behind I still am."

Connar stopped abruptly and swiveled to face me. "You've been doing amazing, Rory. Don't let anyone tell you differently. Who else would even have tried to take on a project like that?" He waved toward the field.

Warmth bloomed in my chest at the compliment, but I found it hard to fully accept. "I think it matters more whether I actually pull it off. Ambition isn't much good without follow-through."

"Without ambition, there's nothing to follow through *on*, is there?" He picked up another rock and brought it over to me. His fingers brushed mine as I took it from him, with flickers of a different sort of warmth that were fanned by the appreciation in his eyes. "You've already gotten pretty damn far. And I'll help you make the rest of it happen. There's no harm in calling on allies." He grinned.

I'd always loved the way that bright smile could transform his chiseled face from something handsome but grim to absolutely stunning. Its effect on him and on me hadn't changed. My pulse fluttered as I smiled back at him. "You really don't have to do this," I said.

"Haven't I made it clear enough that I want to?"

It would have been the perfect moment for him to lean in and kiss me. If all the awfulness between us had never happened, he probably would have. As it was, he motioned for me to sit down next to him. "Shaping conducting pieces definitely falls into my domain. I'll show you the elements you need for a good ward anchor."

He took one of the stones back from me and cupped it in his hands. "We want this part more rounded and hollowed for the right resonance of containment," he said, the enthusiasm of sharing his knowledge animating his voice. "And a point protruding at the bottom to steady it."

I leaned close as he talked me through the process step by step, transforming that one stone carefully before my eyes and then watching while I worked with one myself. His hand brushed mine again when he made a small suggestion. In the midst of my concentration, my shoulder came to rest against his. He nodded, his head bowed close to mine.

"That's perfect," he said softly when I'd finished.

I looked up at him, and an eager quiver ran through me at his nearness, his light blue eyes fixed on mine. The memory of how it felt to be held by him rose up with a rush of eager warmth. I couldn't say I had any doubts left about whether this change of heart was genuine. He'd thrown his lot in with me completely.

But, damn, it'd been bad enough a couple months ago when I'd been grappling with my attraction to both Declan and Jude. Those feelings hadn't faded, not really, even if I was reining them in with both guys, and something in me had sparked with Malcolm, as much as I hated that it had. Now, to feel drawn back to Connar on top of all that… What the hell was wrong with me? How could I be caught up in four different guys all at the same time?

I ducked my head, shame prickling over my skin. "Maybe you shouldn't be here. I'm a mess, Connar. You have no idea… *I* have no idea what I want. Or maybe it's that I want too many different things."

I exhaled with exasperation. "It doesn't really seem fair to pull you into that."

"Rory." He touched my cheek, just lightly, but that gentle touch sent tingles through my whole body. "Look at who you're talking to. You want to talk about messes? You can't get much messier than me. The way we're raised, the kind of people we're supposed to grow up to be—I'd be surprised if there's anyone on campus who isn't some kind of mess. I don't mind. I'm not here because I expect anything from you. However much *you* want me is all I care about—and I'll take that as it is."

The tender warmth that had spread through me before stretched even further, filling my throat, wrapping around my lungs. I rested my hand on his chest tentatively.

Accepting everything he was offering wouldn't hurt him. It shouldn't hurt me either. That was more than I could say for any of the other guys right now. Connar had been the first one to really understand me.

And God, I was getting so tired of having to pull back, to walk away, to tell myself no. I didn't want to go rushing in right back to where we'd left off… but I could allow myself a little indulgence, couldn't I?

"I do want you," I said quietly, raising my eyes. When he dipped his head, I lifted mine to meet him. And his kiss was every bit as sweet as I remembered.

Once we'd started, I didn't want to stop. One kiss slid into another, each deeper and more tender than the last. I hadn't really remembered what it was like to kiss a guy I was *allowed* to want, who I couldn't ruin and who wasn't out to ruin me. The joy of it took my breath away.

I couldn't let it overwhelm me, though. Getting lost in the heat of the moment had gotten me into too much trouble already. I let myself lean into one more kiss, reveling in the press of Connar's mouth, and then I drew back, tipping my head against his shoulder instead. He clasped my hand. For a few minutes, we just sat there in companionable silence.

A thread of tension ran through my sense of peace. I shouldn't be getting comfortable at all. The conflicts of life here on campus had distracted me from my bigger concerns for too long. Professor Banefield's key was still tucked in my purse, unused.

Thanks to Connar, soon my project site would be much better protected. Protected enough that I could risk leaving campus for long enough to do some more investigating.

CHAPTER EIGHTEEN

Jude

As I stood in the entranceway of the New York City brownstone, waiting for the upper apartment to answer my buzz, my heart thumped away at an erratic rhythm. My attempts to will it into evening out had little effect.

My mission here really was a silly thing to get nervous about. Sure, I didn't have the slightest idea whether I really would be able to convince the man living in that apartment to go along with my plan, and if he did and we were found out, we could both be punished harshly under fearmancer law. I might be expelled from Blood U on top of that. And then there was the whole matter of my relationship with Rory possibly riding on this act.

But really, when you cut it down to the core of the matter, I was a Killbrook calling on a close family friend for a favor well within his expertise, and that sort of thing was standard practice. I'd never really liked claiming benefits through the Killbrook name, not since I'd found out it wasn't really mine, but if I was going to lose it soon enough, I might as well take advantage of it while I could.

Since I'd called Dr. Wolfton to arrange this appointment, he was expecting me. The door to the stairway unlocked with a click, no inquiring voice crackling through the intercom. I started up at a brisk pace. If he agreed, we might even see this mission through today.

I'd never visited the doctor at his home before. He was a regular guest at the Killbrook Manor, a close friend of Dad's from college whose placid demeanor always set Mom at ease too. No doubt he'd been dropping in on them even more than usual the last few months while I'd been at school, overseeing the early stages of Mom's pregnancy.

In the years since I'd made my world-upending discovery, I'd sometimes wondered how involved Dr. Wolfton might have been in my parents' initial attempts at producing a child. Did he know just how much they'd struggled, just how clear it'd become that they were unlikely to ever conceive? Had he ever suspected that my arrival, therefore, might have involved some trickery?

I'd studied him closely during many visits since then, and I'd never seen any sign in his attitude toward me that he saw me as a sort of interloper. The cautious insight spells I'd tried on him hadn't revealed any wariness. Actually, he was much more likely to laugh at my more cutting jokes and ask me with genuine interest how my studies were going than many of my parents' friends.

If he'd known the full extent of their difficulties, he must have thought my mother's first pregnancy was as much a bit of unexpected luck as her current one.

Dr. Wolfton opened the door as I reached his floor, smiling his usual calm smile. His whole aura was so soothing I found it hard to imagine how he ever generated enough fear to fuel his magic, but maybe he could turn on the menace as needed. Or he might make extensive use of his familiar. Unlike most fearmancers, he'd opted for a non-predator animal, but in a city mostly inhabited by Naries, a rat could generate plenty of panic just by making an appearance in a nearby apartment.

"Jude," he said in his equally calm voice. "Come on in. I'm curious to hear this mysterious request of yours."

When I'd called him, he'd offered to come by the school so we could talk, but I'd told him I'd thought it'd be better somewhere there was less chance of us being overheard—that the topic was somewhat "sensitive." Now I just had to find the right way to pitch it to him. Thankfully I should be able to count on my magic for that. Insight was my one other true strength, and one from past experience I knew Dr. Wolfton either couldn't or didn't bother shielding against very carefully.

"Thanks for letting me come over," I said, figuring it couldn't hurt to lead with politeness.

He ushered me into an apartment with a weird contrast of grand moldings, fine architectural stylings, and totally modest furnishings. "Can I get you anything to drink?" he asked.

I sank down on his linen sofa. "I think I'm all right. Might as well cut to the chase, right?"

He sat across from me in an armchair, his gaze intent. To him, I wasn't just the son of his best friend but a scion and one of his future barons, I reminded myself. He'd *want* to make me happy if he could.

"What's this about?" he said.

I clasped my hands on my lap. "I have a favor to ask. A medical favor. Someone I'd like you to perform a magical treatment on… but it would have to be done without them realizing any magic was used."

Dr. Wolfton's eyebrows rose. The hesitation that crossed his face made my gut twist.

"It would be for their benefit," I added quickly. "It's only that—the person in question is a Nary. That's why the secrecy."

His eyebrows stayed up. "And how did you become so invested in a Nary that you're going out of your way to handle their medical treatment?" he asked with a hint of bemusement.

"It's a fellow student from the university."

The doctor waited, obviously not considering that enough of an answer. I restrained a grimace. "Seeing this matter taken care of is important to me. I hardly have the skill to do it myself. That's why I hoped you could help."

Dr. Wolfton ran his fingers through his fine gray hair. "I'm assuming if the university medical staff felt they could reasonably intervene, they would have."

"They don't have half the skill you do," I said. "And you know how over-cautious they can be. I wouldn't be here asking if I wasn't sure you could pull it off."

He looked as if he was about to shake his head. Before he could express any more doubts, I leaned on my last gambit. "Actually, I am kind of thirsty. If I could just get a glass of water…"

"Of course." He got up, maybe relieved to have a respite from the awkward conversation, and walked past me through the kitchen's wide arched doorway.

I turned on the sofa to watch him. As he reached for a glass in the cupboard over the sink, I fixed my gaze on the back of his head and murmured an insight spell by way of a question. "*What do you want?*"

It was a nicely broad avenue of inquiry. I slipped into the flow of his thoughts and emotions with only the faintest hitch of a breach. Images washed over me.

Well, I couldn't offer *that*. That was too simple for a situation like this. Ah, there we were.

A smile curved my lips. I'd have him. It was only a matter of putting the offer to him in the right terms.

"Look," I said when he came back with the glass, "I realize this is a big ask. I wouldn't expect you to do it just out of the goodness of your heart. I'll repay you."

The doctor adjusted his glasses as he sat back down. "I couldn't take a fee for something like this."

"Oh, no, that's not what I meant at all." I gave him my most winning grin. "I gather there are some people you're looking to impress. I can cast some very impressive illusions."

Dr. Wolfton paused, but he couldn't hide the flash of hope that lit his eyes. My grin widened. Jackpot.

"What exactly did you have in mind?" he said slowly, leaning forward in his chair, and I knew it was only a matter of negotiation now.

Honestly, it was hard to look at the little town we'd driven into and not think it was awfully drab. Dr. Wolfton didn't look concerned as he parked down the street from the address I'd looked up, but this place was a far cry from both New York City and the elegance of the Killbrook properties.

"She has to think you're a regular doctor," I said, as if we hadn't already been over this, as if he didn't know the consequences of a mistake as well as I did. My nerves were twitching away. "It's better if she thinks the other doctors made a mistake, not that you fixed something they couldn't."

"I know," the doctor said in his usual mild tone, and patted my shoulder. "From what you described, I don't imagine it'll be much trouble. Take a walk around if you'd like to. I expect I'll be a half hour or so."

I didn't think I'd want to wander around this place, but after a few impatient minutes twiddling my thumbs in the car, I couldn't bear to just sit anymore.

My feet carried me off without much sense of direction. I ended up at a park a few blocks away. The sun beamed brightly over the whole place, warming my skin. A woman was walking her dog in the broad grassy area. Children clambered over the playground equipment while their parents or other caretakers watched. I meandered around the fringes, feeling utterly out of place.

This was the right move, wasn't it? Suddenly my entire plan seemed ridiculous.

And yet Rory's voice rose up in the back of my head, repeating the words that had echoed through my mind over and over since the moment she'd said them. *All that matters to me is what you do and what you believe.*

I sucked in a breath, and with it my resolve steadied.

I knew her. I thought maybe I was starting to really understand her. And this—this was *doing* something. Trying to woo her all over again had never been the right tactic. She already knew how I could be with her. My charms had never been the problem.

It might be too late to fix the actual problem, but at least I could give it my best shot. And… even if this didn't change her mind about me, it wouldn't be for nothing. I'd done damage that I hadn't meant to, that the recipient hadn't deserved. Some part of me felt a little relief just knowing I might be able to reverse that. Which wasn't an emotion I'd ever have anticipated experiencing in these circumstances, but…

In the playground, one mother and father clasped their toddler's hands as they eased him down the slide. The child burst into excited laughter when he reached the bottom. I propped myself against a tree to watch, and a hollow sensation opened in my stomach.

Look at these people—these people without magic. *Was* there really anything all that different about them other than that fact? Could I really say that mother and father were worse than my own? That their child deserved less than I did? God, could *anyone* deserve less than the lot my father had inflicted on me?

The thought still jarred uneasily inside me, but it was starting to sink in. The look on Rory's face when she'd said it wouldn't matter if I were a Nary, that my magic didn't even factor into what she thought of me… In that moment, it'd hit me just how much she meant that.

I had less magical skill than everyone around me believed. Did I really believe that made me less of a person than Malcolm or Connar or Declan? And if it didn't… then why would these people in front of me be anything less than some half-assed mage who could barely cast a coherent spell?

Because it let us feel powerful. Because we enjoyed having someone to lord it over. Because we were all full of fucking bullshit.

That was the way my father thought—about appearances, about clinging to status. I'd thought I was nothing like him, but I'd bought into an awful lot of the same ideals, hadn't I?

I watched the Naries go about their lives for several minutes longer, and then I headed back to the car. None of the thoughts that had been whirling around inside my head felt easy. But I'd opened my eyes to something I'd missed before, and that could only mean I was heading someplace better.

I just hoped I hadn't taken too long getting there.

CHAPTER NINETEEN

Rory

It appeared I'd made it to Professor Banefield's home off-campus just in time. Or maybe not quite on time, considering that the truck for some storage company was parked out front and the workers were already prepping it to be loaded. Whoever Banefield's inheritors were, they'd obviously heard about his death by now, and they'd decided to pack up the contents of his house.

I watched from my car down the street, suddenly wishing I'd rented something inconspicuous rather than driving the Bloodstone Lexus from the university garage. None of the workers had glanced my way yet, but the Lexus didn't exactly fit in on this suburban street. My mentor might have been an expert at his craft, but he mustn't have been much for extravagance—or maybe he'd just downsized a lot after his wife's death. The pastel-trimmed bungalow didn't look like anything a fearmancer would want to be caught in, dead or alive.

I needed to look through the contents of that house before these people shipped them off. Something in there might fit the key he'd given me or at least lead me to the place I needed to go. Which meant

I had to find some way of diverting the company for at least an hour or two to give me time for a thorough search.

My back tensed as two of the men walked up to the front door. What would make them leave—and stay away for a while? They were here to move furniture and box up the other possessions… They wouldn't be prepared to deal with anything more fraught than that.

An idea unfurled in my head as one of the workers fit a house key into the lock. As many issues as I'd had with Victory, she'd demonstrated plenty of repulsive spells I could use for inspiration. I didn't have the chance to give the brainstorm a lot of thought. As the guy pushed open the door, I muttered the word "rancid" under my breath with a flick of my hand.

My magic coursed through the air and condensed into a sensory illusion that flooded the front hall. The worker coughed and backed up a step, waving his hand in front of his face.

"What the hell?" he said. "Something's gone *very* bad in there. We can't work in a place like that."

The guy next to him caught a whiff and turned a bit green. "Call it in to the office. They've got to let the owners know to put a cleaning crew through there before we can get on with the job."

They tramped back to the truck and closed the ramp. I exhaled in relief. I couldn't imagine the inheritors would be able to find a cleaning crew in an instant, even if the storage company reached them right away. The gambit should buy me enough of a window.

I waited until the truck had pulled out of sight around a corner farther down the road and then gave it another ten minutes just to be sure. In an ideal scenario, I'd have made myself invisible so no one even saw me walking over to Professor Banefield's house, but from what I'd gathered, hiding one's self from all angles across a significant distance wasn't the sort of thing you should first attempt in potential view of dozens of Naries. Rendering myself invisible on an open street was several orders of magnitude above cloaking my descent ten feet down a solid wall.

Instead, I relied on the illusion of looking like I belonged here. I ambled down the street as if I wasn't in any particular hurry and headed down the driveway to the back of the house like I lived there.

The high picket fence around the backyard meant I didn't have to worry as much about witnesses there. I popped the lock with a quick casting and slipped inside.

My stink illusion had remained at the front of the house. I dispelled it with a word and a wave so I wouldn't have to inhale it and started my search.

The house's interior definitely gave the impression that Professor Banefield hadn't invested much energy in the space since he'd moved here. The pots hanging in the kitchen were coated with a layer of dust; a few pieces of framed art leaned against the walls in the living and dining room, but nothing had been hung. Here and there, moving boxes sat open, some with just a few objects lying in the bottom, some still mostly full.

In the second bedroom, where the mattress was bare, I came across a stack of closed boxes labeled "Delia." His wife's name, I guessed. Looking at them, a lump rose in my throat. She'd died in a car accident several years ago—while pregnant with their first kid. I couldn't imagine how awful that'd been for Banefield. Her absence must have still haunted him.

I didn't come across any safes or lockboxes. The house didn't even have furniture with locked drawers here like he'd had in his office.

After I'd riffled through every room, I came to a stop in the hallway with a sigh. If I didn't find anything here, I had no idea where to look next. This was my last lead.

If the key didn't fit anything here or in his office, then he must have another property, or a storage unit, or a safety deposit box. That would cost money. Money left a paper trail.

There'd been a file box full of receipts and banking statements in Banefield's bedroom closet. I crouched down next to it and pulled out the first few papers. Those were from three years ago. Would he have had whatever the key opened that long? I dug farther, but he seemed to have tossed records in haphazardly. Here was one from this past winter, here one from five years ago.

The growl of an engine right outside made my skin turn cold. I got up and eased over to the window. My pulse hiccupped.

Another van had pulled up outside. The inheritors had gotten their act together faster than I'd anticipated. Shit.

I wavered and then grabbed the box of financial records. These distant family members had been out of the picture so long they were only just taking care of Banefield's belongings. It wasn't likely they'd realize this box was missing… and if they did, they'd have no idea who'd taken it. Hefting it in my arms, I dashed for the back door.

The picket fence created a problem now. There was no easy escape route other than back up the driveway where the van was parked. I braced myself by the back of the building and peeked around the corner.

Four figures were getting out of the van. Two of them retrieved baskets of cleaning supplies from the back. Then they all trooped over to the house.

The door squeaked open and thumped shut behind them. I hustled along the driveway, past the van, and down the street, slowing when I'd gotten a few house-lengths away. As soon as I reached my car, I tossed the box in the trunk.

I wasn't sure I could bring that into my dorm room without raising all kinds of questions… but at least I had it now.

In the end, I opted to leave Professor Banefield's records stashed in the trunk of the Lexus. No one had messed with my car yet. It had an actual lock, unlike my bedroom door, and I enhanced that with an extra casting that should punish anyone who tried to open it by magical means with a sharp electric zap.

I headed up to the dorm intent on grabbing something to eat and then checking on the clubhouse site. When I opened the door, I stopped in my tracks, my jaw going slack.

"Shelby?"

The Nary girl turned with a swish of her mousy brown ponytail. It *was* her, with her usual shy smile as if she couldn't quite believe I'd be happy to see her.

A much wider smile sprang across my face. I grabbed her in a hug and then eased away, joy and disbelief mingling inside me. "Are you really back? Like, back in the program and everything? What happened?"

My reaction had left Shelby beaming. She raised her hand where her wrist had been broken and waggled her fingers. No cast, no sign she'd ever been injured other than a slight pallor to her skin around the joint.

"It was amazing," she said. "Two days ago, this doctor just showed up at my house. He said he looked over the records of my treatment and thought the other doctors made a big mistake in interpreting the X-rays—something about shadow fragments or I don't know what. Anyway, it was about time for the cast to come off anyway, so he took it off and led me through these exercises, gave me a cream to rub into it, and by the next day, my wrist already felt as strong as before. I can play no problem!"

I blinked. A doctor showing up out of nowhere? And her wrist *had* been broken.

The guy must have used magic to make her recover that quickly. But who would have—Ms. Grimsworth had said there was no way the school could interfere—

"The headmistress called me yesterday afternoon," Shelby went on. "She said a 'concerned party' had been following my case—I guess one of the people on the scholarship panel?—and they'd heard I might be able to continue with the courses here after all. I told her I was sure I could, and…" She gestured to herself and her room. "I just got here half an hour ago. I guess it's pretty quiet during the summer, huh?"

"Yeah," I said, still reeling. "Only some people come for the summer session." A suspicion started to form in my head. There were very few mages who knew about Shelby's situation and would have gone out on a limb like this. Declan might have wished he could, but he wouldn't have compromised his position over a girl he hadn't even known. I didn't think I'd ever talked about Shelby with Connar. So…

"It's so great to be back," Shelby said. She snatched up her cello case and hugged the neck of it. "I've got to get going—there's a class about to start and I don't want to fall any more behind—but maybe we can go get dinner tonight? Imogen too, if she's around and wants to?"

"Yeah, that'd be great. You go show them you haven't missed a beat."

I gave her a minute's head start, and then I went out too—down to the fourth floor to the dorm room across from Declan's. When I knocked, a burly guy with a scraggly moustache opened, with a little jolt of nerves that echoed into me when he saw who'd come calling.

"Hi," I said. "Ah, is Jude around?"

The guy looked as if he was afraid of what I'd do to him if he didn't produce Jude instantaneously. "Killbrook," he called over his shoulder. "It's one of your colleagues."

He stepped back to let me in, and I stopped just past the threshold. Jude emerged from his bedroom in the corner looking vaguely irritated until his gaze found me. He brightened so quickly a pang shot through my chest.

I hadn't thought he was capable of caring enough about the damage he'd done to make real amends. I hadn't been sure he could even understand that harm done to a Nary was actual damage.

He strode over, his gaze never leaving my face. "She's back at school?" he said, erasing any lingering doubts I might have had about who Shelby's mysterious benefactor had been. "It all worked out?"

The lengths he must have gone to—my God. And he looked not just pleased with himself but *relieved*, like he'd really been worried about whether his efforts would succeed.

"It worked," I confirmed. "You…"

No words felt adequate. A couple of his dormmates were watching us, and the urge rose up inside me to show both him and them how much I adored him in this moment. I clasped the front of his shirt and tugged him into a kiss.

I'd meant it to be a quick one, not much more than a peck. But Jude made a tight sound and kissed me back hard, and it took me a few seconds to think of anything other than the intensity of his mouth against mine. I managed to swallow a gasp as I drew back.

"How did you—" I started, lowering my voice, and hesitated with the awareness of our small but avid audience. "Is there somewhere we can talk?"

Jude's head twitched toward his bedroom, but he must have had the same awareness of the thin walls as I did.

"Come on," he said, setting a tentative hand on the small of my back to guide me. "There's the scion lounge."

His hand dropped away as we went down the stairs, but he sidled a little closer. "So, that kiss," he said in his teasing tone. "Was that just a one-time, 'thank you so much' kiss, or was that a 'you're the love of my life, Jude, and I never want to stop kissing you again' kiss?"

I elbowed him, but I couldn't help smiling. "Maybe give me a little more time to decide?"

"I suppose that's fair." His cavalier attitude faded for a second, his expression turning serious. "I didn't help her only because I knew you'd appreciate it. It wasn't just some kind of ploy to win you back. I—I wanted to do the right thing. I don't want to be responsible for screwing up people's lives. Maybe that's a little hard to believe—I'm not sure I'd have believed it a few months ago—but, if you want to poke around inside my head to see I mean it, or—"

"It's okay." I touched his arm, the earlier pang coming back at his fumbling earnestness. "I believe you." Something had changed in his perspective, something that hadn't quite clicked all those weeks before. It would've been easier to pull off a scheme like this when Shelby had first been injured, and I'd have been just as happy about it then, but he'd needed time to find his way there.

And after our conversation in the piano room the other evening, we were way past lying and pretense. Maybe it'd been something about the vulnerability of his confession that had opened him up in other ways too.

I hadn't given much thought to the location he'd suggested until I was descending the basement stairs and my chest clenched up. It squeezed tighter as I stepped into the lounge room with its cluster of seating, the pool table, the bar cabinet.

The last time I'd been in this room, the guy standing next to me had made me believe he was feeding Deborah to his familiar. He'd smirked at my panic.

Jude noticed my reaction and stiffened with a wince. "Maybe this isn't the best place after all. We could go outside somewhere..."

I shook my head, letting the emotions well up inside me. "No. What happened here really happened. If we can't face that, then we haven't gotten anywhere."

He turned to me, his head bowed. "I'm so fucking sorry," he said hoarsely. "If I'd known—if I'd seen—" He let out a frustrated sound. "I should have been the one bowing down to you."

He dropped to his knees as he said it, in a motion every particle in my body rejected, especially after what he'd told me about his parentage. I grasped his shoulder with the urgent need to bring him back onto his feet. "No. You're not less than I am. You're never *less*."

I wasn't sure he believed me, but as he got up, his gaze searching mine, it struck me how it must have felt to him back then. What it must have been like for a guy who'd spent the last seven years knowing he was wearing a false crown, that at any moment the rug could be pulled out from under him and he'd lose everything, faced with a girl who'd had all the same handed to her in an instant only for her to try to throw it away.

Of course some part of him had hated me. He hadn't known any of the other things I was going through.

I leaned in again, seeking out his lips, wanting to confirm the connection we had now. Jude cupped my face as he met me. This kiss, I let linger on, soft and tender. The two of us, together. Understanding each other. There was something miraculous about how far we'd come to unite in this moment.

Jude's hand lingered against my cheek as our mouths parted. "Well," he said, "I'm glad to know it was at least a two-time thing."

A laugh tumbled out of me, but I didn't think his question before had been totally in jest. "I'm not making any declarations about the 'love of my life' anytime soon, just so we're clear." I thought of Connar in the forest, the comfort I'd taken from his embrace. "I can't even say you're the only one I'm going to be kissing. You should know that."

"You're a woman who wants to keep her options open," Jude said with a nonchalance I could tell took some effort. "I can respect that.

I'll simply endeavor to continue to be the most appealing option." He paused, and his eyes narrowed slightly. "You and Connar…?"

And Declan. And Malcolm. Although I supposed the former didn't matter since he'd rejected any possibility of a real relationship, and the latter didn't because no way in hell was that happening again. So, Connar. I decided it couldn't hurt anything to admit this much. "To be fair, he was there first, before anything ever happened between us."

"He—*what*?" Jude looked so flabbergasted by this announcement it was almost funny. "When—*how*—you're joking."

"Nope. While you were busy figuring out ways to make me miserable, he and I ended up talking and getting to know each other, and one thing led to another…" I spread my hands.

"But—I saw him lay into you."

My expression tensed. "That was after. I'm not saying there weren't any hitches along the way. But you've had plenty to sort through too, haven't you?"

"Still. Connar."

I socked him in the arm. "I don't think the rest of you give him enough credit. He's more than just a musclehead, you know." How much did the other scions even know about what had really gone down with Connar's parents, with his brother? That part wasn't my story to tell, though.

"Okay, okay. He's a great guy. I just need to be greater." Jude winked at me, having recovered his composure, and I relaxed again.

I nudged him toward the couch. "We'll see how that goes. Are you going to tell me about your grand plan to restore Shelby to Blood U or not?"

He grinned. "Well, I can start by telling you that I'd better not need any *other* favors from Ms. Grimsworth in, oh, the next few centuries or so…"

CHAPTER TWENTY

Rory

I wasn't sure I trusted Lillian Ravenguard and her assistant all that much more than I did my grandparents, but at least brunch with them was a hell of a lot more pleasant than that earlier lunch. Lillian had encouraged me to pick the place and ordered off the menu without any hinting commentary, and she was paying for her and Maggie's meals anyway. Why Maggie had come along when her employer could be present no one had explained, but the younger woman was enthusiastic enough company that I didn't mind.

"So what's your summer project this year?" Maggie asked not long after we'd sat down in the café. "I remember having some pretty intense assignments during my school days." Which, from the look of her, couldn't have ended more than a few years ago.

When I explained the gist of our task, Lillian leaned her elbows onto the table with an intent expression. "And how are you approaching that mission?"

"Oh," I said, feeling abruptly awkward. "My Nary is in the architecture program, and I've got him designing and arranging for the construction of a small building on campus." I hesitated to say anything about the intended purpose of that building or how I was attempting to protect as many other Naries as I could from the other students' influence. From the calm way the blacksuit and her assistant had reacted to the general idea of the summer project, they obviously didn't see Naries as worthy of protection.

"Make use of his strengths." Lillian nodded. "That's a solid approach. I look forward to hearing the final outcome. Your mother won the summer prize at least once during her school days."

"Did *you* ever win?" Maggie asked with a little smile.

Lillian laughed. "No, I don't think I was quite creative enough." She waved a finger at me. "The professors like to be surprised, in a good way. Keep that in mind."

Well, I was pretty sure they'd be surprised by the angle I'd taken when the whole thing was finished, although whether it'd be in a good way by their standards was debatable. If the clubhouse actually *got* finished, that was.

"If there's any aspect you're finding particularly challenging, I'd be happy to talk it through with you," Lillian added as our food arrived with a buttery whiff of fresh-baked breakfast rolls. "You can be sure all the other students are drawing on their parents' and other experienced mages' expertise."

There were probably all sorts of facets of my project that a blacksuit could advise on, but that would mean admitting my intentions. Between my strengths and Connar's, we seemed to have the situation under control.

"Thanks," I said with a smile. "I think everything's going to plan right now, but I'll keep that in mind if I run into any problems."

Besides, I hadn't accepted Lillian's brunch invitation to talk about my summer project. I had another, unofficial project to tackle that was both much more important and much more secret. I'd spent a good part of the night figuring out the best questions to ask that might help me find what I was looking for in those papers I'd stolen from Professor Banefield's house.

"I was wondering," I said carefully, digging my fork into my slice of feta and spinach quiche, "I found a couple of notes in the Bloodstone house that my mother wrote that suggested she'd sent a few valuables to be stored off the property, but I haven't been able to figure out where. Is there sort of a standard company or bank or whatever that fearmancers would normally work with for something like that?"

Lillian considered me with evident curiosity, and I kept my expression as innocent as I could. I hadn't found any notes like that at all, and as far as I knew all of the Bloodstone valuables had stayed on Bloodstone ground, but I didn't think even a best friend would assume she knew every little thing a person had done with her possessions. And I couldn't exactly ask where Professor Banefield might have stashed important materials without raising a whole lot of other questions I wasn't ready to answer.

"What sort of valuables?" Lillian asked.

"There weren't any details—it was all pretty vague." I offered a sheepish shrug. "Maybe she never ended up doing that. I just wondered so I'd have the right context if I stumble on any more information."

Maggie tapped her lips. "Most of us have our accounts with Yewsley," she said. "They've got a few fearmancers in the upper management, so there's that extra level of security. Most of their branches would offer safety deposit boxes."

"You'd have to know which branch to narrow it down," Lillian said. "Do you want me to look into that for you?"

"Oh, it's really not urgent," I said quickly. "I'm sure you've got a ton of much more important things to take care of. I'll see what I can find the next time I'm home and if I'm still stumped then maybe I'll call in that favor."

Yewsley. I did remember seeing that name on some of Banefield's records. I'd have to scrutinize those more closely.

The other question required even more care. My heartbeat sped up as I braced myself, pushing through a moment's doubt. "There was also—do you have any idea what she'd have meant if she mentioned a 'reaper'?"

Maggie frowned with what looked like genuine puzzlement. Lillian… If I'd had any hope of breaking through a top blacksuit's mental shields, I'd have given all the magic in me to use an insight spell on her right then. Her face went blank, but so perfectly it was hard to tell whether she was completely confused or making very, very sure she didn't give anything away.

"A 'reaper'," she repeated, with a quizzical tip of her head. "Where did you see that?"

"It was just—she liked to write thoughts in the margins of her books sometimes, you know?" That much was true, to make this story plausible. "I was looking through the library and one of them said something like 'tell reapers'… I don't remember exactly. It didn't make much sense to me. There aren't actually, like, mages who go around like the grim reaper deciding on deaths or something, I assume?"

I added a giggle to show how absurd that idea supposedly was to me, even though it actually sounded reasonably plausible given how many deaths this community seemed to orchestrate.

"Odd," Lillian said, in a voice as carefully even as the blankness on her face. A prickling sense crept over me that she *did* know something. The blacksuits should know more than just about anyone when it came to the inner workings of fearmancer society, right? But I couldn't even tell whether reapers were a good thing or a bad thing from her response. Damn it.

She swirled her fork in the yolk of her eggs benedict. "You'll have to show me that book some time. Maybe with the proper context there, I'd be able to connect the dots. Your mother had a poetic side—it might have been some kind of metaphor."

"I'll see if I can find it again," I said. There were a few thousand books in the Bloodstone library, so it wasn't likely Lillian would be able to determine I'd been lying about the note in the first place. I didn't think Banefield would have answered my question about who'd wanted him to attack me with metaphors, though. *Some* group literally called themselves reapers. And that group had wanted to destroy me.

I'd have felt a lot better if I'd known whether Lillian was trying to protect me from that fact or protect them from threat of discovery.

The tension that had balled in my stomach while I'd maneuvered through that conversation didn't leave much room for hunger. I forced myself to gulp down the rest of my brunch and switched to talking about some of the videos Lillian had sent, with honest appreciation of the gift. By the time she and Maggie dropped me off back on campus, though, my whole abdomen felt like one giant knot.

I had an hour or so before class, so I figured I'd wind down in my room for a bit. The common room was empty—always a relief. Victory hadn't lashed out at me since our bloody tiff during the illusion demonstration, but I wasn't naïve enough to assume I'd cowed her.

I started toward my bedroom, scanning the door for signs of intrusion, and my gaze slid along the rest of the wall. It stopped at Shelby's room. A ragged bit of red fabric protruded from under the door by about an inch. Just far enough to be easily spotted if you happened to be looking, but not so obvious it looked deliberate. I had the sinking suspicion that was a pretense, though. Someone had wanted me to notice.

If Victory or her friends had gone after Shelby, it wouldn't be because they hated her returning so much. It'd be to strike a blow at me, because they knew she was my friend. Not much different from Victory setting her cat after Deborah.

I knocked on the door tentatively. "Shelby?"

When she didn't answer, I nudged the door open, since of course she didn't have any lock on it at all. The whole school was set up to make the Naries as easy targets as possible even before you considered this year's summer project.

My jaw clenched as I stepped inside. Torn fabric in all sorts of colors and of all kinds of textures scattered Shelby's bed, desk, and floor. And not just random swaths. There was a chunk of sleeve. There a shred with a beltloop from a pair of jeans. And the doors of her wardrobe hung open. Nothing remained inside.

Nausea swelled inside me. This was cruel in so many ways. They'd destroyed every piece of clothing Shelby wasn't wearing. Some of those pieces she'd probably loved. Some might have had special significance, like my charm bracelet had. And even if none of her clothing had meant all that much to her, she was here on scholarship. A fearmancer could have ordered a bunch of replacement outfits without batting an eye. Shelby's family wouldn't have that kind of money.

All the more reason for Victory and the others to hit her like this instead of me.

I closed my eyes for a second as my queasiness rose to the bottom of my throat. Professor Banefield had warned me about this once—that being friends with someone "weaker" than me would make me vulnerable too. But I didn't regret being Shelby's friend because of how it hurt me, seeing this. I just hated that it was my fault she'd been attacked. *She* might have been better off if I'd never given her the time of day.

No. I couldn't let myself believe that. The other girls had been tormenting her long before I'd arrived at Blood U—and if I hadn't finally gotten through to Jude, she'd have lost her spot in the music program forever.

Still, I had to make this mess as right as I could.

I picked up a few scraps that looked like they went together, and hopelessness washed over me. Victory and her crew had shredded the clothing so thoroughly that I wasn't sure I had the skill to put even one item back together, let alone all of them.

Okay. First priority then: reducing how traumatic this would be for Shelby. I could at least clean up the mess so she wouldn't have to walk into this horror show of fashion carnage.

Partly with my hands and partly with gusts of magic, I gathered all the bits into a heap. I nearly threw it all in the garbage, but then it occurred to me that if there was a particularly special item in the mix, Shelby might want the pieces of that. Instead, I stuffed it all into a few bags and shoved those under my bed in my own room.

Now, how was I going to arrange for her to get new clothes? I worried at my lower lip as I came back to her room.

Maybe it didn't have to be all that complicated. There were plenty of assholes at Blood U, but Shelby knew she had at least one benefactor. It might seem totally reasonable that someone could be both at the same time.

I scrawled a quick note on an envelope, tensing my hand to disguise my handwriting. *Your clothes needed an upgrade. Take this and refill your wardrobe.* Then I stuffed it with a bunch of the cash I'd started hiding away in my room in case I decided I needed to make a quick run from the university and didn't want to risk accessing the Bloodstone accounts. I'd accumulated about ten thousand dollars over several withdrawals—I gave Shelby half of that. She should be able to get more than enough clothes to replace what she'd had here with that amount, and it wasn't even a dent in my family's holdings.

She was still going to be at least a little horrified, but I couldn't think of any better way to mitigate the damage. Hopefully I'd be around when she came back to the dorm so I could offer moral support too.

It was a good thing her cello pretty much always left the dorm when she did. Lord only knew what the other girls would have done to *that* if they could have gotten their hands on it.

I wasn't quite done, though. I'd made a promise to myself that I wasn't just going to take anything Victory threw at me… and attacking Shelby was an attack on me, no doubt about it. My queasiness came back as I moved to my nemesis's bedroom door.

How much retaliation would it take before she decided she was better off leaving me and the people I cared about alone? How far was *I* going to have to go, lashing back at her?

Always an equal effect. I wasn't going to hit her with anything she hadn't already hit me with. These were just… natural consequences.

She'd sealed her room more securely than when I'd done the trick with the cat urine, but within fifteen minutes, I was inside. I opened the doors to her wardrobe, looking at the row of hanging silk and linen, and folded my arms over my chest.

"All right," I said to myself, shoving aside my revulsion at the ravaging ahead. "Let's do this."

CHAPTER TWENTY-ONE

Declan

The library in the Fortress of the Pentacle was open to all scions once we reached a certain age, but I was pretty sure I was the only one of the current generation who'd set foot in here. I hadn't encountered even the other barons all that often in the dim room that smelled of stale ink and dust, although some spell kept any particles from accumulating.

To tell the truth, I winced a little to think of how much time *I'd* spent in the dreary space. More than once, though, the historical precedent of some past ruling had given me the authority I needed to overturn one of my aunt Ambrosia's schemes for retaining or regaining power, so that time had been worth it.

The library contained the official documents on fearmancer law, records of every case handled by the blacksuits from inception to outcome, and the minutes from every meeting of the pentacle. Those minutes were somewhat edited—I'd find no proof of the treason the other barons had hinted at toward Rory during recent meetings—but there was still a chance I'd come across something useful.

These "reapers" her mentor had mentioned had apparently been working alongside the barons. They might have been a more legitimate presence in the past, a group that was openly talked about. If there was any mention of them that would help me figure out who they were—and Rory figure out how to protect herself from them—I meant to find it. It was one of the few things I *could* do for her without jeopardizing my family.

I leaned back against the shelves where I'd hunkered down on the floor and flipped another page in the thick volume open on my lap. The stuffy air always made me sleepy, but I kept my focus on the task at hand. It really was too bad we still insisted on keeping all our records physically instead of digitizing them. Imagine if I could simply do a search for "reapers" and have the results in seconds. But no, for this we were stuck in the dark ages, maybe specifically so that anyone searching for inside info on the barons would have to work to dig it up.

I didn't remember coming across the term "reapers" in my previous readings. I hadn't found any mention of it so far today. With a sigh, I turned the page and kept skimming. At least I'd gotten good at scanning for the material I was looking for quickly.

The door squeaked open. I looked up from the book, and my back stiffened against the shelves.

Baron Nightwood stepped into the room with an air of subtle disdain, as if he couldn't see why anyone would bother with the records in here. He came to a stop a couple of feet in front of me and peered down. I debated between standing up so I could look him straight in the eye and staying put as if I didn't feel the need.

Doing this research wouldn't jeopardize my family, no… as long as none of the other barons realized exactly what I was searching for in here and on whose behalf.

"Ashgrave," Nightwood said smoothly, his voice just a touch deeper and more acerbic than Malcolm's. "Hard at work as always, I see. What problem has you holed up in here for hours on end now?"

I opted to stay sitting. Easier than trying to pull off a nonchalant leap to my feet. "I wanted to double-check some of the past rulings regarding young barons without regents," I said, keeping my tone relaxed. "Considering we are going to have to start integrating the Bloodstone scion into the pentacle before too long."

Nightwood hummed with faint approval. "If you find anything interesting, do share it. Although I think we're on our way to having her well in hand."

Were they? Not through any strategies they'd discussed while I was around. I dropped my gaze to the book as if I wasn't all that invested in his answer. "I'm glad to hear that. I didn't realize we had any current plans in the works."

The other baron's hum was more on the dismissive side this time. "Not every action needs to be a group activity. You haven't missed out on any official policy-making, I promise. This summer session should give us a final measure of her, I think. We'll just have to see whether the outcome shakes her or steadies her, and there are ways we can handle either eventuality."

That sounded ominously vague. "If there are any other ways you'd like me to be involved at the university…"

"No, I think at the moment we're best off giving her plenty of free rein with which to hang herself." The corner of his lips twitched upward.

I could only return the smile tightly. "I suppose I'll be waiting to see that outcome too, then."

"I wouldn't waste too much time on the fine details," Nightwood said. "You have your own studies to worry about if you're going to take your full spot at the table."

As if I needed the reminder—which might have also been a veiled threat. "Oh, I'm staying on top of those," I assured him.

He examined a couple of the volumes on the shelf nearest him, possibly waiting to see if I'd reveal anything else in the awkwardness of the silence. When I turned all my attention back to my book, he sauntered out of the room.

He was probably using the Fortress for some sort of business meeting, which was one of the perks of the barony. Even if you weren't acting in your capacity as ruler, meeting a prospective client or partner here cast a long shadow of authority over the proceedings.

I expected that'd be the last I heard from him today, but just as I'd reached the end of my current book and gotten up to pick out another, footsteps came rasping back over the stone floor beyond the door.

"Ashgrave," the baron said as he pushed the door open, "can you think of any particular reason the elder Evergrists might be paying a call here?"

My head jerked around. "Who?" I said, and then hoped feigned ignorance hadn't been a bad gambit.

Nightwood cocked his head. "Our Bloodstone scion's grandparents on the non-Bloodstone side. They've pulled up in the lot a couple of spots over from your car, but they haven't gotten out. Very peculiar."

It was. Very peculiar, and also highly annoying.

Nightwood obviously didn't want anything to do with them, which I supposed worked in my favor. I offered him a puzzled shrug and shoved the book I was holding back into its spot. "I was just finishing up here. I can go out and see what's going on."

"Please do. And let's not have them in the building, all right? They're liable to walk off with the table and half the decorations if they have the chance."

He stepped back for me to leave ahead of him rather than setting off himself. I thought his gaze followed me with a little more scrutiny than normal as I passed him. He hadn't spoken to the Evergrists, but them being here at all was odd enough that it had to be raising questions in his head. What the hell were they thinking?

Who was I kidding? This would be exactly what they were thinking—that showing up at the Fortress would make me uncomfortable and put me in a potentially difficult position. It was a power play, pure and simple. The only real question was what they wanted at this exact moment.

Well, that and how they'd known I'd be here right now. I wasn't able to make the trip very often between classes I was taking and classes I was TA-ing for. Had they paid off someone on staff to let them know if I left the university? Did they have someone watching the likely places they thought I might go?

A chill crept up my back. Whatever the case, my denials and Rory's clearly hadn't shaken their certainty that they were holding something over me. And I didn't think they'd hesitate to call my bluff if I pushed back much harder.

Rory's grandparents had indeed parked their silver-blue Cadillac two spots away from my Honda. I strode over with as casual an air as I could summon.

The Evergrists didn't bother to get out. Stella, in the passenger seat, simply rolled down the window.

"Mr. Ashgrave," she said in a saccharine voice. "What a lovely surprise."

I managed not to snort at that remark. "What are you doing here? We didn't arrange any meeting." And there was no other reason for anyone besides the barons to visit the Fortress, as any fearmancer knew.

Rory's grandmother brushed her fingers over her pale curls. "That's true. Perhaps we should arrange one. We've been getting the impression that you've forgotten about our request. It really wasn't a very large one, was it?"

The business venture they'd wanted approved. I forced a smile. "It's got nothing to do with my memory, Mrs. Evergrist. The pentacle has a backlog of proposals to consider. The one you were interested in hasn't even come up yet. I can't support a venture that isn't on the table, can I?"

"Maybe you can see about having it bumped up, then," Rory's grandfather said, leaning over in the driver's seat.

"We really have been quite patient," his wife added. "And it would be such a shame if a comment happened to slip out that put your conduct into question. If we get impatient, it may be harder for us to stay circumspect."

And there was a direct threat. I guessed it'd only been a matter of time. I crossed my arms over my chest and stared down at her with the baronic glower I'd had years and ample reason to perfect.

"If you have some complaint about my behavior, you're welcome to put it to whoever you'd like. Attempting to skew the proceedings of the pentacle could be considered treason. I'm sure you didn't intend to cross that line."

"It seems as though we'd both be best off if no complaints are made on either side." Mrs. Evergrist tipped her head coyly. "We've waited a long time for our granddaughter to be returned to us, Mr. Ashgrave. Naturally we have a stake in what happens to her. We nearly are Bloodstones ourselves by marriage. That should entitle us to a certain amount of respect."

I was tempted to recite a line of my father's about respect being earned rather than bought, but I didn't expect that would go over well. I just wanted them gone. As they no doubt well knew, the longer we stayed here talking, the more suspicious the interaction would look to anyone taking note. Like Baron Nightwood, for example.

"I've told you I'll see what I can do about your business endeavors," I said. "The reminder wasn't necessary. I'd imagine that proposal isn't too far back in the queue."

As intended, they took that as acknowledgment that I'd move it forward, not that I had any plans of doing so. "I'm so glad we're on the same page," Rory's grandmother simpered. She rolled her window back up and gave me a little wave as her husband pulled out of the spot.

My stomach clenched as I watched them drive away. If I didn't follow through, how far would they go next time? In one escalation, they'd already jumped from calling my house to showing up at my workplace. If it'd been the day of a full meeting—if Aunt Ambrosia had been here, if she'd talked to them—fuck.

I couldn't see any way this stand-off was going to end well.

CHAPTER TWENTY-TWO

Rory

After a string of clear, sunny summer days, it was a little depressing stepping out of Ashgrave Hall into cool, humid air under a sky choked with gray clouds. As I went around the building to the field, I rubbed my arms, wishing I'd picked a warmer shirt than a tank top.

Connar was already waiting by the far corner where we had a good vantage of the clubhouse. He shot me a warm smile as I joined him, and I resisted the urge to sidle right up to his well-muscled body and soak up even more warmth that way. I wasn't here for snuggling.

Across the field, the workers who'd been assigned to the clubhouse were just finishing the new frame with the intermittent whir of their electric screwdrivers. Would they have been putting their magic to use constructing the thing too if they hadn't had Naries watching so eagerly? Benjamin and a couple of his friends were supervising, pitching in by passing along tools or steadying beams where they could.

"Ready?" Connar asked. "I doubt you're going to need much help from me. You're usually a quick study."

"But you promised help, so you'd better deliver it," I said with a teasing waggle of my finger. "Can we check the wards from all the way over here? I don't want the Naries wondering why I'm lurking around the clubhouse."

"It's not a problem at all. Just requires some additional concentration. You remember where we buried them?"

I nodded. We'd planted one shaped stone at each corner of the foundation and a fifth in the center for good measure. They were buried under not just dirt but a thick slab of concrete now. The spells on them must be working, because work on the clubhouse had resumed without any further hitches, but Connar had recommended testing them every few days to make sure the magic was still holding strong.

He touched the back of my elbow as if to form a point of connection. "The easiest way to get at them is to let your magic move through the earth to them rather than trying to leap straight to the wards. I'll guide you to the first one, and if that goes well, you can probably do the others on your own."

"Okay." I trained my eyes on the grassy ground a few feet from one corner of the structure. "Feel," I murmured, because all I was doing, really, was feeling them out.

A spark of magic leapt up from my chest through my mind, and my senses sharpened to take in the dew dampness still clinging to the grass, the grainy dirt flecked with pebbles. Connar said something quietly beside me, and a tingle of energy that must have been his coursed over my skin and wound through my awareness. It urged me on through the soil.

I pictured the stone we'd shaped for the ward, reaching for the curved hollow of it. An earthy but not exactly unpleasant flavor filled my mouth. The impression of darkness momentarily threw me, but Connar's magic nudged my awareness to the side, and the ward's magic flowed into me with a jolt.

The spell he'd helped me plan still thrummed through the stone with a crackling power. The shaping we'd done had worked—the magic was holding steady rather than fading the way it would have in most circumstances. I pulled back into my body with a sigh of relief.

"Still working perfectly," Connar said. "You did a great job with those. Even Viceport wouldn't find anything to criticize."

I let out a short laugh. "I don't know about that. She's very committed to her cause. Okay, let me see if I can find the next one on my own."

The ward at the other near corner wasn't difficult at all to locate now that I knew what sensations I was looking for. The far corners took a little more effort, but I confirmed those wards were functioning properly with a clenching of my jaw as I concentrated. I got a bit lost trying to find the central ward, which didn't have a clear physical marker on the building to guide me, but Connar eased alongside me after a few moments and together we hit on the right spot.

That stone's magic didn't feel as vibrant as the others. "It's fading," I said, half my awareness still trained under the ground. Damn it.

"Four out of five good conducting pieces is a great result for your first attempt," Connar said. "The other four might be more than enough on their own, but we can bolster the spell on the fifth. Consider it useful practice."

I grumbled something under my breath but focused even more tightly on the central ward. More magic fizzed at the base of my throat. I drew it into my words and refilled the stone's well with the effects I wanted to generate.

The tingle of Connar's magical presence stayed with me until I pulled back from the clubhouse completely. I'd never really cast *with* someone else before, and there was something compelling about the act. I could almost feel Connar's dragon form in that essence of him, powerful and fierce but not without a certain grace.

"I don't think anyone will be damaging that building any time soon," he said with a grin. "If you want me to pitch in any other way, just let me know."

"Thank you," I said. "You've done a lot already."

He shrugged, his gaze still holding mine. "I owe you a lot. And I'm looking forward to seeing you win." He paused, and his expression turned stern. "If anyone hassles *you* again, whether it's Malcolm or someone else, you can count on me then too."

I'd seen Connar's protective side come out in full force before. The memory of those times threw me back to my last confrontation with Professor Banefield in his quarters, to the agony in his voice as he'd grappled with the magic controlling him to save me from himself. I swallowed hard.

Connar thought all he had to protect me from was the jabs of the other students. If he took too big a stand, he'd be making himself a target too.

I rested my hand on his arm, giving him a firm look. "I appreciate that, but I don't want you rushing in at the first sign of trouble, okay? I can look after myself pretty well, and anyone who comes at me should have the chance to figure that out. No need to put yourself in the line of fire if I can handle it."

"You shouldn't have to handle it."

No, I shouldn't, but this place and these people were what they were. "That's why you need to look after yourself too instead of just worrying about me," I said with a playful tap of his chest. "The pentacle needs some good barons when it's time for the next generation to take over."

He couldn't know how seriously I meant that sentiment—and how much I really did think I needed to worry about *his* safety if he threw in his lot with me—but the words made his chiseled features soften and his light blue eyes brighten with an emotion that sent a flutter through my chest. He leaned in, and his kiss drove away any lingering chill from the clouded morning. I let the heat and pleasure of it wash through me.

After the kiss, he tugged me into his arms. I leaned my head against his solid chest, reveling in all the strength he wanted to offer me, and my gaze slid across the grounds beside us… to land on Declan, who'd just glanced our way where he was crossing the green.

The moment our eyes met, the other scion tensed. Then he jerked his gaze away and hurried on toward the Stormhurst Building as if it hadn't mattered anyway. There wasn't enough time for me to do anything about whatever he might have thought or felt—and what could I really have done anyway? He'd vetoed any idea of us being together more than once for multiple very good reasons.

Still, my stomach sank at his reaction. I must have tensed a little myself in Connar's arms, because he drew back to look down at me.

I sucked in a breath. There were things I definitely should say to Connar, even if I couldn't say everything.

"You should know," I said, "I—I'm kind of seeing Jude again. Which doesn't mean we can't…" I made an awkward gesture between the two of us to indicate the embrace. "He knows that I'm, er, dating around. But I didn't want to give the wrong impression. I guess… you and I couldn't really get all that serious in the long run anyway, could we? Since you're the only possible heir of Stormhurst."

"Yeah. I've been trying not to think about that." He bowed his head over me again, his chin coming to rest by my forehead. "I guess it's a weird situation all around, isn't it? I can't ask you to go all in on me, considering. If Jude is making you happy, then I can't complain about that."

"You make me happy too," I said softly.

I felt his jaw shift with a smile. "Good. I think… I just want to be with you as much as I can while I can. The barony's a long way off for most of us. It doesn't have to matter yet." He nuzzled my hair. "You make me feel like I don't have to be that guy everyone thought I was, Rory. The guy I didn't want to be anyway. The last few days… I'm starting to believe I can be someone I like better. And that'll mean something no matter what happens in the future."

My heart squeezed. I hugged him again. "It means something to me too. When I first really talked to you, I could tell you weren't that guy."

"I've still got plenty to make up for," he said. "Not just with you. But helping you with projects like this…" He nodded toward the clubhouse. "Maybe I can make up for some of the hurt I've done in the past by stopping other people from getting hurt."

It wasn't you who hurt your brother, I wanted to say. *It was your asshole parents.* But I didn't think he'd ever fully believe that. And maybe it'd be wrong of me to try to take any sense of responsibility away from him. He'd been there. I hadn't been. He needed to do what felt right to him.

I might not have needed to say it. Connar kissed me again, so full of passion and tenderness that I felt a little giddy when he eased back. No, I definitely wasn't looking forward to having to give this up somewhere down the road. Not thinking that far ahead seemed like a perfectly good plan for now.

"Unfortunately, I've got a class to get to now," he said. "You know how to find me if you need me."

I grasped his hand just for a second. "I'll see you soon."

After he left, I lingered beside Ashgrave Hall for a while longer, watching the progress of the construction, willing the clouds not to let loose any rain that would end today's work. A few of my fellow fearmancers wandered by the site, but if they attempted any magic on the structure or the people building it, the wards deflected those spells. Benjamin stepped back to take the whole building in with a satisfied grin that strengthened the resolve inside me.

Whatever else happened to me here at Blood U, at least I'd have made one change for the better.

"Hey, what're they up to over here?" Shelby meandered up beside me, staring at the half-finished clubhouse.

I'd forgotten my friend would have missed all of this. "The scholarship students are building a clubhouse just for their use," I said. "Ms. Grimsworth approved it. A little escape for you guys from the mean girls and the rest."

If Benjamin's grin had buoyed my mood, that was nothing compared to the effect of seeing Shelby's face light up. She beamed at me and then at the structure. If her expression had tightened a bit at the same time, no doubt it was because of her hostile supposed benefactor who'd stolen all her clothes.

"That's amazing," she said. "I guess I missed a lot. I wonder if there's any way I can pitch in."

I couldn't help beaming back, and not just because of her obvious happiness. I also hadn't thought about how much easier my project might become with Shelby back on campus. Unlike any of the other mages, I had an ally among the Naries. I didn't need to use any magic on her to encourage her in the direction I was hoping for. I could be totally open with Shelby about how I felt.

"I'm sure you can," I said. "A bunch of the other scholarship students have been helping out here and there. You should go on over and ask."

She patted the cello case she'd set down beside her. "I have practice right now, but afterward, I'll definitely have to do that. I can't wait until it's done." She paused and gave me a slightly guilty look. "Not that I'm looking forward to excluding *you*..."

I laughed. "It's fine. I know what the people around here are like. You deserve a space where you don't have to worry about any of us. We've got plenty of other places where we can hang out."

"Yeah." Her smile came back, and she bounded off with her ponytail swinging.

Watching her go, my gut tightened. Shelby needed a shelter like that even more than most of the Naries *because* of her association with me. Would the other fearmancer students start targeting her even more if she started contributing to the clubhouse?

I had to make sure I protected her as much as I did the building.

A few possibilities flitted through my mind. I was about to turn away from my vigil to pursue them when a tall, grim man came striding across the field toward the clubhouse.

"We've gotten too many noise complaints from the staff and students," he said with a jerk of his hand. "You've got to stop construction, now."

CHAPTER TWENTY-THREE

Rory

One of the nice things about the town just off campus being so small was that many of the scattered stores carried multiple kinds of merchandise. So it was totally plausible that I could be deciding between sterling silver pendants in one corner, and Declan Ashgrave might just happen to pop in to check out the ties on the rack behind me.

When I heard him come to a stop, I turned partway around, holding a pendant in each hand as if studying them in different light. I hadn't been sure he'd appreciate me dropping in on him—literally—another night, and meeting like this had seemed like the next best option if we were going to talk.

"Thanks for coming," I said quietly. The other shopper currently in the store, a Nary who wasn't from the school, stood at the other end trying on scarfs, but it couldn't hurt to stay cautious.

"I feel like I've stumbled into a spy film," Declan said, but there was enough tension in his voice that the joke didn't quite land. "What's going on?"

His briskness told me I should get straight to the point. "I know you've done a lot of reading on fearmancer policies and so on—do you have any idea of the best way to fight a noise complaint at school?"

He was silent for a moment, no response other than the rustling of the ties as he sorted through them. A fan was whirring on the ceiling, but it barely stirred the summer heat enough to cool the sweat forming on my skin.

"I can't say that's something I've looked into specifically," he said. "But most of the university policies are designed to ensure safety and security within essential bounds, while leaving room for the students to learn. I'd suspect your best bet is going to be coming from the angle that the noise is actually productive to student learning somehow."

Given what I'd see of how Blood U worked, that sounded reasonable. "Okay. I'll see if I can work with that. Thank you. How have you been?" It felt weird that I could consider him one of the people at school I was closest to and yet I had no idea what his life had been like the last few weeks.

"Pretty much the usual. I don't think it's a good idea for us to just chat, Rory."

He moved as if to leave, his tone outright brusque now in a way I hadn't heard in a long time. My gut twisted.

"Wait," I said, as firmly as I could without raising my voice. "Did something happen? You seem more… worried than before." Another thought occurred to me. "Or, if this is about Connar—"

Declan stopped. "No," he said quickly. "It's not that. I told you before—I know I don't have any right to be jealous, no matter who you're with. I just…" He exhaled raggedly. "Your grandparents were nosing around the Fortress of the Pentacle, making threats. I'm lucky it wasn't an official meeting day and only one of the other barons saw them. I'm still working out if I can find any information on the barons' plans or these 'reapers' that would help you, but unless I do, I think it's better we don't take any chances of even seeming slightly friendly for now."

"They followed you all the way out there?" Abruptly I felt twice as sick. My father's parents clearly cared way more about any advantage they could gain from this situation than having a real relationship with me. "I'm sorry. I had no idea."

"It's not your fault. They're just… the way we are." He paused. "It's probably for the better in the long run if we interact as little as possible anyway. I can't keep indulging my feelings for you when it's impossible for us to have anything real—that's only going to make things harder."

"Yeah." It felt awfully hard right now, thinking I might not even talk to him again except as a distant coworker. I dragged in a breath. "I understand. If I can think of any way of getting them off your back, I'll do it."

"I don't want you making yourself a target either. Be careful—not that I need to tell you."

His voice gentled for that last remark. Then he strode over to the counter with a tie he'd picked out, not so much as glancing my way. I forced myself to keep my gaze on the pendants I was holding.

It wasn't as if I'd really lost a friend and ally—and whatever else we'd been—even if my stomach had balled into a knot. He'd be around. He'd said he was still trying to help me.

And I had other allies I could still talk to who needed *my* help. I looked over the pendants one more time, and my fingers closed around the best one. When Declan had left the store, I followed his footsteps to the counter.

Victory and her friends were lounging in the common room when I went over to Shelby's bedroom door. Their gazes followed me with an ominous sensation even though they didn't speak.

Their presence made me twice as glad that I'd decided to take this step. Maybe I couldn't protect every Nary in this school perfectly, but I could put all my power to looking after the one who'd been my friend since my first day here.

"Hey," I said when Shelby opened the door. "Can I come in? I, ah, got something for you."

The other girl looked surprised, but in a pleased way. "Sure! You really didn't have to. I mean, I got the whole clothing situation sorted out."

"Yeah, but I owed you one." I took the little cardboard box out of my purse. "I finally got myself my own chain for that charm bead, so I can give yours back to you. And as a thank you, I saw this pendant I thought you'd like…"

The brightening of her face when she opened the box told me I'd made the right choice. She held up the silver chain she'd lent me months ago to study the pendant: a violin with curves and grooves I'd managed to reshape slightly to contain the magic I'd cast on it. The structure wasn't perfect—I'd probably need to strengthen the ward every week or so—but if I'd worked the spell right, it should deflect any of the usual sorts of spells my fellow students might have cast at a Nary. If someone started up a brute force attack, the one small ward wouldn't be enough, but I couldn't exactly drape her in them. Hopefully it wouldn't come to that.

"It's beautiful," she said. "You *really* didn't have to."

"I'm just glad you like it. I know you play a cello, not a violin, but I figured it's pretty close…"

She laughed. "Close enough. I don't figure there are many cello necklaces out there." Undoing the clasp, she drew the chain around her neck. The charm settled just below her collarbone. "Thank you. I was just happy I could help you out."

"It looks great on you," I said, figuring the more enthusiasm I showed, the more likely she was to wear it as often as possible.

Apparently I'd missed Imogen's entrance—and some disagreement between her and Victory. I stepped back out into the common room to Victory sashaying out the main door with a toss of her hair, Cressida and Sinclair in tow. My nemesis tossed an acidic comment over her shoulder. "Maybe you could just go to your dad about that."

Imogen glared after them where she was standing by one of the sofas. Her shoulders came down with the click of the door shutting behind them. She turned to me. "Don't ask. Just Victory being Victory."

"No surprises there." The fact that Imogen's father ran the maintenance department at the university rather than holding some more prestigious position had apparently made a lot of the fearmancers turn their nose up at Imogen. Victory had already used her relationship with her dad to threaten her into betraying me once.

But… that connection could work the other way too, couldn't it? To my benefit?

I hesitated and then ventured, "Hey, I… actually need to speak to someone in Maintenance about something. Preferably the higher up the better. Do you think you could get me a few minutes with your dad?"

Imogen raised an eyebrow at me. "Is this about the stalled construction on that building in the east field?"

Yeah, my involvement with the clubhouse wasn't much of a secret anymore. I gave her a sheepish smile. "Cat's out of the bag, huh? If you don't want to help the competition, I totally get it."

She waved off my concern. "I told you, I don't have a hope in hell of winning anyway. Just tell me: if you get this done, is it going to make things more difficult for the assholes like Victory?"

I couldn't stop my smile from stretching into a grin. "Yeah, I'd say so."

"Then consider me in. Come on, we can go right now. Dad'll always make time for me if I say it's important."

We set off across the green and over the west field to the squat brown maintenance building. Imogen marched right in as if she worked there too. The hall inside smelled of lemony wood polish, although I didn't know what they'd been polishing since the floor was gray linoleum that squeaked under my shoes.

Halfway down the hall, Imogen popped a door open a crack. "Dad? Do you have a minute?"

"Sure, Genny," said a warm voice from within the room. "Come on in."

"I brought a friend," Imogen said, motioning for me to join her. "She needed to ask you about something."

I'd been a little nervous about approaching Mr. Wakeburn, but the sight of him put me at ease. He had the same dark blond hair as Imogen, a little shaggy as if he were one of those California surfers I'd see at the beach back home, and the corners of his eyes crinkled with his smile. If the other fearmancers thought Imogen was worse off having a dad like this instead of the kinds of parents they seemed to cope with, they obviously had no idea what a healthy family looked like.

"Sorry to interrupt you, Mr. Wakeburn," I said with a bob of my head.

"That's totally fine." He pushed back his chair from his desk, sinking into a relaxed pose. His body tensed slightly once he'd had a chance to take me in. "You're Rory Bloodstone."

"Um, yeah." I hadn't really thought about how my position as scion and almost-baron might give me a certain authority here. But I didn't want to bully him into agreeing. I launched into my pitch. "Some of the Nary students have been working with the maintenance staff to build a clubhouse on the east field. The work was shut down yesterday with a noise complaint. I'd like to challenge that complaint and call for the work to be resumed."

Imogen's dad raised one eyebrow much the way his daughter had minutes ago. "On what grounds?"

"The whole philosophy behind everything we do at Bloodstone University is to prepare us to handle the challenges of the real world. We can hardly expect to never experience a little irritating noise in the background. This gives students the opportunity to practice honing their concentration. The construction work should be finished fairly soon anyway."

Declan's advice appeared to have been on the mark. Mr. Wakeburn nodded as if he could see my point. But he didn't agree right away. "We have gotten *several* complaints. I have to take that into consideration."

"Dad," Imogen said in a pleading voice. "You know that's got to have more to do with the summer project competition than them actually being bothered. Remember the berries two years ago?"

His lips twitched, and he chuckled. "Okay, point taken. I suppose I could make a sort of jam out of this." His gaze slid back to me. "I'll see the Naries get their workers back."

"Thank you," I said with a rush of relief tempered by confusion.

As Imogen and I headed out, I glanced at her. "Berries?"

"It's sort of an inside joke. Long story. He got the picture, and you're back in the game." She offered me a high-five.

I returned it, but the gears in my head had started spinning in a totally different direction.

People used sort-of codes like that all the time—referencing shared experiences or understanding to get their point across quickly… or if they didn't want other people to know what they were talking about. My searching through Banefield's records hadn't turned anything up so far, but I'd been looking for the sorts of clues *anyone* would have recognized as meaningful, like bank names or something obviously labeled as a storage facility.

He must have known there was a good chance he wouldn't be able to tell me everything he had to in the moment. He'd have hoped I'd come searching if I needed to know more. Maybe the answer was in there somewhere—but left for me in a way only he and I would understand.

CHAPTER TWENTY-FOUR

Malcolm

All told, this was a pretty wretched party.

The summer parties often were. With only about a quarter of the usual student population, the crowd couldn't summon the same energy. The summer nights didn't get quite cool enough for the heat of the bonfire to be enjoyable, and the humidity kept the smoke lower to the ground, seeping into our lungs. Not to mention everyone was a little at odds because of the term's project, eyeing each other across the flames or over the beverage table as if trying to determine who their biggest competition was.

Tonight, though, I had to admit that some of the wretchedness was happening inside me.

I circulated through the revelers nursing my beer and making sure everyone knew I was there and keeping an eye on things. I had Victory and a few of the other girls hanging off me at one point, and a bunch of the guys tagging along with their flattering remarks hoping to get in good with the king of the scions. That should have been all I needed.

But about a half hour in, I glanced up to see a couple ducking into the boathouse in mid-kiss, and my next gulp of beer seemed to burn right through the bottom of my stomach. I'd turned away, only to notice Rory standing farther down the shore with that dormmate of hers, the one whose father was in Maintenance.

The Bloodstone scion didn't so much as glance my way. She meandered along the edge of the crowd, slipped over to the tables briefly to grab a wine cooler, and retreated into the shadows beyond the firelight again.

She'd never acted all that enthusiastic about these parties, although maybe that was because of the treatment she'd received at her first ones. Was she being even more hesitant than usual to avoid me? Because she was afraid of what I might try to do in the dark once I had a beer or two in my system?

That question made my stomach churn harder. I ended up setting my beer down by the firepit and abandoning it.

Rory wasn't the only one giving me a wide berth. Declan had dropped in briefly, as was his usual party MO, and offered me a nod. Jude and Connar hadn't acknowledged me at all.

Neither of them were exactly sticking *with* Rory, but Connar always moved when she did, staying where he could keep an eye out for anyone else coming at her, I guessed. Jude wove through the crowd with his usual jokes and pranking illusions, always managing to be on the opposite side of the fire from me.

I could take a little comfort from the fact that he was behaving normally, other than the avoidance thing. Whatever dark mood had gripped him recently, it appeared to have lifted.

My gaze kept returning to Rory, seeking her out as if by a supernatural pull. I must have noted her travels through the party a couple dozen times before I caught a glimpse of her back as she headed up the path toward the campus buildings, leaving early.

Just not her thing, or too many uncomfortable memories?

Victory laughed at something Chandler had said and squeezed my arm as if it'd been my wry remark. Bradley made some comment about how the awesomeness of this party was obviously thanks to me. For just an instant, I wanted nothing more than for a black hole to open up in the ground beneath me and warp me away from here.

A Nightwood didn't run away from his problems, though. A

Nightwood looked them in the face and tackled them head-on. Even if those problems were of his own making.

The thought of running into Rory alone in the night made me queasy all over again. I waited several minutes until I was sure she'd have reached her destination, and then I gave my fans some quick excuses and ducked away to tap a message into my phone.

Meet me in the lounge. We need to talk. Scions are meant to be family.

I set off without waiting for a response. That last line would bring them if the order didn't.

The fresh air farther up the field was a welcome change after the fire's smoky heat. I sucked it into my lungs and let it wash over my skin. I still couldn't say I felt particularly cleansed by the time I reached Ashgrave Hall and descended to our basement lounge.

I went over to the bar cabinet but decided halfway through reaching for a glass that having this conversation as sober as possible was probably the wisest move, if not the easiest. I wandered back to the seating around the TV and dropped into one of the armchairs.

Declan showed up a moment later, the most prompt of the others, of course. He gave me that nod again and sat down on the sofa. I guessed he realized there wasn't much point in asking what I wanted until they were all here to hear it.

Connar arrived next, with a wary glance toward me and then around the room. He stopped by the side of the sofa, not sitting down. Jude sauntered in a minute later with a cooler from the party still in one hand, but the steadiness of his steps told me he hadn't drunk much other than that.

"All right," I said, leaning forward. "We're all here. I—"

"We're not all here," Jude said tartly, dropping into the chair across from me. "Unless you've forgotten how to count. Last time I checked, there were five scions."

I glowered at him. "I wanted *us* to talk, just the four of us."

Connar pulled back from the sofa. "If you're still shutting Rory out, I don't really want to be part of this conversation. If this is about some new scheme to tear her down, you know I'm out, and if it's about something else to do with the pentacle, she has a right—"

"I know," I snapped. "Will you shut up for a second and let me explain?"

Connar went still, but the tendons in his square jaw flexed. I rubbed my hand over my face. "I'm sorry. We were here first, all right? We've known each other way longer than Rory's been in the picture. Whatever… Whatever I have to say to her, it's not the same thing I have to say to you. So I'm keeping them separate for now. That's all."

I didn't even want to think about Rory right now. There was nothing in this room that should remind me of that encounter last week when we—when I—

I closed my eyes for a second, but the images flashed through my mind anyway. Her hair, so fucking soft, and her lips somehow even softer but still fierce as they pressed back against mine, and nothing had existed in my body except fire and wanting until that cold shock of terror had torn through everything.

That wasn't really what had happened, though. The fear had been there before, flowing from her into me. I didn't know when exactly it had started, but it wouldn't have come out of nowhere. I'd been so caught up, so drunk on *her*, I'd tuned out all the rest of my senses until she'd said those words and shoved me back. The look in her eyes, afterward—the strain in her voice…

Shame and horror curdled inside me like they had then, like they had every time I'd remembered it since. Rory thought fearmancers were monsters. That's why she preferred the prissy joymancers on their high horses. But I'd acted just like a monster, hadn't I? I'd been enough of one in that moment for her to think that I'd—that I'd really—

I didn't want her broken, not like that. And sure as hell not by me. I laid down the law. I made sure people got in line. I taught lessons where they needed teaching, so the juniors smartened up, so the seniors remembered where they owed their respect. That was what a Nightwood did—that was what the leader of the scions was meant to do. He didn't *savage* people for his own personal gratification.

But maybe I'd broken a lot of things without really seeing what I was doing.

The other guys had stayed silent as I gathered myself. I raised my head and looked from one of them to the next.

"I *am* sorry," I said. "That's the main thing I wanted to say, to all of you. I let the whole feud escalate way too far, and I lashed out at you when I should have thanked you for trying to snap me out of it, and that's not… that's not how we're supposed to be. We're a family. And however much that's screwed up right now, I recognize it's at least mostly my fault. So let's make it right and move on. I don't want the pentacle to stay fractured like this."

Jude's eyes had widened, as if he hadn't thought I was even capable of making an apology. Connar blinked, and a small smile crossed his face. Even though I'd been the hardest on him, he was willing to let bygones be bygones so quickly.

I'd better be worthy of that loyalty.

Naturally it was Declan who got down to the practicalities. "Does that mean that your whole campaign to knock Rory down a peg is over?" he asked, his tone as even as ever. He hadn't fought with me over the feud, but he'd tried to steer me onto a different course. And I'd ignored him. He deserved the apology as much as the other two did.

"No more fighting," I said. "It wasn't helping anything. I should have seen that sooner."

Connar allowed himself to sink onto the sofa. "I don't think Rory ever wanted to fight," he said quietly.

I could believe that. Her stance on the boathouse floor hadn't been that of a predator readying for the next lunge but a protective hunching in defense. Seeing her in that moment, the battleground I'd thought we'd been waging war over had crumbled away.

If I could have been that wrong, misread her that badly when I had a direct line into the fear I was provoking in her… how many more subtle cues had I missed from her along the way? Dad had been urging me on, and my pride had been stinging from the way she'd tried to cut me down that first day, and she kept singing the praises of those fucking joymancers—

I cut off that train of thought with a tensing of my jaw.

"I'll figure out how to address that with her, between the two of us," I said. "Right now—what do you need from me? I'm not going to assume saying I'm sorry is enough."

"I'm just glad you've thought this through," Declan said.

Connar looked down at his hands and then back at me. "You aren't going to be pissed off about me—or anyone else—spending time with her? I don't want to just not hassle her. She deserves to be a part of the pentacle."

"Cozy up to her all you want," I said, even though my stomach lurched all over again at the thought. That he would touch her—that she would welcome his touch in a way she couldn't mine—

Get back on track, Malcolm.

"And we'll get the pentacle business sorted out," I added. "It's going to be complicated. I made the problem, so can you let me worry about sorting it out?"

Connar nodded.

Jude slung his legs over the arm of the chair and ran a finger along his lips. "Since you're in such a contrite and generous mood," he said lightly, "I *have* always thought that Aston Martin of yours would fit perfectly in my collection."

I narrowed my eyes at him. "I'm not giving you my car."

He spread his hands with a wide grin. "Hey, it was worth a try."

There was something so perfectly Jude about the way he'd said it, the expression on his face, and the fact that he'd tried it at all, that an unexpected laugh careened up my throat. I tipped back in my chair as it spilled out of me, and Connar started laughing too, and after a moment all four of us had cracked up, the sound bouncing through the room.

A good sound. A sound like a family back together again.

Something shifted in the air, and when we settled down, we fell into a natural conversation of trying to suss out what each other's summer project plans were and who'd gotten a scoop on future tests from which teachers, like old times. By the time we got up to head off to our dorms, I was breathing a little easier.

But not exactly easy. I caught Declan before he headed out after the others and waited until the door swung closed.

"What's the matter?" he asked, taking in my expression.

I grimaced and forced myself to spit out the question. "What exactly do you think my father did?"

I didn't need to tell him I was talking about our conversation at his house. Understanding lit in his eyes. I braced myself with the same sickening uncertainty that had been tugging at me since I'd left Rory in the boathouse.

If I could act like a monster… who was to say my parents had never crossed that line? And with far more resources than I had at my command.

Declan's shoulders had stiffened. "I haven't accused any of the barons of anything," he said in a voice that sounded a touch stilted too.

"I know," I said quickly. "That's not what I meant. Just… if someone had taken down Professor Banefield on purpose… what would that have looked like? What would you have to look *for* to know?"

He seemed to work the question over. Then he sighed. "The best thing I can say to you is, if you want to know more about what your father is doing, you should ask him about it. Ask him, and really *listen*."

That was less of an answer than I'd hoped for, but it might have been the most reasonable one he could give me.

He paused with his hand on the doorknob. "How are you going to approach Rory?"

Now that was *the* question. "I'm working that out," I hedged.

I was still a scion. I was still a Nightwood. Maybe I wasn't going to undermine her anymore, but I couldn't cut my own feet out from under me making amends either. It was… a delicate balance.

What would a Nightwood do with her? What would the mage I wanted to *be* do with her, after everything that'd happened between us?

I honestly didn't have a clue.

CHAPTER TWENTY-FIVE

Rory

Deborah scampered off my hand onto the roof of the Lexus. *Ready to stand guard! Do you think you have a better idea what you're looking for now?*

I peered around the shadowy expanse of the school garage, even though I'd just double-checked that I was alone here a second ago. While that hadn't changed, I kept my voice low anyway. "I'm not sure. But I've at least got a new angle to try."

She stayed perched on the roof as I pulled the box of Professor Banefield's records out of the trunk and brought it into the back seat, where I'd been conducting all of my searches through it. Her sharp mouse ears would pick up on anyone coming into the garage before I might notice, especially once I got absorbed in the task ahead of me. No one had come poking around my car yet, but they might if they noticed I was using it for more than just driving places.

I needed to look for a sign Banefield might have left just for me—something the average person wouldn't recognize the meaning of. But something that wouldn't stand out too much as unusual either, since that would draw attention too. I sucked my lower lip under my teeth as I considered.

He and I hadn't really had anything I could call an inside joke. There were things it was possible only the two of us knew about, like how he'd helped me get the hang of generating fear by having me protect a rabbit from a cat, but I wasn't sure how he could convey that in a simple notation somewhere in these documents.

If he'd even left a hint in these at all. Maybe I'd missed something in his office or his apartment that he'd meant to guide me instead. Although I thought I would have noticed a clue left on some random object… Records like these would be the easiest place to hide them.

There was of course the key itself. I dug it out of my purse and studied it. It was printed with a brand name that an internet search had revealed tons of keys had, as well as a few digits on either side that didn't appear to have any meaning. 1307 on the left. C95 on the right.

Generic might be good in this case. No one would know either of those sets of digits referred to a key. They could be just about anything.

I pulled out the first stack of records and started scanning them. Before, I'd focused on the official lists of charges and investments. Banefield had made notations on the edges of several of the papers that might have been references for tax purposes—just a few letters jotted here or there. I'd stopped paying attention to them after I'd realized they were so common.

Now, I focused specifically on the handwritten bits. What might BFR stand for? Or ZP? I still couldn't see how any of them connected to me or this situation at all.

I flipped through the first stack, set it aside, and pulled out a bunch more papers. More of the same, more of the same…

My hand paused over a bank statement from a few months ago. At the bottom, Banefield had written *C95* in faint pencil, followed by a street address.

My pulse stuttered. That had to be it. I moved to tear off the bottom of the paper, thought better of it, and took a photo of it with my phone. Then I tucked all the papers back in the box. All I needed to do was look up that address, and—

Deborah's voice carried faintly through the telepathic connection.

Lorelei, I'm not sure this is anything you need to worry about, but someone's yelling outside nearby. They sound rather distressed.

I went still and then eased open the car door so I could hear better. When I strained my ears, I made out the voice but not the words, filtering through the garage walls. It sputtered something, fell silent, and then abruptly hollered something else.

No, I didn't like the sound of that at all.

"Come on," I said. I shoved the box back in the trunk and leaned close so Deborah could jump onto my shoulder. We hurried out of the garage.

Outside, the sound reached me more clearly. "There's no point," a guy was saying raggedly. "It's all so stupid."

There was something familiar about the voice. And it was coming from around Killbrook Hall—from the east field. I picked up my pace.

As soon as I came around the building, my heart sank. I had a view of the clubhouse now—the external frame complete and the roof just finished—and a figure standing on the peak of that roof. A figure I could recognize even at that distance as Benjamin Alvarez.

Several other students had gathered around the base of the clubhouse. "Come down, Ben," one of his classmates called. "Please."

The steel rungs of the ladder he must have climbed up gleamed in the mid-morning sun. He'd walked to the opposite end of the building though, teetering there on the edge like he was thinking of jumping. It wouldn't have been that far a fall, but he could still hurt himself badly.

My gaze darted across the grounds and settled on a head of ice-blond hair streaked with purple and pink. Cressida was watching the commotion from farther down the field, a small falcon-like bird I guessed must be her familiar perched on her arm. Her lips were curled with just a hint of a smile.

She'd done this. She must have cast some sort of persuasive spell on Benjamin to set him out of sorts and then pushed him toward the clubhouse. The building was protected from magic, but *he* wasn't.

Somehow I doubted he was even her assigned Nary. Everyone seemed to have figured out by now that this construction was my summer project. This was all part of the same campaign to mess with me.

The sight of her predatory familiar sent a flicker of caution through me. I veered toward Ashgrave Hall on my way over and touched the wall. "You can make it to my room no problem from here?" I whispered to Deborah. "I don't know if you'll be safe out here while I'm dealing with this."

Understood. I can find my way back. Take care of yourself too.

"I will." As much as I could.

"Why do you even care?" Benjamin was saying. "I wasted so much time…" He swayed on the roof, his arms whipping out for balance, and my stomach lurched. I had to get him down from there.

I stepped a little closer, but not so close that the gathered students would hear me casting. With my first tentative spell just to feel out his mood, the hum of my wards' magic echoed back at me. Shit. They were going to deflect any spells I cast in that direction as much as they would anyone else's.

Cressida had picked this set-up for more reasons than one. What better strategy than to cast her spell outside the wards and then send him behind them where he'd be harder to help.

But they were my wards, and they responded to my call. I could reach out to them quickly now after the practice I'd gotten. I extended my awareness to the one closest to me and murmured to it under my breath. Just a little opening, enough for me to send spells through without pulling down the defenses completely. Lord only knew what Cressida would do if I gave her that big an opening. Or her friends, if Victory or Sinclair were lurking around too.

With a gap opened in the wards' magic, my insight spell found Benjamin's mind. His thoughts were a storm of pain and shame, so fraught I could hardly focus on any one impression before it whirled away again.

"Calm," I whispered, willing those emotions toward him. "Steady."

He kept ranting, wobbling again on his feet. My attempts at soothing the desperate chaos Cressida had stirred up weren't penetrating the haze. I frowned and made another attempt, but that magic didn't have any noticeable impact either.

"Tricky situation."

My head snapped around at the voice beside me, my concentration slipping from Benjamin. Jude had joined me, his coppery head cocked as he took in the scene, his mouth set in a flat line. "And here our fellow fearmancers are proving just how much the Naries need that clubhouse of yours, hmm?"

"Yeah," I said. "But I'd rather they didn't end up proving it by having my guy break half the bones in his body."

Jude nodded. "Understandable. What have you tried?"

"His mind's all in turmoil. I tried to soothe it, to calm him down, but whatever spell is acting on him already, it's stuck in there pretty tight."

"You know… when a person's caught up in a mental spell like that, sometimes you need to take their mind off the pattern it's stuck in for a moment before you can get a real foothold. A brief distraction, not trying to change anything yet, just giving them a pause." He glanced at me. "Can I try something?"

"Please," I said. "As long as it doesn't involve rampaging bears."

He chuckled and lifted his chin toward the clubhouse. "I've got a lot more range than that. Be ready with your calming spell when he's open to it."

He made a subtle gesture with his hand by his side, speaking a few quiet words, and a form shimmered into being in the air just a few feet in front of us: a bright-feathered bluebird.

It fluttered its wings and flitted across the field, finding the gap I'd opened in the wards. With a cheerful chirp, it swooped around Benjamin.

Its colorful body caught his eye. His head turned, just slightly, following its path. The bird flew around him again and landed on the roof a few feet behind him. This time, Benjamin shifted around to study it with a puzzled look, probably wondering why it was being so friendly.

Well, puzzled was better than his previous state. I cast my calming spell again, finding his mind already less scattered when I touched it. I urged more magic from inside me to settle his thoughts, to wash away the hopeless gloom Cressida has filled his head with. He wavered and seemed to register where he was for the first time.

His hands shot out for balance. "I—what--?"

"Come back to the ladder," one of the Naries below said. "Just walk carefully. We're right here to help you."

I eased closer as he picked his way across the shingles. The other students congregated around the base of the ladder. A couple of them reached to help steady him as he made his way down.

"I don't know what I was thinking," he said. "Everything just felt so… dark for a second." An embarrassed flush darkened his cheeks.

I cast more calm toward the rest of the students, willing acceptance and reassurance. I didn't want this moment haunting Benjamin for the rest of his time here at school, tainting his friends' opinion of him.

One of the girls pulled him into a hug, and then they all drifted away from the building. "Let's go chill out for a bit," someone else said. "You must be putting too much pressure on yourself."

When I glanced Cressida's way again, the other girl had vanished. So had Jude's bluebird. He set his hands on his hips with a satisfied smile. "Nice job. Let's see this clubhouse of yours."

"It's more theirs than mine," I said as he ambled over to the doorway where no door had yet been attached. He stepped inside, his shoes echoing dully on the unfinished wood, and I trailed behind him.

The frame gave off a pungent pine smell that tickled my nose. Light streamed through the two raw windows. It was all one big open-concept room with a few cupboards where a fridge and microwave would be set up at one end and a built-in bench beneath one of the windows. Enough room for a couple dozen students to hang out here without it feeling crowded.

I hadn't seen the inside since the walls had gone up. Looking around, I couldn't help smiling.

Jude swiveled on his feet, taking the space in. "Nice job here too," he said. "Just for the Naries, huh? I'm feeling a little left out."

I smacked his arm. "Says the guy who has a whole basement entertainment room just for him and his three friends."

He shrugged with a grin. "My three friends and my girl. The lounge is open to all scions."

"Yeah, and I feel super welcome there," I said with a healthy helping of sarcasm.

"We'll work on that." He caught the hand I'd swatted him with and twined his fingers with mine as he turned toward me. "We made a pretty good team out there, didn't we?"

"We did." And when he beamed down at me like that, it made me want even more with him. But I didn't know—being with me meant *so* much to him—I couldn't give him the escape he wanted so badly. Not yet, anyway.

As I gazed up at him, I felt the need to say something to that worry, though. "You know that even if I'm not ready to commit to a whole future together, I'm going to do whatever I can to make sure your parents don't make you pay for their mistakes, right? If your dad's going to try to hurt you, or worse, he'll have to get through me first."

A pleased glint lit in Jude's eyes at the vehemence in my voice. He touched my cheek and drew his fingers along my jaw in a caress that sent tingles all through me. "He doesn't stand a chance, then, does he?" he said, and kissed me.

It was the kind of kiss that swept every other sensation away. His lips branded mine and his spicy smell filled my lungs, and everywhere our bodies touched, mine started to melt. I tucked my hand around his neck and tugged him closer. He wrapped his arm around my back with a little groan. It felt like being worshipped and claimed all at once, and I was totally on board with both.

Nothing stirred inside me except heat and wanting. Not a single shred of fear flickered in my chest this time. Maybe I wasn't ready to tie my life to this guy's in a permanent way just yet, but I believed in him. I believed he'd be there for me the way I'd just promised to be there for him.

Jude released my lips to trail his mouth down to the side of my neck, and a sigh quivered out of me. He teased his fingers down over my shoulder toward my chest at the same time.

Things might have gotten a lot more interesting if voices hadn't carried from outside. I tensed, and Jude lifted his head.

"Damned Naries coming to take back their damned clubhouse," he muttered, but with enough amusement in his tone to diffuse the complaint. He kissed me again, quickly. "We'd better give it back to them."

Benjamin wasn't in the group that was strolling over to the

clubhouse, but a couple of his friends were, and some of the other Naries, including Shelby. They gave us an uncertain look as we stepped through the doorway. Jude made a grand salute.

"The inspection is complete," he said. "Continue onward."

I bit back a giggle. The other students still looked apprehensive as we passed them, but Shelby's voice reached my ears, bright and firm.

"You don't have to worry about Rory. She's okay—she's my friend."

I made a mental note to do something particularly nice for Shelby as soon as possible.

"Oh my god, this is seriously the best ice cream I've ever had." Shelby took an enthusiastic swipe at her cone as she, Imogen, and I came out of the shop. "Why haven't we ever gone in there before?"

"I think they just opened this year," Imogen said with a smile at the other girl's enthusiasm. "And I don't know about you, but ice cream during a New York winter isn't super appealing to me."

"If it's this good, maybe it'd be worth it."

I laughed and took a nibble from my own chocolate-banana-almond scoop. It *was* pretty damn good ice cream, creamily sweet with just a hint of salt from the nuts. Although… "There was this amazing place near where I lived in California, where they made their own flavors with fresh fruit in custom combinations…"

I trailed off as a punch of homesickness and grief hit me. The painful loss of my old life, of my parents, had started to numb, but it came back without warning at random moments like this.

Imogen shot me a concerned glance. Shelby only looked curious. She had no idea of the history there.

"I forgot you're from California. I guess it's ice cream weather there pretty much all the time. Must be nice!"

"Yeah," I said, forcing a smile of my own. "There's a lot of nice stuff back there."

Unfortunately, I couldn't say the same for this particular area of the world. Especially right now, when the two figures emerged from a car down the street and hustled over with expectant expressions. I stopped in my tracks.

"Persephone!" my grandmother chirped. "What a wonderful surprise. I'm so glad we happened to cross paths."

My hackles had gone right up. No way was this a coincidental meeting. Why on earth would they have been hanging around in this town other than to see me?

First following Declan to his workplace, then catching me by surprise here—my grandparents were turning into total stalkers, weren't they?

"Good to see you too," I said stiffly. "We, ah, were actually just—"

My grandmother barrelled right over me. "These must be your friends from school! I don't think we've met." Her gaze took in Imogen and then Shelby, with a tightening of her mouth when it crossed the leaf pin on her blouse that marked her a Nary. "Well, it is wonderful to see you out enjoying yourselves. Stella Evergrist, and this is my husband Rupert."

She held out her dainty hand to Imogen, who took the whole thing in stride with a shake, and then to Shelby. As she gripped the Nary girl's fingers, I caught a movement of her lips with the intake of her breath.

A faint vibration shivered through the air—the impression of a spell deflected by the violin charm hanging from Shelby's neck. The taste of it prickled over my tongue with a tinge of queasiness and the flavor of vomit. My whole body went rigid.

She'd tried to make Shelby sick, probably so the girl would leave and wouldn't prevent us talking about any magic-related subjects. Fury rose up inside me so quickly I could barely contain it.

My grandmother's brow knit as she let go of Shelby's hand, realizing her spell hadn't worked, and I snatched her wrist. "You know," I said, fighting to keep my voice even, "there's something I really need to talk to you about now that you're here." I looked to my friends. "Give me a couple minutes?"

"Of course," Imogen said, frowning as she picked up on the tension. Shelby went back to her ice cream without the slightest idea she'd just been under attack.

I marched my grandmother several feet away, letting my grandfather trail behind us. When we reached their car, I stopped and spun on her.

"Don't you *ever* cast magic on any of my friends again," I said, quietly but sharply.

My grandmother's eyes widened. "She was just—she's a feeb. We can't—"

"*Shut up.*" I dragged in a breath and got a hold of my temper. "She's my friend. That's all you need to know if *you* want any part in my life at all. Got it?"

"Your grandmother didn't mean anything by it," my grandfather said, in such a remorseless tone that I wanted to hex them both halfway across the country right then.

"It still happened, and I don't want it happening again. And because it happened, I don't really feel like spending any time with you right now. Go home—and please don't drop in on me out of the blue like this again."

"Now, Persephone," my grandmother started.

"My name is Rory," I gritted out. "*Leave now.*"

I spoke the last words with the heft of a persuasive spell. It cracked right through the mental barriers my grandmother had in place, and she reached for the car door automatically.

"You really didn't have to go that far," she sputtered as she got in.

My grandfather hustled around the car muttering something about respect for elders, but my grandmother was already shifting in the passenger seat as if to move to the driver's side if he didn't get in there to fulfill my command quickly.

"I'll let you know when I'm ready to see you again," I said as he ducked inside, but as the rage continued to radiate through me, I wasn't sure that'd ever happen in my lifetime.

CHAPTER TWENTY-SIX

Rory

I'd been dreading my weekly sessions with my new mentor for most of the summer, and I didn't think Professor Viceport had been all that enthusiastic about them either. Most of the concerns I had, I wouldn't have felt comfortable bringing up with her anyway. I definitely wasn't going to discuss the problems of trying to give the Naries a better footing at the university. So the mentoring sessions had tended to consist of a quick check-in and a perfunctory suggestion or two.

Today, though, I had an actual goal in mind. I settled into the chair across from Viceport's desk, told myself the astringent whiff of herbs in the air was pleasant enough, and looked her straight in the eye. "I'd like to talk about my grandparents."

The professor blinked, clearly startled, before regaining her cool composure. "That hardly seems like a subject related to your schooling."

I shrugged. "Our magical abilities are partly inherited. It seems to me that finding out more about my heritage could be useful. And I got the impression that you know at least a little about them, from the way you acted when we bumped into you in town."

Her jaw worked. "I still don't think it's entirely appropriate for me to discuss your relatives with you. If there's something you'd like to know about them, surely you can ask *them*?"

"Yeah, somehow I suspect I'd only get the answers they want me to hear, not what's actually true. They want something from me. Maybe lots of things. That much is obvious. It'd be really useful to know how much I need to worry about that. Like… am I in any actual danger from them if they don't get what they want?"

Viceport frowned. "Causing major harm to a scion or baron is one of the highest offenses in our society. They'd have to be insane to attempt it, and I haven't gotten the impression from them that they're quite so desperate as that."

"But they are desperate. Why?" When she hesitated, I leaned forward in the chair and played the last but possibly best card I had. "Let's say I'm not asking as your student. I'm asking as the heir and pretty much baron of Bloodstone. I've been out of the loop for a long time, and I need to know everything I can."

She didn't like me invoking my status. I could tell that from the pursing of her lips. But she sighed and folded her hands on her desk, and I knew I'd won.

"I'm not sure there's a very concrete reason why," she said. "The Evergrists have always been a fairly powerful family, but from what I've seen, they're rarely satisfied with what they have. They're always seeking out more influence, more connections, more wealth."

"And they're willing to go to some questionable lengths to get that," I filled in, thinking of their blackmail attempts with Declan, the fact that they'd shouldered their way into my life in the first place.

"Well…" Professor Viceport looked at her hands and then back at me with a hint of a grimace. "There have been rumors. And occasional problems in the past. I would rather not say anything that could be construed as an attack—"

I waved off her concern. "It's fine. I'm sure I said worse things to them the other day than you'd even think of saying."

The corner of her lips twitched into something closer to a smile at that comment. "It was my impression," she said, "that their efforts at heightening their status escalated after your parents' marriage. And that they skirted the line of the law more than once, but the transgressions were small enough that the blacksuits ignored them in favor of avoiding conflict with a ruling family."

"They committed actual crimes?" I said.

"I don't know the details. I simply observed and overheard." Her expression turned grim again. "I trust these comments won't be repeated with my name attached to them."

"Of course." But her need to add that last remark told me a lot about the dynamics that could have allowed my grandparents to get away with who knew how many "transgressions." I wasn't sure how I'd go about finding out details of their crimes or what I'd even do with that information, but it at least confirmed that my instincts to avoid them were one hundred percent correct.

"Thank you," I added. "That's something I'll want to keep in mind."

"If you have any questions about your actual schooling..."

I shook my head and stood up. "No, I think I've got everything else under control. Unless you have any suggestions about my performance in Physicality?"

For a second, I'd have sworn she glowered at me before her face turned impassive again. "You've been doing quite well the last few weeks. Continue in the same vein, and I'll have no complaints."

I guessed that was progress.

I headed out of the staff wing and down the stairs to the main fore-room. I was just coming through the narrower hall between the two sections of the building when Malcolm stepped into view at the other end.

My legs locked automatically. Malcolm froze on the threshold of the hall. His usual expression of cool confidence came over his face, but his stance stayed uncertain.

"Bloodstone," he said in a tone I couldn't read.

"Nightwood," I replied tightly. The thought of squeezing past him, my shoulder nearly brushing his in the narrow space, made my skin shiver.

He wavered there a moment longer, and then he… backed up a couple steps. Out of the hall into the room beyond, so I could walk past with plenty of space.

For a moment, I was too startled to move. Was Malcolm Nightwood actually *giving way* to me? How was that even possible? Then I walked forward cautiously, every sense on high alert in case he tried some sort of magic on me.

He didn't raise his hand or cast a single spell, though. He just waited for me to go by. I slowed as I passed him, not really wanting to leave my back open to him while I walked on, and he cleared his throat.

"You might want to keep an eye out," he said brusquely. "Victory looks like she's on a rampage out there."

Without another word, he ducked down the hall and was gone.

I stared after him, letting the words sink in. He'd stepped aside for me, and he was also warning me about one of his biggest devotees? Had I stumbled into a parallel universe between Viceport's office and here?

Whatever was going on, I should probably go find out what the hell Victory was doing. I'd just proceed with caution, in case this was some kind of trick.

I passed a couple of professors in quiet conversation and slipped out of Killbrook Hall. It only took a second for me to spot my nemesis stalking across the other end of the green.

Victory's expression was taut, her hands moving restlessly at her sides as if waiting for the chance to cast. As I watched, lingering in the shadow of the broad doorway, she glanced toward Ashgrave Hall, then the field beyond where the clubhouse stood, then back to the hall. She stopped and brought her hands to her mouth. It looked like she murmured something into them, her eyes narrowing intently.

I didn't know what she was up to, but the vibe she was giving off and the direction of her attention made the hairs on the back of my neck stand on end. Whether Malcolm had hoped I'd clash with her or been trying to help me avoid a collision, he clearly hadn't been lying about her state of mind.

A couple of Naries left Ashgrave Hall, and Victory's gaze followed them while they gave her a wide berth, either from past experience or picking up on her current mood. They were heading toward Nightwood Tower, though. She made a face and folded her arms as she waited… for whatever she was waiting for.

After Cressida's assault on Benjamin the other day, I didn't think I wanted to give her the chance to act on her intentions. But how could I head her off? The second I started casting any magic on her, she'd notice, and the situation would only escalate.

Another few students came around Killbrook Hall—a couple of fearmancers walking together, and Shelby, trailing a careful distance behind them, clutching a bag of groceries she'd slung over her shoulder. I hurried over to catch her before she walked onto the green into Victory's realm of attention.

"Hey," she said. "What's going on?"

I tipped my head toward Victory. "One of our roommates looks like she's prowling for victims. Here, I'll walk with you over to the dorms. She's less likely to bother you if you're not alone."

"Okay, thanks." Shelby peered toward Victory and shuddered. "I don't know how people like her manage to get away with so much. She's got to be breaking some kind of school rule, the way she hassles people."

I paused, a spark of inspiration lighting in the back of my head. Victory *wasn't* breaking any school rules by harassing the Naries—she was doing exactly as we were taught. But there were other rules she'd be sanctioned for.

I didn't have to cast any magic *on* her at all. I just had to convince an authoritative witness that they had to intervene.

The plan unfurled in my head, but I couldn't do it alone. I touched Shelby's arm to stop her. Victory had noticed us skirting the green, but she hadn't left her spot at the far end. All we got was a sneer that looked way too self-satisfied for my liking.

"What if we could get her in the kind of trouble she deserves?" I said. "I think I can make that happen, if you'll help… but she might figure out it was us."

A slow smile stretched across Shelby's face. "What can she do that's any worse than how she already treats me? Of course I'm in. What do you need me to do?"

Her eagerness steadied me. I tipped my head toward Killbrook Hall. "Run in there and tell the first teachers you see that Victory's saying crazy things, you don't know what's wrong with her. I saw a couple of them talking in the fore-room—they're probably still there. I'll take care of the rest."

Shelby nodded with a sly gleam in her eye and jogged back to the hall. I drew farther back from the green so the buildings blocked me from Victory's view.

As soon as Shelby had disappeared through the door, I started murmuring a spell. An illusion, capturing Victory's voice. I'd heard that caustic tone when she was angry enough times to reproduce it pretty accurately, I thought.

I cast the spell toward the entrance to Killbrook Hall so it would echo through the door, projecting it only in that direction. If Victory heard what I was doing, she'd realize the trick in a second.

"*I can crush all of you feebs if I want to,*" I made her conjured voice screech. "*You think you're so special because you got to come here? You're nothing. We've got all the power. We can bend you to our will just like that. You want to see? This is what we call* magic."

I let the spell fade. At the squeak of the door's hinges a second later, I cast another, brief illusion—a thunderclap of sound intended to make Victory flinch and look unnerved.

The two professors I'd seen burst out of the hall and charged across the green toward her. "You need to come with us," one of them said.

"What the hell?" Victory said, out of my sight around the building. "What are you talking about?"

"The problem is what *you're* talking about," the other said. "A visit with the headmistress is in order, *now.*"

I slunk even closer to Ashgrave Hall as they ushered Victory past, protests continuing to sputter from her mouth. Several seconds after they'd tugged her inside, Shelby emerged with a triumphant grin. She loped over to rejoin me.

"It worked, right?"

"It worked perfectly." I grinned back and raised my fist to bump it against hers.

Right then, it didn't matter that this girl had no magic and couldn't know about mine. She couldn't have been a better friend. And what were friends for other than conspiring together?

Glancing back toward Killbrook Hall, the ploy we'd just pulled off stirred another idea. We'd gotten ahead of Victory's scheming by preemptively bringing down sanctions on her.

What if there was another way that strategy could be put to use to save a whole lot more than one clubhouse?

CHAPTER TWENTY-SEVEN

Rory

It wasn't hard to pick the right time to drop by the teacher's aide office. I'd had enough sessions with Declan there last term that I was familiar with his hours—and which of those hours he usually had there alone.

At least, alone as far as other aides went. When I slipped into the office that afternoon, Declan was sitting at one of the tables in the large room, talking through something with another student.

They both glanced up at me, Declan's expression tensing for an instant and the guy he was tutoring only looking mildly curious. My first instinct was to turn around and hightail it out of there, but then I might as well hold up a sign declaring I was up to something untoward. So I gave a little nod in greeting and went to sit on one of the chairs near the door, as if I was there for the same reason the guy was.

"I can wait," I said.

Declan had a lot of practice at keeping a cool head. He returned the nod, his expression carefully neutral again, and turned back to his student. I tried to relax into the firmly padded chair as the drone of the air conditioner hummed in the background.

To my relief, the other tutoring session wrapped up quickly. Declan got up as the guy headed out. He didn't say anything until the door had closed solidly behind the other student.

"Rory…"

"I know," I said quickly, holding up my hands as I came over. "I just need to ask a couple of quick questions about the Insight work, and Professor Sinleigh is busy with classes this afternoon. It'll only take a few minutes."

I *had* confirmed that I had a good excuse for going to Declan instead of the professor, who'd been giving me some additional instruction as I asked for it during the summer. He made a bit of a face at the cover story, but his shoulders came down a little.

"Fair enough," he said, his hazel eyes intent on my face. "What's the problem?"

I inhaled slowly as I gathered my words. "It's more a possible solution than a problem. To the issue of my grandparents. I was talking to Professor Viceport about them yesterday, and she suggested they've committed some minor crimes in the past that were overlooked because of their connection to the barony."

"That wouldn't surprise me," Declan said. "The blacksuits are going to be a lot more hesitant to pursue leads involving one of the ruling families, in case it turns out they're wrong and there's backlash from the baron."

Or backlash even if they were right, I suspected. "Well," I said, "I know you've studied the laws backwards and forwards to make sure your aunt can't trip you up, and you're obviously good at doing that research… If you looked, you could probably find one of those crimes and some evidence for it, don't you think?"

Declan gave me a puzzled look. "And I'd do that because…"

"Because then you could see them *charged* for that crime, and that would get them off our cases. Or at the very least, once you've initiated that investigation, they can't make accusations about you and me without it looking like retaliation rather than a legitimate concern.

They don't have any proof. And the only Bloodstone around who could get upset about them being investigated is giving you her blessing."

Declan's eyes had widened. "You really want me to try to get your grandparents arrested?"

An uncomfortable twinge ran through my gut. "Don't look at me like that. If they *have* committed crimes, it's their own fault. And they've proven they're dangerous while they're walking free. I'm protecting the people I care about."

Me. Shelby. And the guy in front of me, whose expression softened at the comment. "Okay," he said. "That's actually a pretty good plan. Having seen them in action, I'd be surprised if they haven't left a trail to one illicit dealing or another somewhere. Overconfidence can screw a person over awfully fast." He paused and gave me a little smile. "We'll still have to keep our distance from each other."

"I know," I said. "I just don't want them to be able to threaten either of us—or anyone else."

"Thank you."

I wasn't sure how he'd react, but I couldn't help reaching out to grasp his hand. That one small point of contact, his warm skin against mine while he gazed back at me with the affection he was trying to restrain, brought back the moment in his bedroom not that long ago when I'd gotten to be so much closer to him for the last time. He squeezed my fingers like a promise, and I eased back before he had to break the moment himself.

"You'll know when it's done," he said. "I'm sure they'll be harassing you for support the second they realize they're in trouble."

The corner of my lips quirked up. "And they're going to be so very disappointed."

My grandparents weren't my biggest concern. I still had the matter of a mysterious key to work out.

The traffic on the city street rumbled by as I sat in my parked car. I studied the building on the corner ahead of me, readying myself for what I hoped would be the last step in my quest for answers. A step I had to take completely on my own.

The back of my neck had prickled more than once as I'd driven out here to this spot about halfway between the campus and Professor Banefield's home. Sudden worries about being followed had crept up through my thoughts. But I'd been parked here for several minutes, and I hadn't noticed anyone else stopping nearby. I hadn't seen any car behind me for an unusual amount of time during the drive over.

It was just hard not to be nervous when so much might ride on this moment.

I got out of the car and headed up the street to the post office the address in Banefield's note had led me to. It wasn't the only building with that street address in the whole state, and his note hadn't included any other details, but the others had been a daycare center and a bridal shop in other cities. This seemed to be the most likely of the possibilities.

A bell dinged over the door as I stepped inside. They had the air conditioning up high—my skin broke out in goosebumps within seconds. I resisted the urge to hug myself and veered around the line of customers waiting to mail something.

A wall of PO boxes stood at the far end of the space. And it *was* a whole wall—dozens and dozens of them, some small and some larger. I eyed them from the side of my vision, wandering over to the rack of envelopes and packing materials for sale nearby. My hand dipped into my purse to close around the key Professor Banefield had given me.

I couldn't go sticking the key in every box until I found a match. The post office staff would notice that weird behavior pretty quickly. They might have been able to look up the key in a database from the digits on it… but I wasn't sure what they'd do if they saw it was registered to an Archer Banefield who definitely wasn't me.

But I was a mage, so there had to be a better solution I could think up.

I ran my finger over the ridges on the key and considered the rows of locks. This felt like a physicality problem. Find the matching shapes among those holes.

After several sweeps of my thumb tip over the key, I had a solid image of the pattern in my mind. I reached to the magic thrumming behind my collarbone and molded it into an invisible copy of that pattern. Then I cast it off toward the rows of boxes with a murmured, "Fit."

An echo of sensation rippled over my skin as the spell slipped across the boxes. I felt it twitch into each opening and jerk back out when the grooves didn't match.

Halfway across the second row, a little jolt hit me and the rippling stilled. I stepped toward the wall of boxes with a skip of my pulse.

The spell tugged me toward the right one. I pushed the key in. It slid into place without any resistance, and the lock clicked over with the twist of my fingers.

A large envelope sat inside the box—nothing else. I grabbed it, shoved it into my purse, locked the box up again, and hurried out as quickly as I could without looking frantic.

I scanned the street again as I headed to my car. No one around me looked shady, but it wasn't as if I knew for sure what to look for. All of my enemies had magic too.

I set my purse carefully onto the passenger seat and started the engine. I'd noted a good pull-off spot on my way here. About a half hour outside the city, there was a little diner that appeared to have been closed for years, given the amount of rust on the drooping sign. It wouldn't look too strange for me to be parked in the lot out front, and the open fields all around gave me a good line of sight if anyone approached.

Despite those benefits, after I'd pulled into the parking lot, I also cast a few temporary wards on the ground around the car. Better safe than sorry, especially with the kind of enemies I was clearly up against.

My mouth went dry as I picked up the envelope. It was sealed, with a postage label and mark on the upper corner—Professor Banefield hadn't just stashed it in the box but mailed it to himself. Just before he'd gotten sick the second time, from the date on the mark. He'd been preparing, knowing he probably wouldn't be able to tell me anything useful directly because of the spell on him.

The seal tore easily at the tug of my thumb. I pulled out the sheaf of papers inside, many of them creased and different sizes. A hodgepodge of compiled records.

One of the first papers, lined and frayed at the top as if it'd been torn out of a notepad, held only a list of names, a couple of them crossed out, added to at various times based on the different shades of the ink.

Julian and Dahlia Nightwood
Edmund Killbrook
Marguerite and Quince Stormhurst
Wesley Cutbridge
Alice Villia
Roland Crowford

I paused over that one. Was that Professor Crowford? The professor who'd come up with our horrible summer project? I couldn't remember if I'd ever caught his first name. I'd have to check the plaque on his office door when I got back to school.

There were several more names on the list. I didn't recognize any of the others except *Pierce Darksend*, who might have been the junior Physicality professor based on his last name, and an Ilene Burnbuck, who might have been related to my Illusion professor. A few of the other last names sounded vaguely familiar, maybe from hearing the professors call on fellow students in class, but I couldn't connect faces to them.

Who were all these people? The barons were obvious—were the rest of them the "reapers" Banefield had mentioned? I set the list aside and dug deeper into the collection of papers.

A lot of them were what looked like rough meeting minutes. Last names and hastily jotted point form remarks that referred to ideas I wasn't familiar with: *Faraday transaction* and *Ulverton switch* and so on. The parts I did understand sounded like plans being made, resources shifted around. A few comments gave the impression of some sort of a bribe, promises made to ensure support.

Then there were articles, both newspaper clippings and printouts from online publications. Politicians announcing new undertakings or canceled projects, companies starting up ventures or adjusting old ones, things like that. Things maybe the people on that list had influenced?

At least some of the events must have been connected to those meetings, because I started seeing names I recognized. James Faraday, CEO of this communications conglomerate. Ulverton Pharmaceuticals. My body tensed as I flipped further.

If I'd had all the context, I suspected this collection of information would have pointed to fearmancers purposefully influencing various powerful Naries. I had no idea why, though. There wasn't any clear pattern I could see to the news articles. And I wasn't even sure using that kind of influence was against mage laws anyway.

A realization sank in slowly as I approached the bottom of the pile. There was something bigger than what I could find here that the barons and maybe some other people working alongside them wanted to accomplish. Something they couldn't accomplish without my agreement, either given freely or forced. If this stuff was all that mattered of them, they wouldn't be attacking me—or magicking the people around me into attempting assaults.

Professor Banefield must have been at these meetings. How else would he know so much about what they'd talked about and who'd been there? Had he *agreed* with what the barons were doing some of that time?

I flipped another page, and suddenly that question didn't matter anymore. Because the next article had a large photograph of a man in a suit surrounded by onlookers—and on the fringes of that crowd stood the barons Nightwood and Stormhurst. Behind them, her head just partly visible beside Connar's mother's, was the unmistakeable profile of Lillian Ravenguard.

A cold shiver crawled up my back. I set the papers down and closed my eyes.

Maybe it was just a coincidence? She was a blacksuit—she might have been assigned as a sort of bodyguard in the crowd.

I held onto that hope for a few minutes longer, until I came to another set of meeting minutes. The fourth of those pages had some discussion about the blacksuits. Something about them *coming on board* and *assisting with the transition*. And the initials LR were marked down here and there all through that section.

I hadn't trusted my mother's best friend to begin with. I wasn't even sure I could trust the person my *mother* had been. But Lillian had at least appeared to be kind to me. It would have been nice if she'd turned out to be an ally and not in cahoots with the people Banefield had desperately wanted to warn me about.

Maybe I didn't know what to make of everything here, but one thing was clear—I couldn't tell Lillian anything, couldn't ask her anything that might reveal my intentions. She might have been my mother's best friend, but she was no friend of mine.

CHAPTER TWENTY-EIGHT

Connar

The entire Stormhurst mansion was gloomy, but the hall outside my brother's rooms held so many shadows I felt them pressing against my skin as I walked to his door.

I wasn't supposed to be in this part of the house. Since the fight they'd provoked and his subsequent injuries, my parents had shut Holden away in a small section of the house with a few adjoining rooms. They'd hired a nurse to check on him and see to his needs. Now, they pretended he didn't exist, and they expected me to follow suit.

To care about the loser in our battle was weakness. They didn't want to see any weakness in their scion. But the truth was, it took far more strength for me to make this walk than it did to stay away and avoid the guilt.

I stopped outside the door and whispered to the air around it, tasting the spells cast there. My parents were talented mages, as all the barony families and their chosen spouses were, but I'd started to surpass them in a few areas. There was a ward meant to alert them if anyone other than the nurse crossed this threshold—I could shift it to one side so my coming and going wouldn't affect it. Opening the physical lock was a piece of cake.

The hardest part, really, was opening that door and stepping through it.

"Holden?" I called cautiously as I entered.

Classical music carried faintly from one of the deeper rooms: strains of flute and piano. The room I'd come into was sparsely furnished with a desk by the broad window, an armchair in the corner, and a couple of bookshelves along the walls. Holden had loved to read his whole life, and he still did. The brain injury he'd taken made it difficult for him to express much, both verbally or in writing, but he could still take just about anything in, as far as I could tell.

A sweet smell drifted from a few springs of lily of the valley arranged in a vase on the desk. He must have managed to communicate to the nurse that he'd wanted her to bring some up from the sparse garden on the west side of the house. They were just starting to droop.

"Holden?" I said again, and the music quieted. The whir of the electric wheelchair announced his approach before I could see my brother himself.

He cruised into the room and came to a stop a few feet inside with a tight smile. I couldn't read much into that, since from what I'd seen it was the only kind of smile his face was capable of now. His head always listed slightly to one side. He'd once been as broad in frame and features as I was, but the lack of exercise had slimmed him, turning him into sharper angles. His hair, a darker shade of brown than mine, fell in waves to the tops of his ears.

"Con," he said in acknowledgment. He hadn't been able to manage my full name since the fight.

"I'm just home for the weekend," I said, as if that mattered all that much to him. "I felt like it'd been too long since I came to see you. How are you doing?"

An awkward question, but I couldn't *not* ask it. He gave his closest approximation to a shrug and said, "Ar—Th—Same." Sometimes it took him a few tries before he hit on a word he could force all the way out.

"The nurse is keeping you well-stocked in new books?" I glanced toward the shelves.

"I," he said, the smile tugging a little wider and even tighter, and gestured to the tablet he'd tucked beside his paralyzed legs.

"Oh, you're lowering yourself to ebooks now, huh? I doubt you can get many fearmancer texts that way."

He made a snorting sound, but the flicker of his eyes made me regret the attempt at teasing. A lot of the books on the shelves behind me were magical texts. He'd kept studying them even after he'd lost any real ability to cast. He didn't need his limitations rubbed in, though, especially when I was the one who'd caused them.

"Sorry," I said. "I just—" I made myself shut up for a moment. I never really knew what to say to him. Sometimes I was sure I was only making things worse. That feeling had lengthened the time between my secret visits more than once.

There was one thing I'd decided I *had* to say before I'd even come up here. I took a step toward him, my head bowing.

If I could talk to Rory about this—if I could beg *her* forgiveness for what I'd done to her—I should at least be able to say a few honest things to my own brother.

"I'm sorry for a lot more than that," I said. "We never talk about it, so I don't think I've ever really apologized. I never wanted to hurt you. I hate that I did. I—If I could give the barony to you and have you back the way you were, I'd do that in a heartbeat. You'd be better for it anyway. Our parents have messed up ideas about what makes a good leader. *You* were the one who was stronger. You resisted them longer—you had more self-control."

I braced myself as I raised my eyes again, half expecting anger or disgust on his face. Instead, Holden only looked sad. "There—" he said, and grimaced at the strain of trying to squeeze the words in his head up his throat. "See— Can't—"

With a frustrated sound, he directed the wheelchair past me to the bookshelves. He leaned forward to snatch up a volume he must have known well. After a few brisk flips of the pages, he held the novel out to me with his finger poised over one paragraph.

There was never any going back, not to the good or the bad. The best we could do was move forward carrying those lessons with us. It was hard to remember, but I returned to that thought whenever I drifted too far into regret.

A lump rose in my throat. "I know," I said. "I know I can't actually undo what happened. And I'm trying to do what's right going forward. It's still…" I trailed off, not knowing how to end that sentence.

Mom had brought in doctors to tackle Holden's injuries, but she said they'd declared most of them too severe to heal even with magic. He was never going to walk again. He was never going to be able to speak or write properly. He would never cast more than a hiccup of magic here and there. And there wasn't anything I could do to change that.

"When I'm baron, I'm kicking them out of the house," I said with abrupt certainty. "I'll put in an elevator and ramps and whatever the hell else so you can go wherever you want, when you want. They shouldn't keep you shut away like this."

He gave that sort of shrug again, as if to say he was used to it, which after nearly six years, I guessed he was. That only made the situation worse.

"I mean it," I said, holding his gaze. "That's a promise." Even if it was one I wouldn't be able to fulfill until years from now.

The highway-side restaurant a couple hours away from the university wasn't much to look at. "Dive bar" would probably have been the appropriate term. But that might have been exactly why the four of us scions had come to appreciate it as a stop-off and meet-up spot on the way back to campus.

After the stresses of a visit home, with all the expectations and emphasis on appearances, where better to unwind than a place where nearly everything on the menu was deep-fried and the only kind of button-up shirts the other clientele wore were printed with plaid?

It was usually Malcolm or Declan who arranged those meet-ups, though. I couldn't remember when Jude had ever reached out to me with a specific invitation. I hadn't even realized he'd gone home this weekend too. But he'd texted me while I was saying my goodbyes to my parents, and while I wasn't sure whether this was going to be a friendly conversation, I wasn't going to snub him.

It was easy to tell he was already there when I arrived. His Mercedes was the fanciest car in the lot by several degrees. I parked beside it and headed inside.

A country rock song was twanging over the speakers, and the air had its familiar salt-and-grease flavor. Jude had staked out a booth near the back, his dark red hair catching my eye even with the yellow lighting dulling its vivid color. I walked over and slid onto the opposite bench.

"You made good time," Jude said mildly, and beckoned for a waitress. He already had a drink in front of him, something dark poured over ice. Even when we'd been in our mid-teens, the waitstaff here hadn't given our enchanted IDs more than a cursory glance. Another reason we liked this place.

"I'll have the bacon burger with pepper fries," Jude said, and tipped his head to me.

"A New Belgium if you still have it on tap, and the barbeque wings." I'd been here often enough to skip a glance at the menu.

"I'll get right on that," the waitress said cheerfully, and sashayed away.

Jude tugged at the collar of his shirt as if he were too warm in it, even though the air conditioning blasting from the unit nearby was keeping the space pretty cool. He looked away from me for a moment, the corners of his mouth pulling down.

"Tough visit?" I ventured.

"Ah, I was prepared for that. It's never *fun*." He turned back to me with a wry smile. "As I'm sure yours wasn't either."

"Let's not get into that." The waitress plonked my beer on the table, and I took a large gulp. "Is there any specific reason you wanted us to grab lunch today?" The last time we'd talked one-on-one, he'd been telling me off.

"Can't I just want to hang out with one of my good friends?" Jude said innocently, and shook his head at himself. "I figured if Malcolm of all people can own up to his assholery, I should be able to too. I've been rough on you this summer, mostly because of my issues rather than any real issue with you. So, I'm sorry about that."

It took me a second to process what I was hearing. I'd have much sooner expected Jude to simply pretend any hostility had never happened than to apologize for it.

"It wasn't a big deal," I said by way of accepting the apology, and let a wry note creep into my voice. "I learned a long time ago not to get too offended by anything you say when you're shooting your mouth off."

Jude sputtered with mock-indignation, but his eyes glinted with amusement. "Look at Stormhurst giving the verbal smackdown. Not your usual style. I guess Rory was right."

At the mention of the girl who'd taken up so much space in my head and heart over the last few months, my mood turned more serious in an instant. "Right about what?"

"Oh, don't worry. It was a compliment. She said the rest of us didn't give you enough credit for being more than the brawn. I'm willing to concede that may be true."

The thought of Rory speaking up for me that way sent a warm flush through my chest, only slightly moderated by Jude's cheeky phrasing. "May be true?" I muttered.

He grinned at me. "I'm not finished collecting evidence yet. That is the other subject I wanted to talk about, though. Rory—and our common interest in her."

I raised my eyebrows. "I hope you didn't apologize for laying into me only to warn me off her all over again."

He waved his hand dismissively. "No, no. Really the opposite. For reasons I'm sure no one would be able to fathom, she's clearly fond of both of us. And she's had a rather rough few months since she arrived at Blood U, I'm sure you can agree."

"Yeah." Not least because of our own initial treatment of her.

"So, I simply suggest that we should focus on making the coming months more enjoyable for her, however we can. And if that means both of us fawning over her, well… In this particular case, maybe more can still be merrier."

I studied him. "Is this some weird way of giving me your blessing? Which I didn't actually need in the first place, by the way."

"Hey, you could give *me* the benefit of the doubt too," he said. "I'm just saying… Let's not fight about it. Let's not interfere with whatever she ends up having going with the other. We each do what we can to show her a good time, and she'll end up with double the good time. Maybe we can even make a joint effort of it now and then." His grin came back. "With both of us on a date, I'm fairly certain she'd at least never be bored."

"We'll see about that," I said, but as the idea sank in, my initial balking reaction faded. His main point was solid. Rory deserved better than having us squabble over her. And maybe… it would make her even happier to see we could not just tolerate each other's presence in her life, but embrace the fact. I wasn't sure what a "joint effort" would look like, but anything that'd make her happy, that'd offset the pressure she was under, I was all for.

"If you think of any possibilities along that line, let me know," I added, and Jude's grin turned into a full-out smirk.

"Oh, I'm sure I can come up with something without any trouble at all."

CHAPTER TWENTY-NINE

Rory

The central air in Ashgrave Hall was having some kind of technical difficulties. Even tucked away in a dim corner of the library, I couldn't escape the summer heat. Sweat trickled down my back as I flipped through one of the books I'd gathered. I swiped at my forehead.

The hardest part about researching anything to do with fearmancers was they didn't exactly broadcast their activities to the wider world. I'd tried digging around online for news articles or other records that might help me figure out the connections between the names on Professor Banefield's list and the Nary activities they'd apparently interfered with, but there hadn't been anything beyond the clippings he'd already collected, none of which mentioned the fearmancers themselves anyway.

I *had* determined that the Crowford on the list was my Persuasion professor, and the Darksend was the Physicality professor I'd only seen in passing. The fact that not just one but two teachers on campus were part of this group—the group that presumably had been responsible for Banefield's death—was far from comforting.

In my earlier searches of the university library, I'd discovered a small section that held volumes of fearmancer records: the lines of inheritance within the ruling families, significant events at the university, and other write-ups someone or other had decided were worth committing to paper. Sorting through those, I'd made a few more discoveries.

Lillian Ravenguard was married to Julian Nightwood's second cousin. Ilene Burnbuck was my professor Burnbuck's aunt and had come by the school for occasional special tutorials. Three of the other names on the list, people I hadn't recognized at all, had contributed funds to the restoration of the Killbrook Hall after a bad storm had caused a bunch of damage, which suggested they were fairly prominent and involved in fearmancer society.

So, basically, my enemies were a whole bunch of people with tons of power. Wonderful. I still didn't have any clue what they were after that had made it worth trying to crush me into submission. Or why they appeared to have eased back in their efforts after my mentor's death.

Maybe they were unsure of what Banefield might have managed to tell me, and they wanted to watch what I did next before deciding *their* next moves. Maybe they were worried that launching another assault so soon after his death would be too risky. There had to be people who wouldn't agree with what they were doing—enough people that they felt they needed to go about their attempts as surreptitiously as possible.

Knowing that wasn't much of a comfort either, though. It didn't mean they were done. It only meant I was getting a reprieve before another attack that might come at any time in any way. How could I prepare when I had no idea what was going to come at me or how soon?

I set down my current book with a sigh and picked up another. This one talked about various international tournaments and the winners who'd come from Blood U. I wasn't sure there'd be anything useful in there, but I skimmed the pages just in case.

I'd only made it a little way through when the floor at the end of my aisle of shelves creaked.

"Here she is," Jude said, with a fond shake of his head. "Hiding away in a pile of books. Typical."

Connar had come over with him. "Project research?" he asked me, looking at the stack.

"Something like that," I said. "Not that I'm getting very far." I paused. I didn't know how to broach the subject of the barons' hostility with either of them. Not that Jude or Connar seemed to really *like* the people who'd raised them, but I'd seen how difficult a fearmancer's sense of loyalty could be to shake. Look at how long Connar had ignored his conscience to support Malcolm's plans. And the barons weren't just family to them—they were the leaders of their entire society.

I'd have to talk to them about it at some point… but maybe not quite yet. Not until I was sure it'd help me and not backfire in my face.

I tucked a damp strand of hair behind my ear, wondering what to make of the fact that they'd come looking for me *together*. Jude waved for me to get up.

"Come on," he said. "We're getting you out of this oven. I'm sure you need a break by now anyway. Go get your swimsuit, and we'll cool off in the lake."

The thought of the lake made my chest clench up. I hadn't gone in the water since things had gotten hot—and then chilling—with Malcolm. "I—"

"You'll be able to focus better if you give yourself a breather," Connar said, clearly anticipating my protest even if he didn't know exactly why. "Summer's almost over. You've got to enjoy it while you can."

He looked at me so hopefully that my resistance wavered. It *would* be nice to get out of the heat. And there was something incredibly sweet about the way the two of them had joined forces to rescue me from my study habits, even though they didn't always get along. Even though they had every reason to feel at odds while they were both vying for my affection. I didn't want to discourage that peacemaking.

I'd decided I wasn't going to let Malcolm ruin any part of my life. Why should I let one bad memory stop me from enjoying one of the few things I did actually like at this school?

"Okay, okay," I said, getting up. "I'm sold. I'll meet you down at the dock?"

Jude winked at me. "You'd better be fast about it, or I'll come and carry you over."

I made a face at him, and he laughed. But I did pull on my bikini as quickly as I could once I reached my dorm room, grabbing a tee for more modesty on the walk down.

When I reached the shore, Jude and Connar were already standing on the dock, Connar in swim trunks and Jude in a fitted Speedo that left very little to the imagination. Between that and the amount of toned musculature on display, a different sort of heat fluttered under my skin.

"Why are you two just standing around?" I teased as I dropped my shirt and towel on the warm boards of the dock. "Last one in's a rotten egg!"

I leapt off the end with that last declaration. The splash and surge of the cool water washed away all the lingering sweat on my skin. There was a shout as the two guys joined me, the water rocking me with the waves from them hitting the water.

"I think we can declare that a tie," Jude said, flicking his hair back from his eyes. Wet, it turned so dark it was almost black.

"If you insist," Connar said, smiling.

"The important part is that I beat both of you," I declared, and started swimming deeper into the lake with casual strokes. The vibe of the moment was already totally different from the previous afternoon. The memory faded more with each push through the water.

Jude dove down. A few seconds later, a tug on my ankle nearly pulled my head underwater. I kicked out instinctively to free my leg, and the Killbrook scion emerged with a sputter.

"You almost broke my nose there, Ice Queen."

"A girl's got to defend herself." I arched my eyebrows at him. "You should be careful. I'm told I'm a very powerful mage."

He just laughed.

Connar swam past us, moving east. "Apparently we gave other people the same idea," the bigger guy said with a quick nod to the shore. A few Naries, none of them students I knew well, were heading down to the water in their swimsuits.

"There's a little bay over here that's nice," the Stormhurst scion added.

And a little more private, I guessed. I followed him, watching the rise of the shore from low rocky ground to nearly sheer gray cliff. Giggles and splashes carried from behind us, but the hiss of the waves against the uneven wall of stone gradually overwhelmed them.

Somewhere up there lay the little clearing where I'd first spoken to Connar, where we'd first kissed… Where we'd done a lot of first things.

Jude cruised after us, switching between a lazy front crawl and gliding along on his back, his pale skin stark against the dark water. For a second, with the sun shining off his boyish face, his lips curled into a smile of contentment so pure it made my heart ache.

Maybe he'd needed a break from reality too.

The shoreline curved, the forest peering over the edge of the cliff high above, and the voices of the other students vanished completely. Nothing stirred in this alcove at the edge of the lake other than the leaves overhead and us swimming into the still water. I shifted onto my back like Jude had, staring up at the broad expanse of the blue sky. The same sky that had spilled out over me back in California. So much had changed, but some things I could count on.

Connar swam closer to the cliffside where he could stand on the bottom, the water rippling around his shoulders. "You like it?" he asked with a pleased gleam in his eyes as I joined him. The lake bottom was rocky too, but the stones pressed smoothly against my feet when I set them down to give my muscles a break.

"You know all the best spots, huh?" I said.

He gave me that glorious grin that had made me want him from the first time I'd seen it, and I had to bob up for a kiss. Connar steadied me in the water with an arm around my waist, his lips slick but still warm against mine. We'd only pressed together with this much bare skin once before. Desire shot through my body, sharp and heady.

Jude cleared his throat with a disgruntled sound where he'd come up behind me. I turned, and Connar's arm loosened around me without letting go completely. Before I could rethink the urge, I grasped Jude's hand and pulled him to me.

His mouth collided with mine, and oh Lord, I hadn't known it was possible to feel this much all at once. Jude kissing me, his hand cupping my face. Connar tracing his thumb over my stomach where he held me beneath the water. Both their bodies connected with mine with such delicious friction, turned slick by the lake.

There had better not be anything wrong with wanting two guys at once, because now that I was experiencing it, I couldn't imagine giving it up.

Connar ducked his head to press his lips to my neck. Jude claimed my mouth even more completely, his tongue tangling with mine. His fingers stroked down my side—and back up to the curve of my breast, shifting the current with the motion.

My breath hitched with a jolt of anticipation, but a thread of anxiety wriggled through the haze of pleasure. I drew back just far enough to speak. "What if someone else comes around this way?"

Jude met Connar's eyes over my shoulder. A sly smile curved his lips. "I think we can make sure there's no need to worry about that. A physical barrier to block off other swimmers and stop sound from traveling, and an illusion to prevent any glimpses from a distance?"

"Sounds like a plan," Connar said in a voice low enough to send an eager shiver through me.

Both of them spoke under their breaths as they cast. Their magic flitted through the air with a faint vibration I only picked up for an instant.

Jude turned back to me looking very satisfied with himself. "Now, where were we?"

"In the middle of making sure this is the best swim our Princess Bloodstone has ever had, I think," Connar said, and lowered his mouth to nibble my earlobe.

Jude kissed me again, teasing his fingertips along my collarbone and then the edge of my bikini top. I gave an impatient hum that Connar responded to first. He slid his hands around me to caress both my breasts at the same time.

My body arched with the rush of pleasure, and Jude gripped my hip, aligning our bodies. If I'd had any doubts about how much *he* wanted *me*, the bulge that brushed against my core would have dispelled them. A hungry ache formed between my legs.

He didn't rush, though. He just held me against him and kissed me with so much passion my head spun, already giddy with the bliss Connar was working through my chest and with his lips along my neck and shoulder.

Connar released me for just a second to undo the clasp at the back of my top. The water glided up over my bare skin even more intimately as the fabric drifted free. Jude tugged it right off and, with a cheeky grin, hung it from a notch in the cliffside.

Connar palmed my breasts again, carefully and then with more assurance. He swiveled his thumbs over my nipples until they stood at throbbing attention and then rolled them between his fingers so firmly I gasped against Jude's mouth. The ache between my legs expanded.

With a rough breath, Connar shifted me higher against his frame, setting me in the perfect position for him to lavish even more attention with his mouth on the sensitive spot where my neck met my shoulder. My breasts broke from the water's surface with a fresh lick of pleasure. He tweaked the nipples again. Then, as Jude left my mouth to nip along my jaw, Connar slid his hand underneath one breast as if to offer it up to the other scion.

Jude let out a breathless chuckle. "Now there's a delicacy I can't resist."

He sucked the tip of my breast into his mouth, Connar worked over the other side even more enthusiastically, and all I could do was moan and be thankful their spells had covered any noises we made.

Pleasure rushed through me in waves of sparks. I tipped my head back, and Connar managed to capture my lips from behind, tucking his head over my shoulder. He teased my breast more tenderly and then pinched the nipple so I whimpered. My hips canted toward Jude.

Even as Jude swiped his tongue over the peak of my breast, he tugged me tighter against him. But that friction wasn't enough to satisfy me anymore. I gave Connar one more desperate kiss and then yanked Jude up so our mouths could crash together. At the same time, I ground against him. He groaned, his teeth nicking my lip.

"Are you sure?" he murmured in a strained voice. His hand came to rest on the waist of my bikini bottoms, his fingers hooking around them meaningfully.

I nodded. "God, yes."

He peeled the bottoms off me and tossed them over my top where it was hanging. With another tug beneath the water, the head of his cock traced over my clit. Connar had resumed his attentions to both my breasts and my neck, and for a few seconds that swell of sensation was enough. Then I growled impatiently.

"Jude…"

"Right here." He curled his fingers into my opening first with a quick murmur to make sure this encounter didn't end up with consequences more serious than any of us were prepared for, and then he was sliding inside me, one hot solid inch at a time. He clutched my thigh with a ragged exhalation as our bodies joined. The ecstatic burn of him filling me in combination with Connar's touch and the fact that this was happening at all nearly sent me over the edge right there.

"Fuck," he muttered. "You feel even better than I imagined."

Somehow the thought of him imagining this moment, of him dwelling in his desire for me, made me even giddier. I bucked my hips to encourage him, and with a shaky laugh he plunged even deeper. My head lolled back, which Connar took full advantage of. The other scion scraped the tips of his teeth over the skin along my throat to blissful effect.

I wanted to give him more too. If I could make him feel anywhere close to as good as I did right now…

Jude thrust into me again, and my ass brushed Connar's groin. I gasped as much from the thick erection that nudged my cheek as from the pleasure of Jude's cock lancing through me. It didn't seem Connar minded being a witness to his friend fucking me. He was nothing if not turned on.

I snaked my hand behind me and gripped his cock through his swim trunks. Connar's breath stuttered against my shoulder. He squeezed my breasts as I slid my fingers over him. After a few tentative strokes, partly rocked by the perfect rhythm Jude was setting, I slipped my hand right beneath the fabric to caress him skin to skin.

Connar pumped into my grasp with a groan. He trailed his fingers down my body and pressed them to my clit just as Jude drove into me.

I cried out, pleasure bursting through me, and Jude claimed the sound with a fierce kiss. He thrust faster, my hand tightened around Connar, and Connar kept working over my clit. The wave of bliss surged even higher and crashed over me all over again, in time with a choked breath from Connar.

Heat rushed past my palm as the Stormhurst scion reached his release too. Then it flooded me from the inside, Jude bowing over me with a shudder. He hugged me to him, tucking his head next to mine, and Connar held me too, nuzzling my hair on the other side.

I floated between them, adrift on ecstasy, too blissed out to even speak for the first few minutes. Then I managed to say, "Definitely the best swim ever. It'd be hard to top this."

Connar chuckled, and Jude pecked my cheek playfully. "That sounds like a dare, Ice Queen," he said.

I was a fearmancer, and I wasn't equipped to absorb any emotion other than fear. I'd have sworn in that moment, though, I could feel the joy radiating through all three of us.

Just this once, just for now, everything was right. Even if I knew it couldn't be more than the eye of a storm I hadn't seen the end of.

CHAPTER THIRTY

Rory

About a dozen of the Nary students were working together to lay the final coat of paint on the outside of their clubhouse. Watching them laugh and chatter with each other as they swiped their paint brushes over the wall, a sense of joy came over me for the second time in as many days. I smiled as I leaned against Ashgrave Hall in my usual vantage point.

The clubhouse was essentially done. The door was in place, glass in the windows, and the first batch of furniture had arrived this morning. Whatever my fellow fearmancers' projects had been, they hadn't managed to prevent mine from coming to fruition. And every word and gesture the Naries made showed how pleased they were with what they'd accomplished too.

This triumph wasn't the only one I had to celebrate. A couple hours ago I'd gotten a frantic call from my grandmother cajoling me to intercede on her and my grandfather's behalf in a "misunderstanding" that had brought the blacksuits to their doorstep. "I'll look into it," I'd told her blandly, which wasn't really a lie. I was curious to find out what Declan had dug up on them. But they'd face whatever their due punishment was.

He and his family should be safe from their machinations now. We'd see whether any sanctions laid were enough to get them off *my* back, but they had a lot less to threaten me with now.

"I need a top-up!" Shelby called, bringing around the tub she'd filled with paint for the students around the other side of the building. Benjamin exchanged a grin with her as he poured more in from the bucket. Was that a bit of a blush in my friend's cheeks? Maybe she'd found even more than I'd expected with this project.

"So, you pulled it off," a sour voice said.

My head jerked around. Sinclair had come up beside me, stopping a few feet away. She regarded the Naries with a frown. "Why the hell you want to do them all these favors to screw over the rest of us, I don't know."

"*They've* never been assholes to me," I said. No need to point out the other side of that fact—most of the mage students had been.

Sinclair shrugged. "You've spent so much time coddling them, maybe you haven't looked after everything else you really should have."

I looked at her more sharply. "What are you talking about?" I had no idea what punishment *Victory* had faced for my trick with the voice illusion or whether she'd realized I'd orchestrated it, but her eyes had narrowed every time she'd seen me the last few days. I'd suspected yet another retaliation might be coming.

Sinclair smiled at me—a thin, tight little smile with about as much warmth as an icicle. "Sometimes it's a trade-off. You can't save everything. Let's just say it's the cat's turn to play."

The cat. Panic shot through me, and at the same time, as my thoughts leapt to my familiar, a distant sensation prickled into my chest. Something small and frantic, tinged with the urge to flee.

I was picking up a hint of Deborah's feelings through the familiar bond. I spun around, my gaze snapping to my bedroom window high above us. What the fuck was Victory doing to my mouse now?

My legs tensed to run up to the dorm, but the vague impressions that reached me from my familiar gave me the sense that she was moving downward—toward me. Through the building? I stayed braced where I was, training all my attention on those clues, tuning out Sinclair's gloating presence completely.

At the front of the building, the door swung open. A snicker I recognized instantly as Victory's reached my ears. "Any second now," she said to someone.

I started to storm around the hall to confront her, but I'd only made it two steps before I felt Deborah's presence getting fainter. She was moving in the opposite direction. I backtracked and came around the other side of the building, my pulse thumping. What was going on? If she wasn't coming to me, where *was* she going?

Footsteps scraped the ground on the other side of the building. Then a small white shape sprang from a tiny opening I wouldn't have noticed otherwise between two of the hall's stones. Deborah dashed away across the field toward the garage, her pale body flashing amid the blades of grass.

"Wait!" I called after her—and another furry shape bolted in the same direction. A much larger, cream-and-brown colored shape that dashed after Deborah with a flick of its slim tail: Victory's cat familiar. With a few bounds, it was already closing the distance.

I had no idea how Victory had contrived to get Deborah out of the dorm—some sort of spell targeting her emotions, maybe, given the distress that had been thrumming off her before she'd even emerged?—but I had no doubt at all what she'd ordered her familiar to do if it caught the mouse. I threw myself after them as fast as my legs would carry me.

If casting magic on my familiar was fair play, I could do the same to hers. They were racing ahead of me so quickly, though, that I had to be careful to make sure whatever I cast hit the right target. If I slowed Deborah down instead, I'd be signing her death sentence.

I pushed myself faster, my legs burning. Thumps behind me told me I was being followed, but I couldn't spare the focus to glance back. I narrowed all my attention onto the larger furry shape charging ahead of me.

"*Stop*," I shouted with a surge of persuasive magic, but I mustn't have aimed well enough. The cat ran on. I groped for an alternate strategy. "Box."

Like the walls I'd used to protect me from Malcolm's persuasive designs in the past, the physicality spell was crude but effective. A transparent but solid structure snapped into place around the cat. It was racing along too fast to register the change in time—its face smacked right into one wall. It rebounded with a screech.

Deborah was still running. I could barely make her out in the taller grass behind the garage now, but I didn't want to shout out her real name. My enemies were smart enough to question whether I'd really have named a normal mouse "Deborah."

"Squeak!" I called instead, resorting to the name I'd called her by for the four years before I'd known the mouse contained a human's spirit. "Squeak, come to me!"

Either she'd forgotten that name belonged to her or she was too terrified to process anything. I was just coming up on the garage when her little white body scrambled up the concrete side of that building. Her claws scrabbled against the roughly textured surface, and she skidded halfway down again. I lunged forward and caught her in the middle of her second attempt.

My hands closed around her trembling body. She squirmed in my grasp. "Deborah," I whispered to her. "Deborah, listen to me, you—"

Terror coursed from her into my chest. She flailed around and sank her teeth into my thumb, so deep the spike of pain made me yelp.

I managed to keep my grip on her, but other voices started hollering from behind me. I whipped around to see not just Victory but Cressida and Sinclair loping toward me.

Victory had just reached her familiar. She grimaced and shattered the spell I'd cast around the cat with a snapped word and a jerk of her hand. Then she pointed toward me.

Cressida called out a casting word. I didn't know what her intention was until a bolt of energy smacked into my hands, heaving them apart. Deborah's panicked form plummeted back to the ground.

"No!" I leapt after her, and Victory said something else in a cutting tone. A force like a steel bar slammed into my shins. I tumbled forward onto my hands and knees, a rock scraping my palm.

Deborah was dashing toward the forest now. I didn't think she'd be all that much safer there, where she'd have other predators to contend with. Victory's cat barreled after her in hot pursuit.

I shoved myself back onto my feet, my thoughts whirling as I tried to think of a spell to stop the animal that wouldn't be easily shattered, a way to stop the three girls from stopping *me* yet again.

Too late. The cat coiled its muscles and threw itself into a pounce. A choked cry slipped from my lips—

—and a dark body hurtled out of the woods to slam the cat to the ground.

Malcolm's wolf pinned the Siamese under its heavy paws, its lips pulled back in a growl. Victory and her friends jarred to a halt around me. The cat yowled, the wolf gnashed its teeth in warning, and Malcolm himself stepped out of the forest.

"What the hell, Mal?" Victory protested, half pouting, half seething. "Get your familiar off of mine!"

"We're just making sure no one else's familiar meets an untimely end," Malcolm said, folding his arms over his chest. "Are you going to call off the cat?"

Now I was just as confused as Victory was. Stunned speechless might be more accurate. Thankfully, she had no problem asking the questions I would have for me.

"Are you serious?" my nemesis said, flinging her arm toward me. "I was messing with her. You should be *helping* me, not getting in the way."

"I don't think so." Malcolm stepped forward to stand beside Shadow. "From now on, scion business stays between scions. I don't want to see *any* of you hassling anyone in the pentacle, including Glinda here. Are we clear?"

Victory stared at him. "But— You said— This is fucking ridiculous, Malcolm. You know what she—"

Malcolm's voice cut through hers, cool and firm. "Are. We. Clear?"

There was so much menace in his expression that she faltered. Half of her interest in harassing me had come from wanting to make good with him, I suspected, at least to begin with. And he, for some bizarre reason, was pulling that rug out from under her.

"We're clear," she said tightly.

"And if I call Shadow off your familiar, where are you going to take him?"

"Back to my dorm." Her lips pursed. "Do you really—"

His eyes hardened even more. "Do I really need to remind you that arguing with me isn't a good idea?"

The other two girls stood silent, shocked or wary or both. In the midst of the tension, it occurred to me that while Victory was focused on Malcolm, this was the perfect time for me to remind her just how bad an idea coming at *me* was.

I fixed my gaze on her and rolled a persuasive spell off my tongue like the lash of a whip. "*You will not cast any more magic.*"

Her mental shields had wavered in her bewilderment, and she hadn't been paying attention to me anyway. I felt the spell spear straight through her protections into her mind. Victory flinched and jerked around to face me. "You—"

"Making sure you have to keep any promises you're making," I said as calmly as I could. My hands were still shaking where I'd clenched them at my sides. Deborah was out there somewhere, still in the grip of the magic Victory had possessed her with.

When Malcolm and the other scions had stolen my familiar before, they'd only tormented an illusion of her. Victory had meant to slaughter the real animal. I wasn't so self-confident I believed the all-encompassing spell I'd just cast with my still-developing talents would last very long, but long enough to make Victory regret what she'd done today was all I needed.

She opened her mouth, maybe to try to mutter a spell, because her voice didn't emerge. She couldn't do it. She glared at me and turned back to Malcolm. "I'm going. If you want me to take my familiar with me, call yours off him."

Malcolm snapped his fingers. That was all the command the wolf needed. It bounded away gracefully, and the cat sprang up with its back arched. When Victory clucked her tongue to it, it streaked across the field to her side. She scooped it up with comforting murmurs, aimed one more glower at me as if this whole situation was somehow my fault, and stalked off with her lackeys flanking her.

"That was cold, Glinda," Malcolm said with an amused gleam in his eyes. "Slipping that spell in like that."

"She deserved it." And I didn't particularly want the Nightwood scion's approval. I let out a ragged breath and scanned the field. My thumb throbbed where Deborah had bitten it. I tucked it, welling blood and all, against my palm. "If you wouldn't mind going somewhere else with Shadow, I'd appreciate it. I still have to find *my* familiar and wake her up from whatever Victory cast on her."

"You should be able to get a sense of her through the familiar bond."

"I know. I don't need your help." I paused. "And if you're sticking around waiting for me to thank you for stepping in just now, don't think I've forgotten that you're the one who egged Victory on in the whole 'destroy Rory' campaign in the first place. I don't know why you're telling her off now, but you'll forgive me if I don't trust that it's from the goodness of your heart."

"Rory…" His jaw tensed. At the tap of his fingers, Shadow trotted to his side. "I meant what I said to her. Anyone who takes you on will have to answer to me. Whatever we still have to work out between us, that's between *us*, and we can do it like colleagues, no more campaigns of destruction."

Oh, he'd just decided that, had he? How wonderful for him. I didn't know what he thought we still had to work out. All I'd ever wanted was for him to stay the hell away from me.

"Great," I said. "Maybe next time a new scion turns up, you can follow that philosophy a few months sooner. Can you please leave now? I have no problem with your *wolf*, but I don't think my familiar is going to calm down while there's one around."

Malcolm looked as if he almost said something else, but whatever it was, he thought better of it. He dipped his head to me with an unreadable expression and strode away, Shadow following at his heel.

I took several slow breaths to steady myself, and a thin thread of emotion crept back into my chest. Deborah. I walked closer to the forest, calling out a little louder now that there was no one around to hear me other than her. "Deborah? Deborah, it's okay now. There's nothing hunting you. It's just me here. Rory."

I paced along the edge of the forest for a minute before the underbrush rustled. A little white head poked from between the leaves. Her voice traveled distantly into my head. *Lorelei?*

Relief washed through me. I knelt down and held out my uninjured hand to her, and my familiar scampered onto it, trembling but still in one piece.

"There you go," I said softly. "I've got you. You're okay now."

I tried not to think about the fact that she might not have been if it'd come down to just me—that I might owe her life to the last guy on Earth I'd have wanted to owe anything to.

CHAPTER THIRTY-ONE

Rory

"You know," Jude said, "technically this competition is over. You can stop working on your project now."

I shot him a mock-glower where we were standing in the field outside the clubhouse. "*You* know I didn't work on this just for the competition."

The tang of new paint still hung in the air, but the building was completely finished. A couple hours ago, before the Nary students had headed home for a week's break before the fall term started, happy voices had been carrying through the windows. We fearmancer students had an assembly to announce the winner of the project competition in a few minutes, but I didn't need any official recognition to feel triumphant.

Jude grinned at me. "Yeah, well, it was worth a try. You push yourself awfully hard. I guess it's a good thing you have the two of us around to make sure you take a breather now and then."

"It is," Connar agreed with a chuckle. He straightened up from where he'd been kneeling a few feet from Jude. "I think that ward's completely solid. We'll still want to check on them periodically, but no one's taking this building down without a lot of concentrated effort."

I wasn't sure what warmed me more—his effortless use of "we" to mean the three of us or the memory of the treatment I'd gotten during the last breather these two had arranged for me.

Jude's eyes twinkled as if he knew what I was thinking about. He grabbed my hand and tugged me closer to him. "And I don't think Ms. Grimsworth will look kindly on that kind of destruction once this project is named the winning effort of the summer. Too bad none of the Naries know to thank you."

"I'm okay with that," I said. I wished I'd been able to do more. This was a step in the right direction, giving them an escape from the mage students who preyed on them, but it still gnawed at me that the school encouraged the rest of us to prey on them at all.

That would end once I could dismantle this place with the help of the joymancers. I had trouble picturing exactly what fearmancer society would look like in the aftermath, but at least I could now say there were people ready to lead who didn't prioritize cruelty. And the documents Professor Banefield had led me to would hopefully get me one step closer to *that* goal. We had a week off for the end of summer after this assembly, and I planned to spend all of it tracking down more information to better understand the pieces he'd given me.

Connar glanced at his phone. "We should get going if we want Rory at the assembly to receive her prize."

Jude sighed dramatically. "And here I was hoping we could take the opportunity to break in the new building with a little… action." He waggled his eyebrows at me.

I swatted his arm. "We're not going to go desecrating the place we just finished shutting people like us out of. We've got the whole rest of campus to make use of."

"Hmm. True." He kissed my cheek. "And what do you say we find some part of it to make use of before we all head home."

A flush spread all through my body. "I might be on board with that," I said, my pulse thumping even faster when I saw the hunger that had lit in Connar's eyes too. "But assembly first. We don't even know that I'm going to win."

Jude scoffed. "If you don't, I'll stage a protest. Let's go, then, Ice Queen."

Many students were already heading toward the Stormhurst Building. We merged with that current, letting it carry us along to the gymnasium where our summer project had first been announced. The platform was set up at the far end as before, Ms. Grimsworth standing near the podium speaking with Professor Crowford. At the sight of him, remembering his name on my mentor's list alongside the barons, my skin tightened.

As we waited for the rest of the students to trickle in, my phone chimed. I fished it out to see Lillian Ravenguard had texted me. *I understand the summer project results are being announced today. Let me know how yours turned out!*

All of me tightened seeing those friendly words. I had no idea just how complicit Lillian might be in the horrors I'd faced since arriving here—and I sure as hell wasn't ready to take her to task. Since I'd retrieved Banefield's records, I hadn't spoken to her at all, and things could stay that way for the time being. I shoved the phone back into my purse without replying.

Ms. Grimsworth tapped the microphone, and the chatter around the room fell silent. "It looks as though we have everyone here," she said, gazing over the crowd. "To begin with, I'd like to congratulate you on a successful summer all around. We saw great efforts from many students and minimal overstepping of rules." Her voice turned wry with those last words.

I couldn't help glancing toward where I'd spotted Victory standing in the midst of her closest friends and a few other girls on the other side of the room. She didn't look my way at all. She'd completely avoided me since her attack on Deborah two days ago. I'd imagine my persuasive spell had worn off and she could use her magic just fine, but she probably wasn't in any hurry to risk losing it again.

I might not have exactly *won* there, and whatever success I'd achieved had been partly due to Malcolm's intervention, but if all she did was ignore me for the rest of my time here at Blood U, I'd consider that a real victory.

"I'm sure you're all impatient to hear which student's performance exceeded all others, so I won't leave you waiting," the headmistress went on. "I'm pleased to announce that our judges unanimously agreed this year's prize should go to a young lady who's not only achieved a remarkable goal but done so only a short time after discovering her powers: Rory Bloodstone."

My name rolled over me with a momentary jolt of shock. Jude whooped, and Connar let out a cheer, and that seemed to spur any students who might have been hesitant given the focus of my project into action. Applause echoed around the room.

Ms. Grimsworth beckoned me up to the platform, and I pushed myself forward to weave through the crowd. A smile stretched across my face as exhilaration bubbled up in my chest. I'd *hoped*, but I hadn't really been sure—hadn't known whether the professors judging our work might dock me an awful lot of points for helping the Naries rather than attacking them.

But they hadn't opposed that approach, at least not enough for them to deny how much I'd accomplished. That was a reason for a lot more hope, wasn't it? Maybe I had even more people here who could transform fearmancer society into something less horrifying.

When I stepped up on the platform, Ms. Grimsworth gave my hand a brisk but firm shake with a smile that was warm by her standards. Professor Crowford came up to me with a small gilded certificate.

"Congratulations, Miss Bloodstone," he said. "Have you decided on your chosen object and enchantment?"

Right—the prize. I'd gotten so focused on seeing the project through that I'd forgotten I'd win anything other than seeing it complete.

"I'm going to need a little time to decide," I said.

He nodded. "Whenever you're ready, bring that certificate to the professor you'd like to cast the spell, and they'll be happy to comply."

I turned back toward the room, and Ms. Grimsworth nudged me forward with her hand on my back. "Let's hear a little more appreciation for this year's winner," she said.

Another round of applause and cheers echoed through the room. My gaze found Declan standing off to the side, clapping hard and beaming like he'd never doubted I'd pull this off. If only I could have really celebrated with him too.

Malcolm stood several feet beyond him, clapping too, his own smile crooked. But it *was* a smile. I didn't know what to make of this apparent truce he'd decided on, but I guessed there'd be plenty of time to hash that out next term.

Before I got down from the platform, I scanned the crowd one more time for another familiar face framed by dark blond hair. I'd have liked to acknowledge Imogen—she'd helped me pull the clubhouse together too. She didn't appear to be in the room, though. Maybe she'd headed home early, she'd been so sure she wasn't in the running?

Shelby should have gotten credit as well—most of the Naries should have, really—but they had at least gotten their clubhouse as a prize. That'd have to do for now.

Several of the other professors came over as I left the platform, grasping my hand or patting my shoulder with enthusiastic congratulations. I tensed a little at Professor Viceport's approach, but her expression didn't look as stiff as it usually did.

"An impressive bit of work, Miss Bloodstone," she said, shaking my hand with her cool dry fingers. "I have to say I'm looking forward to seeing how far you can take these skills of yours in the months ahead."

That approving remark felt like a whole extra win. I restrained the urge to do a fist-pump in celebration.

After a few moments, I was caught up in the crowd of my fellow students, with more congratulatory gestures and remarks. I doubted most of them meant that appreciation all that genuinely, but fearmancers were nothing if not pragmatic when it came to sucking up to people. If it meant even fewer of them messed with me next term, I was all for it.

The maintenance staff set out platters of snacks and drinks on tables along one wall, and for the next hour or so, the gym turned into an end-of-summer party. Someone turned on an upbeat pop album that didn't sound fearmancer-y at all, and Jude twirled me around a few times in his approximation of dancing. Connar grabbed the last of my favorite kind of tart before it disappeared.

As people started to drift out of the building, the two guys each took one of my hands. "So," Jude said meaningfully, "about that 'action' we were planning…?"

I elbowed him, but a flicker of heat ran through me. "We could go for a little drive, get right off campus?"

"I'd go for that," Connar said.

"Let me just pop back into the dorm. These aren't the best shoes for driving." I'd worn heels to go with my dressy slacks, but I wasn't so confident behind the wheel I wanted to experiment with advanced types of footwear just yet.

"As you wish," Jude said. "We'll meet you at the garage."

We parted ways on the green. As I headed to the stairs in Ashgrave Hall, Cressida barged past me in the hall with a rigid expression and a swish of her braid, her shoulder jarring against mine. Apparently *she* was in quite a rush to get home.

I hurried up the stairs to the fifth floor, my mind riffling through the possibilities for a peaceful—and private—date spot. Maybe the place where Jude had arranged our picnic what felt like ages ago? Or we could go all the way out to my country property. That might take too long for us to make it home in good time tonight, though…

I pushed open the door to the dorm room and stopped in my tracks. Every thought in my head scattered.

A body lay sprawled on the floor just a few feet into the room. A body splattered with blood and unnaturally still. A body with blond hair held back by a silver clip that glinted beneath the flecks of red.

My stomach lurched, and a rush of images flashed in front of my eyes. Imogen's face, twisted with anger, yelling something at me. Her hand slashing out to slap my face, the impression so real my cheek stung. My throat vibrating with words and power. A hail of razor-edged magic cutting my friend down. *Her* throat, slit. Her chest and stomach gouged.

"No," I said, shaking my head as if I could force the images away. But they weren't coming from inside me. They had to be some kind of spell, an illusion. They started up all over again from the beginning, Imogen yelling at me even as she lay there lifeless on the floor.

I tried to spin, to grope for the door that had hung open somehow behind me. My legs jarred, refusing to budge. I sucked in a breath to scream, and that caught in my throat. Magic gripped me from head to toe as the illusion whirled through its violent imagery in front of me. I couldn't even force my eyes to stay closed. My eyelids jerked back open with every blink.

And Imogen just lay there, the blood seeping further across the floor…

I had to help her. If there was any way she was still alive—*please*, let her still be alive—

There was a gasp and a shriek in the hall behind me. A voice murmured frantically as it faded away down the stairs. The illusions battered me again. I strained at my legs, at my vocal chords. Come on, Rory.

Footsteps thundered up the steps, and just like that, the spell released me. I stumbled around with a ragged inhalation to see four figures in black shirts and slacks bursting into the fifth floor hall. They charged right at me. One of them caught sight of Imogen's body beyond me and grimaced as he nodded to the others. A woman dropped beside Imogen and held her hand over Imogen's chest with a murmur of a casting.

"My friend—" I started.

"She's dead," the woman said, looking up.

The man at the front of the pack wheeled on me. "Rory Bloodstone," he said in a hard voice. "You need to come with us. You're under arrest."

SINISTER WIZARDRY - BONUS SCENE

By popular demand, this bonus scene gives you the chance to experience the infamous lake encounter in Chapter 16 from Malcolm's point of view…

Malcolm

There really was nothing better than a dip in the lake on a hot summer day, and today was absolutely sweltering. As soon as my morning seminar was over, I traded my slacks for swim shorts, grabbed a towel, and cast a quick deflective spell over myself to avoid burning. I'd learned my lesson years ago when I'd ended up with a heap of peeling skin all down my back after a careless couple of hours lounging on the dock.

I'd mentioned my intentions to Chandler and Dermot on our way out of class. They joined me leaving the dorm, Dermot yammering about how brilliant his summer project was and Chandler making snarky remarks about one of our Physicality classmates. I listened and nodded where it seemed appropriate, most of my attention on the thought of that expanse of cool water that would wash the stickiness of the day away.

It turned out that we hadn't been the only ones with a hankering for a swim. As we came down the path, I spotted a couple of figures moving through the water toward the dock. My gaze caught on a familiar head of dark brown hair, turned black as it fell slick and wet across her bare shoulders, and a flicker of heat raced through my veins. My pulse kicked up a notch with a jolt of anticipation.

I hadn't had a chance to mess with Rory since she'd walked off on me during the Illusion demonstration at the Casting Grounds. She couldn't have made a more appealing target than she did right now. Her pale skin glimmered through the rippling water. I could just make out the swell of her breasts beneath the sweetheart neckline of her bikini. What I wouldn't give to be tracing my fingers over those slopes…

Well, in a way, I would be.

When we reached the narrow strip of sand at the shoreline, I pretended I hadn't noticed her at all, shucking off my T-shirt and heading right into the water. Oh, it was good, that crisp chill cutting through the perspiration that had formed just with the walk across campus. But the fun I was going to have next would be even more enjoyable.

I eased down to where the water covered most of my chest, watching Rory's form from the corner of my eye. She'd come to a halt, treading water near the end of the dock with her friend—that girl whose father ran Maintenance, who'd sold Rory out under threat from Victory a few months ago. It figured that Rory would have forgiven her. The heir of Bloodstone deserved better friends than a nitwit who'd roll over the second anyone shot a sharp look her way.

I couldn't do anything about that part of my annoyance with Rory right now, though. Instead, I took careful note of her position in the water relative to me and then turned to face my friends, planting my feet in the soft lake bottom.

Chandler had already sculpted a blob of water into a solid disc. He tossed it to me with a flick of his hand, and I snatched it out of the air with just a slight bob on my feet.

"Nice!" Dermot hollered, as if the move had been all that impression. I threw the disc to him with a snap of my wrist that sent droplets spewing from its edges. He grabbed at it with a splutter, and Chandler cracked up.

"You'll pay for that," Dermot warned, as if the suck-up would ever risk doing anything to remotely offend any scion, let alone the heir of Nightwood. He sent the disc whirling toward me on its edge across the surface of the water, kicking up spray on either side, but all I got was a light dappling before I scooped it up with a chuckle.

"Let's just play an honest game," I said, and tossed the disc to Chandler like a regular frisbee. It'd be easier to focus on the other game I wanted to play if the guys weren't screwing around too much.

As Chandler hurled the disc to Dermot, I spoke a casting word I'd been getting a lot of use out of lately under my breath. I focused on my impression of Rory behind me where I could vaguely make out her voice in conversation with the other girl. My fingers glided through the water, exactly as I'd have liked to tease them across her taut stomach. Then I leapt up to catch Dermot's next throw.

Had she reacted? The one problem with keeping up the plausibly deniability of having my back turned was I couldn't see her responses. I shifted my fingers again, willing the current to sweep back and forth across her belly.

The water lapped my shoulders—and shivered down my chest with a current of someone else's making.

Oh, she'd caught on, all right. The liquid ghost of her touch traced over my sternum and trailed back up to my collarbone. Even in the cool water, heat seared across my skin in the wake of her magic.

I gave my fingers a teasing twist, and Rory retaliated almost instantly. The ripples of her spell sped down over my torso to the more sensitive span of my own stomach, sending a twang of desire straight to my groin—and making my muscles twitch as I reached for the disc Chandler had just tossed my way. The conjured object skimmed just above my reaching hand. Shit.

"Fine, fine, I'll make another one," Chandler said with a mild tut-tutting.

I was more concerned with the girl behind me. I jerked my casting hand upward, swiveling toward my imagining of the breasts I'd admired just minutes ago.

The spell gave me none of the tactile satisfaction of caressing those curves, but the gasp that slipped from Rory's lips was more than enough to stoke the heat building inside me. The sound had me half-hard just like that. Fuck, if I could have really touched her…

I managed to focus enough to catch the disc when Dermot flung it my way. The currents around my torso had stilled. Had the Bloodstone scion really given up? I should have felt triumphant at the thought, but a twinge of disappointment ran through my gut.

I drew back my arm to whip the disc toward Chandler—and a rush of sensation coursed down my belly to stroke right over my cock.

Pleasure sang through my nerves, my erection stiffened from half-mast to full, and my throw went wild, crashing into the water several feet from where Chandler was standing. As I tamped down on my arousal, he raised his eyebrows at me. "You're off your game today, Nightwood."

This game, maybe, but not the other one I'd initiated. I shifted my hand beneath the water more forcefully, down across Rory's belly to those enticing hips and then between her thighs, guiding the water to press right against her sex.

Rory didn't gasp again, but the warble of water around her body suggested she was trying to shake off my touch. I swiveled my fingers to intensify the sensations I was provoking.

At the same moment, the current by my groin cupped tight against me, wrapping around the base of my cock so firmly my vision hazed with a surge of pleasure. A groan reverberated from my chest before I could smother it—I forced a cough, which came out sounding as if I were choking.

My thumb flicked over the spot I imagined her clit must be. There was a faint splash in reaction, but not enough.

None of this was even halfway close to enough. The passion searing all through my body wasn't going to be sated by these stupid pranks. My hands itched to travel over Rory's terrain the way I'd let myself at the edge of the Casting Grounds, but I sure as hell wasn't going to get away with that here with everyone around.

So what was the point?

I waved toward the other guys. “I’m cooled off now. Let’s find something more interesting to do.”

The chill of the water streaming over my swim shorts only softened my hard-on a little. When I got close to the shore, I hustled the rest of the way as quickly as I could without being obvious about my rush and tugged my towel around me, arranging it to hide the lingering bulge.

Thankfully, Chandler and Dermot weren’t the most observant guys around. They gave me a careful ribbing about being a sore loser and then went back to their inane chatter while we started back toward the green.

Chandler stopped before we’d even reached the Stormhurst Building and rubbed his neck. “I wonder if I could talk one of the medics into giving me a massage. That last football match did a number on my spine.”

Dermot snorted. “They’ll probably tell you off for misuse of school resources.”

I glanced back and noticed Rory and her friend had climbed out onto the dock. The Bloodstone scion already wrapped her towel around her, hiding her figure from chest to knees, but just the sight of her naked shoulders and calves stirred my groin again.

For fuck’s sake. She’d gotten me way too keyed up.

Rory didn’t come our way, though. Her friend set off toward us, and the heir of Bloodstone strode past the dock to slip into the boathouse. Huh.

The lust still winding through my body tugged at me. Her detour might as well have been an invitation. Right now, not a single part of me could come up with a reason to decline it.

We couldn’t have fanned the flames in the lake with our classmates looking on, but behind closed doors, just the two of us… Hell, she had to be just as on fire as I was.

Every heated glance we’d exchanged since that first kiss, every caress both magical and literal, had sent us careening toward this inevitable act. Let her try to ignore me when I was right there in front of her. She'd started us on this collision course with that damned kiss; it was time for us to finish it.

"I need to grab something I left by the lake," I said to the guys without even looking at them, and headed toward the boathouse without waiting to hear their response. Just thinking about Rory standing in there, about all the curves and nooks I'd imagined through the water, brought my emotions back to a boil.

No girl had ever gotten to me like this before. She wasn't just any girl, of course, but even the heir of Bloodstone had to know there was a point when she couldn't just walk away.

I tossed my towel onto the railing outside the boathouse, shoved open the door, and stalked inside.

Rory froze where she was leaning against the rack of paddles, staring at me, but she didn't only look startled. Her cheeks were flushed and her dark eyes feverishly intent. Desire crackled through the air between us.

My voice came out hoarse. "You." I didn't know what else to say, couldn't do anything except march right up to her and yank her mouth to mine.

I half expected her to heave me off her, to try to keep up the pretense of disinterest, but apparently she'd lost her grip on her self-control too. She dug her fingers into my hair, kissing me back so hard I groaned at the sensation.

Her hand trailed down my chest along the same course she'd sent her current in the lake, even hotter now that we were skin to skin. I ran my hand up her thigh, her towel falling away as I hefted her against one of the rungs of the rack.

Her legs parted to admit me, just two layers of fabric between my aching cock and her sex. I swallowed another groan and branded the side of her neck with the press of my lips and a swipe of my tongue.

"We can fight more later," I said, inhaling in the caramel-sweet scent of her, practically drunk on it. She had to understand—she had to see this was the only possible conclusion to our latest bizarre battle. "Right now—you've been driving me crazy."

I claimed the crook of her shoulder with a light nip, and her fingers tightened in my hair. "I've been driving *you* crazy?" she retorted with a breathy quality to her voice that somehow made me twice as hard.

I'd show her fucking crazy. The strap of her bikini top gave at my nudge so easily. As it slipped down her arm, I dropped my head to suck the peak of her breast into my mouth.

Her nipple pebbled with a flick of my tongue, and she gasped, her hips swaying toward me. Wanting, wanting, just as much as I did.

And I was going to give her everything she wanted, everything we both wanted. It should have been like this all along. If she hadn't been so goddamned *stubborn…*

I licked her nipple once more for good measure, like a promise to return, and rose up to plant another kiss right on that scorchingly sweet mouth. My hand on her thigh held us locked together; the other rose to cup her breast where my lips had left off.

Everywhere our skin touched, we lit up like an inferno. My groin ached with need. The words tumbled out, a declaration and a promise. "God, I can't wait to be inside you."

Rory stiffened just slightly against me. Then she yanked her mouth from mine, wrenching herself away from both me and the rack so abruptly she teetered on her feet.

Not quite done with the games, was she? Did she really think I'd be willing to go back to playing now?

With a ragged laugh, I grasped her wrist. "Where do you think you're going? I think we've had enough of a chase."

I tugged her toward me, and she slipped on the damp boards of the boathouse floor. I let myself tumble forward with her, keeping just enough control to make sure she didn't hit the ground too hard before I braced myself over her. Tucking my hand behind her head over that silky hair, I nibbled along her jaw again.

"Get off," she protested with a hitch of breath.

"We're nowhere near finished," I retorted, and kissed her again. She waved a hand at me, and I curled my fingers around her wrist.

Her skin was slick and warm against my fingers, and the heat was still flooding through me from head to toe, just like it must be for her. One more kiss, one more caress, and she'd be melting into me again—

A splinter of ice shot through the inferno within, energy quivering down into my chest like a bolt of… fear? I paused with my mouth against her neck, and her voice cut through the haze of lust that'd consumed me with even harsher force. "So you're going to *rape* me?"

Rape? Another shock of frightened energy jolted from her into me, and I yanked back from both it and the accusation. Even as I recoiled, she spat out a word ringing with magic. "Off!"

The spell walloped me in the direction I'd already been heaving myself. I stumbled, nearly losing my balance, and caught a beam to steady my stance. The fear that'd trickled into my reserve of power had become a flood, more and more of it coursing through me in a frigid torrent, dousing the fire that had been spurring me onward.

Rory sat up, clutching her knees. She stared at me as if—as if I'd actually *attacked* her. As if she was terrified of me.

No. That wasn't right at all.

"I—You *wanted* this," I said, trying to set the scene back into a frame I could comprehend. I moved toward her, and she… she *flinched.*

I stopped in my tracks, the bottom of my stomach dropping out. Oh, fuck.

"Not with you," Rory said with a quaver in her voice that didn't belong there, not one bit. And I was the one who'd put it there. "Not like that."

Staring at her tensed and pale on the boathouse floor, there was no convincing myself that she was only pretending now. I could taste how real her fear was.

My chest constricted. She was that afraid of *me*. How long had she really been fighting, when I'd thought— How could I have pushed her to the point where she'd be that shaken?

The Rory in front of me wasn't a girl playing games for kicks. She didn't look like a fighter either. She just looked scared and tired.

Why wouldn't she, after the way I'd beaten her down over and over across the past few months, after how I'd just manhandled her like some kind of hooligan?

"I didn't mean—" I began, but I didn't know how to follow those words. How was I supposed to have known what she could handle when she'd launched herself at me that first time? "*You're* the one who started this."

Rory stood up, snatching her towel and wrapping it around her like a shield. Then she looked at me again, the iron will I'd become so familiar with shining through her eyes despite the vulnerability in her posture.

Was it really defiance, or just a frantic determination to simply *survive*?

"I did," she said in a taut voice. "And I'm sorry I did. So now I'm stopping it. Don't touch me again, in any way, or I'll break every bone in your hands. Are we clear?"

My fingers curled into my palms as if that would hold back the nausea surging up inside me. That she'd felt she needed to make that threat… Shame and frustration twined inside me, but the frustration was mostly with myself.

"I wouldn't have forced you," I said as firmly as I could. "Just so we're clear on *that*. I thought you were into it. I thought it was all more messing around."

Her mouth pulled tight. "Then you weren't paying enough attention. I was fucking terrified."

She was right. It'd been there when I'd let myself feel it, when I'd snapped out of that lust-drunk state. I'd been so busy chasing what *I* wanted, I'd let my desire drown out everything else.

I stepped back, swallowing hard. Rory whipped around and fled the boathouse, the door banging behind her.

Days ago—hours ago—I'd have rejoiced that I'd cracked her rebellious façade enough to send her running. Now the sight left me empty.

This wasn't what I'd wanted, not at all.

HORRID CHARMS

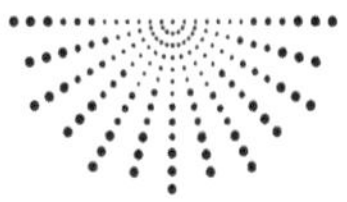

ROYALS OF VILLAIN ACADEMY #4

CHAPTER ONE

Rory

As prison cells went, I guessed the blacksuits' holding rooms met a pretty high standard. I'd stayed in motel rooms drearier than this.

The space was about twice the size of my dorm bedroom back at Bloodstone University, with a double bed complete with mahogany sleigh frame set in one corner, a chaise lounge against the wall next to it, and a narrow bookshelf with a decent variety of novels and nonfiction offerings beside that. A matching table with three chairs dominated the other end of the room by the tiny bathroom. The soft whir of central air cooled the late summer heat, and it carried a sweet lemony basily scent that I'd probably have found pleasant under other circumstances.

But as cozy as my surroundings looked, this *was* a prison. The walls with their ivory-and-gold wallpaper held no windows. The main door wouldn't budge at my tug. I couldn't attempt any spells on it or anything else thanks to the warded cuffs fastened around my wrists.

On the first morning after I'd been taken in, a faint but persistent itch behind my collarbone reminded me of something else I was missing. I'd heard that a mage would start to feel uncomfortable if they stayed far apart from their familiar for very long. Mine was back at the university. I hadn't been this far away from her for this long since I'd gotten her four years ago.

Would Deborah be okay? She'd managed to find quite a network of passages around the dorm building—hopefully she wouldn't have any trouble finding food and water.

Before I could worry about that for very long, two blacksuits stepped into the room, and I discovered why the table had come with three chairs. One was for me, and the two on the opposite side were for my interrogators.

I hadn't seen the man and woman who came in before, although they wore the same black dress shirts and slacks as every member of the fearmancer law enforcement that I'd encountered. The woman's white hair was pulled back in a no-nonsense bun, and the shadow of a beard on the man's face had a silver sheen. Maybe the older agents handled the talk while the younger ones carried out the activity in the field.

"Please have a seat, Miss Bloodstone," the woman said in a flat voice. "We have a lot to discuss."

I came over to the table as they sat down at it, but after nearly twenty-four hours shut up in this place, I didn't have the patience to wait for them to start the conversation. "I didn't hurt Imogen," I said, grasping the top of the chair. "I wouldn't have. She was my friend."

I'd never hurt *anyone*, let alone killed them. The image flashed through my mind of my dormmate's sprawled body, the blood pooling under her, the lacerations gouging her body. My stomach heaved. Who in the whole school would have wanted to do that to Imogen?

Silly question. It *was* my fault, in a way. My enemies, the rulers of dark magic society and their allies, had set out to undermine me from the moment I'd been "rescued" from the joymancers who'd raised me and brought back into the fold. When I finished my schooling, I'd join the ranks of the fearmancers' rulers, and they didn't want anyone who wouldn't kowtow to their ideals gaining that kind of power. They'd already been responsible for my mentor's death a couple months ago.

And now this. It was the only possible explanation. Bespelling someone into attacking me hadn't done the trick, so they were framing me as a criminal.

"Your involvement in Miss Wakeburn's death is what we're here to determine," the man said. "Please, sit down."

I tugged out the chair and sat. The silver cuffs that diffused my magic clinked as I rested my arms on the table.

I had to remember that these blacksuits might not be cooperating with my enemies. They could be conducting a perfectly legitimate investigation. I'd have a much better chance of convincing them of my innocence if I showed I was willing to cooperate.

The woman had taken out a small tablet. She poised her hand over it as if to take notes, but I wondered if she was making an audio recording of the conversation as well. "Let's start with you giving your account of what happened yesterday afternoon leading up to Miss Wakeburn's death and your arrest."

I'd tried to give my account to the blacksuits who'd hauled me away from the university, but they hadn't been interested in listening. They'd basically ignored me from the moment they'd tossed me in the back of their car with these cuffs around my wrists, other than when they'd escorted me up here to this room.

"I was celebrating my win in the summer project competition at the end-of-term party with my friends and the other students," I said. That interlude of snacking and dancing yesterday afternoon felt like it'd happened weeks ago. "We were in the large gymnasium in the Stormhurst Building. After a while, I left with two of the other scions —Jude Killbrook and Connar Stormhurst. We were going to take a drive before we all headed home for the end of summer break. I went up to my dorm to get better shoes for driving, and they were going to meet me at the garage."

What did Jude and Connar think had happened to me? What did *anyone* think had happened to me? I didn't know who had called for the blacksuits or who might have witnessed my arrest or what they were saying about it. The guys knew me pretty well by now, in… a variety of ways. They had to realize I hadn't actually murdered someone, right?

A pang ran through my chest. God, I wished I had Connar's steady strength and Jude's irreverent humor here to help get me through this new ordeal.

"And then?" the man said.

I wet my lips, my mouth going dry. And then everything had gone to hell.

"I went into my dorm, and right away I saw Imogen on the floor," I said. "I could tell she was badly hurt. I tried to call or run for help, but some kind of spell held me in place. I couldn't talk. And I started seeing images of things that hadn't really happened, of some kind of fight—like her attacker had left an illusionary impression of what they'd done."

The illusionary impression had been structured to put me in the attacker's shoes. It'd felt as if the spell that had sliced Imogen up had seared from my throat.

My interrogators exchanged a glance. "That sounds like a strange thing for a criminal to have done," the woman remarked.

"I'm not saying it was normal. There was nothing normal about finding one of my dormmates dead either. You asked me to tell you what happened."

Her eyebrows arched slightly, but she didn't make any further comment on that subject. She glanced at her tablet's screen. "Our team doesn't report any noticeable magic acting on you when they made their arrest."

"No," I said, my stomach knotting. "The illusions faded away, and the spell that was holding me released right before they got there. As soon as I saw them, I tried to tell them that my friend needed help."

"I don't have any record of that."

"They didn't give me the chance. They cut me off."

"Mmhm." The woman tapped a few things and let out a breath. "How had you and Miss Wakeburn been getting along before this incident?"

"Pretty well. We'd hung out a few times over the summer. She helped me get something fixed for my project." I wasn't sure how much to say about our history. "We didn't argue or anything."

"We've spoken to some of your other dormmates," the man said. "They indicated that there had been tension between you and Miss

Wakeburn not that long ago. Because she sided with other students instead of you in a personal conflict?"

Victory or one of her friends had been all too happy to make me look guilty, no doubt. I forced my voice to stay calm even though my mouth tightened. "A few months ago, one of the other girls *blackmailed* Imogen into betraying something I'd told her in confidence. I was upset about it, and I didn't trust her as much afterward, but I mostly blamed the girl who instigated it." They didn't really think I'd killed Imogen over something like that—something that'd happened months before—did they?

"A similar situation could have arisen, then," the woman said. "Another 'betrayal' or conflict of interests, which would have made you similarly upset."

"It's possible that could have happened," I said. "But it hadn't. There wasn't any friction between us this summer. I hadn't even seen Imogen yesterday, let alone talked to her, before I found her body. And even when I was upset about what happened before, I never lashed out at her."

The woman hummed to herself again with what sounded like skepticism. An uneasy prickle ran over my skin.

These people didn't know me at all. They just knew I was a scion and soon-to-be baron, and most of the barons were power-hungry assholes who believed they could get away with whatever they wanted to if they played their cards right. Why would the blacksuits assume I was better than that?

But my position had to come with some privileges. I was the only heir to the Bloodstone barony. They couldn't throw me in their version of jail for years on end without any real evidence… could they?

Or had my enemies managed to produce some sort of evidence that solidified their framing attempt?

The man had tipped back in his chair, watching me. "Can you think of anyone else who would have had a motive to attack Miss Wakeburn?"

I opened my mouth and hesitated. My gut knotted.

I couldn't point the finger at the other barons, claim there was some huge conspiracy they were orchestrating against me, when *I* didn't have any evidence of that. I only knew because of the words of my dying mentor, and no one could ask Professor Banefield to confirm his story now. He'd managed to get a bunch of documents to me that might lead me to concrete proof, but I hadn't fit the pieces together clearly enough yet. I hadn't had time.

If I tried to accuse the barons, I'd only look desperate and possibly insane.

"I don't know," I said finally. "She'd mentioned to me that some of the other students hassled her now and then because she came into her magic late and they didn't respect her father's position as head of Maintenance, but I'm not aware of anyone on campus who would have wanted to really hurt her."

"You didn't notice anything unusual in or around the room when you found her?"

I'd been so shocked by the sight of her body and then panicked as the illusion caught me up that I hadn't had much chance to take a careful look around. "No," I admitted. "I wish I could tell you more."

The woman cleared her throat. "And no one else was in the dorm or nearby outside when you arrived, to confirm that when you went in, Miss Wakeburn was already injured?"

The fifth floor hall had been empty. We'd been the only two people in the dorm—that I'd seen, anyway. No doubt the murderer had taken steps to ensure there were no witnesses. "No, not that I know of."

"Well," the man started, and the door to the holding room swung open again.

The sight of the woman who strode in should have been a relief. Lillian Ravenguard, like a muscular, tawny lioness even with the hint of gray in her hair and the faint lines around her eyes and mouth, had been my birth mother's best friend. She'd come to me a couple months ago offering any help she could give during my transition into fearmancer society, and she'd given me a glimpse into my mother's life through a bunch of letters and media she'd put together for me.

I'd also seen evidence of her collusion with the barons and their allies in the papers Professor Banefield had left me. If she was helping them, she couldn't *really* want to help me.

"All right," she said briskly, setting her hands on her hips. "I think you've badgered Miss Bloodstone enough. She's unfamiliar with our procedures and ought to have a proper debriefing before any interviews are conducted. I'll handle that. You get on with the rest of your jobs."

Even though my interrogators looked old enough to have seniority over Lillian, they leapt from their chairs immediately, a hint of a flush coloring the man's cheeks. As they headed out, Lillian glanced at my warded cuffs and grimaced.

"I'm sorry about those. It's policy. If all goes well, we'll have you out of them and out of here soon. I got here as fast as I could after I heard."

I couldn't take any comfort from her words when I wasn't sure how much I believed them. Had this plot really taken her by surprise, or was she putting on a front so she could screw me over even more thoroughly later? I didn't know what to say to her.

It'd probably be safest for me if I pretended to trust her while I was in such a precarious position.

"This whole situation seems crazy," I said. "I found Imogen's body—that's all. I'm not a killer."

"Of course you're not." Lillian leaned against the side of the table. "There'll be an official hearing once the agents are finished gathering evidence and testimony, and then we can easily set the record straight. All it'll take is one insight spell conducted by the judge for you to show that nothing violent happened while you were there. Those kind of memories always leap out if they're present."

My heart sank. All at once, the illusions that had battered me when I'd seen Imogen's body made sense.

The tactic wasn't strange after all. The killer had given me images of Imogen angry as if we were arguing, of my own body and voice casting a murderous spell at her. Now those impressions were etched into my memory as if they'd actually happened. From what I knew of insight spells, the sensations that the caster took in were imprecise and muddy even when they were real. Would the judge be able to tell the difference between fact and illusion?

I didn't trust Lillian even enough to ask her that. I wished I hadn't even mentioned the illusions to the other blacksuits. The last thing I wanted was to confirm to my enemies how well their gambit had worked.

"Okay," I said in a voice that felt as if it came from a long distance inside of me. "How long will it be until the hearing?"

"I'll see if I can rush things along. A few days, I think we can hope for. And my colleagues will make sure you're well looked after while you're here, or there'll be hell to pay." She straightened up. "I should appeal to the judge for haste right away. I'll check on you again as soon as I can. You've been through so much already… This just isn't right."

She gave my shoulder a quick squeeze that I managed to restrain a flinch at, and then she swept out of the room. I stared at the closed door with a hopeless sensation expanding inside me.

The barons had locked me up in a trap far smaller than this room, and right now I didn't have even a glimmer of an idea of how to get out.

CHAPTER TWO

Rory

I expected Lillian or maybe the interrogators to return later that day, but no one came through the door except for the impassive woman who delivered my meals and gathered the dishes from the previous one. The blacksuits didn't want me starving, but I couldn't say I had much appetite given the circumstances.

It was almost a relief when the door opened in the middle of the next afternoon, after lunch but way too early for dinner. I sat up on the chaise lounge where I'd been sprawled trying to think my way out of this mess—and immediately stiffened at the sight of the guy in the doorway.

Malcolm Nightwood, the heir to the most powerful baron family other than the Bloodstones, had stopped on the threshold to say something to the blacksuit who'd let him in. He drew his golden-haired head even higher, his muscular shoulders squared with an aura of authority, and the guy nodded and backed away. Malcolm came in alone.

He drew to a halt just a few steps into the room as the door clicked shut behind him. Something in his stance shifted, uncertainty tempering his usual cocky confidence. We eyed each other from across the room.

Malcolm and I… Well, calling our relationship fraught was putting it lightly. He'd struck me as an asshole from the first time I'd seen him, divine good looks notwithstanding, and he hadn't cared for my more compassionate attitude at all. He'd spent most of the last few months trying to bully my defiance out of me by every means at his disposal.

But during the summer, things had taken a turn for the strange. I'd realized he was jealous of the interest Jude and Connar had taken in me, and I'd thought I could turn the tables on him by reminding him of what *he* was definitely never going to have with me. The trouble was, it'd turned out some part of me was attracted to him despite his assholery, and wow, did he know how to fan those flames.

Our attempts at provoking each other to get the upper hand had ended in catastrophic fashion. We'd collided in a sudden desperate make-out session that Malcolm had gotten so wrapped up in, he hadn't registered when my reactions had switched from desire to fear.

He'd backed off when I'd forced him to, and he'd seemed genuinely horrified that he'd pushed things farther than I'd wanted. Ever since that incident, he'd been more careful around me, even intervening when a few members of his unofficial female fan club had tried to hurt my familiar. It had seemed as if he was offering some sort of truce, but I wasn't sure yet how much faith to put in it—or how much I wanted to interact with him ever again regardless. A couple of small kindnesses didn't make up for months of torment.

"What are you doing here?" I demanded.

My voice prompted Malcolm into action. He looked away for a second to mutter a few words under his breath and made a quick sweeping motion with his hand. A quiver of cast magic rippled past me. "To make sure no one's spying on us," he said in reference to the spell, and then, "I told them I had urgent scion business I needed to discuss with you."

That explained why they'd let him in here but not what he actually wanted. "Do you?" I said pointedly.

He gave me a smile with a glint in his dark brown eyes and spread his hands innocently. "It's all scion business between two scions, right? I thought you'd want—" He cut himself off and opened up the messenger bag he had slung over his shoulder. When he drew his hand out, his fingers were cupping a small white form with a black splotch on its hip.

My heart leapt. I jumped up as he held the mouse out to me, and Deborah scrambled from his grasp onto my palm in an instant. She darted up my arm to perch on my shoulder, hiding in the waves of my hair.

She didn't say anything, but then, I wasn't surprised she'd keep quiet while Malcolm was so close. Even the few people who'd met my familiar had no idea that Deborah wasn't just a mouse. The joymancer authorities had arranged for a dying woman's spirit to be transferred into the animal so she could watch over me—and watch out for any threat I might begin to pose if my magical powers awakened.

Deborah's human aspect meant she could telepathically communicate with me in actual words, unlike most familiars, but if the fearmancers ever found out what she really was, we'd both be in deep trouble. My new community saw the mages who worked with happiness instead of terror as mortal adversaries.

"She wasn't all that enthusiastic about coming with me, but I made a case she must have understood the gist of," Malcolm said. "It's ridiculous that you're here at all. I figured you'd at least be able to cope better if you had her with you. I know it can feel pretty awful being far apart from your familiar for longer lengths of time."

I guessed he'd have discovered that from experience. Despite all the things I could have criticized about the Nightwood scion, I'd seen him show real caring for his own familiar, a wolf named Shadow that I'd ended up befriending as well.

"How do you think the blacksuits are going to feel about you bringing her?" I asked.

"Who gives a shit what they want? She's small. I'm sure you can keep her hidden." He paused. "If you're really worried, I could take her back to school."

"No." Every bone in my body balked at the idea of losing this one small ally now that I had her with me. Deborah *was* very good at staying out of sight.

The rest of what he'd said sank in. I sat back down on the chaise lounge, bracing my hands against the firm cushion. "What's ridiculous about me being here?"

Malcolm gave me an incredulous look. "You obviously didn't kill anyone, Glinda."

He'd taken to calling me "Glinda the good witch" after I'd made it clear how much I disliked the way he bullied the other students. If that was the worst way he could insult me, I'd take it.

"What makes you so sure about that?" I couldn't help saying, even as relief fluttered through me. If the guy from school who'd most wanted to tear me down could see that this case was a load of bullshit, I might have some hope of proving my innocence after all.

"Oh, I don't know, maybe the fact that I've never seen you be the slightest bit physically violent with anyone, even when violence might have been sorely deserved." He crossed his arms over his chest, his smile turning wry. "Somehow I doubt that pushover dormmate of yours managed to piss you off *so* much more than any of the rest of us ever have."

I rolled my eyes. "So, you're sure because if I were that kind of person, I'd have already murdered *you*." There was a certain logic to that reasoning, I'd give him that.

Malcolm chuckled, relaxing a little at the mild humor in my tone. "That's one way of putting it."

He grabbed the nearest chair at the table and spun it around to sit on it with his arms resting on the back. When we were on the same level, his presence wasn't so imposing.

"I think the feeling is unanimous within the pentacle of scions," he said. "Declan is running around looking up every court case he can get his hands on, and Jude and Connar insisted on staying at school into the break to poke around for evidence."

I let myself lean back in the chaise, some of the tension wound inside me dissipating when I exhaled. I did have other allies, even if they weren't right here. Declan Ashgrave had been keeping his distance from me because our attraction while I was a student and he was working as a teacher's aide could put his career and his family's security on the line, but he'd spent most of his life using policies and precedents to get his way. If there was anything in fearmancer law that could help me, he'd find it. I didn't know if Jude or Connar would be able to turn up anything the blacksuits hadn't, but it sure as hell didn't hurt having them try.

I rolled the question around in my mouth for a moment before deciding to say it. "What about the pentacle of barons?"

Malcolm's father was the most powerful current baron. Professor Banefield had implicated both him and his wife. How well did they bother to keep their attitudes hidden from their heir?

Malcolm's expression tensed. "I haven't been part of those discussions," he said.

I couldn't tell whether he was dodging the question or just frustrated that he was on the sidelines. He ran his hand through his hair, bringing out the hint of curl in the short locks. Then he glanced around the room, speaking another casting word I didn't know the meaning of, maybe testing the protective spell he'd put up earlier. When he turned back to me, he looked both hesitant and grim.

"Declan suggested your mentor might have been murdered too."

My pulse stuttered, but from Malcolm's phrasing, Declan had been careful to make it sound like the theory was his own idea and not a fact that I'd told him. The Ashgrave scion knew how to be careful when it came to internal politics.

"Are you bringing that up because you're thinking I might actually be a serial killer?" I said with forced nonchalance.

Malcolm made a face at me. "I'm bringing it up because this latest murder makes the possibility sound a whole lot more plausible. That someone else did it, not that you did."

How far had he gotten with speculating about who that someone else might be? Would he have believed his parents were involved? It didn't seem worth taking the gamble that he'd accept my story and not give away to them how much I knew.

"Well, if you figure out who this murderer is and turn them in so I can go free, I'm all for it."

"Rory…" He studied me for a long moment. His smile had fallen away completely, and there was something weirdly vulnerable in his expression with the cocky front stripped down. "I'm not here to hurt you, okay? I know what happened in the boathouse was awful. I never should have gotten so caught up that I wasn't paying attention to how you were responding, and I'm sorry. I'm so fucking sorry. That's not— That was never— I don't want to keep fighting with you. I'm done with that."

His voice had gone raw with the apology. I couldn't cast any spells myself, but even without supernatural insight, I felt the truth in his words. It might be the first time he'd ever been completely honest with me, without any posturing or calculation.

That fact made my heart squeeze in an uncomfortable way, because the apology was completely unexpected and yet wasn't quite enough all at the same time.

"Are you sorry about any of the rest?" I said. "I never wanted to fight in the first place."

"I'm… still sorting all that out. Can we table that discussion for now? Until you're no longer under suspicion of murder, say? I don't expect you to absolve me of whatever all you think my wrongdoings are. I'd just like us to be able to work together while we figure out where we stand on everything else."

He might have had a point. And if he wasn't asking me to forgive him, I didn't see why I should argue about it, especially when "working together" right now was mainly going to mean "get Rory out of this goddamned jail."

I dragged in a breath. "Okay. I accept the apology given and will be patient about the ones that had better be forthcoming eventually."

The corner of his mouth twitched upward, even though otherwise he still looked serious. "Spoken like a Bloodstone." He got up from the chair. "I don't know how long I can get away with staying. Mostly I wanted to deliver your familiar and let you know the pentacle is on the case."

Mostly. He'd also wanted to ask me about Banefield's murder. I hesitated as he headed for the door. I didn't have to tell him anything that would definitely get me in trouble, only enough to plant a seed, if he was already open to it. He'd put himself out there for me by coming here, by saying what he had. I could repay that with a little honesty of my own.

"Malcolm," I said, and he stopped to look back at me. I spoke cautiously but evenly. "What if I told you I *know* my mentor was murdered?"

His jaw tightened. I braced myself, but all he said was, "Then I'd say someone has a lot to answer for."

He let that statement hang, watching me. Waiting for me to offer more detail if I was ready to? I wasn't going to point the finger at his parents right here, right now. I wavered and then said, "If you come up with those answers, I'd be happy to hear about them."

He tipped his head to me. Then he stepped out of the room, leaving me feeling suddenly exhausted.

Deborah scampered from one shoulder to the other with a faint prickling of her tiny claws behind my neck. *Thank goodness. I've been so worried about you, Lorelei. They haven't hurt you?*

I wasn't sure if Malcolm's privacy spell had lingered or how long it would. To stay on the side of caution, I simply shook my head, as if to myself.

My familiar must have caught on to my apprehension. She tucked herself close to the crook of my neck, still enveloped in my hair. *I wasn't sure about that Nightwood boy, but he seemed like my only chance to get to you. Better not to put too much trust in him after the way he's shown himself to behave in the past.*

No kidding. I gave a slight nod to show I'd heard her and agreed. Her dry, steady voice wrapped me in a thin but welcome sense of comfort, even though there wasn't much she could do for me. I lay back down on the chaise lounge, careful not to put pressure on her perch.

Maybe she *could* help. She'd often left my bedroom to scoop out unusual sounds or magic. I groped for the right words.

"I wish I knew what really happened to Imogen," I murmured.

Yes, of course, that's why the blacksuits brought you here, isn't it? I can tell you what I know. I saw a fair amount of the altercation.

My heart leapt with more hope. If she knew what'd really happened…

Deborah snuggled closer. *I heard voices in the common room—not yelling, but they sounded terse. I slipped out to a spot behind the baseboard where I have a view of a good part of the room. Your friend was there, and a woman—she had a shadowy spell around her to obscure the identifying details of her face and body, so sadly I can't tell you anything useful beyond that. If I was near her again, I think I'd know her by smell.*

A woman. One of the barons was a woman—Connar's mother—and there'd been several others on Professor Banefield's list. That didn't narrow it down terribly much.

She forced your friend to stay in one place, Deborah went on. *She must have had some way of knowing when you were on your way to the dorm. All of a sudden she lashed out at Imogen with a spell that hurt her the way you saw. It was only a few minutes before you arrived. She slipped away into one of the bedrooms before you came in. I tried to warn you, but the second you opened the door, this wave of magic hit me…*

"It's okay," I whispered. I hadn't been able to fight the magic that had attached me to Imogen's murder, so I certainly couldn't blame Deborah for being incapacitated by it. I tucked my legs higher, my stomach twisting.

Nothing in Deborah's story gave me much of a lead toward the actual killer. I had a witness to the murder, but she was a witness that no one other than me could interrogate.

One the other fearmancers would have seen as a crime in itself if they'd found out who and what she was.

CHAPTER THREE

Malcolm

Saying I was "home" when I was at the Nightwood mansion never quite sounded right to me. The truth was the first time I'd felt a place was really my own was when my first-year mentor at Blood U showed me to my bedroom in the junior dorm. That room was *mine*, no one dared to even try to breach the spells securing the door, and after a few weeks I finally discovered what it was like to sleep a full night in total relaxation.

Everything in the mansion belonged to my parents. There was no inch of it they couldn't touch if they wanted to. A fact that had been drilled into me to painful and occasionally explosive effect for as long as I could remember. When I drove back through that gate, my armor automatically went up.

Dad and Mom had appeared to be in decently good moods since I'd arrived for this visit during the end-of-summer break, though. As they assembled their breakfast plates from the spread on the buffet before heading to work, I could have sworn I heard my mom briefly humming a melody to herself. A *cheerful* melody.

It was hard not to wonder if the recent incarceration of the Bloodstone heir had anything to do with their sudden high spirits.

I sliced my knife through a sausage as they sat down at the broad dining table. The smells of fried pork and buttery eggs normally would have made my mouth water—we had a damn good cook—but this morning the scents only made my stomach clench up. I forced down the chunk of sausage anyway, savory juices filling my mouth. If I was going to find out anything from my parents, I had to keep every appearance of cool.

If you want to know more about what your father is doing, you should ask him about it, Declan had said when I'd questioned him about the uncomfortable insinuations he'd been making about Professor Banefield's death. *Ask him, and really* listen.

I'd talked with my parents about Rory before. I'd have said I'd been listening. But the events of the last month had proven I'd missed a lot of things I should have seen because I'd been so focused on my own assumptions and goals. What might I have misheard or ignored because I'd taken for granted that my parents were approaching the problem the same way I was—firmly and aggressively but not murderously?

I wasn't getting answers anywhere else, that was for sure. Things had been less tense with my friends since I'd extended the olive branch for my earlier assholery, but they were still cautious about discussing anything to do with Rory's situation. When I'd asked Connar about his and Jude's investigations around campus, his response had been vague and wary. Which I supposed made sense considering how I'd treated Rory for most of her first couple semesters at Blood U.

That was fine. I'd just have to conduct my own investigations, my way.

"Quite the mess the Bloodstone scion has gotten herself into," I remarked casually as I speared another piece of sausage.

My father sat down with a flick of his napkin over his lap. "I'm sure the blacksuits will sort it out to everyone's satisfaction."

"There are certain standards of behavior even a soon-to-be baron should be expected to maintain," my mother put in, taking the chair beside him.

By which she meant, if Rory had been going to murder someone, she should have made sure she wasn't caught. I swirled the sausage briefly on my plate and wished I had ketchup to dip it in. My parents saw the condiment as too "pedestrian." If I'd brought some with me, it'd no doubt have been rancid before I took a single bite.

"Seems like an odd victim, if she was going to snap," I said in the same offhand tone. "Some of the other girls had really been giving her hell."

Dad made a noncommittal sound. "She was undisciplined and lacking in training. Justice will be carried out in any case."

"Better we see what she's capable of now, especially after her attempts to present herself as some sort of peacekeeper." My mother sniffed disdainfully.

"A loose cannon needs reining in," my father added, with just the slightest note of triumph.

I looked up in time to catch the glance he exchanged with Mom—a glance with a quick flicker of a smile. My breakfast stirred uneasily in my stomach. Yes, that was exactly why they'd have wanted this to happen to Rory. It offered a perfect excuse to limit her powers and bring her solidly under the other barons' control.

That was why they might have orchestrated the entire situation. It'd be awfully convenient if someone else had framed Rory with no involvement from the people who stood to benefit most, wouldn't it? And the Wakeburn girl made a much better victim than Victory or her friends from *their* perspective. A mediocre mage from a middling family—not someone who'd be especially missed, no risk of pissing off the powerful figures they wanted to maintain good relations with.

Was that what Nightwoods did now? Not just attack our enemies to keep the upper hand, but slaughter random innocent mages if it served our plans? Who the hell wanted to be ruled by barons like *that*?

No one. Which was why they were staying so close-lipped about it even with me.

I had dozens more questions clamoring for attention inside me, but I couldn't ask any of them directly. I did let myself venture a mention of their other possible crime.

"I've heard that the professor who got sick and ended up offing himself was her mentor. Wonder if that really was a natural death or she had something to do with that one too."

Dad had a poker face with the best of them, but I felt him perk up from across the table. "Have you heard someone speculating about that?" he asked.

What, because then they'd try to spin that story around on Rory too?

"No," I said blandly. "It just occurred to me, considering the current situation."

"Well, let me know if anyone else starts talking. If there are leads pointing in that direction, we'd want to know."

Or if he thought they could sway public opinion toward pinning Rory with that death too, he would. I poked at my scrambled eggs before managing to gulp down another mouthful.

What the fuck had happened to family honor? Where was the strength they'd insisted I learn to show from the moment I was old enough to follow their orders? It wasn't *strong* to kill some nobody girl and put the blame on your opponent because you couldn't manage to take the real threat on directly.

They'd decided Rory was too tough for them to handle, so they'd taken a coward's route.

My fingers tightened around my fork, but I plowed through the rest of the food on my plate while my parents cleared theirs. Dad had a new investment to go over with his business partners, and Mom had a meeting for some board she was on. They headed out one after the other before I'd left the dining room.

I wouldn't have considered myself to be under my parents' thumb. I made my own decisions; I had my own mind. But there were some rules I'd never contemplated violating. For example, Dad's home office had been off-limits for as long as I could remember.

Before, I wouldn't have violated that rule out of respect. Now… I was finding I couldn't summon quite the same level of deference I might have in days past.

If Dad really was involved in more horrifying machinations than I'd ever have suspected, I wanted all the proof I could find. He might not have left even a hint around the house anywhere, but if there was going to be some, it'd be in that office.

He didn't simply trust family and staff to stay out of the office. The door had a complicated magical repulsion spell on it too. I cast a quick bit of my own magic to make sure no one was nearby, and then I studied the threads of energy surrounding the doorway. If I stepped more than a few inches away from the opposite wall, a shiver ran over my skin and down into my muscles, urging me to flee.

So I kept close to the wall and murmured a testing word and then another to get a deeper feel for the spell. I'd used something like one part on my dorm bedroom plenty of times. Another aspect reminded me of a project we'd worked on in Persuasion last year.

A small smile crossed my lips. I could disarm it. Dad's areas of magical strengths were the same as mine, and he'd underestimated how much my skills had grown.

I knew Dad well enough to realize the defenses outside the door wouldn't be the only protections. After I nudged the door open, I identified an alarm spell tied to the floorboards just inside. I didn't need to remove that, only to take a good hop over it. Then I stopped and swiveled to take in the room.

The furniture was styled like the rest of the house—lots of old, fine wood and thickly embroidered fabrics. The space was more open than I'd expected, though. A huge desk dominated one end of the room, backed by a stately wingchair, but the other half held nothing but a rug and a single armchair, with bookshelves along the walls and a heavily curtained window.

No one came in here other than Dad, but I didn't see a hint of dust or smell a wisp of must. He must clean it himself and air it out regularly.

The chair at the desk squeaked faintly when I sat on it, and my nerves jumped, but no catastrophe descended on me. I already knew his computer was a lost cause—I couldn't magic my way into knowing his password, and he'd have chosen something not at all obvious. Like all the other fearmancers I knew, though, he still did a lot of work on paper.

I flipped through his leather-bound agenda, lifting the pages carefully. The meetings and appointments were mostly written in short form I couldn't fully decipher, but it wasn't as if he'd include something like "Frame Rory Bloodstone for murder" in there anyway. I didn't see any suspicious-looking items around the day of her arrest or of Professor Banefield's death.

The document sorter on his desk held various bills and invoices and other business-related paperwork. Somehow I doubted he'd requested a formal receipt for any murders either. I riffled through those quickly anyway and then turned to the drawers.

Nothing in there linked him to Rory or to the professor. Nothing pointed to any violent plans. I grimaced at myself as I pushed the last drawer back into place. Maybe it'd been stupid taking this risk.

My gaze fell on the small metal trash can under the desk. I tugged it out and peered at its contents. The few crumpled papers that I smoothed out, I found unhelpful. Then there was an invitation to some fearmancer gala that Cressida Warbury's parents hoped mine would attend. Obviously Dad hadn't been interested.

I was about to flick the cardstock rectangle with its silvery lettering back into the can when marks on the back caught my eye. I turned it all the way over and tipped it to the light filtering through the window.

Dad must have had this on his desk when he'd taken some notes on another paper. His pen had pushed impressions into the card underneath. I could make out some of the letters just squinting at them.

With a whisper of magic, I filled in the shallow grooves with thicker shadow. The text swam into sharper focus.

Pers – Wed, 2pm

Phys – Thurs, 11am

Illu – Fri, 4pm

I stared at the notes for a moment, my chest constricting. It wasn't hard to guess what this was. He'd been writing down someone's university schedule.

Two of those classes I'd been in this summer. They were the ones I'd shared with Rory. I'd be willing to bet everything I owned in this house the other class was hers too.

At the beginning of the summer, he'd told me to back off her at school. Apparently he'd been keeping track of her movements by other means. For other purposes.

It didn't scream murder, but it wasn't a good sign, either.

I dispelled the magic and tossed the invitation back into the garbage. As I set everything into the right places, the constricting sensation expanded from my chest up to my throat.

Was there really much question? If Dad *hadn't* wanted Rory in the blacksuits' custody, he could have gotten her free by pulling a few strings. He was in on the plot, regardless of his exact level of involvement. I knew that, even if I hated it.

I dodged the alarm by the door again and tugged it shut behind me. As I was rebuilding the repulsion security spell, the floor down the hall creaked. My nerves jumped, and I spat out the rest of the casting as quickly as I could under my breath. I stepped away from the door and started ambling down the hall just as my little sister slipped around the nearest corner.

Agnes slowed, peering at me with her big brown eyes as she tucked her blond hair behind her ears. Her gaze slid past me down the hall and then back to my face. I tensed instinctively, bracing for questions I'd have to dodge. But she just ducked her head, her own shoulders tense. Maybe she was worried about what *I'd* say to her about her coming down for the morning this late.

She was only thirteen, for fuck's sake. We were in the exact same boat, always on our guard around our parents, always waiting for the next test. I'd never tried to test her too—I'd never wanted to take part in that vicious aspect of our lives… but maybe I should have offered her a little more support along the way. Could I really say I completely agreed to our parents' approach to toughening us up?

Not anymore, not knowing what I did now, that was for sure.

"Hey," I said carefully. "Have you had breakfast yet?"

Agnes shook her head. "I slept in," she said, her voice meek but her mouth tightening defiantly.

She'd definitely picked up a lot of their lessons in caution and keeping one's own counsel. But maybe there were a few things I could teach her that'd serve her better than anything our parents had inflicted on us.

I stepped closer with a tentative smile. "You know, it's been a while since we went to that pancake place you like in town. Mom and Dad went out—they won't even know. You want to go grab a stack?"

Agnes's face brightened in an instant. Our parents disdained the Nary-run pancake place the same way they looked down their noses at ketchup and nachos. I'd always been the one to take her out there when the coast was clear.

"That'd be great," she said. "It's been a while."

It had been, I realized as we headed for the door, Agnes with more of a bounce in her step now. I wasn't sure we'd gone out there since I started in the senior class at Blood U. Our parents' tests had ramped up, and Dad had been watching for the slightest slip to hold over my head… All my attention had narrowed down to surviving and maintaining the authority I had.

Not anymore. I was done dancing to his tune.

CHAPTER FOUR

Rory

I was just getting up from the dinner of roast beef and buttered beans my jailors had brought me when a knock rapped against the door. I froze. No one had bothered knocking before they'd come in before.

"Um," I said. "Come in?" Was telling them to go away even an option?

When the door swung open, I was grateful I hadn't tried that. Declan strode into the room with an authoritative air lent even more power by his tall frame. His bright hazel eyes flashed with a hint of anger as they took in my holding room. Then his gaze came to rest on me, looking me over with obvious concern.

My heart had started thumping twice as fast. I could have kissed him just for being here, except that would have been an exceptionally bad idea with two blacksuits hustling into the room behind him.

"She's been held according to proper procedures," one of them was grumbling.

"Maybe as far as where and how," Declan said, folding his arms over his chest. "As I've already pointed out to your supervisor, any mage never before charged with a crime has a right to continue their day-to-day life with minimal restrictions. She shouldn't be here at all."

"When the crime is murder—"

Declan turned to the man with a glower. "Nothing in the statutes makes exceptions based on type of crime. Do we need to go back and run through the entire law book with your supervisor again?"

"It's fine," the other blacksuit snapped. Apparently having a scion barge in on their operations and tell them how they were doing things wrong had put them in a bad mood. Somehow I couldn't summon much sympathy.

"I can leave?" I said as Declan walked over to me.

He nodded, with a hint of a smile at the relief that must have been written all over my face. "Until your hearing. Which isn't going to happen for at *least* ten more days, because the law also says you're allowed a minimum of two weeks to gather evidence and testimony for your defense." He shot a pointed look over his shoulder at the blacksuits.

"Not when the accused has appointed a representative to investigate in her stead," the first blacksuit protested. "That's already being handled, and her representative—"

"Did you appoint anyone as your representative in this case, officially?" Declan asked me.

"No," I said immediately. "That—I didn't even know it was a thing."

Lillian must have claimed that role without telling me about it or asking whether I wanted her taking charge. I resisted the urge to clench my hands. She'd told me she was going to defend me—all the while speeding my hearing along so there'd be *less* chance to find proof that I was innocent and denying me the chance to look into anything myself.

"There you go," Declan said. "Do the blacksuits have any signed documents that contradict the accused's own statement?"

From the scowls we got, they obviously had simply taken Lillian's word for it. I supposed I couldn't blame them for that.

I rubbed my wrists instinctively, shifting the warded cuffs I was starting to get used to, and Declan frowned.

"Those need to come off too," he said, pointing to the cuffs. "You can monitor her magic usage, but you can't cut it off completely. She'll need it to continue her studies and conduct whatever inquiries she needs to before the hearing."

"That never came up during the negotiations," the second blacksuit protested.

"Because no one bothered to tell me you'd cuffed her like this. I've got photographs of the relevant documents right here." He fished his phone out of his pocket. "And if you need the source material, I've got more books in my car I can bring for you to go over."

The first blacksuit sighed. "You stay here and keep an eye on things," he said to his colleague. "I'll check with Sootbane."

It didn't seem wise to say much of anything to Declan with the other guy eyeing us. I took the opportunity to sit down on the edge of my bed, tucking my hand slightly behind me.

Deborah, who'd found an opening in the box spring that let her use it as a hiding spot, must have been following the conversation. Several seconds later, her small warm body darted onto my palm. I closed my fingers gently around her and lifted her as if I were reaching to scratch the back of my neck. She scrambled beneath the collar of my shirt where both the fabric and the fall of my hair would conceal her.

I was going to get to leave this place—this prison. I'd have ten days to try to break the case against me. It wasn't a lot, but it was so much more than I'd had before.

The first blacksuit reappeared a few minutes later and beckoned for Declan to come with him. "I'll be right back," the Ashgrave scion assured me. I stayed where I was, with the second blacksuit standing guard, the seconds ticking by with the thud of my pulse.

Finally, Declan and the woman blacksuit who'd been part of my first interrogation marched into the room. She was carrying two cuffs that were slimmer and detailed with different etchings than the ones I was currently wearing. These looked more like matching bracelets.

"Please come here, Miss Bloodstone," she said in a terse voice. I didn't think she was very happy about this turn of events either, but obviously the precedents Declan had presented couldn't be argued away. Thank God I could count on him.

I came over, and she motioned for me to sit at the table. "Lay your arms out," she instructed. When I had, she clicked the new cuffs around my wrists before unfastening the old ones with a couple of quiet casting words. The reduced weight on my arms brought a fresh wave of relief.

"The monitoring cuffs will take an impression of every spell you cast," the woman said. "Certain types of more aggressive magic will set off an alert and result in your returning to custody. Is that understood?"

I nodded, tucking my hands onto my lap. I didn't think that'd be a problem… I'd just have to hope none of my fellow students pushed me into a situation where I needed to use force to defend myself. Lord only knew how the blacksuits would respond to that. I didn't suppose the cuffs conveniently recorded magic that was cast *on* me.

"She's free to go?" Declan prodded.

The woman nodded. "We'll notify you when the hearing date is settled on."

Even more tension stripped off me as I stepped through the doorway into the hall, leaving my lovely but suffocating prison cell behind. I curled my fingers into my palm against the urge to grasp Declan's hand. That wouldn't be a good look here either.

He didn't speak until we'd left the entire three-story facility behind. Outside, evening was falling, a cool breeze washing over the nearly empty parking lot and the shadows stretching long across the asphalt. Traffic whirred by along the highway I could see in the distance.

"I'm sorry it took me this long," Declan said. "I had to make sure I had every possible argument covered, and then it took a whole day before they even gave in to having the meeting." He swiped his hand through the smooth black strands of his hair with a jerky movement.

"You don't have to apologize," I said. "I had no idea there was any way to get out at all. Thank you so much for going to all that work on my behalf."

He looked at me, so much emotion in his eyes in that instant that a flutter ran through my chest. "Of course I did. I know you had nothing to do with Imogen's death. I wasn't going to leave you in there to be treated like a murderer."

"That's what they think I am."

"Well, we'll just prove them wrong."

He opened the passenger-side door of his car for me before going around to the driver's side. As I sank into the leather seat, the familiar cedar-sweet smell of him that lingered inside filled my lungs. I had to work twice as hard not to reach for him as he settled into the seat beside me.

As he started the engine, Deborah scurried down my arm to nestle in my hand. She hadn't spoken to me since I'd picked her up. The truth was, while I trusted Declan more than any other fearmancer I'd met, I still wasn't completely sure how he'd react to the idea that I'd brought a miniature joymancer into their midst. It seemed better not to find out when there was no reason to give away that secret. *I* knew Deborah wouldn't—and honestly, couldn't, seeing as she'd lost her magical abilities with the transition—hurt any of them.

Declan turned the car toward the winding road that led to the highway. "Are you all right?" he asked. "I mean, other than the obvious problems. They didn't push you too hard with the interrogations or anything like that?"

I shook my head. "They mostly left me alone. I think—my mother, the Bloodstone one, had a close friend in the blacksuits. She's been 'looking out for me.' I think she's involved with the barons' plans, though. Part of that looking out for me must have included claiming I'd made her my representative, even though she never told me I had a right to leave."

"They'd need conspirators among the blacksuits to pull something like this off." Declan shot me another concerned look. "I also mean—you found your friend's body—after what happened with your mentor, too, I can't imagine how horrifying that must have been."

"It… wasn't fun." My throat closed up at the memory of Imogen's savaged form. "I haven't had much else to do except come to terms with it, though. And be really pissed off at the people who actually murdered her."

"They won't get away with it," Declan promised, although I didn't think he had any more idea than I did how to make the other barons pay. He exhaled slowly. "You've got a few more days before school's back in session. Did you want me to make arrangements to get you home?"

Home—that big old house in Maine? I hesitated. "If I need to be building a case to prove I didn't hurt Imogen, nothing out there is going to be much use to me, is it? I'll be able to accomplish more on campus. Malcolm came by—he brought my familiar… He said Jude and Connar have stuck around trying to help with the investigation?"

Declan nodded. "They went home yesterday, I think more to see if they'd hear about anything from their parents' circles than because they really wanted to be there, but as soon as they know you're out, they'll come back." One side of his mouth curved up in a crooked smile. "You've inspired a lot of loyalty all around."

I didn't know how to talk about the other guys with Declan. He knew I was… dating them, or whatever exactly you could call what we had. I knew he had similar feelings for me—feelings I returned. But he was the one who'd vetoed any possibility of him and me having a relationship even after he was finished with the teacher's aide job. It wasn't as if I'd picked them over him.

To be honest, I'd have taken all three of them given the opportunity.

That thought sent a not entirely welcome flush of warmth under my skin. I swallowed and groped for a change of subject. "So, we have to assume the other barons are behind this whole setup—them and the 'reapers' or whatever their allies call themselves. Do you have any idea why they'd do something like this? I can't be there to support whatever it is they want to do in the pentacle if I'm in fearmancer prison, can I?"

Declan's smile disappeared. "It actually makes a lot more sense than you'd think. More than I like to think about. We don't really lock people up for extended periods of time—no one's committed a crime the authorities felt warranted that punishment in as long as I've been alive. If you're convicted, the most likely consequence will be that you'll have a spell placed on you that'll restrict your ability to cast."

Uneasiness prickled over me. "Restrict it in what way?"

"You wouldn't be able to cast certain types of spells. There'd be a limit to how much power you could draw on for any individual casting. But that's not the real issue."

It sounded like an awfully big issue to me. "What is, then?"

He was silent, watching the road, for a few moments before he spoke. "Placing a long-term enchantment on a person puts them in a very vulnerable position. Once the spell is attached to you, it'd be easy for the original caster to adjust the workings in various ways without you even knowing. If the person doing the casting is in the barons' pocket… they could use it to control what you do, what you say, what you *think*… and there'd be nothing you could do about it."

CHAPTER FIVE

Rory

The dorm was completely silent. Even after Declan and I walked in and I flicked on the light in the common room, an ominous ambiance filled the empty space. Everyone else in the whole building had gone home for summer break. I hadn't really thought about what that would mean.

As I set Deborah down on the floor, my gaze slid automatically to the spot where Imogen's body had been sprawled when I'd found her. Just as with Professor Banefield, the maintenance staff had removed all traces of her death. I'd never have known any blood had been spilled there if I hadn't seen it a few days ago.

During the chaos of the discovery and my arrest, it seemed the full impact of her death hadn't really sunk in after all. Now it hit me like a punch to the gut.

I was never going to walk into this dorm and see her careful smile and the flash of her silver hair clip again. Never hear her urge me on in my attempts to push back against the more vicious students. Never head into town together for a little company while we grabbed some groceries or a quick meal.

She might not have been a perfect friend, but she *had* been my friend. Maybe if I'd forgiven her faster for her one betrayal, the barons wouldn't have targeted her. If they hadn't thought they could make a real case for me being angry with her…

I closed my eyes as if that would shut out those guilty thoughts. I couldn't have known my enemies would go this far. If I'd gotten closer with Imogen again, they could have used her in some other way.

Still, the thought of going to sleep amid this silence with the images of her murder floating in my head made my skin crawl.

"Hard being here again?" Declan asked from behind me.

"It just… feels kind of haunted, with no one else here." A lump rose in my throat. "I tried to save her, you know—I wanted to call for help, I fought the spell as well as I could—"

"It wasn't your fault," Declan said firmly. When I drew in a shaky breath, he slipped his arms around me in a gentle embrace. I couldn't help leaning back into the warmth of his body just a little, soaking in the comfort he was offering.

He swallowed audibly. "If it's too much, staying here alone, you could spend the night in my dorm. I mean, there are the couches, and one of the bedrooms has been vacant since that guy graduated in June. But I'd be in shouting distance if you need anything."

The desire to take him up on that offer rang through me from head to toe, but at the same time my throat tightened even more. Already, with his arms around me and his head ducked close to mine, a whole lot more desire was welling up inside me—to be even closer than this, to feel his kiss, to rediscover every inch of the lean frame aligned with mine. How much self-control could either of us really count on alone in the night with only a single thin door between us?

I didn't want to ruin another life.

"I'm not sure that's the best idea," I said. "Even if we stick to different rooms… if someone on staff came by and saw I'd stayed in your dorm… it could still cause a problem, right?"

"It could." He sighed. His head dipped over my shoulder, his breath tickling over my cheek and his arms hugging me a little harder, and for a second I thought he might turn that short distance to brush his lips against my skin. The warmth where our bodies touched flared into a sharper heat.

If he started kissing me here, right now, I wasn't sure my good intentions would hold. I wanted him too much.

His stance tensed, and then with obvious effort he drew away from me. "If you do need anything, I'll be right downstairs."

"Thank you. For everything."

When he left, the space felt even emptier. I hurried over to my bedroom, where at least I had all my familiar things. And Deborah, who'd squeezed her way in through the various mouse-sized passages. While I pulled the curtain shut against the darkness outside and changed into a pair of pajamas, she curled up in a nook on the bedcovers.

"Do you want anything to eat?" I asked her, able to talk to her freely for the first time since Malcolm had delivered her to me. With Declan's interruption coming right after my dinner, I hadn't gotten the chance to slip her the morsels I'd saved from my prison meal.

I had enough at lunch that I think it'll hold me over, Deborah said. *I can't say this situation has left me with much of an appetite.*

"No kidding." I flopped down on the bed and she cuddled next to my arm. Seeing the blank floor with all trace of the crime wiped away had stirred up other uneasy emotions as well. "I don't know how I'm going to get out of this, Deborah. What evidence am I going to find? Whoever did this will have taken all kinds of precautions to make sure there were no witnesses. And they messed with my mind, so even *I* can't be a witness to my innocence."

The real attacker didn't count on me as a witness, she reminded me.

"Yeah, but it's not as if I can present your observations at the hearing."

She paused for a moment. Her cool nose nudged my skin. *I could present my own observations. You tell them you believe your familiar may have seen at least part of the altercation, and they could take a peek into my memories.*

I tipped my head to look at her. "Do insight spells work on animals?"

Joymancers use similar sorts of magic, and they can allow you to delve into any conscious mind. As I recall, the impressions you get from an animal tend to be vaguer and more jumbled, but that'll be less of an issue in my case.

Or more of an issue. "They'd notice it's strange that your memories are so clear, though, won't they? They might even see something that shows you're more than just a mouse, like a memory of us talking together."

A small risk. If it prevents these barons from putting you under their control… I was made your familiar so I could protect you, Lorelei, and I intend to do that however I can.

She'd always said that, but she knew as well as I did that the joymancer Conclave had assigned her to me more to protect everyone else *from* me rather than the other way around. As much as that fact made my skin crawl, so far it certainly seemed as if I was more of a danger to the people around me than they were to me, if indirectly.

"No," I said. "It's not just a small risk; it's a huge one. The barons are going to be pulling out all the stops to make this charge stick. Who knows how deep they'll poke into your brain if we give them the chance? Then I'd lose you… and I'd still be charged with a major crime. It wouldn't help anyone."

Perhaps you're right. I wasn't thinking about how you would be threatened by the discovery as well. She paused. *I'd do it if you decided it was worth the risk after all, though. I want you to remember that. If those miscreants take you over for their awful purposes, then I'll have failed both you and the Conclave.*

A thought that might have been unfair passed through my mind—was she more worried about failing me or failing the Conclave? I shoved it away. Deborah had supported me as well as she could, stuck in that mouse body and unable to cast.

"I appreciate that," I told her. "We'll just have to find another way." With three—or maybe even all four?—of the other scions working alongside me, I had to have some kind of chance, didn't I?

I nestled my head in the pillow with my hands tucked by my face. The cuffs pressed against my wrists, not letting me forget them even when I closed my eyes to try to sleep. It was a long, uneasy time before I finally drifted off.

The fridge had been cleared out after all the summer students had departed—some of us less willingly than others—and the cafeteria wasn't running during the break, so the next morning I made the twenty-minute walk into the town down the hill to make sure Deborah and I wouldn't starve. I returned to the dorm loaded down with bread, cheese, fruits, and various other essentials, and nearly gave a woman standing in the common room a heart attack.

She flinched at the swing of the door and jerked her hands down from where they'd been raised to cast a spell over the sofa's upholstery. A jolt of fear shot into me from her. When she saw me, her eyes widened. Her stance shifted but didn't exactly relax, smaller whiffs of anxiety tickling past my collarbone from her to join my stores of magic.

"I'm so sorry, Miss Bloodstone," she said. From her simple blue dress shirt and gray slacks, I figured she was part of the maintenance staff. "I didn't know you were back. I was assigned to deep clean the common seating areas today. If you'd rather I came back later..."

"No, no," I said with a wave of my free hand. "It doesn't bother me, as long as it doesn't bother you if I make myself some breakfast."

"Of course not," she said, but I felt her gaze follow me as I headed into the kitchen area.

The woman went back to her cleaning spells, but I caught more than one wary glance aimed my way—and more tingles of nervous energy passing into me—as I toasted a couple slices of bread, fried an egg, and chopped up an apple to share with Deborah. Suspicion wormed its way under my skin.

Was she *really* here just to freshen up the rooms, or was she yet another person the barons or their allies had brought under their sway? They might be setting new plots in motion now that I was temporarily free, even with the hearing looming. She might have intended to cast some kind of harmful spell in here. She might still mean to do it and was worried I'd realize.

I trained my eyes on the back of her head and murmured a general insight spell as I spread butter on the toast, my low voice covered by the scrape of the knife. The woman didn't have much in the way of defenses up. I tumbled into her thoughts in an instant.

As always, the impressions flowed around me without much rhyme or reason. I tasted her determination to see her job done well to make her boss happy… while he was so torn up in grief over his daughter's death. Her boss was Imogen's dad, of course. A simmering discomfort at my presence ran through her consciousness too, but it had nothing to do with any nefarious plans she was part of. Her heightened awareness of the knife in my hand only solidified that fact.

She was afraid she was in the presence of a murderer. And not just any murderer—one who might fly off the handle without much warning.

Nausea gripped my stomach as I pulled back into my own head. I had to force myself to add jam to my toast before I carried it into my bedroom.

Ever since my assessment had shown I was strong in all four domains of fearmancer magic, my fellow students had regarded me with a certain amount of caution. I hadn't *liked* it, but it'd conveniently replenished the fear I relied on to power my magic without me having to actually hurt anyone. Now, though… How many of the students and staff outside the few who knew me well believed I'd killed Imogen in a vicious fury? Was this the kind of reaction I'd have to expect across the board once school was back in session?

I relaxed a little when I heard the click of the main door as the woman left—and tensed up all over again when a knock sounded on it a few minutes later. Then a familiar playful voice carried in from the hall.

"Oh, Ice Queen, don't leave me hanging here."

My spirits lifted in an instant. I leapt up from my desk and all but ran for the door.

Jude's tone might have been light, but when I threw open the door, his green eyes met mine, even darker than usual with worry. I grabbed him in a hug, and he squeezed me back with a pleased chuckle.

"Now that's the kind of welcome I'm talking about. Are you okay?"

He eased back just far enough to examine my face. "The blacksuits didn't manhandle you too much, did they?"

Seeing that much concern from a guy who rarely showed he was anything other than absolutely carefree made my heart squeeze. Jude had plenty of his own problems weighing on him, but he'd dashed back to campus to be here for me without me even asking.

"No one hurt me," I reassured him. "It just wasn't exactly a vacation."

"They never should have taken you in the first place," he muttered, and traced his fingers along my jaw. "We'll just have to make whoever set you up like this regret it, won't we?" He gave me a wicked smirk and tipped up my chin for a kiss.

He made it sound so much easier than I could imagine fixing this mess would be, but it was impossible to focus on that with his mouth claiming mine. I kissed him back hard, letting myself get lost just for a moment in all the desire and adoration that radiated from his touch.

Someone cleared his throat from the top of the stairs. I broke from Jude to see Connar watching us with one eyebrow cocked.

"You just had to get in there first," he said to Jude, but his low baritone had a teasing note to it.

He strode over as I turned to meet him, and in an instant I was engulfed in his brawny arms. I lifted my head to kiss him too. Even with the horrible situation I'd found myself in, a wave of gratitude washed through me—that I had these guys who were not only willing to fight for me against my enemies but to share my affections with each other as well.

"All right," Connar said, after pressing another kiss to the top of my head. "Let's see what we can to do make sure justice is served."

As much as I appreciated that sentiment, my gut twisted at the comment. The two scions didn't know yet that any real justice I got for the attacks against me would tear apart both their families.

CHAPTER SIX

Declan

I'd known from the moment I started digging into fearmancer murder law that my efforts wouldn't go unremarked on. So when Ms. Grimsworth summoned me to her office, I had no doubt what the meeting was going to be about. The only question was exactly how it'd play out.

"Come in, Mr. Ashgrave," the headmistress said in her cool voice when she answered my knock. She didn't look especially happy about having to deal with this business before the end-of-summer break was even over, but then, I rarely saw much emotion color her primly professional demeanor. She rarely appeared happy about good news either.

I stepped into her office, the sharp scent of incense tickling my nose, and discovered we had company for this meeting. A blacksuit was leaning against the bookshelves to one side of Ms. Grimsworth's desk—a fairly high ranking one, from the cut of her dark clothes and her apparent age, though I hadn't encountered her during my work to get Rory out of their custody. She didn't say anything as I took the chair in front of the desk, but her intent gaze followed me beneath the sweep of her short tawny hair. Maybe this was the family "friend" Rory had mentioned.

Ms. Grimsworth sat in her usual chair without introducing the onlooker. Apparently the blacksuit wanted to be a relatively silent partner in this conversation. The headmistress folded her hands on the top of the desk and leaned forward. When she spoke, her tone gave the impression that she'd suppressed a sigh.

"Concerns have been raised regarding your involvement with Rory Bloodstone. You've assisted with her Insight seminar in your capacity as teacher's aide as well as offering her tutoring, if I'm correct?"

"That's right," I said calmly, although my stomach had knotted. I'd expected this, but I also didn't know exactly how the accusations might play out. The last I'd heard, Rory's paternal grandparents had fled the country in the wake of the criminal investigation I'd set in motion, off to Europe somewhere to hope they could simply wait out the inquiries. That didn't mean they couldn't have tried to take one last jab at me by sharing their theories about my and Rory's personal relationship as they'd left. Hell, for all I knew, someone else had witnessed an incriminating interaction between us without us even realizing.

"It appears you've gone to great lengths to assist Miss Bloodstone in the face of her recent incarceration," Ms. Grimsworth went on. "Certainly beyond what we'd consider in the scope of a teacher's aide's responsibilities to one of his students. Questions have been posed about potential bias interfering with your ability to do your job."

That all sounded pretty vague so far—and while it was difficult to read Ms. Grimsworth's mood, my increasing impression was that she found this entire interview rather ridiculous. Not that I could afford to relax with the blacksuit looking on.

I schooled my expression into one of bemusement. "I can understand why that issue might be raised, but all I can say is that I don't see my efforts on Rory's behalf as having anything to do with my role as teacher's aide. Regardless of our positions within the school, we're colleagues within the pentacle. I supported her as a fellow scion."

The blacksuit opened her mouth for the first time. Her voice had a slight edge to it. "You'd go to these lengths for your other 'colleagues' as well?"

I shifted my gaze to her, my shoulders squaring. "I would. Thankfully, none of the other scions have been involved in a crime on this level, so I can't point to direct evidence of that fact, but if you look over my history, you'll find plenty of instances when I've used my understanding of our laws and formal procedures to help them in smaller ways."

I didn't know whether she'd already investigated that history, but if she hadn't, she'd find out it was true soon enough. Of all the questionable things I might have done when it came to Rory, defending her legal rights wasn't one of them. When it came to those actions, at least, I stood on perfectly firm ground.

Unless the blacksuits had something else up their sleeves. Or unless my fellow barons had decided to throw me under the bus along with Rory. Apprehension prickled down my back.

Ms. Grimsworth shifted back in her chair. She glanced at the blacksuit. "I can confirm that Mr. Ashgrave has generally led any petitions involving formal policy when it comes to the other scions, here at the university at least."

"It seems to me there is some conflict of interest there all the same," the blacksuit said.

"School wasn't in session at the time," I said before she could go on. "And if it would be a problem for me to continue contributing to Rory's case once classes start up again, then I'll resign as teacher's aide. I'm sure the blacksuits would agree that the pentacle must come before a temporary teaching position."

I said the last bit as evenly as everything else, but it was meant as a parry. No blacksuit would want to suggest, especially in front of a respected witness, that they opposed solidarity among their future leaders.

The woman frowned, but she mustn't have had any other ammunition—or none that she was prepared to use just yet. "I don't think that will be necessary," she said. "At least not from our perspective."

"Nor from ours," Ms. Grimsworth put in. "The matters appear to be quite unrelated. Though while you're particularly engaged in Miss Bloodstone's legal affairs, I expect you to ensure that any evaluations of her class performance are conducted by Professor Sinleigh rather than yourself."

"Of course," I said, and with that, it seemed the interview was over.

I only had a few minutes to feel relieved. As I headed out of Killbrook Hall, my phone buzzed in my pocket. I pulled it out, and my heart sank.

I'd gotten a single, brusque text from Marguerite Stormhurst—Connar's mother and the Stormhurst baron. *Urgent meeting, 1pm, the field. Your presence is mandatory.*

That was less than an hour from now. Which wouldn't have given me enough time to drive out to the Fortress of the Pentacle if the barons had tried to hold the meeting there… and perhaps they hadn't wanted there to be any risk that what we were about to discuss could be overheard or recorded by the pentacle's official administrative employees.

I'd only met the other barons at the isolated field where we occasionally assembled for emergency meetings twice before, once while I was still technically only in training with my aunt Ambrosia as acting baron. The only good thing about the way they'd called this get-together was the fact that she'd almost certainly been left out. On the other hand, if they didn't like the answers I gave them today, they might be inviting her back into the position that should be mine soon enough.

I switched directions to veer toward the garage, ignoring the impulse to text Rory—or, hell, even Jude or Connar—and tell them why I was leaving campus. It wasn't as though, if the barons decided to turn their murderous intentions on me, the other scions would be able to do anything about it without putting themselves in even more danger. And I didn't really think my older colleagues would go to those lengths just yet.

That didn't mean this conversation was going to be at all enjoyable, though.

The possibilities of what they'd say and how I'd answer whirled through my head as I drove, although I'd already thought through my arguments before I'd first contacted the blacksuits on Rory's behalf. The issue wasn't so much what I'd say as how the barons would take it… and if the last few months had taught me anything, it was that for all I knew about them, I was still capable of underestimating them.

The field in question lay a few miles from any habitation, stretches of pine forest shadowing either end. The country road that led to it was full of potholes that jolted my car's suspension. An even rougher lane branched off, petering out into overgrown grass after some ten feet. It was there that three other cars were already parked when I pulled into the field. The three full barons—Julian Nightwood, Edmund Killbrook, and Marguerite Stormhurst—were leaning against the hoods. Their gazes followed me.

I stopped the car with the uneasy impression that they'd been talking for quite a while before I'd turned up. That they might even have already been together when Baron Stormhurst had called me to this meeting. Together and discussing *me*.

"Ashgrave," Nightwood said the moment I'd opened the door. "Glad you could make it." His steady voice was laced with just enough venom for me to register it, but hardly enough that I could have called it out.

"Of course," I said. "The pentacle calls, I answer." They weren't going to dock me any points on loyalty to *this* job, that was for sure.

I came around the front of the Honda and propped myself against the hood as the others had, keeping my movements as loose as I could manage to despite the tension wound inside me. Nothing would be worse than revealing *I* knew I'd done something they wouldn't approve of.

Distant thunder rumbled in the cloud-choked sky, and a damp wind licked over the field. If we didn't keep this meeting short, we'd all end up soaked.

"What do we need to discuss?" I asked, as if I had no idea.

Killbrook narrowed his eyes at me, which only amplified the serpentine impression his angular face always gave me. "We were informed that the Bloodstone scion has been released from blacksuit custody, on your request. Something you should have discussed with *us* before going ahead, don't you think?"

I blinked at him as if startled by the idea. "I was simply ensuring proper procedures were followed. I didn't realize there'd be any debate about that."

Nightwood shifted, with a tiny gesture of his hand that might have signaled something to his colleague. "Naturally we expect the law to be followed," he said. "But I would trust the blacksuits were in the process of handling it. Bloodstone has finally made a misstep that may benefit us. Surely you could see that?"

A "misstep." As if murder were a simple mistake. As if they hadn't orchestrated the entire thing rather than Rory stepping wrong.

I reined in my irritation. "Of course that factor occurred to me," I said, letting my voice get slightly tart. When dealing with venomous snakes, sometimes you had to show you could respond in kind, or they'd take your apparent weakness as an opening. "It also occurred to me that convicting the sole heir of a barony might be a rather difficult task. If she's given the full amount of time to mount a defense and still can't establish her innocence, the judge will be even more… open-minded in the extent of the sanctions, don't you think?"

He'd be more inclined to lay down harsher punishments—and to give the barons more rein to impose them, I meant.

The other barons were silent for a moment. Stormhurst cocked her head. "How can you be so sure she won't manufacture some proof in her favor while she's walking free?"

I raised my eyebrows at her. "Considering the blacksuits are tracking every bit of magic she casts, I'm not sure how she could manage that. If she tries to, she'll only dig the hole even deeper. I can't imagine how she'd start even if she had unrestricted use of her magic. With the carelessness of the crime, there must be ample evidence against her already, assuming she's responsible."

I watched the faces around me carefully. Killbrook exhaled wearily and rubbed his mouth. Nightwood only kept his usual imposing demeanor. Stormhurst gave a snort that sounded just a touch forced. The figures in front of me had far too much practice at holding their cards close.

"She has dug herself quite a hole," Stormhurst said. "Her access to the barony will depend on our good graces once she's convicted."

"As it should have all along, considering the outside influences that have muddled her understanding of the world," Nightwood put in, the closest he'd likely ever come to admitting he'd not only wanted but intended for this outcome. "The balance will be right within the pentacle, and we can move forward without further distractions." He fixed his dark gaze on me. "As long as your gambit doesn't backfire in some way you haven't anticipated."

"I'll be right there to keep an eye on her process," I said. "I can't see any way she'll get herself out of this fix unless somehow she's honestly not guilty. How much chance is there of that?"

The question might have been a smidge too pointed. Nightwood's mouth tightened, and Killbrook shot me a brief glance that was just shy of a glower. I kept my expression impassive as if I'd meant it as an honest question.

"I expect we have no need to worry about that," Nightwood said. "But we *would* like to be kept informed of any further action you take as it involves Bloodstone. All of our fates are connected to hers."

"I'll take initiative as I see the need," I said. "But I'll make sure you stay updated."

Stormhurst's voice dropped low, to almost a growl. "Before you take any more initiatives on your own, remember *you're* not quite full baron yourself. Your fate depends on us as well."

"I'm only attempting to live up to the role," I said with a smile, but my stomach balled tighter as I got back into the car. That was as close to a direct threat as I'd ever gotten from them. The line I walked had just gotten twice as precarious.

But it still wasn't anywhere near as fraught as the path Rory was on. I tried to stir more sense of triumph in me as I started the engine, but it was weighed down by the dread pooling in my chest.

As much as I hated it, what I'd told the other barons was true. If Rory couldn't prove she hadn't hurt her dormmate even with the time and freedom I'd bought her, she'd be worse off than if I'd left her to stew in the blacksuits' holding room.

CHAPTER SEVEN

Rory

"If only the school had bothered to invest in security cameras," Jude lamented, stroking his fingers over my hair where he was sitting next to me on the sofa in the scion lounge.

"They wouldn't have done us much good," Connar pointed out at my other side. "Anyone who could pull off the level of magic needed for the rest of the crime could have blocked them off or cast an illusion to change the recording."

Jude hummed to himself. "True. All right, scratch that complaint, let's keep all cameras away."

I resisted the urge to pull both him and Connar closer, to snuggle into them like a shield against the awful situation I was facing. Just because Declan accepted that I was involved with other guys didn't mean I liked the idea of rubbing it in his face. Besides, the four of us had come down here to the private basement lounge area to figure out the right strategy to tackle that situation. I had to stay focused.

Thankfully, Malcolm wasn't back from the break yet, so we didn't have to deal with any interruptions from him.

Declan shifted in his armchair with a frown. "The two of you didn't come up with anything useful when you were poking around while I was researching the legal aspect?"

Connar shook his head. "Nothing that would prove Rory wasn't behind the attack or that someone else was." He gave my knee a gentle squeeze. "What about Victory and her friends? They've had it in for you for a while, haven't they? And they knew about the tension between you and Imogen—they had easy access to the dorm…"

I took a sip of the Coke that Jude had poured for me, the fizzing of the liquid going down my throat sharpening my focus. "They *were* at the party in the Stormhurst Building."

"I stayed longer than you did," Declan said. "I remember seeing Victory and Sinclair there afterward—I was keeping an eye on them in case they tried something. But Cressida…"

I'd seen Cressida, I realized. She'd bumped into me, literally, in the first floor hallway when I'd been heading for the stairs that led to the dorms.

A chill washed through me for just a second before I remembered Deborah's account. She'd said the real attacker had still been in the dorm room when I'd come in.

"Cressida couldn't have been involved either," I said. Besides, I knew I hadn't been framed by students, although I guessed it was possible the barons had made use of them somehow. I hesitated, debating for the hundredth time whether this was the right moment to drop that revelation in my lovers' laps.

Declan redirected the conversation before I had to decide, maybe sensing my discomfort. He didn't appear to be in any hurry to accuse his friends' parents of treason either. "If it wasn't for the illusion spell, your memories would be enough to absolve you," he said, and rubbed his mouth. "Will you let me do an insight spell on you—just to look at that moment? Maybe there's something about the illusion that we'll be able to point in comparison to your actual experiences, so we can prove it isn't real."

My spirits leapt with a jolt of hope. "Okay. I couldn't really tell if there was anything really off about the illusions—but I was pretty distracted in the moment, panicking over Imogen."

With a deep breath, I willed down the mental shields that had become instinctive. Even though I was surrounded by people I knew wanted nothing more than to help me, my pulse thumped a little faster as Declan leaned forward, his gaze intent on my forehead. Through everything that'd been thrown at me since I'd entered the fearmancer community, I'd managed to keep my thoughts and memories reasonably secure. Leaving myself vulnerable made my nerves jitter.

"*What happened when you found Imogen Wakeburn's body?*" Declan asked with the slight lilt of a casting. A tingle raced through my head as he must have delved into my thoughts. I had no sense of what he was seeing. Jude took my hand as if suspecting I needed the extra reassurance.

All I could do was sit still and wait for Declan to finish sorting through whatever impressions had risen up to meet his question. When he sat back with a sharp exhalation, my mental protections sprang back into place before I even needed to think about it. A ripple of relief passed through me having that wall of defense around me again.

Declan's expression had turned pensive. "It's going to be hard," he said. "That was a skilled illusion—it mimics actual memories too well to distinguish the difference with insight. The whole process is always so jumbled as it is…" His gaze rose to meet mine. "There might be something, though. Most of the words were blurred, but with the spell —you haven't been using your own casting words yet, have you?"

I shook my head. "It's easier using actual words. I haven't been confident enough to start making things up on the spot or relying on invented phrases. There's a word I've been using for general insight spells, but that's it."

"And your professors would be able to confirm that?"

"They should. They've all seen me cast for classwork recently—honestly I've felt a little embarrassed that I'm still using literal words."

The corner of Declan's mouth crooked upward. "You should be thankful for it. It might help solidify your defense. Whoever cast the illusion clearly didn't realize that about your own magic use. The spell that appears to kill Imogen in your memories was directed by a word I've never heard before."

"Really?" The hope I'd felt before bubbled higher. I hadn't noticed that aspect in the chaos. "That's pretty good evidence that I didn't cast the spell, isn't it?"

"It should be," Connar said.

"It *should*," Declan agreed. "And I expect it'll help sway the judge. I don't think it'd be smart for us to assume it'll be enough on its own. Your accusers could argue that you purposefully came up with a casting word for that kind of spell to sow doubt if you had to use it."

Jude made a face. "That's a huge stretch. If Rory supposedly lost control in a fit of anger, why would she have a spell for that situation?"

Declan held up his hands. "I know it's ridiculous. We all know it's ridiculous to think that Rory would have attacked anyone in the first place. But we also know that scheming isn't exactly an uncommon occurrence among fearmancers, don't we? It wouldn't be a hard story to sell. *If* that's the only proof we offer. We've got at least a week to come up with more."

"They could use insight to help determine whether she planned a casting word in advance, couldn't they?" Connar said.

"Maybe," Declan said. "It'd be hard to phrase a question that specific in a way that gives definitive proof. Especially when the truth is that she didn't."

And I didn't really want the judge poking around in my head any more than he or she needed to. The fear that had gripped me when Lillian had talked about the judge viewing my memories shivered through me again.

"They'll probably want to use a lot of insight on me at the hearing, won't they?" I asked. "It'd be hard for me to refuse without looking guilty."

Jude elbowed me teasingly. "If you don't have any murderous secrets to hide, I think you'll be fine. You put the rest of us to shame."

"Not by regular fearmancer standards, though, right?" I looked at each of them. "There are things I've thought, things I've said, that the authorities might see as treason. I still miss my joymancer parents. I still… I still wish I were back with that community instead of here sometimes."

A lot of the time, even if not quite as much now that I had the support of these three guys. And then there were the plans I'd made to bring down the whole school, the conversations I'd had with Deborah that would reveal who she really was… My mind could incriminate me of crimes the judge would probably see as worse than a murdered friend.

"I've never seen a judge request an all-encompassing insight spell during a hearing," Declan said softly. "But it's true, we don't know for sure what questions they'll ask—and it's possible they'd ask something that would brush up against those feelings. They'll be looking for signs of animosity…"

Connar sat up straighter, his expression fierce. "We'll make a good enough case that they don't have any grounds to do an extensive insight interrogation."

Declan and I exchanged a glance. We both knew that the people pulling the strings behind the scenes would take the opportunity of the hearing to undermine me any way they could. I couldn't count on any amount of evidence sparing me that intrusion.

But maybe there was a defense I could use that didn't involve any magical shields. If my enemies could mess with my memories using an illusion… there were other ways I could disguise the reality of my thoughts, weren't there?

"Just in case," I said to Declan, "why don't— Before, you passed on some reports to me about cases involving the joymancers, conflicts between them and the fearmancers. I'm guessing there's more material like that you could give me? If I've been reading that stuff before the hearing and have it fresh in my mind, it should help cloud any of the positive feelings I have about them."

Declan paused. "There is more. If you're sure you want to read it. The joymancers… I don't doubt that your adoptive parents treated you well, Rory, but you didn't know any of the others. The reports I gave you before were true. Their community has done some pretty awful things."

Awful by fearmancer standards, maybe. I still wasn't convinced there was no bias in the accounts I'd read. Even if the Conclave had been afraid of me and denied me my magic… even if the circumstances of my birth parents' deaths had been questionable…

how could anything they'd done compare to the horrors the fearmancers had treated me to in just five months?

"That's fine," I said. "I want to know the truth. If it unsettles me, well, then it'll stick in my mind even more, right?"

Jude chuckled. "That's the spirit," he said, ruffling my hair.

By the time we headed up to the main floor, we each had tasks to do, if not a definite plan for proving my innocence. Declan went off to get those records for me, and Connar gave me a quick kiss before heading into the library, where he was going to look up some advanced physicality approaches that he thought might reveal something in the crime scene. Jude ambled out onto the green with me, intending to chat up the few teachers currently on campus.

My job was to take a walk around the university and see if anything jostled free a memory that could point me in a useful direction—something I might not have noticed the significance of before Imogen's murder. It didn't feel like a lot, but it was a starting point, anyway.

As we came out of the building, one of the general education professors was leading a small group of students our way. The glints of the leaf pins by their shirt collars revealed that they were all scholarship students: Naries. Blood U admitted a handful of nonmagical students each year to give the rest of us practice at keeping our magic secret—and easy targets for generating the fear we needed to fuel that magic.

"This is Ashgrave Hall, where you'll be staying," the professor was saying. "Each of you should have received a dorm assignment with your letter."

"The new batch of senior Naries," Jude said by my ear as the professor led the group into the building. "Or at least the newly senior ones. They always start their school year here in the fall to mimic the regular school system. The staff have them arrive a little before classes start to get settled in… so they have a little time to acclimatize before the mage students will really go after them."

"Lovely," I muttered.

"Hey, they'll have more of a respite this term thanks to you."

I'd almost forgotten the summer project I'd been celebrating right before Imogen's death. With my help, a group of Naries had designed and overseen the construction of a clubhouse solely for the scholarship students. The wards I'd laid down with Connar and Jude's help would give them one place safe from malicious castings.

That victory seemed like a small one in the face of everything that had happened since.

Jude leaned in to kiss me, letting his lips linger a few seconds longer than Connar had—maybe on purpose—and shot me a grin before setting off toward the teachers' offices in Killbrook Hall. The guys might have been willing to share my affection, but I didn't think their competitive instinct had completely faded.

I was about to meander toward the Stormhurst Building, figuring I should retrace my steps from right before the murder first, when a few more figures came around the hall from the main parking lot, one of them a completely welcome sight.

Shelby, the Nary girl from my own dorm room and the first person on campus who'd been truly friendly to me when I'd arrived, was hauling a small wheeled suitcase over the grass to the paved path. She had her cello case, which was nearly as tall as she was, slung over her shoulder. Her mousy brown hair bobbed in its usual ponytail, and her expression was as earnestly determined as ever. Keeping her spot at the music program at this school meant the world to her, especially since she'd nearly lost it once.

My first impulse was to hustle right over to welcome her back, but something in me balked. I didn't know what she'd heard about Imogen and my supposed involvement in the murder. The Nary students had left the morning before it'd even happened. Maybe she had no idea? But surely the administration would have notified them somehow, if only to pre-empt the talk that would be circulating among the fearmancer students on their return.

Shelby spotted me right then and bounded toward me as fast as her luggage allowed with a smile that didn't leave any room for doubt. Whatever she *had* heard, she was still perfectly happy to see me. I let a smile stretch across my own face as I met her halfway.

"I'm glad you're already here," she said after we exchanged a quick hug. "Weird as it might sound, I'm glad to be back."

"Even when you've got more hassling from people like Victory to look forward to?" I said.

"Ah, really, there are people back home who can be just as mean. At least here I'm making sure I'll have a good enough career that eventually I'll never have to go back." She gave a sheepish laugh. Then her smile faltered. "Is it really true—the school sent around this official notice that Imogen *died*?"

My chest tightened. "Yeah," I said. "They're still investigating exactly what happened." She obviously didn't know the whole story. I fumbled for the right words. "I—People are saying, because I was the one who—"

"I didn't know they allowed murderers to come back to school," someone said from across the green.

I stiffened, my head jerking up. It wasn't only Naries arriving today. A few of the senior fearmancer girls, ones I didn't know that well, had just come onto the green, carrying their posh tote bags. If they had larger luggage, no doubt their chauffeurs or the school staff would be carrying that.

The three of them were staring at me, hostility in their eyes, fear wafting off them to congeal in my chest. The aggressive posturing was a front. They saw me as just as dangerous as the maintenance staff woman had the other morning.

"I didn't hurt anyone," I said, willing my voice not to shake. "I found her body—that's all."

"That doesn't seem to be what the investigators think," one of the girls said. Her gaze dropped to my arms, and I could tell she'd noted the recording cuffs, although she couldn't comment on them in front of Shelby. "I think I'll steer clear, thanks."

She raised her chin with a faint sniff, and the girls started to march on, giving me a wide berth. I'd have left it at that, but Shelby took a step toward them, her voice unexpectedly taut.

"You obviously don't know Rory at all," she said. "She's the last person who'd ever attack someone, let alone—let alone *that*."

"Shelby," I said quietly, even though her defense made my heart squeeze with gratitude. The last thing she needed was for her friendship with me to make her an even bigger target.

"What the hell do you know?" the first girl snapped.

"A lot more than you do. She's the only non-scholarship student in this place who's *never* been an asshole to me." Shelby gave the girls a pointed look as if to remind them of the times when they'd probably been assholes too. "So why don't you shut up about things you don't know anything about?"

The girls looked from Shelby to me, and another quiver of fear seeped into me. They turned and went into the building with an audible huff but no other comment. Shelby drew herself up a little straighter.

"That felt good," she said. "I'm tired of just putting up with them talking crap—especially when it's about you too. How could anyone think *you'd* murder someone?"

You have no idea, I thought but couldn't say. I wasn't allowed to tell her anything about magic or fearmancer politics… and even if I could, at this point my life was such a mess I wasn't sure she'd have been able to wrap her head around it.

"People look for the easiest person to blame," I offered, and she nodded as if that was explanation enough. As she hefted her cello, I noted the silver chain with the violin charm I'd given her still hanging around her neck. I'd warded that charm to defend her from any spells cast her way.

"Let me help you with your stuff," I said, reaching to grab her suitcase. As I bent down, I murmured a few words under my breath to propel more magic into the charm. After a week away, its effects would have faded.

And as much as I appreciated Shelby's growing confidence, I knew just how much trouble it could get her into too.

CHAPTER EIGHT

Rory

I discovered Malcolm was back in residence when I stepped out of my dorm room that evening. He was standing in the hallway outside, in the process of cuffing a boy who didn't look more than sixteen across the head while two other junior students looked on.

My lips parted with an automatic protest. The juniors had all glanced up the second the door had opened, even the one Malcolm was harassing, and three waves of terror coursed into my chest. At that sensation, my mouth snapped shut before a sound had left it.

"I'd better not see you skulking around the senior dorms again," Malcolm said, aiming a menacing glower at all three of them. With bobbed heads and meek postures, the juniors fled for the stairs.

By the time they'd disappeared from view, my nerves had settled. I gave Malcolm a skeptical look. "Is it really necessary to resort to physical violence just because they wanted to check out the place?"

I got the impression he'd only just held himself back from glowering at me too. "That's not all they were doing, Glinda. I caught them whispering to each other about some big plan to see if they could provoke you. Two of the nitwits had dared the other to bang on your door and pick a fight."

To see whether they could get me to attack him like I supposedly had Imogen? My stomach turned. I guessed I shouldn't be surprised. It was just like fearmancers to goad each other on like that, and the juniors weren't quite as careful in their attempts at bravado.

"Well, you didn't need to step in," I said, pulling the door all the way shut behind me. "I'm pretty sure I could have sent them off no problem on my own, without maiming anyone in the process. Or are you rethinking your stance on my innocence and you were hassling them for their own protection?"

Malcolm's jaw worked. "This is my job as the heir of Nightwood. I know you don't like it, Rory, but the scions are meant to exercise their authority—to keep the rest of the community in line. If you don't start now, no one's going to listen to you when you take your spot at the barons' table."

I wasn't in the mood to get into an argument with him about this of all subjects. "I think I'll find other ways to 'exercise my authority'," I replied, and headed for the stairs.

"It's for their good too," Malcolm called after me. "If no one lays down the law when they're breaking it in small stupid ways, imagine how much trouble they'll get into the next time around."

Unfortunately, that logic did have at least a little sense to it, even if the last thing I wanted to do was *agree* with Malcolm on his approach to student relations. I settled for ignoring him as I left him behind.

Jude had texted me asking me to meet him in "the music room." Nightwood Tower, which held all of the university's classrooms, had at least a few different spaces for rehearsing music, but I knew from past experience which one the Killbrook scion would have meant.

The room with the piano was right up near the top of the tower. A graceful melody seeped out as I nudged open the door.

Jude was already sitting at the piano, his fingers dancing over the keys with an easy confidence. He didn't look up in acknowledgement, but a few additional flourishes crept into the tune with my entrance. A satisfied smile curled his lips. I leaned back against the door and let the music wash over me. It was a shame, really, that he kept this talent a secret. He was very good.

He finished with a chain of finger work that sped through the notes so quickly his hand became a blur. Then he turned with a little bow. I laughed as I gave my applause. "Show off."

"If you've got it, flaunt it," Jude said with a wink. He scooted over and patted the bench beside him. "Come here?"

I sank down next to him, and he tucked his arm around my waist. Sitting there in the small but airy room, I couldn't stop my mind from slipping back to the last time I'd spoken to him here. The time when he'd confessed that he knew he wasn't really the heir to the Killbrook barony—that he wasn't a Killbrook at all. When his parents had failed to produce an heir, they'd arranged for his mother to get pregnant with another man under the influence of magic.

And now his parents were expecting a new baby, one that would be the real heir. One that made Jude not only expendable but a liability. His father wouldn't want anyone finding out about his deception.

I was the only person Jude had dared to tell. Not even the other scions knew. Being with me wasn't just about having a good time for him, despite the carefree airs he feigned so well. I might be the only fearmancer he knew who wouldn't shun him when they found out the truth of his parentage.

Maybe Jude had guessed the direction my thoughts had wandered in. He rested his free hand lightly on the keys and played a few soft notes. "If I've got any natural talent, it came from my real father," he said, looking at the piano rather than me. His floppy dark copper hair fell forward to shadow his eyes. "That's actually why I started teaching myself in the first place. I figured out who he was not that long before I started here, looked him up, and found out everything I could about him."

I scooted closer and tipped my head to Jude's shoulder. "Do you think you could ever tell him what happened—who you are?"

He shook his head. "It'd just make a bigger mess. And I don't think he'd want to know. He was married when it happened—he's got his own kids. I don't want to ruin his life, for what? He'd probably hate me because of what my parents did to him to make it happen."

"It wasn't your fault."

"No, but it's the only reason I'm here." He reached and shut the keyboard cover before turning to me. "Let's not dwell on that, though. I had much more enjoyable reasons for asking you to meet me here."

I raised an eyebrow. "Did you?"

He smiled slyly and touched his nose to mine as his breath warmed my lips. "Who do you think you're talking to?" His fingers teased into my hair and traced over my scalp, sending a giddy shiver through me. "You've had to spend your summer break worrying about all kinds of crap. I think you deserve a chance to leave all that behind." He brushed a kiss to my cheek, then my jaw, then the corner of my mouth, until my lips ached for contact. His voice dropped to a murmur. "I've never been with a girl up here before."

"No?" I said, just barely holding back a gasp when he nipped the crook of my neck.

"You're the only one who's ever gotten to see my musical side." He paused and looked me straight in the eyes. "The only one I would have wanted to share that side of me with."

The emotion in those words made my pulse skip a beat. Before I could answer, he was kissing me the way I'd wanted, his mouth capturing mine, his hands in my hair and on my waist pulling me even closer to him.

Jude had bragged to me once about his extensive experience in this area, and while I couldn't say I enjoyed thinking about the many other girls he might have gotten hot and heavy with, I had no complaints about benefiting from all that practice. With each kiss, my lips tingled hotter. They parted, and his tongue slipped past them to duel with mine. An eager flush was already spreading through my entire body.

Maybe this was only a temporary escape from the problems looming over me, but damn, it was a thrilling one.

Jude turned his attentions to my neck, making each inch of my skin light up with pleasure. His fingers danced up my side as if playing a melody on my ribs and stroked my breast through my silk blouse. A whimper worked from my throat at the rush of sensation.

I slid my hands up under his shirt, ignoring the wobble of the thin silver cuffs at my wrists, wanting to feel as much of him as I could. His lean muscles shifted at my touch. I swept my palms over his nipples, and he groaned with a sear of breath against my neck.

"I never knew it was possible to want someone this much until I met you," he said in a rasp.

My agreement came out as a shaky chuckle lost in the crash of his mouth against mine. As we kissed even more hungrily, his hand eased my skirt up my thigh, his fingers tracing patterns on the sensitive skin as they climbed. A throbbing heat built where my legs met.

An urgent sound escaped me that was almost a growl, and Jude grinned against my lips. He cupped my sex, somehow relieving the ache of need and sharpening it at the same time.

With each swivel of his fingers, bliss pulsed up from my core. My breath trembled between kisses. Jude rose off the bench, tipping me over so I lay on my back and tugging my panties off at the same time. He bent over me to claim my mouth once more, but before I could do more than run my hands down his chest, he was pulling back.

"I haven't gotten to taste you yet," he said with a mischievous gleam in his eyes. Tugging at my hips, he slid me to the far end of the bench. My knees bent to keep my feet on the wooden surface for balance—and splayed around his head as he knelt between my thighs.

"Fuck," I muttered as he pressed his lips to a tender spot just inches from my sex. Jude hummed with satisfaction and charted a scorching path the rest of the way to my core. His mouth closed over my clit with a skillful flick of his tongue, and I couldn't hold back a moan.

My hips rocked with the movements of his mouth. Every thought fled my mind except the awareness of the waves of pleasure rushing through me. He sucked hard on my clit and then grazed it with the tips of his teeth, and I outright bucked with a cry of longing. My head tipped back against the bench.

Jude devoured me with renewed intensity, his tongue slicking right inside me, and I came apart with a shudder of limbs and breath. The ecstasy rolled through me all the way up to my head and down to my toes.

It wasn't enough. When he raised his head, I tangled my fingers in his hair and urged him back up over me. "I want everything," I said.

"Who am I to deny you?" he said with a rough laugh. He snapped his belt open and made short work of his pants, leaning over me. As he kissed me again, my taste tart on his lips, his hand slid under my ass to pull me even closer to the edge, raising my hips at the same time. My ankles crossed behind his waist instinctively. He dipped his head just long enough to speak the quick protective casting, and then he plunged into me so hard and fast I moaned again.

I was so ready, and the angle he held me at sent his cock through me with the perfect sear of pleasure. He kissed my mouth, my shoulder, my breasts through my blouse, his free hand branding me everywhere as the other held my hips in place. I caressed his lean body everywhere I could reach, but it was hard to focus on anything except the peak I was hurtling toward with each thrust.

I arched into him, he adjusted my hips against him just slightly, and his cock hit a spot inside me that set off an even more electric burst of pleasure. "Faster," I pleaded. He complied with a groan. He filled me again and again, pressing that blissful spot over and over, and I lost myself completely.

My back bowed, my legs quivered, and pleasure crashed over me so forcefully that sparks went off behind my eyes. "Oh," I mumbled, with another quake as Jude came shuddering with me.

He rocked to a stop, still holding me to him, bent over me where I lay on the bench. Pleasure had hazed his eyes and softened the sharp angles of his face. I touched his cheek with a rush of affection. He gazed down at me with a smile I couldn't have called anything but joyful.

In an impressive show of physical maneuvering, he managed to collect me against him so he could sit down on the bench with me straddling him, barely breaking the contact between our bodies. He leaned back against the closed piano and wrapped his arms around me. I nestled my head against his shoulder with a contented sigh. His arms tightened.

"I know we talked about it before," he said quietly, "but I want to say it again, just to be clear. I don't care about being part of the barony. I just want you in my life, any way I can have you. If some secret Bloodstone sibling appeared tomorrow and proved themselves the real scion, that wouldn't change a thing. If you ever have any doubts—if you need to look inside my head—"

The earnestness of his tone made my heart skip a beat. I lifted my head to meet his eyes. "I believe you. *You* don't have to prove anything to me."

A look came over his face that was hopeful and hesitant all at once. "That's why— Everyone and everything here is bullshit. *I've* been bullshit my whole life. But now, being with you… I feel like I'm figuring out how to be someone real." A tiny bit of fear shivered from him into me. His voice came out even lower than before, "I love you, Rory."

An ache spread through my chest at the nervousness he'd felt admitting those three words. My emotions were too cluttered for me to say them back with the certainty he'd have deserved, but I answered him the best way I could, with a kiss so tender it took my own breath away.

Jude kissed me back, holding me close, not seeming to need more than that. As he adjusted me against him, my sex brushed against an unexpected hardness in his lap. I kissed him once more and eased back with an amused smile. "Ready to go again already?"

Jude beamed at me, any anxiety he'd been feeling before gone. He shifted his hips so his erection slid against me again. "I do bring a *few* talents to the table, if not a title."

A giggle tickled up my throat. I leaned close, slipping my arms around his shoulders, and murmured in his ear, "Then make love to me."

He laughed a little breathlessly. "I've never wanted to do anything more." And as he slid inside me, I couldn't let myself believe that I'd ever have to give this up.

CHAPTER NINE

Rory

Being back in class should have made my life feel more normal, but reminders of how much had changed in the past week surrounded me. Except for Connar, the students in my current Persuasion seminar reacted with varying tremors of fear when I walked into the room. The girl at the desk next to the one I took scooted farther away on her seat. I heard someone behind me murmuring to a friend that they didn't need to worry because of the blacksuit "bracelets" I had on.

And then there was our teacher. Professor Crowford strode in looking like his usual aging ladies'-man self, his mostly silver hair falling artfully on either side of his heavy-lidded eyes. In his particular case, the problem wasn't that anything about *him* had changed. I simply knew more about him than I had before. Like that he'd thought it was a great idea to encourage all the fearmancer students here for summer term to manipulate the Nary students as far as they could.

Like the fact that Professor Banefield had included him on a list of people involved with my biggest enemies, the barons.

Crowford didn't appear to pay any special attention to me when he came to a stop in front of his desk. He leaned against it and rubbed his hands together with a smile of anticipation.

"Good to see you all back. I hope you enjoyed your break—longer for some of you than others—and that you're ready to dive back into your learning."

Heads nodded along the rows of desks. Crowford pushed off the desk again and started to pace at the front of the room. I let my gaze follow him, which was totally normal for a student. What I'd really like to learn today was not his lesson but what was going on inside his head. But a man adept in Persuasion must have also built up some pretty solid mental walls.

"I thought we'd try something a little different today," he said. "All of you are more than familiar with the most common use of persuasion spells, which is to influence another person's mind. But for those of you who aren't particularly strong in some other domains, you may be interested to hear that a talent in persuasion can be adapted to compensate for certain other skills. For example, you may not be able to conjure an object out of thin air, but with enough practice you can 'persuade' something already there to move or alter its shape in basic ways."

To supplement a person's abilities in Physicality. I had to admit that was kind of interesting, even though I already enjoyed working in the Physicality domain more than Persuasion. That kind of flexibility must apply to other skills as well. Jude had told me he was only actually strong in two areas, not three, but he'd managed to convince the professors that he had the same three strengths as the other scions all this time.

As Crowford drew in a breath, I said my insight casting word under my breath with just the slightest nudge of power. I wasn't launching an assault yet, just testing the terrain.

My awareness tapped against a barrier around the professor's mind. To my careful prodding, it felt firmer than any I'd encountered before.

I drew my focus back. Getting in there, especially getting in unnoticed, would take a lot of work. Maybe not something I could risk while the blacksuits' cuffs were recording every spell I cast.

Crowford motioned to us. "Let's start with a small test you can all participate in. Take out some small object you have on you—a pen, a coin, a keycard—and set it on your desk. See if you can persuade it to move from one side of the desk to the other, using *only* your persuasive abilities. No physicality spells allowed."

The first thing in my purse that my fingers closed around was a pack of gum. That seemed small enough. I set it at the left side of my desk and considered my approach.

A pack of gum didn't have a mind to cast on. How was I supposed to direct my spell?

Professor Crowford chuckled. "I see many of you looking puzzled. As an additional tip, let me remind you that all magic is about the transfer of energy. When you persuade someone's mental state, your magic is acting on the energy in their brain. Every object contains a certain amount of energy down to its atoms. Convince that energy to act."

Right. I frowned at the pack of gum and drew some of my magic into the back of my throat. When I concentrated, I could sense a faint hum of… not awareness, but *presence* from the little cardboard case.

"*Slide*," I ordered it in my best persuasive tone, willing the energy be inclined to shift sideways. The box twitched and traveled half an inch to the right. A smile crossed my lips. Not bad for a start.

It took ten minutes or so, but I managed to compel the gum all the way across my desk. From the whispered voices around me, everyone else was intent on the assignment as well. Professor Crowford strolled between the desks, offering words of encouragement and assistance as needed. When he reached me, he watched for a few seconds and then said only, "Nicely done."

As the rest of the class finished with their attempts, he took his position at his desk again. "Let's try something a little more substantial. Miss Scarlow, you've worked from this angle before, clearly. Would you like to show the class just how large an effect you can pull off. Say…" He glanced around and pointed to the wooden cabinet in the corner. "Lift and rotate the cabinet."

"I think I can do that, sir," the girl said, her cheeks flushing eagerly at having been singled out as a worthy example.

I guessed she'd have to persuade the air around the piece of furniture that it was meant to push upward and then around? Using that type of magic to move something that big and heavy seemed absurd to me, but presumably showing the limitations of this kind of spell was the point of this lesson.

It was possible to move that large an object, in any case. The girl said her casting under her breath, and then added a few more words, and the cabinet wobbled a few inches into the air. It edged up inch by inch until it hovered a foot off the ground.

Triumph lit her face as she spoke again with more casting words that meant nothing to me. The cabinet swayed and began to turn in a slow but steady circle. Someone behind me drew in a breath in awe.

Then the classroom door opened with a squeak of the hinges and voices in mid-conversation.

Everyone startled and looked over. Professor Crowford made a cutting gesture with his hand, and the girl who'd been casting blanched. The cabinet thudded to the floor as she released the spell. We all stared at the four figures in the doorway who were now staring back at us.

They were Naries. I recognized a couple of the guys from my summer project activities, and there was Shelby just behind them with another girl. All Naries… and they'd almost walked in on us in the middle of a magical demonstration. My heart started to thud almost as loud as the cabinet's fall. Weren't there supposed to be protections against that kind of intrusion?

"I believe you've come to the wrong room," Crowford said in a cold tone.

"I—the schedule said—" the boy at the front of the group stuttered. He looked down at the paper in his hand and winced. "Crap. I could swear I re-checked this three times because we don't usually go to this room. I'm really sorry about the interruption."

They retreated together, Shelby shooting me a quick smile when she spotted me just before the boy yanked the door shut again.

"*That* could have been disastrous," the professor muttered, which didn't do anything to settle my nerves. Or those of my classmates, from the look of the faces around me. "They're getting awfully bold."

I didn't see what boldness had to do with it when it'd been a mistaken reading of a schedule. But a shadow flickered across most of the other mages' faces at those words. "Should we do anything?" one of the guys asked.

Crowford cocked his head. "Perhaps it would be good to leave them with a negative impression of this intrusion, if anyone has an appropriate idea?"

"I'll knock one down the stairs," another guy volunteered, sounding way too eager, and leapt right into his casting. My pulse hiccupped for a totally different reason. Any of the Naries could get really hurt if he pulled that off.

There wasn't time to protest. As soon as he used his magic to sense their position, he'd attack. I swiped my hand across my mouth to hide the word I spat out in a whisper with a sharp breath. "Shield."

With every ounce of my concentration, I flung my protective spell through the door, willing it to fill the entire stairwell. It snapped into place an instant before the guy's casting hurtled into it. A jolt ran over my skin as the contrasting magic dissipated against each other.

The guy sat back in his seat with a smirk. Clearly he hadn't been able to tell that his spell had been blocked before it'd reached its target. Better for me.

Crowford gave an approving nod that made my stomach turn. "We offer them so much already," he said in apparent scorn, and switched back into teaching mode.

As he talked further about the manipulation of inanimate objects using persuasion, I stayed tensed in my seat. The entire sequence of events ran through my head on repeat. With each iteration, my heart sank a little more.

When class let out, I hung back so I could leave with Connar, who'd been sitting in the back. He caught my eye with a slight tip of his head in acknowledgment. I walked slowly to give the other students the lead, waiting until they'd disappeared around the bend in the stairs.

"That was weird, right?" I said in a low voice. "The Naries coming in—the way Professor Crowford reacted… I know I haven't been here that long, but it's been a couple terms, and that's the first time I've seen something like that happen."

"I've never seen a mistake like that either," Connar said. "I guess everyone makes mistakes from time to time, and it isn't surprising that Crowford might have forgotten to put the protections in place at the beginning of class…"

His doubtful tone bolstered my conviction. "But it'd be an awfully huge coincidence for him to forget at the exact time a Nary somehow repeatedly misread the number on his schedule, wouldn't it? And… it all happened really fast, but I'd swear he motioned for what's-her-name to drop the cabinet before he had a chance to see who it was. Why would he have assumed the people at the door were Naries?"

Connar considered me. "Are you saying you think that he knew it would happen ahead of time? That he *meant* for it to happen?"

"I don't know. That seems awfully weird too." I rubbed my arms, even though the dry tower air was only pleasantly cool, not cold, compared to the lingering summer heat we'd face outside. "I just don't like it. It felt… like it happened as an excuse to hurt them."

"Yeah," Connar said quietly. He scowled at the steps. "You've got enough to worry about as it is, Rory. I'll keep an eye on him and watch for anything else that seems strange. I don't think that incident had anything to do with you, at least."

Thank God for small mercies? I forced a smile. "True. What are you doing now? Maybe we could—"

We stepped out into the sunlit green outside, and my voice halted at the sight of the woman waiting just beyond the tower. Lillian Ravenguard had been standing with her hands on her hips, her stance poised but not tense with that leonine grace of hers. She moved to meet me the moment I came into view.

"Rory," she said with a warmth I no longer trusted. "I was told you should be out of class soon. Can I talk to you for a few minutes?"

Her gaze passed over Connar's brawny frame with what looked like professional attention, as if she were sizing him up. Even though he could have handled a hell of a lot more fight than I could, I bristled instinctively inside. I didn't want anyone targeting my guys in the plot against me.

"Sure," I said, and shot Connar a quick smile. "I'll see you later."

He nodded with a wary glance toward Lillian. I suspected he wasn't going to stray too far from where he saw us go.

Lillian started to amble toward Ashgrave Hall, and I fell into step beside her. "What's going on?" I asked. "Is there news about the hearing?" A nervous quiver raced through my chest. They hadn't arranged it early despite Declan's efforts, had they?

"It's been set for next Wednesday," Lillian said. "You'll have a little more than your two weeks to prepare… however you intend to prepare." She peered at me sideways. "Are you sure coming back to the school was the wisest idea? I wouldn't tell you what to do, of course, but I promise you my own investigations will cover every aspect of the situation."

She wouldn't tell me what to do, no. She'd only lie to me about the authority she was claiming and what my rights were. I caught myself before I gritted my teeth in annoyance.

"Even if I can't find anything useful myself, I'd rather be living life as normally as possible as long as I can rather than be shut away in that holding room."

She chuckled. "Spoken as your mother would have. Fair enough. That wasn't actually the main reason I wanted to talk to you. Have you experienced anything unusual in the last few days?"

Was that question some new part of their plot to establish my incompetence? "Unusual how?" I asked.

"Just a sensation in or around your body, maybe quite faint, that you didn't recognize and couldn't see a cause for. Maybe something you'd have taken for a spell."

My brow knit as I thought back. "Not that I can remember. Why? Do you think someone might have been casting on me?" Had they and she was confirming that they'd done it subtly enough that I hadn't noticed?

Lillian didn't look comforted by my answer, though. She rubbed her mouth. "You never know, when you've drawn this much attention… Have you seen any other illusions, even if not on the same scale as the ones around the murder, that appeared to be aimed at you?"

"No, nothing like that either." My throat had started to tighten. I stopped before we'd finished passing the hall. "Is there something I need to be worried about—to watch out for?"

I wasn't sure she'd tell me if so, but I got the impression she was actually bothered by this line of questioning. She might have wanted to help speed along my downfall, but only her way. If someone had other designs on me, she could very well decide to protect me from those.

But Lillian shook her head. "I just wanted to be sure. If anything like that does come up, you get in touch with me right away, all right? And I'll keep tracking down our leads to make sure you come out of that hearing with the right verdict."

She turned and patted my arm. Her hand brushed my skin with a faint prick as if from the rough edge of a ring. It faded before I'd even registered it, and then she was hurrying away with one last wave.

I studied my forearm, but the skin appeared unbroken. There wasn't even a pink spot as if it'd been pinched. I might have only imagined the hint of pain after all her talk about odd sensations. Given the circumstances, though, I'd ask one of the guys to check my arm just to be sure she hadn't cast some covert spell on me.

Whatever that sensation had been, I had no doubt at all that she hadn't told me the real reason behind her questions.

CHAPTER TEN

Jude

I'd never enjoyed calling home—really, I'd avoided doing it unless absolutely necessary. Since my mother's announcement about her pregnancy, any contact had gotten even more uncomfortable, on my end at least. So, I might have procrastinated for around a half hour, tidying my room and reviewing my most recent class assignment, before I finally convinced myself to pick up the phone. But I did pick it up.

My body sank into the plump feather pillow I'd braced against my bed's headboard. The fresh breeze slipping through the half-open window carried a pleasant hint of the autumn to come, but every muscle in my body tensed as I placed the call.

It was Mom who answered, of course. If Dad was in the vicinity of a phone, he'd have taken one look at the call display and promptly turned away. I was counting on Mom to get me access.

"Jude!" she said in her typically over-exuberant way. "I didn't expect to hear from you so soon. Is everything all right?"

She'd always acted as if she thought she could make up for Dad's coldness by showering me with appreciation, and that hadn't changed even with the baby on the way. Had she even thought about what the new arrival was going to mean for me? She'd stuck with Dad all this time despite what he'd made her do and how he'd treated her and me afterward… Had she convinced herself that they'd somehow quietly swap heirs without any harm coming to me?

"Nothing's wrong," I said. No need to make her anxious. "School's the same old school. How are you doing?"

I didn't really *want* to hear about my impending sibling, but showing an interest would make her more likely to advocate for me after.

"Oh, you know, this is the easy part, really. The baby's been kicking a little harder the last couple days. She's obviously a strong one."

I had to partly tune out her voice while she rambled a little more about the kid who was essentially my death sentence, but I needed that space anyway to gather my resolve. My mind traveled back to yesterday night with Rory, to the terrifying but exhilarating release of telling the heir of Bloodstone how much she meant to me.

Our interlude in the piano room had been amazing in so many ways. The truth was, though, that the moment I thought back to with the most satisfaction was simply holding her in my arms and feeling her relax in my embrace. To know that she trusted me to support her, that I'd somehow *earned* that trust… No sexual bliss could top that.

I could do this for her. Even if it made me feel sick to my stomach; even if it was going to take every ounce of my self-control. She needed me to fight for her in every way I could. I might have let down an awful lot of people in my life, but she wasn't going to be one of them.

When Mom's chatter fell into a lull, I drew in a breath, my free hand clenching around the bedspread.

"Could you get Dad? There's something I wanted to ask him about."

The question startled Mom into a few seconds of silence. I was pretty sure I'd never asked to speak to my father in all the years I'd boarded at the university. "Yes," she said, wrenching herself out of her shock. "Yes, of course, I'll— I'm sure he'll have a moment. Let me go get him."

She hadn't been able to hide the uneasiness in her voice. She knew as well as I did that it didn't matter how many "moments" Dad had, he wouldn't want to give any of them to me. I was counting on her being tenacious enough—and him being softened a little by the heir on the way—to get him on the line.

The dead air while I waited stretched across one minute and then another. I shifted restlessly on the bed. I didn't have much of a backup plan if he refused to talk to me at all.

There was an abrupt rustling as the phone on the other end was lifted. Dad's voice carried to my ear, distant and brisk. "Your mother said you wanted to speak to me."

With less than ten words, he could make me feel like I was barely worth the dust on his shoe. I closed my eyes and reminded myself of why I was doing this. Of the caramel sweet smell of Rory's hair and the way she smiled at me.

To her, I was someone who mattered.

"Yes," I said in my most pleasant tone. "I mean, we haven't really talked since…" *Since ever.* "…since all the plans for the new baby started. How was your tennis match yesterday?" I might not have a remotely close relationship with my father, but I still listened well enough to know what he was up to.

"Fine. I'm assuming there's something else."

Okay, so making friendly conversation wasn't going to get me anywhere. I hadn't figured it would, but it'd been worth a shot. Down to business then.

I sat up straighter, as if I could convey my posture over the phone. "Yes. But it's not for me. You know I handle my own affairs just fine." As he preferred. "It's about Rory Bloodstone."

"What about the Bloodstone scion?" Dad asked, sounding more attentive all of a sudden. That seemed like a good sign.

I launched into my pitch. "Obviously you know about the accusations she's facing. I've gathered since she's been released temporarily to the school that there are complications with proving her innocence. From what I've seen of her, there's no way she could be responsible for the attack, but she doesn't have many resources on her own. If one or more of the barons spoke up on her behalf, I'd imagine—"

Dad cut me off, twice as cold as before. "If she's to be baron, she needs to learn to fend for herself too."

My throat tightened. "She's only known fearmancers *exist* for a few months. Her entire family is gone. The barons have gone to bat for each other before—it's hardly unprecedented. Wouldn't it be better for all of you to have her unencumbered by—"

"What makes you so concerned about her future?"

I'd been prepared for a question along that line, but my back stiffened anyway. If he thought I was asking for personal rather than professional reasons, he'd never want to agree.

"I'm concerned about the barony," I said. "Shouldn't I be? It's my future too. Strong, united leadership is what keeps our society in line."

Either Dad didn't buy that explanation or he didn't care what my reasons were—it only mattered that I was the one asking. "If Bloodstone has the strength to be part of that unity, this hearing will determine that," he said firmly. "No scion or baron should need to send others begging on their behalf."

"I'm not— She didn't—" I started, but the phone hung up with a definitive click.

My fingers squeezed around my own phone. I forced myself to lower it without hurling it across the room in frustration, glaring at the wardrobe across from me the way I should have been glaring at my father.

The barons had the perfect opportunity to solidify Rory's role in their midst. If they stood up for her now, she'd see being part of the pentacle had some benefits, the way she'd come to trust me after I'd shown I'd be there for her. How the hell did they expect to accomplish anything if they never found a way to accept her into the fold?

But I'd heard it in Dad's voice. He cared more about thwarting my request than about what it would mean for his career. Fuck, I might even have made him *less* inclined to help Rory by asking.

Even with a real heir on the way, even when he was the one who'd created our family situation in the first place, he hated me that much.

I dropped my head into my hands and pressed my palms to my

forehead. Why did I even let myself care what he thought? I knew who he was and what he'd done. I'd tried my best… and this was where it got me.

Why was I waiting around for him to sever me from his life when I could decide what I did with mine all on my own?

A tenuous but hopeful sense of resolve rose up inside me. I didn't have a solution to any of the larger problems Rory and I were facing, but I could at least pull myself completely out from under Dad's thumb for as long as I had until he upped the ante.

I got off the bed, glanced out the window, and was diverted by a scene that appeared to be in the process of unfolding. A couple of Naries were just heading out of view in the direction of Rory's clubhouse… and a few of my fellow fearmancer students were slinking along a careful distance behind. I didn't like the look of that at all.

When I strode out of the building, the mages I'd seen were still lurking several feet away from the clubhouse. Connar and I had checked the wards Rory had buried beneath the place when we'd returned to school, so I knew their magic had been holding steady, but they were still small in the grand scheme of things. A concentrated assault could break them.

I sauntered over to the other students—seniors, but newly promoted ones, the guy on the right sporting straggles of hair he must be attempting to call a moustache. I didn't think any of them had been here for the summer session.

"Hey," I said in a casual voice as I joined them. Their murmured conversation fell silent as they all turned wary but respectful gazes on me. I might not know them well, but they knew who I was. Everyone recognized the scions.

I nodded toward the clubhouse. "You know that was Rory Bloodstone's summer project, don't you? If you mess with it… you're messing with her. Maybe not the wisest idea, just as a tip."

I didn't like the fact that my warning would have twice as much impact given the crime Rory had recently been accused of, but the end result was worth it. The guys paled, mumbled acknowledgment, and backed away with enough wide-eyed worry to convince me they wouldn't be striking at the Naries' new safe spot any time soon.

Footsteps hissed through the grass behind me. I looked around to see Sinclair coming over. She glanced after the retreating guys and gave me a tight smile.

"Still fighting her battles for her, huh?" She flicked her sleek black bob back from her shoulder. "You've made yourself into a real knight in shining armor. It's kind of pathetic."

Did she really think I'd ever cared what *she* thought of me? We'd barely talked outside of our occasional tumbles into bed. At most we'd been acquaintances with benefits, and since I'd set my sights on Rory, even that small connection had ended.

"You're entitled to your opinion," I said nonchalantly. "In my role as knight, I should probably let you know that you and Victory and the rest had better keep your distance if you want to keep *any* favor with the pentacle."

She let out a huff. "You don't want to worry about that. Malcolm made it very clear to Victory that he expected her to back off, and you know what she's like about him. She still thinks she's going to marry him someday." Her tone made it clear how ridiculous she found that idea.

I hadn't known that Malcolm had not only reconsidered his approach to Rory but been publicly enforcing a cease-fire too. With a jab of uneasiness, my mind tripped back to the claim he'd tried to stake on the Bloodstone scion not long after she'd arrived here. Even when he'd been determined to tear her down, he'd wanted first dibs on picking up the pieces and winning her heart. He'd torn into me when I'd made my intentions to pursue her clear.

Rory had only proven herself more spectacular since then. What were the chances he didn't still want her? Ha. The question was more… what were the chances she'd want him, if he made his amends thoroughly enough? She'd forgiven *me*, after all.

How much room would be left for me if he made a move? As an actual fucking scion, with all the strength and clout that came with that, he had a hell of a lot more to offer than I did. And I didn't think he'd like the idea of sharing.

I shook those worries away. Rory would do what made her happiest, and that was the way it should be. I couldn't dwell on uncomfortable hypotheticals.

Especially when I had a very definite malicious force right here in front of me.

I studied Sinclair. "And you'd never go behind Victory's back?"

"No," she said tartly. "I wouldn't. I happen to know what loyalty is."

Was that supposed to be a jab at *me*? I raised my eyebrows as I crossed my arms over my chest. "I didn't make you any promises I didn't mean, Sinclair. I didn't make you any promises at all. We had a little fun—and you were having plenty of fun with other guys at the same time—and now that's done. I never owed you more than that."

She sniffed. "I guess I just expected that if you ditched me, my replacement would meet a higher standard."

A flicker of anger shot through me at the implication that Rory was somehow less than the girl who'd made the remark—or that what I had with her was only a replacement for the scrap of a relationship before. I held it in check with a sharp smile of my own.

"All that proves is you don't know very much at all, Sinclair. I'm so glad we could have this chat."

I set off for the hall that bore my father's last name without a backward glance. If Sinclair wanted to stew in bitterness, let her, as long as she left Rory alone.

It'd been months since I'd last paid a visit to the professor who was assigned as my mentor. Regular meetings were only scheduled during a student's first year, and after that you talked only as either party deemed necessary. I hadn't made much use of that opportunity in general. It was no wonder that surprise was the first reaction that flashed across Professor Burnbuck's face when he saw me at his office door.

The senior Illusion professor recovered quickly. "Mr. Killbrook," he said, motioning me in. "To what do I owe the unexpected pleasure?" Burnbuck could give all due deference without being afraid to work in a subtle criticism about my neglect of this resource. That was one of the reasons I liked him, as much as I liked any of the staff.

I dropped into the seat in front of his desk and folded my hands in my lap. "One time you mentioned a friend of yours who does independent work with her illusion magic. I was hoping you could tell me more about that."

Burnbuck gave me a curious look. "Any particular reason why?"

I shrugged and grinned at him. "Let's just say I was thinking it might be good to expand my horizons."

And if those horizons didn't involve Baron Killbrook being anywhere in sight, so much the better.

CHAPTER ELEVEN

Rory

I settled in on the scion lounge sofa, my legs stretched across the pliant cushions and the welcome silence of the basement room wrapping around me, and for the first time I felt like the space could really be mine. I'd avoided coming down here for most of my time at Blood U because it'd been too much Malcolm's domain. Too much a reminder of the other scions' initial hostility.

But most of that hostility had transformed into anything but animosity by now, and even Malcolm appeared to have suspended his campaign against me. There wasn't any better place on campus to meet up with other scions in private. And, hell, I *was* a scion too. I had every right to use the lounge.

I got to enjoy that comfortable sense of confidence for about two minutes. Then Malcolm walked into the room.

I tensed automatically. He blinked as if making sure he was seeing right but then strolled on past me without any further indication that he thought it was strange I was down here. I watched him make his way to the bar cabinet, tucking my feet closer to me so I could easily jump up if I felt the need to escape.

"What are you up to down here?" he asked in a mild tone. Ice from the little freezer next to the cabinet rattled into his glass, followed by a hiss of poured alcohol.

"I'm supposed to be meeting Declan," I said. "He wasn't sure exactly when he'd get back."

"Am I allowed to ask what you're meeting him about?"

Declan had said he'd have some reports on the joymancers for me —hard copies, like before, so there wouldn't be any electronic trail suggesting I'd had to work to skew my testimony. Knowing how Malcolm felt about the magical opposition, I wasn't inclined to find out what he'd think of my current strategy. For all I knew, he'd tip off his dad.

"It isn't any of your business," I said.

He turned with the glass in his hand and took a sip of the amber liquid. "Fine. You don't have to sit there all tense like I'm going to spring an attack. I told you, I don't want to fight anymore—and I remember very well what you said you'd do if I so much as touched you again." He gave me a wry smile. "But I'm also not going to leave just because you're here."

I guessed that was fair. And I cringed a little remembering my threat to break every bone in his hands. We'd *both* gotten carried away that day in the boathouse, and with everything that had happened after, I didn't really believe he'd intended to force me into anything I didn't want.

It was kind of hard to hold the intensity of that moment against him when half of the reason his presence unnerved me was how much I'd enjoyed… well, having him against me, for the brief time before logic and panic had set in.

I let myself sink into the back of the sofa, but I kept my legs bent close. "I'm not asking you to leave, but I think I'm justified in a certain amount of caution, no matter how many white flags you're waving. You've put me through a lot more than just that moment by the lake. I hope you don't think my memory's that short."

He shrugged and, with a casual ease that made my skin itch, sat down at the other end of the sofa. It was a three seater, so a few feet of empty space remained between us, but I'd have preferred a few dozen.

"You came into the university guns blazing, insulting me and everything I care about," he said. "I can admit that I should have realized sooner that you didn't understand what you were getting into. Like I said before, we can hash out what I should be apologizing for when everything's simmered down. But I'm *not* going to apologize for defending myself, the scions, or fearmancer society in general when it seemed necessary. Just so we're clear."

Damn it. With every word he said, I wanted more and more to smack the cool self-assurance out of him, but at the same time he made it sound so fucking *reasonable.* As if he hadn't already proven himself to be an asshole before I'd said a single word to him.

"You can see it however you want," I said. "But I'll just point out that the first time I ever insulted you, it was after *you* had just mocked the people who raised me—my parents, who I'd watched murdered in front of me that morning. I wasn't exactly in the clearest state of mind, and I don't see why your insults get a pass while mine were some horrible offense."

Malcolm's expression darkened for a second. He turned his gaze to his glass. "So, you're still calling the joymancers who stole you your 'parents'."

"They *were* my parents." I pushed myself straighter, keeping my eyes trained on him. "Do you still think they kept me in a cage and tortured me or something like that? The worst thing they did to me was suppress my magic and not tell me that I had it. Otherwise, as far as I can tell, they did a hell of a lot better by me than the parents of most people around here. They took care of me like I was their own kid, they comforted me when I was sad, they celebrated everything I accomplished, they tried their best to make sure I was happy and safe. I never, for one second, doubted that they loved me and wanted me to have the best life they could give me."

Malcolm's head had come back up. He stared at me for a long moment, apparently lost for words. Then he made a pained grimace and took a bigger gulp of his drink. "Well, no, I wouldn't have expected that's how they'd have treated you."

Because his own parents didn't treat him anywhere near that well? I'd been horrified by Connar's story of how his parents had compelled him and his brother into a near death match to decide who'd inherit the barony, and he'd indicated that he thought Malcolm had it even worse. I'd only met Malcolm's dad once and briefly, but he'd struck me as brutal in that short time.

If it was normal for fearmancer parents to be harsh on their kids—whatever excuses they gave about preparing them for the wider world—why would any of them imagine their enemies would treat a fearmancer with more kindness rather than less?

I didn't want to delve into the fraught relationship Malcolm might have with his parents. Maybe he could shed some light on the less personal dynamics I was still grappling with, though.

"My parents were the only joymancers I knew," I said tentatively. "They always talked positively about the magic they worked and the mages they worked with, but I never met any of the others—not while I was aware of it." Representatives from the Conclave might have observed me from afar surreptitiously. "So while I can speak up for the two of them, it's true that I don't really know their community all that well. Why do you hate them so much? Have joymancers actually *done* anything to you, or is it—"

Malcolm interrupted with a rough chuckle. "Have they done anything? Rory, they killed your fucking parents—your real parents."

My stomach twisted at the memory of the burnt bodies in the photograph. "We don't know exactly what went down that day. Maybe my parents were planning to do something harmful and that was the only way the joymancers could stop them. It's not like the barons always tell everyone else what their real plans are."

"I don't know whether they were doing more than they'd told people they were. But it wasn't just them. Declan's mom was there, and she wouldn't have been scheming with your parents. From what I've heard, the other barons saw her as a pain in the neck, always arguing against any harsher policy they were considering. And *you* were there. Maybe our ideas on parenting are different from joymancer ones, but I can tell you there's no way in hell a baron would bring her only heir into a remotely dangerous situation at two years old."

I thought of the video Lillian had shared with me of my birth mother cuddling my infant self, of the gold-encased baby shoe I'd found in the Bloodstone mansion's storage room. No, I didn't think the former Baron Bloodstone had seen me as expendable.

"My mother must have been involved in other questionable plans before," I said. "The joymancers might have gotten the wrong idea, but not out of nowhere."

"They still didn't have to kill them. They didn't have to kill Declan's mom. How the hell do you think he feels every time you sing their praises, by the way? And they didn't have to drag you away and raise you on lies. No matter how nice the people who raised you were, they stole your power and your heritage from you. That's sick."

I didn't totally disagree—and the comment about Declan made me wince. "Is there anything else?" I had to ask. "In your whole lifetime, is that the only way the joymancers have attacked fearmancers?"

Malcolm snorted. "Are you kidding me? No matter what we do, even the mages as powerful as the barons have to take all kinds of precautions to make sure the joymancers don't interfere. They cost my dad a major business deal just last year. There've been skirmishes—I'd swear the blacksuits spend at least as much time protecting all of us from joymancers as they do policing within the community. The 'Conclave' always has people skulking around up here, trying to figure out what we're doing and messing it up any way they can, even when it's totally legitimate work."

"Well, what have the fearmancers been doing to them at the same time?"

"Nothing," Malcolm shot back. "That's the one principle all the barons have agreed on for as long as I can remember. We don't engage. We stick to our territory up here and leave them to do whatever they want off at the other end of the country. If they left us alone, there'd be no fighting at all."

I wasn't sure I totally believed that. There'd been other things Malcolm hadn't known about his father's activities. But… I couldn't think of any good reason to keep it *secret* if the fearmancers launched a counter-attack. It sounded like pretty much every mage around here would have cheered on an assault.

"They've decided everything we do is evil, and that any means are acceptable when it comes to screwing with us," Malcolm went on.

"You have no idea… My grandfather, the baron before my father, he's got a huge scar where his eye should be." He drew his finger from his brow down to his cheek. "Joymancers caught him when he was coming out of a consult with his *accountant.* The fact that we exist at all is a crime to them. So, who are the really bloodthirsty ones?"

I was saved from having to try to answer that question by the soft squeak of the door's hinges. Declan stepped into the lounge and paused at the sight of us in what must have been an obviously tense conversation. He caught my eye with a questioning look as if to ask if I needed help.

Malcolm shoved himself off the sofa, setting his glass with its remains of ice on the coffee table. "Don't worry, no one's been eviscerated. A little faith would be nice."

"I didn't say anything," Declan said calmly.

"Doesn't take any insight to read that face sometimes." Malcolm gave him a light clap on the shoulder as he passed the Ashgrave scion, with no sign of being actually offended. "I'll leave you to your 'meeting'."

As soon as Malcolm was gone, Declan turned to me. "Was he hassling you?"

I shook my head. "No. He was actually… okay for once. I was just asking him what he knows about joymancers."

"Ah. I'm sure he had plenty to say about that." Declan drew out a thick envelope from his shoulder bag. "I've got plenty of official material for you to look through. Take it slow. There's some stuff in there that's pretty… upsetting."

So considerate of my feelings even when it came to the people who'd murdered his mom. I swallowed hard as I stood up to take the envelope. Malcolm had made a good point on that subject. In his hostility against my parents' people, he hadn't just been defending fearmancer ideals but his closest friends as well. Maybe I'd been a little callous when it came to the Ashgrave scion's past.

"I hope you know—no matter what else I think about joymancers, I hate what they did to your mother," I said. "I'm not absolving them of that. It was awful."

Declan's mouth twitched with a hint of pain. "I know, Rory. And

I'd never say every one of them is a horrible person. Your parents obviously raised you well. I just think… it's good for you to understand exactly where you came from."

"Yeah." I looked down at the envelope, its weight ominous in my hand. "I guess I'd better get on with that."

When I'd retreated to my bedroom, though, I didn't open the envelope right away. I lay down on the bed and let my thoughts stew about the information I'd already gotten from Malcolm.

Deborah's furry body scurried along my arm, coming to a stop by my shoulder. *Hard day, sweetheart?*

"You could say that." I frowned at the ceiling, debating even asking the question. But if anyone could give me an answer unbiased by fearmancer principles, it'd be her. "Deborah… The joymancers do come up here to the northeast and try to meddle with fearmancer business quite a bit, don't they?"

Well, I suppose a few take up that duty at any given time. It's not something the Conclave talks about widely. But it's the only way we can stay abreast of what they're planning and intervene as necessary.

As necessary. How did the Conclave define that? Deborah had admitted to me that they'd wanted to take down this school for as long as she could remember… but did they even *know* how the place worked if they'd never been able to observe it, or were they simply operating under that principle that all fearmancer things should be shut down?

"What about the other way around?" I said slowly. "I mean… Did the fearmancers ever come to California or wherever to attack the joymancer community down there? Other than when they found out where I was and came for me? I don't remember my parents ever seeming nervous, like they'd heard about some altercation and were worried my real people might be coming for me."

Deborah made a dismissive noise in my head. *The fearmancers know better than to tackle us on our home ground. Perhaps the Conclave became over-confident because of that, and that's how they ended up finding you. The attack on your home is the only breach of our security I know of.*

She sounded proud of that fact. Even though, from what Malcolm had just told me, the success wasn't because the joymancers were so good at protecting their own… It was because the fearmancers hadn't *tried* to break down those defenses until they'd had an unavoidable reason to.

I rubbed my forehead. I didn't even know if I objected to people interfering with the fearmancers in general. A lot of them did do a lot of awful things. But… how did killing the ones who actually pushed for moderation, like Declan's mom, or throwing off legitimate business deals do anything other than stir up more resentment?

What if my parents hadn't been typical joymancers? What if their attitudes of compassion and acceptance had made them as much outliers in their community as Declan's family was in his?

CHAPTER TWELVE

Rory

With no one but the four of us in it, the main gymnasium felt twice as big as usual. Our voices bounced off the high ceiling as we walked over the colored lines marked on the wooden floor.

"I checked with all my usual professors," I said. "They'll all confirm that I haven't been using my own casting words with my spells." I'd half expected my current mentor, Professor Viceport, to refuse. She'd acted chilly toward me since I'd started at Blood U for no reason I'd been able to determine. But she'd actually been the most emphatic in her agreement. Maybe she was finally getting over her grudge now that she'd talked with me more and seen my skills develop over the summer.

"That's something." Declan stopped where the platform had been set up on the day of the summer project announcement and turned on his heel. "You'd have had the best view of the room when you were up here getting your certificate. See if you can settle right into that memory—watch for anyone you didn't recognize, especially someone who couldn't have been a student."

I let my mind slip back to that moment, my senses detaching from the present the way Declan had coached me. It wasn't exactly a spell, but the technique was related to Insight—a way of sharpening one's own mental impressions.

"I recognized all the teachers," I said, my voice sounding oddly detached as I focused on the memory. "And all the students there looked familiar. I don't remember seeing anyone else. I was looking pretty carefully too, because I was wondering where Imogen was."

"I didn't see anyone unexpected either," Connar put in from where he stood at my other side. "I was keeping a close eye out in case anyone tried to interrupt Rory's moment. If there was someone who didn't belong, I think I'd have noticed."

Declan sighed. "It was a long shot. It wouldn't have been smart for the culprit to make an appearance here."

We'd already tried the same trick with my memories outside and by Ashgrave Hall, on the theory that someone might have been standing watch to alert the murderer of my impending arrival. But if that'd been the case, they'd kept themselves well out of view.

Jude caught my attention with a trailing of his fingers halfway down my back. "You're still owed a prize, aren't you, Ice Queen? Unless you claimed it without telling us about it."

"No." I let out a raw laugh. "I almost forgot." For winning the summer project contest, I had the right to pick any object in my possession and bring it to the professor of my choice to ask for them to use their expertise to imbue it with a spell. I'd been caught up in the murder before I'd had much time to think about my options. "I don't suppose there are any innocence-detecting spells I could ask for?"

"Wouldn't that make life easier?" Declan gave me a crooked smile. "I'd already been considering whether your prize might come in handy, but I can't think of any spell you could request that'd make a difference to your hearing. There are ways of identifying illusions, for example, but they only work in the moment, not from memory."

"Save it for when you're sure of how it can help you the most," Connar suggested.

Lord knew there'd probably be some new problem I could use help with soon enough.

"Do you know who the judge will be now that the hearing date is set?" Jude asked Declan as we meandered back toward the entrance. "Anyone we could find some way to sway toward more sympathy?"

Declan shot Jude a look. "I don't think we want to get Rory off the hook through bribery or threats. Something like that could come back to haunt her so easily."

"I know, I know. I'm just tossing ideas around." Jude grimaced. He paused for a few seconds and then met my eyes. "I tried to convince my dad to step up on your behalf—for the good of the pentacle and all—but he was being his usual asshole self and didn't want to hear any ideas coming from *me*."

My heart skipped a beat. He'd gone to his dad asking for support for me—his dad who was part of the conspiracy to see me sanctioned in the first place?

But Jude didn't know that. Because I'd balked at telling him—my chest clenched up at the idea even now. I wasn't even sure why anymore. It wasn't as if he or Connar could have much worse opinions of their parents than they already held. Did I really not trust them with the information, after everything?

I had to trust them. I couldn't let them keep fighting for me without knowing exactly what—and who—we were up against.

"It wasn't because of you," I said. "I—There's something we really should talk about." My gaze found Declan's. His jaw had set, knowing what I was about to do and maybe dreading it, but not objecting. "Not here in the gym, though." Was even the scion lounge secure enough to have this conversation?

"I know a good place," Declan said. "Somewhere no one would expect students to bother with."

He led us down the hall and around the corner toward the change rooms that led to the pool. A faint chlorine scent laced the air. He murmured a quick spell to open a maintenance door halfway down the hall, and the smell thickened as we descended a set of stairs into a dim room full of pipes and valves and a mechanical hum. Declan spoke another few words that I assumed were intended to guarantee our privacy and nodded to the space.

"One of the benefits of having studied the school blueprints, among many other things."

Jude touched one of the larger pipes gingerly to make sure it wasn't hot and then propped his shoulders against it, crossing his arms loosely over his chest. "What's all the secrecy about?" His tone stayed light, but a worried crease had formed on his forehead. No doubt it hadn't been lost on him that I'd mainly reacted to his comment about his dad.

I looked down at my hands and then at Jude and Connar. The Stormhurst scion had stayed near the bottom of the steps as if to guard the door.

"I wasn't sure how to tell you this, and I wasn't sure it was even a good idea, so… maybe I let it go longer than I should have." I swallowed thickly. "You know that my first mentor, Professor Banefield, died. I was there when it happened. It was a spell that'd been cast on him—first to make him sick when he tried to warn me about people who were out to hurt me, and then to make *him* attack me when I managed to dispel the first part. He killed himself because it was the only way he could stop the magical compulsion."

Jude's eyes flashed. "It must be the same people who set you up to take the fall for Imogen's murder. Fucking bastards."

"That's what I'm assuming," I said quietly. "And that's the part I haven't known how to bring up with you. Banefield was able to tell me who'd cast the spell on him before he died. He said it was the older barons. And some people called the reapers, who I guess are working with them."

All other emotion vanished from both guys' faces in the wake of stunned shock. Connar recovered first, the muscles in his arms flexing as fury radiated through his voice. "You're saying our parents are behind all this—that they tried to have you *killed*—"

"I don't think they want me dead," I interrupted. "Not that it makes things much better, but they might have even bigger problems if the Bloodstone line passes to someone they can't predict. Banefield said they wanted him to destroy my magic. I guess… to hurt me enough so I couldn't really cast anymore, like what happened with your brother."

Connar winced at the comparison, but his anger didn't fade. "Competition within a family in the pentacle is accepted. Barons trying to sabotage an heir to another family on that level, especially conspiring together, is the worst kind of treason. If they were exposed…"

"There's nothing to expose at this point," Declan said as the other guy trailed off. "I've been watching for the slightest hint, but the barons are keeping their cards close even when they're talking with me. It's no wonder they haven't let anything slip to either of you."

Jude's hands were clenching and opening at his sides. "I thought I knew just how low he'd stoop. Fucking hell. He doesn't deserve the goddamn barony."

"If it helps at all, I don't think your mother has been part of the plots," I said. "Banefield was able to leave some papers for me, including a list of people I'm assuming are these 'reapers'… and the barons. Both of Malcolm's parents are on there, and both of yours." I tipped my head to Connar, and then turned back to Jude. "But only your dad. Whatever meetings they were having to plan out this stuff, he never saw her getting involved."

"She wouldn't stand up to him if she found out, though. She's never been able to argue with him." Jude kicked at the floor. His expression stiffened. "You don't think—will it have made things worse that I talked to him about you?"

"You didn't mention any of the ideas we've talked about for proving my innocence, like the casting word, did you?"

He shook his head vehemently. "Even without knowing he's a full-out traitor, I wouldn't have trusted him with that."

"Then I think it should be fine. For me." My heart squeezed as I gazed back at him. "If he thinks you're on my side, I'm not sure what that'll mean for you—or you, Connar."

Connar's face was grimmer than I'd ever seen it before. "If my parents want to take me to task for standing by a fellow scion, they can try. I don't think they'll enjoy the results."

"I doubt my father believes I'd be able to accomplish much anyway," Jude said with a flippancy I could tell was forced. "He may use it as an excuse to turn on me later—but if he didn't have that one, he'd find something else. Don't worry about that when you're the one on the chopping block."

I choked up for a second before I managed to speak. "I just don't want anyone else getting hurt because of me."

"Hey." Connar stepped forward and set his hand on my waist, looking down at me intently. "It's never been because of *you.* It's because they're power-hungry jackasses."

It was hard to shift the blame that easily when I'd had to watch blood spill from so many people I cared about. I closed my eyes and dragged in a breath. "Whatever it is, both of you should be careful how you talk to them about the case and about me… Until we have real evidence that they're scheming against me, they have so much more power than we do." And even if we got that evidence, would the blacksuits really act against three of their rulers? I had my doubts.

Connar made a disgruntled sound, and Jude grasped my hand to give it a squeeze. "I'm not sure I'll be speaking to my father ever again," he said. "But I'm still here for *you*, whatever you need."

Declan exhaled slowly. "Right now you need to be getting to our Insight seminar, Jude." When the other guy started to protest, the Ashgrave scion held up his hand. "If they can make a case for Rory being a disruptive influence when it comes to our studies, do you really think they won't make use of that?"

Jude muttered a stream of scathing words to himself, but he followed Declan in tramping up the stairs. Connar and I trailed behind them, out of the Stormhurst Building and along the path to the main triangle of the tower and the two halls. He took my hand, running his thumb over my knuckles in a gentle caress.

It was getting late in the afternoon, though the late summer sun still shone brightly, and the green was bustling with students heading to their last class of the day or chatting with friends after just having gotten out. Walking among them, apprehension prickled over my skin. I shifted my hand away from Connar's instinctively.

Jude had declared his affections in public before, but Connar hadn't made any romantic gestures quite that overt. If word got back to his parents that he'd not only defended me to Malcolm but was actively intimately involved with me…

Connar caught my hand before it'd strayed more than an inch

from his. He glanced at me and tugged me around to face him when he saw my expression.

"Listen," he said, leaning close. "I've spent too much of my life letting other people decide what I should be doing, what I should care about… And that's led me to making the worst decisions of my life. I'm with you, no matter what my parents will think about it. That's *my* decision. Let me have it."

I choked up all over again. "Of course," I said.

He touched my cheek and closed the last short distance to kiss me, there in the middle of the green with at least a dozen spectators. My pulse thumped, but it was at least as much giddy as it was nervous. I kissed him back hard. If he wanted to show everyone what I meant to him, let them see that I returned those feelings without reservation.

He drew back just a smidge, his nose bumping mine, and gave me a smile that was almost shy. "I told you ages ago that I wanted to take you out someday. It's really taken me too long to follow up on that idea. Can I treat you to dinner in town?"

I had to smile back. "Are you asking me on a date, Mr. Stormhurst?"

"If you can't tell, then I'm obviously doing a bad job of it."

A laugh spilled out of me, a little bittersweet because of the circumstances but happy all the same. "Not at all. I think that's just what I need right now."

I needed the reminder that people could change. That no matter how awful a situation seemed, it could still turn around into something wonderful. Even if I couldn't see just yet how either of those facts would apply to the murder charge hanging over me.

CHAPTER THIRTEEN

Connar

Heading up to the dorms after our date, Rory and I had to part ways in the Ashgrave Hall stairwell at my floor. I wasn't ready to let the evening end just yet. I guided her past the door and nudged her up against the wall as I kissed her.

Rory smiled against my mouth with a pleased hum. The sweet smell of her and her soft form against mine returned me to the backseat of my car less than an hour ago, when her breath had broken as she'd arched beneath me.

A twinge of longing to do that all over again shot straight to my groin. I willed my desire to stay in check. I had no problem being open about my feelings for this girl, but getting caught in the act in the dorm stairwell wasn't a good look on anyone.

At least I'd taken her away from all the stress that had been dogging her for a little while. I'd given her a little slice of normality in the middle of the chaos. That was what mattered more than anything.

I kissed her again, catching a hint of the red wine we'd had with dinner still lingering in her mouth, and then forced myself to draw back. Rory beamed up at me, even more gorgeous than usual with her eyes bright and her cheeks flushed. I couldn't resist leaning in to claim her mouth just once more.

"I'll see you tomorrow," she said like a promise as she headed for the stairs up to her own floor.

"As much as I can," I replied. I watched her disappear up the steps before pushing past the door to the hallway outside my dorm.

The common room light was on, but none of my dormmates were around. The first week back at school, it wasn't unusual for most seniors to stay out late enjoying the freedom of being away from home before the workload started to pile up. On the other hand, a droning snore carrying from one of the bedrooms told me at least one of the guys had already crashed for the night.

I ambled over to my corner room, said a few quick words to disable the security spells I had in place, and stepped inside.

I froze on the threshold with my hand halfway to the light switch. The moonlight seeping past the window silhouetted two figures standing by my desk. Figures familiar enough that I knew them before I flicked the light on, but that didn't stop my stomach from sinking.

"Hello, Connar," my mother said in a low, blunt voice. "Let's take a walk."

When I'd talked to Rory about my parents this afternoon, I'd dismissed them completely. It was a lot harder to summon that certainty facing them just a few feet away.

These two people had witnessed me at my absolute worst. They'd *pushed* me to my worst… and I wasn't completely sure they couldn't do it again. Baron Stormhurst was used to getting things her way, regardless of who fell beneath her feet.

Whatever they wanted to say to me, I at least agreed with them that it was better to do it away from here. I didn't need my dormmates hearing the way they'd speak to me.

"Sure," I said, keeping my cool as much as I could. With a burst of confidence fueled by my growing sense of conviction, I added, "You could have just called."

"I felt this discussion would be best had face to face."

They followed me out of the building, my mother stalking after me and my father striding along with heavier steps. Even though he was built like I was and she was much thinner, her wiry frame exuded even more power than his bulky body. I might be able to look down at her from a few inches, but she hadn't lost the ability to make me feel small with one cutting glance.

When we'd left Ashgrave Hall, my mother took the lead without hesitation, knowing I'd come along. She veered across the east field, considering the Nary clubhouse with narrowed eyes, and marched straight into the thicker darkness within the forest. I followed her more by sound than sight as the cool night breeze shivered past us. It wasn't that cold, but goosebumps rose on my bare forearms.

It didn't take long to figure out where she was going. She stopped and motioned my father and me past her, and then activated the key ward that protected the Shifting Grounds. Physicality had been her primary strength too, the talent running in the family as magical skills so often did. I'd never seen her shift forms, but no doubt she'd made plenty of use of the private clearing when she'd been a student here some thirty years ago.

No one except one of the two Physicality professors could disable that ward once activated. We'd have no witnesses for this conversation.

Dread swelled in my gut as we walked the rest of the way to the clearing. The moon was only half full, but it cast enough light across the cleared circle of grass for me to see my mother's expression when she spun on me. Her sinewy features were tensed.

"I hear you've taken up with the Bloodstone scion," she said. "Some sort of romance? Really, Connar?"

The things Rory had revealed to me about my parents tickled through my mind, making my jaw tighten. My gaze slid away from my mother for a second, taking in the clearing.

Not that long ago, I'd been here with Rory. I'd let her watch me shift, trusted her not to be unnerved by my dragon form. And she hadn't been. She'd shown so much faith in me, then and since… I had to be worthy of it.

I met my mother's eyes again. "Is there any particular reason I shouldn't get involved with her? It's not as if I'm going to let it interfere with my duties as scion."

"Oh, no? So you haven't forgotten that you can't have her if you still want to be baron."

"Of course not." That fact weighed on me every time I looked at Rory.

"The girl is a threat to the stability of the pentacle and your mother's work there," my father said darkly. "You know we want to see her beaten down, not *wooed*."

"I thought you were taking care of that aspect yourselves now."

That tossed-out comment might have been too careless. My mother's gaze sharpened. "What exactly do you mean by that?"

If she knew that Rory had found out about the barons' involvement, they'd pull out all the stops to utterly crush her before the hearing even happened. My pulse hiccupped.

"I understand the barons are all refusing to support her in challenging the charges against her," I said, fumbling for an answer she'd believe. "Normally you'd stand by a fellow baron."

"She's not baron yet." My mother sucked in a sharp breath. "Has she been speaking against the rest of the pentacle, then?"

Shit. "No," I said quickly. "Jude mentioned that his father said something along those lines." And hopefully I hadn't just landed my friend in a heap of trouble too. I might have the physical strength and the magical power to more than hold my own among my peers, but I'd never been known for quick wits. I couldn't match my mother in verbal sparring. How the hell could I get through this confrontation without turning it into a catastrophe?

The answer came to me in a rare flash of brilliance—so brilliant that I hesitated as I turned the idea over in my head to make sure I wasn't tricking myself. But no, that should work to get my parents off my back *and* protect Rory from their prodding. And the strategy was simple enough that it only required one lie.

I adjusted my stance, cocking my head to one side. "I thought you'd be happy about the progress I've made. I'm in the perfect position, don't you think?"

My mother raised her eyebrows. "The perfect position for what?"

"To find out what Rory *is* thinking about, how she plans to fight the charges—what she decides to do afterward. To undermine the decisions that would put her in a better position to oppose you. She trusts me now. She'll listen to me. I can get a lot more mileage out of that than bullying her."

A slow, cruel smile crept across my mother's face. I had to restrain a shudder at the sight of it. She glanced at my father. "Look at our heir, coming into his own. I was starting to think I wouldn't see the day."

The implied criticism in those words would have stung more if I'd actually wanted to live up to their example. With everything I knew about them, after everything they'd put me through, I was happy to be charting my own path.

I would have felt satisfied that the gambit had worked so well if my mother hadn't turned to me a moment later with a calculating gleam in her eyes. I'd learned a long time ago to be on guard whenever I saw that expression on her face.

"You can do something for us right away, then," she said, raising her chin. "Put a worm in your new girlfriend's ear."

I hadn't bargained on having my bluff called this quickly. But maybe I could still work around her request. "What kind of worm?" I asked.

She ambled a little ways into the clearing and then back toward me, the strength in her movements turning the stroll into more of a prowl. "The barons *have* discussed lending our support to Bloodstone's cause, *if* she concedes to our very reasonable requirements. Baron Nightwood will be coming to put the proposal to her tomorrow. It would be in everyone's favor, including hers—and yours—if she accepts the deal. So use this influence you've gained to advise her in the right direction. That shouldn't be too difficult for you, should it?"

The slight edge in her voice told me she hadn't totally meant her praise about me coming into my own. She might believe I'd seduced Rory with malicious intentions, but she wasn't confident I could follow through. She knew I wasn't a skilled schemer just as well as I did.

"Encourage her to take the deal?" I said. "I should be able to manage that. She doesn't want to have to go through with the hearing as it is." That much was true but vague enough that I couldn't see it hurting Rory any for me to have said it.

My mother's smile grew. "Excellent. Let's see how well your powers of persuasion—magical and otherwise—have grown. And here I was thinking you might need a little more motivation to really find your footing as scion."

Something in her tone turned my blood cold. "More motivation?"

She nodded casually and rested her hand on my father's arm. "We've worried that you've been held back by qualms about the past. You won your position fair and square. There's no shame in how it happened. But maybe it would be easier for you to focus on where you are now if the last traces of that past were gone. We've been looking into facilities that take people like Holden when it's no longer ideal for them to remain at home."

Every particle in my body stiffened in resistance. "I don't think that should be necessary," I said carefully. To my relief, my voice came out steady, even though my heart was thudding. "I barely think about Holden anymore as it is."

Please, let them not know about my periodic visits to my brother's quarters in the Stormhurst home. Please, let this be only a threat they don't see the need to follow through on. Lord only knew what would happen to Holden if they decided to cut him off from the family completely.

"I'm glad to hear it," my mother said. "In that case, I suppose there isn't any rush. It's an option we can keep on the table if it seems necessary in future." She nodded in satisfaction. "I'm so glad we could have this talk."

I wished I could feel half as pleased with it. As we set off back toward campus, the full impact of the threat sank in.

I'd bought myself a little time with Rory—but how long would I need to pretend to be double-crossing her to ensure my brother's safety? And what would happen to all of us if I couldn't pull the ploy off convincingly enough?

CHAPTER FOURTEEN

Rory

The only thing worse than having to get up for an early class after a fantastic date was having that class with your most disapproving teacher. I showed up for the Physicality workshop with a minute to spare and my clothes and hair pretty well in order considering I'd only woken up half an hour ago, but Professor Viceport followed my trek to the last remaining worktable with a look of disdain. She might not have been eager to see me convicted of murder, but she still didn't exactly *like* me.

She cleared her throat to begin class, but a guy farther down the same row as me raised his hand in the air with a question. One of Viceport's eyebrows arched, but she nodded to him. "Yes?"

"I was trying to fix something in my dorm this morning using a Physicality spell," the guy said, "but I had to stop because the feeb who's—"

"I'd prefer we stay above base slang in this class," Viceport interrupted. "You mean a Nary dormmate of yours?"

The guy gave a brief grimace that could have been in embarrassment at a misstep or annoyance that he wasn't allowed to use the insult—it was hard to tell. "Yes. Exactly. Because he was hanging out in the common room, I had to stop. It got me wondering about why we try so hard to keep our powers secret from the—from the Naries in the first place. I know all the stuff everyone says about caution and so on, but we're way more powerful than they are. Would it really be so awful if they knew that?"

Viceport offered a considering nod, leaning her slimly elegant frame back against her desk. "An interesting question, Mr. Cutbridge. Somewhat beyond the usual scope of my teaching, but certainly relevant to every area of magic. We can take a little time to discuss it."

My back stiffened at his name. *Cutbridge*. There'd been a Cutbridge on Professor Banefield's list of the barons and their allies. Could it have been this guy, even though those notes had gone back years and he didn't look any older than me? Probably not, but almost definitely a relative—his dad or grandfather or an uncle… even an older cousin.

Which didn't mean my classmate necessarily had nefarious intentions, but his use of the derogatory term for Naries and his general attitude had already raised my hackles.

Professor Viceport glanced around the room. "Can anyone share their understanding of our policy of discretion?"

At the back of the room, Victory raised her hand. My long-time nemesis hadn't spoken to me—had barely looked at me—since Malcolm had told her off a couple weeks ago, but her presence still made my skin twitch warily.

"We have more freedom if we don't have to navigate Nary rules or expectations about magic," she said in a pert voice. With the teachers, she was always on her best behavior. "Our powers allow us to work around them pretty easily, and if they knew about us, it'd just cause a whole lot of extra stress."

"Yeah, but we're letting that policy restrict us too," the Cutbridge guy said. "Families aren't supposed to have more than two kids so our society doesn't get too big to stay hidden. We're always having to keep a look out and disguise or hold off on using magic if we're anywhere outside fearmancer properties."

"Both of those points are true," Viceport said. "It's very rare that there's one obvious right way of handling a societal issue. What usually happens is we decide on what causes the fewest problems for the greatest number of people, and staying hidden has accomplished that goal so far. If we *were* to start using magic openly, how do you think the much larger Nary population would respond?"

"They'd be scared," the girl behind me said. "They'd think we're monsters or mutants or something like that."

"Yeah," the guy beside her piped up. "They'd try to… to exterminate us or at least imprison us to make sure we couldn't hurt them."

"I'm pretty sure we'd come out of that fight on top," Cutbridge said. "I mean… we do have magic."

"But why have some big war at all?" Victory asked. "And then, what, we'd have to be constantly watching our backs afterward in case they tried to attack us again?"

Cutbridge shrugged. "We could convince them it's in their best interests to let us do our thing. Then we'd be the ones in charge, calling the shots. We wouldn't have to hide from anyone."

Professor Viceport gave him a wry smile. "I'm not sure the scenario you're proposing would be all that simple to achieve. And many of us have no interest in ruling over the entire population of Naries. Let them live their lives, and we live ours, governing our own. If the barons felt we'd be better off otherwise, I'm sure they'd propose as much."

Her gaze slid to me for just a second, as if she thought I might contribute some political comment. I was still getting used to *being* a fearmancer—I wasn't really qualified to weigh in on global issues just yet.

"Well, *I* think it'd be amazing," Cutbridge said, apparently needing to get the last word, and then let the subject drop so Viceport could get on with the actual class. I made a mental note to pay extra attention to what he was up to around campus.

The workshop was almost over when Viceport's phone pinged with an alert. She took a brief glance at it, and her mouth tightened.

"Miss Bloodstone," she said, shooting me a narrow glance with no effort at all to keep the message private. "Ms. Grimsworth would like to see you once class is out."

Why would the headmistress want to see me right now? I fumbled my final conjuring a little in my distraction, which didn't win me any points with the professor. As soon as she dismissed us, I hurried over to Killbrook Hall.

Ms. Grimsworth had generally been a supportive if distant figure since I'd arrived on campus. I hadn't seen any reason to consider her an outright enemy. So I wasn't feeling *that* nervous until she answered her office door and I saw it wasn't just the two of us.

Malcolm's dad, Baron Nightwood, was standing by the other side of her desk, his arms folded over his chest. Seeing him was just as disorienting as the first time. He looked so much like his son, only a little tighter in the face and grayer in the hair with age.

The last—and first—time I'd talked to him, he'd frozen me in place and made it clear he intended to make me regret any disrespect. And since then, of course, I'd found out he was part of, if not the leader of, the plot to crush me into subservience. If I were making a list of people I least wanted to talk to, he'd be right at the top.

I gave him a slight dip of my head as I came in, figuring a minor show of respect couldn't hurt anything, anyway. I was hardly in a position to do battle with the most powerful fearmancer in the country, as the thin weight of the silver cuffs on my wrists gave extra evidence to.

"Thank you for coming so quickly, Miss Bloodstone," Ms. Grimsworth said. "Baron Nightwood wished to have a conference with you, and I'm lending him the use of my office." Her tone gave away no sign of whether she liked the idea of this meeting. She turned to the baron. "Naturally, the room is fully warded to ensure all conversation within stays private."

"I'd expect nothing less," Baron Nightwood said.

He waited until she'd disappeared into her private quarters before sinking into her chair behind the desk. I wavered on my feet, not sure whether I should sit too or keep standing there awkwardly. At least standing I could more easily make a run for the door if I felt the need to flee.

"It appears you've found yourself in something of a quandary," the baron said, leaning back in the chair in a casual pose. His expression was contemplative but not hostile. "Have you made much progress toward building a defensive case for your hearing?"

As if I intended to discuss my progress with him of all people. "I've gained some ground," I said vaguely. The truth was I still wasn't sure I had a hope in hell of getting through the hearing unsanctioned, especially with him and the other barons pulling the strings behind the scenes, but I wasn't going to admit that.

The baron hummed to himself as if he could guess what I wasn't saying. "It does seem to be a rather complicated situation. Unfortunate that you've made so many enemies in your short time here that someone would go to such lengths to besmirch you, assuming that's your story." Even though it was just the two of us, and he knew I was innocent as well as I did, he worked a clear note of skepticism into his voice.

I fought to keep my teeth from gritting. "I didn't kill anyone."

"The other barons and I don't much care whether you did or not," Baron Nightwood said. "The Wakeburn girl was no one of consequence. Your carelessness, if you were responsible, is a separate matter. Our main concern is for the pentacle. So, I've come in my official capacity to extend an offer of support."

I controlled my reaction as well as I could, but I was pretty sure my eyes bulged. "I—what?" Hadn't Baron Killbrook just dismissed Jude's request for help? There had to be a catch.

And here it came. Baron Nightwood smiled coolly at me. "We're willing to intercede on your behalf to ensure the hearing is decided in your favor. However, in consideration of those efforts and in light of your potentially reckless conduct, we would expect you to make some concessions to us in return."

Of course they would. I finally let myself sink into the chair across from him. "And what concessions would those be?"

"Nothing all that involved. As is reasonable regardless of the charges, given how new you are to the community, we'd ask that you pick one of the three of us established barons as an advisor, established by official contract, for the next five years. Your decisions as baron would need to be discussed and agreed on with that advisor."

How very convenient for them. They wouldn't be able to force me into a ruling I didn't want, but I wouldn't be able to outright object to or present proposals of my own unless they approved. Fuck that.

"And?" I prompted, because he had said "concessions," plural.

He nodded to my arms. "And you would continue to wear those cuffs for the next year, with the monitoring of your magical usage handled by us."

So they'd also be able to keep track of every spell I cast, even those I was using to protect myself. My stomach knotted.

"It isn't very much compared to what you'll face if you're judged guilty of the murder of a magical peer," Baron Nightwood said without any apparent concern. "But if we're going to intervene, we have to begin proceedings now. So I'll need your answer before I leave."

My pulse stuttered. They were really putting the pressure on. I looked down at my hands, willing my mind to focus despite the whirling of my thoughts.

What he'd said was true. Giving one of the barons veto power and letting them monitor my magic for a set period of time was a hell of a lot better than the fate Declan had described, where they might take over my thoughts and actions completely. I *didn't* have much of a defense yet. What if I gambled and said no, and then I lost? Wouldn't it be smarter to take the safe route?

But every part of me balked at the idea of giving in. They'd set me up in this situation, and now they were going to play savior?

Why would they be making this offer at all if they were sure I couldn't prove my innocence?

I grasped onto that thought with a surge of resolve. They *weren't* sure. That was the only explanation. They were worried I'd come out of this scenario without any sanctions placed, free to keep doing things my way, so they were willing to take a lesser advantage to ensure they won something.

They'd orchestrated the trap. If they thought there might be a way out… I had to believe there was too. I still had a week to find it.

I raised my head and looked Baron Nightwood straight in the eyes.

"Thank you, but if I'm going to be judged innocent at the hearing, I'd prefer it to be because I proved I actually am."

A hint of surprise flickered across the baron's face. He hadn't really expected I'd decline.

"Wait a moment," he said. "I don't think you've fully thought this through."

I got up from the chair. "I have, and that's my final decision. When I'm absolved of the crime, then we can discuss my place in the pentacle."

Before he could argue more, I walked out of the room with a thudding heart, hoping I hadn't just risked my freedom and my magic in vain.

CHAPTER FIFTEEN

Rory

Shelby was in the dorm room kitchen when I came in. She startled at the sound of the door so badly the glass in her hand slipped. It hit the counter with a thunk, water splashing out. She checked it for cracks and let out a sigh of relief.

"Sorry," she said. "I guess I'm a little jumpy this morning."

I frowned, coming over to join her. "Is everything okay?"

"Yeah. I mean, it's pretty much normal." She grabbed a dish towel from the knob of a cabinet and swiped it over the puddle on the counter. "I feel like the regular students are being a little more… pushy than before with people like me here on scholarship. Maybe they don't like that we have the clubhouse now? I don't know. It's nothing major, more just a vibe."

I didn't think "just a vibe" would have her flinching at the sound of the door. Shelby had a habit of downplaying her problems. And between the weird incident in Persuasion class and the discussion that guy in Physicality had brought up today, *I* was also noticing some kind of shift in attitude toward the Naries compared to the past two terms.

It could be about the clubhouse—that made a certain kind of

sense. Seeing the Naries have a safe space to escape to could have rubbed a lot of the fearmancer students the wrong way, diminished their sense of power. I really hoped my attempt at helping the Nary students hadn't backfired spectacularly.

"Let me know if anyone in here hassles you, all right?" I said, motioning to the bedroom doors around us. "You shouldn't have to put up with that kind of crap, and… they're all a little scared of me because of the rumors about Imogen. I might as well put that nervousness to use getting them to back off on you."

I didn't like the way most of my peers looked at me now, but at least that way I'd get something good out of the whole mess.

The corner of Shelby's mouth twitched with what looked like amusement, but she shook her head. "I think it's better if I fight my own battles—or don't, when it's better to keep my head down. They'll just be worse when you're not around. That's what bullies are always like."

Having been homeschooled most of my life before now, I didn't have much direct experience to go by, but she sounded as if she did. "Fair enough. If you change your mind, just give me a shout."

"For sure." She perked up. "Oh, one of the guys came around looking for you about an hour ago. Connar? I told him I was pretty sure you'd gone to a class. He wanted me to tell you to meet him at the 'lounge' if I saw you before he did." She gave me a speculative look.

That request sounded more urgent than him just wanting to spend time together. "Thanks," I said to Shelby. "I'd better go find him now."

When I opened the door to the scion lounge, Connar was standing by the pool table with Jude and Declan, his expression stormy. "I know it can't be anything—" he was saying. He stopped and turned at my entrance, relief washing across his face. Jude set down the pool cue he'd been fiddling with.

"Hey," I said, taking in the worry they were all exuding. "What's going on?"

"Malcolm's dad is going to come to make you an offer to do with the murder charge today," Connar said. "I'm not sure exactly what the barons are going to try to arrange, but—"

Was that all? I gave him a wry smile. "I know. He was already here. I talked to him after my class."

Connar tensed. "What did you tell him?"

I waved off his concern and walked over to the alcohol cabinet to grab a pop. It was way too early in the day still for anything alcoholic. "It's fine. I told him thanks but no thanks. They wouldn't be trying to bargain with me if they didn't think there's a decent chance I could pull through this, right?" I hoped I sounded more confident saying that than I felt.

"What did they want?" Declan asked, putting his own cue back on the rack.

"For me to hand over veto power for my decisions as baron to one of them for five years, and let them monitor my magic through these for one." I wiggled one of the cuffs. As I took a gulp of the tart cola, the fizz bubbling down my throat, I glanced over at Connar. "How did you know Baron Nightwood was coming?"

His chiseled jaw tightened. "My parents paid me a visit last night. They were hoping I could help convince you to take the deal. The fact that it mattered that much to them makes me pretty sure that going along with it would have been a bad idea."

His parents had dropped in out of the blue last night—rather than just calling him or something. I studied him. "Is that all they wanted to talk about?" Yesterday had also been the day of his big public show of affection toward me. It was possible word about that had gotten back to them quickly.

He shrugged. "Nothing else worth mentioning."

I'd take his word for that. I dropped onto the sofa's cozy cushions with my drink. "I know the barons think I can beat the murder charge… but *I* still don't know how I'm going to do that. I've only got a week left before the hearing. What else is there we haven't tried?"

Jude took the chair next to me, his eyes bright. "I've been doing some additional research on illusions," he said. "Tricks for differentiating between magic and reality. There are a couple factors I hadn't realized that might apply even via an insight spell into your memories."

My spirits lifted. "Like what?"

"Did Imogen have any small but distinctive features the illusionist would have had to duplicate? Like… a dark mole on her face, or an obvious scar, or maybe she was wearing something that day that had a pattern or image that wasn't totally symmetrical?"

I knit my brow as I thought back to the memories, fighting the urge to cringe at them. "Nothing on her body or her clothes that I noticed, but she was always wearing a silver hair clip on one side."

Jude leaned forward. "How big?"

I formed an oval between my thumb and forefinger. "Around that size. Not tiny."

"Hmm. That might not be small enough. Apparently when casting under stress—which I'm going to assume the mage who was working against you was operating under, at least a little—there can be a faint mirror effect in an illusion meant to copy an actual being or object. But it centers on small, high-contrast details. The pins wouldn't have been that much lighter or darker than her hair either, would they?"

"No. I don't remember seeing any mirroring of the pin, but I was probably too distracted to pick up on things like that."

Declan sat down on the sofa beside me. "I can take an objective look at the memories again, if you're okay with that, and see if anything shows up to an outside viewer." He tipped his head to Jude. "You said there were a couple factors."

"Yeah. The same thing with stress and copying an existing thing—there may be a small vibration visible on areas of fine detail—like hair, or eyelashes, or if she had a particularly intricate design on her clothes." Jude motioned from his head to his shirt.

My hopes had started to deflate. "All of this is assuming the murderer was feeling stressed. The barons would have sent someone who'd be cool under pressure for a job like this, wouldn't they?"

"It can't hurt to try," Declan said. "Will you let me take a look?"

"Of course." It was easier the second time around. I exhaled slowly and willed my instinctive shields down at the same time.

As before, Declan asked about what happened when I'd found Imogen, and a faint tingle rippled through my head with his intrusion. It felt like even less time had passed than before when he pulled back out. His frown told me enough.

"I didn't pick up on either of those effects," he said. "I don't think we're going to make a case that way, at least not from Rory's memories."

"Who else's could we use?" Connar muttered. "She was the only one there."

No, I wasn't. I had to catch a laugh as a rush of inspiration hit me.

Deborah couldn't act as a witness at the hearing. Her perceptions of the illusion wouldn't help me. But she'd told me that a mage could look inside an animal's head using insight. Just as Declan had been peering inside my memories to get a more detached outside perspective… maybe *I* would recognize something from my familiar's memories that would connect a few dots. There were all sorts of fearmancers I'd met that she hadn't. Spells I'd seen cast that she wasn't familiar with.

Jude was watching me. "You look like a lightbulb just went off in that head of yours, Ice Queen."

I wrinkled my nose at the nickname—and to deflect from the point he'd made. The truth about Deborah was the one secret I still had to keep, for her sake more than anyone's.

"I just remembered a technique I read about a while back for clarifying memories," I improvised. "I should go back to the scene and see if I can prompt anything else loose by looking around my dorm." I pushed myself onto my feet.

"Do you want us to come with you?" Connar said from where he'd stationed himself behind the sofa, looking like he very much wanted to be with me on guard duty.

"You all aren't really supposed to be in the girls' dorms, are you? Maybe there are other illusion clues you can find, or—" I glanced at Declan. "Professor Crowford is involved with this group somehow. I haven't gotten a good opportunity to take a peek inside his head, but maybe you'd be able to."

He nodded. "I'll watch for an opening. You let us know if you turn up anything you think we could work with, okay?"

"Of course."

As soon as I'd left them behind, I dashed up the stairs to my dorm room. Deborah must have sensed my urgency, because she came scampering out of one of her nooks in the wall seconds after I'd burst into my bedroom. I sat down on the bed, and she scurried up it to hop onto my palm.

Did something happen, Lorelei?

"Not exactly," I said quietly, mindful of the thinness of the walls now that the other girls were back in residence. "I just realized there's one important avenue I haven't tried. You said you'd let a judge use insight on you to view your memories of the murder—will you let me see them?"

Deborah answered without hesitation. *Of course. I've told you everything I saw already, though.*

"Yeah, but… we're not always the best judges of our own memories. And I've met a lot of fearmancers you haven't had any contact with. Maybe I'll recognize the murderer, or see some other clue that'll help us prove my case. It's worth a shot, right?"

It certainly can't hurt. You go right ahead, whenever you're ready. Without my magical abilities, I couldn't block anyone from taking a peek even if I wanted to.

I peered down at her furry white head. *Please* let this get me somewhere. I couldn't let the barons take total control over my life. I couldn't be branded as a murderer.

"What did you see when Imogen was murdered?" I whispered, and fell into my familiar's head.

As expected with an insight spell, the impressions that washed over me were jumbled rather than a clear replay of those events. I tasted the dry, woody air from the tight passages inside the wall, heard the faint squeak of the dorm's door opening and a startled gasp. I saw a figure cloaked in shadow, even her edges blurred so it was impossible to tell her height or much about her frame other than she had a woman's shape, whipping a spell that sliced into Imogen's skin. I watched the figure duck into one of the bedrooms as footsteps sounded outside the door.

The fragments jumped back and forth. I was dashing to the opening to see what the fuss was. Then blood sprang from the wounds all across Imogen's body. Then she was uninjured again, protesting in a choked voice. Then she fell and hit the floor with a limp thud.

And something thumped faintly in the distance, like an echo.

The disjointed memories swept over me again. I could piece together the sequence in my head. The murderer had taken too much care to ensure she couldn't be identified on the off-chance someone was watching. But there was that distant thump again, just after Imogen's dying body slumped on the floor.

I yanked myself out of Deborah's mind and swayed with momentary dizziness.

Did you notice anything? my familiar asked anxiously.

"I think… maybe." I gathered my thoughts. "After Imogen fell because of her injuries, there was another sound, farther away, like something being hit or dropped. Do you remember that?"

My familiar rubbed her paw against her nose. *Yes. Now that you mention it, I did catch that at the time. It came up through the floor—someone in the dorm below, I assumed. Not anyone who could have seen or heard anything from your room, I don't think. Those floors are quite thick. I barely heard the sound from down there even with my sharper hearing.*

"It came *right* after, though," I said. "There's a chance someone heard something. If they could even cast a little doubt on when Imogen was attacked—if their testimony could suggest it happened before I was even at the room— I've got to find out who was down there."

CHAPTER SIXTEEN

Rory

My eyes popped open, and I gasped for air. For the first few seconds, I couldn't seem to pull more than a fragment of a breath into my lungs. My pulse thundered in my chest, and my mind scrambled to make sense of the shadowy room around me.

Lorelei?

Deborah's familiar dry voice penetrated the haze of panic. I clenched my hands and found them grasping the sheets on my bed in my dorm room. My breaths started to even out as the pressure on my chest eased.

Nothing was attacking me, at least not right in this moment. I was here in my bedroom alone, other than my familiar. It'd just been a nightmare.

A nightmare like the ones Malcolm had used to send into my head: dark and formless, shot through with terror but with no sense of what was so terrifying when I woke up. A chill ran down my spine.

I didn't appear to have torn up anything like I often had in those fits during spring term. "Deborah," I whispered. "Was I yelling?"

No. My familiar's voice became clearer as she scampered across the bed to rest her front paws on my arm. *You murmured a little in your sleep—you sounded distressed—but I don't imagine anyone heard you other than me.*

Thank God for that. I gave her a quick stroke of my thumb down her back and slipped out of bed to my open window. Leaning out, I checked the stone wall of the building between my room and Malcolm's at the opposite end. The early morning light was thin but bright enough for me to see no unusual protrusions had appeared. Last time, he'd been using an amplifying piece to store and intensify the spells he'd been aiming at me in my sleep.

All that meant was he'd decided to be more subtle about it. My jaw clenching, I yanked myself back into my room and grabbed the first halfway decent outfit I could assemble out of my wardrobe. With a rake of my fingers through my hair, I pulled the messy waves into some kind of order. Then I marched out of my dorm and across the short hallway to Malcolm's.

The guy who answered the door was tall and freckled with a mop of dark brown hair. He blinked at me over the top of the toasted wrap he was in the middle of eating, and a quiver of fear shot into me. He recognized the supposed murderer from next door.

I gave him a tight smile. "Is Malcolm here?"

"Just a second." He dashed across the common room as if I'd threatened to fillet him if he didn't hoof it fast enough. The other two guys eating breakfast at the dining table watched me with equal wariness. I decided I didn't much care whether they saw me as some horrible threat if it meant they cared more about appeasing me than potentially pissing off Malcolm by summoning him.

The Nightwood scion emerged from his bedroom a minute later in a shirt and slacks that looked just thrown on, with a frown and slightly bleary eyes. He gave them a quick rub when he saw me and drew his posture straighter as he sauntered the rest of the way over.

"What's going on, Bloodstone?"

My awareness of our audience prickled over me. I backed up, and he followed me into the hall. As soon as the door had shut behind him, I jabbed a finger at him.

"It's not much of a truce if you're still messing with my head."

Malcolm's expression turned puzzled. "What are you talking about?"

"Those nightmares you sent at me before—I just had another one."

His frown came back. "I didn't have anything to do with that. I haven't cast any magic at you since… since that day when we were in the lake." He gathered his composure after that momentary faltering. "I didn't hear anything from your room."

"I didn't freak out the same way," I said. "I just—I woke up in the same kind of panic, without remembering the dream at all—that's not how my regular nightmares usually go."

Something shifted in his face at my comment about "regular nightmares." Maybe he hadn't realized how many others I had to compare to. He looked down at his hands and then at me again, his eyes searching mine. "I don't know what to tell you. I honestly had nothing to do with it."

He sounded genuine. Maybe it was just a coincidence that this nightmare had felt so much like those past ones. Maybe it'd been inspired by those past ones rather than directly caused by the same source. In which case I'd dragged Malcolm out of bed for nothing.

On the other hand, he could be lying. It wasn't as if he hadn't jerked me around plenty of times in the past.

I crossed my arms over my chest, just shy of hugging myself. "How do I know I can believe that?"

Malcolm opened his mouth with an exasperated look and then closed it again. His brow knit. He contemplated me for a moment, possibly realizing what a tall order proving himself would be considering our history.

"Ask me whether I cast any magic at you. Or when the last time was. Or however you want to phrase it," he said abruptly. "Make it an insight spell. I've got nothing to hide. I *am* telling you the truth."

I stared at him. *Malcolm* of all people was voluntarily letting me inside his head. Of course, I had to assume that if I tried to take a more general dip into his thoughts and memories, he'd punt me out faster than I could blink. But even for a specific question, it was a greater show of trust than I'd have thought he was capable of.

The fact that I'd misjudged him sent a twinge of guilt through me, but I had to take the opening he'd given me, just to be sure. "All right," I said. "Ready?"

His jaw tightened, but he nodded. If he was going to offer me this much trust, I could show him I wasn't the kind of person who'd abuse it. I fixed my gaze on his forehead and said, "When was the last time you cast any kind of magic to affect me?"

My awareness flipped and mingled with his. The impressions washed over me in a shifting wave of images and sensations. I caught a glimpse of me bobbing in lake water up to my neck with my hair slicked wet and sleek, a flash of desire, a murmured spell shaping the currents in the hopes of stirring the same desire in its target, the flush of my cheeks and an answering flare of heat in Malcolm's body—

I jerked myself out of his head, my face flushing too. A tingling that was awkward but not entirely uncomfortable spread through my chest and farther down, to all the places that wouldn't have minded indulging in that sensation again if I'd been willing to let myself.

He hadn't been lying, anyway. It took me a second to find my tongue. "Okay. Thank you. I'm sorry I jumped to conclusions."

Malcolm shrugged, his gaze a little more intent on me, maybe a little more heated with the thought of the memory I'd just dipped into. "I suppose I can't really blame you. I did do quite a number on you with those spells before." He paused. "I'm sorry about that. I think it's safe to say that was one tactic I took too far. I thought… I don't know." He rubbed his forehead with a grimace.

A second apology from the heir of Nightwood in as many weeks, on top of the vulnerability he'd just offered in opening up his mind to me? I found myself speechless again.

The other scions had assured me that Malcolm had plenty of positive qualities, but it'd been pretty hard to see them in the midst of his campaign against me. Now that he was lowering his guard, trying to make peace and even understand where I was coming from… It was hard not to wonder how much differently our association might have played out if I'd gotten this version of him to begin with.

I still disagreed with plenty of his ideas, but less of them than I'd have expected. I couldn't claim anymore that he was a full-out villain.

Who was to say how I'd have acted if our positions and histories had been reversed?

As I groped for an appropriate answer to his apology, one of the dorm doors behind me opened and a couple of the other senior students ducked out, talking quietly as they walked to the stairs. People were starting to head off to classes or whatever other responsibilities they had this morning. A different sort of panic jolted through me.

I turned on my heel. "Well, I— I've got to get going."

"What's the big hurry all of a sudden?" Malcolm took a step after me. "Is something else going on?"

It might have been the way he'd just opened up to me or the fact that he sounded honestly concerned—probably some of both. Before I could second-guess the impulse, I told him the truth.

"I wanted to talk to the guys in the dorm under mine. It occurred to me that one of them might have been in the room when Imogen was attacked and could have heard something that would help my case."

Malcolm gave a brisk nod, looking completely alert now. "I'll come with you. I can encourage them to… speak up if any of them aren't so keen."

That wasn't the outcome I'd been going for. "I'm sure if I need any help, Declan—"

"Declan will already be off in the library or consulting with Professor Sinleigh or God knows what," Malcolm said dismissively. "The guy has never heard of the concept of sleeping in. Come on. Let's see who's around. I don't know all his dormmates off the top of my head, but when I see them, I should be able to at least tell you who was around for the summer session."

That could actually be useful. I wasn't sure I trusted my memory with the students I didn't know all that well and hadn't known for very long.

"Okay," I said. "But let me ask the questions. It's *my* case."

A teasing note came into Malcolm's voice. "If you insist, Glinda."

We tramped down one flight of stairs to the hall beneath ours.

True to his word, Malcolm hung back a couple steps behind me as I knocked on the dorm door.

I *did* recognize the guy who came to answer it: Alex Rutland, who'd tried very ineffectively to ask me out a few months back, after everyone had found out I was the most powerful mage currently attending the school and before anyone had thought I was a murderer. I suspected the new development might have put a damper on my marriage prospects. An unexpected bonus.

He paled a little when he saw me, as if he thought I might be going to murder him for daring to flirt with me two terms ago. I fixed him with a firm look. "Rutland, get all your dormmates who are around into the common room. I need to talk to everyone. Scion business." If that excuse had worked for Malcolm with the blacksuits, it'd damn well better work for me here.

"Yes—yes, of course," Alex mumbled, and hustled across the common room, leaving the door open for us.

A couple of the guys were already sitting on the sofas, and a few more were at the dining table. Alex rapped on two of the other doors to bring the inhabitants out and stopped a guy who'd just emerged from the bathroom in a bathrobe.

Malcolm had been right—Declan, who had the bedroom right under mine, was gone. I knew he'd still been at the end of summer party when I'd left it anyway, and it wasn't as if he'd have failed to mention he'd come back to the dorm during the time of the murder.

I scanned the faces in front of me. Alex had been around during the summer, and I was sure two of the other guys had been in some of my classes. The other five I couldn't have said.

Malcolm leaned closer and spoke under his breath. "Mr. Bathrobe, the two on the sofas, and that guy just coming out of his room weren't here for the summer."

I tipped my head in acknowledgment with a rush of gratitude. "You four don't need to be here for this," I said, pointing to them. Even the ones who'd already been out in the common room when I'd arrived scattered to their bedrooms at my dismissal. My chest jittered with fresh jolts of fear. I was building quite a store of magic today.

In the momentary silence as the remaining guys gathered warily, I couldn't help noticing that no sound at all traveled to me from the room above. My own dormmates must be walking around up there with their morning preparations now, but I wouldn't have known it from down here. *Was* there any chance someone had heard Imogen's fall—and that they could say exactly when it'd happened?

I had to try.

"You were all here for the summer session," I said, looking at the four guys still in front of me. "What time did you each of you leave the end-of-term party?"

"I was there until the end," Alex said. From Malcolm's nod at the corner of my vision, he remembered well enough to confirm that.

"Same here," the second guy. Another nod.

"I left right after the prize announcement," said a guy holding a mug of coffee. His gaze darted nervously not to me but to Malcolm before he added, "My parents wanted me home right away for a family business meeting."

"I left somewhere in the middle," the last guy said. "I wasn't really paying attention to the time."

I focused on the final two. "Did either of you come back to the dorm after you left the party?"

They both hesitated. Malcolm cleared his throat, and the coffee guy shook his head with a jerk. "I'd already packed the things I needed in my car. I went straight to the garage and drove home."

The last guy sighed and offered a crooked smile. "Eventually, sure, but by the time I got here there were blacksuits all over the place. I took a detour with my girlfriend into the woods."

The room had been empty until after the murder, then. Except—it *couldn't* have been. I didn't know whether anyone down here could have heard what was happening over their heads, but Deborah had definitely heard a noise from down here.

"Thanks for your time," I said quickly. "That's all I needed to know."

"You're giving up just like that?" Malcolm asked when I'd retreated into the hall.

I shook my head. "There was someone in that room when Imogen was attacked. I—I was able to figure that out." Regardless of the new side of him I was seeing, I sure as hell wasn't telling *him* Deborah's secret. "Would the cleaning staff have started work before the session was even over?"

"Not likely," Malcolm said. "They have a whole week afterward to get everything in order. Maintenance prefers to keep out of students' way as much as possible. But you're thinking too much like a good witch." He raised his hand as if to tap my head but stopped just shy of brushing my hair. "You're assuming whoever was in there was supposed to be. Breaking and entering is fair play around here."

My heart sank. "Then it could be literally *anyone*. If I just had some idea—"

I cut myself off in mid-sentence as the pieces clicked in my head.

I did have an idea. I'd dismissed the possibility that Cressida knew anything because I'd seen her leaving the stairwell before I'd even started up from the first floor, and the real murderer wouldn't have shown herself to anyone in my dorm.

But… if Imogen's attacker had been holding her in place for a little while before I even showed up, like Deborah had said, then Cressida couldn't have gotten into *our* dorm room in the first place. So where had she gone up there? What had sent her hurrying out of the building so quickly she'd practically run into me?

"What?" Malcolm said, studying my expression.

"I know who else to ask," I said, without much boost to my spirits. "But even if she does know I'm innocent, I think she might be happy to see me go down for the crime anyway."

CHAPTER SEVENTEEN

Jude

It was a long drive to the main Killbrook home from Blood U, but I jumped at the first chance I got to make the trip. The funny thing about coming to a major decision was that once you'd arrived there, no matter how gradual the process would be, the impatience to get on with it would keep itching at you. I was going to make a clean break, and I wanted it to start now.

I had no classes after my morning seminar until my business course the next afternoon, so I didn't really need to hurry. The Mercedes's engine purred as I zipped along the highway past trees and farmland. My familiar, who I hadn't wanted to leave cooped up in my dorm bedroom for ages, bounced between the floor and the passenger seat with ferret chortles that were a lot more pleased than I felt.

After a while, to distract myself from thoughts of the task ahead, I put on my playlist of my favorite modern piano tracks. Too bad the music industry was even more of a clusterfuck than the fearmancer community, or maybe I'd have considered trying to build a career for myself there.

The complex melody that filled the interior of the car didn't quite overwhelm my nerves. I drummed my fingers against the steering wheel. Mischief cocked her head at me with a questioning sound, and I reached over to give her a quick scratch under her chin.

"It'll be fine," I told her and myself. "In and out. No big deal."

This early in the afternoon, I could hope no one would be home except the staff, who wouldn't hassle me. Dad should be off tending to his various business concerns, and Mom often visited with her friends or looked in on the local shops she'd invested in during the day.

Still, my chest tightened when I finally turned down the winding drive that led to the mansion. The tall gate with its dark bars loomed ahead of me. I punched in the code on my dashboard control that would unlock the gate and drove on in toward the sprawling stone building beyond.

One of the grounds staff was trimming the hedges along the driveway. Otherwise there was no sign of activity. I parked the Mercedes in the loop outside the front door, not bothering with the garage. "Wait here," I told Mischief, who for once in her life decided to be obedient and curled up on the leather seat. Lord only knew how much of my uneasiness she was picking up on.

Ideally this really would be a quick in-and-out. I didn't have much here I was interested in hanging on to.

"Hello, Mr. Killbrook," our butler said as I crossed the foyer to the stairs. A look of consternation crossed his face. "We weren't expecting you home."

"Don't worry, Cravers," I said. "I'm not staying for dinner. I'll be out of your hair in less than an hour."

I jogged up the stairs and veered across the expansive hallway to the east wing. My shoes thumped against the worn but polished hardwood. It was a familiar sound, but the matching thud of my pulse turned it somehow ominous.

I threw open the door to my set of rooms and paused for a moment when the door closed behind me, letting out my breath. A faintly floral smell tickled my nose—the housekeeping staff had come through with their cleaners and air fresheners. Otherwise, the sitting room attached to my bedroom and private bathroom looked the same as it had when I'd left last week: cushy leather couch across from the huge TV, shelves packed with an equal number of books and video games, the old arcade consoles I'd been collecting standing along the opposite wall.

The other scions and I used to have a blast here when I'd invite them over. I hadn't done that in a while. Not since I'd realized how little this all belonged to me, actually.

But I figured my father who wasn't really my father owed me a few things for dragging me into this world and this wretched situation. I just had to figure out what in this place I cared about enough to bother taking with me.

I didn't have the means to transport large items, and anyway, the apartment I'd managed to rent on short notice came furnished. Better not to have any major reminders of my old life there anyway. The whole point was to leave this all behind.

Wandering the room, I grabbed the newest game console and my favorite games. The rest I could live without. I tossed those into one of my suitcases and took another look around the room. The tightness in my chest dug in little claws.

How much had *any* of this stuff really mattered to me? It'd all been its own kind of distraction from my dad's chilly treatment and the reasons for it I'd discovered.

I left the sitting room for my bedroom and checked my closet for any clothes I'd want to hold onto that I hadn't already brought with me to school. This formal suit had always suited me particularly well, if I ever had a good occasion to wear it again. I tossed a few sweaters and thicker pants for the winter after it. A nice pair of Oxfords that felt too fancy for most school functions. My wool coat. Some diamond cufflinks I doubted I'd ever wear but that might be useful if I burned through my money too quickly.

There really wasn't much else. I stepped out of the bedroom with an empty feeling expanding inside me, just as the door from the hallway opened.

"Jude." My mother stopped on the threshold, staring as she took in me and then the suitcase, her eyes widening. "The staff said you'd come home. What's going on?"

At five months along, her pregnancy was starting to become

obvious. The silk blouse she'd chosen flowed over her rounded belly. The life growing in there had the potential to utterly destroy mine—through no fault of its own, of course. I focused on Mom's face, on the red hair just a couple shades lighter than my own falling in loose curls around her features. My stomach clenched.

I didn't want to blame Mom for her part in the conspiracy to bring me into this world. She loved Dad; she'd only been trying to make him happy. She'd believed him that producing an heir by whatever means necessary would accomplish that. She'd showered me with affection when that promise had proven to be a lie.

But she had to have realized that eventually the truth would come out, one way or another, and I'd pay the consequences. She'd never stood up to him about the way he'd treated me. And how could she not realize what her current state meant for my future? Was she just willing that knowledge away, letting herself pretend it wasn't true because as far as she knew, I didn't have any idea?

"I'm just getting a few of my things," I said in a voice that came out oddly detached to my own ears. "I decided to get a place of my own."

She blinked at me. "A place of your own? But—if there's something you're unhappy with at the house— You can always make use of one of the other properties—"

"I wanted a place that's just mine," I said, calmly but firmly. "That's all. You can tell Dad not to worry—I'm not going to come asking for anything. I can handle it all on my own."

I'd already spoken to the bank to make sure my account there was only in my name. My parents couldn't touch my accumulated "allowance" and the chunk of my inheritance that had transferred over to me at eighteen. The funds in there should last me a good long while, definitely long enough to finish school and establish myself in some kind of paying work.

My parents would never need to think about me again. I'd fade right out of their lives… and maybe Dad could let that be enough.

Mom's mouth twisted at a pained angle, and her hand came to rest on her belly, as if somehow my soon-to-be baby sister was affected by this situation. "I don't understand. Did something happen, Jude? Please, if something's wrong, you can tell me."

Looking back into her worried eyes, I was struck by the urge to take her up on that offer. To tell her just how much I knew and how scared I was. To go back to those childhood years when getting a hug from her was almost enough to offset the sting of Dad's cold shoulder.

It had been a long time since then, though. I wasn't sure I'd even get a hug. More likely, her stare would turn horrified, and she'd plead with me to stay… so that she could contact Dad and find out how *he'd* want to deal with me.

I swallowed hard. "I'm fine, Mom. Just feeling the need for a little independence. *You* don't need to worry about me either, I promise."

There might have been a thing or two in the bathroom I'd have taken, but now that Mom was right here, I didn't want to linger. I moved toward the doorway, pulling the suitcase on its wheels, and she backed out, her expression still distraught. She touched my shoulder as I passed her.

"I'm here for you if you do need anything," she said. "I *want* to worry about you if there's reason to."

For a second, I completely choked up. Maybe she meant that, but not enough. Not enough to save me. As far as I could tell, I was the only one who could do that.

"Okay, Mom," I said, because I wasn't here to be cruel to her either. Then I hurried out to my car before the mix of guilt and resentment could grip me any harder.

I had another long drive ahead of me, and this one came with a new set of troubled thoughts. Mom might not have guessed why I was taking this step in the moment, but once she'd had time to mull it over, to talk with Dad about it… would they suspect I was onto their secret? Would Dad decide I was a threat that needed to be eliminated right away after all? Presenting a false heir to the entire community, including the other barons, was an offense a hell of a lot worse than anything Rory was accused of doing.

I couldn't control what they thought or decided to do, only what I did for myself from here on.

Evening set in during my drive. The lights of New York City glowed in the distance long before I passed through the suburbs and crossed the bridge to Manhattan Island. Traffic slowed to a crawl, and Mischief squirmed impatiently beside me, but the bustle of city energy was weirdly soothing. In a place like this, I could disappear at least temporarily.

When I reached my apartment building, I left the car in the underground garage and hauled my suitcase and the bag I'd brought from school to the elevator. My familiar bounded along ahead of me. The elevator dropped me off on the second highest floor, and my ferret and I walked into the apartment together.

Crisp filtered air wafted over me in the sparse modern space that belonged to no one but me. Mischief let out an excited chortle and scurried across the hardwood floor to make a full exploration. A smile crossed my lips as I stopped by the broad windows overlooking Central Park. It wasn't a huge apartment, but I'd been willing to splurge a little for this view.

The combined living-dining room had enough seating for six around the TV and at the dining table. Maybe someday I could invite all the scions over *here* for a proper hang-out. The thought of Rory nestled on the corner of the sofa made me giddy.

I wasn't sure how I'd explain this move to the others, though. The thought of telling them the truth about my parentage still sent a shudder of panic through me.

Why the hell would they want to hang out with an imposter, a guy who wasn't even one of them? Would they have given me the time of day in the first place if I hadn't been thrust into their midst under false pretenses?

I inhaled slowly, letting the clean lines of the furnishings calm me. I didn't have to find out the answer to that question yet. Maybe I never had to. For now, I needed to take every step I could to make sure I kept this new life.

As I opened my bag, the conducting pieces I'd carefully shaped clicked against each other. I picked up the first one, sat down on the sofa, and began the slow process of casting a protective ward strong enough to buy my escape if Dad happened to come calling.

CHAPTER EIGHTEEN

Rory

As soon as I started looking for Cressida instead of avoiding her the way I normally did Victory and her best friends, it became very obvious that *she* was avoiding me. Very effectively, too. No matter what time I left my bedroom in the morning or popped back into the dorm during the day, I never bumped into her. Our paths never crossed on the green or elsewhere around campus. So far she hadn't even been in any of my classes.

After getting nowhere for a day, I knocked on her bedroom door the next morning. No one answered, but I had no idea whether that meant she was in there ignoring me or had already headed out. At this point, both possibilities seemed equally plausible.

As I went about my day, still without so much as a glimpse of her white-blond French braid, the sense grew that this couldn't be coincidence. She was staying away from me on purpose. And why would she be keeping such a careful distance from me unless she knew something to do with me that she didn't want to have to face?

I couldn't believe she was simply terrified that I might really have murdered Imogen. She'd seen just as much as Malcolm had that I wasn't the type to lose my temper violently even under extreme circumstances.

Her two cohorts, Victory and Sinclair, hadn't taken any jabs at me since they'd gotten back from break, but they weren't dodging me either. I came into the common room in the middle of the afternoon to find the two of them sitting on one of the sofas murmuring over a fashion magazine, and a prickle ran up the back of my neck. Normally Cressida would have been perched there with them. Was she just not around… or had she been alerted to my arrival somehow and ducked away before I'd walked in?

The last thing I wanted to do was ask my long-time nemesis for help, but I could bite the bullet when my ability to prove I wasn't a murderer was on the line. I strode up to the sofa and waited until Victory raised her eyes to meet mine.

"Where's Cressida?" I asked. Might as well cut to the chase and keep this conversation as brief as possible.

Victory wrinkled her nose. "I'm not her keeper. And why should I tell you even if I know—so you can go harass her?"

I restrained myself from rolling my eyes. I'd never done anything remotely close to "harassing" Victory and her friends, unless you counted paying them back in kind for the ways they'd harassed me.

"I need to ask her about something important," I said. "I'm not looking to argue with her or whatever."

Victory shrugged and turned back to her magazine. "You really should ask your fellow scions for help, since you're all so close these days."

Obviously she was still pissed off at me because Malcolm had interrupted her plan to feed Deborah to her cat familiar. I wavered, wondering if there was any other tactic I could try, but the only things I knew Victory wanted from me were to see me crushed or disgraced, neither of which I could offer up. She'd probably rejoice if I failed at the hearing.

In the end, I grabbed a book on insight magic from the library and took it out onto the green to read where I could watch for Cressida coming or going. She had to have classes sometime. I didn't think she could make it from the dorms to Nightwood Tower without me spotting her.

The first hour or so passed pretty uneventfully. Other students claimed spots on the grass between the paths, some of them eyeing me before moving a little farther away, but no one interrupted my reading. Cressida didn't make any appearance either, though. I'd gotten through a couple chapters with my broken attention when mocking laughter reached my ears from across the green.

I shifted position surreptitiously and peered toward the sound with my head still tipped toward the book. Shelby and two other Nary students from the music program had just left Nightwood Tower, and a few fearmancer students had closed around them. One of them was the Cutbridge guy who'd argued for fearmancer world domination in Physicality the other day.

The girl beside him made a subtle gesture with her hand, and Shelby's feet flew out from under her as if she'd tripped. She sprawled on her hands and knees, her cello case landing with a thump that made me wince. Cutbridge laughed again.

"Leave us alone," one of the other Naries snapped at the mages.

"We didn't do anything," Cutbridge said in a sly voice. "It's not our fault if just being around greatness makes you clumsy."

Behind the Naries, another of the fearmancers twisted his fingers. The Nary guy's ankle jerked at the same time, and he stumbled.

I scrambled onto my feet with a hiccup of my pulse. The fearmancer students liked to hassle the Naries, sure, but I'd never seen them toe the line of revealing their magic so blatantly. They were *pointing out* the fact that they hadn't needed to touch the other students to assault them. Was Cutbridge trying to force some kind of reveal with his talk about greatness?

Shelby had said the vibe between the scholarship students and the regular ones had become more tense. How long had stuff like this been happening?

I wasn't sure how much I cared whether Naries knew magic existed or not, but I wasn't going to sit around while a bunch of bullies tormented my friend and her classmates. I shoved the book under my arm and marched over.

Shelby was just pushing herself upright when she looked around and saw me. A relieved smile touched her lips even as she blushed with embarrassment. The fearmancer girl who'd tripped her, currently leaning over the cello case, caught her glance, raised her own head, and yanked herself backward at the sight of me.

"It's Bloodstone," she murmured. "Holy shit." Her face paled, and her shoulders came up defensively. A waft of fear rolled off her into my chest.

The smack of emotion made me queasy. I held up my hands to show I was coming over peacefully, but the movement made the girl flinch. The other guy was backpedaling too with another wave of panic. Cutbridge held steadier, but his jaw had clenched tight.

"I'll just remind you that there are witnesses," he said stiffly.

Witnesses? So that I'd think twice if I'd been planning on murdering him? Frankly, that comment made me *want* to murder him more than anything else this bunch had done. I settled for letting my voice come out sharp and tart.

"Why don't you all go find something more productive to do? You've got better ways to make yourself feel big than this, don't you?"

I waved my hand vaguely toward the other buildings, and the girl lurched away with a yelp as if I'd cast something at her. Fresh fear raced into me so swiftly it quivered all the way up my gums.

"I didn't—" I started, not knowing how to deny I'd done something that I wasn't allowed to admit was even possible in front of Shelby and the other Naries, but the girl was already spinning and dashing away.

"Bitch," Cutbridge muttered, and stalked after her. The other fearmancer guy fled in the opposite direction.

Shelby straightened the rest of the way up, brushing off her clothes. "Thanks. I don't know what trick they were pulling there. That was almost spooky."

"Seriously," the guy said with a shudder.

My gut twisted, but I didn't know what was disturbing me more—how blatantly the other mages had flouted university rules or how terrified they'd been of me. I'd known people were more nervous of me than before, but… were there really students who'd seen how I'd behaved in the five months I'd been going to school here and still thought I might slaughter one of them in the middle of the green?

The worst thing was, they weren't even completely wrong, were they? Being my friend, helping me in any way, could get you killed. Ask not just Imogen but Professor Banefield too. Could I even keep the Nary girl in front of me safe, really?

"I'm glad you're okay," I said quickly, and swiveled to hurry off in the direction of the Stormhurst Building, for no particular reason other than I was sure the Naries wouldn't be heading there too.

I was about halfway there when I noticed the thud of footsteps behind me. A moment later, Declan caught up with me, his black hair windblown. When he stopped, his hawk familiar circled overhead and dropped from the sky to perch on his shoulder. I guessed he'd been out letting it stretch its wings.

"Hey," he said quietly. "I caught the end of that confrontation on the green. You looked pretty upset."

"I wasn't going to hurt them," I blurted out.

Declan gave me such an incredulous look that I immediately felt ridiculous for even saying that. "Of course you weren't," he said. "I wanted to make sure *you're* okay."

"Yeah, I mean, I guess. I'm a lot more okay than Imogen is." I managed a weak laugh. "Which is obviously what's on everyone else's mind too."

He glanced around and motioned for me to follow him. "Come on. Let's go somewhere quiet, and you can talk about everything that's bothering you. You're going through a lot."

I didn't have the wherewithal to argue with him. I wasn't sure I really wanted to.

We wandered down toward the lake, where the breeze carried the fresh watery scent and a chilly tinge that had put an end to most swimming expeditions. Declan made for the boathouse, giving his familiar a gentle rub to its chest that must also have served as a command. As he opened the boathouse door, the hawk lifted off him with a flap of its wings and soared over the roof.

My heart skipped a beat before I followed Declan inside. He had no idea about the heated and then chilling encounter I'd had with

Malcolm in here. That was weeks ago now, though. I *wanted* to move past it.

The dim space felt different now with the cool of the approaching autumn instead of mid-summer humidity. The boats creaked in their moorings with the lapping waves. Declan pulled a couple of plastic crates away from the wall and pushed one toward me. He sat down on the other.

"It's getting to you," he said. "The way people are reacting because of the accusations."

I sank onto my makeshift stool. "I know there was the arrest and everything, but it's hard to see how people could think I'm this violent person after everything I've done *not* to lower myself to really fighting since I got here. Even if I'm acquitted at the hearing… do you think they'll assume I just cheated my way out of the sanctions? Will they still be scared of me?"

Maybe they'd be even more scared, thinking I'd not only murdered a fellow student but gotten away with it.

"They might," Declan admitted. "But it's fearmancer nature to assume the worst of people, to always be suspicious and wary. No one knows you all that well except for, well, us scions I suppose. You'll have more chances to show them the longer you're here."

I lowered my head into my hands. "I just wish all this craziness was done already. It feels like every time I think I've found my footing here, someone pulls the rug out from under me in some new way. I'm *tired*, Declan."

His crate scraped against the boards as he scooted closer. He touched my shoulder with a reassuring stroke of his thumb. "I know. I'm trying to make it easier for you any way I can. We'll get through this, and when we're both in the pentacle of barons, we can start changing things. That's why they're pushing so hard at you now, you know. Because they're scared of what will happen when you really have power."

That idea provided a comfort all of its own, but only a small one, considering I wasn't sure I'd make it to that future. It seemed awfully distant right now.

"I guess I shouldn't be complaining to you," I muttered. "You've had to fight to keep your position for *years.*"

"I worked up to it. You were thrown into the deep end. And I've never had to deal with attacks as intense as they're aiming at you."

"So, I'm just special."

"Yes," he said with a smile I could hear. "You are."

I looked up at him so I could see that smile, a little crooked on one side. The affection shining in his eyes wasn't quite enough. I shifted forward on my crate so I could lean into him, giving him what I'd meant to be a quick hug. But once his arms came around me, it was incredibly hard to let him go. I pressed my face into his soft shirt and drank in the cedary smell of him.

One of his hands came up to brush over my hair. An electric tingle shot through my skin. Heat pooled in my lips, and I pulled myself back before I was any more tempted to act on that attraction.

"I'm sorry," I said. "I just—I needed that."

"It's okay," Declan said, but I saw the conflict in the tensing of his face. He stood up a little abruptly. "I think I've found a source for some more information on the joymancers, if you still think that would help."

It took me a second to catch up with the abrupt change in subject. "I—Yeah. Yeah, it still might. And I'd like to know everything I can about them anyway." If I was going to turn to these people, I'd better know who I was really dealing with.

Declan nodded. "I'll meet you in the scion lounge tomorrow morning at nine?"

"That works."

He tipped his head to me again and headed out, so briskly I couldn't help feeling I'd somehow ruined the moment between us on top of everything else.

CHAPTER NINETEEN

Declan

I ended up in the scion lounge a half hour before I'd told Rory to meet me. Restless, I managed to kill several minutes fiddling with the espresso machine Jude had requested a couple years ago. It finally produced a cup of coffee that tasted like coffee. As I sipped the bitter liquid, I wandered through the room.

The envelope I'd left on the sofa felt way too flimsy to really help Rory. It was good for her to know what the people who'd stolen her away were capable of, but I wasn't sure reading those horror stories would block enough of her long-held sympathies for her to get past the judge's scrutiny if he started along that line of questioning. She shouldn't have to be worrying about how much she might have misjudged the community she'd grown up in on top of everything else going on.

And even if the material did protect her from accusations of treason, it wasn't going to do anything to absolve her of the murder charge. We only had a few days left, and I hadn't made much progress at all.

I couldn't let the other barons win against her. It was that simple. I just… didn't have any idea how I could ensure that *we* won yet, and that fact niggled at me more and more with each passing day.

I'd finally sat down on the sofa when Rory slipped into the room, just before nine. She smiled at me, so goddamn grateful for the little I'd managed to accomplish—grateful that I was here at all—and my stomach clenched up even as my heart skipped a beat.

"So, what have you got for me this time?" she asked in a casual tone that I suspected took some effort. She dropped onto the other end of the sofa.

I nudged the envelope toward her. "These files took a little more digging to uncover. Not because they're top secret or anything, but because the authorities didn't consider them to be of the same level of concern. But… I think you might find them even more concerning than what I've shown you before. They're reports on incidents when the joymancers' efforts to interfere with fearmancer activities didn't result in any of us being harmed, but bystanders were."

The envelope creased where Rory's fingers tightened around it. "They hurt Naries?"

"Sometimes, if those people were in the way to getting at us. Looking over the reports, I'd say it was accidents or carelessness in the moment, not planned callousness, but still. The ones who stalk us think screwing us over is worth a little collateral damage."

I could tell how much that thought disturbed her from her hesitation before she opened the envelope. The uneasy sense crept over me that I should leave her to do her reading in private, but she hadn't given any sign she wanted to be alone. The least I could do was be here for her if she needed someone to talk with to process everything in those files.

As she looked over one report and then another, I returned my attention to my coffee. Her mouth pursed tighter with each page she read. After several, she set the sheets down and pressed the heel of her hand to her forehead.

"There'd be no reason for them to lie about or exaggerate those accounts, would there?" she said, her voice gone hollow. "The fearmancers writing the reports obviously didn't care about what happened to the Naries either—they were just being thorough in noting everything that happened."

"That would be what I'd assume." I didn't believe the blacksuits and other authorities who'd written up attacks where fearmancers *had* suffered would have exaggerated those accounts either, but I couldn't say it wasn't possible a few liberties had been taken here or there to emphasize a case. With the Naries… No, most of my fellow mages saw them on the same level as public property that'd been damaged.

"Some of those situations were so pointless." Rory let out a rough breath. "If they'd just waited for another opportunity, they might have gotten a better one, *and* there wouldn't have been any Naries around. What's the point in trying to stop harmful fearmancer activities if you're going to cause a bunch of harm yourself along the way? Those people who ended up in the hospital… That family whose store was destroyed…" She shook her head.

I grimaced in sympathy. "I know. I'm sure not all joymancers would be that single-minded, just like not every fearmancer is a total asshole, as I hope you're convinced of by now. From what you've said about your adoptive parents, they were good people. I'd never try to convince you that their entire community is evil or something like that. But some of them have gotten so caught up in their campaign against us, I'm not sure they're really thinking things through anymore. Kind of like how Malcolm got in his feud with you."

Rory winced at that reminder. "Okay. That kind of single-mindedness can obviously happen on both sides." She gazed down at the papers with a sort of hopeless expression that squeezed my heart. Maybe there really wouldn't be much loyalty to the joymancers left in her by the time the judge might be poking around inside her head. In this moment, I was finding it hard to consider that a victory.

"Are there *any* mages who don't go around wreaking havoc on regular people?" she asked. "Is that just what all kinds of magic do to you—make you power-hungry and arrogant?"

"I don't know," I admitted. "That seems to be how it works around here, anyway. I'm not sure if the mages in other cultures around the world approach the situation differently… We don't have very close contact with other fearmancer communities outside of a few in western Europe."

"I guess there are mages all over the world, huh?"

"As far as I know." I rubbed my mouth and then let myself add, "That's something I've always wanted to do—travel around and get to know the different communities, find out how they work, see if there are things we could learn from them."

An eager light came into Rory's eyes. "Why haven't you?"

I made a sweeping gesture with my hand to indicate the responsibilities all around me. "I can't afford to take my attention off the barony for that long. Maybe once I'm full baron and more established—once the older barons have retired and I don't have to worry about them undermining me as much... Of course, there'll still be my aunt to keep an eye on. Lord knows how long she'll keep coveting the role."

"I don't suppose she's had any criminal dealings we could sic the blacksuits on her for like we did with my grandparents?"

My lips twitched with a wry smile. "No, she's too careful for that. Which I should probably be thankful for, because if she were bolder with her attempts at sabotage, I might not still be here."

"I won't argue against that." Rory sighed and shoved the reports into their envelope, which she tucked inside her purse. Then she tipped her head back against the sofa. She frowned at the ceiling. "It seems like every time I turn around, there are fewer people I can count on."

"You've got the scions," I said. "Well, maybe not quite Malcolm yet, but Jude and Connar. And me. I'm not going anywhere."

"As long as the barons don't ramp up their scheming to try to crush you too."

There was so much guilt in her strained words that my throat closed up. I eased closer to her on the sofa, my knee brushing hers with a faint warmth. "Not going to happen. I've got way too much practice at dodging those kinds of threats."

She turned her head to face me, her brow knitting. Her hand slid across the cushion to find mine. An eager quiver shot over my skin at the feel of her fingers twining with my own. "But who's going to look after you while you're so busy looking after me?"

I couldn't have said exactly what broke the dam inside me. Maybe it was the compassion glowing in that gorgeous face of hers, part of what had drawn me to her in the first place. Maybe it was the fact that she could still worry about what happened to me even when her entire future was on the line. Or maybe I'd simply been holding myself back so long my self-control had worn thin.

"I happen to be very good at multitasking," I said, my voice dropping low of its own accord, and before I could think better of it, I'd brought my mouth to hers.

How many weeks had it been since I'd last had this pleasure? I'd forgotten what kind of heaven kissing Rory was. Especially when she kissed me back, with a soft little sound of encouragement that sent a jolt of lust straight to my groin. Her fingers teased into my hair, and her warm lips moved against mine, deepening the kiss. Just like that, I was lost in the taste of her, in the berry sweetness lingering in her mouth.

Her other hand clutched my shirt, tugging me closer. My breath stuttered with the press of her chest against mine. I gripped her waist, a thrill racing through me as the silky fabric shifted to offer a strip of bare skin.

In that instant, I wanted nothing more than to lay her back on the sofa and rediscover the blissful rush that came with the joining of our bodies. So what if the door to the lounge wasn't locked? Let the other guys stumble on us and see that she wanted me too.

My hand slid higher up her side, her fingers tightened in my hair, and a spark of warning finally penetrated the haze of my desire. I could fuck everything up if just one person stepped over that threshold and saw us—fuck it up not just for me but for her.

I yanked myself back, my nerves raw with the sudden loss of contact and my chest heaving. Rory stayed where she was, even more beautiful with that flush in her cheeks and the hungry glint in her eyes.

"I'm sorry," she started.

I cut the rest of her apology off with a shake of my head. "No. You didn't do anything wrong. I shouldn't have— *I'm* sorry."

It wasn't just for school policy, I reminded myself. I couldn't have her. Not in the long run, not the way I already wanted her, not without losing the barony and throwing my little brother into the fray. It was easier if I never got involved with her this intimately in the first place.

That was the logic I'd been using from the moment I'd realized I wanted her. Suddenly it struck me as absurd. I *was* involved—Rory Bloodstone was tangled all through my mind and my heart, and I'd be lying to myself more than anyone if I denied it. Sure, it'd be painful letting her go later if I gave in to those feelings wholeheartedly now… but every time I stopped myself, every time I pulled away, was plenty painful too. What was I really sparing myself from?

None of that mattered right now, though. Rory needed a friend, someone to help her through the awful situation she was facing, not another lover. The rest of those thoughts… the rest I could sort through later.

I exhaled slowly and brought my attention back to the reason for this meeting. "Do you think you'll want more of those reports?"

Rory looked down at her purse. She hesitated for a second before accepting the change of subject. The flush was already fading from her cheeks. "No, I think—I think this is enough to color my opinions in the right direction."

"Is there anything else I can look into or try to dig up that would help?" The need shot through me, sharp and searing, to do *something* more than I'd managed so far. "Really, anything at all, even if you're not sure I'd be able to. I do have more access to the professors and the administration in general…"

Rory's face brightened abruptly. "There actually is something. Can you get your hands on a student's class schedule for me? There's someone I'm having a lot of trouble tracking down."

CHAPTER TWENTY

Rory

"I feel so stupid," I said to Deborah as I flopped back on my bed. "I never even met any joymancers other than Mom and Dad, and I just assumed they were all peaceful and kind and, I don't know, focused on joy."

Deborah scurried along my arm to nestle her warm furry presence against my shoulder. *You weren't wrong. The Conclave's main objective is to see us spread as much joy as we can.*

"And to get in the way of the mages who are stirring up fear instead, by whatever means necessary, no matter who's in the way."

I don't know much about the active hostilities between our people and the fearmancers, but I'm sure they always weighed the risks carefully—

"How can you be sure if you don't know much about it?" I reined my temper in and sighed. I had to remember to keep my voice quiet when I was talking to her to make sure no one overheard. If I concentrated, I could make out the murmur of a few of my dormmates talking in the common room on the other side of my door.

"I'm sure they believe they're doing the right thing," I went on. "They probably have all sorts of justifications. I'm just starting to think they weigh the factors in the situation differently than I would. At least, when it comes to the ones that come up here basically hunting fearmancers, even though the fearmancers leave them alone."

They don't come after the fearmancers to protect themselves. It's for the Naries' sake.

"Then I don't see why they're so reckless about hurting the Naries who happen to be nearby."

Maybe the joymancers who fought those battles told themselves it was on behalf of people without magic, the people the fearmancers exploited… but the records I'd seen made it hard to believe that. How much were they trying to make the world more joyful, and how much did they simply take joy in eliminating mages they disagreed with, no matter who else paid the price along the way?

I wasn't going to say the fearmancers were *better* on average, but…

"How can I go to them to take down the school when I don't know how they'll handle that fight?" My throat tightened. "They might decide even the people who want the fearmancer community to be better, like Declan, are a threat. They might hurt the Nary students while they're destroying everything here they can. I don't want to cause some kind of slaughter."

If you laid it out for them—if you explained things—they'd understand.

"Maybe. How much will they even listen to me, when I'm one of those fearmancers?" I grimaced. "They didn't even trust me staying with my parents once I got old enough to come into my magic, when I'd never done anything wrong and they were suppressing my powers the whole time."

Deborah didn't seem to have any answer to that. She nuzzled my shoulder.

Whatever happens, I'll stand up for you however I can. I know you're more joymancer than fearmancer at heart.

That reassurance only made me queasy. I wasn't so sure anymore that I *wanted* to be more like the joymancers. I wanted to be like my adoptive parents—but as people, not as mages. When it came to my magic, I wanted to be *me*.

A fearmancer could do good for the world. A fearmancer could care about other people. I had more than one example of that just among the scions.

The peal of my phone's ringtone broke through my uneasy reverie. I rolled over to grab it out of my purse.

"Rory!" a cheerful voice said when I answered. "It's Maggie. I'm glad I could catch you."

It took me a second to recognize the voice and the name. Then my body tensed against the bedspread.

Maggie was Lillian Ravenguard's assistant. I hadn't heard from Lillian since our tense conversation on the green. I'd found her employee pleasant enough to talk with in the past, but now the brightness of Maggie's voice, as if we were all such good friends, rubbed me completely the wrong way.

"Hi," I said warily. "What are you calling about?"

Maggie's tone became more subdued as if she'd noticed my hesitance. "Oh, it's kind of silly." She let out a brief self-deprecating laugh. "I was just wondering if Lillian had come by to see you in the last couple days."

Wasn't knowing Lillian's schedule part of her job? The inquiry set my nerves even more on edge. "I haven't seen her since Monday."

"Ah. All right. Did she mention anything she was planning, maybe to do with your case, when you saw her then?"

"No, not really." And if she'd worked any magic on me, the other scions hadn't been able to detect it.

I wasn't inclined to give Maggie the details of our conversation if she didn't already know them anyway. I frowned at the phone. "Shouldn't you be asking Lillian this stuff?"

Maybe my tone was a little more brusque than was necessary. Maggie paused for a moment before answering, and her voice came out with a slight edge to it beneath the brightness. "I would, but she hasn't been in touch for a few days. I'm a little worried, considering her line of work, that's all. I thought she might have said something to you."

Lillian was probably off figuring out all the ways to ensure my murder charges stuck. "Well, she didn't, so I can't help you," I said. "And actually, I've got to get to class."

My jaw clenched as I tucked the phone away. Maggie was worried about *Lillian* and asking me for help, when I was the one just a few days away from losing the whole rest of my life? She had to have some idea what her employer was involved in even if she didn't know all the specifics. I didn't like being rude, but if I'd offended her and she didn't call again, I couldn't say I minded.

I hadn't been lying about having a class to get to soon, although it wasn't my own. Thanks to Declan's consultation of the student records, I happened to know that Cressida would be getting out of an Illusion seminar in just fifteen minutes.

"Wish me luck getting some answers," I murmured to Deborah, who bobbed her head encouragingly.

I got to the classroom on the fifth floor of the tower several minutes early, but that was fine. For all I knew, Cressida might have tried to sneak out early. I waited, leaning against the wall outside, until the door swung open and the students filed out.

Cressida was in the middle of the pack. She was just opening her mouth and raising her hand in what looked like the start of a casting when I snagged the sleeve of her blouse. Her mouth snapped shut at the sight of me.

"Hi," I said with a tight smile. "I think we need to talk."

Her lips pressed into a flat line. "I don't think we have anything to talk about," she said stiffly as we headed down the stairs together.

"Well, why don't I ask you a few questions, and we'll find out whether that's true. Consider it a request from one of your future barons."

I didn't expect that angle to necessarily work. As we left Nightwood Tower, I kept a casting on the tip of my tongue in case I needed to hold onto her magically. But Cressida apparently wanted to keep a certain appearance of dignity, because now that I'd found her, she made no moves to bolt for the hills.

"Where are we having this conversation?" she asked.

I wanted privacy, but I didn't want to have to travel very far while counting on her compliance. After a moment's deliberation, I headed toward the kennel. No one was hanging out on the field nearby, and

Malcolm's familiar was the only animal currently residing in the small building.

After a quick peek into Shadow's stall to confirm the Nightwood scion wasn't around—which earned me a pleading whine from the wolf—I turned to Cressida. Her nose had wrinkled as if the incredibly faint doggy smell offended her.

"You were in Ashgrave Hall when Imogen was killed," I said. "I passed you on my way to the stairs—and she was already dead when I got up to the dorm."

Cressida lifted her shoulders in the most subtle of shrugs. The dim daylight that streaked through the kennel's few windows washed out the purple and pink streaks in her white-blond hair. "That doesn't sound like a question."

She sounded as if she didn't care about the topic at hand, but a flutter of fear passed from her into me. She'd seen something she was afraid to talk about.

I willed my hands not to clench in frustration. "What were you doing up there? I'm going to assume the actual murderer didn't let you wander into our dorm while she was toying with Imogen."

"I was going to grab something from my room but realized I didn't really need it. Nothing particularly shocking about that."

I studied her expression. She'd kept a casual air, but her stance had tensed. Under my scrutiny, she narrowed her eyes at me. "I hope you're not trying to accuse *me* of killing her."

"No," I said quickly. "Of course not. I know it wasn't you. The point is, I think *you* know it wasn't *me*. And it's kind of important to me that I don't end up sanctioned for a murder I didn't commit."

"Well, I can't say I care either way." Cressida flicked her braid over her shoulder with obvious contempt.

Keeping my cool was getting harder by the second. "Maybe you'd care if you realized how much I already know. You went into the dorm room under ours, didn't you?"

Her eyes didn't give away more than a twitch, but a sharper jolt of anxiety hit me at the same time. I'd been right. She'd been the one who'd made that sound right after Imogen's attack. And why would she be scared of me revealing that if she hadn't heard evidence of the murder?

"What makes you say that?" she hedged, crossing her arms over her chest.

Of course, I didn't have any evidence I could put on display. "I put the pieces together," I said. "Other people might too. Won't you get in trouble if it turns out you were keeping quiet about important evidence that could exonerate a scion?"

"Is that a threat now?" She cocked her head. "I think if you had any real leverage, we wouldn't be talking about this in the doghouse. I have no idea what the hell you've gotten yourself into, Bloodstone, but you obviously have a lot of people out to tear you down. It'd be pretty stupid of me to do anything other than stay as far away from that mess as I possibly can, don't you think? Why the hell should I put my neck out for you? What the hell have *you* ever done for me?"

I hadn't hit back at her for all the ways she'd tried to undermine me with Victory or on her own, which I thought was pretty generous. Clearly Cressida didn't agree.

"Why make this about me?" I tried. "The whole fearmancer community is going to be affected if a soon-to-be baron goes down for a crime they had nothing to do with. Do you really want the kind of assholes who'd set me up like this to win?"

"If they win, then you don't deserve to be baron anyway," Cressida said tartly, and spun with a swing of her braid. "You asked your questions, and I answered them. We're done."

"Cressida." I took a step after her, but I really didn't have anything else I could say. All I could do was glower at her back as she sashayed away.

Her testimony could be the deciding factor in my hearing. The confirmation that she knew something gave me hope, but not enough to lift my spirits.

How the hell could I convince her it was worth the risk of giving that testimony?

CHAPTER TWENTY-ONE

Rory

"I don't know much about Cressida's family," Connar said as we ambled together across the green. "The Warburys are definitely respected, but they're a little distant from the other top families. They always give off a vibe like they prefer to stick to their own inner circle."

I made a face at the building in front of us. "So you don't have any idea what they might want that they don't already have."

"They seem to have pretty much everything they could want. I mean, maybe they'd want to mingle with a barony if they had the chance, but Cressida's never pushed the flirting all that hard, so I'm not sure—and anyway..." He trailed off awkwardly.

I gave him a playful tap of my elbow. "Don't worry, I won't try to marry off you or the other scions to clear my name. There's got to be something other than that."

"The trick will probably be getting her to tell you. If you could get a peek in her head with an insight spell, that might help."

"I don't think I'm going to win any points with her if I start stealing her thoughts without permission. She'll only hate me more."

"I don't think she hates you," Connar said quietly. "The crap she and the other girls pulled—it's all the same power struggle, you know. Jockeying for position, making themselves look powerful to anyone watching. Pretty much everyone here does it if they can get away with it. She thought she could lord it over a scion." He shot me a quick grin. "Clearly a major miscalculation."

It was hard to get into that fearmancer mindset—to understand the ways they might think automatically that were so different from how I'd been raised. I rubbed my forehead as the warm September sun beamed down on us.

The day was gorgeous, between that sun and the woody scents of the forest carrying in the air. I'd have been able to enjoy it a lot more if the problem of convincing Cressida to speak up for me hadn't been gnawing at me.

We came to a stop by Killbrook Hall, Connar tucking his hand around mine. We'd just left an early afternoon class, and I didn't have another today, but I couldn't summon any enthusiasm for heading back to my dorm—where Cressida would be hiding from me again, no doubt. There wasn't any point in making another attempt at talking to her until I'd figured out a better strategy anyway.

As I stood there waffling, Declan came out of the building with a couple of the professors. He nodded at something one of them was saying and then offered a remark that made the other chuckle, carrying himself with ease. But I recognized the strain in the slight stiffness of his posture, the flicker of fatigue that crossed his face when it was partly hidden as he swiped his hand up over his hair.

If I felt trapped by this situation, how much more confined must he feel, working himself to the bone to keep up appearances and prove himself every second of every day since he'd been a child. Even the brief respite I'd given him at the nearby Bloodstone country property had ended with more stress.

He deserved better than that.

The idea sparked in my head and traveled to my tongue before I had a chance to second-guess myself. "Connar," I said, squeezing the Stormhurst scion's hand, "I think we could use an escape, don't you? And Declan could definitely use one too. Why don't we all go up to the cliff for a little while and leave this place behind? Maybe getting away will give my mind a chance to come up with some brilliant plan."

Connar hesitated. The cliff where the two of us had first talked—and first a lot of other things—had been his private place for a long time, from what I'd gathered. I didn't think any of the other scions had ever joined him there before I'd stumbled on the spot. But he only balked for a second, and then he nodded. "Yeah. Why not? I'm sure a little time away would be good for him. I'm still impressed he managed to talk circles around the blacksuits to get you out of their custody in the first place."

Declan had just parted ways from the professors. Connar raised his hand with a quick wave. "Declan! We're going down to the lake. Why don't you take a break and come along?"

The Ashgrave scion's expression turned a bit puzzled at the invitation. As he seemed to waver, I smiled at him. "You don't have any classes to run off to, do you?"

"No," he admitted. "I'm not in much of a mood for a swim, though."

"We're just going to take a walk," Connar said, lowering his voice as we came up beside Declan. "There's a great spot a little ways down the shore that's great for just… thinking, and putting all the campus's tensions aside for a while."

The other scion didn't look any less bemused, but he nodded. "All right. You've been holding out on the rest of us, huh?"

The teasing was gentle, but a faint flush colored Connar's face. "None of us have many places we can feel are just ours."

"No denying that. I guess I didn't realize…" Declan trailed off as if recognizing that he couldn't end that sentence in a positive way. He hadn't realized that Connar was sensitive enough to be bothered by a lack of privacy? None of the scions had really seen the big guy as anything other than a musclehead. The Ashgrave scion course-corrected quickly, though. "You don't have to share it now."

"I want to," Connar said firmly. "I think… the last few months have proven that we have to be able to count on each other if we're going to get through this."

Declan gave him a longer, considering look, and a more relaxed smile crossed his lips. "Yeah." He caught my eye for a second, extending the smile to me, and I had the urge to reach for his hand too. But I knew better than to attempt that when we were in full view of the green.

We meandered past the campus buildings toward the lake and then veered down the path that rambled through the east woods. Connar walked with the confidence of a guy who'd taken this route dozens of times in the past.

He left the path with an assured turn of his heel, and Declan and I followed through the brush, up the forested slope. The leaves rustled overhead, and birds called to each other in the distance. As we neared the top, I made out the hiss of the lake's waves washing against the base of the cliff now far below us.

When he stepped from the line of trees at the edge of the clearing, Connar let out an audible breath. The brightening of his face made me wonder how much *he'd* needed a break too.

Declan stopped beside me, taking in the stretch of grassy ground along the cliff, the fallen log that bisected it, the warble of the water below, and the warm waft of the breeze. His stance relaxed by increments.

"This is nice," he said with a bit of awe in his tone. "I can't believe I didn't know this clearing was here."

Connar smiled with obvious satisfaction. "I stumbled on it when I was hiking around burning off steam. I'm sure I'm not the first person who's ever come up here, but most people don't go far off the paths."

"No, I guess they don't." Declan moved forward cautiously, as if he thought he might overstep in some way, but after a moment he headed over to the log and sat down on it to gaze across the lake. Something in my own chest released seeing him relax, if only for a short time.

"We should cast a spell to make sure we have this place to ourselves right now," I said to Connar. "I don't really trust the appearance of privacy these days."

"I'll cast it," he said. "Who knows what the blacksuits would make of that spell if you did?" He tipped his head toward the cuffs circling my wrists.

"Good point."

As he murmured a spell to block anyone from roaming this way, I wandered farther into the clearing, soaking in the sunlight and the fresh air. Other than the light weight of the cuffs, there was nothing here to remind me of everything I wanted to escape back in the real world.

Declan glanced over at me, his expression turning thoughtful. "You've been up here before," he said, not even a question.

"Just a few times." Who knew what he'd make of that.

Connar hunkered down in his favorite spot with his back against a tree trunk, and I walked all the way to the cliff's edge. I sat down there with a little thrill at letting my legs dangle over the distant water beneath. If the most nerve-wracking thing in my life had been this thirty-foot drop, I'd have been ecstatic.

After a while, the tug of the wind right over the water became too insistent. As I got to my feet, Connar did too. He came to join me in the middle of the clearing, setting his hand on my waist. I let myself lean back into his solid frame at his soft tug, but my senses sprang into sharper awareness of Declan several feet away. I didn't want to remind him of what he'd decided he and I couldn't have.

Connar touched my jaw to turn my face toward him and leaned over my shoulder to steal a kiss. I couldn't help melting into it for the few seconds before I eased away. My gaze twitched toward Declan, who'd turned to look at us. Connar followed my gaze.

"It's okay," Declan said. "Don't worry about me." That last bit he obviously meant more for me than Connar. His tone had stayed even enough, but his throat bobbed with a thick swallow, and there was enough hunger in his eyes to heat my skin. My mind slipped back to the other day in the lounge, the delicious burn of his kiss, over too soon.

Maybe I made some motion I wasn't aware of, or maybe Connar could pick up on at least some of what'd passed through Declan's expression. It wasn't as if he hadn't seen how much I enjoyed having the attentions of two guys at the same time before. The Stormhurst scion considered his friend for a long moment, and then he said, low but steady, "You could always join in."

A deeper flare of heat unfurled inside me at the thought, with a pang at the thought that Declan would refuse. His eyes widened, and he wet his lips, the brief movement of his tongue setting off all kinds of sparks through my nerves even across that distance.

To my surprise, he got up. "You're sure no one's going to make their way up here?" he said.

"If someone breaks the spell I put up, I'd feel it well before they got to the clearing," Connar said.

Declan's attention shifted to me. Our gazes locked, a quiver of anticipation racing through me. I lifted my hand toward him. If he'd changed his mind about what he was willing to let himself get into with me, I was totally on board.

He crossed the last distance between us and twined his fingers with mine. "Rory," he said, his voice raw, before he dipped his head to kiss me.

It wasn't like our kisses before. So many of those had been hasty, lust on the verge of being reined back in again. Even when we'd had sex in the country house, every caress had come with the sense that our time together was strictly limited.

This kiss captured my lips with a tender pressure that spoke of an expanse of pent-up desire, desire that could go on and on without fading away or being tamped down. As if Declan were offering himself up to me as he was, no boundaries or restrictions—all of him. A heady flutter passed through my chest.

Another set of lips brushed my skin. Connar kissed his way across my shoulder, adjusting the neckline of my dress for better access. His fingers trailed over my stomach. As he stepped around me, Declan pulled back from the kiss with a wildness in his bright hazel eyes that I'd never seen before. He seemed to waver for a second and then pressed his mouth to the side of my neck, leaving my lips for Connar to reclaim.

As their mouths sent heat searing through my body, I released their hands to curl my fingers into both of their shirts. Just having them on either side of me—these guys I wanted so much and was coming to care about so deeply—made me tingle from head to toe.

Connar's tongue slipped past my lips, and his hand came up to cup my breast. The swipe of his thumb pebbled my nipple in an instant with a jolt of pleasure. Declan grazed his teeth across the crook of my neck. At my ecstatic shiver, he stroked his fingers over my other breast.

The contrasting sensations of Connar's firm caresses and Declan's light teasing brought a gasp to my throat. The tingling condensed between my thighs. I wanted so much more than this—I wanted all three of us gasping—I wanted the pleasure to carry me away from my worries completely if only for a few moments.

My grip on their shirts tightened. As if picking up on my growing urgency, Connar reached for the hem of my dress and eased it up, letting the smooth fabric trace a path over my thigh. He released my mouth to nibble along my jawline, and Declan was there to catch my lips with his.

Connar's fingers settled over my panties. Bliss careened from my core. I made a hungry sound against Declan's mouth and stroked my hands down both guys' chests, wanting to pay back the sensations they were provoking in every way I could. They both stood several inches taller than me, but their differing frames, brawny and slim, felt like the perfect combination.

When my hand brushed over the bulge in Connar's slacks, he growled against my neck. The circular motion of his fingers between my legs intensified, each pulse of pleasure making my knees wobble. I traced my thumb over Declan's erection, taut against his fly, and his breath stuttered as he deepened our kiss.

Connar gave my clit one last flick of his thumb and yanked down my panties. I squeezed him through his pants encouragingly. His next growl turned a groan.

"Down," he murmured, half command and half plea, with a guiding nudge of his hand. I sank onto a grassy bit of ground on my knees, and he dropped with me, slicking his fingers over my arousal from behind. I rocked into his touch.

"Yes," I gasped out as his forefinger dipped right inside me. At the same time, I gripped Declan's pants, tugging both him and them down to my level. He knelt in front of me. As I flicked open the clasp and delved inside to free his cock from his boxers, he inhaled sharply.

"Rory?"

I gazed up at his face, reveling in the bliss thrumming from my core with each pump of Connar's fingers, in the silky stiff feel of the cock I held in my grasp. Nothing in Declan's expression looked anything but eager other than a hint of concern about me. As if I hadn't wondered what he'd taste like from the first moment I'd touched him like this months ago.

Slowly, deliberately, with a smile of anticipation, I brought my mouth to his cock. His hips jerked at the slide of my lips over the head. "Fuck," he muttered, the curse a strangled sound. He grasped my hair, his fingertips skimming my scalp in giddying ways.

The sound of a zipper opening behind me made me quiver with my own eagerness. I took more of Declan into my mouth, swiveling my tongue around his sweetly musky length, and Connar's cock grazed my entrance. Need throbbed through my sex. I pressed back toward him in encouragement.

He murmured the necessary spell, ran his hands over my ass, and then gripped my thighs as he thrust inside me. I cried out over Declan's cock. Riding the surge of pleasure that filled me, I closed my lips again and sucked even harder.

We rocked together in a perfect symphony of bliss, Connar plunging in and out of me with deeper and deeper strokes that fanned the flames inside me higher, my body swaying with his rhythm and carrying it into the bob of my head over Declan, Declan's hips pumping in time, his fingers stroking over my head.

As I felt the wave of release building inside me, I squeezed my mouth tighter around Declan's cock and sped up, urging him to join me. His fingers tightened in my hair. "Fuck," he said again in a strained voice. "I'm almost there. Rory, you don't have to—"

But I wanted to. I slicked my tongue around him as firmly as I could, and his voice broke. He came with a salty flood in the back of my mouth. As I swallowed, he drew back and urged my head up so he could kiss me.

As our breath and tongues twined, Connar sped up his thrusts too. A sound escaped me that was almost a whine. Connar's cock pumped into me even deeper, and he tucked his hand around me to rub the sensitive nub just above where we joined. The mastered strength in his powerful body radiated through me.

I shattered, leaning forward into Declan, every muscle shaking. In the rush of ecstasy, the hitch of Connar's chest told me he'd followed me over.

My head slumped against Declan's shoulder, my body slack in the aftermath. He slipped an arm around my back, and Connar hugged me from behind with a kiss to the base of my neck. All I could do in that moment was wonder at the fact that I'd gotten so lucky to have moments like this at all—and whether I could really hope for that luck to last much longer.

CHAPTER TWENTY-TWO

Rory

The vines rose up around me, clutching my limbs, squeezing my chest. Their thorns jabbed through my skin. I winced and gritted my teeth, willing myself not to yelp at the pain.

Professor Razeden's voice reached me distantly. "None of it is real. You can fight them off. How can you destroy them or slip free?"

That was the question, wasn't it? I had no doubt at all about what was being symbolized by the tangled thicket I'd found myself in for this Desensitization session. The dark chamber around me was meant to use a combination of insight and illusion to throw my worst fears at me so that I could practice tackling them. And yeah, I was plenty afraid of forces beyond my control constraining me and dragging me down. I was just glad the chamber hadn't produced a more literal illusion this time.

Well, other than the cool chuckle that echoed off the walls, mimicking Baron Nightwood's voice.

I'd slowly been getting better at fending for myself in these sessions, after the initial few when Razeden had needed to rescue me from my own mind. Conquering the agonizing sensations still wasn't anywhere near *easy*, though.

Dragging in a breath, I retreated farther into my head. The pain dulled with the distance. The vines squeezed tighter, but they weren't really there. They were just illusions—illusions I *could* change with the right spell.

They wanted to strangle me? I'd loosen them right up.

"Expand and open," I murmured, focusing on the tight coils. I pictured the loops stretching and releasing. Magic danced behind my collarbone, but at first the vines didn't budge. My pulse stuttered with the suffocating pressure.

Frowning, I spoke the words again, imbuing them with a harder push of magic. Sweat beaded on my forehead—and the friction around my limbs released. I scrambled away from the illusionary brambles before I lost control and they snatched at me again.

My feet skidded on the smooth floor, and I tripped onto my ass. Not my most graceful moment. But the prickly vines dissolved once I'd gotten my distance. The light blinked on overhead, revealing the domed room with every surface painted black, and nothing around me except Professor Razeden in his spot near the door.

"That one took you a little longer than last time," he said, checking his watch, "but not by a lot."

"I feel like it's a success any time I don't need you to step in," I said with a weak laugh as I pushed myself to my feet. "That's enough of a victory for me right now."

"Fair enough." He gave me a mild but genuine smile. "You've needed increasingly less intervention as we've gone on. Do you think you're ready to return to the usual group sessions?"

A twinge of guilt shot through my gut. Normally Desensitization was run with four students at a time, three observing while each struggled through their fears. Dealing with the potential distraction and embarrassment of those witnesses was part of the learning experience.

Because I'd had so much trouble with my initial sessions—and maybe because the images summoned up, like those of my parents' murder, had been so traumatic—the headmistress had switched me to solo sessions. But that obviously meant extra work for the professor.

The thought of my peers getting a glimpse of the things that terrified me made my stomach knot. But really, that was even more reason I should come to grips with the idea. They all had their fears exposed to each other on a weekly basis. And mine had been coming out more metaphorical recently, which was a small comfort.

"All right," I said. "If you think I'm ready."

"I'm sure you are, Miss Bloodstone," Razeden said. "But I don't resent giving you time to catch up at your own pace. It's hardly your fault you came to your studies so late and with so little preparation."

No, it was the joymancers' fault. Razeden didn't belabor that point, which I was grateful for. I nodded. "I appreciate it. I think I can handle group sessions now. I guess I should talk to Ms. Grimsworth about adjusting my schedule?"

"I can bring it up with her." He motioned me over to the door. "You obviously have much larger matters occupying your mind for the coming week."

Today's metaphors hadn't been particularly subtle, had they? Razeden must have been able to read between the lines.

He paused as I reached him, his hand resting on the door handle but not turning it. For a few seconds, he just studied me, his gaunt face even more solemn than usual.

"I can't imagine the pressure you're under at the moment," he said. "So I don't know if this will provide any comfort. But I'd like you to know that there are many of us in the school and farther abroad in the community who have certain standards of fairness and justice, even if they're not quite what you grew up with, and who wish to see you acquitted of this crime. If I can contribute toward your hearing, or if there's any other way I can assist you with this or future troubles, it would be my honor to serve my future baron."

He spoke in his usual measured voice, no outburst of emotion, with a matter-of-fact tone about the "future troubles" as if he took it as a given those would appear. Still, the unexpected declaration of loyalty brought an awkward flush to my cheeks.

How much did he know about the scheming behind the scenes? How much was he risking by making this statement to me?

Unless he was with my enemies, and this was a ploy to get past my guard? I didn't get that impression, though. He wasn't being pushy about helping or prying for information, just stating his position for the record.

"Thank you," I said past the tightness in my throat.

Razeden dipped his head in response and opened the door for me.

The Desensitization chamber was located in the basement of Nightwood Tower, and it had a typical basement vibe. As I climbed the stairs to the main floor, the air turned crisper and warmer, and more sunlight splashed across the walls from the windows above. The knowledge that I might have more supporters than had spoken up warmed me a little too, but it was hard to get much relief when there was no concrete way for those people to get me through the week ahead.

Jude had suggested we grab lunch in town after my session, so I headed around the tower toward the road into town. I expected to meet him at the path that ran through the woods alongside the road, but instead I spotted his dark copper hair halfway across the west field, where he was striding toward a cluster of students.

It only took a second and a gleam of the leaf pins on a couple of the figures' clothes for me to figure out that the fearmancers were up to their usual bullying tricks. Or the not-so-usual tricks, actually. A group of fearmancer students were surrounding the two Naries. As I veered over to intervene, one of the bullies stepped to the side to reveal another boy sprawled on the ground. The Nary guy was trying to push himself up, but his arms kept giving as if a force was pressing him down.

A force the fearmancer student was directing with subtle flicks of his hand. As the other Naries knelt to try to help their friend, the bully's lips moved with a softly spoken spell. Just like the bunch who'd harassed Shelby and her classmates the other day, these fearmancers were toeing the line of just how much magic they could get away with using without making their supernatural powers totally obvious.

Jude reached the group several strides before me—and caught the main bully's wrist in mid-flick. As the Killbrook scion faced the guy, I caught Jude's expression: jaw clenched and eyes dark with anger.

"I think that's enough," Jude said in a cuttingly flippant voice. "If you pump your ego up any bigger, it just might pop, and then everyone will see how small you actually are."

The other guy flinched, shifting into a defensive stance but shrinking a little just staring down the scion. When I caught up, his posture deflated even more.

"I wasn't *doing* anything," he said, giving us a pointed look as if *we* needed reminding that we weren't supposed to acknowledge the existence of magic. "The kid is such a weakling he couldn't manage to get himself up."

The "kid" in question, who looked about seventeen, had scrambled onto his feet now that he wasn't being magically restrained. "You were doing *something* to me," he accused, looking a little terrified at his own daring.

A chill shot through me. The fearmancer students really had stepped awfully close to the line for him to speak with that much certainty.

The main bully paled slightly himself, but he raised his chin with a snort. "I was just pointing out feebleness where I see it." He strode off without another word, his friends hurrying after him.

Jude and I exchanged a glance. He didn't look any happier about the situation than I was. I'd known he'd been working on his attitude toward the Naries, that he'd gone out of his way to help Shelby after the accidental injury he'd caused her, but I still wouldn't have expected him to defend a bunch of strangers from fellow mages. A flutter of affection rippled through my uneasiness.

The Nary guy was wiping off his jeans, his friends standing close with concerned murmurs about his wellbeing. I wasn't sure there was anything else we could do for them now. Would the professors care if we reported how bold some of the mages were getting with their magical harassment? I could just picture Ms. Grimsworth saying, "If we haven't heard anything worrisome from the Naries, then the other students must have disguised their magic well enough."

Jude was obviously thinking along similar lines. "Hey," he said to the Naries when their hushed conversation fell into a lull. "Has that kind of thing been happening a lot since the term started?"

"People have been pretty weird," one of the guy's friends said, hugging herself, her gaze and her tone wary.

"I've seen it before," I said quietly.

Jude frowned. His expression turned oddly contemplative for a moment. Then he snapped his fingers. "I've got a strategy you could try if the regular students get 'weird' like that again."

The guy considered him with narrowed eyes. "Why should we listen to *you*? Maybe you're setting us up for some other trick."

I shook my head. "We want to help. If Jude's got an idea, it's probably a good one." I didn't think he'd be offering it if he wasn't fairly confident it'd help.

The guy stayed skeptical, but his other friend cleared his throat and tipped his head toward me. "She's okay. I've seen her standing up for us to the assholes around here. I think we should at least listen."

Jude spread his hands. "You can give it a shot, and if it doesn't work, well, you at least shouldn't be any worse off."

"Okay, let's hear it, then," the guy said.

"It's very simple. Bullies are cowards underneath, you know. They like seeing you scared or upset. So what you do, next time someone's messing with you—stare right at them. Don't stop looking at their face. Show them you're not going to cower, and I bet you they'll back down."

Understanding clicked in my head. "Yeah," I said. "Stare them down. They'll hate that."

"Worth trying, I guess," the girl said with a shrug.

They all ambled back toward the green. Jude beamed at me. "You get it."

"If the Naries are watching their faces, they can't cast anything without giving themselves away. They've got to speak to get a spell out."

"Exactly! That doesn't mean they won't go back to old methods, but I think it'll cut down on some of that really overt torment." He glanced at the spot where the Nary guy had been pinned down and grimaced. “The general jerkishness of the student population does appear to have escalated. Something in the water?”

“I wish I knew,” I muttered.

“Well, I hope the next time the bastards try that on our scholarship students, they find themselves unpleasantly surprised.” He grinned again, looking incredibly pleased at the imagined triumph he might have manufactured for the people that just a few months ago he’d sneered at.

The flutter came back into my chest. I stepped closer to him and pulled him into a hug. Jude’s arms came around my shoulders, his voice amused but happy. “What’s that for?”

“Do I need a reason?” I mumbled into his shirt, my nose filling with the spicy smell of him, like peppered coriander. But the truth was, I did have a reason. A very big one.

He hadn’t done any of this for me. He’d already been charging over to the Naries’ rescue before I’d been nearby. Protecting them really had mattered to him for their own sake.

He wasn’t the same guy who’d mocked me during my first month here, not at all, and there was something miraculous about that transformation.

I lifted my head, and he pressed a quick kiss to my forehead. Emotion swelled in my throat. It wasn’t just for him—Lord knew I felt a hell of a lot for Connar and Declan too—but I was completely sure about these words in this moment.

“I love you too,” I said.

A wider smile leapt across Jude’s lips. His embrace tightened around me, and he ducked his head lower to capture my mouth. Right then, all I could feel, taste, and smell was him, and I was okay with that.

“Of course you do,” he said, but he couldn’t quite smooth the tremor out of his voice. “I’m eminently lovable.”

I swatted him, and he laughed, his eyes shining with affection. He pressed one last kiss to my temple, holding me as if he couldn’t convince himself to let me go just yet.

“If love were enough to protect you from the assholes after you, I’d have you covered,” he murmured. “You’d never have to worry again.”

If only we had a solution that simple when it came to my enemies.

CHAPTER TWENTY-THREE

Connar

Up in the cliff-side clearing, the morning breeze was a little biting, but I got all the warmth I needed from Rory nestled against me. She leaned her head on my shoulder, gazing out over the rippling expanse of the lake and the clear blue sky above, and sighed.

"It's too bad I can't just hide away up here for a few weeks and have the hearing blow over."

"Not much chance of that," I agreed with a grimace. I pressed a kiss to the back of her head in a way I hoped was comforting.

Having her like this was bittersweet. I couldn't think of much I enjoyed more than the simple pleasure of getting to hold her in my arms, inhaling her scent as sweet as toffee, knowing she had enough faith in me to completely relax in my embrace. But at the same time I was sharply aware of how ineffective all the muscles I'd built in those arms and the rest of my body were when it came to defending her from the greatest threat she was facing.

I could hold her right now, comfort her right now, but I couldn't fight or intimidate her enemies into fleeing. Why should she rely on me when I couldn't offer anything better?

I shoved those uneasy thoughts down and focused on the softness of her body against mine. Rory stayed cuddled there, the tree I was leaning against shading us, for another few minutes. Then she checked her phone. With a groan, she pulled away from me.

"I've got my mentoring session with Professor Viceport. She'll never forgive me if I'm even two seconds late."

Guilt jabbed through my chest. The Physicality professor hadn't exactly been warm toward Rory from the start, but the way I'd subtly sabotaged some of Rory's spells a couple terms ago hadn't helped the situation.

"Has she at least lightened up on you now that she's gotten a better idea of your abilities?"

Rory smiled crookedly. "She's not as overtly hostile as she used to be. I still don't think she likes me very much, for whatever reason. I guess there's not much point in worrying about that with everything else going on."

Before I could apologize again for the crap I'd put her through, she twisted around to kiss me, so tenderly I didn't need to hear the words to know she'd completely forgiven my transgressions. I wasn't sure I'd ever completely forgive myself, but I shouldn't put the burden of my guilt on her.

"I'll see you later," she said, getting up. As she moved toward the forest, another figure slipped through the trees toward us. My eyebrows rose at the sight of Declan hesitating at the edge of the clearing.

He glanced from me to Rory, his stance a little awkward, no doubt thinking about the unexpected intimacy we'd shared up here just a couple days ago.

"Hey," Rory said easily, as if it wasn't any big deal, and his shoulders came down. "I've got to get back to campus."

He nodded. "Can you meet me at the Stormhurst Building this afternoon? Let's say two? There are some things about your hearing I think we should discuss."

Rory's smile fell at the mention of the hearing, but she dipped her head in agreement. "I'll be there."

She brushed her hand against his before heading down the slope.

Declan ventured farther into the clearing, some of his earlier awkwardness coming back. He cleared his throat and looked at me. "I wanted to talk with you too."

I shrugged. "Sure. This is as good a place for a chat as any."

The corner of his mouth quirked up. He cast around and ended up sitting down against a tree a few over from mine, his long legs sprawling in front of him. His gaze drifted toward the horizon as he ran a hand through his hair.

"I probably don't need to tell you this, but what happened up here the other day—no one can know that there's anything going on between Rory and me. Not while I'm still an aide, anyway."

Something about his phrasing made me wonder how much had been "going on" between the two of them before that afternoon. It'd been clear from the way he looked at her that some kind of feelings had been developing for a while, and Rory had seemed nothing but eager about him joining in, but I hadn't seen any hint of a more than friendly connection between them before. I wasn't sure whether that was my own obliviousness or Declan's usually excellent self-discipline.

"Of course," I said. "Even if you weren't working for the university, I'm not really the type to go around gossiping."

"I know. Discretion just seems particularly important right now." He let out a ragged breath. "Maybe I should have walked away. But it was starting to feel so pointless, pretending not to want… what I want."

He fell silent. Declan didn't talk about his feelings in general all that much, at least not with me, so I didn't have a clue what kind of response he'd be looking for. I fumbled for the right words and finally settled on, "She's something special."

His whole mouth curved with a smile then. "Yeah, she is."

It was an awfully strange situation when you looked at it, him and me and Jude all caring about Rory the way we did, and her seeming to share that affection, but none of us really being in a position to make anything permanent out of it. Maybe that was why it only raised the smallest prickle of jealousy to think that she might have had something going with Declan that I'd had no idea about. We were all in the same boat. And we were all on her side.

"The things you need to go over with her about the hearing…" I said. "Have you come up with a new strategy that could help?"

"Not exactly. More like damage control." His smile turned pained. "These aren't the easiest opponents to go up against."

As I knew from personal experience. I hadn't meant to say anything about it, but his comment brought out the ache in my stomach that I'd been suppressing since I'd gotten the text last night. In some ways, Declan had a better idea of how to deal with the barons than the rest of us scions, even if they were family. Maybe he'd have some wisdom that would bolster my confidence.

"I'm supposed to meet with my parents later today," I said. "They're going to hassle me about Rory not taking their deal, I assume, and who knows what else." Just saying it aloud made my gut clench tighter. I'd stonewalled their suspicions briefly, but I wasn't used to playing mind games. What if I fucked something up this time? I hadn't forgotten my mother's clear threat about Holden. Of course she'd drag my brother into this situation too.

"And you're obviously not looking forward to that meeting," Declan said mildly. He looked down at his hands where he'd rested them on his knees and then glanced over at me. "You know, I think I've made assumptions about you over the years that weren't really fair, based on seeing what *they're* like. Malcolm was right about at least one thing—we need to stick together as scions. I should have paid more attention to *you*, and I'm sorry about that. For what it's worth, now that I am paying attention, it couldn't be clearer that you're nothing like them."

The words might not have given me an answer to my most pressing problem, but they were worth a lot all the same. Some of the uncertainty I'd felt about him and his apparent wariness of me crumbled away. I couldn't really blame him for keeping a certain distance given my parents, the stories about me, and the aggressive front I'd often let myself put on.

"I appreciate that," I said. "Hopefully you won't ever need to testify to that effect on my behalf."

He let out a rough bark of a laugh. "I'll be happy if the word 'hearing' never comes up again in the rest of my life in relation to any of us."

He'd been open enough with me that I decided to press the issue a little further. "Why the need for damage control for Rory? What's going on with her hearing?"

Declan paused, and for a few seconds I thought he might decide he couldn't trust me enough to tell me. Then he sucked in a breath. "The blacksuits have assigned a different judge at the last minute. Under pressure from the other barons, I have to guess. The new one—he's known to insist on extensive insight interrogations of the accused, often going far beyond the boundaries of the case to seek out other possible crimes."

A chill trickled through me. "We already figured it was possible they'd dig deeper into Rory's thoughts and memories."

"Yeah, but now it's basically certain. I think her attitudes about the joymancers have shifted, but the wrong piece of a memory, the wrong emotional impression in a situation… The barons want to dredge up anything incriminating they can. It's going to be awful for her, and I think it's pretty likely they'll find something they can spin against her with the lengths this judge goes to."

"Fuck. And she can't get some kind of exemption for privacy's sake, being the only heir of Bloodstone?"

He shook his head. "I get the sense there are a fair number of people even in the blacksuits who are wary of her because of her upbringing. I don't think the barons have had much trouble getting their way with the hearing. A lot of fearmancers would rather have one point of the pentacle dulled than potentially 'contaminated' by attitudes they don't approve of."

The idea set my teeth on edge. "If they'd just give her a chance…"

"We didn't really when she first got here, did we? It's only because we had to interact with her so much that we started to see her as she really is instead of through the biases we've had ingrained in us. I'm not sure how we'd get the wider community to that point. I'm not saying everyone's against her or anything, only that it's not going to be the smoothest road. If we can even get her past the current roadblock."

"Yeah." That was the problem right there.

We just sat, quietly contemplative, for a little while. Declan got up with a sigh and said, "I'll leave you to it. Good luck with your parents."

As he left, my spirits sank again. I focused on the glimmer of sunlight on the water and thought back over everything he'd told me.

A flicker of inspiration lit in my mind. Maybe there was something there I could use to my advantage. The meeting with my parents might not be a total disaster. I just had to play it right… and I had managed to play them once before, if on a smaller scale.

I turned the possibility over in my head as I lingered in the clearing, and kept mulling it over on my way back to campus. Was it really the best choice I could make? I could be shooting myself in the foot.

But I had to come to my parents with something, or God only knew how they'd take out their disapproval and frustration on me—and my brother.

My heart thumped hard as I drove through town and onward to the country inn restaurant farther down the highway where my father liked the food. I got there early, but their car was already in the parking lot. I squared my shoulders and strode inside.

My parents had only just gotten their drinks: a Bloody Mary for my mother and a whisky sour for my father. The thought of adding alcohol to the churn of my stomach made me queasier. I sat down at their table and asked for a root beer.

They didn't even give me a chance to pick up the menu. "You appear to have overestimated your influence over the Bloodstone scion," my mother said in a low but caustic tone, ripping one of the bread rolls in half. "Given the evidence, I wouldn't be surprised if she's learning more from your slips than you're managing her behavior. At this point, the most useful thing you could do is break her heart the morning before the hearing and let her go with that shaking her up."

She watched me from the corner of her eyes as she jabbed butter across the roll, evaluating my response to that suggestion as much as waiting for my agreement. My skin prickled.

"Rory had already talked to Baron Nightwood before I had a chance to see her that day," I said. "Once she'd made her decision, it'd have been humiliating for her to run back to him begging to take the deal after all. I don't think *anyone* could have influenced her that far."

"Nonetheless—"

I barreled ahead before she could pitch her heart-breaking plan again. "I might not have been able to talk her into accepting your deal, but acting like I'm on her side means she lets all kinds of things slip to *me*. I don't think that's a benefit we should be so quick to throw away."

My mother snorted. "And what great insights have you picked up that would be of any use to us, Connar?"

I forced myself to smile. "Just today I found out something I think you'll want to hear about this new judge who's been assigned to her case."

CHAPTER TWENTY-FOUR

Rory

The chlorine smell tickled my nose as I followed Declan down to the boiler room near the Stormhurst Building's pool. The hum of the pipes filled the dim space. It felt even more eerie than when we'd come down here with Jude and Connar to tell them about their parents' role in the conspiracy against me. Declan hadn't said yet what he wanted to talk to me about, but it was obviously something perilous if he felt the need to bring the conversation here.

He crossed the small room and came to a stop by the large pipe at the far end. One of the maintenance staff had left a bucket there. He flipped it upside down and nudged it toward me with his foot. "You can sit if you want. This will probably take some time."

"*What* will?" I asked. "What's going on?" The worries that had been nipping at me ever since he'd asked me to meet him here clamored louder. "Have the barons come up with more made-up evidence against me or something?"

Declan shook his head. "It's not exactly a new threat, just one that's escalated. The original judge has been replaced with one who's known for extensive insight interrogations. I'm sure the barons set that up to maximize their chances of uncovering something damaging in your own thoughts or memories. We have to assume at this point that the questioning will go far beyond the scope of the case."

"Shit." I rubbed my face with a rising sense of exhaustion. "I think… I think I should be okay now as far as the joymancer stuff goes. Unless they're going to hold the fact that I still care about my parents against me, but there's nothing I can do about that. There might be other things, though." Deborah, in particular. "The judge or whoever's doing the interrogation will ask specific questions, though, right? Not just go rummaging around at random?"

"It'll definitely be a directed questioning. We just don't know for sure what questions they'll ask—or what might come up in your mind in response. That's why I thought we could try a practice run, if you're okay with that. I've come up with a list of the questions I think they might use that would pose the most risk, and I can ask you them using insight to see what they provoke. If anything shows up that I think could be a problem, we have a few days to figure out how to handle it."

My pulse stuttered at the thought of even Declan making a thorough exploration of my mind. There were things he still didn't know about me, things I didn't think he'd approve of. But… If *anyone* out of all the fearmancers I'd met was going to accept the secrets I'd been keeping, it'd be him. Better I found out what might emerge now in his company than during the hearing.

"I guess there's not much chance I could simply decline the interrogation altogether?" I said without any real hope.

Declan made a face. "Not without looking incredibly guilty. The best defense we have is the use of the casting word in the illusion, and we've got no proof of that unless you let the judge see it. If you refuse to allow other questions, the barons or the blacksuits on their side will spin that hesitation against you in an instant."

"Okay." I exhaled slowly. "Let's try the practice interrogation then." I wasn't sure what a judge might ask that would uncover any sign of Deborah's true nature anyway. Maybe it'd turn out I was safe after all. The questioning might reveal some of my antagonistic feelings about the fearmancers, but only in the context of my parents' murder or the harassment at the hands of students here. It wasn't as if I'd taken any active steps toward taking down the community so far.

I sank onto the up-turned bucket. The ridged plastic surface pressed through my dress pants in a way that wasn't exactly comfortable. Declan took a step toward me, just close enough to graze his fingers across my forehead and brush my hair farther aside. It'd been a perfunctory gesture, but a tingle of warmth shot through me anyway. For an instant, I was back by the lake with his mouth and hands—and Connar's—on me.

A question of my own tumbled out. "Are we ever going to talk about what happened on the cliff?"

We'd left the clearing in a sort of blissful daze, and I hadn't seen Declan the day after. Since meeting up today, he hadn't made any mention of the encounter or any move to touch me other than that brief motion just now. I wasn't even sure whether he was glad he'd surrendered to the moment or full of regret.

Declan's body went still. His mouth opened, closed, and opened again. "We will," he said, in a slightly rough tone that sent a flutter through my stomach. "But I think maybe we should leave a discussion that potentially intense for after the hearing. And… it's better not to mix any of that part of our relationship with preparing for the hearing."

Because we wouldn't want the judge stumbling on *those* memories either. Concern shot through me. "You don't think—he won't ask about my dating life, will he?"

Declan gave me a crooked smile. "I'd say it's unlikely. But even if he does, anything he sees of us will only reflect badly on me. By the time you're in the hearing, I'll already have supported you every way I can. Even if you lose my testimony, you've got Jude and Connar too."

"I don't want you getting in trouble either," I muttered.

"It was my choice. On the off-chance it does come up, you can always say those were only daydreams."

My lips twitched in amusement. "I just fantasize about you a lot. Got it." It wasn't even a total lie.

"Are you ready?" he asked.

I steadied myself on my makeshift seat. "I'd better be."

I closed my eyes to try to focus on my own internal sensations, not that I'd be able to detect exactly what Declan picked up. He stayed where he was a couple feet away from me, a solid presence even when I couldn't see him.

The lilt of spell-casting came into his voice. "How did you interact with Imogen Wakeburn in the months before her murder?"

A quiver of magic rippled through my head. Then there was only stillness. I trained my attention on the rhythm of my breath until Declan must have seen everything he thought he'd get and moved on.

"What was your relationship like with your other dormmates?"

My enemies might get some mileage out of that, but not anything I could imagine anyone seeing as a criminal act. Victory and the others had done a lot worse to me than I'd ever done to them.

Declan went on through his list of questions, and I gradually relaxed. Nothing he thought the judge might ask seemed to bump too closely against the things I'd rather keep hidden. I was just starting to feel a little relieved when he said, "Have you ever intended to cause anyone at the school harm?"

My body tensed instinctively for a second before I willed myself calm again. What could he see in my impressions that would give away any of the plans I'd only considered, without any chance to put them into action? And I'd never really wanted to see anyone *hurt*, only… stopped.

But that might not be good enough. Declan was silent for a longer stretch than before. When he spoke, there was a note in his voice that made me nervous all over again.

"Rory."

I opened my eyes and looked up at him. He was studying me, his brow knit, the brightness of his eyes shadowed with concern.

"When I asked that question, I mostly got fragments of times when you pushed back against Victory's hassling," he said quietly. "Nothing unusual there. But there was also—some time when you were with Connar, at night—I think it might have been up on the cliff—you were asking him about the school's wards. About the joymancers trying to find us. Why would that have come up?"

My heart sank. It'd come up because when I'd asked Connar those questions, I'd been trying to figure out how I could help the joymancers get past the wards and attack the school. I'd forgotten about that short conversation—forgotten that I'd pursued the idea of destroying the school that far in an overt way.

Declan has asked whether I'd intended to cause anyone harm. Could I explain away that memory somehow without admitting why I'd really brought up the subject of the wards? I groped for an excuse, but nothing came to me. The drone of the pipes echoed through my head.

Declan crouched down in front of me, taking one of my hands. His voice stayed gentle—as gentle as it'd been the first time I'd met him, when he'd tried to reassure me in the midst of my parents' murders.

"Whatever it was, we need to talk about it now. If you freeze up during the hearing like you just did with me, the judge will double-down on the questioning in an instant. I know it couldn't have been anything that bad, Rory. I know *you*. You can tell me."

I swallowed thickly. He didn't know me as well as he thought. Looking back on those moments when I'd been so sure that bringing the joymancers charging into the university was the right thing to do, I had to suppress a cringe. The situation, the people here and there, the history between the mage communities—it was all so much more complicated than I'd realized.

I could tell him that too, along with everything else. He deserved to know, didn't he, before he tangled his life even more with mine? Maybe it was wrong that I'd let him stick his neck out so far for me without telling him how many traitorous thoughts I'd entertained.

"It is pretty bad." My gaze dropped to my hands. "I— You have to remember that when I first got here, all I'd seen was fearmancers murdering people and then acting like bullies. As far as I was concerned, calling this place 'Villain Academy' was totally accurate. Compared to that, and knowing what my parents were like, I had to think the joymancers were the heroes."

"That makes sense," Declan said. "You didn't exactly get the most pleasant welcome into the community."

A halting laugh made its way up my throat. "No. And I—all I

wanted to do was get back home to California. To be with people like my parents again. And to get justice for my parents against the people who'd killed them—to get justice for the Nary students here for the way everyone seemed to treat them—to stop all the lessons about how to terrorize people..."

My throat closed up for a second. Declan waited patiently, his grip steady on my hand.

I made myself look at him again. "I decided I was going to find a way to give the joymancers access to the school: figure out how to disable the wards, or something like that. And then I'd run back to California and use what I could tell them as proof that I wasn't a villain like the rest of you. And let them take down the school."

I had to suck in a breath before I could go on. "But I never thought—I had no idea the joymancers might be so *vicious*, that they might kill people indiscriminately just for being fearmancers. I didn't want some kind of slaughter here. And I was going to make sure people like your family were protected. But after seeing all the reports, and remembering how my parents kept me apart from the rest of the joymancers, I don't want even that anymore. That conversation with Connar—it was months ago. I haven't done anything to undermine the school."

Declan's expression had tensed. My gut knotted at his reaction. "I'm sorry," I added. "I just wanted to *stop* more people from being hurt."

"Oh, Rory," he said in a tight voice. I braced myself for an accusation or recrimination, but instead he simply leaned forward and hugged me.

I hugged him back automatically, burying my face in his shoulder. "I don't want anything to happen to you," I said. "Or Jude or Connar or... so many people here. I'm not sure what I want to do if I can make it through this hearing, but I'm not running back to the joymancers. I promise you, I wouldn't put you all in that kind of danger."

"I know." Declan eased back a bit so his head bowed next to mine. He paused, his jaw working.

"I never told even my father about this," he said. "Back when I was around fifteen, when I was getting more access as baron-to-be and I saw the full report on our parents' deaths… There was a while when I kept picturing how I could encourage the other barons to launch some kind of assault on the joymancer community. It ate at me so much that they were getting away with what they'd done and with so many other attacks on us too."

A lump rose in my throat. "That makes sense."

"Well, once my anger settled down, I felt ashamed that I'd let that impulse for revenge get a hold on me. But if I'd had the opportunity, I might have acted in the moment."

"You were younger. Fifteen's practically still a kid."

He shook his head. "That's not the point. *You* saw the people you think of as your parents killed right in front of you and had people at school pushing you around. All I did was read a report and look at some pictures. If your response means something awful about you, then I must be the most wretched human being ever."

Every particle of my body balked at that judgment, which I guessed had been the point Declan was trying to make. "So you don't hate me for what I wanted to do?"

"Not at all." He pulled back completely to look me in the eyes. "But the other barons and the blacksuits won't see it that way. We need to come up with a reasonable answer if they stumble on that memory."

"I couldn't think of anything except the truth to tell you."

He gave me a wry smile. "I appreciate the honesty. What if… what if we lean into the protectiveness you feel now for at least some of the people here? You could say you were imagining that if joymancers came onto the campus, you'd have to hurt them to defend us. That's still harming someone who in the scenario would be at the school."

The idea of joymancers storming the school did send a jab of anxiety through me now. "Do you think they'd buy it?"

"If you let your real emotion come through, yes. Nothing else emerged that would suggest you were sabotaging the school. You didn't take any concrete steps toward putting that plan into motion, did you?"

I shook my head emphatically. "It was just asking about the wards, and, I mean, I thought about how I could do it. But you can't read specific thoughts in memories, right?"

"Definitely not." He sat back on his heels and then straightened up. "We'd better make sure nothing else jumps out like that. Are you good to keep going?"

"Yeah," I said, but as I adjusted my position on the bucket, an ache crept through my chest.

Declan had accepted the plans I'd been making in this moment when he was set on exonerating me. Would he be so forgiving when he'd had more time for what I'd told him to sink in after the hearing was over?

CHAPTER TWENTY-FIVE

Rory

Staying in the university library instead of studying in my dorm had plenty of upsides. I got immediate access to all the books in the place without hauling them up multiple flights of stairs. If I found a good nook, it was often quieter. And there was something soothing about the high ceilings in the expansive room. Sometimes my little bedroom started to feel claustrophobic.

Of course, the library also had its downsides. Not least of which was the fact that if someone noticed me in whatever secluded corner I'd holed up in, the illusion of privacy could vanish in an instant.

It started with the page I was looking at in the book open on my lap abruptly slipping from my fingers. As I flinched at the sudden movement, more pages started flipping over as if in a strong gust of wind, though I didn't feel anything on my skin. I stared for a second before my brain caught up. It was a spell, obviously.

I jammed my hands down on the book to try to hold it still, but jerked them back at the first sound of tearing paper. I didn't want to ruin this magical text because of someone else's stupid prank. Instead, I settled for tipping it off my lap onto the floor. As soon as the cover thumped shut, it lay still.

Before I could decide whether it was worth trying to pick the book up again—or try any other—a slim, leather-bound volume tumbled off a shelf above me and smacked me right on the top of my head.

Pain spiked through my scalp, and a yelp slipped from my lips. I scrambled onto my feet, just as a heavier volume careened toward me. I jerked my arm up just in time, wincing at the slam of the edge just below my elbow. That was going to leave a bruise.

What asshole had thought it'd be a good idea to pull this stunt? Assaulting a scion and supposed murderer didn't seem like the wisest move ever. Another dare between junior students who were immature enough to ignore the possible consequences?

I braced for another blitz from above as I marched down the aisle toward the open area of the library, but the next projectiles came from the opposite shelf instead. Three books hurtled at me in quick succession from slightly different angles. This time, at least, I was prepared enough to snap out a spell to form a protective barrier around me. The books bounced off it and thudded to the floor.

When I emerged from my aisle, it was just in time to see a familiar but unexpected figure charging into the row of shelves next to mine. In the brief glimpse I got of him, Malcolm's eyes were so fierce beneath his golden hair that you could forget about the divine part—that was all devil. A second after he'd barreled out of view, someone let out a squeak of pain.

I hurried over to find him holding a girl, who did look young enough to be a junior, by the collar of her blouse.

"What the hell family did you grow up in that you figure attacking a scion is a good way to make a name for yourself?" he demanded, glaring down at her.

The girl had blanched. "I'm sorry," she mumbled. "I was just—my mother said everyone would be safer if someone proved the Bloodstone scion would lash out again, so she'd have to leave school—"

Her gaze flitted to me, and a rush of fear hit me from her, so sharp I almost bit my tongue with the impact.

"Let her go, Malcolm," I said evenly. "She was just trying to impress her parents. You should know something about that."

Malcolm grimaced at me, but he released the girl's shirt, still glowering at her. "Didn't you ever think that if *you're* the one throwing books around, if someone did lash out, it'd be at *you*? I don't think anyone will be impressed if you get yourself killed. Not that Rory would have done that anyway. In case you haven't noticed, she's a hell of a lot more forgiving than I am."

The girl cringed against the shelves as if expecting him to hurl a spell at her. I slipped past him to face her. The comment about her mother had sent my thoughts spinning. I couldn't help remembering Cutbridge and his campaign against the Naries.

"What's your name?" I asked her.

She wet her lips nervously, hugging herself. "Penelope Villia," she said after a moment's hesitation.

Villia. That name had been on Professor Banefield's list too. Yeah, provoking me into a show of force, especially against a junior, would only have solidified the case against me, which of course the barons' allies would want. This kid was only a tool.

"I'm not going to hurt you," I said, and shot a pointed glance at Malcolm. "And neither is he. But I'd appreciate if you didn't dive bomb me with books any more in the future, all right? Go study for your classes or something."

"Yes. I'm sorry." She bobbed her head and bolted past Malcolm out of the aisle.

The Nightwood scion shook his head. "You go easy on them, and they'll just come back worse."

I narrowed my eyes at him. "Where the hell did you come from all of a sudden anyway? Have you been following me around?" Interrupting the guys outside our dorm rooms had been reasonable enough, but this situation was more of a stretch as a coincidence.

"Why would I do that?" Malcolm said. "I was walking by, and I heard the commotion. You're welcome, by the way."

"I don't think yanking her around solved anything. And I'm really supposed to believe you just *happened* to be passing by at the right moment?"

Malcolm let out a huff of breath. "If we're going to argue about this, can we at least do it somewhere less public? You can tell me exactly how horrible it is that I saved you from an avalanche of textbooks in the scion lounge just as easily as here."

He might have a point. An argument between scions, especially when one of those scions was me, could draw attention I didn't really want just two days before my hearing. I gritted my teeth and nodded.

Malcolm didn't say anything else until we'd descended the stairs to the basement room. The lounge was empty, but the hint of coffee scent in the air suggested someone had been enjoying the space recently.

The Nightwood scion ambled around the pool table with a drum of his fingers against the wooden edge. He tucked his hand into the shoulder bag he was carrying and drew out an ancient-looking book.

"I do actually care about my classes. I was in the library grabbing this book for a Persuasion theory essay I'm supposed to write."

"Oh." A significant portion of my annoyance dissolved. I rested my hands on the end of the pool table, keeping several feet of distance between us. "Sorry for the stalking accusation, then. You do still need to back off if you notice someone hassling me, though. I'd much rather handle it my way—and I *can* handle it."

Malcolm frowned. "We're scions. That means we look out for each other."

"Because you think if I look weak, somehow that'll make you look bad too?" I restrained myself from rolling my eyes. "I don't totally know why you've decided *you're* not going to attack me anymore, but heroics on my behalf really aren't necessary."

"Even if I want to jump in and give you a hand?"

"Why would you? You don't even like me."

For a second, Malcolm just stared at me. Then he let out a sputter of a laugh. "For Chrissake, Rory."

He snatched up one of the nearby balls and dropped it on the table with a thunk. The other balls rattled as it connected with a cluster. His gaze followed them across the green surface.

"You've got official confirmation that you're the most powerful mage in the school," he said, his voice dropping lower, "but you still blush a little whenever any professor compliments your spellwork.

When you're concentrating hard on figuring out what to cast, your mouth sets with a little crease at the corners, and that's when anyone who's been tangling with you should know to watch out. When you're scared, you lift your chin as if you can intimidate the feeling into going away. But the best moments are when you totally commit to whatever cause you're championing next. There's this light that comes into your eyes, so fierce and unwavering…"

He looked at me then, with an expression I couldn't read but an intensity in *his* eyes that made my breath catch in my throat. "I don't *like* you. I fucking adore you, Rory."

It was my turn to stare. My jaw had gone slack, but I couldn't have missed the affection that had run through every observation he'd related. He meant it.

I had no idea how to react to that. Confusion and wariness, sure, but the idea that I'd provoked that much fond emotion in him also sent a weird sort of thrill through me.

I snapped my mouth shut, and then managed to say past the thumping of my heart, "You haven't acted like it."

His mouth twisted. "You could say it crept up on me. And it's not as if you haven't been incredibly frustrating at times too. Maybe I tried so hard to break you because I thought we needed to remake you before I could let myself really want anything. But I don't believe that anymore. I'm starting to think you might be exactly what I need as you are."

My fingers had curled around the lip of the table, clutching it tight. I forced them to release. So many feelings were colliding inside me that I could hardly identify all of them, let alone tell which was winning out.

This was Malcolm Nightwood—the bully, my tormentor, hater of joymancers and mocker of good intentions. But… I kind of understood his rancor toward the joymancers now. I even sort of understood how he could see his treatment of the other students as a guiding and strengthening force, as part of his role as scion, rather than real attacks, even if I didn't agree with his approach.

He'd recognized at least some of his mistakes and taken steps to make up for them. He was trying to protect me now, with the same passionate loyalty he had for the other scions. Within the vicious bully was a devoted friend, a determined leader, an affectionate master to his familiar… and just remembering kissing him set off a flare of heat over my skin.

So no, Malcolm wasn't evil. But he was still that bully at the same time. He *had* still tormented me, in all kinds of ways I couldn't forget.

"Why are you telling me?" I said finally. "What are you expecting to happen?"

"Because it seemed like something you should know. And I'm not expecting anything. I'm *hoping* that you've got enough goodness in your heart to give us a chance to be whatever we could be, together."

His dry tone with the last sentence brought back all the times he'd called me Glinda as a jeer. I sucked in a shaky breath.

"I don't know if that's possible. I don't trust you—I'm not sure I'm ever going to really trust you, after everything."

"I can work with that." He took a careful step toward me. "I've spent my whole life so far proving myself every way I can to a man who's never satisfied and barely deserved the effort. Proving myself to you sounds like a much better deal. I broke your trust—I'll rebuild it just like I figured I'd rebuild you. You'll see."

He took another step, almost close enough that he could touch me now. A quiver ran through my body in awareness of him. Part of me clamored to flee, but a larger part was determined to see how far he'd try to take this moment.

I was just as much a scion as he was, and the heir of Bloodstone didn't run away.

"There goes that chin," he said softly, with so much tenderness my throat closed up. "All glorious defiance. I swear, the last thing I want to do now is hurt you, Rory."

Maybe some part of me *wanted* him to convince me, to prove to me that all that past between us didn't have to matter. That the good in him could override the rest. In that moment, I could imagine that being possible, even if I wasn't there yet.

With a click, the lounge door opened behind me. I glanced back to see Jude on his way in, his stride casual until he caught sight of the two of us. Something about the vibe in the air made him hesitate.

Then he started to backtrack, reaching for the door. "Never mind, I can see you're busy."

My head jerked around in time to catch the glower Malcolm had been shooting his way. My hackles rose with my own protective instinct. I marched across the room to catch Jude's arm.

"This is your lounge too. *I* don't want you to leave."

He stopped, his gaze flicking to Malcolm and back to me. At my expression, his shoulders came down. He eased closer, taking my hand. "Well, in that case…"

Malcolm cleared his throat with a disgruntled sound. I gripped Jude's fingers and turned to glare at the other scion.

"You want to prove yourself?" I said. "The first thing you've got to demonstrate is that you can handle me having other guys in my life. Because if you try to tell me who I'm allowed to care about or make out with or anything else—if you try to make me choose between you and everyone else—then I'm going to choose the guys who aren't making up rules about how I live my life."

Jude ducked his head. "Well said, Ice Queen," he said in an amused tone, but the squeeze of his hand told me how much the declaration had meant to him. I didn't imagine he was used to being valued over the Nightwood scion.

I bobbed up on my toes, and he met my kiss, no hesitation in him now. My other hand slid around his neck as I leaned into the embrace. The thought of Malcolm watching, of him deciding how he was going to respond to my statement, somehow made the kiss even hotter.

If Malcolm still had any illusions of me kowtowing to him, he'd better get rid of them fast.

Jude slipped his arm around me as I pulled back from the kiss. I tipped my head against his chest and looked toward Malcolm.

He was watching not me but Jude, with an expression that looked almost startled. Had he ever seen his longtime friend look actually content? I wasn't sure Jude had ever *been* content from the moment he'd discovered his father's secret until finally admitting that secret to me. It had burned too deep a hole in him.

Jude gave my hair an affectionate ruffle. "It's no good loving a wild thing if you're going to stick it in a cage."

"Wild?" I said in mild objection, and he chuckled.

"Only in the best possible ways."

Malcolm's gaze had come back to me, with a heat in it that was nearly scorching. "No, I suppose it isn't. I can handle starting on the sidelines." He folded his arms over his chest and nodded to Jude. "Let's see how well you can drive her wild, then."

Jude hesitated. "What do you mean?"

Malcolm tipped his head, considering. "Go down on her. Get her off."

Jude's eyebrows leapt up. He wavered for a second and then glanced at me in question. Desire had already lit in his eyes.

An unexpected giddiness ran through me. I'd been with two guys at the same time before, but they'd both been participating. To have Malcolm, lord of the scions, exercising the self-control to stand back and watch his friend do what I suspected he'd have liked to do himself… I guessed that would prove something. It made the temptation to go along with his suggestion that much more delicious.

Why not? What did I have to hide? If he was going to melt down over seeing me with Jude after all, it'd be better to find that out now and lay any question of us getting together to rest.

Okay, maybe I was a little wild.

I teased my hand down Jude's chest, and he grinned, obviously taking that as answer enough. As he captured my lips again, he walked me a couple steps backward so my shoulders touched the wall. He held me there, kissing me so thoroughly my mouth tingled, while he trailed his fingers down my side and over my thigh, and then around to the already eager place where my legs joined.

My hips swayed toward him as he stroked my clit through my clothes. He smiled against my mouth. With tantalizing slowness, he undid the zipper of my pants and drew them down until they fell the rest of the way to puddle around my ankles. Leaving my mouth to kiss my neck, he hooked his fingers around my panties. With each inch he tugged them down, he descended twice as quickly.

He pressed his lips to my sternum and my belly button through my blouse. When his breath spilled over my sex, I tipped my head back. Anticipation hummed through me, almost as heady as the pleasure to come. I braced one hand against the wall and curled the other into Jude's hair.

He lowered his mouth to me with a swipe of his tongue that sent a bolt of bliss through me. A moan vibrated from my throat. He worked me over gently and then more determinedly, increasing the pressure with every sound that escaped me. Pleasure rippled up from my core in sharper and sharper waves.

As he teased his tongue around my clit, Jude stroked his hands over my thighs and then up to my opening. He suckled hard and dipped a finger inside me at the same time, and I let out a noise like a growl, all wanting. My hips jerked.

Oh, fuck, that felt good—but somehow not good enough at the same time. I wanted to be really full, full of him.

Malcolm didn't get to call the shots, not in any of this. I had the final say in how my lovers came to me—and how they made me come.

My fingers tightened in Jude's hair and urged him up. "Jude. I need more."

He caught my eye, his smile coming back with a flash. In an instant, he'd straightened up. His hand dropped to help me as I fumbled with his zipper. I wriggled my panties the rest of the way down to my feet.

Malcolm let out a wordless sound of protest, but I didn't give a damn. I clutched Jude's shoulders, and he lifted my thighs, molding them around his hips as he plunged into me with a hastily cast spell. I cried out at the burst of pleasure. My legs squeezed around him, holding me up and holding him to me. With each rock of his hips, fresh bliss swept through me.

Jude kissed me roughly on the mouth, his control starting to wobble. I arched into him, and he thrust deeper to hit just the right spot to send me spiraling higher.

"Love you," he murmured in a hot rasp by my ear. "Love you so fucking much."

With those words, I shuddered right into ecstasy. The crackling of pleasure raced through me, jolting another moan from my throat and setting every nerve singing.

As I clutched onto Jude, his breath broke, his rhythm turning jerky. With a groan, he spilled himself inside me.

We came to rest against the wall, my legs still clasped around Jude's hips, his head tucked against mine. I touched his cheek and turned his face for another kiss, long and lingering. Only after that did I look to where Malcolm was still standing.

The Nightwood scion's hands and jaw had clenched, but his eyes were outright blazing, and not, from the feel of them, with anger. Especially not when paired with the bulge that had formed against the fly of his slacks.

Without letting myself rethink the impulse, I reached out to him. After a second, he stalked over. I let my feet sink to the ground, but I kept my other arm around Jude. He nuzzled my neck as I held Malcolm's gaze.

"Not what you asked for, I know," I said. "You might be the king of Blood U, but you don't rule over me."

"Point made, loud and clear," Malcolm said, with a rawness that sparked one more wave of desire through me. That and the fact that he'd accepted our deviation from his orders with relative grace brought my hand to the front of his shirt. I grasped it and pulled him to me.

If Malcolm objected to kissing me while I was still partly entwined with another guy, he didn't show it. His mouth claimed mine with all the searing confidence I remembered. I was breathless when he eased back, but from the hitch of his chest, so was he.

"I'll take that for now," he said, with a look so heated it promised a hell of a lot more to come, if I decided I'd take him.

If I was free enough in two days' time to take anyone at all.

CHAPTER TWENTY-SIX

Rory

The dynamic between Malcolm and I might have been shifting, but the lines drawn in the past hadn't completely dissolved. When Declan called a last-minute meeting of the scions to discuss my hearing, this time over breakfast in a corner booth at one of the restaurants in town, he didn't include the Nightwood scion in that invitation.

As I slid onto the bench next to Connar, I couldn't say I wished Malcolm were there. He could talk all he wanted about "adoring" me, but I hadn't seen any evidence yet that he'd risk his standing in his father's eyes to help me in any public way. Sharing one kiss with him was a heck of a lot less risky than sharing the details of my planned defense.

The waitress started bringing over plates and glasses a minute later, the rich doughy smell of fresh waffles filling my nose along with the savoriness of crisp bacon. Declan, who'd arrived just after me, blinked at the spread as he sat down across from me next to Jude.

The Killbrook scion leaned back in his seat with a smirk at his neighbor. "I took the liberty of ordering for all of us. I figured once you got here, you'd be all talk and forget about the fact that breakfast generally includes eating. Grab whatever looks good. I think we can share."

He rolled the last word off his tongue with a sly glance at me. Warmth tickled through me despite the anxiety balling my gut, but only for a moment.

My hearing was tomorrow. This was our last chance to prepare. But Jude was right—better not to do it on an empty stomach.

I lifted one of the waffles onto my plate and garnished it with a dollop of syrup. The anxious pressure inside me made me stick to only a small bite to start, but the fluffy sweetness offset some of my queasiness.

Declan gave Jude a bemused look, but that didn't stop him from taking toast and bacon for his own plate. "I've actually got good news," he said as he scraped butter over the toast. "I still think the practice session we did was worthwhile, Rory, but your judge has been replaced *again*. The new one is much less Insight-leaning."

"Really?" Connar perked up, avid interest gleaming in his light blue eyes. A smile slipped across his face that looked more triumphant than I'd have expected.

Declan lifted his gaze to contemplate the other guy. "Do you know something about this? It's pretty unusual to have a change like that so close to a major hearing, let alone two."

Connar's grin stretched a little wider. "I wasn't sure it would even work. It was a gamble." He glanced at me. "My parents insisted on meeting with me a couple days ago. They still think I'm going to help them undercut you. So… I told them you were glad to hear about the new judge because you thought what he'd glean from intensive insight would push the case in your favor."

Jude let out a low whistle and a laugh. "Look at the heir of Stormhurst turning schemer. The rest of us better watch out."

Connar started to glower at him, but I grabbed the bigger guy's arm with a grateful squeeze. "Thank you. Obviously they bought your story. You might have just saved me a whole lot of trouble." I paused. "Are you going to get in trouble with them when you speak for me at the hearing?"

He shook his head. "I already prepared them for that. I told them I'd need to testify on your behalf to keep up the 'ruse' of being on your side, but that I wouldn't say anything too concrete." His mouth slanted. "Unfortunately that's mainly because I don't have any concrete testimony I *can* give."

"I still appreciate it. Every little bit has to help."

Looking at him and around the table, an unexpected sense of conviction settled over me even though I still had a long, uncertain day ahead of me tomorrow. The four of us were working as a real unit now, not just as lovers but as the colleagues we were meant to be for the rest of our lives. Despite our rocky beginning, our goals had ended up aligning. Even Malcolm was starting to reject his father's ideals, if only in private.

For the first time, the sense of what it might be like to rule alongside these men really hit me. We could do a hell of a lot when we were all barons. We could change the whole direction of fearmancer society into something much less villainous.

It didn't matter what the joymancers had done or how much I could trust them—I didn't need them. I didn't *want* them involved. I had all the support I needed to tear down the toxic parts of the community right here with me, ready to work from the inside.

As long as I was still free to do that work after tomorrow.

A thought that was obviously on Declan's mind too. "Not that you're out of trouble yet," he said. "But you definitely have one problem off your plate. Have you made any progress with Cressida? If she did hear or see something, *her* testimony could be all you need."

I grimaced, poking at my waffle. "She's still avoiding me. I don't know how I could convince her to stick out her neck. She obviously doesn't see any benefit in it for her, and it's not as if I have anything she doesn't have that I can offer her." Money meant nothing to someone whose family was already rolling in it. I hadn't established any real connections in business or politics yet. Mostly what I brought to the table were enemies.

Jude waved his fork at me. "You have the barony. She's got nothing like that."

"I can't exactly give *that* to her," I replied. "And I don't have much official power yet anyway."

"You will, though, if you get through the hearing. Maybe you can work with something there."

"There was—" I cut myself off, hesitating. I'd come across some magical theory in yesterday's studying that could apply to this situation. A way of guaranteeing Cressida a future reward dependent on future needs. But it'd been so open-ended that my instinctive reaction had been to reject the idea.

She'd helped Victory with the other girl's campaign of harassment against me. She clearly didn't have any interest in supporting me for my sake or doing the right thing. How the hell could I trust *her* with any kind of open-ended deal?

But maybe it was time to take that gamble, just like Connar had with his parents. Owing Cressida some uncertain price was better than becoming the other barons' virtual slave.

And really… a few months ago, I hadn't trusted any of the guys sitting around me. As I'd just been thinking, they'd changed so much, revealed depths I hadn't suspected.

Most of my fellow students had to be more than simply villains. I could be cautious, but maybe I should give more of them the benefit of the doubt. These were my people. I was going to lead them one day —soon, as long as I didn't let the older barons win.

That girl in the library yesterday had outright attacked me to try to get me re-arrested, and I'd been willing to forgive her. I had no idea what pressures Cressida might be operating under, did I? *What have you ever done for me?* she'd asked, and from a fearmancer perspective, that was a totally valid question regardless of the stakes.

The guys were watching me with open curiosity, waiting for me to finish. I pushed a piece of my waffle across my plate. "I think I'm going to have to take a leap of faith."

Since our initial talk, Cressida hadn't been going to quite the same lengths to stay away from me. This time, waiting for her to come down from her afternoon class, I lingered in the first floor landing rather than right outside the door.

Despite the lesser intrusion, she stiffened as soon as she saw me standing there. She picked up her pace as if to stride right past me, but I stepped over to block her as unaggressively as I could manage.

"You said I've never done anything for you," I said quickly, pitching my voice low to avoid the curious ears of the students filing past us. "And that's true. What if I could do something that would make it more than worthwhile for you to get involved in my 'mess'?"

She stayed tensed, but something shifted in her expression, a hint of eagerness that gave me hope. I motioned her to the side, away from the other students. "We could talk downstairs? There's no Desensitization session going right now." I'd checked.

Cressida's mouth tightened before she exhaled in a rush. "All right, fine. Let's hear this. But it'd better be good. People will notice that you're even talking to me, you know."

Exactly why I'd already planned a nearby private spot for that conversation. We tramped down the stairs into the cool basement air and its thicker silence.

The waiting area outside the Desensitization chamber wasn't exactly comfortable, not much more than half a room with a wooden bench on either side. With a little luck, this conversation wouldn't take very long. I said a few words in casting to make sure no one would follow us down while we were there and sat on one of the benches.

After a moment's hesitation, Cressida sank down opposite me. "So?"

"Have the other barons ever done anything for you?" I asked. "Is screwing me over going to get you anything from *them*?"

She scowled at me. "What does that matter? I'm not staying out of this to get some reward—I'm trying to make sure whoever has it out for you doesn't put me and my family in their crosshairs too."

Nothing about her response gave me the impression that the barons had approached her or that she knew they were the ones who wanted to undermine me. Her family's name hadn't shown up on Professor Banefield's list. That wasn't any kind of guarantee, but it gave me the confidence to continue.

"It matters because if I make it through this hearing, I'm going to be a baron soon too. And I've got to think that having one baron in your corner is better than none."

Cressida let out a scoffing sound. "That's an easy thing to say when you're backed into a corner. We're not friends. I've got no reason to think you'd actually follow through on any promises once you're past this."

I swallowed hard and clasped my hands together. "What if you didn't have to count on promises? What if we magically sealed the deal?"

That flicker of eagerness came back, but her skepticism hadn't vanished. "What do you mean? You can't give me anything right now, and you don't know what you'll be able to offer in future."

"No. So you could think of it as me writing you a blank check. I think I found an approach that'll let me offer you one favor if you testify at the hearing tomorrow. You'd be able to come to me at any time during the rest of your life and ask for one thing, and I'd have to do that for you, whatever it is."

Just saying the words made my chest clench up. Cressida's eyes widened as the enormity of what I was proposing sank in. "Are you serious? You lay down magic like that, and—I could ask you to actually murder someone. I could ask you to give me your entire estate."

Of course she'd immediately see the ways the spell could be exploited. I gave her a slanted smile. "I was planning on including a couple of caveats about the favor not being a criminal act and not doing me or anyone else direct harm, so the really questionable stuff would be out. But yes, I know it's a risk. I'm willing to take that risk, because I'm asking a big risk of you. It's only fair, don't you think?"

Disbelief lingered on her face. I'd be surprised if most fearmancers would ever have considered putting themselves at another person's future mercy like this. But I wasn't an average fearmancer, as she should know by now.

"Do I have to decide right away?" she asked.

I shook my head. "We can cast the spell now—you need to contribute a little to confirm your end of the deal—but it's conditional. If you don't show up at the hearing tomorrow and share everything you know that would help my case, then I won't owe you the favor. You can make up your mind on your own schedule."

She paused for a moment, her gaze going distant as she took that information in. Her lips pursed and relaxed again. She shifted her focus back to me.

"All right," she said. "What do we have to do to work this spell?"

Relief washed over me. I got up, infinitely glad that I'd spent all my time between breakfast and this meeting studying the magical techniques involved.

"We can cast it right here. All we have to do is agree on the exact wording of what we'll each offer, and the rest is actually pretty simple."

"And you won't tell anyone else we made this deal, whether I go through with it or not?"

She was still nervous about the repercussions. I couldn't blame her for that. "I won't," I said. "I know you don't have the highest opinion of me, but I think you've at least seen that I'm not in the habit of publicly airing private business."

"Then we'll put the spell in place," she said, getting to her feet. "And I'll decide about the rest… when I'm ready to decide."

CHAPTER TWENTY-SEVEN

Rory

The hearing room in the blacksuits' building looked a lot like a regular courtroom, at least from what I'd seen of those on TV. A raised seat with a sort of podium for the judge stood in the middle of the far wall, two lower seats on either side of it, and several rows of benches filled the other end of the room. All of the furnishings gleamed with dark hardwood. An inoffensive beige hue colored the walls.

Someone had cranked the air conditioning even though it was a cool September day outside. I'd worn a jacket over my blouse and dress pants, and I left it on, restraining a shiver, as I walked with Declan to the judge's end of the room. Our shoes tapped eerily loud on the polished floor. I curled my fingers around the hem of my jacket, resisting the urge to hug it closer around me.

Several people were already taking spots on the benches: Jude and Connar, the professors who'd agreed to testify about my temperament and approach to casting, and a number of blacksuits, including a few I recognized from my arrest. How many of them really believed I was guilty?

I dragged in a shaky breath as we came to a stop at the seat to the left of the judge's spot.

"This is where you'll sit for the entire hearing," Declan said in a low voice. "Anyone else giving testimony will come up on the other side. You've got about fifteen minutes before they'll get started—the blacksuits are usually pretty prompt. We'll get through this."

I wished the steadiness of his voice was enough to reassure me. I nodded and sank into the chair, resting my forearms on the narrow desk-like protrusion in front of me. My thin cuffs clinked against the wood.

Declan went to join the other two scions. A few more blacksuits arrived, including Lillian. She caught my eye and strode over. I tried not to tense too much at the thought of talking to her.

"Is there anything you need before we get started?" she asked. "Even a glass of water?"

I grasped my purse. "I brought a bottle of water. I can't think of anything else at this point." I hadn't been sure I could trust anything the people here might give me to consume. And really, I just wanted this day to be over. I didn't think Lillian could give me that, at least not with the outcome I wanted.

A woman built like a football player marched into the room and up to the judge's podium with barely a glance around. She didn't even seem to make note of me. Maybe this one wasn't an Insight enthusiast, but she still looked awfully intimidating.

The next figure to step through the doorway unsettled me even more. Baron Nightwood stalked over to a bench at the back of the room and settled onto it, resting his hands on his lap. Apparently he wanted to watch over the proceedings he and his colleagues had set in motion first-hand. I was probably lucky I didn't have to stare down all three of them.

A different venomous trio arrived a couple minutes later: Victory and her two best friends. I couldn't take any comfort from the sight of Cressida in the room when it was in the company of my long-time nemesis. I guessed the blacksuits had wanted them here to give their account of my earlier conflict with Imogen.

I watched Cressida cross the room, waiting to see if she'd give me any sort of sign of whether she meant to go through with the deal we'd set up, but she kept her gaze averted. That alone made my heart sink.

Reflections of the assembled figures wavered in the mirror that stretched along one side of the room. Declan had told me that observers, mostly blacksuits, often watched from behind that one-way glass, some of whom the judge might consult with for a second opinion if she felt she needed one. The thought of the gazes that might be following me from behind that surface made my skin itch.

The judge clapped her hands together, and the murmured conversations on the benches fell completely silent. "Judge Blazehed, bringing the proceedings to order. We're here today to consider the case of the murder of a Miss Imogen Wakeburn, contended to have been carried out by Miss Rory Bloodstone." Finally, she turned her dark gaze my way. "That would be you, I assume."

"Yes, Your Honor," I said, falling automatically into courtroom lingo.

I thought the corner of her mouth twitched at the title, but so briefly I couldn't tell whether it had shifted up or down. She set a sheaf of papers on the podium area in front of her.

"I've read over the written reports, but I'd like to hear directly from those involved. I also understand both the prosecutor and the accused have witnesses to offer support to either side of the case." She turned to the blacksuits sitting on the front bench. "Let's begin with your account of the discovery of the murder and the arrest."

The blacksuits got to give their version first? That didn't strike me as particularly fair.

I willed myself to sit still without fidgeting as one of the men who'd arrested me took the seat on the other side of the judge, where I couldn't even see him. Maybe that was the point of this layout—to ensure the witnesses couldn't be influenced by anything they saw of the accused. But the situation gave his voice an oddly disembodied quality as he recounted the call they'd received from a fellow student, their arrival at the scene, their observations of Imogen's body and my behavior, and how they'd taken me into custody.

The judge took all this in with nods here and there and an

occasional question. When she was satisfied, she dismissed the blacksuit and turned to me.

"Miss Bloodstone, can you give me your account of the events leading up to and around Miss Wakeburn's death?"

My chest constricted with nerves, but I cleared my throat and started speaking. I gave her the same story I'd given the blacksuits—the party, noticing Imogen was missing, going back to my dorm to get better shoes for driving, finding her body, being gripped by magic as illusions bombarded me.

"I see," the judge said, with no indication in her expression of whether she believed me. "And will you allow me to verify this version of events as well as I can with an insight spell?"

"Yes, I'll allow that," I said, and remembered to add, "One thing you should make note of that I realized afterward—in the illusion of me casting the killing spell, I use a casting word. That's part of my evidence that those are illusions and not memories. Because I only came into the magical community recently, I'm not yet at the point where I feel comfortable working magic by using my own invented words. I pretty much always use literal words to fit the intent of the spell. Some of my professors are here today to confirm that."

"Noted for the record."

The judge's seat swiveled with her so she could face me straight on. I kept my head turned toward her, my pulse thudding as I willed down my instinctive mental shields. She focused her gaze on my head and asked the question charged with magic: "How were you involved in Imogen Wakeburn's death?"

Like with Declan, I had no sense of her intrusion into my mind other than a faint shiver of energy. I held still and tried to keep my breath even. After several uneasy minutes, the introspective haze cleared from the judge's eyes, and she leaned back in her seat.

"All right," she said. "I'll hear from your professors next. Before I do, is there anything else you'd like to offer in your defense?"

I'd rehearsed this speech in my head over and over. To my relief, it spilled out easily.

"Imogen was my friend. Even if I'd been arguing with her, I wouldn't have hurt her. I haven't hurt *anyone* since I arrived at

Bloodstone University, even though people have done a lot worse to me than argue. A few of my fellow scions who are also my classmates have come to vouch for that."

The judge's expression stayed impassive. "I'll hear from them after the professors, then. Thank you, Miss Bloodstone."

My fingers twisted together in my lap as Professor Viceport, Professor Burnbuck, and then Professor Crowford went to the other side of the podium and testified that during class, they'd only heard me using real words that literally fit the spell I was casting. Viceport even submitted herself to an insight question so the judge could check her memories. I couldn't tell how much weight this one detail was being given, though. It sounded so small when they talked about it.

The judge called the scions up next. Declan came first and gave a firm, articulate declaration that he'd never seen me to be anything but fair and even-tempered, sometimes to my own detriment. Jude followed and said he agreed with everything Declan had mentioned.

"I gave Rory a hard time when she first got to the university," he added. "The fact that she not only took that treatment in stride but had the generosity to set the past behind her and consider me a friend is all the proof *I* need that she'd never lash out at someone in violence."

He shot me a quick smile as he went back to the bench. Connar passed him to take the same spot.

"I haven't always been the kindest to Rory either," he admitted in his statement. "There were times I was horrible to her. But when she was hurt or angry with me, her reaction was to stay away from me, not to attack me. I've never seen her show any aggression that wasn't in immediate self-defense, and even then, she's moderate about it."

As he returned to the others, one of the blacksuits stood up. The judge nodded to him.

"I'd like it noted on the record that by multiple accounts from their peers, Mr. Killbrook and Mr. Stormhurst have both appeared to be romantically involved with Miss Bloodstone, and as such their opinion of her is likely to be biased."

The judge glanced toward the guys. "Would you dispute that fact?"

"That my feelings for Rory go beyond friendship?" Jude replied.

"No. I dispute the bias. I'm hardly so starry-eyed I'd somehow miss murderous rages."

Connar nodded. "I don't feel my relationship with Rory has affected my ability to see her actions clearly."

"All right. I'll take that all into account." The judge shuffled a few of her papers to the side and looked to the blacksuits again. "You have your own witnesses to make statements?"

"Yes," the man who'd given the initial testimony said. "I'd like to establish the underlying tension that had existed for some time between Miss Bloodstone and Miss Wakeburn, and I have three of their dormmates here to recount their experiences."

This should be fun. I clasped my hands together tighter as Victory came up to speak.

She and Sinclair didn't say anything I couldn't have expected. Victory explained how Imogen had spilled the beans about my familiar, leading to Deborah's being stolen by the scions—playing down the threats she'd used to get that result, unsurprisingly. They both commented on the chilliness between us in the days right after that incident and the distance that had never quite disappeared. None of it sounded like the prelude to a violent murder, at least.

When Cressida walked over, my heart pounded faster. She vanished from my sight on the other side of the podium. I waited, forcing my breaths to stay even. If she was going to speak up about what she'd observed during Imogen's murder, this would be the time to do it.

"Tell me about what you saw of Miss Bloodstone's associations with Miss Wakeburn," the judge said.

Cressida inhaled audibly and repeated most of what the other girls had said in her own words. Then she paused.

The judge cocked her head. "Is there something else you'd like to add, Miss Warbury?"

I braced myself. And Cressida said, "No. That's all."

My spirits sank as she sauntered away without a backward glance. She'd decided even with my "blank check," telling the truth to save me wasn't worth the risk.

My freedom depended on the testimony of three guys the judge could easily dismiss as biased and one minor detail of the illusion.

I swallowed hard, fighting down a swelling sense of hopelessness. Baron Nightwood hadn't stirred from his spot at the back of the room, where he was watching the proceedings with a small smile. He thought he'd already won. He might be right.

"Have you found any evidence of anyone else who might have been present in the room during Miss Wakeburn's murder?" the judge was asking the blacksuits, with a shake of the lead guy's head in response, when a door at the opposite end of the room swung open.

Malcolm Nightwood stepped in and strode right up to the judge's podium, his handsome face set with total determination. I stared at him for a second before my gaze darted to his father… who was no longer smiling.

The judge looked a little startled too. "Mr. Nightwood," she started.

Malcolm lifted his head at a typically cocky angle. "I apologize for the delay, Judge Blazehed. I have a few things to say in regards to Miss Bloodstone's character." He didn't so much as look at me.

A chill crept over my skin. Had all that fuss about wanting to prove himself to me been a front? Was this some kind of coordinated assault arranged with his father?

But as the judge waved Malcolm to the testifying seat, the baron's face only tightened. He was keeping his cool, but I'd swear he was upset. He definitely didn't look as if he'd expected this.

"Go ahead," the judge said to Malcolm.

I caught a flicker of movement, as if the Nightwood scion had waved his hand in the direction of the benches. He must have been indicating the scions, because the first thing he said was, "Those two told you how harsh they were on Rory when she arrived at the school. But they'd have to admit that the way they cracked down on her was nothing compared to my offensives. The truth is, Miss Bloodstone challenged me and insulted me on her first day at the school and refused to back down, and I couldn't let that kind of disrespect stand."

"I see," the judge said. My stomach churned with the uncertainty of where he was going with this. His testimonial didn't sound all that complimentary yet.

Malcolm's voice stayed confident, but I caught a hint of rawness creeping into it, like the other day in the lounge. "I intended to break her down, and my actions in pursuit of that goal were undeniably cruel. As a few examples, I forced her to walk to a high window using persuasion and threatened to make her jump out. I organized the stealing of her familiar and the trick to make her think it'd be killed. I conjured nightmares so wrenching she woke up screaming several nights."

The memory made me cringe inside. Malcolm kept talking.

"Through all that, no matter how badly I hurt her or terrorized her, she never *once* inflicted the slightest harm on me. Not a single bruise or scratch, not the slightest emotional scar. She refused to back down, but she also refused to fight on my terms. Even when I mocked her to her face, I never once had to fear for my safety."

"With all due respect, Mr. Nightwood," the judge said, "your situation and Miss Wakeburn's may not be entirely the same."

"Of course they aren't," Malcolm said, his voice turning derisive. "I'm the heir to a family second only to Rory's. The Wakeburn girl couldn't possibly have dealt the same kind of damage I'm capable of. There's no doubt in my mind that it's impossible for Rory to have injured her, let alone murdered her."

I couldn't help glancing at Baron Nightwood again. He kept strict control over his expression and stance, but he couldn't completely hide the furious glint in his eyes. No, this hadn't gone according to his plan at all. My stomach listed with a nauseating combination of gratitude and fear.

Malcolm's father looked ready to rip *someone* apart. And I didn't think it'd be me this time.

Malcolm got up to sit on the bench behind the other scions without acknowledging his father. He met my eyes for just a second, with the slightest tip of his head as if to say, *I owed you.*

It probably wasn't enough. The judge hadn't sounded convinced. But it might make a difference—and it mattered more than I could say that he'd even tried.

And it seemed his show of courage had affected more than just me. As the judge shifted in her seat as if to call an end to the hearing, Cressida shot to her feet.

"I have something else to say," she blurted out, ignoring Sinclair's gape of bewilderment beside her. "I know that Rory didn't kill Imogen."

The judge's eyebrows leapt to the fringe of her bangs. "And you didn't think to include this information earlier?"

"I… I'm including it now," Cressida said, her hands clenching at her sides.

"Well, come up here and let's hear it, then."

There was a stirring among the blacksuits as Cressida recrossed the room. Her face was nearly as pale as her hair, but she walked steadily enough.

"This is what I know," she said after she sat down. "The day Imogen died, I left the end-of-term party early because I was tired and wanted to head home. I just needed to get a few things from my room. When I tried to go up the stairs to the fifth floor, a strong emotion came over me that I needed to be somewhere else. As I backtracked, I realized it had to be a spell compelling me away."

She paused and then soldiered on. "I was suspicious. I—I actually wondered if Rory had something to do with it, because the three of us had been hassling her quite a bit, and maybe she was taking some kind of revenge. I went into the dorm room under ours and cast a spell to bring out any sounds from above to try to hear what was going on up there."

The whole room was dead silent when she stopped to gather herself. "I assume you did hear something," the judge said, with an unexpected softness.

"I did," Cressida said, quietly but clearly. "At first there wasn't anything I could really make out, but then I heard a sort of scuffing noise like shoes on the floor. All of a sudden, someone cried out, and there was a heavy thump. It startled me so much I flinched and hit the coffee table behind me. That made me nervous that whatever was going on upstairs, the person or people responsible might realize I'd heard. So I hurried out of the building as quickly as I could… and I passed Rory after I came out on the first floor. There's no way she could have been the one who did it. She wasn't anywhere near our room when it actually happened."

Her voice had turned strained with the finale of her confession. The judge peered down at her. "Would you allow me to verify your statement using insight?"

"Yes," Cressida said, even more quietly. That had been part of our deal—that she had to offer direct proof of her statement for it to count. "I'm ready."

I fought the urge to squirm in my seat as the judge delved into Cressida's mind. While my dormmate had spoken, Lillian had disappeared from the gathering of blacksuits. Interestingly, Baron Nightwood was gone as well. Had they slunk off somewhere to brainstorm urgent damage control?

If they had, they didn't make it back in time. The judge straightened up and dismissed Cressida back to her bench. She turned to me with the first glimmer of sympathy I'd seen from her.

"I apologize for everything you've been through, Miss Bloodstone," she said.

The realization that this horror show was actually finished swept through me so suddenly tears sprang to my eyes even as I smiled.

The judge turned toward the rest of the room. "I've now been faced with overwhelming evidence that Miss Bloodstone had no part in Imogen Wakeburn's murder. Which means I do hope the blacksuits will quickly apply themselves to discovering who not only killed one of our own but attempted to damage the reputation of a soon-to-be baron at the same time. Rory Bloodstone is innocent. This hearing is over."

CHAPTER TWENTY-EIGHT

Malcolm

Watching the blacksuits detach the silver cuffs from Rory's wrists gave me a sense of elation that overwhelmed even the dread expanding in my stomach. I held on to that feeling as they escorted her, with due deference this time, to the exit, but the moment she passed through the doorway, my relief had already started to fade. The other scions were heading over to follow her. I got up too, but more slowly.

My friends glanced back at me, obviously assuming I'd join them. That subtle show of solidarity nearly broke my resolve, but I gave them a brief shake of my head. Though Declan looked a little concerned and Connar hesitated a beat longer, they went on without me when I didn't move toward them.

The dread rose up to fill my chest as well. I'd done what I could for Rory here, however much difference it'd made. Now I'd face the consequences. I'd rather not face even a fraction of them in front of her, especially when that might make both our situations worse.

Dad had left his seat at the back of the room at some point during the final testimony. I wasn't sure where he'd gone, though no doubt he'd find me the moment he wanted me. He had to be fuming about this outcome. Maybe he'd stalked off to take his first round of hostility out on his blacksuit co-conspirators?

One battle for Rory's freedom was won, but the war was hardly over. It'd be useful to know which of the blacksuits or other leading fearmancers the barons had far enough in their pocket to involve them in the highest level of treason.

Rory and the others had disappeared by the time I came out into the hall. A few blacksuits lingered near the office doors farther down the brightly lit space with its khaki-green walls, but my father wasn't among them. I strolled over as if I had every right to be nosing around the blacksuit headquarters.

"I don't suppose any of you know where my father wandered off to?" I asked in a blasé tone.

One of the women motioned toward the other end of the hallway. "I think I saw Baron Nightwood going into Ravenguard's office."

I bobbed my head in thanks and ambled on. Blacksuits were trained to pick up on suspicious body language or any other sign of ill intentions. I didn't want them to see anything besides a scion looking for his dad.

"...was quite a mess," one of the other blacksuits muttered behind me as they went back to their conversation. "Can you believe— Someone should have found that witness before the hearing."

Yeah, I'd bet this catastrophe would haunt the blacksuits who actually cared about justice for quite a while. Now they had to sit with the fact that they'd wrongly accused and almost wrongly sanctioned a baron-to-be. Was it too much to hope that a few sanctions be laid out on some employees around here?

I found the office labeled with a Lillian Ravenguard's name just around the corner. The murmurs of the other blacksuits had faded away—this stretch of hallway was empty and silent. No sound filtered through the closed door either, unsurprisingly. If blacksuits couldn't handle their own security, what the hell was the point of them?

None of them could quite match a Nightwood's power, though. We were a ruling family for a reason.

I glanced around, weighing my options. If someone came by,

which was totally possible, they'd catch me eavesdropping in an instant. Maybe I should take a page out of Cressida's playbook. Making use of available nearby space had worked for her, even if what she'd heard hadn't been what she'd have wanted to.

I moved to the office next to Ravenguard's and sent a quick querying spell inside to confirm it was empty. Then I tested the lock with a casting. The physical mechanism had a complicated winding of magical strands reinforcing it, but not quite as treacherous as the wards I'd disabled on my father's home office. I could handle this one as long as no one interrupted me.

I bowed my head next to the door and murmured one casting word after another, gradually unwinding the spell. At the sound of footsteps in the distance, I froze and edged to the side so I could pretend I'd just been standing here waiting, but the person stopped before they reached the bend. With a thankful exhalation, I returned to my work.

God willing, my father and the blacksuit and whoever else might have joined their meeting wouldn't already be done talking by the time I made my way inside.

Finally, the lock clicked over with the twist of my fingers. I ducked into the dark room, leaving the light off in case it'd be visible from beneath the door. A thin illumination seeped through the closed blinds on the tiny window at the far end.

I moved to the wall between this office and Ravenguard's and came to a halt beside the shelving unit against it. Training my gaze on the bare stretch of wall, I cast my way through the plaster.

Ravenguard had a silencing spell embedded in the boundaries of her room. My awareness nudged against it cautiously. I didn't want to *break* it, because she'd definitely notice that, but if I could just scrape a little gap in it…

I worked at it as slowly as I had the patience for, my skin prickling in recognition of the minutes slipping away from me. It took at least ten before I'd worn the silencing spell thin enough that the amplifying cone I conjured in the air brought faint voices to my ears.

The first one I heard I easily identified as my father's. "…taken due precautions."

A woman's voice answered. "We've been over this. It was a delicate balance. The more variables you control, the more likely your control will be noticed."

"That's simply not good enough."

"Well, what do you expect me to do, baron? I can hardly arrest her all over again for a crime it's been proven she didn't commit."

"Perhaps you should have had a more extensive back-up plan."

"There wasn't any sign we needed one until the last minute."

Any last lingering hope I'd had that Rory and Declan's insinuations were wrong, that my father hadn't crossed the line into overt treason and murdering random mages after all, crumbled away. The murder and the false arrest had been *his* plan, clearly. And the blacksuit he was talking to was one of those who'd helped him carry it out.

"What about the other avenue you said you were investigating that might solve our problems?" Dad asked, and I perked up again, shoving down the admittedly rather feeble flicker of disappointment. I didn't hear any indication of others in the room, just him and this Ravenguard woman. Was she his main contact here, then?

"I'm continuing to pursue it," she said. "I don't have definite information yet, but we're getting closer. I'd rather not raise expectations until I know for sure what we're dealing with."

"I'd better be the first to hear all the details."

"Of course, baron. I'll actually be taking the next step shortly."

Her tone indicated that she had nothing else to say on the matter. The conversation was winding down. I'd better get going before they came out and potentially noticed the nearby intrusion.

I slipped out of the office and engaged the physical lock with a jerk of magic. There wasn't time to reconstruct the rest, but I could hope the caster's comings and goings had become so automatic that they wouldn't notice if their dispelling casting had nothing to catch onto. I strode off down the hall, slowing at the click of the other door behind me.

Dad's voice carried to me, managing to contain an edge with just two syllables. "Malcolm?"

I turned and gave him a mild smile. "There you are. I wasn't sure where you'd gone off to."

He was alone—Ravenguard had stayed in her office. Which might have been worse for me, because there were no witnesses as the baron stalked along the hall to meet me. I drew myself up a little straighter, bracing myself.

I could have run back to the school and waited him out. I could have bought myself some time. But over the years I'd decided that when the axe was going to fall, it was better to get it over with as quickly as possible rather than wallow in the dread.

I came up with a quick excuse for why I'd been looking for him, but apparently Dad had too much on his mind to care about those technicalities. He gripped my elbow for one painful moment to spin me around and push me forward.

"I think you'd better come back to the house with me. We've got a lot to talk about."

His voice was flat and sharp as a razor. I kept pace with him, keeping up my oblivious front. "I drove here from school. My car—"

"You'll ride with me. We can have someone deal with your car later."

I shrugged. "All right, if you think that's really necessary."

Perhaps the shrug was a little too much. The tendons in Dad's jaw flexed. He marched me out into the cool, gasoline-tainted air of the parking lot just a hair's breadth from looking as though he were taking *me* into custody. Although in a way he was.

"In," he said when we reached the car.

I dropped into the passenger seat, he got in behind the wheel, and the doors slammed closed. His knuckles stood out against his skin as he grasped the wheel. But my father was nothing if not conscious of appearances. He didn't lay into me until we'd left the blacksuit headquarters behind.

"What the hell was that display during the hearing about?" he snapped. "Why would you get up there and speak *for* that girl?"

I gave him my best puzzled look. Having a plausible story wouldn't prevent retribution, but it would make the difference between him seeing me as inept rather than an active opponent.

"From what I saw and heard around campus and my own experiences with her, it was obvious she couldn't be responsible.

Obviously we wouldn't want one of the barons handicapped unnecessarily. You want to be able to bring her around so you can use her power, not have it suppressed."

Because I wasn't supposed to know that he'd intended from the start to use the unjustified sanctions to get her under control. That he might actually prefer her weak and out of the way after the defiance she'd already shown. He hadn't trusted me enough to fill me in on his real plans, and he could hardly blame me for not reading his mind.

He couldn't even tell me now exactly why he was so furious. "You couldn't have known for sure," he bit out, taking a turn just a tad too abruptly. The engine roared as we sped onto the freeway. "If you'd been wrong and your testimony had swayed the judge—"

"But I wasn't wrong," I said matter-of-factly. "It's a good thing I showed solidarity."

I shouldn't have rubbed it in. Dad's eyes flashed with an anger that crackled through the car.

"Your job is to focus on solidarity with your own family first. I shouldn't have been finding out that you meant to step in when it happened in the middle of the hearing."

All right, valid point. Even if he hadn't been a traitor, he'd have a right to be upset about me surprising him like that. Of course, *I* hadn't known I was going to burst in there until seconds beforehand.

I hadn't known if I'd need to. I'd come just to watch, to see how the hearing would play out from the observation room. But it'd been obvious that the other guys hadn't convinced the judge, and Rory must have known Cressida was keeping something vital to herself, because she'd looked so hopeless in the moment after the other girl left the witness chair…

There'd been a small chance my words would tip the balance, would make the difference between Rory continuing to grow into her power as the magnificent mage she was already becoming and seeing her greatness cut off at the knees, and in that moment it hadn't really been a choice at all. I knew which woman, which baron, *I* wanted to stand beside when it was my turn at the table of the pentacle.

And having that woman would be worth whatever Dad intended

to do to burn my regret over my "mistake" into my memory. I owed Rory, didn't I, after all the unnecessary pain I'd caused her?

"I'm sorry," I said to Dad, not meaning it at all. "I wasn't thinking."

"Clearly. I'm going to make sure that next time you will."

CHAPTER TWENTY-NINE

Rory

Professor Burnbuck raised his eyebrows when he answered his office door and found me standing outside.

"Miss Bloodstone," he said, flicking his scruffy hair farther out of his eyes. "It's good to see you unencumbered." His gaze dipped to my now bare wrists and back to my face. "Is there something I can help you with?"

I resisted the urge to rub the unencumbered skin, to revel in my new freedom as I had a whole bunch of times since yesterday's release. As I drew in my breath, my nerves jittered.

There'd been a Burnbuck in Professor Banefield's notes, but she was his aunt, not even part of his immediate family. If the Illusion professor had been conspiring with the barons, surely my mentor would have known?

In any case, I'd have Jude examine the spell I was about to ask for before I trusted it completely.

"I've decided on my prize for the summer project," I said. "At least, I think I have, if it's possible. And I'd like you to cast it."

"Something to do with illusions, hmm?" His eyes lit with eager interest. "I don't usually get asked since the winners tend to be looking for permanent effects. Come in and tell me what you're thinking."

Like his hair, his office had a scruffy look to it, books stacked in front of other books on the shelves even though there were gaps here and there where they could have been tucked in, the desk's finish worn down in patches. The pendulum on the dusty grandfather clock in the corner clicked as it swung. The room smelled fresh enough, though, with a grassy scent that carried through the half-open window from the field beyond.

I sat down on the slightly lumpy armchair. "I'm hoping you can cast a sort of charm for *detecting* illusions. A spell that would allow me to tell when something I'm seeing or hearing or whatever isn't actually real."

It wasn't the kind of spell I'd have most wanted as a prize. If one of the professors could have given me an "out to destroy the Bloodstone scion" detector so I knew exactly who to trust and who not to from here onward, that would have been perfect. But since there was no chance of that, I'd stick with something that could have come in handy multiple times since I'd arrived here. Even if I'd have to keep using my wits to figure out *who* to trust, at least I'd have a tool to help me figure out *what* to.

If I was going to stay here and fix the toxic parts of the fearmancer community myself, I had a feeling I'd need a tool like that.

The professor rubbed his narrow chin. "I can imbue an object with a spell for that purpose, but I should warn you that it wouldn't operate on a continual basis. You'd need to activate it to test a particular stimulus, and each test would drain some of its power, because the function requires that the magic leave the enchanted object to interact with the outside world."

"How many uses would I get?"

"It depends on how big and subtly cast the things you're testing are. Several at least, perhaps even dozens, depending. Is that adequate?"

I hadn't thought of any other prize I could ask for that would be half as good. I could accept what he was proposing. Hopefully by the time I'd used up the spell's magic, I'd be advanced enough in my studies to re-cast it myself.

"That's fine." I reached to undo the clasp on my necklace and slipped my glass dragon charm off the chain. My chest clenched as I handed it to Burnbuck. It was my last remaining token of my life with my real parents, and I hadn't let it out of my sight since I'd arrived here. But it was also the only object I could be sure of having on me when I needed it. "This is what I'd like you to place the spell on."

Burnbuck nodded. "I can have that ready for you by our class tomorrow morning. I'll attempt to give it as much potency as possible. It'll be an interesting challenge." He gave me a smile as if he was pleased to tackle that challenge.

When I left the Illusion professor's office, Declan was heading my way from farther down the hall. When he saw me, his gaze darted around us, instinctively checking for witnesses, but he gave me a little smile and didn't object to my waiting for him so we could walk together.

"Who were you calling on?" I asked.

"Professor Sinleigh." He paused. "I stepped down from my position as teacher's aide."

"Oh?" My heart skipped a beat. I hadn't expected that—he hadn't even hinted he was considering it. "Any particular reason?"

Declan's smile turned a bit wry. "I told her I felt as though I needed my full focus on my other responsibilities for my last few months here. There certainly have ended up being… many more factors demanding my attention than I anticipated when I took the job."

I might have laughed if another part of his comment hadn't struck me. "You're only here a few more months?"

He nodded. "I'll have finished my full education by the end of January. Then I'll take over the Ashgrave barony completely."

How long was *I* going to have to stay at the university, considering all the catching up I needed to do? Were they going to make me continue classes even after my twenty-first year since I'd missed so many before? That was, assuming I made it through the next year without finding myself in cuffs either literal or metaphorical again. As relieved as I was to have the hearing over and my innocence established, I found it hard to believe the battle between me and the barons was anything close to finished.

Declan couldn't answer those questions, though, and his decision mattered in other ways. I smiled back at him with a tingle of warmth. "I'm sorry your life has gotten so hectic, but glad you'll have fewer... constraints on your time." Not to mention on who he spent that time with and how.

We came down the staircase to the main floor of the building and veered out a side door onto the green. "I was thinking now that I've settled that and your most immediate problem is dealt with," Declan said, "maybe we could have that talk about—"

He cut himself off at the sound of my name called across the green. Shelby was bounding toward us, grinning.

"Guess what!" she said. "One of the restaurants in town invited the music students to perform tonight. They're even paying us!" Her ponytail bobbed with her excitement. Then her eyes widened. "I don't know what to wear for something like that. They're probably expecting everyone who's from the university to dress all fancy."

The conversation with Declan about what exactly we were doing with our relationship could wait until this minor friend crisis was over. I caught his eye, and he nodded with obvious amusement.

"Let's take a look in your wardrobe, and I'll help you pick," I told Shelby. "And that's awesome! I guess you were right about the program here being good for your career."

"One more year and then I can start making applications to orchestras."

She practically bounced up the stairs to our dorm room. As she pulled out her key card, my gaze caught for a moment on the door next to ours that led into Malcolm's dorm.

I hadn't seen the Nightwood scion since yesterday at the hearing. Maybe he'd needed a little space to figure out how he was going to proceed now that he'd put himself out there in opposition to his father's interests.

A twinge ran through my chest. I wasn't totally sure what I'd say to him, but we definitely needed to talk. At the very least, so I could thank him. Taking that stand couldn't have been easy. And I'd been suspicious of him even after he'd started his testimony…

This once, I might owe *him* an apology. If I was coming to know anything about Malcolm Nightwood, it was that he kept his word, and he'd said he'd prove himself to me. I couldn't really have asked for a clearer show of loyalty.

Shelby tugged me into our room, away from those conflicted thoughts. As we examined her clothing options, I let myself become absorbed in her giddy chatter. After the weeks of worrying and uncertainty, there was something blissfully normal about hanging out with a friend who had no part in the conspiracies around me and talking about something as mundane as appropriate work attire.

In the end, we settled on a pearl-pink blouse and dark wash jeans, since Shelby didn't have any dress pants or skirts. "I'm sure they care a lot more about how the music sounds than what you're wearing," I reassured her. "Anyway, who'll be able to see your pants past the cello?"

"Good point," she said with a laugh.

My good mood lingered as I crossed the common room—and vanished when I opened my bedroom door to find Lillian Ravenguard standing by my desk. My pulse hiccupped, and my fingers tensed around the doorknob. I hadn't even noticed that the magical defenses on my room had been breached. But then, this was a top blacksuit I was dealing with.

"I'm sorry for the sudden visit," Lillian said, obviously noting my surprise. "It's a rather urgent matter… and one too discrete to discuss by traceable methods or in public." She stepped away from the desk and raised her hand. "I'll make sure we won't be overheard here."

As she cast the silencing spell, I sank down on the edge of my bed. Deborah darted across the bedspread a moment later, tucking herself behind me. I moved to gesture to her to hide herself somewhere farther away, since we couldn't be sure how sensitive Lillian might be to my familiar's unusual state.

Before I could, Deborah's voice traveled into my head, faintly as if at a whisper. Whatever she had to tell me, it was important enough for her to risk discovery.

Watch out, she murmured. *I got a whiff of that woman as she was waiting for you. I'd swear she's the one who murdered your friend.*

My stomach lurched. I'd known Lillian was almost certainly involved in the plot to frame me, but the possibility that she'd killed Imogen herself had never occurred to me.

Deborah scurried away. Lillian turned, finished with her casting, and my mouth went dry.

The woman aiming that concerned look at me hated me so much that she was willing to kill to cut me down.

"What's going on?" I said, scrambling to think of an excuse to get out of this room, somewhere we wouldn't be alone. Somewhere I'd have a chance of getting help if she launched another attack of some sort.

Lillian leaned against my wardrobe, partly blocking my way to the door. Not that I could have made a run for it without revealing a whole lot more about what I knew than I wanted to just yet. She lowered her head with a ragged sigh. Then she looked at me again.

"I don't know how to tell you this," she said. "If it's true, I'm ashamed that I missed it for so long. Rory… We've found evidence that your mother is still alive."

ABOUT THE AUTHOR

Eva Chase lives in Canada with her family. She loves stories both swoony and supernatural, and strong women and the men who appreciate them. Along with the Royals of Villain Academy series, she is the author of the Flirting with Monsters series, the Cursed Studies trilogy, the Moriarty's Men series, the Looking Glass Curse trilogy, the Their Dark Valkyrie series, the Witch's Consorts series, the Dragon Shifter's Mates series, the Demons of Fame Romance series, the Legends Reborn trilogy, and the Alpha Project Psychic Romance series.

Connect with Eva online:
www.evachase.com
eva@evachase.com

www.ingramcontent.com/pod-product-compliance
Lightning Source LLC
Chambersburg PA
CBHW030344310726
48979CB00001B/185

* 9 7 8 1 9 9 8 7 5 2 0 3 4 *